# *STAR TREK*®

# RIHANNSU
## THE BLOODWING VOYAGES

Diane Duane with Peter Morwood

Based upon *Star Trek*®
created by Gene Roddenberry

POCKET BOOKS
New York   London   Toronto   Sydney   ch'Rihan

POCKET BOOKS, a division of Simon & Schuster, Inc.
1230 Avenue of the Americas, New York, NY 10020

This book is published by Pocket Books, a division of
Simon & Schuster, Inc., under exclusive license from
CBS Studios Inc.

ISBN-13: 978-1-4165-2577-6
ISBN-10: 1-4165-2577-7

This Pocket Books trade paperback edition December 2006

1   3   5   7   9   10   8   6   4   2

POCKET and colophon are registered trademarks of
Simon & Schuster, Inc.

Manufactured in the United States of America

These titles were previously published individually by Pocket Books.

For information regarding special discounts for bulk purchases, please contact
Simon & Schuster Special Sales at 1-800-456-6798 or business@simonandschuster.com.

# STAR TREK®

# RIHANNSU
## THE BLOODWING VOYAGES

# ACKNOWLEDGMENTS

Sometimes people can be of incredible assistance to you without saying a word. This is the place to acknowledge one such contributor, whose simple existence made writing this book easier: the stately, sharp-minded, wonderful Dorothy Fontana (or "D.C." Fontana, as some of you may know her). Dorothy has in the past done me many amazing and undeserved kindnesses—but the one most in my mind at this writing is one she did for you too (if you love *Star Trek*) during her stint as the series' story editor, and as writer of some of its best stories.

Dorothy knows Vulcans and Romulans better than anyone else, having been intimately involved with their creation. Much of her vision of those enigmatic and delightful species—as creatures as complex as any other hominid, not mere logic-boxes or disposable hostiles to be shot up and forgotten about—informs this work, and I delight to add that influence to the list of my glad debts to her. When we think of the power that Leonard Nimoy and Mark Lenard have brought to the Vulcans and Romulans they've played, let's not leave D.C. out of the reckoning. Without her, Spock and Sarek and both the original Romulan Commanders would have been very different people. My own feeling (and even Vulcans these days seem to admit that feelings have value) is that the Vulcans and the Romulans are as marvelous as they are partly because they take after Dorothy. So—to the Lady Who *Knows*—great thanks and love.

Also:

Inside the Franklin Institute in Philadelphia (to the right of the statue of the Great God Franklin, and three flights up) is the Fels Planetarium.

Hidden away in the Planetarium is a door with a very odd doorbell attached to it. And working behind that door are Don Cooke, the Director of the planetarium, and his staff—a group of people very sanely devoted to that study of the Earth's backyard that we call "astronomy."

These people share with the author the conviction that "Thataway" is not an appropriate set of course determination coordinates for the flagship of the Terran branch of Starfleet. The Fels group's eager (though sometimes bemused) assistance with some thorny astronomical questions ("George! *B minus V?*" "Yes, what about it? . . .") made it possible to plot not only the positions of major stars for several thousand light-years from Sol, but also the real positions and shapes of the Galactic Arms, in enough detail so that the structure of the Galaxy itself made it obvious where the Romulans and Klingons lived. To Don and all his happy people, and to their doorbell (a never-ending source of merriment), affectionate thanks, still air, and good seeing.

# CONTENTS

# PART ONE

# My Enemy, My Ally

To Ael's godmother—

*"—cara mihi ante alias;*
*neque enim novus iste Dianae*
*venit amor, subitaque*
*animum dulcedine movit—"*

*—arma eraeque canō!*

. . . Then none was for a party;
   Then all were for the state;
Then the great man helped the poor
   And the poor man loved the great;
Then lands were fairly portioned;
   Then spoils were fairly sold:
The Romans were like brothers
   In the brave days of old.

Now Roman is to Roman
   More hateful than a foe,
And the Tribunes beard the high,
   And the Fathers grind the low.
As we wax hot in faction,
   In battle we wax cold;
Wherefore men fight not as they fought
   In the brave days of old. . . .

                                   —Macaulay


*Daisemi'in rhhaensuriuu*
   *meillunsiateve*
      *rh'e Mnhei'sahe yie ahr'en:*

*Mnahe afw'ein qiuu;*
   *rh'e hweithnaef*
      *mrht Heis'he ehl'ein qiuu.*

(Of the chief Parts of the Ruling Passion, only this can be truly said: Hate has a reason for everything. But love is unreasonable.)

                    —V. Raiuhes Ahaefvthe [of Romulus II],
                       *Taer'thaiemenh,* book xviii, par. 886:
                             J. Kerasus, translator

# Chapter One

Her name, to which various people had recently been appending curses, was Ael i-Mhiessan t'Rllaillieu. Her rank, in the common tongue, was *khre'Riov*: commander-general. Her serial number was a string of sixteen characters that by now she knew as well as she knew her fourth name, though they meant infinitely less to her. And considering these matters in such a fashion was at least marginally appropriate just now, for she was in a trap.

How long she would remain there, however, remained to be seen.

At the moment her patience was mostly intact, but her spirit had moved her to rattle the bars of the cage a bit. Ael propped her elbow on her desk, rested her chin on her hand, and said to her cabin's wall screen, *"Hwaveyiir. Erein tr'Khaell."*

The screen flicked on, and there was the bridge, and poor Antecenturion tr'Khaell just as he had been twenty minutes ago, still hunched over and pretending to fiddle with his communications boards. At the sight of Ael he straightened quickly and said, "Ie, khre'Riov?"

*Don't play the innocent with* me, *child,* thought Ael. *You should have had that dispatch decoded and translated ten minutes ago . . . as well you know.* "Erein, eliukh hwio' 'ssuy llas-mene arredhaud'eitroi?"

She said it politely enough, but the still, low-lidded look she gave him was evidently making it plain to tr'Khaell that if Ael had to ask him again about what was holding up the dispatch's deciphering, it would go hard with him. Sweat broke out on tr'Khaell's forehead. "Ie, khre'Riov, sed ri-thlaha nei' yhreill-ien ssuriu mnerev dhaarhiin-emenorriul—"

*Oh indeed! I know how fast that computer runs; I was building them with my own hands before you knew which end to hold a sword by. Of course, you can't just come out and tell me that the security officer ordered you to let her read the dispatch before I saw it, now can you?* "Rhi siuren, Erein."

Poor tr'Khaell's face gave Ael the impression that t'Liun was going to take rather longer than "five minutes" to read the dispatch. Tr'Khaell looked panic-striken. "Khre'Riov—" he started to say. But *"Ta'khoi,"* Ael said to the screen, and it flicked off.

*Pitiable,* Ael thought. *Truly I could feel sorry for him. But if he chooses to sell his loyalty to two commanders at once, who am I to deprive him of the joy of being caught between them? Perhaps he'll learn better.* And after a second she laughed once, softly, as much at herself as at tr'Khaell. *Perhaps the galaxy will stop rotating.*

She pushed away from the desk and leaned back in her comfortable chair, considering with calm irony how little her surroundings looked like the cage they actually were. *They truly think they've deceived me,* she thought, amused and contemptuous, looking around at the spare luxury of her command cabin. *Pad the kennel with velvets, they say to each other; feed the old* thrai *on fat flesh and blood wine, put her in command of a fleet, and she won't notice that the only ones who pay any attention to her orders are the ones stuck inside the bars with her.* Ael's lips curled slightly upward at the thought. *"Susse-thrai"* had been the name bestowed upon her, half in anger, half in affection, by her old crew on *Bloodwing;* the keen-nosed, cranky, wily old she-beast, never less dangerous than when you thought her defenseless, and always growing new teeth far back in her throat to replace the old ones broken in biting out the last foe's heart. You might cage a *thrai*, you might poke it through the bars and laugh; but it would find a way to be avenged for the insult. It would break out and tear off your leg and eat it before your face—or run away and wait till you had died of old age, then come back and excrete on your grave.

Then Ael frowned at herself, annoyed. "Crude," she said to the room, eyes flicking up to the ceiling-corner by the bed as she wondered whether t'Liun had managed to bug the place already since last week. "I grow crude, as they do." *Chew on that, you vacuum-headed creature, and wonder what it means,* thought Ael, getting up to pace her cage.

The most annoying part was that it was true. That courtesy, honor, noble behavior should be cast aside by the young, perceived as a useless hindrance to expediency, was bad enough. But that she should begin to sink to their level herself, descending into brute-beast metaphors and savagery instead of the straightforward dealing that had been tradition for four thousand years of civilization—that was galling. *I will not fight them with their own methods,* Ael thought. *That is the surest way to become them. I will come by my victories honestly. And as for Sunseed—*

She stopped in front of another of her cabin's luxuries, one better than private 'fresher or sleeping silks or key lighting. Beyond the wide port, space yawned black, with stars burning in it—stars that at *Cuirass*'s present sublight speed hung quite still, apparently going nowhere. *As I am,* she thought, but the thought was reflex, and untrue. Ael grimaced again and leaned her forehead against the cool clearsteel.

In one way, she had no one to blame for where she was right now but herself. When she had heard about the Sunseed project based at Levaeri V, and had begun to realize what it could do to Rihannsu civilization if fully implemented, shock and horror had stung her into swift action. She had taken leave from *Bloodwing* and gone home to ch'Rihan to lobby against the project—openly speaking out against it in the Senate, and privately making the rounds of her old political cronies, all those old warrior-Senators and those few comrades in the Praetorate who owed her favors. However, Ael had not realized the extent to which the old warriors were being outweighed, or in some cases subverted or cowed, by the young ones—the hot-blooded children who wanted everything right now, who wanted the easy, swift victories that the completion of Sunseed would bring them. Honorless victories, against helpless foes; but the fierce young voices now rising in the Senate cared nothing about that. They wanted safety, security, a world without threats, a universe in which they could swoop down on defenseless ships or planets and take what they wanted.

*Thieves,* Ael thought. *They have no desire to be warriors, fighting worthy foes for what they want, and winning or losing according to their merits. They want to be robbers, like our accursed allies the Klingons. Raiders, who stab in the back and loot men's corpses, or worlds. And as for those of us who remember an older way, a better way, they wait for us to die. Or in some cases, they hurry us along. . . .*

She pushed herself away from the cool metal of the port, breathed out once. Somewhere among those stars, out in that blackness, ch'Rihan and ch'Havran hung, circling one another majestically in the year's slow dance around amber Eisn; two green-golden gems, cloud-streaked, sea-girt, burning fair. But she would probably never walk under those clouds again, or beside those seas, as a result of that last visit to the sigil-hung halls of the Senate. The young powers in the High Command, suspicious of Ael from the first, now knew for sure that she was opposed to them, and their reaction to her opposition had been swift and thorough. They dared not exile her or murder her, not openly; she was after all a war hero many times over, guilty of no real crime. Instead they had "honored" her, having Ael sent out on a long tour of duty, into what was ostensibly a post of high command and great peril. Command she wielded, but with eyes watching her, spies of various younger Senators and Praetors. And as for peril . . . it came rarely, but fatally, here in the Outmarches—the deadly peaceful space that the power surrounding most of it called the Romulan Neutral Zone.

*Names,* Ael thought with mild irony, *names . . . How little they have to do with the truth, sometimes.* The great cordon of space arbitrarily thrown about Eisn was hardly neutral. At best it was a vast dark hiding-place into which ships of both sides occasionally dodged, preparing for intelligence-gathering forays on the unfriendly neighbor. As for "Romulan"—after first hearing the word in Federation Basic, rather than by universal translator, Ael had become curious to understand the name the Empire's old foes had given her world, and had done some research into it. She had been distastefully fascinated to find the word's meaning rooted in some weird Terran story of twin brothers abandoned in the wild, and there discovered and given suck by a brute beast rather like a *thrai.* It would take a Terran to think of something so bizarre.

But whether one called Eisen's paired worlds ch'Rihan and ch'Havran or Romulus and Remus, Ael knew she was unlikely to ever walk either of them again. *Never again to walk through Airissuin's purple meads,* she thought, gazing out at the starry darkness. *Never to see that some loved one had hung up the name-flag for me; never to climb Eilairiv and look down on the land my mothers and fathers worked for a thousand years, the lands we held with the plowshare and the sword . . .* For the angry young voices in the Senate, Mrian and Hei and Llaaseil and the rest, had put her safely out of their way; and here, while they held power, she would stay. They would wait and let time do what their lack of courage or some poor tattered rag of honor forbade them.

Accidents happened in the Neutral Zone, after all. Ships far from maintenance suddenly came to grief. That was likely enough, in this poor secondhand warbird with which they'd saddled her, this flying breakdown looking for a place to happen. Crews rebelled against discipline, mutinied, on long hauls . . . and that was likely too, considering the reprehensible lot of rejects and incompetents with whom she was trapped here. Ael thought longingly of her own crew of *Bloodwing;* fierce, dogged folk tried in a hundred battles and faithful to her . . . but that faithfulness was why her enemies in the High Command had had her transferred from *Bloodwing* in the first place. A crew that could not be bought, the taste of the old loyalty, made them nervous. It was a question how long even Tafv, so far innocent of the Senate's suspicion, would be able to hold on to them. And it was no use thinking about them in any case. She was stuck with the ship's complement of *Cuirass,* half of them in the pay of the other half or of her enemies in Command, nearly all of them hating nearly all the others, and all of them definitely hating *her;* they knew perfectly well why they'd been cut orders for so long a tour.

And if those problems failed to wear her down to suicide, or kill her outright, there were others that surely would. Those problems had names like *Intrepid . . . Inaieu . . . Constellation.* If Ael survived too long, she knew she would be ordered into the path of one of them. Honor would require her to obey her orders; and since *Cuirass* was alone and far, far from support, honor would eventually be the death of her. Her unfriends in the Senate would find the irony delightful.

*Well,* Ael thought. *We shall see.* She shifted her eyes again to the desk screen and reread the letter coolly burning there, blue against the black.

FROM THE COMMANDER TAFV EI-LEINARRH TR'RLLAIL-
LIEU, SET IN AUTHORITY OVER IMPERIAL VESSEL *BLOOD-*

*WING,* TO THE RIGHT NOBLE COMMANDER-GENERAL AEL T'RLLAILLIEU, SET IN AUTHORITY OVER IMPERIAL CRUISER *CUIRASS,* RESPECTFUL GREETING. IF MATTERS ARE WELL WITH YOU, THEN THEY ARE WELL WITH ME ALSO. HONORED MOTHER, I HEAR WITH SOME REGRET OF YOUR RECENT ASSIGNMENT TO THE OUTMARCHES, IN THAT I SHALL FOR SOME TIME BE DENIED THE PRIVILEGE OF PRESENTING MY DUTY TO YOU IN PERSON. BUT WE MUST ALL BOW WILLINGLY TO THOSE DUTIES EVEN HIGHER THAN FAMILY TIES WHICH THE IMPERIUM REQUIRES OF US; AS I KNOW YOU DO.

PATROLS IN THIS AREA REMAIN QUIET, AS MIGHT BE EXPECTED, OUR PRESENTLY-ASSIGNED CORRIDOR BEING SO FAR FROM ANY ENEMY (OR COME TO THINK OF IT, ANY FRIENDLY) ACTIVITY. HIGH COMMAND TELLS US LITTLE OR NOTHING ABOUT HAPPENINGS IN THE OUTMARCH QUADRANTS WHICH YOU ARE PATROLLING— SECURITY UNDERSTANDABLY BEING WHAT IT IS—BUT I CAN ONLY HOPE THAT THIS FINDS YOU SAFE, OR BETTER STILL, VICTORIOUS IN SOME SKIRMISH WHICH HAS LEFT OUR ENEMIES SMARTING.

MASTER ENGINEER TR'KEIRIANH HAS FINALLY MANAGED TO DISCOVER THE SOURCE OF THAT PECULIARITY IN THE WARP DRIVE THAT KEPT TROUBLING US DURING *BLOODWING*'S LAST TOUR OF THE MARCHES NEAR THE HA-SUIWEN STARS. EVIDENTLY ONE OF THE MULTISTATE EQUIVOCATOR CRYSTALS WAS AT FAULT, THE CRYSTAL HAVING DEVELOPED A FLUID-STRESS FAULT THAT MALFUNCTIONED ONLY DURING MEGA-GAUSS MAGNETIC FIELD VARIATIONS OF THE KIND THAT OCCUR DURING HIGH WARP SPEEDS—AND NEVER IN THE TESTING CYCLE, WHICH IS WHY WE COULD NOT FIND THE SOURCE OF THE PROBLEM BEFORE. I HAVE RECOMMENDED

TR'KEIRIANH FOR A MINOR COMMENDATION. MEAN-
WHILE, OTHER MATTERS ABOARD SHIP REMAIN SO UN-
REMARKABLE AND SO MUCH THE SAME AS WHEN I LAST
WROTE YOU THAT THERE IS LITTLE USE IN CONTINU-
ING THIS. I WILL CLOSE SAYING THAT VARIOUS OF
*BLOODWING*'S CREW HAVE ASKED ME TO OFFER THEIR
OLD COMMANDER THEIR RESPECTS, WHICH NOW I DO,
ALONG WITH MY OWN. THE ELEMENTS LOOK ON YOU
WITH FAVOR. THIS BY MY HAND, THE ONE HUNDRED
EIGHTEENTH SHIP'S DAY SINCE *BLOODWING*'S DEPAR-
TURE FROM CH'RIHAN, THE EIGHTY-NINTH DAY OF MY
COMMAND. TR'RLLAILLIEU. LIFE TO THE IMPERIUM.

Ael smiled at the letter, a smile it was well that none of *Cuirass*'s crew
could see. Such a bland and uncommunicative missive was hardly in
Tafv's style. But it indicated that he knew as well as Ael what would
happen to the letter when Ael's ship received it. It would be read by
tr'Khaell in communications, passed on to Security Officer t'Liun, who
had tr'Khaell so firmly under her thumb, and avidly read for any possible sign of secret messages or disaffection—then put through cryptanalysis as well by t'Liun's tool tr'Iawaain down in data processing.
Much good it would do them; Tafv was not fool enough to put what he
had to say in any code they would be able to break.

Oh, t'Liun would find *something* in cryptanalysis, to be sure. A stiff
and elegant multiple-variable code, just complex enough to be realistic
and careless enough to be breakable after a goodly period of head-
beating. She would find a message that said, PLAN FAILED, APPEALS TO
PRAETORATE UNSUCCESSFUL; FURTHER ATTEMPTS REFUSED. Which,
being exactly what t'Liun (and the High Command people who paid
her) wanted to hear, would quiet them for a little while. Until it was
too late, at least.

Ael leaned back and stretched. Tafv's mention of repairs to the warp
drive told her that he and Giellun tr'Keirianh, Elements bless both their
twisty minds, had finally succeeded in attaching those stealthily-acquired
Klingon gunnery augmentation circuits to *Bloodwing*'s phasers—an addi-

tion that would give the valiant old ship three times a warbird's usual firepower. Ael did not care for the Klingon ships that the Empire had been buying lately; their graceless design was offensive to her, and their workmanship was usually hasty and shoddy. But though Klingons might be abysmal shipwrights, they did know how to build guns. And though the adaptation to *Bloodwing*'s phasers had bid fair to take forever, it had also been absolutely necessary for the success of their plan.

As for the rest of the letter, Tafv had made it plain to Ael that he was close, and ready, and waiting on her word. He had also told her plainly, by saying nothing, that his communications were being monitored too; that Command had refused to allow him details on Ael's present location, which he evidently knew only by virtue of the new family spies still buried in Command Communications; that there was some expectation of the enemy in the quadrant to which Ael had been sent; and that her old crew was willing and ready to enact the plan which she and Tafv had been quietly concocting since the "honor guard" had come to escort Ael off *Bloodwing* to her new command on *Cuirass*.

Ael was quite satisfied. There was only one more thing she lacked, one element missing. She had spent a good deal of money during that last trip to ch'Rihan, attempting to encourage its presence. Now she had merely to wait, and keep good hope, until time or Federation policy produced it. And once it did . . .

The screen chimed quietly. *"Ta'rhae,"* she said, turning toward it from the port.

Tr'Khaell appeared on the screen again, his sweat still in evidence. "Khre'Riov, na'hwi, reh eliu arredhau'ven—"

*Four and a half minutes,* Ael thought, amused. *T'Liun's reading speed is improving. Or tr'Khaell's shouting is. "Hnafiv 'rau, Erein."*

The man had no control of his face at all; the flicker of his eyes told Ael that there was something worth hearing in this message indeed, something he had been hoping she would order him to read aloud. "Hilain na nfaaistur ll' efwrohin galae—"

*"Ie, ie,"* Ael said, sitting down at her desk again, and waving a hand at him to go on. News of the rather belated arrival in this quadrant of her fleet, such as it was, interested her hardly at all. *Wretched used Klingon*

*ships that they are, they should only have been eaten by a black hole on the way in. "Hre va?"*

"Lai hra'galae na hilain, khre'Riov. Mrei kha rhaaukhir Lloannen'-galae . . . te ssiun bhveinu hir' Enterprise khina."

Ael carefully did not stir in her chair and kept most strict guard over her face . . . slowly permitting one eyebrow to go up, no more. *"Rhe've,"* she said, nodding casually and calmly as if this news was something she might have expected—as if her whole mind was not one great blaze of angry, frightened delight. *So soon! So soon! "Rhe'. Khru va, Erein?"*

"Au'e, khre'Riov. Irh' hvannen nio essaea Lloann'mrahel virrir—"

She waved the hand at tr'Khaell again; the details and the names of the other ships in the new Federation patrol group could wait for her in the computer until her "morning" shift. *"Lhiu hrao na awaenndraevha, Erein. Ta'khoi."* And the screen went out.

Then, only then, did Ael allow herself to rock back in the chair, and take a good long breath, and let it out again . . . and smile once more, a small tight smile that would have disquieted anyone who saw it. *So soon,* she thought. *But I'm glad. . . . O my enemy, see how well the Elements have dealt with both of us. For here at last may be an opportunity for us to settle an old, old score. . . .*

Ael sat up straight and pulled the keypad of her terminal toward her. She got rid of Tafv's letter, then said the several passwords that separated her small cabin computer from the ship's large one for independent work, and started calling up various private files—maps of this quadrant, and neighboring ones. *"Ie rha,"* she said as she set to work—speaking aloud in sheer angry relish, and (for the moment) with utter disregard to what t'Liun might hear. *"Rha'siu hlun vr'Enterprise, ir-rhaimehn rha'sien Kirk. . . ."*

# Chapter Two

CAPTAIN'S PERSONAL LOG, **Stardate 7504.6:**

*"Nothing to report but still more hydrogen ion-flux measurements in the phi Trianguli corridor. Entirely too many ion-flux measurements, according to Mr. Chekov, who has declared to the bridge at large that his mother didn't raise him to compile weather reports. (Must remember to ask him why not, since meteorology has to have been invented in Russia, like everything else.)*

*"Mr. Spock is 'fascinated' (so what else is new?) by the gradual increase in the number and severity of ion storms in this part of the galaxy. He will lecture comprehensively and at a moment's notice on the importance of our findings as they relate to the problem—the implications of a shift in the stellar wind for the sector's interstellar 'ecology,' the potentially disastrous effects of such a shift on interplanetary shipping and on the economies of worlds situated along the shipping lanes, etc., etc., etc. However, even Spock has admitted to me privately that he looks forward to solving this problem and moving on to something a little more challenging. His captain agrees with him. His captain is bored stiff. My mother didn't raise me to compile weather reports, either.*

*"However, it's an ill wind that blows nobody good . . . or however that goes. At least things have been quiet around here.*

*"Now why is it that, when I say that, my hands begin to sweat? . . ."*

"Jim?"

"Now now, Bones."

"Medical matter, Captain."

James T. Kirk looked up from the 4D chesscubic at his chief surgeon. "What is it?"

"If you make that move," said Dr. McCoy, "you'll live to regret it."

"Doctor," said the calm voice from across the chesscubic, "kibitzing is as annoying to the victims in chess as it is in medicine . . . which is doubtless why you practice it so assiduously."

"Oh, stick it in your ear, Spock," said McCoy, peering over Jim's shoulder to get a better view of the cubic. "No, I take that back: in your case it would only make matters worse."

"Doctor—"

"No, Spock, it's all right," Jim said. "This'll be a lesson to me, Bones. Look at this mess."

Bones looked, and Jim took the opportunity to stretch and gaze around the great recreation deck of the *Enterprise*. The place was lively as usual with crewpeople eating and drinking and talking and playing games and socializing and generally goofing off. There was a merrily homicidal game of water polo taking place in the main pool: amphibians against drylanders, Jim judged, as he saw Amekentra from dietary break surface in a glittering, green-scaled arc, tackle poor Ensign London amidships, and drag Robbie under with her in a flash and splash of water. Closer to Jim, in the middle of the room, a quieter but equally deadly game of contract bridge was going on: a Terran-looking male and a short, round Tellarite lady sat frowning at their cards, while the broad-shouldered Elaasian member of the foursome peered at his hand, and his partner, a gossamer-haired Andorian, watched him with cool interest and waited for him to bid. Nearest to Jim, some forty or fifty yards away, a Sulamid crewman leaned against the baby grand, with a drink held coiled in one violet tentacle, and most of his other tendrils and tentacles draped gracefully over the Steinway. Various of those tentacles wreathed gently, keeping time, and the Sulamid's eight stalked eyes gazed off into various distances, as the pianist—someone in Fleet nursing whites—wove her way through the sweetly melancholy complexities of a Chopin nocturne. That was appropriate enough, for it was "evening" for Jim, and for about a fourth of the *Enterprise*'s crew; delta shift was about to go on duty, alpha shift's day was drawing to a quiet close, and all was right with the world.

*Except here,* Jim thought, glancing at the chesscubic again, and then, with wry resignation, back up at Spock. The Vulcan sat in his characteristic chess-pose, leaning on his elbows, hands folded, the first two fingers steepled—gazing back at Jim with an expression of carefully veiled compassion, and with what Jim's practiced eye identified as the slightest trace of mischievous enjoyment.

Jim became aware of another presence at his side, to the left. He looked up and found Harb Tanzer, the chief of recreation, standing there—a short, stocky, silver-haired man with eyes that usually crinkled at the corners with laughter . . . as, at the sight of the chesscubic, they were beginning to do now. Jim was not amused. "Mister," he said to Harb, "you are in deep trouble."

"Why, Captain? Something wrong with the cube?"

With some difficulty Jim restrained himself from groaning out loud, for the whole thing was his own fault. He had mentioned to Harb some time back that 3D chess, much as he loved it, had been getting a little boring. Harb had gone quietly away to talk to Moira, the master games computer, and shortly thereafter had presented the ship's company with something new—4D chess. Spock had objected mildly to the name, for hyperspace, not time, was the true forth dimension. But the Vulcan's objections were swiftly lost in fascination with the new variant.

Harb had completely done away with the form of the old triple-level chessboard, replacing it with a hologram-style stack of force-field cubes, eight on a side, in which the pieces were "embedded" during play. The cubic was fully rotatable in yaw, pitch and roll; if desired, parts of it could be enlarged for closer examination, or for tournament play. The pieces themselves (the only physical element of the set) were handled by an exquisitely precise transporter system, with a set of controls on each player's side of the gametable. This innovation effectively eliminated "you-touched-it, you-have-to-move-it" arguments, illegal "behind-the-back" moving, and other such minor excitements. Not that either of the *Enterprise*'s premier chess players would ever have had recourse to cheating. But the new design opened up possibilities as well as removing them: and it was one of these newer variations that Spock was presently inflicting on the captain.

Harb had programmed the table's games computer so that a player could vanish desired pieces from the cubic, for a period of his own determination, and have them reappear later—if desired, in any other spot made possible by a legal move. Pieces "timed out" in this fashion could appear behind the other player's lines and wreak havoc there. But this innovation had not merely expanded the usual course of play. It had also completely changed the paradigm in which chess was usually played. Suddenly the game was no longer about anticipating the opponent's moves and thwarting them—or not merely about that. It was now also a matter of anticipating a whole strategy from the very start: a matter of estimating with great accuracy where an opponent would be in fifteen or twenty moves, and getting one's pieces there to ambush him—while also fooling the opponent as to where one's own weak and strong areas would be at that time.

As a result, Jim now found himself playing with a deadly seriousness he hadn't been able to bring to the game in a long while . . . for everything was changed. All the strategies he had laboriously worked out over the years for play against Spock—strategies that had finally begun working—were now suddenly useless. And worse than that, Spock was still walking all over Jim in the game—which said uncomfortable things to the captain of the *Enterprise* about his ability to tell what his first officer was thinking. Once again Jim found himself wondering whether Spock's dual heritage was giving him an unfair advantage . . . whether the Vulcan half of him, so coolly analytical, was better at understanding his own human half, and thereby, the actions of the full humans around him.

Though Jim remembered McCoy, some time back, warning him against such generalizations: "As if you could chop a mind in half like an apple," Bones had said, derisive and amused. "He's one whole being—a *Spock*—and the sooner you armchair shrinks get that through your heads, the better you'll be able to deal with him." *Still* . . . Jim thought. But it was late for theorizing, and at any rate no amount of it was going to get him out of this one. He tilted his head back to look at Harb Tanzer. "Couldn't you have stuck to shuffleboard?" he said.

"I can see where it might have been wiser," said Harb, looking down at the cubic.

Regretfully, Jim had to agree with him. He had tried one of his favorite offenses from 3D chess—an all-out, "scream-and-leap" offensive opening that in the past had occasionally succeeded in rattling Spock slightly with its sheer bloody-minded enthusiasm. Unfortunately, mere howling aggressiveness was of no use in this game, not even briefly. Spock had merely sat in calm interest, watching Jim's game unfold, responding calmly to Jim's screams and leaps. Spock had moved rather conservatively, moving first one queen and then his second into mildly threatening mid-level positions, counterbalancing Jim's double-queen pin on the king's level (four, at the time) from levels three and eight. Jim had run merrily amok for a while, inexorably pushing Spock into what looked like a wholly defensive position in the center-cubic upper levels, then timing out both his rooks, one of his knights, and several pawns in rapid succession, in what was meant to be a nettling display of security.

That was when Spock had lifted his head from a long scowl at the board, and very, very slowly put that one eyebrow up. Jim had stared back at Spock, entirely cheerful, not saying anything but mentally daring him to do his worst.

He had. Jim's half of the cubic now looked like the Klingon half of the Battle of Organia at the end of the fourth quarter . . . not that his pieces even held as much as half the cubic anymore. Spock had not even needed to wait for his own timed-out pieces to return. Not that there were many of them; Jim now suspected that Spock had purposely restrained himself there, to keep Jim from feeling too bad—or perhaps to keep the win from looking too much like mindreading. Jim, looking in great annoyance at his poor king penned up in the upper levels with queens above and below him—in Spock's silent demonstration of his own brand of poetic justice—considered that he would have preferred mindreading to the implication that Spock could anticipate him this completely *without* it. The situation elsewhere was no better. Spock's king was redoubtably fenced around by knights and rooks; his bishops were so perfectly positioned in the center cubic that they controlled it practically by themselves. And Jim had nothing available with which to attack them even if they had been more poorly positioned. Both his queens were gone now, and almost everything else was timed out in preparation for what was supposed to have been the closing of a cunning and totally unpredictable trap. . . .

*When will I learn,* Jim thought. He looked up over his shoulder. "What do you think?" he said to Harb.

"Sir," said the chief of recreation, "I think you've got a problem."

"Thank you very much, Mr. Tanzer. *I* think that as soon as I finish this, you're being transferred to hydroponics. Head first. Bones?"

McCoy looked down at the cubic. "As it stands now, mate in six."

"Five," Spock said, in that cool dry voice in which no one was meant to hear arrogance, or kindness either.

Jim stared calmly into the cubic, trying to look deeply thoughtful. He was actually hoping for a broken glass somewhere in the room, a call from the Bridge, a red alert—any distraction that would get him out of this mess before it proceeded to its inevitable conclusion. But nothing happened. Finally he sighed, and looked up at Spock with as much good grace as he could muster, reaching for the "resign" touchpad. "I have to admit, Mr. Spock—"

Bones laid a hand on Jim's arm, stopping his gesture. "Wait a minute, Jim. Would you mind if I played this one out for practice? Would you, Spock?"

Jim looked up at McCoy in mild surprise, then across at his first officer. Spock's eyes widened in carefully simulated concern. "I would think," he said to Jim, "that such a sudden impulse toward masochism would be the symptom of some deeper disorder—"

"Oh, come on, Spock. Just to keep my hand in."

"Doctor," Spock said almost pityingly, having caught Jim's slight nod, "you could hardly keep your hand in the cubic unless you had first *put* it in—and despite our many past differences, I must say I cannot recommend such a course of action."

"I take it that means yes." Bones slipped into Jim's seat as the captain stood, smiling, and got out of it.

"I believe the appropriate phrase is 'Be my guest,' " said Spock, leaning forward to study the cubic with renewed interest.

McCoy settled down and gazed into the cubic too. "All right, where's the damn memory on this—Oh," he said as Harb reached down over his shoulder to touch the retrieval control, bringing up the small shielded "status" hologram with its readouts of locations of timed-out pieces and their schedules for reappearance.

"You understand, Doctor," Spock said politely, glancing up, "that for each piece whose status you now alter, you must forfeit a real-time move."

"Mmmhmm," McCoy said, not looking up. Spock lifted one eyebrow and went back to his own examination of the cubic. Jim exchanged a bemused glance, over McCoy's head, with Harb, then became aware of movement off to the right of him, and glanced that way. The pianist, finished with her Chopin, was making her way toward them. It was Lia Burke, one of the newer additions to McCoy's staff; a whip-slender woman with dark culy hair, a cheerful grin, and the devil in her eyes. "You still here, Commander?" Jim said, bantering, as she joined him and Harb beside McCoy. "You were recalled from leave for that last mission of ours; I thought you were going to go pick up your vacation where you left off. . . ."

She shrugged, a quick amused gesture. "Sir, I thought so too. Problem is, I find that working on the *Enterprise* is more fun than taking a vacation anywhere else." That made Jim grin back at her appreciatively; he felt the same way. She peered over McCoy's shoulder at the cubic. "Looks like there's shortly going to be plenty to do tonight, though. He always gives us more work when he's upset. . . ."

"Lia," McCoy said, delicately touching one cubic-control surface after another and still not looking up, "hush up before I put r-levosulamine in your coffee and give you cerebral hemorrhoids." Lia hushed, though not without a look of tolerant merriment at Jim and Harb. " . . . Spock? Ready for you." McCoy looked across at the Vulcan. "Three moves."

"Very well," Spock said, and touched several controls one after another, taking his three permitted moves in rapid succession. First one of his bishops, then the second, moved out of their positions in the center cubic—not entirely relinquishing control of it, but drawing the noose around Jim's king just a bit tighter; and the third piece, a knight, came in and sat on the one spot on the seventh level that Jim had been praying Spock would overlook. "Check," Spock said calmly, tilting his head just a bit and gazing into the cubic as if to celebrate the lovely knight fork.

Jim groaned softly. Without a word Spock was commenting on what happened to people who set traps for their opponents and then purposely waved the fact in their opponents' faces. "Your move, Doctor," Spock said to Bones, with the same mostly-hidden sympathy he had shown Jim.

McCoy scowled at the control pad, touched one section. One of Jim's few remaining useful pieces, a knight, slipped up from the second level where it had been protecting several pawns on a diagonal from Spock's white-cube bishop. It took the secondary knight option, three levels straight up and one cube over, blocking the check and threatening one of Spock's queens.

"A valiant choice, Doctor," Spock said. "But I would not have expected you to make a move that would so prolong the game's suffering." He reached out a hand to his pad. "The response is obvious, though unfortunately rather crude. Queen to level eight queen's-rook three, resuming the pin and now threatening your knight on the vertical diagonal."

Spock rested his head on his folded hands again. "Your move," he said calmly—

—and all hell broke loose in the cubic. One of Jim's rooks appeared in the cube occupied by Spock's whitecube bishop, sacrificing itself in their mutual annihilation. The other rook appeared in the cube to which Spock's first queen had moved, and took her out too.

Both Spock's eyebrows went straight up. "'Kamikaze' chess, Doctor?" he said, sounding—to Jim's ears—as if he were fighting down astonishment very hard. "Marginally effective. But inelegant—"

"Mr. Spock," Bones said, gazing into the cubic, "generally I prefer to work with protoplasers and light-scalpels. But for some things—knives are still the best."

A pawn timed back in and blew up Spock's second queen, the only piece on the board left in a really threatening position. And two other pawns timed in—one in the unprotected eighth file of Spock's ground level, one in the eighth file of his eighth level—then both sizzled with transporter effect, and with charming simultaneity turned into queens.

Very slowly, Spock reached out and touched a control on his side of the cubic. Black's king fell over onto its side, fizzed briefly bright with transporter effect, and vanished.

Jim and Harb and Lia all stared.

Spock's absolute expressionlessness was more eloquent than any words. McCoy gazed into the cubic, lifted his arms to stretch, and as he did so, said very softly, as if to himself, "So. One whole being . . ." He stood up. "Thank you, Mr. Spock," he said, nodding gravely at the Vulcan. Then McCoy turned away and grinned at Jim, leaning slightly toward him. "You really must stop underestimating yourself," Bones said in Jim's ear. And the chief surgeon straightened, and strolled off toward the rec deck doors, whistling.

The intercom whistled as he went, a note a third higher than McCoy's. *"Bridge to Captain Kirk,"* said Uhura's voice out of the air.

Jim simply looked at Harb Tanzer for a moment before answering. Harb shook his head at Jim and went off across the rec deck to find something to tend to. Lia Burke, staring in astonished delight after McCoy, realized what she was doing, excused herself, and strode off in the doctor's wake. "Yes, Uhura?" Jim said.

*"Sir, we have a dispatch in from Starfleet that needs your command ciphers for decoding. Do you want it in your quarters?"*

"No, that's all right. I'll be up on the bridge in a few minutes."

*"Yes, Captain. Bridge out."*

Jim just looked down at the cubic for a moment, then across at Spock. The Vulcan, somewhat recovered, quirked one eyebrow at his captain. "Jim," Spock said, "perhaps you will wish to make a note of the date and time. I admit to astonishment."

"I admit to a damn sight more," Jim said softly. "Spock, did I miss something?"

The soul of tact as always, Spock hesitated. "Various opportunities— yes. Yet the winner of a game does so no less than the loser. And where one mind may find a way out of a position, another may see no plain way—yet be no worse a player for it. The motivations and patterns within a living mind, the endless diversity of the ways those patterns deal with new occurrences—and one's success at understanding those patterns, or not—those are what make play delightful. Not expertise alone. One of your Terran artists said it: 'There is hope in honest error—none in the icy perfection of the mere stylist.'"

Jim heard the message, and smiled, knowing better than to thank Spock openly for it. "True. But I made enough 'honest errors' in that game to last me a month; and specifically, I never even saw the possibility of McCoy's whole final scenario. I *should* have seen it. Was the table recording? I want to take that endgame apart later, with you looking over my shoulder and pointing out my mistakes."

"Certainly, Captain. The analysis will be beneficial to your play."

Jim nodded. "At this point, I suspect anything would be an improvement." And he smiled again, this time at catching the amused flicker of eyes that said Spock appreciated not having any such statement made about *his* own game. "Come on, Mr. Spock—let's see what miracle Fleet wants us to pull off today."

"The question is," said Uhura, gazing down at the communications station's screen, "what's really going on out there? You don't send such a collection of firepower—along with a destroyer, no less—all out together on a routine patrol. Who does Fleet think it's fooling?"

Those were fair questions, for which Jim had no answer. He shook his head and looked down at the dispatch burning on Uhura's screen. To James T. Kirk, commanding NCC 1701 *Enterprise*, blah, blah, blah . . .

. . . YOU ARE ORDERED TO ABORT PRESENT MISSION (REF: DISPATCH SFCC/T 121440309 DATED SD 0112.0) AND PROCEED WITH ALL DUE HASTE TO GALLONG 177D 48.210M/GALLAT +6D 14.335M/DISTARBGALCORE 24015 L.Y. FOR RENDEZVOUS IN PHI TRIANGULI OUTER PATROL CORRIDOR WITH SHIPS OF TASK FORCE ENUMERATED BELOW. ONCE ASSEMBLED YOU WILL TAKE COMMAND OF THE TASK FORCE AND PROCEED IN GOOD ORDER TO THE SECTOR

DEFINED BY A HUNDRED-PARSEC SPHERICAL RADIUS SURROUNDING ∑285 TRIANGULI/NR 551744, THERE TO PERFORM STANDARD PATROL MANEUVERS OF STRIN-GENCY AND SECURITY LEVELS CONSONANT WITH THE STRATEGIC CLASSIFICATION OF SURROUNDING SPACES. FOR THE DURATION OF THIS OPERATION YOU ARE GRANTED "UNUSUAL BREADTH OF DISCRETION" AS DE-SCRIBED IN STARFLEET REGULATIONS VOL 12444 SECTION 39.0 FF. OPERATION TO CONTINUE UNTIL FURTHER NO-TICE. (SIGNED) WILLSON, K., ADMIRAL, SFC DENEB.

(CC: WALSH, M., CPT, CMDR NCC 1017 CONSTELLATION: RIHAUL, NHS., CPT, CMDR NCC 2003 INAIEU: SUVUK, CPT, CMDR NCC 1631 INTREPID: MALCOR, K., ADMRL, SFC SOL III/TERRA: T'KAIEN, ADMRL, SFC 40 ERI IV/VULCAN)

Uhura frowned down at the dispatch, then glanced up at Kirk, look-ing wry. "It reveals a lot more by what it doesn't say than by what it does, Captain. I haven't seen such a roundabout way of referring to the Neutral Zone in years. Do you suppose Fleet's afraid someone's cracked our command ciphers?"

"Maybe. Though that's supposed to be impossible. . . ." Jim looked up from the message. "But you're quite right, Uhura. There's not so much as a hint about whatever's going on out there."

"Romulan trouble, certainly," Uhura said. "And what exactly is 'un-usual breadth of discretion' supposed to mean?"

Spock glanced up at the bridge ceiling, a resigned gesture, and for a Vulcan, an exasperated one. Jim shook his head. "It doesn't mean any-thing *exactly*," he said, "and that's the problem. The section is a catchall reg for use in unstable situations. It means that if I need to go into this situation and break one or more directives, and if by doing so I keep the situation from blowing up, and Fleet likes the way I handled things, they'll probably give me a medal. It also means that if they *don't* like the way I handle the situation, they'll probably court-martial me . . . whether I solve the problem or not."

Uhura sighed. "Thus saving their own precious reputations, as usual."

"Yes," Spock said. "And thereby indicating that there is something afoot from which the higher echelons of Fleet feel their reputations must be saved. The situation must be grave indeed."

"Speculating without data, Spock?" Jim said. "That's a surprise."

Spock made the gentle you-must-be-joking expression that Jim knew so well. "Sir, I am the *Enterprise*'s science officer. And politics is a science . . . no matter how clumsy, crude, and emotion-riddled a science I may find it. There is not much data, but enough to indicate this at least—that there is trouble of some kind occurring, or about to occur, in the Neutral Zone."

"And that Starfleet wants its resident experts in things Romulan on the scene to deal with the problem," Uhura said. "Meaning the *Enterprise* . . . and you two."

Jim made a face. Having officers so sharp made for pleasant work much of the time, but it also meant that unpleasant truths came right out into the open. "Unfortunately, I have to agree with you both. But— that business aside—Spock, I can't help being annoyed that, just as you're starting to get some results, we have to break off our researches here, without even the courtesy of being given a good reason why, and go warping off on some fleet maneuver two thousand light-years away. . . ."

"One thousand nine hundred sixty-eight point four five light-years," Spock said. "Eight point three three days at warp eight."

"Right. Dammit, just for once I'd like to start a mission, and take it right through to the end, and then stop, without being called away to do something else. . . ."

"It is true," the Vulcan said soberly, looking down at the dispatch, "that the data were finally beginning to correlate. But I am sure they will continue to do so in our absence."

"Certainly . . . if some other ship continues the research. Heaven only knows if Fleet will bother to assign another. And besides, if what you've found so far is any indication, this isn't just some dull little research that can be dropped and then come back to. If the stellar ecology in this part of space is really changing, the effects will be much more far-reaching than we even suspect now. *This* is the time to do something about it— not a month or a year from now, when it might be too late."

Spock looked at Jim with an expression of ironic resignation. "Sir, we are entirely in agreement. But Starfleet, as we have noticed many times before, has its own priorities. And we have our duty."

"Yes. I just wish their priorities and ours coincided more often. However, entropy is running, and things are the way they are. . . ." Jim tapped a finger on Uhura's console, thinking. "Well. Uhura, have the computer pull out the last several months' Fleet dispatches and abstract everything that might be relevant to this business: intelligence reports, logs from ships on Neutral Zone patrol, what have you. Routine and classified information, both. Send it all through to my terminal and I'll look at it before I go to bed."

"Those data have been in your computer for the last twenty minutes," said Uhura with a slow, mischievous grin, "and since you gave me your command ciphers, the classified materials have been there for about five."

Jim smiled down at her. "Uhura, are you bucking for a raise?"

The smile she gave him back was amused, but weary. "Captain, gamma shift on this run has not exactly been Wrigley's Pleasure Planet, if you catch my drift. I've been over my board from translator circuits to logic solids about a hundred times, out of sheer boredom." She stretched a bit, cracking her knuckles. "Not a bad thing, actually; I've stuffed this station's comm circuitry so full of neoduotronic upgrades that the main board can probably hear other ships *think*. But having something else to do is a delight. Which reminds me—" She turned back to the board. "Here's something that came in just before that dispatch did. It should be done transcribing now." She reached out to one of the comm board's recording slots, pulled a slim cassette out of it, and handed the cassette to Spock.

"Mail?" Jim said.

Spock turned the cassette over, reading the labelstrip that burned bright at his touch, then faded slowly. "Not precisely, Captain. This ap-

pears to be some additional data I requested from the Federation Interstellar Commercial Transport Authority—a master list of all ship losses
in known space over the past several years. It should be most helpful in
ascertaining whether some trends I have been detecting in the data
we've previously amassed are in fact real trends, or statistical artifact."

The Vulcan was already moving to sit down at the library computer,
his eyes alive with that old familiar look of interest. *There goes the endgame
analysis for tonight,* Jim thought with amused regret. *Oh well* . . . "Very
well, Mr. Spock. Let me know how it works out. In the meantime,
Uhura, have your computer give the rendezvous coordinates to the
helm. Mr. Chekov, get a move on and plot us a course. We're not getting any closer to phi Trianguli just sitting here. . . ."

"Begging the captain's pardon," said Chekov, straight-faced, as he
touched various controls on the helm and passed Uhura's coordinates
on to the navigations computer for a course. "But both local starstream-
ing and galactic rotation are carrying us roughly toward the phi Trianguli patrol corridor at a velocity of some eighteen kilometers per
second. . . ."

Greatly amused, Jim looked from Chekov over to Spock. "Mr.
Spock," Jim said with mock severity, "you are corrupting this man."

"Indeed not, sir," said Spock, glancing up from his science station
and speaking as innocently as Checkov had. "I have merely been encouraging Mr. Chekov's already promising tendency toward logic. A
characteristic, might I mention, that is entirely too rare in Terrans . . ."

"Yes, Mr. Spock," Kirk said, unable to resist. "So I noticed earlier this
evening. . . ."

All over the bridge, faces turned away in every possible direction,
and hands covered mouths, to spare Spock the sight of much smiling.
Jim took no official notice of this, while once more noticing the truth
of the old saying that the only thing faster than light in otherspace was
starship gossip. Spock merely gazed across the bridge at Jim, one more
look of tolerant acceptance in a series of thousands. Very quietly,
Chekov said, "Course plotted and laid in, sir."

"Very good, Mr. Chekov. Get us going—warp eight: Fleet seems to be in a hurry. Uhura, if you would be so kind, log me off the bridge. Thank you for a pleasant game, Mr. Spock, and a good night to you. Good night, everyone."

"Sir," Spock said, and various " 'Night, sir's" and "Good night, Captain's" came from about the bridge as Jim stepped into the lift wall and let out a tremendous yawn.

*"Please repeat,"* the lift's computer said sweetly. *"That did not make sense."*

Jim laughed. "Oh, yes, it did! Deck five." He yawned again, thinking for the moment less about the vagaries of Fleet than about his bed.

Much later in the evening he was still yawning, but the thoughts behind the yawns were very different. Jim sat as he had been sitting for nearly an hour now, with the twelfth page of Uhura's report burning on the screen in front of him. An annoying document, this; like the dispatch from Starfleet, what it did say was less revealing than what it didn't.

The first part of it concerned civilian and military shipping, and was utterly unilluminating. Fleet ship movements in the sectors bounding the Neutral Zone, and in the sectors farther away, were routine and undisturbed. And business was progressing as usual in the Neutral Zone, as far as long-range sensors based in the Zone inspection stations could tell. . . .

Those few agents whom the Federation had managed to insinuate into the Empire knew that their chief value lay in staying alive and unnoticed; so they dared do nothing that would attract attention to themselves—such as pry too closely into areas of real interest, including the seats of government and the counsels of the great. As a result, their reports tended to be brief and scanty of detail. But in the reports for the last three months, Jim found more than enough to interest him.

He had long been fascinated by the "modifed tri-cameral" or threehouse legislative-executive branch of this Emperorless Empire. The Tricameron was comprised of a "Senate"—evenly divided against itself into a half that proposed and passed legislation, and a half that vetoed it—and a "Praetorate," a sort of quadruple troika or duodecimvirate: twelve men and women who implemented the Senate's decrees, declared war or peace, and (it seemed to Jim) spent most of the time squabbling amongst themselves for power. That was partially due to the nature of their office, since a Praetor could be "made," by election or manipulation of influence. But a Senator could only be born—the senatorial office was hereditary, passed from father or mother to eldest sister's-son or -daughter: and the only thing that could remove a Senator from office was death.

That was what interested Jim right now. For over the past few months, it seemed several Senators had lost their posts in just that fashion. Considered by itself, this fact was unremarkable. Often enough, some Senator or Praetor would antagonize another one possessing more influential alliances, and pay the price by being publicly executed, or ordered to commit suicide, by a majority of the Twelve. But four different senators, from both the proposing and vetoing sides of the Noble House, had died recently . . . of what were reported as natural causes.

Jim sat there thinking that an inability to live after being poisoned was natural enough. Yet at the same time he was disturbed, for as he understood it, assassination was not the Romulan style. It was supposed to be disdained as a dishonorable act, a sign of barbarity and weakness in the person who hired the assassin: the type of "irresponsible" behavior that made the Romulans despise the Klingons. One more thing that made no sense.

*Irrational. Illogical. And the Romulans are still culturally close enough to their parent Vulcan race not to have given up logic entirely. . . .*

*Four deaths are hardly enough to allow me to deduce logically that all hell is about to break loose over there. But the Romulans are so . . . so consistent . . . that the irrationality seems huge.*

*Damn Fleet! They won't give me even a hint of what's going on. Postulating worst case . . . always a wise course of action, where Starfleet's concerned . . . how am I supposed to prevent a war, or at worst win one, if they won't tell me how they expect it to start?*

*Unless . . .* Unless what? Some piece of information hand-carried to Fleet, not yet disseminated? Some highest-level intelligence too sensitive to declassify or openly transmit? What could be that sensitive?

*Or . . . unless they don't know what's going on either . . . and want us to find out* . . . Jim breathed out, thinking of old stories of how the great cats were once hunted on Earth; with "beaters" who would run into the brush where the tigers were hiding. There the beaters would hoot and shout and hit around them with sticks, banging on pots or on shields, so that the noise would panic the tigers and make them break cover, revealing themselves. Or else make the tigers, in understandable annoyance, attack the beaters. *And there we'll be, three starships and a destroyer, parading up and down outside the borders of the Neutral Zone, shouting and beating on pots. . . .*

The sudden, bizarre image of Spock banging with straight-faced efficiency on a saucepan abruptly made Jim realize how very late it must be getting. He leaned forward, elbows on the desk, and rubbed his eyes—then rested his chin against his folded hands and stared once more at the screen. Page twelve of the report stared back at him, burning there golden and still. Jim had read Uhura's careful compendium backward and forward several times now, but page twelve kept pulling him back. On page twelve were listed the Romulan vessels patrolling the far side of the Neutral Zone, and their schedules. The ships were maintaining those schedules to the minute, as usual. Jim would have been very surprised indeed if they hadn't; Romulans were always punctual as clockwork, in peace as in war. And there on the list were the old familiar names—*Courser, Arien, Javelin, Rea's Helm, Cuirass, Eisn, Wildfire. Enterprise* and her crew knew those names well from many brushes in the Neutral Zone, many skirmishes, many long dull patrols spent pacing one another on either side of the line. Jim leaned slowly forward, propping his chin on one fist, and stared at the screen.

The usual names . . . in the usual places.

All the names but one.

*Where the hell is* Bloodwing?

Unnoticed by its owner, the fist clenched.

# Chapter Three

*"Khre'Riov?"*

Ael stretched in her center-chair in the bridge, and turned her head just enough to show she was paying attention to Centurion t'Liun, without actually having to look at her. *"Ie?"*

*"Nniehv idh ra iy'tassiudh nnearh."*

*What you mean, of course, is that my gig is allowed to be "ready" because your security people have checked it and failed to find anything that would confirm your suspicions of me. Fool! Do you think you're dealing with someone who works on your level?* Aloud, all Ael said was *"Khnai'ra rhissiuy, Enarrain";* and if the thanks was rather warmly phrased, so much the better. It would confuse t'Liun into a standstill.

Ael got up from her hard seat and headed for the lift, and sure enough, t'Liun was standing there at her post when she could have been sitting, and gazing at Ael with what t'Liun doubtless thought was perfectly faked respect. *How I detest you!* Ael thought as she went past the narrow, dark, cold-faced little woman. *You would sell your sisters'-sons and -daughters to Orion slavers for a quarter-chain of cash if the deed would buy you power. No matter, though; you and yours will be rid of me soon enough.* Ael stepped into the lift. *"Ri'laefv'htaiell, Enarrain,"* she said, and waved the lift doors shut.

T'Liun headed down toward the center seat as ordered, but rather hurriedly. That was the last thing Ael saw as the doors closed on her; and it made her laugh. *How she wishes I would leave her that seat forever!* And she laughed softly about it all the way down to engineering, where her gig was kept.

It was a pretty little ship—a one-man scout, actually, very sleek and lean, with a high-absorption black coating and warpdrive capacity. It was many years newer than *Cuirass* or any of her sorry equipment; and this was because it was Ael's own, brought with her from *Bloodwing*—the one thing she had insisted on taking. Privately she called it *Hsaaja,* after the first *fvai* she had demanded to ride as a child—a cranky, delicate, annoyed and annoying beast that was eternally hungry. This *Hsaaja,* like the first, was a glutton where fuel consumption was involved. But also like the first, nothing of his size could match him for speed . . . and neither could some larger craft: *Cuirass,* for example. *Hsaaja*'s presence made t'Liun acutely nervous. That suited Ael very well.

The ship stood with his forward cockpit open. She went up the ladder, settled and sealed herself in, then called the upper engineering deck and told tr'Akeidhad to go ahead and exhaust the smaller, lower deck where *Hsaaja* stood. His instrumentation came on and the power came up at the sound of her voice; air hissed out of the deck, the sound of the pumps becoming inaudible. The doors rolled away, and the lights went down, leaving Ael in starlight and the flashes of the landing beacons set in the floor. She took *Hsaaja* out on chemical jets, and once well clear of the ship, cut in the ion-drivers and headed for her fleet.

They were all at the prescribed distance for fleet maneuvers, about a hundredth of a light-second from each other and from *Cuirass*—well out of visual range. Ael considered kicking in just a touch of warpdrive, then decided against it. Not from any concern about panicking t'Liun, who was certainly monitoring her course—that would in fact have been a minor pleasure. But she saw too little of realspace these days; and the otherspace in which ships moved while in warp was a wavering, uneasy vista, not pleasant to look at at all. She sat back, handling the controls at her leisure, and took her own good time.

*Hsaaja*'s computer already was displaying the three new ships' ID signals—strings of numbers and the code for their class type. Klingon ships, all right. *I do wish Command would stop buying those flying middens,* Ael thought. But then Command couldn't, as Ael well knew. The Rihannsu had entered into a trade agreement with the Klingons: an agreement that was nothing but a fair scabbard over a sharp sword—the threat of war if the Rihannsu should fail to buy a certain number of ships every year. It was the old story, the old saying: "Buy a murderer once and you will get lifetime service." And the Klingons, with their present economic problems, would like nothing better than the excuse of a broken treaty to justify raiding the Rihannsu outworlds. So ch'Rihan fulfilled its half of the agreement, more out of fear than integrity. And the Fleet was now about half a collection of poor old warbirds falling into ill repair, because spare parts for them were no longer being made, and half Klingon ships which could be repaired—with spare parts sold at extortionate prices—but which immediately malfunctioned again anyway.

*Planned obsolescence,* Ael thought bitterly, as her ship coasted closer to the nearest of her fleet. *Or maybe it's true what they say, that the Klingon government contracts for its ships to be built by the lowest bidder. . . .*

Still, her curiosity got the better of her. She tapped her console for more information from the ID signals. Names came up along with the numbers: *Arakkab, Kenek, Ykir.* Ael stared at her datascreen; but there the names hung in black and blue, with no alternate Rihannsu naming, no extra information. *Klingon names?* she thought, in some bemusement. *Maybe they simply haven't had time to assign them decent names yet?* But that seemed ridiculous. No Rihannsu ship was allowed into service without being properly named; it would be terribly unlucky, not to mention an insult to the Elements and to the ship itself—one that the ship would surely avenge on its crew at some point.

Ael's unease did not show on her face: it never did. But it was down in her stomach already, clenching there like a fist. On an uncomfortable hunch she told her ship's computer to scan behind her, read the ID of the ship she had just left.

KL *Ehhak,* said her datascreen.

And it was all suddenly and horribly plain. Ael did not need to go any nearer to the other ships, though she did, for completeness' sake and to prevent anyone from becoming suspicious. She found, on final approach to the first ship, exactly what she knew she would: a brand new *K'tinga*-class warship, with Klingon markings on the exterior. Before she had even set foot out of *Hsaaja* onto its hangar deck, she knew exactly what was going to happen to her and this fleet in the next few weeks. She was going to be ordered to lead them across the Neutral Zone and into Federation space, there to start a "Klingon" war with the

Federation. She and her fleet would, of course, not survive the experience; she would be permanently out of the Senate's way. And while the Klingons and the Federation were busy blowing one another to plasma, for months—years it might be—the Rihannsu would be off doing other things.

*What?* Ael thought, while the obsequious, annoying commander of *"Arakkab"* welcomed her and escorted her around his ship; while her body did all the proper things, smiled, or laughed in a reassuring fashion at nervous jokes, or made appreciative remarks about new (and ill-made) equipment. *What will they do? Raid both sides, most likely. Do something about our sorry economy in the most direct and dishonorable way possible. Pillage those worlds where the war has passed, scavenge about behind Klingons and Federation like a* sseikea *skulking behind a* thrai, *picking up scraps. They will take advantage of the disorganization and mistrust of such times, use them to expand, to enlarge the Empire at the cost of both sets of enemies. And when one of the great powers has reduced the second to slavery or powerlessness, then the new voices in the Senate will cry out for war.* "Hit the winner now, while he is weak," *they'll say. More war, more death. Perhaps even victory—but, O, dishonorable, vile—*

The tension of the fist clenching her insides got no less as time went on, as she beamed over to *Ykir* with some of the officers from *Arakkab*, and was greeted in turn by another commander, whose thick-featured face she later thought of with grim pleasure—for these people and these ships deserved one another. *O Fire above us and Earth below,* she thought. *Convicts, failures, the castoffs of Command. No doubt very proud of being given new ships, and a mission. How far will that get them?* For *Intrepid* was out there waiting, along with *Constellation,* and worse still, the destroyer *Inaieu;* and worst of them all, *Enterprise.* Even with *Bloodwing,* with a crew both skilled and utterly loyal to her, she had survived her encounters with *Enterprise* with the greatest difficulty. And some of her own relatives had not been so lucky. What would happen to *this* poor lot?—newly assigned, from the look of them, and incompetents all, in ships falsely named? And what would happen to *her,* for that matter—in a ship full of paid help, already busy with treachery to her, a ship itself wearing an alias? Not all her skill could save her from a ship whose name had been taken from it. There was no tampering with names.

She went right through *Ykir*, and then through *Kenek*, extrapolating at furious speed, while the bland or confused or malicious faces around her never noticed a thing. *Forget staying on* Cuirass *and surviving,* she thought. *And even if I should—what then? Capture by* Enterprise *or one of the other ships. Processing, and release—back to the Empire. A shameful death, and a protracted one, while the Senate laughs. No indeed; I shall die before it comes to that.*

*Yet my young friends would like that, would they not? They think they have me netted. Honorable suicide would suit them nicely. My death in battle would suit them too, or my execution in disgrace back home. Perhaps they even think I might suicide rather than carry out my dishonorable orders to cross the border in the first place. Surely the question of honor would come up—should I receive those orders.* And Ael smiled just once at a moment she did not need to, while looking up some ugly conduit full of circuitry in *Kenek*'s engine room. She silently blessed the bureaucracy, just this once, for getting her orders stuck in itself. She resolved that when she got back to *Cuirass,* she would help those orders stay stuck for a while.

"*Hra'vae?*" she said in apparent wonderment, while some under-officer explained to her (inaccurately) some detail about the marvelous new Klingon gunnery conduits. She was thinking of *Bloodwing*'s new equipment, and her anger was turning humorous—her most dangerous mood, as Ael knew well. She made no attempt to abate it. She would need to be dangerous for the next few days. *Treachery,* she thought. *I cannot abide treachery. As they shall come to know. . . .*

Eventually the tour was done. Ael beamed back to *Arakkab,* and bade its commander a very cheerful farewell—strongly intending that the two of them should not meet again until they had both passed out of this place where the Elements were physical. She got back into *Hsaaja* and took off for *Cuirass* again, noting as she approached how very worn the bird-of-prey shadows along its underbelly were, in what bad shape the ship appeared to be. At one time, this would have scandalized her. Now she did not worry. It would shortly be none of her concern.

One thing she did, before she came about where *Cuirass* could scan her. In the shadow of *Kenek*'s deflector screens, up at minimal power, she hit a control in *Hsaaja,* and felt the slight bound of the ship as explosive bolts knocked something out of a concealed hatch. She could not see the object—it was covered with the same nondetectable coating as *Hsaaja* was—but her datascreen came alive as it went, reading out the readiness of the little probe's engines, the status of its tiny computer. In an hour or so it would have maneuvered its way around behind *Kenek* on shielded impulse drive. In the nightwatch of the four ships, it would burn out its little primary pod in a single one-second warp eight burst. Tafv would find it, and its message, before the ship's night was over.

Then it would all begin.

Ael went back to *Cuirass* to get ready.

# Chapter Four

The space around sigma-285 Trianguli was, to put it baldly, dull. Not one of the stars in the area had a name; and hardly any of them seemed worth naming anyway. They were, generally speaking, a weary association of cooling red dwarfs—little Jupiter-sized stars of types N and R, and here and there a sputtering S-type "carbon" star with water-vapor in its atmosphere. ("Running out of steam," Uhura remarked, looking over Spock's shoulder at the data-breakdown on one of them.) Some of the stars had planets, but those were dull too—bare rocks, where life might have been, millennia ago, but certainly wasn't now. There was nothing on those worlds that anyone wanted. Which was just as well; right next door to the border with the Neutral Zone would have been an uncomfortable place to live.

It was dark space to fly in—a bad place for seeing who was getting close to you, but a good spot for a quiet rendezvous with people whose looks you already knew. So *Enterprise* found it when she came out of warp and coasted down into 285's feeble little gravity well, settling into a long elliptical orbit around the star. Other shapes, barely illuminated, broke their orbits and gathered slowly in around her. Two of them kept to the usual five-kilometer traffic limit: *Constellation* and *Intrepid,* ships of *Enterprise*'s own class. The third ship held itself ten kilometers away, but for all the extra distance, it looked the same size as *Intrepid* and *Constellation* did. This was even more of an illusion than the dim space alone could have caused, for the third ship was *Inaieu.*

*Inaieu,* as one of the destroyer-class starships, had been built large; built to carry a lot of people on very long hauls, and built to carry more power and more armament than any three starships—just in case. Her upper-hull disk was three times the size of *Enterprise*'s; her engine nacelles twice as long, and there were four of them—one above, two on the sides, one below. Her central engineering hull was a quarter-mile in diameter, and a mile long. Having been built at the Starfleet shipyards at Deneb, she flew under Denebian registry, and had been named for the old High King of Deneb V who, as the song said, "rose up and smote her enemies." Jim watched her now on the bridge screen— massive, menacing and graceful, a great, glowing, blood-red shape in 285's simmering light—and felt glad to have her along on this business, in case some heavy-duty smiting should be necessary.

"How long, Mr. Spock?" he said.

Spock glanced up from his station. "The meeting is not scheduled to begin for another twenty-five point six minutes, sir. Captain Rihaul is obviously already aboard *Inaieu;* Captain Walsh is in transit via shuttle-craft; Captain Suvuk has not yet beamed over."

McCoy, standing behind the helm and watching everything as usual, looked surprised. "Shuttlecraft? Why doesn't Captain Walsh just beam over like everybody else?"

Jim looked with wry amusement at McCoy. "That's right, you don't know Mike Walsh, do you? You two are going to get along just fine. Mike hates the transporter. Remind him to tell you about the time on Earth when he was heading for the Sydney Opera House and wound up instead in Baltimore Harbor. Or on second thought, don't remind him. He'll tell you anyway."

McCoy humphed. "Two sensible men in this crazy Fleet, anyway— Jim, do I have to go to this silliness? This is supposedly a strategy and tactics meeting. Why should I scramble up my stomach and my brain-waves in that thing to sit and listen to—"

"Sorry, Bones. All the section chiefs have to be there. Regulations."

"—bloody battle plans on one side and a whole horde of overlogical Vulcans on the other—"

Jim started to laugh. "Oh, Bones! The truth will out, I see. . . ."

"Indeed," Spock said, without looking up from his work. "The thought of a whole starship full of Vulcans, all doing perfectly well without one single human to leaven the deadly weight of their logic, in-tellection and sobriety, obviously has shocked the good doctor into the unwelcome thought that he might possibly not be necessary—"

"Careful, Spock," McCoy grumbled. "You're up for a physical in a couple weeks. . . ."

Spock merely raised an amused eyebrow at McCoy, letting the expression say what he thought of such a déclassé retort. Jim sat back, looking past *Inaieu* on the screen to where *Intrepid* hung, glowing like a coal. It was several years now since the first *Intrepid* had run afoul of the spacegoing amoebalike creature that *Enterprise,* with a lot of help from Spock, had managed to destroy. The Vulcans had naturally gone into the expected restrained mourning for their many dead; but the monument that they found most fitting was another Vulcan starship.

She was built along the usual heavy-cruiser design, but with details of construction so much improved that Fleet had decided to use the Vulcans' design, later, to refit all the heavy cruisers. Years ago, Jim had looked at the plans and pictures of *Intrepid,* and had found the design surprisingly pleasant—not only more logical than the original starship design, but very often more pleasant to look at, and sometimes downright beautiful. McCoy had looked over the plans mostly in silence, only commenting at the end of his perusal that the Vulcans had at least made the bathrooms larger. But Jim had noticed that all through, McCoy had been making the "hmp" noises that meant he approved even if he didn't want to admit it. At any rate, there hung *Intrepid* herself, and whether it was logical or not, Jim was glad to see her. Her captain, Suvuk, was a briefly retired admiral whom Jim was looking forward to meeting—a veteran of decades of cruises, and the kind of man Terrans would call a hero, though the Vulcans insisted that he was just doing his job.

"Pretty ship," he said. "Look how they've trimmed her nacelles down. . . . Spock, did they sacrifice any power for the weight they dropped there?"

"They improved power generation fifty-three percent before they made the alteration," Spock said; "so those engines run at a hundred thirty-three percent of the best level the *Enterprise* could manage. I fear Mr. Scott is probably deep in that ugliest of emotions, envy. . . ."

McCoy groaned softly. "Can we get on with this?" he said under his breath. "I've got a sickbay to tend to."

"Momentarily, Doctor," Spock said. "I am waiting for a final piece of data for this research of mine. While we are off on *Inaieu*, the computer will process it and provide us with a solution—"

"That ion-storm business?"

"Affirmative."

The bridge doors hissed open, and Ensign Naraht shuffled in with a sound like someone dragging concrete blocks over the carpet. Jim smiled. He always smiled when he saw Naraht; he couldn't help it.

Naraht was one of the thirty thousand children born of the last hatching of the Horta, that now-famous silicon-based creature native to Janus VI. The *Enterprise,* early in her five-year mission, had been called to Janus VI to exterminate a "monster," and instead had wound up first injuring, then saving, the single surviving Horta who was about to become the "mother" of her whole eggbound race. Once out of the egg, the hatchlings grew with the usual speed; they were tunneling rock within minutes of their birth, and all the thirty thousand who hatched reached latency, and high intelligence, within standard days.

Any race so strange, and yet so adaptable to "bizarre" creatures like hominids, was naturally of immediate interest to the Federated Worlds. And the Hortas—curious creatures that they were—returned the interest with interest. Nothing could have kept them out of the Federation; and as for the political formalities, a creature used to moving easily through solid rock will be only slightly slowed down by red tape. It took no more (and in some cases much less) than the four years in which a Starfleet Academy class graduates for Hortas to start appearing on starships.

Naraht had come to the *Enterprise* highly qualified, with an Academy standing in the top tenth of his class. ("He" was an approximation; his official Fleet "arbitrary gender designation" was "orthomale type B-4A," which McCoy usually described as "close enough for jazz.") The Horta had chosen to specialize in biomaths, that peculiar science claimed by both psychiatry and interactional mesophysics. This put him, at least nominally, in McCoy's department. But engineering and analytical chemistry both wanted to get their hands, fins or tentacles on him; not surprising, since Hortas eat rock, deriving both nutrition and flavor from the metallic elements and silicates found in it. Naraht could take a bite of any metal or mineral you pleased, and seconds later give you a readout of its constituent elements, with the expert precision of a gourmet reporting on the ingredients and balance of a wine sauce.

Jim had watched the intradepartmental squabbling over Naraht with amusement, and hadn't allowed himself to be swayed by it; the *Enterprise* was made for the entities who rode in her, not the other way around. He left Naraht happy in biomaths, and simply kept an eye on his progress. Meantime, Spock apparently found it illogical to waste his talents, and had been calling him up to the bridge for consultations now and then. Jim didn't mind this at all; he had long since confessed to himself that he never got tired of being earnestly "Yes, Captain"ed by someone who looked like a giant pan pizza (sausage, extra cheese).

"I have the data you wanted on the meteoric debris, sir," Naraht said to Spock, drawing himself up to his full height in an approximation of "attention." Behind him, Jim heard McCoy most carefully preventing his own laughter; Naraht was basically a horizontal creature, and his "full height" was about half a meter at best.

"Report, Mr. Naraht," Spock said, beginning to key data into his library computer.

"Yes, sir. In order of greatest concentration—iron-55 forty-five point eight zero percent, nickel-58 twelve point six one percent, lead-82 nine point eight eight percent, mercury-201 nine point four six percent, gallium-69 nine point three zero percent, gold-198 eight point one one percent, samarium-151 three point one zero percent, rhodium-101 one point two three percent, palladium-106 zero point two zero percent, iridium-193 zero point three zero, and trace amounts of neodymium, yttrium, strontium and tantalum making up zero point zero one percent."

Spock was staring at his station with great interest. "Mr. Naraht," he said, "are you quite certain of that figure for the iridium?"

"To six decimal places, sir! Zero point three zero four one four one two two."

"That is *eight* decimal places, Ensign," Spock said; but he said it so mildly that McCoy looked at him very oddly indeed.

"Oh," Naraht said. "I'm sorry, sir! I thought you might like some more."

"'Liking' is one of the humanities' emotions to which Vulcans are not generally prone," Spock said, in that same mild voice. Jim held his own smile out of sight, particularly noticing that Spock hadn't said at all that *he* might not occasionally like something. "Nevertheless I am inclined to overlook the error—just this once."

McCoy looked down at Jim, who had swiveled his chair around to look at the screen—and to have something to do besides laugh. Bones's look said, very plainly, *Is it just me, or is Spock teasing that boy!* Jim shrugged and took Bones's clipboard away from him, pretending to study it while the lecture went on behind him. "Enthusiasm about science is to be commended," Spock was saying, "but enthusiasm *in* science is to be avoided at all costs; it biases the judgment and may blind one to valuable observations. Guard against it."

"I'll remember, sir," said Naraht. "Will there be anything else?"

"Not at the moment, Ensign. You may go."

Naraht went shuffling off toward the bridge doors.

"Mr. Naraht," Spock said, just as Jim thought it might be safe to turn around again. Behind him he heard Naraht pause.

"Sir?"

"That was well done, Mr. Naraht. Keep working and we will make a scientist of you yet."

"Sir!"

"You are dismissed."

Off went Naraht, rumbling and shuffling, into the lift. Spock went back to his work at his station, ignoring Uhura's quizzical look at him, as well as Jim's and McCoy's. Bones couldn't stand it. "Mr. Spock," he said, deadpan, and somehow sounding only slightly interested, "did I hear you compliment that lad?"

Spock was still touching pads and switches on his library computer, so that he didn't look up. "I accurately assessed his performance, Doctor. Feedback is most important for continuation of optimum performance, as even you must know."

"I take it then," Jim said, equally nonchalant, "that you find his performance generally satisfactory?"

"Oh, quite satisfactory, Captain. In fact, he exhibits many of the most positive traits of a young member of *your* branch of humanity—being by turns, or all at once, cheerful, conscientious, obedient almost to a fault, courteous, enthusiastic, respectful of superiors—"

"And he's probably thrifty, brave, clean and reverent, too," McCoy said. "In other words, Mr. Spock, we've got a genuine 'space cadet' on our hands."

"Bless 'em all," Jim said. "Where would Fleet be without them?"

"But the point is, Jim, that Spock approves of him! Can I stand the strain!"

"Doubtful," Spock said with a sigh, turning away from his work. "Doctor, Mr. Naraht has an eminently logical mind—unsurprising: so did his mother. If his emotional tendencies—"

"Aha! The truth *will* out!" McCoy said jubilantly. "That's it! You like that boy because you knew his mother the Horta—*and she liked your ears!*"

Spock simply looked at McCoy. Jim started to whoop with laughter. Unfortunately, Uhura's board chose that moment to let out one of its more strident whistles. She put her transdator back in her ear, looked off into space for a moment, then said, "Captain, it's *Inaieu*. They're ready for you."

Jim got up out of the helm, still shaking with laughter. "Tell them we're on our way. Gentlemen, the defense against the charge of nepotism-by-association will have to wait till this is over with. Uhura, call the transporter room."

"No shuttlecraft?" McCoy said, a little sorrowfully.

"Sorry, Bones, we're late."

"One of these days," McCoy growled as the three of them stepped into the lift, "that damn transporter'll glitch, and we really *will* be."

*Inaieu* was if possible even huger than it looked. Jim at first wondered if some slippage in protocol, or confusion on the part of his own transporter chief, had sent him to the cargo transporters instead of the one for staff and crew; for the room they beamed into seemed almost the size of a small hangar deck. But the Eyrene transporter officer on this side reminded Jim forcibly that not only ships, but people, came in rather different sizes.

Deneb was a large star with more than one planet. The Klaha, the first Denebian race that Fleet had made contact with, lived on Deneb V; it was that species which Federation nomenclature meant when it referred to "Denebians." But the peoples of the other worlds, the Eyren and the !'hew and the Deirr, were Denebians too—not simply because of sharing a star. The worlds of this huge blue primary were all big, and dense, and had heavy gravity, for which their various versions of the humanities were equipped. So the *Inaieu* had been built to accommodate the primarily "Denebian" crew who would be handling her—such as the Eyrene transporter officer. She was typical of her people, looking very much like an eight-legged, circular-bodied elephant with no head and four trunks—a squat, golden-skinned, powerful person, and one (with her six-foot diameter) rather too large for any merely hominid-sized transporter platform.

When they were all materialized she came out from behind her console and bowed by way of respectful greeting—a Denebian bow, more of a deep knee bend. "Captain, gentlemen," she said, "you're expected in main briefing. Will you follow me, please?"

"Certainly, Lieutenant," Jim said, noting the stripes on one of the four sleeves; noting also, with mild amusement, that all there was to the uniform was those sleeves. The Lieutenant led the way out into the hall, moving very quickly and lightly—and understandably so; the common areas of the ship were apparently kept at light gravity for the convenience of a multispecies crew. "Hi-grav personal quarters?" Jim said to McCoy.

"So I hear. They had to do quite a bit of juggling with the power-consumption curves to make it work out. But this ship's got power to burn."

"That's no joke, lad," Scotty said, peering in an opening door as they went past one of *Inaieu*'s six engine rooms. "That one warp-drive assembly in there is by itself half again the size of the *Enterprise*'s."

Jim glanced at Scotty, who was now nearly walking backward, and looking hungrily back the way they'd come. "Later, Scotty," he said. "I think we can spare you time for a tour. We have to do a routine exchange of ships' libraries anyway; you might as well stop in to see the chief engineer and exchange pleasantries."

"And equations," McCoy said.

Scotty smiled, looking slightly sheepish, as the group entered a turbo-lift about the size of a shuttlecraft, and their Eyrene escort said, "Deck eighteen. Low-grav." The lift went off sideways, then up, at a sedate enough pace; but even so Jim had to smile to himself. All the Denebian races, it seemed, love the high accelerations and speeds they were so well built to handle; and the thought of the speeds the lifts in this ship probably did when there were only Denebians aboard them made Jim shudder slightly. But that was part of their mindset, too; no Denebian would ever walk anywhere it could run, or do warp three if it could make warp eight. Life was too interesting, they said, to take it slowly; and certainly too short—if you have only six hundred years, you must make the most of them! So they plunged around through space, putting their noses (those of them who had noses) into everything, and thoroughly enjoying themselves; the galaxy's biggest, merriest overachievers, and a definite asset to the Federation. Jim was very fond of them.

"Here we are. This way, gentlemen," said the Eyrene lieutenant, and hurried out of the lift. The four of them went out after her, hurrying only slightly, and were relieved to see her turn leftward and gesture toward an open door. "Main briefing, gentlemen."

"My thanks, Lieutenant," Jim said, and led his officers in.

Main briefing, as he suspected, was about the size of a tennis court. The table was of that very sensible design that the Denebian races used when dealing with other species; a large round empty space in the middle, where Klaha and Eyren and !'hew would stand—they never sat— and chairs or racks scattered around the outside of the table for hominids, along with bowl chairs for the Deirr. This way everyone, whether they had hominid stereoscopic vision or multiple eyes or heat sensors, could see everyone else; and of course everyone was wearing intradermal translators, so that understanding was no problem. At least, no more so than usual . . .

The company seated at that table rose, or bowed, to greet Jim and his party as they entered. One of them got up out of her bowl chair with the sucking sound that Jim remembered so well; and he started to grin. "Nhauris," he said, holding out his hands, "you haven't changed a bit."

"Neither have you, flatterer," said the Captain of *Inaieu,* flowing toward him and reaching out a tentacle to wind in a comradely grip around one of his wrists. Nhauris Rihaul was a Deirr, from Deneb IV; half a ton of what looked like wet brown leather, all wrinkles and pouches and sags, shaped more or less like a slug that had half mastered the art of standing upright—but a slug eight feet long and five feet across the barrel. One long multipupiled eyeslit ran across what would have been a forehead, if she had properly had a head. Under the eyeslit was a long vertical slash of a mouth, lipless and apparently toothless, though Jim knew better. From beneath the mouth sprang the cluster of handling tentacles, ranging from tiny ones to huge thick cables. It was one of the smaller ones that was holding him, pumping his arm up and down in Nhauris's old mocking approximation of a handshake. "Jim, how are you?"

"Fine, Captain," Jim said—the old answer—"as soon as you stop that!"

She did, though not without bubbling briefly with Deirra laughter, a sound like an impending gastric disturbance. "Well enough. Captain, I have to apologize for asking you to hold this meeting here; properly it should have been on *Enterprise,* since she's flagship for this operation. But I think we might have crowded your briefing room a bit."

"I think you're right," he said, looking at the two Klaha, three Eyren and one !'hew standing at the center of the table, each one of them nearly the size of half a shuttlecraft. "In any case, let's get introductions over with so that we can get down to business. Captain Rihaul, may I present my first officer and science officer, Mr. Spock"—Spock bowed slightly—"my chief engineer, Montgomery Scott; my chief surgeon, Leonard McCoy."

"Honored, gentlemen, most honored," Captain Rihaul said, taking them each by the hand, though foregoing the jump-start motion she had used on Jim. "Welcome aboard *Inaieu*." She led them toward the table. "I present to you my officers: first officer and chief of science

Araun Yihoun; chief of surgery Lahiyn Roharrn; chief engineer Lellyn UUriul. And our guests; outside the table, from *Constellation*—"

"Jim and I have met, Nhauris," said Mike Walsh, reaching out to grip Jim's hand warmly. "Academy—then posts together on *Excalibur,* ages back. When did we last see each other? That M-5 business, wasn't it? Horrible mess, machine getting out of hand . . ."

Out of the corner of his eye Jim could see McCoy getting very interested indeed. "This meeting's a lot better than that one," he said, looking Mike up and down. Long ago, Jim and his classmates had used to tease Mike that it was a good thing Starfleet didn't have the old space agencies' maximum height requirement; otherwise Walsh would never have made it past atmosphere. He was six foot six, a slim man with sandy blond hair, a long, loose-limbed lope, and a look of eternal, friendly calculation, as if he were doing odds in his head. Probably he was; Mike had a reputation among his friends for being the biggest gambler in Starfleet. It might have been a problem, if he didn't always win. Nobody played poker with Mike Walsh—at least, not twice—but people fought to get aboard *Constellation*. Her command record since Mike took her was almost the equal of *Enterprise*'s for danger, daring, and success not only snatched from the jaws of failure, but afterward used to beat failure over the head. It was easy enough for Jim to understand. Mike Walsh hated to lose as much as Jim did; and he had carefully surrounded himself with people who felt the same way. It was a good way to stay alive in a dangerous galaxy.

Mike waved at his officers—a Terran Oriental, and two handsome, intense-looking women, one a Tellarite. "My first, Raela hr'Sassish; my chief surgeon, Aline MacDougall; my chief engineer, Iwao Sasaoka."

"And here is the Captain of *Intrepid*," Rihaul said from one side. "Captain Kirk, may I present Captain Suvuk."

"Sir," Jim said, bowing slightly—not just because Vulcans were not handshaking types. This was, after all, the man who had saved nearly thirty other ships and the lives of thousands of Starfleet personnel by willingly delivering himself into the hands of the Klingons during their last brief war with the Federation. That war had been won on another front, at Organia. But Suvuk, even after being physically tortured, and then subjected to the Klingon mind-sifter, had still, in rapid succession, broken free of his captors on the Klingon flagship *Hakask* at Regulus; disabled the ship's warp-drive and melted down its impulse engines, strewing unconscious, injured, and occasionally dead Klingons liberally along the way as he went; made solid-logic copies of everything of interest in the Klingons' library computers, then dumped the computers themselves; and had finally made it back aboard his own ship in a stolen Klingon shuttlecraft, well before the Organians' ban fell and both Klingons and Federation suddenly found their weapons too hot to handle. The Federation had later given Suvuk the Pentares Peace Commendation, with the extra cluster for conspicuous heroism.

But it did not take decorations to make it obvious that this was a man to be reckoned with. Suvuk was much shorter than Spock, and slighter; that Jim had known from holos he'd seen, and had wondered at, hearing the reports of what he did on *Hakask*. Now Jim didn't wonder. What the holos didn't adequately express was the sheer force of the personality living inside that rather ordinary-looking body. This was someone Jim had suspected might exist, without ever having seen confirmation of it—a full Vulcan so powerfully certain of himself that he had no need to be bound any more than he desired to be by the conventions of his homeworld. The face was sharp, set and cool, like that of almost every Vulcan Jim had ever seen. But it was also still, from within, in some way that most younger Vulcan faces only imitated. There was slight wrinkling around the eyes and mouth, an almost lazy droop to the eyes; a look of ease and relaxation, though the body held itself erect and alert, its power ready, but leashed. *This is what Spock might look like in sixty years or so,* Jim thought. *I hope I live to see it. . . .*

"Captain," Suvuk said. Jim was surprised again; who would have thought such a powerful voice would come out of such a small person? He held up one hand in the Vulcan parted-hand salute. "I greet you, for my world as well as for myself. We have had cause to acknowledge your contributions to us before this; nor would it be speculation to state that we doubtless will again." He turned to Spock and Scott and McCoy. "Long life and prosperity to you, Spock," he said, and Spock lifted a hand and returned the salute and the greeting. "To you also, Mr. Scott, and Dr. McCoy. Doctor," Suvuk said, letting his hand fall, "I read your recent paper on conjoint enzyme adjustment and cryotherapy as applied to the traumatized Vulcan simulpericardium. May I compliment you on it? It is precise, comprehensive, and conclusive."

McCoy's face was so still that Jim knew he was concealing absolute astonishment under it, saving it for later. "Captain," he said, "I'm gratified to hear you say so. All I need to know now is whether the technique will work as well in the field as it did on paper and in the lab."

"Oh, as to that, you may make your mind easy," Suvuk said, "for the T'Saien Clinic at the Vulcan Science Academy is already using it on their patients. I should know; I was one of them, some months back." McCoy's eyebrows went up; that was all he allowed himself for the moment, though Jim strongly suspected the Saurian brandy would be flowing in sickbay when they got back. "But we may discuss that later," Suvuk said. "My chief surgeon will also desire to hear what more you may have to say; the syndrome is a problem for us. My chief surgeon, Sobek; my chief engineer, T'Leiar; my first officer, Sehlk." One after another his officers nodded in acknowledgment—the slightly stout doctor, Sobek; the willowy, blue-eyed T'Leiar, with her long black hair; and Sehlk, a man much like Suvuk, but younger—small, darker skinned than the others, and with a keen, ready, intense look about him, all very much controlled. "Captains, gentlebeings all, shall we sit? Captain Kirk no doubt has a great deal to discuss."

Everyone found his, her or its place. Jim heard Rihaul sit down with the usual bizarre noise in her bowl chair, and had to repress a laugh again. Deirr weren't really wet—their smooth, slick skin just looked that way, and in contact with some surfaces, acted that way. Rihaul had been complaining since the long-ago days at the Academy, where Jim was her math tutor, that the Fleet-issue plastic bowl chairs were the bane of her existence; sitting down in one invariably produced noises that almost every species considered embarrassing, and getting up against the resultant suction required mechanical assistance, or a lot of friends. Nowadays Nhauris and Jim had a running joke that the only reason she had become a captain was to have a command bowl chair that was upholstered in cloth.

"I think the first matter before us," Jim said, "is to briefly discuss the strategic situation. Tactics will follow." Spock handed him a tape; Jim slipped it into the table and activated it. The four small holoprojection units around the table came alive, each one constructing a three-dimensional map of the galaxy, burning with the bright pinpoints of stars. The map rotated until one seemed to be looking straight "down" through the galactic disk, and the focus tightened on the Sagittarius Arm—the irregular spiral-arm structure, thirty thousand light-years long and half as wide, that the Federation, the Romulans and the Klingons all shared. From this perspective, the Sag Arm (at least to Jim) looked rather like the North American continent; though it was North America missing most of Canada, and the United States as far west as the Rockies and as far south as Oklahoma. Sol sat on the shore of that great starry lacuna, about where Oklahoma City would have been.

"Here's where we stand," Jim said. The bright "continent" swelled in the map-cube, till the whole cubic was full of the area that would have been southwestern North America, Mexico and the Californias. "Federation, Romulan and Klingon territories are all marked according to the map key." Three sets of very lumpy, irregular shapes, like a group of wrestling amoebas, flashed into color in the starfield: red for the Klingons, gold for the Romulans, blue for the Federation. There was very little regularity about their boundaries with one another, except for one abnormally smooth curvature, almost a section of an egg shape, where the blue space nested with and partly surrounded the gold. "Disputed territories are in orange." There was a lot of orange, both where blue met red and where red met gold; though rather more of the latter. "These schematics include the latest intelligence we have from both Romulans and Klingons. You can see that there are some problems in progress out there. The alliance between the Klingons and the Romulans is either running into some kind of trouble, or is not defined the way we usually define alliances. This gives us our first hint as to why we're out here, gentlebeings—unless Fleet was more open with one of you than it was with me."

Suvuk shook his head slightly; Walsh rolled his eyes at the ceiling.

"I've rarely seen them so obtuse," Rihaul said. "Surely something particularly messy is coming up."

"Indeed," Jim said. "Which is why we will be needing to keep in very close touch with one another. Any piece of data, any midnight thought, may give us the clue to figuring out what's going to happen. My staff has done some research involving recent Romulan intelligence reports; I'll be passing that data on to you for your study and comment. Anything, any idea you may come up with, don't hesitate to call me. My intention is to keep this operation very free-form, at least until something happens. For something *will* happen."

"I wholly agree, Captain," Suvuk said. "Our mission here is as surely provocatory as it is investigatory. One does not waste a destroyer on empty space, or space one expects to stay empty. We are expected to force the Romulans' hand, as Captain Walsh would say."

Jim looked with carefully concealed surprise at Suvuk, who had flashed a quick mild glance at Walsh. *Is it just me?* he thought. *But, no, Vulcans don't make jokes. Certainly this one wouldn't*—"Yes, sir," Jim said. "With that in mind, here's our patrol pattern as I envision it; please make any suggestions you find apt."

The map's field changed again, becoming more detailed. The long curved ellipsoid boundary between the two spaces swelled to dominate the cubic; stars in the field became few. "Here we are," Jim said. "Sigma-285 and its environs. I suggest that we spread ourselves out as thinly as we can—not so far as to be out of easy communication with one another, but far enough apart to cover as much territory as possible with any given pattern."

"The ships would be a couple of hundred light-years or so apart," Walsh said.

"That's about right; the boundaries I was considering for the whole patrol area, at least to start with, would be defined by 218 Persei to the galactic north, 780 Arietis to the south, and the 'east-west' distance along the lines from 56 Arietis to iota Andromedae; about half a galactic degree. This way, any ship in need of assistance can have it within from a day to an hour, depending on what the situation is."

"*Inaieu* should at all times be at the heart of that pattern," Rihaul said, "so that she will have minimum response time for the other ships."

"That's right," Jim said. "That was my intention. I don't propose to hold *Enterprise* at flag position, out of the way, during the operation; firstly because she'll better serve us running patrol like everyone else, and secondly because she has something of a name among the Romulans. While out by herself, she may draw their attention, draw them out and give them an opportunity to let slip what's going on, on the other side of the Zone; either by communication among themselves, or with us. We have experts in Romulan codes and the Romulan common language aboard, awaiting such an opportunity. And should there be an engagement, all steps are to be taken to preserve and question survivors . . . if any Romulans allow themselves to survive."

"Noted," Suvuk said. "Captain, have you yet assigned patrol programs?"

"They're in the table for your perusal. Positions in the task force rotate."

"I see that *Enterprise* is flying point for our first run down the length of the Zone," Rihaul said, with a merry look at Jim, after she had studied the screen on the table before her. "Well, we could hardly grudge you that, could we? Your campaign, Captain. But do leave us something to do. We, too, get these sudden urges to save all civilization."

"Captain," Jim said to her, grinning, "I have a nasty feeling that this operation will provide every one of us with ample opportunity to indulge those urges. Meanwhile I give your request all the attention it deserves. . . . Anything else, gentlebeings? Comment? Suggestions?"

"Only that it would be logical to implement patrol immediately," Suvuk said.

"So ordered, sir." Jim got up; the others rose with him. "Everyone is dismissed to their commanders—would the captains remain? Bones," he said to McCoy over the bustle in the room, mostly caused by Denebians running out as if to a fire, "no need for you to hang around if you don't want to—"

"Jim, are you kidding?" McCoy was obviously far gone in self-congratulation. "Did you hear what that man said about my—"

"Oh. Well, as long as you feel that way about it—" Suvuk came up to them at that point, along with the Vulcan medical officer, Sobek. "Captain," Suvuk said, "you wished to see me?"

"Only to deliver McCoy into your company, sir. He is so retiring that if I didn't order him to, he would certainly never allow himself the vanity of discussing one of his papers at any length. In fact, I'm sure he'd love to see your sickbay—in detail. Please accompany Captain Suvuk, Bones. Don't worry about us: we won't wait up for you."

Jim watched in amusement as the Vulcans led McCoy away, politely talking medical terminology at him at a great rate. Bones had no time for more than one I'll-get-you-for-this look over his shoulder before they had him out of the room. "Spock," Jim said softly to the Vulcan, who had been solemnly watching the whole process from behind him, "I haven't had time to read it. Was the paper really that good?"

Spock looked at him sidelong. "After the spelling had been corrected," he said, "indeed it was."

Mike Walsh came over to Jim with that old calculating look on his face. "How about it, Jim? Got a few free hours for poker this evening?"

"No," Jim said firmly. "But I have twenty credits that say you can't beat our ship's chess champ with a queen handicap."

"Oh really? You're on. When do we start?"

Jim looked at Spock, eyed the door, put an eyebrow up. Spock looked thoughtful, nodded fractionally, and headed out for the lift and the transporters. "Right now," Jim said. "Come on, let's get Nhauris up."

*"You two get out of here!"*

"Dangerous business, coming between a captain and her ship. Obviously this chair isn't doing too well at it. . . . Why, Captain, I do believe you've put on a bit of weight!"

# Chapter Five

According to a widely-held Rihannsu military tradition, the best commanders were also often cranky ones. Normally Ael avoided such behavior. The showy, towering rages she had seen some of her own commanders periodically throw at their crews had only convinced Ael that she never wanted to serve under such a person in a crisis. Pretended excitability could too easily turn into the real thing.

Now, however, she saw a chance to turn that old tradition to good advantage. She came back from her tour of her fleet not positively angry, but looking rather discommoded and out of sorts when she reentered her bridge. T'Liun noticed it instantly, and became most solicitous of Ael, asking her what sort of condition the other ships were in. Ael—hearing perfectly well t'Liun's intention to find out the cause of the mood and exploit it somehow—told t'Liun what she thought of the other ships, and the Klingons who had built them, and the Rihannsu crews who were mishandling them, at great length. It was a most satisfying tirade, giving Ael the opportunity to make a great deal of noise and relieve some of her own tension, while leaving t'Liun suspecting her of doing exactly that—though for all the wrong reasons.

Then off Ael stormed, and went on a cold-voiced rampage through the ship, upbraiding the junior officers for the poor repair of equipment that was generally in good condition. Late into the ship's night she prowled the corridors, terrorizing the offshift, peering into everything. The effect produced was perfect. Slitted eyes gazed after her in bitter annoyance, and in eavesdropping on ship's 'com, after she had theoretically retired for the night, Ael heard many suggestions made about her ancestry and habits that revised slightly upward her opinion of her crew's inventiveness. Ael felt much amused, and much relieved by the discharge of energy. But far more important, no one had noticed or thought anything in particular of a small interval she spent peering up a circuitry-conduit—an inspection from which she had come away frowning on the outside, but inside quite pleased. Ael fell asleep late, her cabin dark to everything but starlight—thanking her ancestors that the most immediate of them, her father, had once made her spend almost three months taking his own old warbird apart, system by system, and putting it back together again.

In the morning she took things a step further. She called together t'Liun and tr'Khaell and the other senior officers and instructed them that they were to begin a complete check of all ship's systems. Her officers, not caring for the prospect of trying to do several weeks' work in the several days she was ordering, did their best to reassure Ael that the systems were in perfect working condition. Ael allowed herself, very briefly, to be mollified—thus setting up for a rage that even her worst old commanders would have approved of, when a message came in from Command later that day, and t'Liun's communications board overloaded and blew up.

Ael had been restraining herself the day before. Now she let loose, resurrecting some of the savagely elegant old idioms for incompetence that her father had used on her the day she forgot to fasten one of the gates of the farm, and three hundred of the *hlai* got out into the croplands. She raged, she flushed dark green-bronze (an inadvertent effect; she still blushed at the memory of that long-ago scolding, but the effect was fortuitous—it made the rage look better). She ordered the whole lot of them into the brig, then changed her mind: that was too good for them. They would all work their own shifts, as well as extra shifts doing the system analysis she had ordered in the first place. But none of them would touch the Elements-be-blessed communications board, which had probably been utterly destroyed by t'Liun's fumblings. Who knew what orders Command had had for them, and must they now send messages back saying, "Sorry, we missed that one"? She would let t'Liun have that dubious pleasure, and served her right; but in the meantime someone had best bring her a tool kit, and the rest of them had best stay out of her sight and make themselves busy lest she space them all in their underwear, *now get out!*

Afterward, when the bridge was quiet except for one poor antecenturion too cowed to look up or speak a word, Ael lay on her back under the overhang of the comm station and called silently on her father's fourth name, laughing inside like a madwoman. *Possibly I am mad, trying to make this work,* she thought, first killing all power to the board so that none of the circuit-monitoring devices t'Liun had installed in it would work. *But how then—should I lie here and do nothing? No, the* thrai *has a few bites left in her yet.* . . . Ael gently teased one particular logic solid out of its crystal-grip, holding it as lovingly as a jewel. The equipment she had been brought naturally included a portable power source; this she attached both to the solid and to the board, bringing up only its programming functions.

Reprogramming the logic solid, which held the ship's ID, was delicate work, but not too difficult; and she thought kindly of her father all through it. *Ael,* he had said again, *times will come when you won't have time to run the program and see if it works. It must be right the first time, or lives will be lost, and the responsibility will be on your head when you face the Elements at last—probably long before that, too. Do it again. Get it right the first time. Or it's the stables for you tomorrow.* . . .

She sat up with the little keypad in her lap, touching numbers and words into it, and thinking about responsibility . . . of lives not merely lost, but about to be thrown away. *Bitter, it is bitter. I am no killer.* . . . *Yet Command sent me here to be a prisoner; to rot, or preferably to die. What duty do I owe these fools? They've pledged me no loyalty; nor would they ever. They are my jailers, not my crew. Surely there's nothing wrong in escaping from jail.*

*Yet I swore the Oath, once upon a time, by the Elements and my honor, to be good mistress to my crews, and to lead them safely and well. Does that mean I must keep faith with them even if they do me villainy?* . . .

The thought of the Elements brought Ael no clear counsel. There was little surprise in that, out here in the cold of space, where Earth was far away, and water and air both frozen as hard as any stone. The only Element she commonly dealt with was Fire—in starfire and the matter-antimatter conflagration of her ship's engines. Ael had always found that peculiarly agreeable, for she knew her own Element to be Fire's companion, Air, and her realm what pierced it: weapons, words, wings.

But even the thought of that old reassuring symmetry did nothing for her now. *Loyalty, the best part of the ruling Passion, that's of fire: if any spark of that fire were alive in them, I would serve it gladly. I would save them if I could. But there is none.*

*Besides . . . there's a larger question.* She sat still on the floor of her bridge for a moment, seeing beyond it. There was the matter of the many lives that would be lost, both in the Empire and outside it, should the horrible thing a-birthing at Levaeri V research station come to term. Thousands of lives, millions; rebellion and war and devastation lashing through the Empire itself, then out among the Federation and the Klingons as well. For the Klingons she cared little; for the Federation she cared less—though that might be a function of having been at armed truce with them for all these years. Still—theirs were lives too.

And beyond mere war and horror lay an issue even deeper. When honor dies—when trust is a useless thing—what use is life? And that was what threatened the spaces around, and the Empire itself, where honor had once been a virtue . . . but would be no more. Tasting the lack of it for herself, here and now, in this place where no one could be trusted or respected, Ael knew the bitterness of such a lack right down to its dregs. Even the knowledge of faith kept elsewhere, of Tafv on his way and her old crew coming for her, could not assuage it. She had led a sheltered life until now, despite wounds and desperate battles; this desolate tour of duty had dealt her a wound from which she would never recover. She could only make sure that others did not have to suffer it.

She could only do so by sacrificing the crew of *Cuirass* to her strategem. There was too much chance that they would somehow get word back to Command of what was toward, if she left them alive. But by killing them, Ael would make herself guilty of the same treachery she so despised in them; and with far less excuse (if excuse existed), for she knew the old way of life, knew honor and upright dealing. There was no justifying the spilling of all her crew's lives, despite their treachery to her. Ael would bear the weight of murder, and sooner or later pay their bloodprice in the most intimate possible coinage: her own pain. That was the way things worked, in the Elements' world; fire well used, warmed; ill used, burned. All that remained was the question of whether she would accept the blame for their deaths willingly, or reject it, blind herself to her responsibility, and prolong the Elements' retaliation.

She remembered her father, standing unhappily over one of the *hlai* that Ael had not been able to catch. It had gotten into the woods, and there it lay on the leafmold, limp and torn; a *hnoiyika* had gotten it, torn its breast out and left the *hlai* there to bleed out its life, as *hnoiyikar* will. Ael had stared at the *hlai* in mixed fascination and horror as it lay there with insects crawling in and out of the torn places, out of mouth and eyes. She had never seen a dead thing before. "This is why one must be careful with life," her father had said, in very controlled wrath. "Death is the most hateful thing. Don't allow the destruction of what you can never restore." And he had made her bury the *hlai*.

She looked up and sighed, thinking what strange words those had seemed, coming from a warrior of her father's stature. Now, at this late date, they started to make sense . . . and she laughed again, at herself this time, a silent, bitter breath. Standing on the threshold of many murders, she was finally beginning to understand. . . .

*Evidently I am already beginning to pay the price,* she thought. *Very well. I accept the burden.* And she turned her mind back to her work, burying her wretched crew in her heart while instructing the logic solid in its own treachery. First, she pulled another logic solid out of her pocket, connected to the first one and then to the little powerpack. It was a second's work to copy the first solid's contents onto the blank. Then, after the duplicate was pocketed again, some more work on the original solid. A touch here, a touch there, a program that would loop back on itself in this spot, refuse to respond in that one, do several different things at once over here, when *Cuirass*'s screens perceived the appropriate stimulus. And finally the whole adjustment locked away under a coded retrieval signal, so that t'Liun would notice nothing amiss, and analysis (if attempted) would reveal nothing.

Done. She went back under the panel again, locked the logic solid back into its grip, and closed up the panel again, tidying up after herself with a light heart. No further orders would reach this panel from Command. It would receive them, automatically acknowledge them, and then dump them, without alerting the communications officer. It would do other things too—as her crew would discover, to its ruin.

Ael got up and left the tool kit lying where it was for someone else to clean up—that would be in character for her present role, though it went against her instincts for tidiness. She swung on the poor terrified antecenturion minding the center seat, and instructed him to call t'Liun to the bridge; she herself was going to her quarters, and was not to be disturbed on peril of her extreme pleasure. Then out Ael stalked, making her way to her cabin. In the halls, the crewpeople she met avoided her eyes. Ael did not mind that at all.

She settled down to wait.

She did not have to wait long. She had rather been hoping that Tafv would for once discard honor and attack by ship's night. But it was broad afternoon, the middle of dayshift, when her personal computer with the copied logic-solid attached to it began to read out a ship's ID, over and over. She ripped the solid free of the computer and pocketed it, glanced once around her bare dark cabin. There was nothing here she needed. Slowly, not hurrying, she headed in the general direction of engineering. The engine room itself had the usual duty personnel, no more; she waved an uncaring salute to them and went on through to where *Hsaaja* stood. As the doors of the secondary deck closed behind her, the alarm sirens began their terrible screeching; someone on the bridge had visual contact with a ship in the area. Calmly, without looking back, Ael got into *Hsaaja,* sealed him up, brought up the power. It would be about now that they realized, up in the bridge, that their own screens were not working.

"Khre'Riov t'Rllaillieu urru Oira!" the ship's annunciator system cried in t'Liun's voice, again and again. But Ael would never set foot on *Cuirass*'s bridge again; and the cry grew fainter and fainter, vanishing at last with the last of the landing bay's exhausted air. Ael lifted *Hsaaja* up on his underjets, nudged him toward the opening doors of the bay, the doors that no bridge override could affect now. Then out into space, hard downward and to the rear, where an unmodified warbird could not fire. *Cuirass* shuddered above Ael to light phaser fire against which the ship could not protect herself. Space writhed and rippled around *Cuirass*; she submerged into otherspace, went into warp, fled away.

Ael looked up with angry joy at the second warbird homing in on her, its landing bay open for her. She kicked *Hsaaja*'s ion-drivers in, arrowing toward home, and security, and war.

# Chapter Six

"How's the focus, Jerry?"

"Mmm—can't see any difference. Here, change places with me."

They were the first words Jim heard that morning as he passed through recreation in search of a cup of coffee and Harb Tanzer, the rec chief; but Jim forgot the search for a moment and paused in the middle of the room. The place was as busy as always—the gamma workshift had gone off duty some six hours before, but was still playing hard; and delta shift would start tickling in shortly, as soon as alpha relieved them. Jim was alpha shift right now, all the department heads of the various ships in the task force having gone over to that schedule to make meetings and communications easier. That was why he was slightly surprised to find Uhura, apparently long awake and sprightly, stretched out more or less under the control console for the holography stage and tinkering with its innards. Standing over the console was Lieutenant Freeman from life sciences, making swift adjustments and scowling at the results.

"How's that?"

"Uh-uh. Come on, Nyota, let me do it."

"Heading up to the bridge?" said a voice by his shoulder. Jim turned around. There was Harb Tanzer, holding two cups of coffee, one of which he offered to Jim.

"Do you read minds?" Jim said, taking a careful sip.

"No, I leave that to Spock." Harb grinned. "Vulcans might think it was an infringement on their prerogatives. Or I'd probably get in trouble with their unions or something. Do Vulcans have unions?"

"Only by mail," Jim said, and took another drink of coffee, watching with satisfaction as Harb spluttered into his. "What're these two up to?"

"I was about to come find out myself; they've been in here since the middle of delta. Uhura's up early, and it has to be the middle of the night for Freeman. . . ."

"It can wait. I was looking for you. You're up early, too, now that I think of it."

"Talking to the computer, that's all. Checking out the crew efficiency levels."

"You *do* read minds."

"No, just my job description."

"How are they?"

Harb actually shrugged. "They're fine, Captain. Reaction time to orders is excellent—very crisp. The crew as a whole is calm, assured—very unworried. They trust you to bring them through this without any major problems."

"I wish I had their confidence in me."

"You should."

"So McCoy tells me . . ."

"Yes, I saw that game. Jim, the computer's analysis shows no department aboard this ship exhibiting signs of an anxiety level higher than plus-one. It's the unknown that frightens people. This is just Romulans."

"'Just . . .'" Jim gazed over at Freeman, who was now lying under the console, and Uhura, who was adjusting the controls on top. "Oh, well. How are the other ships?"

"*Constellation*'s fine. Randy Cross, the rec officer over there, tells me they're about on a par with us—plus-ones and an occasional plus-one point five. By the way, why do they call Captain Walsh 'Mike the Greek'? I thought he was Irish or something."

"Reference to an old Earth legend, I think. The Greek either invented democracy or handicapping, I can't remember which." Harb snorted into his coffee again. "But do a little discreet snooping for me and see if there's a betting pool going on over there."

"Certainly, Captain. Want a little action?"

"Mr. Tanzer! Are you accusing me of being a gambler?"

"Oh, *never,* sir."

"Good—I think. What about the Vulcans?"

"Well, *Intrepid* doesn't have a recreation department per se, though they have the same sort of rec room as we have. Recreation's handled out of medicine, and gets prescribed if someone needs it. But Sobek tells me that no one does. They're all running the usual Vulcan equivalency levels, plus-point five or so. *Inaieu,* though—"

"I bet they're having a good time over there. They love trouble."

"Plus-point fives and point sevens, right across the board."

Jim glanced at Harb in concern. "That's *too* good a time."

"Not for Denebians. The Deirr are the most nervous, generally. But they're not very worried either."

Jim gave silent thanks that Rihaul was a Deirr; nervous captains tended to be better at keeping their crews alive. "Something should be done to harness levels like those, nevertheless. I'll talk to Rihaul. Anyway, you've answered all the questions I had for you." Jim glanced up at the wall chrono. "About ten minutes, yet. No harm in being early . . ." He trailed off. "What *are* they doing?"

"Okay, try it now," Freeman's voice said, slightly muffled since his head and shoulders were up inside the console. "That first tape."

Uhura picked a tape up from the console, inserted it and hit one of the console's controls. Immediately the holography stage lit up with the figure of a seated man, with another man beside him. They both looked bitter. "I coulda *been* somebody!" the first man said angrily. "I coulda been a con*tenda!*"

"No, the other one," Freeman's voice said from inside the machinery. Uhura pulled the tape, and the two men vanished.

Realization dawned. "Harb," Jim said, "*this* is the crewman who's been rechanneling all that archival stuff and showing it on ship's channels in the evenings? I thought he was in life sciences."

"Xenobiology," Harb said. "This is his hobby, though. It's useful enough. The data have been digitized and available for flat display for years, but no one's cared enough about a lot of this material to rechannel it for 3-D and ambient sound. Freeman, though, loves everything as long as it was made before 2200. It took him about three months to get the image-processing program running right, but since it's been up he's enlarged the entertainment-holo library by about ten percent. He mentioned to me yesterday that he wanted to do some fine-tuning on the program so he could rechannel some of the old Vulcan dramas and send them over to *Intrepid*."

Jim stepped closer to the console, followed by Harb, and stood there watching the proceedings along with several other curious crewpeople. "Captain," one of them said to him, knotting several tentacles in a gesture of respect. "Well rested?"

"Very well, Mr. Athendë," Jim said absently. "How's Lieutenant Sjveda's music appreciation seminar coming along?"

"Classical period still, sir. Beethoven, Stravinsky, Vaughan Williams, Barber, Lennon, Devo. Head hurts."

"Bet it does," Jim said, wondering where the Sulamid, who seemed to be nothing but a tangle of tentacles and a sheaf of stalked eyes, might consider his head to be. "Not overdo it, Mr. Athendë. Take in small doses."

"Here we are," Uhura said, and dropped another tape in the read slot, hit the control. For a second nothing seemed to be happening on the stage. Then a peculiar grinding, wheezing sound began to fill the air. On the platform there slowly faded into existence a tall blue rectangular structure with doors in it, and a flashing white light on top, and what appeared to be the Anglish words POLICE PUBLIC CALL BOX blazoned on the front panel above the doors. There was a pause, during which the noise and the flashing light both stopped. Then one of the box's doors opened. To Jim's mild amusement, a hominid, quite Terran-looking, peered out and gazed around him in great interest; a curly-haired person in a burgundy jacket, with a floppy hat, a striped scarf of truly excessive length, and sharp bright eyes above a dazzling smile, ingenuous as a child's. "I beg your pardon," the man said merrily in a British-accented voice, apparently looking right at Jim, "but is this Heathrow?"

*Brother, have you ever taken a wrong turn!* was Jim's first thought. "Harb," he said, "is that man happy in xeno?"

"Very."

"Pity. With a talent like this, we could use him in communications."

"Uhura thinks so too."

"Speaking of which—" But Uhura had been watching the chrono.

She reached down and thumped on the side of the console. "Jerry, I'm on duty in a few minutes." She glanced up, caught sight of Jim and Harb standing there, and grinned a little. "Keep up the good work," she said. "I'll see you later."

She left him there with his head still inside the console, and crossed to Jim and Harb. "You really must be bored if you're getting up early to watch old sterries, Uhura," Jim said. "Maybe I should find you some more work to do. . . ."

She chuckled at him. "Harb," she said, "I think we've got the last bugs worked out of it. Mr. Freeman wanted to be very sure—he knows how picky Vulcans are. Once he's done with that last batch for *Intrepid*, though, he's ready for requests."

"Good enough. Thanks, Lieutenant."

"My pleasure. Coming, Captain?"

"After you."

They headed for the bridge lift together. "Are you taking up this hobby too, Uhura?"

"Oh, no, sir. Bridge," she said to the lift as the doors closed. "This is professional interest. Mr. Freeman has some novel ideas in image and signal processing, computer techniques that a communications special-ist might not think to try. He's been doing some specialty programs for the xeno labs that might actually be of some use in cleaning up sub-space communication. Interstellar ionization is always a problem, it mangles the highest and lowest bandwidths and slows down transmis-sion speed. The sub-ether carrier wavicles—"

The doors opened onto the bridge. "Uhura," Jim said, "I'm still working on my coffee. . . ."

She smiled wryly at him. "Noted," she said. "I'll write you a report."

"Do that. And log me in, please."

"Yes, sir."

"And a good morning to you, Mr. Spock," Jim said, stepping down to the center seat as Spock stood up from it. "Report, please."

"Your initial patrol pattern is running without incident," Spock said, "and the Neutral Zone appears quiet. *Intrepid* is at 'point' position at this time, two hundred eighty-four light-years ahead of us on bearing one-eighty mark plus six, in the vicinity of 2450 Trianguli. We have dropped back to pace *Inaieu*, which is at two-seventy mark zero, one hundred fifteen light-years away; and *Constellation* is flying rearguard at zero mark minus three, two hundred ninety-two light-years behind. The whole task force is maintaining an average speed of warp four point four five."

"Very good. How's the weather?"

Spock looked grave. "Generally unremarkable so far. However, Captain, the computer has presented me with some very unusual figures regarding the ion-flux research we were pursuing before this operation."

Jim nodded at Spock to continue. The Vulcan looked down at the clipboard he was carrying with an expression that suggested there was something distasteful about the data on it. "You remember the analysis of a meteoric debris sample that Mr. Naraht carried out at my request."

"You were interested in the figure for the iridium, weren't you?"

"Affirmative. The amount of the isotope—for it was not 'normal' iridium—was abnormally high, indicating that the piece of matter in question had been bombarded with extremely high levels of hard radiation in the recent past. That sample was taken from one of the areas we passed through on the way to maneuvers, an area on which I had other data and desired a fresh sample. The peculiar thing is that other samples from approximately the same area, older ones, do not reflect the same bombardment. And there has been ion-storm activity in that area since."

"Any conclusion?"

Spock looked as unhappy as he ever allowed himself to in public. "None as yet, Captain. It would be possible to indulge in all kinds of flights of speculation—"

"But you are refraining."

"With difficulty," Spock said, quietly enough for only Jim to hear him. "The situation is most abnormal. Mr. Naraht is running further studies for me."

"Yes. How *is* my favorite pan pizza doing?"

"Sir?"

"Sorry, I couldn't resist. How is he?"

Jim never found out, for at that moment Uhura's board beeped for attention. She put a hand up to the transdator in her ear, listened briefly, then said, "Captain, it's the *Intrepid,* if you want to talk to them."

"Put them on."

Uhura flicked a switch. The main screen's starfield blinked out—to be replaced by a screen full of static.

"Bloody," Uhura said under her breath. "Sorry, sir, I can't raise them now. The *Intrepid*'s comm officer was reporting the bow-shock edge of an ion storm—force four, he said, and it looked to be worsening."

"Were they all right?"

"Oh, yes, he said it wasn't anything they couldn't ride out. It was just their routine hourly report."

"Very well. Pass the information along to the other ships and have them take precautions." Jim sighed in very mild annoyance, then looked up at Spock and saw him still wearing that uncomfortable look. "Well," Jim said, "here it comes. It's not as if you didn't warn Fleet that the climate around here is changing in a hurry. Looks like our operation's going to get caught right in the middle of it."

"So it appears," Spock said. "Though, truly, Captain, I am uncertain what we could do about the problem even if Starfleet Command decided to dedicate all of Fleet to the problem. Relocating entire populations is hardly desirable, or feasible. And there is still something. . . ." He trailed off.

"What?"

"Unknown. I am missing data, Captain. Though I find it most interesting that the subject of our research extends eighteen hundred light-years past the area of the galaxy where we were studying it."

"*Intrepid* again, Captain," Uhura said, working hard over her board to hold the signal. "Their comm officer managed to get a squirt through between storm wavefronts. It's up to force six, but they predict it'll stabilize at that force and then break somewhere in the neighborhood of 766 Trianguli. They'll leave further reports with the unmanned Zone monitoring stations as they pass them—that way they won't have to waste time trying to punch through the interference. Their status is otherwise normal; the area's clear."

"Eminently logical," Jim said.

—and the ship abruptly went on automatic red alert, lights flashing and sirens whooping. All over the bridge, people jumped for battle stations. "Ship in the area, Captain!" Uhura said. "Not Federation traffic."

"Identify it!"

"No ID yet. Power consumption reading, nothing more—"

"Warship, Captain," Spock said, back at his post and looking down his hooded viewer. "An extravagant power-consumption curve. Approaching from out of the Neutral Zone at warp eight."

*Bingo,* Jim thought. *At last it's beginning.* "Course?"

"Not an intercept. I would say it has been unaware of us until now."

"ID now, Captain," Uhura said, looking both excited and puzzled. "It's a Klingon ship!"

"The Klingons have been selling the Romulans ships for a long time now—"

"Noted, sir. But the ID is unmistakably Klingon code and symbology. KL 77 *Ehhak.*"

It was a name Jim recognized from accounts of the Battle of Organia: one of the ships that had invested the planet. "What the hell are they doing here? Mr. Chekov, arm photon torpedoes, prepare to lock phasers on for firing. Mr. Sulu, prepare evasive action but do not execute."

"Aye, sir."

"Phasers locked on, sir."

"Excellent. Hold your fire until my express order, Mr. Chekov."

"Aye, sir."

"Intruder's range—"

"Not a Klingon ship," Spock said abruptly. "ID is in fact Klingon. But the power-consumption curve is inconsistent with either the old *Akif*-class or new *K'tinga*-class warships. Range now six hundred eighty light-years and closing. Course is still not an intersect. If this continues they will pass far above and ahead of the task force—"

"Another contact!" Uhura said. "Romulan this time. ChR 63 *Bloodwing*—"

Jim's fist clenched, hard. "Course?"

"Following the first ship," Spock said. "Closing on it at warp nine."

"Uhura, messages to *Inaieu* and *Constellation*. All screens up, and battle stations. But if either ship comes within range, do *not* fire unless fired upon! Let them pass."

"Yes, Captain."

"We'll see what they're up to," Jim said. "I am willing to be forgiving of an accidental intrusion into Federation space—always supposing the intruders tell me why they've come without calling first."

"Indications are that the first ship will shortly be unable to tell you anything, Captain," said Spock. "The ship with the *Bloodwing* ID is closing on it very—More data; the ship ID'ing as *Ehhak* is actually a ship of the old Romulan warbird class. Cloaking device in place but not functioning. *Ehhak* is beginning evasive maneuvers, but they are proving ineffectual. *Bloodwing* continues to close."

"Range—"

"Two hundred fifteen light-years. Two hundred—Better readings on *Bloodwing*, now. Its power-consumption curve too is atypical. Warp engines have been boosted, and other alterations are indicated—One hundred fifty light-years—"

"Time till they cross the Neutral Zone—"

"At this speed, four seconds." Spock watched in silence. "*Ehhak* has crossed. Now *Bloodwing*. Visual contact—"

The screen leapt to life with their images—two Romulan warbirds, both screened, screaming out of the Neutral Zone high above the plane of the *Enterprise*'s travel. The pursued ship veered suddenly, trying to shake its pursuer; to no avail. *Bloodwing* would not be shaken. "Still closing," Spock said. "One hundred light-years from us. Seventy-five. They will pass within twenty-two point six three light-years of the *Enterprise* at closest. *Bloodwing* continues to close on *Ehhak*. Within firing range. Firing."

"Gently, Mr. Chekov," Jim said, noticing his weapons officer's twitch. "They're not shooting at us, not yet."

"Noted, sir."

"Good man. Result of fire, Mr. Spock—"

"None as yet. *Ehhak* is turning again. Toward *Bloodwing*, this time. Firing now—No effect. Standoff. Firing again—"

The blast of blinding light that suddenly filled the screen lit the whole bridge like lightning. When it faded Spock said quietly, "Evidently some of the alterations installed in *Bloodwing* have been to its phaser systems. Their intent was apparently to draw *Ehhak* into range for quick and certain destruction. Obviously they succeeded."

"Noted," Jim said softly. "*Bloodwing*'s location and course, Mr. Spock."

"Its old course took it somewhat past us, Captain. Turning now: fifty-three light-years away on bearing one-ninety-nine mark pluseighteen. Approaching us."

"Status," Jim said, beginning to twitch a little himself.

"Slowing," Spock said. "Screens up, but no sign of further belligerence. Down to warp six now; warp five; holding at warp five exactly, and coasting in toward us. If the Romulan continues along this course, *Bloodwing* will be paralleling our course at a distance of one lightsecond from us."

"Neighborly," Jim said. "Hold the screens as they are. We'll wait and see what they do."

And they waited, the bridge becoming very still indeed. Closer and closer *Bloodwing* glided to them. After about a minute she had no motion relative to *Enterprise*, but was soaring along beside her in neat formation, a hundred and eighty-six thousand miles away.

Ten seconds passed, and three hundred sixty million kilometers of empty space, and several breaths' worth of silence.

Uhura's board beeped.

She listened to her transdator, then said, "They're hailing us, Captain."

"Answer the hail. Offer them an open channel if they want it."

Uhura spoke softly to her board. The screen shimmered.

They found themselves looking, as they had looked once before, at the cramped bridge of a warbird-class Romulan vessel. A man in the usual Romulan uniform—dark-glittering tunic and breeches, with a scarflike scarlet half-cloak fastened front and back over one shoulder—stood facing the bridge pickup. He was of medium height, dark skinned for a Romulan, with even features and a slightly hooked nose; young and well built, with auburn hair cropped short in a style reminiscent of the Vulcan fashion, and light, narrow, noticing eyes. He spoke in Romulan, which the translator in Uhura's board handled with the usual disconcerting nonsynchronization of mouth movements. "Enterprise," the Romulan said, *"I am Subcommander Tafv tr'Rllaillieu, second in command of the Romulan warship* Bloodwing. *Do I address Captain James Kirk?"*

Jim stood up, feeling an odd urge to match the young man's courteous tone, even if there might be a trick behind it. "You do," he said. Then he paused a moment. "Sir—may I ask if by chance you are related to a commander by the name of *Ael* t'Rllaillieu?" He said it the best he could, hoping the translator would straighten out his mangled pronunciation.

The subcommander smiled very slightly. *"You may, Captain. I am the commander's son."*

"Thank you. May I also ask what brings you into our space under such—unusual—circumstances?"

*"Again, you may. The commander's business brings us here. I am directed to express to you Commander t'Rllaillieu's desire to meet with you and any members of your staff you find appropriate, to discuss with you a matter which will be as much to your advantage as to ours."*

"What matter, Subcommander?"

*"I regret that I may not say, Captain. This is an unshielded channel, and the business is urgent and confidential in the extreme."*

"What conditions for the meeting?"

*"The commander is willing to beam over to your vessel, unescorted. As I have said, the matter is urgent, and the commander has no desire to stand on ceremony at the moment."*

"May I consider briefly?"

*"Certainly."* The young man bowed slightly, and the screen went dark, showing stars again, and *Bloodwing* hanging there, silent.

Jim sat down in the helm for a moment, swung it around to face Spock. "Well, well. What now? Recommendations, ladies and gentlemen?"

Spock stood up from a last look down his viewer and folded his arms, looking very thoughtful indeed. "This is a vessel we know, Captain."

"No kidding," Jim said. "She's singed our tail a few times. Of course we've singed hers too. . . ."

"However," Spock said, "while we have often been at enmity with *Bloodwing,* the ship has never acted in a treacherous fashion toward us. In fact, often very much the contrary. Ael t'Rllaillieu, whoever she may be, has dealt honorably enough with us, though we have never seen her."

"True enough," Jim said. He remembered the shock after their first engagement, over by 415 Arietis it had been—on fighting a whole week's fight-and-run battle with *Bloodwing* and finding out afterward that the "t'" prefix on the house-name denoted a woman. *Oh God, not another one,* he had thought at the time. But he had changed his mind since, after a few victories, and a couple of defeats. He wanted to meet this old fox, very much indeed.

And now he had the chance.

"Well, Mr. Spock," he said, "we came all this way to gather information about the Romulans, and now it seems they've got some for us. Let's see what the commander wants. Uhura?"

She nodded. The screen came back on again; Jim rose. "Subcommander," he said, "if you will be good enough to come within transporter range, and provide my communications officer with the commander's coordinates, we will be delighted to receive her. Beaming in three hundred seconds precisely. Uhura, give the subcommander a five-second tick for his reference."

*"Thank you, Captain,"* said Tafv, *"we have that information. I will confer with your officer.* Bloodwing *out."*

Jim turned his back on the star-filled screen. "Uhura," he said, "when you've finished that, page Dr. McCoy and have him report to the transporter room. Come on, Spock. We mustn't keep the lady waiting."

# Chapter Seven

Five minutes later, Jim said to the transporter chief, "Energize."

Light danced and dazzled on the platform, settling into a woman's silhouette. The silhouette grew three-dimensional, darkened, solidified. The dazzle faded away.

Jim stood very still for a second or so, simply regarding her. She was little. Somehow he had always thought of her as being tall, lean, and ascetic; or else tall, muscular, and athletic. He was not prepared for this tiny woman, smaller even than the other female Romulan commander he and Spock had dealt with. If she was five foot one, that was granting her an inch or so; if she weighed as much as a hundred and ten pounds, that was on a dense planet. She was wearing her hair braided and coiled at the nape of her neck; exposing the upswept and pointed Vulcanoid ears; there was gray in those neat, tight braids. The woman's build and facial structure were so delicate that she looked as if she could be broken between one's hands—but knowing Romulans, Jim knew much better. She had great dark eyes and a mouth with much smiling behind it, to judge by the few wrinkles that showed there; and looking at her, Jim could see where Subcommander Tafv had come by that proud nose. But probably the most striking thing about her was her age, and the way she bore it. Jim had never thought to see a woman with such an aura of power, or one who seemed to take that power so much for granted. She carried herself like a banner, or a weapon: like something proud and dangerous, but momentarily at rest. Jim found himself wondering whether he would look that good when he was—how old was she? Romulans were of Vulcan stock, after all. She could be well up in her hundreds—

"Permission to come aboard," the commander said.

"Permission granted." Jim stepped around from behind the transporter console, Spock pacing him. "And welcome."

She stood there quite relaxed, looking Jim up and down, then favoring Spock with the same calm, unthreatening examination. Jim used the moment to continue his own. "They've changed the uniform," he said.

The commander glanced down at her tunic and breeches and boots, then smiled; a wry expression. "It was well changed," she said. "The kilt on the old uniform was a drafty bit of tailoring, and difficult to work in." She stepped down from the transporter platform, looking around her with curiosity. "Is my translator functioning adequately?" she said. "It was a hasty business, reprogramming it for Federation Basic."

"So far it seems to be doing well enough," Jim said. "If you like, though, Dr. McCoy here will help equip you with one of our intradermal models."

"I would appreciate that," said the commander. "We have talking to do, and there must be no chance of imprecision or error; too much rests on it."

She looked at Jim with such perfect ease that for a moment he was envious. *Would I be so calm after I had delivered myself into the hands of the enemy? What cards is she holding?* "So here at last," she said, "is my old friend Captain Kiurrk." Doubtless some flicker of reaction got out despite Jim's best intentions, for she smiled again. "Perhaps I will just call you 'Captain'; for it does not do to mishandle names." She turned to Spock. "Yours, though, I think I can say, estranged though our languages are. And yours," she said, glancing toward Bones, "might almost be Romulan. But 'Doctor' is an honorable title, so if I may, I will call you that. Gentlemen, may we go where we can talk? Handsome as this room is, it hardly looks like a reception area."

"This way," Jim said, and led the group out and down the hall to the officers' lounge. He bowed the commander in; and the first thing she responded to was not the elegant appointments, or the artwork, or the refreshments laid out, but the large port that looked out on the stars. That starlight was wavering, the uncomfortable starlight of unfiltered otherspace. Nevertheless she looked long and hard at it before she turned away. "The view must be marvelous," she said, "when the ship is not in warp."

"It is," Jim said. "Commander, will you sit?"

"Gladly." Without a moment's hesitation she slipped past the two couches set by the low refreshment table, and sat down in the single chair that faced them both, the chair commanding both the best view of the couches' occupants and the best access to the table—the chair Jim had intended to sit in. He smiled, said nothing, and made himself comfortable on one couch; but McCoy, fishing around in his medikit for a translator implant and the spray injector to fit it into, caught Jim's eye and raised one eyebrow before turning his attention back to business.

"Commander," Jim said, "what can we do for you?"

"For the moment, listen," said the commander. "More strenuous service may come later, however, if you agree with what I have to say. First, though, I have given you no name. I am Ael."

Spock, who had seated himself beside Jim, looked momentarily startled, and immediately composed himself. "Your first officer understands, perhaps better than most, that we are chary about giving others even our first names, even when they are already known," Ael said. "And there are other names more private yet. But I can think of no other way to demonstrate my sincerity to you from the start, since many of the things I must now say to you will sound incredible. I urge you, study to credit them. The whole Romulan Empire, and the Federation, and the Klingon Empire as well, rests on how seriously you take me."

"Tell us your problem, madam," Spock said.

"It will not be simply told." Seeing that McCoy was ready, Ael held out her arm to him; he took it, picked a spot on the inside of the forearm, and used the spray injector to install the translator's neutral implant up against the brachial nerve. "How is that? All right?—Well enough. Captain, have you ever heard of a place called Levaeri V?"

Jim considered for a moment. "Levaeri is a star in Romulan space, if I remember right. I would assume the 'V' refers to a planet."

"It does. Actually, the planet itself is uninhabited; a space station, built for research purposes, circles it. The Empire has been doing research there for some fifteen years into the nature and exploitation of genetic material, particularly the building-block molecule that governs and transmits life, along with its various messenger segments."

"DNA and RNA," said McCoy.

"Correct. The research has been secret, for reasons you will come to understand. But it is very nearly complete now. If the fruit of that research is allowed to escape into our civilization, it will destroy it—and eventually yours. The research has specifically involved the genetic material of Vulcans."

Spock sat up very straight. Jim glanced sideways at him—knowing that putting-it-all-together look from long experience—but for the moment said nothing but, "Toward what purpose?"

"The scientists at Levaeri V have been correcting Vulcan DNA and messenger RNA for the genetic drift that has occurred over the years between Romulan and Vulcan genetic material—so that the drift-corrected material can be used to give Romulans the paramental abilities of trained Vulcans."

"My God," Bones said softly.

Jim sat there wondering if he had missed something. Certainly it sounded dire. . . . "Bones, explain."

McCoy looked as though he would rather have done anything else. "Jim, this research—if I'm understanding Ael correctly—had its earliest antecedents on Earth in some very primitive mind experiments concerning planaria. Flatworms, as they're called. If you teach a flatworm something—takes awhile, I can tell you—and then chop it up and feed it to other flatworms, the worms that ate the first one will learn the same trick the first worm learned, but much more quickly than normal. This is a terrible oversimplification, but RNA and DNA can be passed from one creature to another by numerous means, even simple ingestion. It caused a lot of poor jokes for a while about how 'you are what you eat.' But some of our own chemical-learning techniques that we commonly use in Starfleet for speed learning are based in the same technology, considerably updated and refined."

"We understand one another," Ael said. She looked somewhat relieved, but also unnerved, as if actually discussing the subject in public frightened her. "The process I speak of is even more refined than the chemical-learning techniques, which we also possess—"

"Stolen from us, I believe," Jim said mildly.

Ael gave him a sharp look, then smiled, that wry expression again. "Yes, we are always stealing things from one another, are we not? I would like to come back to that later, Captain. But for the moment let me say that the scientists have refined the techniques to dangerous levels. Some bright creature—the Elements should only have taken him back to Themselves—got the idea that, since we are brother stock to the Vulcans, surely they could teach us what they know of the arts and disciplines of the mind, to our great benefit—"

"Madam," Spock said, leaning forward and looking at Ael with great intensity, "those techniques of the mind were not developed until long after the Vulcan colony ships bearing your remote ancestors had left. In the warlike state of the pre-Reformation civilization, before the Peace of Surak, the techniques could never have been developed at all. And the Romulan civilization as we know it preserves to this day almost exactly the same combative atmosphere as existed on Vulcan before the Reformation—unless you can give us some better news."

"If I could, Mr. Spock," Ael said, laughing with a trace of bitterness, "I would not have had to blow up my old ship to keep word of my actions from getting back into the Empire. I would not have been exiled to the Neutral Zone at all. Perhaps there would be no Zone. But those are all wishes, and I am wandering from my story. The researchers at Levaeri determined that such abilities, the mind-techniques such as mindmeld and mindfusion and touch telepathy, and such lesser physical techniques as the healing trance and controlled 'hysterical strength,' could in fact be successfully passed on to the nontalented, and quite simply—by a procedure involving, among other things, selective neutral-tissue grafts to the corpus callosum and spinal cord, and a series of injections of the DNA and RNA fragments into the cerebrospinal fluid."

"It could be done," McCoy said, looking rather upset. "Certainly it could. But you would need—"

"Donor tissue, yes," Ael said. "Brain tissue, both 'white' and 'gray,' and cerebrospinal fluid cultures, from mentally talented Vulcans. A great deal

of it, at first, until cultures had been perfected that were sufficiently innocuous not to be rejected outright by the recipient's autoimmune system. Naturally the researchers at Levaeri could not simply take ship
across the Zone to Vulcan and ask for some good-quality live Vulcan
brain tissue; any more than the Vulcans would have given it to them for
any reason whatsoever. So the researchers began—borrowing—Vulcans."

Spock looked at Jim. "Captain," he said, "this is the reason why I
asked the Federation Intersellar Shipping Commission for the data on
all recent ship losses. My preliminary studies were showing an odd
jump in the curve—a nearly statistical probability that spacefaring Vulcans were going missing more frequently than were travelers of other
species. I had hoped very much that I was wrong—"

"But you were not," Ael said. "Romulans were taking them, Mr.
Spock. They were taken to Levaeri V—as many Vulcans as the researchers thought could be kidnapped without anyone really noticing—
and there they were used as experimental subjects and tissue donors."

Jim looked across at McCoy, who was practically trembling with
rage. "This is monstrous, Commander," he said, controlling himself
very tightly.

"Certainly it is, Doctor," she said. "What honor is there in taking
one's enemies by stealth, giving them no chance to fight back, and then
binding and torturing and slaughtering them like animals? But there's
worse to come. Surely you must realize the purpose of the research. The
Empire's High Command greatly desires the Vulcan mind-techniques
for a weapon against its enemies—against you, and eventually against
the Klingons, who are swiftly becoming a garment too tight for us. And
the High Command has been an unscrupulous lot for some time now.
The Command, and the Praetorate and Senate, will demand to be the
first to use the newly developed techniques. The implementation
would not take long, I understand; a clinic-type surgery, followed by
several injections and a very brief period of training. Then— Can you
imagine, just by way of example, the kind of place Vulcan would be if
its people at large, and its rulers in particular, had never developed the
logics of peace and ethical behavior that Surak brought—and had the
mind techniques anyway?"

Spock looked more grave than Jim had seen him in a long time. Evidently the thought had occurred to him at one time or another. "A culture of ruthless opportunists," he said, "violating one another's minds for gain, or for power, or even for the mere pleasure of the act. Turmoil among the great as they struggle for preeminence and domination, trying to keep the techniques for themselves. Rebellion among those who do not have the techniques, and desire to, at any cost. War . . ."

"Worse than war," Ael said. "A world in which no thought that did not agree with the present political 'gospel' would be safe—where a chance whim, a moment's disaffection, could mean death at the hands of those who were listening to your thoughts. A world in which honor and trust would swiftly become devalued coinage, and personal integrity a death warrant, if it crossed the desires of those who controlled the technique, those in power. The process has already started. Right now on Romulus and Remus there is already considerable political infighting going on over who will first get the technique when it becomes available. Who will first read all the others' minds? Who will first learn his enemies' secrets? And of course there are people who must be prevented at all costs from learning one's own secret business. A lively trade in assassination is springing up." Ael said the word as if it tasted bad. "We have already lost four Senators to the ambition or fear of people in high places."

Jim nodded slowly, now fully understanding those deaths by "natural causes."

Ael sat silent for a moment, as if gathering her thoughts. "Gentlemen," Ael said, "I will be open with you. I am a warrior, and I find peace very dull. But honor I cherish; and I see, with the completion and release of this technique, the rise of a new Romulan Empire that will have lost the last vestiges of the glory and honor of the old one. I have sworn oaths to that Empire, to serve it loyally. To stand by and do nothing about the destruction of the ancient and noble tradition on which that Empire is based, is to put the knife into it oneself. I will not. The research station at Levaeri V must be destroyed before the information and materials stored there can be disseminated throughout the Empire."

Jim and Spock and McCoy looked at one another. It was now very plain what Starfleet's problem had been—for there was no hinting at this situation in the open. If the Klingons heard so much as a word about it, they would be at war with the Romulans instantly, trying to get their hands on the same technology. It might not work as well for them, but that would hardly matter; once they had subordinated Romulan space, which was the buffer between them and the Federation, the next step would be to cross the former Neutral Zone and attack the only remaining enemy. *And*—the thought sent a cold chill down Jim's back—*how many officials in the Federation, on any one of a thousand planets, would be willing to pay any price for such an advantage over their opponents? Even benevolent motives couldn't be trusted. They might start out that way, but they wouldn't stay there. Any power of this magnitude corrupts absolutely. . . .*

"Commander," Jim said slowly, "this is information we've come a long way to hear. And we thank you very much for warning us of this danger. But there's something I don't understand. Why are you telling us this? I can't be said to know you well; we've only just met. But I've fought you often enough to know that you never do anything without a good reason."

Ael looked at him tranquilly for a moment, and again, very briefly, Jim had a flash of combined admiration and envy of her composure. She then tipped her head back to look around the room. "Captain," she said, "do you have any idea how many times I've dreamt of blowing this ship up?"

It seemed a moment for honesty. "Probably about as many times as I've dreamed about blowing up yours." That sounded a little bald, and Jim added, "Of course, it would have been a great pity. . . ."

"Yes," she said absently, "it would have been a shame to blow up *Enterprise,* too. The workmanship appears excellent." She flashed a smile at him: Jim became aware that he was being teased. "Captain, I come to you because I see my world in danger—and incidentally yours—and there's no more help to be found among my friends. At such a time, with millions and billions of lives riding on what is done, pride dies, and one has recourse to one's enemies. Of all my enemies I esteem you highest; you are a fierce combatant, but you've never been less than courteous with me—valorous in the best sense of the word, a warrior who deals in hard knocks or careful courtesy, nothing in between. Excluding, for the moment, various small subterfuges and thefts in the past." Now she did not smile; this was not teasing. "I too have been ordered in the past to do things I found hateful, so I understand the necessity of what you once did to my sister's-daughter—"

"The other Romulan commander—she's your *niece*?" McCoy said.

"Was," said Ael. "I agree that sooner or later we shall have to deal with that old business, Captain. But right now there is new business far more pressing. Levaeri V must be destroyed!"

"I agree," Jim said. "But if preventing war is one of your aims, Commander, then we have a problem. While I am willing to overlook the presence of your ship on this side of the Zone, your High Command would never overlook that of *Enterprise* in Romulan space. I suspect you want *Enterprise* to come in and assist you in the destruction of this base, is that right?"

"Yes."

"But our crossing the Zone would be a breach of the Federation-Romulan Treaty, and an act of war."

"Not necessarily."

"Ael," McCoy said, "we're unmistakably a Federation craft. There's no disguising the *Enterprise* as a Romulan warbird, no matter what you suggest we do to our ID! How do you propose to get us into Romulan space without getting us discovered and shot at?"

She leaned back in her chair and favored them, one after another, with a look that Jim could only call mischievous. "I was thinking of capturing the *Enterprise*," she said to Jim. "Would you mind? . . ."

# Chapter Eight

Jim looked quietly at Ael. "If that was a joke," he said, "it was a poor one. And if this is a trap of some kind, good workmanship or not, I am going to reduce *Bloodwing* to its component atoms—or die trying."

Ael smiled at Jim, as if seeing a response she had expected, and enjoyed. "It was no joke," she said. "And it is no trap. I may be desperate, but am I mad, to threaten you under a destroyer's guns? Do you think I don't know *Inaieu* is hanging five kilometers off your starboard side, and *Constellation* is closing in fast as per your orders? Give me credit for intelligence if nothing else, Captain."

"That," he said, "if nothing else, Commander. What exactly are you proposing?"

"That you join with me in a bit of subterfuge that will be, as my son has told you, as much to your advantage as to mine. Working together, we will set it up so that it will appear, to any Romulan observer, that the *Enterprise* has been bested in an engagement—disabled, boarded, manned by Romulans from my crew. We will so advertise the situation to Romulan High Command, and prepare to tow your 'conquered' ship in to the Romulus-Remus system. Even if Command should send us an escort— which possibility is difficult to predict, ships for Neutral Zone patrol being grudged right now, due to our problem with the Klingons—there would still be no real difficulty in maintaining the ruse. There is no way to sort the types of life-readings, Romulan from hominid or alien, using our ships' sensors; only numbers can be counted. Your crew would remain aboard your ship, running it possibly from the auxiliary bridge, where control would reside . . . and the bridge would be full of Romulans, who would handle all communications with other Romulan ships and otherwise maintain the illusion."

"Now, *wait* a moment!" McCoy said.

"Bones, hold your thought. Ael, assuming I should agree to this outrageousness—what would be our justification for passing by Levaeri V on our way in to Romulus-Remus? Such a high-security establishment as you're describing would surely have traffic routed away from it normally—"

"Normally," she said, "of course it does. But what would be normal about capturing the *Enterprise?* Questions of revenge aside—and there are various people at Command who would be only too delighted to tear you apart limb from limb—there are also the legates, who have multiple warrants out for the arrest of you and Mr. Spock on those old espionage charges. Don't look so left out, Doctor; there are writs out on you too, as I understand it, for aiding and abetting an act of espionage, complicity in the impersonation of a Romulan officer, various other things. . . . But in any case Command would want the *Enterprise* brought in by the swiftest and most straightforward route, to reduce your chance of having time to improvise an escape. From this part of space, our course in to Romulus-Remus lies right past Levaeri V. I planned it so. We drove the destroyer Romulan ship *Cuirass* to this location before engaging it, for that very purpose. Now we have an excuse to be here—and radiation trails that conform to the story we will be telling."

Jim leaned forward a bit, grinning. It was a treat to hear this wicked mind working out loud. The only problem was that there was no way to tell whether what Ael was proposing was on the level. Unless . . .

"Commander," he said, "I make you no promises, but you're beginning to interest me. Tell me 'our story.'"

"Why, only this," she said, smiling back at him, "that *Cuirass,* which I command—at least it will seem to be *Cuirass,* for I have a copy of that ship's ID solid aboard *Bloodwing,* ready to be installed—that *Cuirass* detected *Enterprise* violating our space, and followed her out into the Zone, where she attempted to bring us to battle, but suffered mechanical difficulties—which I suspect your chief engineer, whom we also know well, can fake without too much difficulty. That, unable to run, and with damage to your warp engines, we had only to draw you into exhausting your firepower, and then wear your shields down with fire of our own, to reduce you to a position where you (with your well-known compassion for your crew) were left helpless enough to be unable to repel a boarding action. With your bridge taken and your crew under the threat of having your own intruder-control systems used on them—a swift killer, that gas—you surrendered the ship to buy their lives. My crew manned control positions on your ship, placed her in tow, and headed for home."

It was plausible. It was even doable. "There have been other ships in the area, though," Jim said. "Anyone tracing your iontrail and ours would also note the passage of first *Intrepid,* then *Constellation* and *Inaieu*—"

"True. But it's difficult to accurately place such residues in time, is it not? Their decay is not regular, especially in the space hereabouts, where you have noticed the weather has been bad lately." Ael tipped her head to one side, regarding Jim. "And by the time anyone follows our trails out this far and returns within subspace radio range of Levaeri V, it will be too late. We will already have done what we came for. *Enterprise* and *Bloodwing* will break away from the escort, if any—"

"You mean take them all on and blow them up?" McCoy said incredulously. "How many ships come in an escort, anyway?"

"For *Enterprise,* they would hardly send fewer than two. Four, at the most, would be my guess."

Bones looked incredulously from Spock to Jim and back again. "We're just going to 'break away' from four fully-armed Romulan cruisers, probably those Klingon-model cruisers—"

"You gentlemen will not fail me," Ael said, perfectly calm. "This *is* the *Enterprise,* after all. . . . Once we have scrapped the escort, destroying Levaeri V should not be too much of a problem."

"I imagine not," Jim said. "But, Commander, what about the loss of life?"

"The Romulans doing the research have not been too concerned about that," Ael said coolly, "especially where the Vulcans have been concerned. I did not think that would be so much of an issue for you. Perhaps I miscalculated."

"Perhaps." Jim thought of about seventy things he wanted to shout at her, none of which would have done him or her any good; this woman might look almost Earth-human, but he had to keep reminding himself that their respective branches of humanity had very different mores indeed. "Mr. Spock," he said after a little while, "opinions?"

Spock looked distinctly uncomfortable. "Commander," he said, turning to her for a moment, "I would ask you not to take anything I say as a slight against your honor."

She bowed her head to him, the gracious gesture of nobility to one almost a peer. Jim started to get very annoyed.

"Captain," Spock said, "the plan is an audacious one. Its odds for success in its early stages are very high. However, I advise you most strongly against it. There are too many variables, unknowns, things that can go wrong at the plan's far end. Even should one of our allies suggest such an operation, having a spare Romulan ship with falsified ID on hand, Starfleet would have no mercy on the plan if it miscarried. And with the suggestion coming from a representative of a power with whom the Federation has long been on the fringes of war—"

"Amen to that, Mr. Spock," McCoy growled. "Whole thing's a pack of nonsense."

"No, Doctor," Spock said, eyeing him, "that it is not. The commander's plan is excellently reasoned—but the risks in its later stages become unacceptably high. For a Vulcan, at least. Captain?"

Jim looked at Ael. "You say that you are willing to forgo pride for the time being," he said. "Then I hope you'll pardon me, but this has to be said. How do we know you're not lying? Or worse—how do we know you haven't been brainwashed into thinking this is the truth you're telling us, so that you can safely lay your honor on the line?"

Ael breathed out once, leaving Jim to wonder whether a sigh meant the same thing to Romulans as it did to his branch of humanity. "Captain," she said, "of course you had to say that. But there is a way to find out, one that strikes to the heart of this whole matter. Ask Mr. Spock if he will consent to subject me to a mindmeld."

Jim looked at Spock. Spock was still as stone. "It's true," McCoy said. "There are ways of blocking or tampering with a mind that won't show up under verifier scan—but will in mindmeld. It would be conclusive, Jim."

"I had thought of it," Jim said. "But I didn't want to suggest it." And he said nothing more.

A few seconds went silently by. Finally Spock looked at Ael and said, very quietly, "I will do this, Commander." He glanced over at Jim. "Captain, somewhere more private would be appropriate."

"Your quarters?"

"Those would do very well. Commander, will you accompany me? The captain and the doctor will join us shortly."

"Certainly."

Out they went together, the Vulcan and the Romulan, and Jim had to stare after them. There was something so alike about them—not just the racial likeness, either. "Well, Bones," he said, "get it off your chest."

McCoy leaned forward on the couch, elbows on knees, and stared at Jim. "How much I have to get off," he said, "depends on what you're going to do."

"Nothing, until we have Spock's assessment of what the inside of her mind looks like."

"And what if she *is* telling the truth, Jim? Are you tellin' me you're going to go off on some damn fool chase into interdicted territory, probably get us surrounded by Romulans again like the last time—but this time on purpose? We're just going to *sit* there and be towed into Romulan space under escort! Why don't we just tie ourselves up and jump out the airlocks in our underwear? Save us all a lot of—"

"*Bones,*" Jim said, not angrily, but loudly; sometimes when McCoy got started on one of these it was hard to stop him. Bones subsided.

"I am *not* seriously considering it," Jim said. "Even if she *is* telling the truth. What I'm trying to figure out is what to do about what she's told us. This information is too sensitive to do anything but whisper in a Fleet Admiral's ear; I wouldn't dare send it via subspace radio, buoy, or any other means that might be intercepted, decoded, anything. Too much rests on it—as far as that goes, she's not understating. None of the ships can leave the task force, and I'm sure as Hell not going to send an unarmed shuttlecraft or one of *Inaieu*'s little couriers off with it. Plus I have other problems on my mind." He reached out to the table and hit one of the 'com switches on it. "Bridge. Mr. Scott."

*"Scott here."*

"Scotty, how're our Romulan friends?"

*"Quiet as mice, Captain. Back on their original course, holding steady at warp five and one light-second."*

"Any communications?"

*"None, sir."*

"Very well. Give me Uhura."

*"She's offshift, sir,"* said another voice. *"Lieutenant Mahasë."*

"Oh. Fine. Mr. Mahasë, call the Romulan ship. My compliments to Subcommander Tafv, and we are still conferring with the commander. No progress to report as yet, should he inquire."

*"Right, sir. By the way, Captain, we have another message from* Intrepid."

"Live message, or canned?"

*"Canned, sir. They left it recorded in a squirt on the satellite zone-monitoring station we just passed—NZRM 4488. The ion storm was holding steady at force six; they expected it to begin tapering down any time. Sensors still show a lot of lively hydrogen up that way, though. We'll be running into it ourselves shortly."*

Jim rubbed his eyes. *Damn weather . . .* "Well, keep trying to reach them in realtime—they ought to be appraised of what's going on back here. Anything else I should know?"

*"Mr. Chekov wants to take just one shot at* Bloodwing, *Captain. Just for practice."*

"Tell him to go take a cold shower when his shift's over," Jim said. "Kirk out. Come on, Bones, let's go see if the truth really *will* out."

# Chapter Nine

Ael followed Spock silently through the corridors of *Enterprise,* trying to understand the people walking those corridors by studying their surroundings. She could make little of what she saw, except that she found it vaguely unpleasant. The overdone handsomeness of the transporter room and the ridiculous luxury of the officers' lounge had put her off; she had found herself thinking of her bare, cramped quarters in *Bloodwing* with ridiculous nostalgia, as if she were hundreds of light-years away from it, marooned in *Cuirass* again. But the situation was really no different. *Here as there,* she thought, *I am among aliens—and if what I plan succeeds, I will have to live so for the rest of my life. I had better get used to it.* And she followed Spock into his quarters expecting something similar—something Terrene-contaminated, overdone, something that would make her even more uncomfortable than she already was.

But she got a surprise. For one thing, the room was warm enough to be comfortable. For another, except that they were bigger, the quarters might have been a twin to her own for the general feel of them. The place was utterly neat; sparsely furnished, but not barren; and if it accurately reflected its owner, she was going to have to revise her estimation of Vulcans upward.

There were some things there, such as the firepot-beast in the corner, that she knew enough about Vulcans not to inquire of; like a good guest she passed them by. But other things drew Ael's attention. One was a stereo cube, sitting all alone on the ruthlessly clean desk. In it a dark stern Vulcan man stood beside a beautiful older woman, who wore a very un-Vulcan smile. Ael put out a hand to it, not touching, thinking of her father. "This would be Ambassador Sarek, then," she said, "and Lady Amanda."

"You are well informed, Commander," Spock said. He had been

standing behind her, not moving—holding very still, as Ael fancied someone might who had a dangerous beast at close range and did not want to frighten it.

She laughed softly at his words, and at her own thoughts. "Too well informed for my own comfort, perhaps." She turned from the portrait toward the wall that adjoined the panel dividing the sleeping area from the rest of the room, and looked up at the very few old weapons adorning it . . . and breathed in once, sharply.

"Mr. Spock," she said, "am I mistaken? Or is that, as I think, a S'harien up there?"

The look in his eyes as she turned to face him was not quite surprise—more appreciation, if that closed face could be said to express anything at all. "It is, Commander. If you would like to examine it . . ."

He trailed off. Ael reached up with great care and took the sword down from the wall, laying it over the forearm of her uniform so as not to risk fingerprinting the exquisite sardonyx-wood inlay of the scabbard. The sheath's design was lean, clean, necessary, brutal logic and an eye for beauty going hand in hand. The hilt was plain black *kahs-hir*, left rough as when it had been quarried, for a better grip: logical again. "May I draw it?" she said.

Spock nodded. Whispering, the steel came out of the sheath. Ael looked at it and shook her head in longing at the way even a starship's artificial light fell on the highlights buried in the blade. No one had ever matched the work of the ancient swordsmiths who had worked at the edge of Vulcan's Forge, five thousand years before; and S'harien had been the greatest of them all. The pilgrims to ch'Rihan had managed to take five of his swords with them. Of those, three had been broken in dynastic war, shattered in the hands of dying kings and queens; one was stolen and lost, thought to be drifting in a long cometary orbit around Eisn; one lay in the Empty Chair in the Senate Chambers, where no hand might touch it. Certainly Ael had never thought to hold a S'harien. The sword in her hand spoke, by its superb balance, of things Ael couldn't say; of history, and home, and treasures lost forever; of power, and the loss of it, and the word there was no one to tell. . . .

She looked up at the Vulcan in unspeakable envy and admiration, her voice gone quite out of her. *A fine showing you're making!* Ael thought bitterly. *Struck dumb by a piece of metal—*

"It is an heirloom," he said, as if sensing her momentary loss. "It would be illogical to leave it locked in a vault, where it could not be appreciated."

"Appreciation," Ael said, in a tone that was meant to be light mockery; but her voice shook a bit. "That's an emotion, is it not?"

He looked at her, and Ael saw that without meld, without the use of touch or anything else, Spock still saw her nervousness with perfect clarity. "Commander," he said to her, innocently matching her tone, "'appreciation' is a noun. It denotes the just valuation or recognition of worth."

She stared at him dubiously.

"I believe you are telling the truth," he said. "And if you are, I cannot say how much I honor you for daring to do what you have done, for peace's sake. But for both the captain and myself, belief will not be enough. We must be utterly certain of you and of what you say."

"I understand you very well," Ael said. "Understand me also; I have given up pride—though not yet fear. However, I demand that you do to me whatever will best convince the captain."

Spock lifted his head, hearing footsteps in the hall. Ael, considering that it might not be wise for the captain to come in and find her facing his first officer while holding a sword, gave Spock a conspiratorial glance and turned her back on him, savoring the feel of the S'harien in her hand for just a moment more. . . .

The door-buzzer sounded. "Come," Spock said quietly. In came the captain and the doctor, and as the door shut behind them, they stood uncertainly for a moment, looking at Ael. She turned to face them, and her fear fell away from her at the bemusement on the doctor's face, the surprise on the captain's.

"Gentlemen," she said to them, picking up the S'harien's scabbard from the desk and sheathing it again, "I had no idea that the *Enterprise* would be carrying museum pieces. Can it be that all those stories about starships being instruments of culture are actually true?"

And to her utter astonishment, she saw that her cautious flippancy was not fooling the captain, either. He was looking at her with the small wry smile of someone who also knew and loved the feel of a blade in the hand.

"We like to think so, Commander," he said. "You should come down to recreation, if there's time . . . we have some interesting things down there. But right now we have other business." And he glanced at Spock much as Ael might have glanced at Tafv when there was some uncomfortable business to be gotten over with quickly.

She bowed slightly to him, sat down in the chair at Spock's desk. The Vulcan came to stand behind her. Ael leaned back and closed her eyes.

"There will be some discomfort at first, Commander," said the voice from above and behind her. "If you can avoid resisting it, it will pass very quickly."

"I understand."

Fingers touched her face, positioning themselves precisely over the cranial nerve pathways. Ael shivered all over, once and uncontrollably; then was still.

Her first thought was that she couldn't breath. No, not that precisely; that there was something wrong with the way she was breathing, it was too fast. . . . She slowed it down, took a longer deeper breath—and then caught it back in shock, realizing that she couldn't *take* that deep a breath, her lungs didn't have that much capacity—

*Do not resist,* her own voice said in her head without her thinking any such thing. Surely this was what the approach of madness was like.

*No! They are breaking faith with me, they are going to drive me mad—no! No! I have too much to do—*

*Commander—Ael—I warned you of the discomfort. Do not resist or you will damage yourself—*

—oh, bizarre, the words were coming in Vulcan but she could still understand them—or rather she heard them at the same time in Rihannsu, and in Federation Basic, and in Vulcan, and she understood them all. Her own voice speaking them inside her, as if in her own thought—but the thought another's—

*Better. Our minds are drawing closer. . . . Open to me, Ael. Let me in.*

—impossible not to; the self/other voice was gentle enough, but there was a strength behind it that could easily crush any denial. *Would* not, however—she realized that without knowing how—

—*closer now, closer*—

—Elements above and beyond, what had she been afraid of? What an astonishment, to breathe with other lungs, to see through another mind's eye, to journey through another darkness and find light at journey's end. . . . That was no more than she did on *Bloodwing,* than she had done all her life; how could she possibly fear it? She reached out for the other, not knowing how: hoping will would be enough, as it had always been for everything else—

—*we are one.*

She was. Odd that there were suddenly two of her, but it seemed always to have been that way. With the odd calmness of a dream, where outrageous things happen and seem perfectly normal, she found herself very curious about the events of the past few months, the whole business regarding Levaeri V, from beginning to end. Luckily it took little time, in this timelessness, to go over it all; and she took herself from beginning to end in running commentary and split-instant images—the crimson banners of the Senate chambers, the faces of old friends in the Praetorate who solemnly said "no," or said "perhaps" meaning "no." There were the faces of her crew, glad to see her back, outraged nearly to rebellion at the thought of her transfer from *Bloodwing.* There were the hateful faces of the crew of *Cuirass,* and there was t'Liun's voice shouting over ship's channels for her to come to the bridge. There was Tafv, dark and keen, reaching out to take her hand as she boarded *Bloodwing* again, raising her hand to his forehead in a ridiculously antique and moving gesture of welcome. And her cheering crew, all of them like children to her, like brothers and sisters. There was *Bloodwing*'s transporter room. And there was another transporter room entirely, with men in it. One fair and lithe, with an unreadable face and a very unalien courtesy; one dark and fierce-eyed, with hands that looked skilled; and one who could have been one of her own brothers, if not for Starfleet blue, and the memory of old enmities. . . .

Her sudden curiosity invited her to look more closely at those enmities. She resisted at first—they were old history, and their consideration bred nothing but anger. But the curiosity wouldn't be balked, and finally Ael gave in to it. That image of her sister's-daughter standing before the Senate after her defeat at the captain's and Spock's hands, after the loss of the cloaking device to the Federation. Ael's impassioned, desperate defense of her before the Senators—useless, fallen on hearts too obsessed with vengeance and fear for their own places to hear any plea. Ael stared again down the length of the white chamber, looking toward the Empty Chair, while around her the voices proclaimed her sister-daughter's eternal exile from ch'Rihan and ch'Havran, the stripping of her honors from her, and worst, the ceremonial shaming and removal of her house-name. Ael had protested again at that, not caring how it would endanger her own position. The protest had gone unheeded. She stood at marble attention while the name was thrice written, thrice burned, and watched bitterly as her sister-daughter went from the chambers in the deepest disgrace—no longer even a person, for a Rihannsu without a house was no one and nothing.

*And where is she now?* she cried to that curious, silent part of her that watched all this. *Wandering somewhere in space, or living alone on some wretched exile-world, alone among aliens? How should I not hate those who did such a thing to her?* Nor was there any forgetting Tafv's bitter anger at the exile of his cousin, his dear old playmate. Yet he had come to know cool reason, as Ael had, just as this sudden new part of her had learned it when he was young and occasionally angry. Hate would have to wait. Perhaps some kind shift in the Elements, at another time, would allow her a chance to face her enemies and prove on their bodies in clean battle that they were cowards, who had consented to deal in trickery to achieve their means. Now, though, she needed those enemies badly. Personal business could not be allowed to matter where the survival of empires was involved.

The new part of her agreed silently and said nothing more for a moment. Ael seized that moment, for she had her own curiosity. Here was one of those enemies, inwardly linked to her. Becoming "curious" in turn, she reached out to it; and the other part of her, in a kind of somber acknowledgment of justice, suffered her to do so. Ael reached deep—

She had for years been picturing some kind of monster, a half-bred thing without true conscience or sense of self, the kind of person who could work a treachery on her sister-daughter with such cool precision. But now, as in her estimate of what his rooms would be like, she found herself wrong again, so very wrong that her shame burned her. Certainly there was the vast internal catalogue of data and store of expertise that she would have expected from a man whom even among the Rihannsu was a legend as one of Starfleet's great officers. But what she had not suspected was someone as torn as she was, and as whole as she was, and in such similar ways. Someone who had sworn himself to a hard life, for what seemed to him a greater good more important than his own, and who had suffered for the oath's sake, and would again, willingly; someone who was also powerfully rooted in another life, a heart's life—based around a planet where he could hardly ever walk, and relationships he could never fully acknowledge, because of what he had chosen to be. No oaths were attached to those choices—just simple will, rock-steady and unbreakable. *That* person she had not suspected. Alien he might be, but there was that very Rihannsu characteristic, the unshakable, unbreakable loyalty to an idea, a goal, a man who embodied it. The best part of the ruling Passion, a banked fire, but burning this man out from within, and never to be relinquished, no matter how much it hurt—

*That* man she could open to, as she might open to Tafv or Aidoann or tr'Keirianh. And she did, feeling suddenly for the terrible suppressed passions in him, and for one of them more than any of the others—for homesickness. She showed him Airissuin, and the barren red mountains of her home, so like his own; she showed him the farmstead, and the place where the *hlai* got out, and her father, so very like his; the small dry flowers on the hillside, and the way the sunlight fell across her couch the day after her son was born, and she held him in her arms for the first time without the distraction of pain, wishing his father had lived to see—oh, Liha, lost to the Klingons in that ridiculous "misunderstanding" off Nh'rainnsele! Could there never be an end to such misunderstandings—worlds to walk safely, an end to wars, other ways to avoid boredom and find adventure? Must the innocent die, and must she keep on killing them? *An end to it, an end!*

Her second self was in distress; but so was Ael, and for the moment she had no pity on either of them. This was after all the most important matter, the only one that ranked with truth and hearts and names. Life must go on, and with the implementation of the project at Levaeri, there would be an end to it. Truth would become deadly, hearts would become public places, and names—Better that small wars should flare up and take their inevitable toll, better that she and Tafv and all the crew of *Bloodwing,* yes, and that of *Enterprise* too, should die before such a thing happened. For these were honorable people, as she had always suspected and now found that she had not known half the truth of it. Just the image of the captain that her otherself held was enough to convince her; his image of the doctor, very different but held in no less loyalty, was more data toward the same conclusion. Such people, whatever her hatreds, hinted at the existence of many more on the other side of the Zone. They must not be allowed to become obsolete, or dead, as honorable people everywhere would should this technique be carried to its logical conclusion; they must not, *they must not*—

—and her mind abruptly came undone. Not a painful sensation, but a sad one, as if she had been born twins and was bidding the twin good-bye.

Ael opened her eyes. The Vulcan she could still feel behind her— some thread of the link apparently remained; she could feel the stone-steady foundations of his mind shaken somewhat. But of more interest to her was the look the captain was giving her, both compassionate and bleak. The doctor was turned toward the wall and rubbing his eyes, as if something ailed them. She realized abruptly that her face was wet.

Spock came around from behind her, his hands behind his back, physically standing at ease; but Ael knew better. "Commander," he said quietly. "I apologize profoundly for the intrusion."

"I thank you," she said, "but the apology is unnecessary. I am quite well."

Glancing up at him, she saw that Spock, also, knew better. The captain was looking from one to the other of them. "I also apologize, Commander," he said. "If it will do any good . . ."

"It will do none to the exiled or the dead," Ael said, as levelly as she could, wondering how much she and the Vulcan might have spoken aloud in this meld, and fearing the worst. "But for myself, I thank you."

"If you would excuse us a moment," the captain said, "I must discuss this business with Mr. Spock and Dr. McCoy."

She bowed her head to him; they went out into the corridor together, all three moving as separate parts of one mind. *We are more alike than I imagined,* she said to herself, rubbing briefly at her face and thinking of those times in battle and out of it when she and Tafv and Aidoann functioned as one whole creature in three different places. *If I am not careful, I will forget to hate these people for what they did to my sister-daughter . . . and what will become of me then?*

"*Captain,*" she distinctly heard Spock saying, "*every word she has told us is the truth. She is under no compulsion save that of her conscience—which is of considerable power; her resolve and fear of lost time was what broke the link—I did not.*"

"*Any sign of tampering with her mind at all?*" the captain said.

"*None. There were areas I could not touch, as there might be in any mind. And one piece of data with unusually powerful privacy blocks around it—an area somewhat contaminated with emotions that I consider similar to human types of shame and regret. But my sense was that this was a private matter, not concerning us.*"

"*I don't like it,*" the doctor said. "*Did you get a 'sense' of any associational linkages to that block that might reach into the areas that* do *concern us?*"

"*Some, Doctor. But this blocked material had linkages to almost every other part of the commander's mind as well. I do not think it is of importance to us.*"

"Well," said the captain, and let out a long breath. "*Spock, I hate to say this, but Fleet is not going to buy what the commander's proposing. It's too farfetched, too dangerous, and even though the commander is an honorable woman, I can't possibly trust all those other Romulans. She tells us herself that the Romulans as a whole are becoming more opportunistic, less attached to their old code of honor. What do we do if some one of them, while aboard the* Enterprise, *gets the idea to try a takeover? Granted that we outnumber them incredibly—if so much as one of my crew should die in such an incident, Starfleet would have my hide. And rightly. I agree with her that we have a moral responsibility to the three great powers—but if we tried to carry off the operation she suggests, and then botched it somehow so that word of what's going on at Levaeri leaked out without our managing to destroy the place—No. I'm sorry. Strategically it's a lovely idea, but tactically, with our present force and numbers, it's a wash. I am going to send for more ships—quietly—and then act."*

The captain let out another unhappy breath. *"Come on, gentlemen. Let's tell her the bad news as gently—"*

The small viewer on Spock's desk whistled. *"Bridge to Captain Kirk."*

Ael reached out to flick the small switch beside it. "If you will hold one moment, I will get him." *Mr. Spock,* she said through the rapidly fading mindlink, *would you please tell the captain he has a call?*

A flash of acquiescence reached her. The door hissed open, and in the three came again. "Sorry to keep you waiting, Commander," the captain said. "Let me handle this first. Kirk here," he said to the viewer.

*"Captain,"* said the communications officer, a gray-skinned hominid who had apparently replaced the lovely dark woman Ael recalled from Tafv's earlier call to *Enterprise, "we have another squirt from* Intrepid. *They were passing by NZR 4486 when they were apparently attacked."*

"By what?" the captain said, glancing sharply at Ael.

*"That's the problem, sir. They didn't know. The ion storm suddenly escalated to nearly force-ten—enough to leave them sensor-blind. It was just after that that they were fired upon. But the odd thing is that they didn't fall out of communication with the relay station until almost a minute and a half after the storm escalated. Then they just cut off communication in the middle of transmission—not a storm-fade, or a catastrophic loss of signal, as if they'd been—as if something had happened to the ship. Just a stop."*

"Keep trying to raise them, Mr. Mahasë. And call red alert. All hands to battle stations. Alert *Inaieu* and *Constellation;* they're to go to red alert as well."

*"Aye aye, sir. Any further orders?"*

"None at present. Kirk out."

Outside Ael could hear the ship's odd red-alert siren whooping, and people hurrying past the room "Commander," the captain said, "what do you know of this?"

"That the attacking ship is almost certainly Rihannsu," she said, "and the ion storm almost certainly our doing. I wish you had told me of this earlier; I have had no news of it from my ship. Unfortunately your sensors seem to be rather better than ours—"

"What do you mean the ion storm's 'of your doing'?" the doctor said.

"I am sorry, gentlemen," she said, "but it is hard to tell you everything presently happening in Rihannsu space while standing on one foot. Mr. Spock, if you look into your memories of our meld, you will find this information accurate. One research that has been complete for some time now is a method for producing ion storms by selective high-energy 'seeding' of stellar coronae. The High Command has been using it for some time as a clandestine weapon to keep the Klingons from raiding our frontier worlds. Their economic situation has been very bad recently, as you may know, and their treaty with us has been honored more in its breach than in its keeping. However, the technique has also been used on this side of the Zone—to cover the tracks of those who have been stealing Vulcans. How better to spirit away small ships, without anyone noticing, then to have them vanish in ion storms? Everybody knows how dangerous those are—"

"Then the change in the stellar weather hereabouts," Spock said, "has not been natural, but engineered."

"To some extent. There was some concern that changing it in one place would also cause changes elsewhere; so the climatic alterations of which you speak may be secondary rather than primary. However, things now look even worse than they did, gentlemen. The research at Levaeri must be even further along than I thought, for the researchers to take such a large group of Vulcans—and right out from under the noses of a Federation task force. They must be about to start production of the shifted genetic material in bulk, to need so wide a spectrum of live tissue." Ael looked grave. "Captain, if you do not do something, shortly half the Imperial Senate will be reading one another's alleged minds, courtesy of the brain tissue of the crew of the *Intrepid*. . . ."

Spock stood still, appearing unmoved—but again Ael knew better; and the other two stared at her in open horror. "Commander," McCoy said at last, "this is ridiculous! If the Romulan ship tries to capture the Vulcans, they'll die sooner than let that happen—"

"They will not be *allowed* to die, Doctor," Ael said, becoming impatient. "Don't you understand yet that this technique not only reproduces in its users the mental abilities of trained Vulcans, but raises those abilities to a much higher level than normal? What use would it be making touch-telepaths out of the Senate? Who among them would allow anyone to touch him? The technique was designed to enable mindreading and control at a distance for short periods—even control over the resistant minds of Vulcans already knowledgeable in the disciplines! Three or four people aboard a Romulan ship could easily hold the bridge crew of *Intrepid* under complete control for the short time it would take to make them stop firing, lower their shields and be boarded. Or there are other methods equally effective. Then the Rihannsu would simply take ship, Vulcans and all across the Zone, under cover of the ion storm, and do their pleasure with them."

"But Vulcans with command training—" the captain said,

"Command training will make no difference to this artificially augmented ability, Captain," Ael said. "We are dealing here with an ability that if developed much further will be able to take on even races as telepathically advanced as the Organians and Melkot."

The captain's face went very fierce. "We've got to go after them—"

"You cannot. If you do, you and your whole crew will suffer the same fate as *Intrepid*—one not so kind, actually. Your minds will fall under control far more swiftly than those of *Intrepid*'s Vulcans did—and after the Rihannsu move in and arrest you and Spock and the doctor, they will kill your crew and take the *Enterprise* home to study. The same thing will happen if *Inaieu* or *Constellation* follow you in. No, Captain, if you want the *Intrepid* and its crew back, my plan is the only way. And we will have to be swift about it. They will not wait around, at Levaeri, now that they have the genetic material they need. Processing of the Vulcans will begin at once."

Ael sat still, then, and watched the captain think. A long time she had wanted to see this—her old opponent in the process of decision, ideas and options flickering behind his eyes. And it was very quickly, as she had suspected it would be, that he looked up again.

"Commander," he said, "I think, for the moment, you've got an ally. Spock, have Lieutenant Mahasë call Rihaul and Walsh. I want a meeting of all ships' department heads in *Inaieu* in an hour. Bones, bring Lieutenant Kerasus with you."

"Yes, Captain."

"Right, Jim."

And out they went. Ael found herself alone and looking at an angry man—one who was going to have to do something he didn't want to, and was very aware of it.

"Commander," he said to her, "am I going to regret this?"

"'Going to'? Captain, you regret it already."

He frowned at her—and at the same time began to smile.

"Let's go," he said.

# Chapter Ten

It turned into the noisiest staff meeting Jim could remember in many years of them. The number of people in attendance was part of the reason—all eighteen of *Enterprise*'s department heads, along with Janíce Kerasus from linguistics, Jim's Romulan culture expert, and Colin Matlock, the security chief; and the captains and department heads of both *Constellation* and *Inaieu*. There they were, crammed into *Inaieu*'s main briefing . . . hominids and tentacled people and people with extra legs, all three kinds of Denebians and very assorted members of other species, in as much or as little Fleet uniform as they usually wore.

In the middle of all the blue and orange and command gold and green was a patch of color both somberer and more splendid; Ael and her son Tafv, both in the scarlet and gold-shot black of Romulan officers. They did not bear themselves like two aliens alone among suspicious people. Ael sat as unshaken among them as she had in the officers' lounge; and Jim, looking across at the calm young Tafv leaning back in his chair, decided that he had inherited more from his mother than his nose.

He had beamed across from *Bloodwing* at Ael's request, and had looked around *Enterprise*'s transporter room with the hard, seeing eyes of someone checking an area for weaknesses, assessing its strengths. Jim had looked curiously at him, wondering how old he really might be; for Romulans, like Vulcans, showed little indication of aging until they were in their sixties. The man looked to be in his mid-twenties, but might have been in his forties for all Jim knew. Then he found himself being examined closely by those eyes, so pale a brown they were almost gold; an intrusive, disconcerting stare. "Subcommander," he had said, and courteously enough the young man had bowed to him; but Jim went away disquieted, he didn't know why.

The department heads of the three ships had been making noise about the Romulans' presence at their council; politely, but they had been making it all the same. Jim was letting them run down. It seemed the wisest course; that way there would be slightly less noise when he told them what he and Ael were planning.

He glanced down past McCoy and Sulu and Matlock toward Lieutenant Kerasus, raising an inquiring eyebrow at her.

She glanced back, shaking her head ever so slightly at some response of one of the Eyrene Denebians to something Spock was telling them about the Levaeri V researches. Janíce Kerasus was chief of linguistics, the person primarily responsible for programming of the translation computer and translation of alien documents received by the ship. She was a tall, big-boned, strikingly handsome woman with dark curling hair and calm brown eyes that slanted up at the corners, making her look like a lazy cat most of the time—excepting when she was very interested, as she was now; then she got the look of a cat waiting patiently by a mousehole, eyes a bit wide and a faintly pleased look on her face.

She was waiting for something now, that was plain. The room had settled down somewhat from the restrained uproar that had occurred when Jim had first introduced Ael and Tafv. Mike Walsh has stared at Jim as if he'd gone nuts, and Rihaul had slitted her eye at him in a later-for-you gesture he knew too well from the old days, after some particularly painful tutoring session. But now the other officers were beginning to get the idea that these Romulans might actually have come to do them a service. It was taking a while to sink in, unfortunately, and Jim grudged the lost time.

It was time to kick things in the side. Spock had done the "dirty" work, filling the meeting in on the news Ael had brought them and his confirmation of it. Now Jim stopped Spock from taking another question from one of Rihaul's people. "Gentlebeings," he said, "we've got to get moving here. You've heard what the commander proposes—"

"It would break almost every reg in the book," Mike Walsh said. "Allowing hostiles into classified areas. Entering into private alliances with foreign powers. Espionage again. Destruction of private property . . ."

"I have those powers, Mike," Jim said quietly. "That's what 'unusual breadth of discretion' is for, after all."

Mike grimaced at him, knowing as well as Jim the pitfalls that awaited him should this operation somehow get botched. "I know. But we're quite literally in an untenable position. We can't stay here; the Romulans monitoring the Zone will get suspicious. We can't leave—certainly not without determining the fate of the *Intrepid*. We can't send for help, communication isn't secure; and we can't send ships to carry a secure message—we need all our strength here. We have to act, and we have to do it now, and much as I hate to admit it, Ael's idea is the best we've got."

Ael threw Jim a glance that reminded him a great deal of one of Spock's appreciative-but-don't-tell-anyone expressions. "Gentlefolk," Tafv said from beside her in his light tenor, "I assure you that the commander is as little sanguine about offering you this plan as you are at the thought of accepting it. If it succeeds, the commander and I have nothing to gain but disgrace, irrevocable exile for both of us and for the rest of her crew, and the permanent possibility of being hunted down and killed by Romulan agents for revenge's sake." He looked grave. "We are all willing to risk that for her sake. It's a matter of *mnhei'sahe*." There were curious looks around the table at the word the translator had failed to render, but Tafv didn't stop. "However, we face far, far worse if the attempt fails. If caught in Romulan territory, we and *Bloodwing*'s crew will assuredly die. You and your ships could conceivably fight your way out again—and whatever difficulties you may have with Starfleet Command afterward, you will still be alive to have them."

"Noted, Subcommander," Jim said. "One moment. Lieutenant Kerasus—'mneh'-*what?*"

"'*Mnhei'sahe,*'" she said promptly. "Captain, I'm sorry, but you would ask me to render one of the most difficult words in the language. It's not quite honor—and not quite loyalty—and not quite anger, or hatred, or about fifty other things. It can be a form of hatred that requires you to give your last drop of water to a thirsty enemy—or an act of love that requires you to kill a friend. The meaning changes constantly with context, and even in one given context, it's slippery at best."

"In this one?"

Kerasus glanced across at Tafv. "If I understand the subcommander correctly, they are returning the favor that Commander t'Rllaillieu has done them by commanding them, by being in turn willing to be commanded. That sounds a little odd, I know, but their forms of what we call 'loyalty' do not always involve compliance. These people will follow her to death . . . and beyond, if they can . . . because they acknowledge that what she's doing is right, no matter what High Command says."

There was a little silence around the table at that. "Commander," Captain Rihaul said quietly, "I hope you will excuse us both our ignorance and our caution. But none of us have ever seen Romulans do anything but make war, and that savagely. That you would also wage peace . . . if forcefully . . . comes as something of a surprise."

Ael smiled at the Deirr captain, a rueful look. "Oh, I assure you, Captain, we know more arts than those of war. But our position between you and the Klingons has left us little leisure to practice them. So we tend to leave their development to others. Our allies . . . or our subjects."

Lieutenant Kerasus lifted her head at that, though she said nothing. Jim caught the look, though. "Comment, Lieutenant?"

"Yes, sir." She looked down the table toward Ael and began to speak, and her quiet voice suddenly had steel in it. "'Other peoples may yet/ more skillfully teach bronze to breathe,

> "'leading outward and loosing
>    the life lying hidden in marble;
> some may plead causes better,
>    or using the tools of science
> better predict heaven's moods
>    and chart the stars' changing courses.
> But Roman, remember you well
>    that your own arts are these others:
> to govern the nations in power;
>    to dictate their rule in peace;
> to raise up the peoples you've conquered,
>    and throw down the proud who resist. . . .'"

Jim saw Ael looking at Kerasus with an expression that looked like surprise, or hope, or both. "That is very well said. But the language sounds old. Those people are no longer with you, I think."

"Their descendants only," Jim said. "Though many of Earth's major languages were powerfully affected by theirs. For the most part, their way is one we've left behind us. But they were a great people."

"If they became less than great," Ael said, glancing around the table at the many sorts of listeners, "it is because they forgot those words and handed their rule over to others—perhaps to onetime enemies, whom in their contempt and laziness they tried to absorb, and forgot to fear. Or else to those who paid lip service to the ancient laws without understanding the vision on which they were founded. Am I wrong?"

The stillness of their faces evidently told her she was not. "That is the danger in which my Empire now stands, gentlefolk. And I will not see five thousand years' civilization fall, as it seems other empires have, due to some paltry cause, to mere sloth, or folly—or the death of honor! I have said to *Enterprise*'s captain that there was no help to be found in my friends, so that I needs must turn to my enemies. Your Federation says it wants peace among the great powers. Now it shall be seen how much it wants that, by the actions of you its representatives. For if you fail to act now on the information I bring you, with the power to hand, peace will fail you forever."

The room was quiet for a few seconds, and into that quietness came the whistle of the intercom. "Main briefing," said Captain Rihaul.

*"Captain,"* said the foghorn voice of one of Rihaul's bridge crew, *"we're now in the area from which* Intrepid *made its last report. The meson residue of her engines comes this far, then stops . . . as if the matter-antimatter converters had been shut down. There's a faint meson trail leading away from here, though—shutdown residue, nothing more."*

"Where does it lead?" Mike Walsh said.

*"Bearing ninety mark plus-five, sir. Into the Neutral Zone."*

People all around the room looked at one another. "Anything else, Syill?" said Rihaul.

*"No, madam."*

"All right. Main briefing out."

"There it is, gentlebeings," Jim said. "One of our starships is missing—and we know where it's gone. If we needed an excuse for crossing the Zone, we've got one now. Not even Fleet will be able to argue with what our sensors show us. And the question of committing an act of war is now also moot. What would you call shanghaiing the *Intrepid?*"

"No argument there, Jim." Rihaul looked across the table at him with great concern. "Unfortunately. Now it falls to us to keep this war from escalating into a full-scale conflict."

"And the only way we're going to manage it is Ael's plan," Jim said. "I'm sorry to have to command you to do things you can't fully support—but I see no alternative."

"Jim," Mike Walsh said, "you misunderstand us. We support you to the hilt. But we don't like this!"

"Bad odds?" Jim said gently.

Mike looked rueful. "They'd be better if you'd take *Inaieu* and *Constellation* along."

"Sorry, Mike, but that's out of the question. At the slightest warning the people on Levaeri will dump their computers and escape with the genetic material—and take *Intrepid* along with them, so deep into Romulan space that none of us would ever get out again."

"We could be taken along in tow, 'captured' as you would be," Rihaul said. But she said it so wistfully that Jim wanted to reach over and pat her tentacles.

Ael, seated not far from Rihaul, laughed very kindly. "Captain," she said, "you do *Bloodwing* such an honor as she has never been done before. But it would never work. One starship I can barely justify catching, on my own reputation as a commander. But with *Cuirass,* and the idiot crew that Romulan High Command knows is aboard her—*three* starships, and one of those a *Defender*-class destroyer? They would know upon detecting us that something was amiss, and flee Levaeri as *Enterprise*'s captain has said. . . . And besides all that, if I tried to tow so much tonnage, I would burn out *Bloodwing*'s engines. I fear it will not work. But I am sorry to have to answer such *mnhei'sahe* with cold counsel. . . ."

The people around the table were quiet, looking at Jim. "Well, we'd best get started," he said. "Mr. Spock has detailed the commander's plan for you. We will be following it quite closely. I want *Inaieu* and *Constellation* to continue routine patrols—being careful to avoid this area for several hours on the next sweep; we mustn't have any more muon trails through here than Ael's story will account for—and the phaser fire of the 'battle' we're going to stage will obliterate the trails left by your presence here and now. Ael will be beaming about forty Romulans aboard to man key posts in case the escorting ships decide they need proof of what's going on. Subcommander Tafv will be remaining on *Bloodwing,* while Ael supervises her people's settling in over here. What's our ETA at Levaeri V?"

"At towing speed, about warp two, two days and five hours in your time system," Tafv said. "We will hit their sensor boundary at about one day twenty hours. An escort, should Command decide to send us one, would doubtless scramble and meet us about one day into the journey."

"Couldn't we just sneak in?" Sulu said, from beyond Spock.

"Besides the lack of honor in such an approach," Tafv said with a slight smile, "no. Our side of the border is as thickly sown with sensor satellites as yours is; and should we try to reenter the Zone without reporting our presence, Command would know immediately that something was amiss. The ships sent to intercept us would fire first and ask no questions, whether we had *Enterprise* in tow or not—in fact, they would be glad to blow you up and take the credit for it. And as you already know, they count the commander a nuisance better dead than alive. No, we must declare ourselves, and then prepare to deceive the escort."

"So we'd best get started," Jim said. "Commander, Subcommander, will you beam over to *Enterprise* with Dr. McCoy and Mr. Spock and work out quartering arrangements for your crewpeople with them? We don't have a lot of space in crew's quarters proper, but those who need to be aboard for the ruse should be comfortable enough. And, Uhura, I want you to see if there isn't some way to temporarily block subspace communication in our neighborhood—or at least interfere with it."

"Aye, sir."

"Captain Rihaul, I leave you in command of the task force—what's left of it. Be very clear about this: should something go wrong with this operation, under no circumstances are you to mount a rescue attempt of any kind. You must disavow us if approached. Understood?"

"Jim—"

"No 'buts,' Mike. Acknowledge and comply."

"Acknowledged," said Captain Walsh.

"Yes, Jim," said Rihaul.

"Very well."

"And good luck, Captain," Walsh said.

"If there is such a thing," Jim said, "I accept with thanks. Dismissed, all."

Jim stood; the room emptied—swiftly of Denebians, more slowly of the other species. Finally only the three of them were left—the two hominids and the brown, baggy Deirr, looking uncomfortably at one another.

"It's hardly a pat hand, Jim," Mike said. "I would much rather you cheated."

"I am considering tucking you two up my sleeve," Jim said. "Nhauris, let's go down to your quarters and talk."

Much later, Jim leaned over the helm console and said, "How about it, Mr. Sulu? Do you think you can make it work?"

"No question, Captain." Sulu was seated at the console, making minute adjustments to a set of programmed flight instructions. Beside Jim, looking over Sulu's other shoulder with great interest, was Subcommander Tafv. He and Sulu had been consulting for nearly an hour now, "choreographing" the "battle" they would fight in Romulan space.

"It's just like the wargames simulations back at the Academy," Sulu said, "except with real ships. We'll have to use phasers at higher-than-minimal power in order to wipe out our muon trail properly and leave the right heat and photon residues to fool any investigator. Screens will be up at normal power on both ships for the first few passes—but see, here in the fourth pass *Enterprise* will 'take a hit' on number four screen, which will go down and allow the damage to the port nacelle that Mr. Scott's arranging—"

"Will be arranging," Jim said, his ears still burning slightly from

Scotty's private conversation with him, in one of the turbolifts, about what Jim was planning to do to his precious engines. "I don't think he can bear to start just yet. Go on, gentlemen."

"We will use a separate burst of phaser fire to make the actual cut in the nacelle," Tafv said. "That way there will be less chance of hurting the reinforcement your chief engineer will be installing on the inner hull, so that the matter-antimatter converter in the nacelle can still function. That is probably the most delicate part of the operation. After that, Mr. Sulu has programmed the *Enterprise*'s navigations and gunnery computers to make another pass at us and do us some damage—a 'missed shot' at our own port nacelle that will instead hull us in one cargo hold, causing the usual explosive decompression and scattering various supplies all over the area. However, it will not be enough to stop us; *Enterprise* will be 'limping' badly at that point, and we will chase her until she's forced to turn and fight because of 'overheating' in the remaining, overstressed nacelle. We will answer with more phaser fire, while *Enterprise*'s, due to the fueling of phasers from the already over-taxed nacelle, drops off. Then screens will go down, and the commander will send her message ahead to Fleet Command. At this distance from Romulus we will have some six hours' grace before it reaches them—during which time we will jointly fake whatever else needs faking; the use of the intruder control system, various burn marks and damages from 'fighting in the corridors,' and so forth."

"At the same time," Sulu said, "we'll be transferring control to the auxiliary bridge, and coaching the Romulan 'invaders' in how to handle communications and so forth, for when the escort comes along and demands to know what's *really* going on." He stopped then, looking a little disconcerted. "Captain—one problem. What if they want to board, rather than just examining us by ship-to-ship communication?"

Jim shook his head. "The commander thinks she can prevent that," he said, "but if they do board—well, we'll get some acting practice, that's all. There shouldn't be too many Romulans to fool, anyway—it's not as if a whole crew would beam over and inspect every bit of the ship. We shouldn't have to deal with any more than twenty or thirty Romulans tops—and if we can't fool thirty Romulans—" Jim stopped

abruptly, grinned at Tafv. "Sorry, Subcommander. Some habits are hard
to break."

"Yes, I agree," Tafv said, smiling slightly. "But the effort is interesting.
Captain, will there be anything else? I am going to be needed on *Bloodwing* shortly."

"If you gentlemen are finished, then by all means go ahead," Jim
said. Tafv bowed slightly to Jim, waved two fingers at Sulu in a small
saluting gesture, and hurried off the bridge.

When the lift doors had closed behind him, Sulu sat back in his chair
and looked up at Jim with an expression both worried and bemused.
"Sir," he said, "is it all right to say that I trust you completely—and I
wish I could say the same for them?"

"Absolutely," Jim said, "because that's exactly the way I feel about it.
However, the only way to prove someone trustworthy is to trust them.
I just wish it wasn't my ship and my crew I had to trust them with. . . ."

Sulu looked up at Jim and nodded. "Captain," he said, "we're with
you. It's not only the Romulans who have mneh—whatever-it-is."

"Yes, Mr. Sulu," Jim said. "I know. And thank you." He sighed. "I
suppose I'd better get down there and see how poor Scotty's doing with
'blowing up' his engine. . . ."

"I bet he's doing most of the 'blowing up' himself," Chekov said
quietly from beside Sulu.

"Mr. Chekov," Jim said, "amen to that. Mind the bridge, gentlemen.
We won't be in it for long. . . ."

And so it was that, several hours later, a lone Federation starship ventured out of its own space into the proscribed space of the Romulan
Neutral Zone, and was found trespassing there by a ship whose ID read
ChR *Cuirass*. The Federation ship tried to escape, but it was too far into
the Zone to make it back into its own space before being caught by
*Cuirass* and brought to battle. The engagement was brief and fierce,
characterized by a virtuoso set of evasive maneuvers by the *Enterprise*'s
helmsman, and the dogged, never-say-die pursuit of *Cuirass;* but in the
end virtuosity was not enough to save the Federation ship, one of whose

engines overloaded during a particularly high-power turn-and-fire maneuver. *Cuirass* was quick to exploit the problem, and though she took some hurt herself in the exchange of fire that followed, she blew a hole eighty meters long in the *Enterprise*'s starboard nacelle. "Oh, m' poor bairn!" someone was heard to moan on the *Enterprise*'s bridge; but the Romulans who heard the exclamation only laughed softly, and those who didn't began raining phaser fire on the *Enterprise*'s weakening screens. Number four went down, and others followed; a great many Romulans beamed aboard the beleaguered ship, right into the bridge, securing it before the *Enterprise*'s own security or intruder-defense systems could act. They took that intruder-defense system and used it to their own advantage—gassing most of the crew into unconsciousness and locking them up, then confining the captain and bridge crew and threatening him with the death of his whole crew unless he unconditionally surrendered his ship.

Faced with the inevitable, he did so. For only the second time in Federation history, a living captain gave up his command and was locked away to await trial with various of his officers. And a Rihannsu commander stood proudly on a Federation starship's bridge, called Rihannsu High Command, and informed them that she had captured the *U.S.S. Enterprise.*

High Command had not yet heard from three other Rihannsu ships, in another part of homespace, concerning the sudden disappearance from their area of *Cuirass,* pursued by another warbird. The three commanders of the ships with the Klingon names were still in conference aboard *Ehhak,* trying to figure out what story to tell Command that would save their necks.

So there was celebration at Command when the message came in; and a three-ship escort was detached from other duty to help *Cuirass* bring the *Enterprise* in. Judges were selected from the Senate for the war-crimes trials, and various people in the science and shipbuilding departments of Command became abnormally cheerful at the thought of the happy months of analysis ahead of them. Some Senators and Praetors grumbled bitterly among themselves. There was nothing to be

done about t'Rllaillieu; throw the cursed woman into a dungheap and
she came up covered with dilithium crystals. There had to be another
way to get rid of her.

They would have been pleased to know that there were already various people working on the problem.

# Chapter Eleven

She could not get used to it—she knew she would never get used to it—this business of standing on the bridge of a Federation vessel, not as a prisoner, but as an ally.

It was bizarre to look around her and see the captain sitting there as calm in his center chair as she might be in hers, looking around at a bridge where Rihannsu worked alongside Terrans and other odd creatures. Her own crewpeople were rather bemused about it themselves, but they applied themselves to their work, and saved their wondering for their few off hours. They had a lot to learn in a very short time.

They were her best. *Bloodwing* had been through its share of trouble over the last three years, and several times had had to be not only refitted but supplied with new people to replace those lost in this or that battle. Of her two hundred crew, only about fifty had been with her for more than ten years—an assortment of canny old creatures who lived almost wholly by their wits, and crazy young ones who had survived this long mostly by trusting her blindly and doing everything she told them. Some of them, by keeping their eyes open and learning from what she did, had become prime command material—though they usually loudly claimed that they would never be as good as she was, did the subject ever come up. Among this latter group were many of her officers; and she loved them dearly, feeling that she had more than one child. They looked up to her like a mother. It was to this younger group that Ael was *"susse-thrai"*; the elder group just called her "our commander," and smiled at the youngsters.

"Commander," said the captain, breaking her out of her thoughts, "anything from *Bloodwing*?"

"Nothing new," she said. "But your Lieutenant Kerasus was busy translating the last communication from Command a little while ago. She should have it for you shortly. Oh, Captain, it was choice."

He looked oddly at her smile. "How so? I thought it was fairly dry, from what you told me."

"Well." She sat down opposite him at one of the auxiliary science stations. "That is why I suggested the lieutenant translate it into Basic for you; there were nuances that I am incompetent to render. I am a thorn in the Senate's side, you see; a major annoyance to them. Command likes me no better, since it's the Senate that appropriates their funds, and the retirees holding down desk jobs in Command all study to dance to their masters' harps. They sent me out on Neutral Zone patrol in the first place in hopes I would be killed—an 'honorable' duty assigned for a dishonorable purpose. Lieutenant Kerasus called it 'being sent to Gaul.' Where *is* Gaul, by the way? Some kind of prison planet?"

The Captain shook his head, smiling. "No, it's on Earth, and the wine there is very good . . . but don't drink the water."

She knew a joke when she heard one, even if she didn't understand it. "I shall not, then. But at any rate, the tone of the communication was, shall we say, rather sour. They had to do me honor—but it annoyed them to do so. Nor did Command dare send me too much 'help' in bringing you home. I might take offense—and should my star rise again in the Senate, as may now seem likely to them, they would be slitting their own wrists in angering me. You will see when you read the communiqué. Lieutenant Kerasus strikes me as a very skilled officer, and I'm sure you will find the text amusing."

Jim nodded. "Three ships, you said?"

"Yes. *Rea's Helm* and *Wildfire,* which I think you know, have been pulled off Neutral Zone patrol in other areas to attend us; and *Javelin,* which usually does courier runs between Eisn and the Klingon borders, was out this way on an errand to Hihwende and is also being dispatched. This is good luck for us, Captain. Two of these, the commanders of *Helm* and *Javelin,* are old unfriends of mine—too politic to argue with me, though, when I am obviously in a position of power. The third, *Wildfire*'s commander, I don't know—but that may work to our advantage as well."

"I've wondered ever since I heard the name," the Captain said, "who 'Rea' was. . . ."

Ael looked at the captain from under her brows, a mischievous expression. "You would have liked him, Captain. He was a magician whose enemies captured him and forced him to use his arts for them. They told him they wanted him to make a helmet that would make the person who wore it proof against wounds. So he did—and when one of those who captured him tried it on, the demon Rea had bound inside the helmet bit the man's head off. A corpse will not care how you wound it. . . ." She laughed at his wry look. "Enough, Captain. Soon you will be asking me what a 'bloodwing' is—"

"That would have been the next question, yes. . . ."

"Later," said Ael, standing, as Lieutenant Kerasus came in. "And you will tell me what great 'enterprise' your ship is named for. . . ."

She went over to stand by the gorgeous dark-skinned woman, Uhura, and her own crewwoman Aidoann, while the captain, with occasional snickerings, read the document the lieutenant had brought him. Aidoann t'Khnialmnae was Ael's third-in-command, a tall young woman with bronze-fair hair and a round, broad face that could be astonishingly complacent or astonishingly ferocious, depending on the mood that rode her. "How are you doing, small one?"

It was their old joke, and here as anywhere else Aidoann flicked her eyes sidewise, stifling a reply until they should both be off duty. "Well enough, *khre'Riov,*" she said. "Lieutenant Commander Uhura has been very patient with me. I don't doubt I will have the more important features of this board mastered by the time the skill is needed."

"I haven't much needed to be patient, Commander," said Uhura. "The antecenturion is very quick—"

Aidoann cocked her head. "All right, Aidoann, then," Uhura said. "It's a pity she's not—no, I beg your pardon, I mean—"

"Not one of your crew?" Ael said. "No offense taken, Lieutenant Commander. For the moment, at least, she is." She glanced at Aidoann. "How has Khiy been doing with the helm?"

They all three glanced down at the small, slim, dark man sitting beside Mr. Sulu, with Mr. Chekov looking over his shoulder and giving advice. "Rather well, I think," Aidoann said. "At least the ship has not crashed into anything yet."

"Commander?" said the captain, looking up from his center seat. "What's this about this other ship?—*Battlequeen,* is it?"

"That's the one that will not be here," Ael said, turning away from Aidoann and stepping down into the center again. "Be glad of it. *Battlequeen* is commanded by Lyirru tr'Illialhae, and Lyirru is a reckless, bloodthirsty idiot who would certainly want to beam over here at first sight of you. He has done enough stupid things in the past to be deprived of his command if he were anyone else—but unfortunately he has friends among both Praetors and Senators, and he's the delight of the expansionist lobby in the Tricameron. However, the kind Elements have put him safely out of our way for the moment—there's a rebellion going on out on one of the colony planets, as you see, and he's off putting an end to it. I just hope he leaves the planet there when he's done; it would be just like him to blow it up in a fit of pique."

She saw on the captain's face what he thought of such tactics, and was heartened. "Fine. As long as he stays out of our way . . ." He handed the report back to Lieutenant Kerasus, who took it around to Mr. Spock. "I see what you meant about the tone of that thing. Bureaucracy doesn't change, does it?"

"Apparently not. —Captain, I want to make the rounds and see how my people are settling in; would you care to come with me?"

"I'll join you later, Commander," he said. "I have some work to finish up here. Just tell the lift where you want to go; once it dumps you out on a given floor, ask it for directions—it'll answer, all the lifts have been put on the translator network."

"Thank you, Captain."

She stepped into the lift. Its door closed on her, and Ael stood for a moment irresolute, wondering where to go. Then she remembered that Tafv had gone off with Hvaid t'Khaethaetreh, one of her subalterns, to see about accommodations near the recreation department. "Recreation deck," she said to the lift, and obediently it whooshed off.

The amiable sound of many voices down the hall told Ael which way to go as surely as the computer could have. She went down toward it, her usual purposeful stride slowed to a stroll, as it had again and again over the past few hours. She could not get used to how large this ship was. *Bloodwing* was a hole by comparison, cramped, dark and barren. *I am getting spoiled,* she thought. *If I am not careful, I will begin to covet this ship. And even thinking that thought is dangerous. . . .*

The doors to recreation were open. She stepped in and was astonished to see how very many people were in there. People of all kinds. That was another thing she was having trouble getting used to. When the Rihannsu had left Vulcan, astronomy had been old, but spaceflight was still in its infancy; and generation ships had been all they had. They had met no other species in their travels, and ch'Rihan had had plenty of animal life, but no other intelligence. For thousands of years the Rihannsu had not dreamed of any other life in the universe; even Vulcan had become almost a legend. But then came the days of starflight, the rediscovery of other species, and the First War that resulted in the setting up of the Zone. What had been mere ignorance and isolation turned rather suddenly into a politically-based xenophobia, the idea that anything not Rihannsu would most likely either shoot at you or steal from you. The Klingons had not helped this impression. Now, though, Ael looked around this bewildering collection of aliens—all these Terrans and Tellarites and Andorians and Sulamids and three kinds of Denebians, and whatnot else—and was bewildered. Four hundred kinds of 'humanity,' the ship's library computers called them. She found that bizarre. There was only one kind of humanity, everybody knew that. But to judge from the way these people worked together, one would think *they* didn't know it. . . .

It would have been the rankest discourtesy, of course, to display that attitude among hosts who thought otherwise. So Ael walked on through the room looking with cool and (she hoped) polite interest at all the weird things with tentacles and the odd-colored men and women, eating and drinking and playing together, and privately wondered how they stood one another.

"Can I help you, ma'am?" said a very polite, very clear voice from her left and down by her feet—a voice that sounded rather like rock grinding on rock, a most peculiar noise. Ael turned and looked down, and Elements have mercy on her, there was one of Them personified—a rock talking to her. At least it looked like a rock, if rocks had shaggy fringes, and if any mineral ever mined came in such odd colors—orange and ocher and black, bizarrely crusted together. The creature glittered as if it were gemmed, and the *Enterprise*'s parabolic insignia gleamed on the small, flat black box fitted into a hollow between excrescences on its back. A voder, possibly.

Ael got hold of herself as best she could and said, "Surely you may, Ensign." The rock wore no uniform, but there were no stripes on the voder, and Ael knew from her study of Fleet protocol that 'ensigns,' equivalent to Rihannsu subcenturia, had no stripes at all. "I am looking for the officer in charge of the billeting of the visiting Rihannsu. Would you know who that might be?"

"Mr. Tanzer and Dr. McCoy are working on it, Commander," the rock said to her, its fringe rippling on one side of it. "May I take you to them?"

There was a cheerful eagerness in the voice that Ael almost smiled at; this was a very young officer, if she was any judge. She thought fondly of Tafv when he was that young, and of Aidoann a few years ago, before battle and friendship had shaken some of the rawness out of her. "Yes, Ensign, thank you."

The rock rumbled off through the big room, and Ael went after him at a leisurely pace, looking around her as she went. A swimming bath, for pity's sake! and banqueting tables surrounded by people eating what would have been a feast by Rihannsu standards, but what Ael suspected was probably just ordinary fare. *They have so much,* she thought. *No wonder they understand us so little, who are so poor. Perhaps they don't even understand the anger that the hungry feel when the full go by, unthinking. . . .* But the anger, the thought of her poor cramped crew who deserved so much better, was shaken out of her somewhat by the sight of her crewpeople themselves. They were standing and sitting, most of them, off in one corner of the great room, looking quite brave and aloof and self-sufficient, and (to Ael's trained eye) rather lost and scared. Dr. McCoy was making his way busily among them, talking to them as kindly as her own ship's surgeon might, as he installed intradermal translators in their forearms. Indeed, Surgeon t'Hrienteh was at McCoy's elbow, carefully watching what he did; and there was an unaccustomed smile on her grim dark face as McCoy patted the forearm of poor nervous tr'Jaihen, spoke some reassuring (though not yet understood) word to him, and slipped the implant in.

"Doctor," Ael said, and to her amusement both McCoy and t'Hrienteh turned to see who called them.

"Oh, there you are, Commander," McCoy said, giving her the casual look someone back on the farm might have given a strayed *fvai* that had finally come back to the stable. "I see Ensign Naraht found you."

"Indeed he did," said Ael, tipping a quick smile down at the youngster. "Are the arrangements about complete, Doctor? My people and I have a lot of work to do."

"Almost done, Commander. Just a few more translators to go in." McCoy looked around at the corner of the room. "The recreation chief has gone off to see about partitioning this area off for your people's sleeping quarters. We didn't have enough room to put them in crew quarters, unfortunately; we're just about full up with our own people right now."

"Doctor, this will suit us very well," Ael said. "We are used to barracks living, all of us, and there's much more room here than even back on *Bloodwing*. Is there a visitor's mess?"

"Not as such, but Mr. Tanzer's reprogrammed the food processors in the lounge adjacent to this area. I've already told most of your people, but now I should tell you; when you use the processor, stay away from anything with a red tag on it—those are the foods that won't agree with your metabolism. Last thing you people need to worry about right now would be coming down with the Titanian two-step."

"Pardon?"

*"LIhrei'sian,"* said t'Hrienteh.

"Oh. Thank you, Doctor, you're quite right. . . ."

"Len?" someone said from behind her. Ael turned to find herself looking at a short, well-muscled, silver-haired man with such calm wise eyes that her first thought was *senior centurion.* But of course that couldn't be the case; the Captain had not even introduced him at the department heads' meeting, though the man had been there. He looked at her in return, weighed her, and accepted her utterly, all in one swift glance; then said, "I beg your pardon, Commander."

"Please don't," she said, though his courtesy pleased her as much as his assessment had unnerved her.

"This is Lieutenant Harb Tanzer, Commander," said McCoy. "He'll be handling your people's needs, since he's in charge of this whole area. If they need anything at all while they're here—anything nonmedical, that is—they should see him."

"I'll be on call at all times, Commander," said Mr. Tanzer. "We should have enough time before the other Rihannsu ships arrive for your crew to get at least one shift's worth of sleep. When they're ready, call me and I'll block this whole area off for them. I'm sorry we don't have solid walls; we normally use opaque force-fields with a high-positive soundblock."

"Those sound fine," Ael said, wondering what in the worlds the man was talking about. "If there's a problem, we'll let you know."

"Meantime, once they've handled what they have to do aboard ship, they're most welcome to our facilities," Mr. Tanzer said. "In fact, Commander, if I may say so, a lot of the people in here are rather hoping your crew will join them. They're incredibly curious. None of us have ever had the chance to talk to a Rihannsu before."

Ael noticed, to her considerable surprise, that the translator was not merely rendering it from the Basic word "Romulan"; the man was actually saying "Rihannsu"—and with a tolerable accent. "If they wish to," she said, looking more carefully at Mr. Tanzer than she had at first, "they certainly may, and thank you kindly. Will you excuse me? I need to talk to them."

"Certainly."

The doctor and the recreation officer and the rock all went off together, leaving Ael with her little group. With their usual cool discipline they all sank down together, sitting cross-legged on the strange, soft floor as they would have after workout in *Bloodwing*'s little gym.

"What of it, my own?" she said. "Are you well, or will you shortly be that way? And can you hold to your oaths in this place, under the eyes of strangers and under these circumstances? For surely none of us have ever been this sorely tested, or will be. Anyone who thinks that he or she might be tempted to do our old enemies evil in an unguarded moment, say it now. I will not hold it against you. You will go back to *Bloodwing* in honor for a bitter truth told, and courage in telling it."

They all looked at her soberly, her faithful group—the many familiar faces that had followed her into battle so many times before. Fair little N'alae with her placid eyes and deadly hands, silent Khoal, great lanky Dhiemn with his farm-child's hands and his sword-sharp mind; Rhioa and Ireqh and Dhiov and Ejiul and T'maekh, and many another—they all watched her, quite silent, and no one moved. "Be certain," Ael said softly. "This is to our everlasting shame and my own dishonor should we fail. Poor tattered rag that my honor will be, once Command finds out what we're up to—yet I would not tear it any worse."

Dhiov, who was always timid except when it came to slighting herself, or killing, said abruptly, "Those things with the tentacles—"

"Are people," Ael said. "Never doubt it. They look horrible to me too, but I make no doubt that their gorge rises somewhat at us." There was soft laughter over that. "They have their own version of the Passion, too; they will defend their ship and their shipmates as brilliantly and as bravely as you will. The same for the blue people and the orange ones and the brown ones and the ones who look like *hlai*."

"And the rock?" said Dhiemn, with his usual dry humor.

"Especially the rock, I think. Elements, my children, what a start that one gave me. May I be preserved from seeing any more of that kind of thing; if Air or Fire should walk up and speak to me, I doubt I could bear it."

More laughter. They were relaxing, and Ael was glad to see it. "So, we're merry. Have you learned your duties well enough to be sure of them?"

Various heads bowed "yes." "It's not hard, *khre'Riov*," said Ejiul. "Most of the positions we're being taught involve only communications. Any consoles we need to read have been reprogrammed for Rihannsu, and the instructions usually coach you along."

"Be certain, now. There will be no room for mistakes once *Javelin* and *Rea's Helm* and *Battlequeen* get here."

There was a sound of indrawn breath. Ael looked over at little dark Nniol, who was suddenly staring at the carpet. "O Air and Earth, *khre'Riov*," he said. "My sister was serving on *Javelin* last I heard."

Ael looked at him. "Nniol, that's hard. Will your oath hold?"

He looked up, stricken. "*Khre'Riov*—I don't know."

"Who must we ask to find out?" she said, very softly.

He stared at the carpet again. "We were close," he said. And after a long pause, he said, "I think I had best go back."

She looked at him, then nodded swiftly. "There's *mnhei'sahe* indeed—painful, but pure. Stay with us for the moment, Nniol: I'll speak to the captain. Anyone else?"

No one spoke.

"Very well. Shall we work out? We haven't had time to stretch as yet today, and we'll need to be limber tomorrow." Ael grinned at them. "Let's show them how it's done, shall we?"

There were answering grins all around, even from Nniol. They rose again, all together, and after reverence done toward ch'Rihan, in the Elements' direction ("That way," Dhiemn said, pointing at the floor; he always knew), Ael led them through the preliminary stretches and focusing. By the time they had gotten through the first few throws and choke-breaks and had broken into small freestyle groups to work out, some of the *Enterprise* people had drifted over, very casually, to watch them. Ael stepped away from her people as a cheerful free-for-all was starting among them—N'alae and Khoal dominating it as usual, everyone leaping at them and being thrown halfway to the horizon for their pains.

Ael wiped her brow and looked, under cover of the motion, at the *Enterprise* people. They were maintaining very carefully their pose of casualness; but Ael saw plainly enough that some of them wanted to dive into that fight too and try their luck. At least some of the hominids did; there was no telling what that tall purple-tentacled thing with all the writhing eyes might be thinking about—or, for that matter, young Ensign Rock, who was standing next to it. None of the hominids, at least, looked hostile. They looked hopeful, like children waiting to be asked to play . . . though their faces pretended mild interest and their conversation was calm.

She felt eyes on her, looked up. *Enterprise*'s captain was coming toward her, along with Lieutenant Tanzer. The captain was in fact looking slightly past her, at the free-for-all, and if she was any good at reading Terrans, Ael thought she caught a kind of itchy expression on his face that indicated he, too, would like to get in on it. But there was regret there, too. *Poor man,* Ael thought, *he doesn't have the leisure either. . . .*

"Commander," said the captain, and paused beside her, watching the madness going on in the corner, as little N'alae picked up Dhiemn bodily and tossed him at Lhair and Ameh. They caught him, barely.

"Captain," she said. "Just a workout; *'llaekh-ae'rl,'* we call it."

"'Laughing murder'? Very apt . . . My people tell me that yours have been picking up the parts they'll play very fast indeed."

"I have no time for slow learners, Captain," Ael said. "And to tell you truth, few of them survive long on Neutral Zone patrol, or on our frontier with the Klingons. —I'm glad you came now; for I have a problem. My crewman Nniol t'AAnikh has kin on one of the incoming ships, *Javelin.* I cannot allow him to be at or near a combat station when we engage that ship. I am sending him back to *Bloodwing.*"

He looked at her narrowly. "Certainly, Commander. Is it a matter of trust?"

Ael restrained herself from frowning at him, though it annoyed her that he should instantly think the worst of one of her people. "Yes, it is," she said. "He trusts me enough to tell me that he does not know whether he can trust himself in such a situation. It is my responsibility to guard his honor, just as by speaking he guards mine."

Perhaps the captain got a sense of how nettled she felt, for his face changed quickly. "Of course, Commander. Do as you think best. When he's ready to go back, just send him down to the transporter room; I'll see to it that they expect him."

"Thank you. Oh, now, see that. . . ." She had glanced away from the captain at a sudden lull in the scrapping behind her. There were several of the *Enterprise* crewpeople among her own—a couple of hominids, one blue-skinned and one fair like the captain—and one of the strange violet-tentacled things with all the eyes. The fairer of the two hominids, a small slim man, was making gestures that approximated N'alae's last throw, evidently asking her something about it; and Ael smiled as N'alae reached out to the man with that demure little expression of hers. The crewman set himself as well as he could to prevent her, Ael gave him credit for that; but all his preparation did the poor fellow no good. He went flying, came down hard and slapped the floor—then bounced up again, none the worse for wear but looking downright delighted.

"Can you all do that?" the captain said from beside Ael, watching the business with the same rueful delight as his crewman.

"No," Ael said, not without some rue on her own side. Many a time poor N'alae had tried to teach her some of the finest points of *llaekh-ae'rl,* the delicate shifts of balance that required a mind that could root itself in earth, or the metal of deckplates. But Ael had too much fire and air in her, and could not root. She had become resigned to defending herself with a phaser, or her mind. "N'alae is our specialist in the art."

"Uh-oh," said the captain, a sound that Ael's translator refused to render. Nevertheless, she understood it, for the tall purple sheaf of tentacles glided over to N'alae and was saying something to her, gesturing with liquid grace and many arms.

"That's a Sulamid," the Captain said. "Mr. Athendë from maintenance. Hand-to-hand combat is one of his hobbies. . . ."

*That* joke Ael understood, and she laughed hard for a few seconds, enjoying the sensation immensely. How long had it been since she laughed for pure merriment, not out of bitterness? She saw various heads turn among her crew; evidently it was a sound they were glad to hear, too, and some of the stiffness and formality seemed to fall away from them on hearing it. N'alae laughed also—that dangerous sound Ael knew very well—and held out her arms to the Sulamid, which obligingly wrapped numerous of its tentacles around them like thick-vine running up a tree's branches. There was a moment of swaying and straining, long seconds when nothing seemed to happen; and then with startling suddenness N'alae was standing all by herself again, and Mr. Athendë was sailing through the air, eyes and tentacles waving and whipping around. He hit the deck without a sound—evidently the tentacles made good shock absorbers—and bounced up again.

All Ael's people were cheering N'alae, who looked flushed and surprised. But, surprisingly, the *Enterprise* people standing around—and there were quite a lot of them now—were cheering her too; and Athendë swayed and bent double in a deep bow to her, saying something Ael couldn't quite catch, but something that made N'alae laugh.

Ael glanced sideways and saw the Captain's look, thoughtful and impressed. "We could learn a lot from her," he said. "None of us have ever been able to pull that on Athendë—not even Mr. Spock. After we finish our business at Levaeri, would you consider lending that lady to us for a little while? . . ."

"I am not sure we would want to give up the advantage," Ael said soberly. "I shall ask her, however."

The two of them turned away from the rapidly growing group in the corner, strolling away across recreation. "Your people have been very kind to ours since we came here, Captain," she said.

The captain raised his shoulders and let them fall again in a careless gesture. "Simple interspecies amity," he said. "The spirit of brotherhood."

The translator made little sense of the last word; but Ael understood why—it having been one of many oddities she had noticed long ago when working on her own translator program. "There is a question you might answer for me," she said. "Why does the word imply male siblings and not female as well?"

"It's an old word," said the captain, looking slightly embarrassed. "'Kinship' would be closer to the meaning."

"But a word's true meaning, its intended meaning, is always implicit in its structure," Ael said. "Evidently there were those who thought, when your language was forged, that only men were capable of that brand of kinship—and that by implication it was impossible between two women, or between female and male. How did they justify that in the face of evidence otherwise? Or did they simply wish half your species to think that it could *not* set back to back and fight for life and the things that mattered?"

He said nothing, and there was something about his silence that troubled Ael, so that she pressed her advantage to see what lay under the silence. "What about it, Captain? How is it that only brothers may fight, be valiant, persevere, defy deaths great and small—while judging half your race outside of that burden, that privilege, from the beginning?"

"I have no answer for you," the captain said, all tact, refusing to be drawn.

"Indeed. One wonders why the other half of your species put up with yours for so long."

"Perhaps they got their revenge," the captain said, "by letting my half of the species think it was right about them—and letting it go to Hell as a result."

Ael's eyebrow went up in surprised and pleased acknowledgment of the captain's shot across her bows. He looked oddly at her, as if even through his anger seeing something familiar in her, though Ael had no idea what and at the moment didn't care. "Besides," the captain said, "there's one characteristic of being a brother that you didn't mention. Liking. Brothers have that for one another, generally. I'm not sure I could have that much of that kind of liking for a woman."

Ael briefly considered the steady, sure relationship she had sensed between the captain and Uhura—the flashes of humor, the utter trust—and realized with wry amusement that she was being insulted. Why, she wasn't yet sure; so for the moment she put the matter aside and merely considered the captain's premise. "Liking. Well. Brothers may certainly develop it. It may make living with one another easier. But it's hardly necessary to brotherhood proper. Say my brother and I quarrel: then he falls in danger of his life. Do I let him lie there, because I no longer 'like' him? Or do I save him—simply because he is my brother, because I have said that he is forever someone important to me—and I'm bound by what I have said?"

"I'm not sure that's what I meant."

"Neither am I. But in any case it is *mnhei'sahe.* The bondage beyond reason, beyond hope or pain or escape. The bond that not even betrayal can break—only snarl around the heart until the betrayer's heart scars. The bond of word, of choice. Unbreakable."

"Death—"

"Death avails nothing against it. Your parents, your own brother who is dead—oh, yes, we know. What use is intelligence but for the knowing of one's enemies? Have you come to love your relatives any less for their being dead? Or perhaps more?"

The captain said nothing.

"So you see the nature of this bondage between beings who fight the same fight," Ael said. "A going in the same direction, for a little while, or for a life, that's all that's needed. The decision to go in company. Liking—" Ael shrugged one shoulder. "What need have allies of such a thing?"

"None," the captain said, "I'm sure."

They walked along in silence a moment longer. Then Ael paused by a curious thing—a table with a holographic projection above it of a cube divided into many smaller cubes, eight of them to an edge. "What is this?"

"Four-dimensional chess," said the captain. "Are you familiar with the game?"

"No."

The captain smiled at her, and a very odd smile it was, one that made Ael curious. "If we have time—"

"I would be delighted to learn. Now, if you like; I dare say I can spare a few minutes to learn the rules."

That smile got wider, and the captain pulled out one of the chairs that stood by the table, offering it to her. But neither of them had time to sit down; that infernal whooping began again. Heads went up all over the room, and a lot of the people who had been talking to Ael's folk excused themselves hurriedly and ran out.

*"Red alert,"* the Vulcan's calm voice said, made gigantic over the ship's annunciator system. *"Battle stations, battle stations. This is no drill."*

The captain slapped one hand down on a switch on the game table. "Kirk here."

*"Captain, we have a Romulan vessel at extreme sensor range. K'tinga-class vessel, ID'ing as Romulan ship* Javelin."

"They're early," Ael said, alarmed.

"Have they hailed us?" said the captain.

*"Not as yet, but they will soon be within range to do so."*

"We're going to need some more of your people up on the bridge, Commander. Mr. Spock, are Antecenturions Aidoann and Hvaid up there?"

*"Affirmative, Captain."*

"Have them handle any communications that come in. No visual until everyone on the bridge is covered by an armed Romulan. Transfer control to the auxiliary bridge immediately and send Mr. Sulu and Mr. Chekov down there to handle things."

*"Done, sir."*

"Good. Give me allcall. Commander—"

"This is t'Rllaillieu," Ael said, astonished at how her voice echoed in this flying cavern. "Rihannsu, report at speed to your assigned posts. Helmets all, and make sure any distinguishing insignia of *Bloodwing* about you are removed. If in doubt about any necessary action, consult with your 'prisoners.'" She allowed herself a slight laugh on the word; the captain looked grim, but his eyes danced all the same. "Remember, you are *Cuirass* crew; do nothing to attract attention to yourselves when we are monitored! Honor to you—and *mnhei'sahe.* Out."

The captain was looking at her quizzically. "I wished them luck," Ael said.

He shook his head. "I thought that word meant 'love.'"

Ael quirked half a grin at him. "What use is a word that means only one thing? Besides, in this context, they are nearly the same. . . ."

He looked bemused, but only for the instant; then he was all officer again, hard and ready. "You may have something there. In the meantime, I think you'll be needed on the bridge. Mr. Spock," he said to the intercom, "our presence has been requested at a little theatrical. Would you care to join me in the brig?"

*"My pleasure, Captain. Bridge out."*

The humor in the Vulcan's voice was so little concealed and so dry that Ael had to laugh again; but the laugh lasted for only a breath, fading at the captain's look. "Madam—" he said.

"I will care for your bridge," said Ael. And she turned and was off, hurrying, and feeling his eyes in her back like the points of spears.

★   ★   ★

Very strange, it felt, to sit there in that soft chair at the heart of airy openness, staring at the big screen and waiting. Ael's heart pounded and her hands were sweating, as they always did before an engagement. She cursed them, as she always did, and rubbed them on her breeches. Around her, her own people failed to notice this business, as usual, and made themselves useful at strange consoles and odd instruments. The only thing missing was Tafv, but he was on *Bloodwing,* lying low for the moment; after all, *Cuirass* was not a place where he belonged. Aidoann was on *Bloodwing,* pretending to be commanding it in Ael's absence; the commander, Aidoann would be telling *Javelin,* was aboard *Enterprise* making it secure and supervising the tapping and recording of its computer library. Hvaid and N'alae sat at the helm console; Khoal manned the science station, and Lhian the communications board. How cool they all looked, how very competent . . . a shadow of the look they had been wearing down in the recreation deck, while the *Enterprise* people had been watching them. *And how I sit here and twitch like a broody* hlai, Ael thought. *Fire burn it, we can build a device that can cloak a whole starship, but we can't find a way to keep people's hands from sweating—*

"Communication from *Javelin, khre'Riov,*" said Lhian, exactly as if they were back on *Bloodwing.*

"Accept it," Ael said.

The screen wavered and settled down, and Ael took a long breath and relaxed. Oh, that bland, round, foolish, familiar face. It was LLunih tr'Raedheol, and the Elements had been kind to her after all, for if anyone in space needed killing, it was this one. A coward and a fool, and one who thought everyone else was just like him, too lazy to do more than exhibit just enough energy to keep Command off his back. "Commander tr'Raedheol," Ael said, companionably enough, "welcome to the Outmarches. You see we have found something rather interesting floating around out here. . . ."

"*Yes,*" LLunih said, and the greed, jealousy and hate distilling behind LLunih's eyes should have killed the man on the spot. Unfortunately, he was immune to his own venom, like the *nei'rrh* he was. "*So Com-*

*mand said. I should appreciate the opportunity to beam over and examine this tremendous prize for myself."*

*And try to figure out a way to cheat me out of it, you mean,* Ael thought. "Oh, LLunih—may I call you LLunih?"

*"Do,"* said the repulsive creature, and smiled.

Ael kept herself from shuddering in loathing. "I couldn't allow that as yet. We are still in the process of learning to handle the command systems aboard this ship. Its officers are understandably annoyed with us, and they have not been as cooperative as would have been wise. These screens, for example; we were working with raising and lowering them, this morning, and we thought they were down—but in an evil moment someone from *Cuirass* tried to beam over and hit a 'phantom' screen of which our intelligence had failed to warn us. An outgrowth of the cloaking device, actually; quite clever." She smiled whimsically. "But unfortunate, since one of my minor officers is now floating around this part of space, reduced to his component atoms." *Oh, I will pay for that one sooner or later. . . .* "Until we're sure, I would rather you didn't take the chance. . . ."

*"Oh, Ael, I quite understand. . . ."* She lost his next few words, thinking of the old saying that a soiled name may only be washed clean in blood. *He has enough of it in all that flab to wash all four of them clean, I'll warrant. We shall see.*

*". . . find it hard to not want a look at the famous Captain Kiuurk. . . ."*

"Oh, as to that," Ael said, looking wicked, and not having to try too hard this time, "I dare say I could let you see a bit of what would please you. In fact, I have been hearing complaints from the captain concerning his present lodging; I was about to go down there and settle them with him when you called. If you will hold a moment, you may watch the proceedings."

*"Surely."*

Ael rose and nodded at Lhian: the screen went blank. "Warn them," she said.

*"Khre'Riov,"* Lhian said, with one of his dark-browed looks, "we're being scanned. Shields are up, but there's some signal leakage, and anything on ship's channels might be overheard—"

"True," she said. "Well thought. Wait till I'm about halfway down the deck eight hall, going toward detention; then pick me up on visual and pipe it over to *Javelin,* following me. Hvaid, come along."

Young Hvaid leaped up from his post, and the two of them hurried into the lift. "Detention, deck eight," Ael said. "Hvaid, when the lift stops, run ahead and warn the captain and his officers. Tell them who has called and that we must play this very broadly; LLunih is stupid and unsubtle, and nods and winks will not do. If we do convince him, though, he'll convince the other ships when they arrive, and save us the trouble of doing all this again. Then you'll have to run about to the various departments and tell everyone not to say anything damning on the ship's intercom until we are sure we're not being scanned, or can find a way to plug the leaks. Find some others of us to help you. Pull Lyie and K'haeth and Dhisuia off their posts; they're quick on their feet." The lift stopped. "Go now!"

Hvaid ran off down the hall. Ael leaned against the open door of the lift for a long, easy count of twenty, doing her best to slow her breathing down. It did not slow much, but finally she had to get out and walk, and found that the trembling in her knees wasn't nearly as bad as it had been. "Are you with me, *Javelin?*" she said cheerily to the air, using her upward look to disguise a glance around the corner she was approaching. Scan could not see it, but Ael could see Hvaid hurrying out of the door to detention, around another corner and out of sight.

"We see you, Ael," said LLunih.

"Good. Here we are—"

She swung around through the door into detention and saw the sight that many of Rihannsu had long desired to see: the captain of the *Enterprise* and his formidable officers, one and all, crammed into a cell in the brig and every one of them looking ready to commit murder that would have no laughing about it. There was the good doctor, his strange blue eyes flashing, and handsome Uhura looking as if she wanted a knife; and Mr. Scott with arms folded and eyes narrowed. He turned away from the sight of Ael as she came in; *a pretty touch,* she thought, *and probably based on reality*—for Mr. Scott had not yet forgiven her for the wounding of his precious engines. Even the Vulcan looked murderous—though in a restrained and decorous fashion. And the captain, the courteous, genteel captain, was from the look of him far gone in a cold rage that would have done the best of Ael's old commanders proud. Ael nodded the outer guards away from the forcefield controls on the door—poor Triy and  Helev, looking as grimly triumphant as they knew how, and, Ael suspected, ready to break up laughing as soon as they knew they were no longer watched.

"Captain," Ael began, courteously enough; but the captain didn't let her get any further.

"It is about time you found your way down here, lady," he said, with a stateliness of language that sorted bizarrely with his anger. *"What are you doing with my ship!* And my crew! You are in violation of—"

"You are in a poor position to be talking about violations, Captain," said Ael, motioning Triy to kill the forcefield. "You were the one we caught in the Zone—"

*"Surely you would not mind if my crew watched this, Ael,"* said LLunih's voice from the intercom.

"Who the devil is *that!*" the doctor shouted.

"Of course not," Ael said, as she stepped into the room and her eye fell on Nniol, who was doing inside guard duty.

*O, by my Element,* Ael thought, for Nniol's sister was on *Javelin,* and there was no possible reason for him to be on *Cuirass*—and there he was, his face shielded by a fortuitous angle for the moment, but the instant he moved a breath's worth, or she did, the pickup would catch him all too clearly. Her back was to it, at least; her eye flashed alarm at Nniol—there was nothing else she could do—

Then the fight broke out. At least it would have looked like a fight to any observer who did not stand where Ael did, who did not see the captain swiftly cock back one fist and turn a little in the doing, just enough to exchange glances with the doctor. The doctor instantly put his head down and economically, savagely, butted Nniol in the gut with it. Nniol doubled over, his face safely out of the way of the pickup; but on the way down he clubbed McCoy two-handed and sidewise in the legs, and the doctor came crashing down on top of him, concealing him further. Mr. Scott and the Vulcan got in the way, but Triy and Helev, shouldering in past Ael and the captain, shoved or slapped them back out of trouble—rather easily, in the Vulcan's case, though the phasers pointed at his midsection and at the captain, and their meaningful looks, might have had something to do with it. And as for the captain's punch, that had started all this, it never fell. Ael blocked it, hard, blocked the second one harder, heard something snap, and didn't dare hesitate, but carried through, slamming the man backhanded across the face. He went flying, crashed up against the wall, sagged down it, didn't move.

Ael glared at Uhura and Scott and Spock, who stood at bay in the corner of the cell, with phasers held on them. "I had thought to offer you honorable parole," she said, "but I see now it would have been a fool's act. Have them bound," she said to Triy. "All their other people, too; I dare say this boorishness and treachery is typical. And tend to this one." She nudged Nniol with her boot. Nniol, who lay sprawled face down under the doctor, stirred and groaned, but very prudently did not move otherwise.

Ael stepped over the carnage and out of the cell, dusting herself off. "LLunih," she said, while Helev assisted the doubled-over Nniol out of the cell and Triy sealed the cell up again, "I would stay for conversation, but you see that I have business to be about—interrogations and so forth; and these people are not going to make it easy for me, that's plain. I do hope you'll excuse me."

*"Any assistance I can offer, Ael—"*

"LLunih, I will surely ask. In the meantime, I would count it a kindness if your navigator and mine would consult together, so that yours can match my course."

*"Certainly."*

"Then a good day to you; I will pay you a courtesy call tonight or tomorrow, if you would be so gracious as to receive me. Perhaps we might have dinner." *Though I say nothing of keeping it down for long.*

*"Ael, I would be delighted."*

"Until later, then." She turned back to the glaring group in the cell and eyed them until Lhian said from the bridge, *"They have closed channels, khre'Riov. Shall I send a security detachment?"*

"No, we're secure," Ael said. "As you were, Lhian."

*"Commander."*

—and she stepped forward and killed the forcefield, and bent down hurriedly to the captain, as the others did. "That crawling slime," she said bitterly as she helped the captain to his feet. "He so loves the sight of others' shame that he cannot resist spreading it around for the delectation of his whole crew. Captain, I have done you a great discourtesy! I shall do you a better turn some other time."

The captain, for the moment, found nothing to say but a groan. She helped him stand from one side, while Spock assisted him on the other, being very careful of the injured arm. "There's this good at least come of it all," she said. "LLunih will gossip so to the commanders of *Rea's Helm* and *Wildfire* of how he saw *Enterprise*'s great captain struck down that they will give us no trouble. In fact, I would lay money on the creature's having recorded it to show them. —Doctor, I heard something break, I didn't mean to hit him that hard—"

The doctor was running a small whirring scanner up and down the captain's left arm. "Greenstick fracture of the ulna, Commander; that's this forearm-bone here. Nothing serious. Jim, are you slipping in your workouts? Since when do you cross-block backward like that?"

"You could do it better?" said the captain, looking humorous through his pain.

"Well, I—"

"Never mind. Commander, that *was* the youngster you were going to send back?"

"Yes. I had no idea he was going to be here, though, else I would have warned him out. . . ."

"Murphy's Law," the Captain said. "At least we managed to cover for him. Nice work, everyone. —Bones, how long is it going to take to regenerate this thing?"

"About an hour. Less if you don't squirm when it itches."

"Captain," Ael said, "who was Murphy, and what was his Law?"

"One I should have learned the last time," said the captain. "Never eat at a place called 'Mom's'; never play cards with a man called 'Doc'; and don't start fights with Romulan commanders."

That was when the punch came that the captain did *not* telegraph; and it slammed Ael back against the nearest wall so hard that the effect was the same as being hit twice, once in front and once from behind. She rebounded from the wall, tried to stand, staggered. Things spun.

"But if you *do* start one," the captain said with an absolutely feral grin, "always finish it."

The room would not stop rotating; and Ael's mind was in such a whirl of rage, relief and merriment that she scarcely knew what to do. "Captain, your hand," she said, holding hers out and considering—just briefly—showing him that trick of N'alae's that he had so admired. But there would be no honor in doing it to an injured man. . . . He took her hand, and then grinned.

"Yours sweat too, huh?" he said.

"Captain," she said, "what a pity you're not Rihannsu. . . ."

"I bet you say that to all your prisoners. Let's get back up to the bridge."

# Chapter Twelve

Jim sat in his center seat and wondered at the strangeness of the world.

Here he was, deep into Romulan space, surrounded by Romulan ships; not even under way, his engines only producing enough power to run ship's systems and keep themselves alive. Another eighteen hours would see the *Enterprise* towed into a Romulan starbase. Yet he sat in his chair, and turning to one side, he could see Scotty leaning back in his station's chair, grumpily eyeing the nonexistent power conversion levels in the not-really-blown-up port nacelle, while delivering a rapid-fire lecture on the difficulties of the restart procedure to the slim dark Romulan man looking over his shoulder. Hvaid, that one was. Turning the other way, there were Mr. Spock and Lieutenant Kerasus and young Aidoann, Ael's third-in-command, deep in conversation about Old High Vulcan linguistic roots and their manifestations in modern Vulcan and Romulan. And Uhura would be—

She wasn't, though. Jim's train of thought was temporarily derailed. "Mr. Spock, where's Lieutenant Uhura?"

"She went down to recreation, Captain," Spock said. "I did not catch the entire conversation, but there was some communications problem to which she felt Mr. Freeman from life sciences had the answer."

"Fine. Where's the commander?"

"I believe she is also down in recreation, Captain. Lieutenant Commander Uhura requested the commander's presence there shortly after she left."

Jim got up, stretched—and stopped the gesture abruptly; his neck muscles still ached from the backhand the commander had given him. "All right, Mr. Spock, mind the store till I get back."

"Acknowledged," Spock said. He moved down to the center seat, and

Kerasus and Aidoann moved with him, the analysis of Vulcan pho-
nemes missing hardly a beat.

"Sickbay," Jim said to the lift, and off it went. He leaned against the
wall, rubbing his neck.

There was something bothering him about the whole business. Not
a feeling that Ael or her people might betray him—not that *specifically*.
But the whole matter of where the *Enterprise* was, of both capture and
escape being out of his hands . . . Out of his control. That was it.

*The old problem,* Jim thought, with some chagrin. He remembered all
too vividly that little incident back on Triacus with Gorgan the *soi-disant*
"Friendly Angel," in which that fear, his worst one, had been inflamed
to paralyzing proportions. *This isn't nearly that bad,* he told himself severely. *And I did choose to do this. It was my decision.* But all the same, it had
been Ael who came to him with the idea all ready-made; and even
when he had been ready to refuse her, damned if circumstances didn't
force him to accept her plan.

*Circumstances. Very convenient circumstances, too . . .*

*Oh, stop that! That's paranoia!*

Still, it was difficult not to be paranoid about this woman. A Romulan, to begin with . . . Well, that by itself wasn't reason to mistrust her.
But she had admitted to Jim that she had rigged most of the circumstances that had brought the *Enterprise* here—even to the point of paying a considerable amount in bribes to have the information about
"something going on in Romulan space" smuggled out to Starfleet
Command, planted where they would hear it. She had angled specifically and with great precision for *Enterprise* to be sent here—and she
had managed it. And now his bridge was full of her officers, and his rec
deck was full of her crew . . . and his neck ached.

She had him right where she wanted him . . . wherever that was. It
was the not knowing that made him crazy.

Loss of control . . .

The lift slid to a stop. Jim stalked out of its open doors and down the
hall toward sickbay, brooding. It might have been slightly easier to handle if the woman were at least likeable . . . if she weren't so relentlessly

manipulative, as sharp and cold as the sword she had been admiring in Spock's quarters. If only she didn't constantly seem to be maneuvering events with the same cool virtuosity that Spock exhibited while maneuvering pieces in the chesscubic. Though not *quite* the same. Spock's terrible expertise was always tempered, at least with Jim, by that elusive, almost mischievous compassion.

Then again, he couldn't set aside that wicked, merry, understanding flash of Ael's eyes at him, just after he had punched her out. . . .

He breathed out in disgust, gave the problem up as something he couldn't do anything about but would be pleased to see ended, and swung into sickbay. And there it all was again, for here was Ael's chief surgeon, t'Whatever-her-name-was, those Romulan words were pretty to hear but impossible to remember—with Lia Burke beside her, showing the Romulan woman how to use an anabolic protoplaser in regenerative mode. They were working on the Romulan's own arm, apparently removing and regenerating the tissue of an old scar a little bit at a time, so that the Romulan surgeon could get a feel for the instrument's settings. "No, watch that, you'll involve the fascia and get the cells all confused," Lia was saying, her dark curly head bent down close together with the Romulan's bronze-dark, straight-haired one. "Try it a little shallower. One millimeter is deep enough where the skin is this thin. Good afternoon, Captain; how's the neck?"

"I have a pain in it," Jim said, thinking more of the figurative truth than of the literal one. "Where's Dr. McCoy?"

"In his office, sir. Paperwork, I think. Can I be of assistance?"

"Possibly. Would you excuse yourself, Lieutenant?" Jim walked on through sickbay to Bones's office in the back; Lia came after him.

"Bones?"

McCoy looked up from a desk cluttered with cassettes and computer pads. "Come on in, Jim. What can I do for you?"

"Close the door after you, Lieutenant. Would you mind," Jim said to the nurse, "telling me what was going on out there? My orders were that our 'guests' were not to be given any nonessential information. We are still going to have to answer to Fleet after we get out of this mess— always providing we *do.*"

Bones opened his mouth to say something, but Lia beat him to it. "Captain, with all due respect, complete healing of the wounded, no matter how old the wound is, hardly strikes me as 'nonessential.' And in this area at least, my oaths to Starfleet—and other authorities—are intact."

"'Other authorities'?"

"'I shall teach my Art without fee or stipulation to other disciples also bound to it by oath, should they desire to learn it,'" Lia said, that dry, merry voice of hers going soft and sober for the moment.

"'. . . and this I swear by Apollo the Physician, and Aesculapius, and Health and Allheal His daughters, and by all the other Gods and Goddesses, and the One above Them Whose Name we do not know. . . .'" Bones said, just as quietly. "The Romulan version turns out to be a lot shorter—but the intent's the same. Some things transcend even the discipline of the service, Jim."

Jim's neck throbbed worse, and he opened his mouth—then closed it again. *Gently. Gently. Loss of control . . .* "Sorry, Lieutenant," he said. "You're quite right. Bones, my apologies."

McCoy raised both eyebrows. "For what? Nothin's normal around here just now—no reason for *us* to be. Lia, get the captain ten mils of Aerosal, all right?"

"Better make it twenty," Jim said.

Lia looked from McCoy to Kirk and back again—then, significantly, up at the ceiling. She nodded. "Fifteen it is," she said, and went out.

McCoy looked after her with rueful amusement. "They don't make nurses like that anymore," he said.

Jim sat down and laughed at him. "Just as well, huh Bones?"

"Well," McCoy said, "I *was* about to say fifteen. I think that woman's been taking lessons from Spock—though I don't want to know in what. Don't get comfortable, Jim; I was just going down to recreation."

"Isn't everybody?" Jim said. "Can't keep the crew away from the Romulans. . . ."

"I didn't think you would want to. We're going to be working pretty closely with those people over the next twenty-four hours or so, on some pretty crucial business. The more comfortable the crew gets with them, the better."

"Theoretically, at least . . ."

"Misgivings?" The small transporter pad on McCoy's desk sang and sparkled briefly, and a spray hypo and an ampule of amber liquid appeared on it. McCoy picked it up, checked the label on the ampule three times, almost ceremonially, slipped it into the hypo and came around the desk to Jim. "Stop twitching."

"The arm still itches."

The hypo hissed, and McCoy tossed it onto the desk. "If I were anything but an old country doctor, I would suspect your itch of being elsewhere."

The throbbing in Jim's neck went away. "I'm nervous," he said.

"See, the truth *will* out after all. Guess what? So am I."

"And who do you tell about it?"

"Christine. Or maybe Lia. Then they tell Spock, see, and Spock tells the ceiling. A carefully arranged chain of confidences. The nurses talk only to Vulcans, and the Vulcans talk only to God. . . ."

Jim snorted. It was a lot harder to be paranoid when he wasn't in pain. "That explains where he gets his chess strategies, anyway. . . . Bones, there's a question I wanted to ask you. Where'd you learn to play like that?"

"Watching Spock, mostly. And watching you."

"With a talent like that, you should be in tournament play."

McCoy started to laugh quietly as the two of them left his office, heading down the hall to the lift for recreation. "Jim, you haven't looked at my record since I was assigned, have you? . . . My F.I.D.E. rating is in the 700's somewhere."

Jim stared at McCoy as they got into the lift. 'The F.I.D.E.' was the Federation Intergalactique des Échecs; its members got their ratings only through Federation-sanctioned tournament play, and the 700's, while hardy a master's level, were a respectable neighborhood. "No kidding. Why don't you play more often?"

"I'm a voyeur. —Oh, stop that. A *chess* voyeur. I use it mostly as a diagnostic tool."

"Come again?"

"Jim, chess isn't just good for the brain. It's a wonderful way to get a feeling for someone's attitude toward life and games and other people. Their response to stress, their ability to plan, what they do when plans are foiled. Their attack on life—sneaky, bold, straightforward, subtle, careless, what have you. Humor or the lack of it, compassion, enthusiasm, the 'poker face,' all the different things that go toward 'psyching' an opponent out . . . A string of five or six chess games can make a marvelous précis of a personality and the ways it reacts in its different moods."

"An intelligence test?"

The lift stopped and they got out. "Lord, no," McCoy said. "On this ship intelligence is a foregone conclusion . . . and in any case, it's hardly everything. It's hardly even *anything,* from some psychiatrists' point of view. You want to get a feeling for where someone's personal style lies, their 'flair.' Spock, for example. Why do you think he gets so many requests for standard 3D tournament play when we're close to home space? It's not because he's brilliant. There are enough brilliant chess masters floating around the Federation to carpet a small planet with. But Spock's games have elegance. My guess would be that it comes partly of his expertise in the sciences—the delight in the perfect solution, the most logical and economical one. But if you look at his games, you also see elegance—exquisitely laid traps that close with such precision, it looks like he micrometered them. There's a great love of the precision itself: not just of its logic and economy, but of its beauty. Though Spock'd sooner die than admit it. Our cool, 'unemotional' Vulcan, Captain, is a closet aesthete. But you knew that."

"I did? Of course I did."

"I should make you figure this out yourself," Bones said. "Still, none of this is anything you haven't already noticed from long observation of him in other areas. That aestheticism is a virtue; it shows up in his other work too. But it's also a hint at where one of his weak spots might be. He will scorn blunter or more brutal moves or setups that might produce a faster win. Why do you think he has that sword on his wall? But this is where you get lucky sometimes, because you tend to go straight for the throat. Spock gets busy doing move-sculpture—and enjoying himself; he loves watching people's minds work too, yours especially—

and he gets lost in the fun. And then you come in with an ax and hack his artwork to pieces with good old human-brand unsubtle craziness. Note, of course, that he keeps coming back. The win is obviously not the purpose of the game for him."

"Obviously. Bones, is this something I can take a correspondence course in?"

McCoy grinned. "Psychology by mail, huh? You might have trouble. Not that many med schools teach diagnostic chess, and they wouldn't be able to help you with 4D anyway. In fact, Lia is one of the few people I know who's managed to find a course in even 3D diagnostic. She routinely plays at least a game or two with her patients whenever she can. She's not much of a tactician, but she says she doesn't mind losing . . . she's more interested in finding out about other people."

Bones chuckled as they stepped into recreation together. "You should have seen her playing with Jerry Freeman the other week . . . poor Lia found out a little more about him than she wanted to. Jerry wasn't paying attention to the game at the beginning, and Lia put him in a bad position pretty quickly. So he bided his time and fought a holding action until she got up to answer a page, and while she was gone, he quietly programmed the cubic for 'catastrophic dump.' When she got back, she tried to move a piece, and the cubic blew up. Pieces flying everywhere . . . I wish you could have seen her face."

Jim wished he could have too. "And what did she deduce from that?"

"If she's smart, the same thing I did after I played with him a couple of times; that Mr. Freeman is quite bright, and knows it, and occasionally gets incautious. What is *not* occasional about him, though, is his extreme dislike of looking dumb in front of people—and he will sometimes resort to very unorthodox solutions to save his game."

"You call that a save?"

"It was for him. The next game he played with Lia—"

"There was a next game? I would have killed him."

"They used to call them 'the gentler sex,' didn't they once? Let's wait and see if Freeman can still walk after his yearly injections next week. Anyway, next game, he wiped the rec deck up with her. Then he fetched her a drink and was the picture of gallantry. He's a very good winner."

Jim chuckled. "Bones, do me a favor, will you?"

"What?"

"Play 4D with Ael."

At that Bones looked somber, and pulled Jim a bit off to one side, well away from the freestyle demonstration of Romulan hand-to-hand combat that seemed to have resumed over in the far left corner of the room. McCoy eased himself down into one of a pair of chairs in a conversation niche, and said, "I already did, a few hours ago."

Jim had a sudden sinking feeling that that line of Ael's about learning the game in "a few minutes" had not been mere casual braggadocio. *Damn* the woman! "And?"

"She blew me to plasma."

"She beat *you!*"

"Don't look so shocked. Don't go all sorry for me, either! I learned lots more from the loss than I would have from the win. But it wasn't a pretty picture."

"What did she do?"

"Oh, no, Jim. I leave that as an exercise for the student. You'll find a recording of the game in my office running files under the password 'Trojan Horse.' She knew I was recording it, by the way."

"And?"

"She didn't care. She knew what I was up to and just didn't care. Chew on *that* one, Jim."

"Later. There's Uhura and your demolitions expert; I was looking for them."

"Not for Ael, of course."

"Of course. Come on, Bones."

"One thing, Jim, before we go over there."

"What?"

"Get some sleep this afternoon. You're looking a bit raw . . . and besides, a brain full of lactic acid by-products and short on REM sleep makes for poor command performance."

"Noted. . . ."

They walked together over to the massive control console for the holography stage. Very little seemed to have changed since several days ago. There was Uhura, working at the controls on top of the console; and there was the lower half of Lieutenant Freeman, sitting cross-legged between the pedestal-legs of the console. The upper half of him was inside the works of the console; as Jim and McCoy came up, one arm came out from inside, felt around for one of the tools littered about, grabbed a circuit spanner, and went back inside again. The only addition to the scene was Ael, looking over Uhura's shoulder with an interested expression.

"Got it, Nyota," said the muffled voice from inside. "Try it now."

"Right." Uhura looked up at Jim, grinned happily, and said, "Say something, Captain."

"Certainly. Aren't you supposed to be on the bridge?"

*"HEUOIPK EEIRWOINVSY SHTENIX GFAK HU MMHNI-NAAWAH!"* the console said, or at least that was what it sounded like.

"What the devil was that?" said McCoy. "Sounds like you've got a problem there, Lieutenant. A malfunction that shouts."

"No, Doctor. It's taken us the last half hour to get it to do that." Uhura beamed at Jim. "Captain, I'm on my break at the moment. But this is the answer to that little poser you handed me the other day. And also the antidote, incidentally, to the trouble we had with signal leakage while Ael's people were running communications."

"I'm all ears," Jim said. "One moment, though. Mr. Freeman, are you just shy, or did Lieutenant Burke finally lose her temper and do a hemicorporectomy on you?"

The half-a-person whooped with that very distinctive laugh of his—an even funnier sound than usual, smothered as it was inside the console—and carefully came out from under, brushing himself off as he stood. Regardless of his age (in the mid-thirties), his six-foot height, and his silver-shot hair (now somewhat disarranged from being inside the console), Jerry Freeman always struck Jim as one of the youngest of his crew. The man was eternally excited about something—for example, right now, those old sterries—but though the subject of the enthusiasm might change without notice, his total commitment to the subject of the moment never did. "What are you two up to?" Jim said.

"Words of one syllable, please," said McCoy.

"Oh, come on, Bones. You have to learn some big words sooner or later. E-lec-tron. Can you say that? *Sure* you can. . . ."

Freeman took a moment to smooth his hair back in place. "We're confusing the intercom system, Doctor," he said. "Among other things. But what the captain needed was a more effective jamming system for subspace communications than Fleet has bothered to design for wide-area use. Mostly they've tried to handle the 'beam-tapping' problem in deepspace communications by avoiding it . . . defeating it at sending and receiving ends with 'unbreakable' codes, hypercoherent wavicle packets, all that silliness. But what technology can produce, technology can sooner or later decode or unravel."

Uhura was leaning on one elbow beside Ael with a humorous look on her face, watching her protégé lecture. "You can't solve a problem that way," she said. "Fleet has been ignoring the medium through which the messages travel, considering deepspace too big and unmanageable to handle. And it's true that 'broadcast' jamming of the sort done in a planet's ionosphere is impossible out here; while the relatively small-scale jamming already available to us is useless for our present purposes. So what Jerry and I have been doing is finding a way to make space itself more amenable to being jammed . . . a method that's an outgrowth of the way Jerry's been making digital documents more amenable to being rechanneled."

"Mr. Scott helped," Jerry said. "We used material from the parts bank to build a very small warpfield generator of the kind used in warp-capable shuttlecraft. We attached that to one of the little message buoys that the ship jettisons in jeopardy situations. Then we adjusted the warpfield generator so that it would twist space just slightly over a large cubic area, causing the contours of surrounding subspace to favor randomly directed tachyon flow along certain 'tunnels' at a certain packet frequency—"

"Good-bye," McCoy said. "I'm off to do something simple. A hemicorporectomy, possibly."

"It makes subspace much easier to jam," Mr. Freeman said, sounding rather desperate. "That's all."

"Why didn't you say that?" McCoy muttered.

"I did."

"It also takes a lot of power," Jim said thoughtfully. "Even a hefty warpfield generator would only have a limited life expectancy."

"Yes, sir. Four hours is our predicted upper limit. But for those four hours, nobody trying to use subspace communication is going to hear anything but what sounds like a lot of 'black noise'—stellar wind and so forth. And whatever they try to send will be perverted into the same noise."

"Range?"

"Presently about a thousand cubic light-years, Captain. If you want more, you can have it, but the life of the generator becomes inversely shorter in proportion to the extension of the jamming buoy's range."

Jim nodded—he had rather expected that. "All right. How many of them can you put together for me in the next four hours?"

Uhura and Freeman looked at each other. "We'll need more people—"

"Get Scotty and the engineering staff on it."

"We don't dare overdrain the parts bank, sir," Freeman said. "Will three more be enough?"

"They'll have to be. Ael, how about it? How fast are your people likely to understand this if they come up against it?"

The commander looked dubious. "Hard to tell, Captain. They are not all idiots like LLunih, or as complacent as t'Kaenmie and tr'Arri-ufvi, who're pacing us in *Helm* and *Wildfire*. I would delay as long as possible before deploying such a device; that would give any interested observer less time to become suspicious and start deducing what was going on."

*Yes,* Jim thought, *you would say that, wouldn't you? No matter what you were up to.* But he put the thought aside for the moment. "Agreed," he said. "At our present rate we should be hitting the 'breakaway' point, where we drop our pursuit, in about five hours, correct?"

"That's so, Captain."

"Fine. We'll drop one of those buoys there as we begin the engagement, to keep your three friends from yelling for help. One we'll drop in the area of Levaeri when we reach it. To the third one I want the fourth warp generator attached so that it has starflight capability as well as the subspace alteration function. We'll send it off past Levaeri, along the likeliest vector of approach for an unexpected ship. Think about that, Commander, and let me know."

Ael blinked at Jim. "But if the ship is unexpected—" Then she smiled. "Ah, Hilaefve's Paradox, eh Captain? Very well. I will think about it for you."

"Good. Uhura, Mr. Freeman, take what people you need and get on it. One thing before you go: *why* have you taught the holography console to shout gibberish?"

Uhura chuckled. "Captain, it takes months of practice and skill to handle a ship's communications board so that there's no signal leakage through the shields. The problem is, after working with a board for awhile, a comm officer does that without thinking of it—and I didn't think to warn poor Aidoann. Not that she would have known what to do about it—I haven't had time to teach her all the board's little tricks. So Jerry took the same random number generator he used in the jamming buoy's tachyon-switching protocols and adapted it to the multiuse programmable logic solid that every intercom in the ship has inside it. The solids will now encode and decode voices and data at their sending and receiving ends; signal along the circuitry, which is where the leakage comes from, will now only manifest as that gibberish you heard—so that even while Ael's people are handling our intercoms, we can say anything we have to without worrying about being overheard, or needing people to run around with notes. . . . "

"Nice work," Jim said, and both Uhura and Freeman looked exceptionally pleased. "Now I need another four hours of it. Uhura, have Lieutenant Mahasë cover for you on the bridge till you're done. Both of you scoot!"

They did. Jim watched them go, and Ael moved around to join him and McCoy. "If we're to be in battle in four hours," she said, "I'd best go see to *Bloodwing* and make sure my people are ready."

"Sounds good to me, Commander. Bones, I'm about ready for my nap. Have me paged at point six, unless something requires my attention sooner."

"Right."

Ael went off in one direction, and the doctor in another. Jim just stood there for a moment, watching them both out of sight—then headed down to his cabin, via engineering, thinking very hard about chess.

He was still thinking about it two hours later, after his nap turned into a tossing-and-turning session, and even one of McCoy's mild soothers left him completely awake. On Jim's desk screen, the ship's computer had obligingly translated the chesscubic's holographic display of McCoy's game with Ael into a 2D graphic, and displayed it for him. It made a fascinating study—the first moves sure on McCoy's part, tentative on Ael's; then roles reversing—McCoy moving with more of an outward show of caution, apparently seeing what Ael would do if offered the run of the cubic. There was a point at which the computer recorded a long interval between moves; she had hesitated. Jim could almost see those cool eyes of hers across the cubic, suddenly lifted to assess not only the tactical situation but the man who sat across from her—who was, at the moment, himself a tactic. And then came a series of moves that were, to put it mildly, insulting. She became "polite" to McCoy. She moved out into the cubic, but genteelly, almost as if not wanting to beat him, almost as if they were playing on the same side. McCoy put up with it for about ten minutes, then timed about half his pieces out, preparing to dump them on her like a ton of neutronium in six very visible moves. He could seem insulting too, when it suited his purposes.

And she derailed Bones as totally as Bones had derailed Spock. Three of her pieces timed out, not even critical ones. Three moves later, McCoy's pieces all came back—into cubes that were suddenly no longer vacant. Annihilation, all over the board. McCoy had one stronghold left for his king and both of his queens.

Ael sacrificed both her queens to his—and checkmated his king with three pawns and a knight fork.

Her first game.

*She didn't even care, Jim. Chew on* that.

He did. It tasted awful.

—and the red alert sirens started whooping, and there was no time to waste worrying anymore. *Trust her,* he told himself bitterly as he leapt up from the chair, pulling the velour on over the undertunic. *Or don't. But make up your mind.*

He ran out, seething. The corridors were alive with his people, and with Romulans, too, scrambling for posts. He dashed into the lift at the end of officers' country and found tall pretty Aidoann already in there, breathing hard. "Where's the commander?" he said, as the doors closed on them.

"Beamed back over to *Bloodwing,* Captain," Aidoann said. She looked at him with those big brown eyes of hers, and Jim had a sudden thought that she looked rather like Uhura, the same slant to the eyes. . . . "Sir—" she said.

It was the first time any of them had called him anything but "Captain." *Something cultural?* he wondered. But whatever, suddenly she wasn't a Romulan anymore; she was a young crewperson, looking nervous before a major engagement. "Antecenturion?"

"Do you have things you believe in?"

Impossible not to answer such directness. "Yes," Jim said.

"I hope They're with us now," Aidoann said. "Those three will blow us all to Areinnye if they can."

"Aidoann," he said, grateful that he could pronounce that word at least, "your commander and I have other plans."

She grinned at Jim, a quick flash through the otherwise Romulan intensity. The bridge doors opened for them.

*I just hope they're the same ones,* Jim thought, and swung down toward the center seat.

Spock got out of it with his usual quick grace and hurried back to his station. "Captain, we are running slightly ahead of schedule," he said over his shoulder as he went. "Registering a group of large masses at most extreme sensor range. Their location and arrangement agree closely with *Bloodwing*'s estimates for ephemerae of Levaeri V and its primary. The station is not yet detectable. On the revised schedule, we are now five minutes from scheduled 'breakaway.'"

"Good. Mr. Mahasë"—Jim turned to the gray-haired, gray-skinned

Eseriat who was holding down Uhura's post, with Aidoann standing by if she should be needed. "Get me engineering."

"Aye, sir."

"*Engineering, Scott here . . .*"

"We're running fast, Scotty—in range a bit early. How are Uhura and Freeman doing?"

"*They're just helping my people put the finishing touches on the last buoy,*" Scotty said.

"Fine. Load one of them up; we're about to lay an egg."

"*Already in photon torpedo tube one, Captain.*"

"All right. Hold on to it, Scotty; I'll let you know when. Thirty seconds tops. Out. Aidoann, please call *Bloodwing* and give them the pre-arranged signal."

"Yes, sir," she said. And then, after a moment, "*Bloodwing,* this is *Enterprise;* t'Khnialmnae."

"*Tr'Rllaillieu,*" said Subcommander Tafv's voice, cool and calm as usual.

"Subcommander, we have an emergency," Aidoann said, not having to fake a small tremor in her voice. "A small party of Federation personnel have broken out of group detention—"

Mahasë killed the frequency between the two ships. Jim hit the intercom button on his chair. "Okay, Scotty, *now!*"

The ship held steady as always, but there was a small muffled noise, much quieter than the usual dull thump of a photon torpedo on the way out. "Buoy away, Captain," Chekov said, "heading one eighty mark minus twenty."

"Activate it."

Chekov hit a control on his board. "Operational, Captain. Subspace communications are jammed."

"Allcall," Jim said to Mahasë; and when he spoke again his voice rang through the ship. "Battle stations, battle stations! Secure for warp maneuvering!" He made a kill-it gesture at the Eseriat. "Screens up, gentlemen, deflectors on full. Mr. Sulu, kick the engines up to warp three. Break out of *Bloodwing*'s tractors and maneuver at your discretion. Closest Romulan vessel—"

"*Rea's Helm,* sir."

"Lock on phasers. Fire at will. Mr. Chekov, photon torpedoes—"

"Tubes three through six charged and ready—"

"Mr. Sulu, why aren't we moving!"

"*Bloodwing* has increased power to her tractors, sir—"

*Why that—! She was supposed to—* "Break them," Jim said tightly.

"Engine overheat, Captain—"

"Risk it. Break free!"

Sulu's hands swept over his board. "No good, sir—"

"Increase warp."

"Sir, no result, *Bloodwing*'s too close—"

"*Rea's Helm* has put its shields up, Captain," Spock said, staring down his viewer. "Hailing us."

"Ignore. Mr. Chekov, fire on *Bloodwing*."

Aidoann's head jerked up; her face was ashen. "Shielded, Captain—" Chekov said.

"I note that. Scan for weakest point and fire phasers right there. Look for areas of screen overlap, those spots are sometimes poorly protected—"

"Shields going up on *Wildfire* and *Javelin,* Captain," Spock said. The ship shuddered as something hit the screens. "Fire, Captain," Spock added. "From *Bloodwing*. Phaser fire, clean hit on number six screen, screen efficiency decreased to sixty percent—"

*Damn! Damn! DAMN!* "Return fire at will, Mr. Chekov. Mr. Sulu, if you don't break those tractors in about a second, I'm going to tell Lieutenant Renner who stole her clothes from poolside last month!"

Next to Chekov, who was firing the phasers in blast after blast, Sulu went pale. Jim didn't see what he did, but the ship lurched mightily, and suddenly space on the screen in front of them was clear again. "Damage?" he said.

"Minimal," Spock said. "A very quick burst at warp eight, most precisely angled. Well done, Mr. Sulu."

"Yes," Jim said, sweating and grim, but grinning nonetheless.

"Four clean hits on *Bloodwing,* Captain. Her forward screen is down to thirty percent efficiency, and her port screen has failed altogether. Further fire—"

"Forget her," Jim said. "Sulu, Chekov, *get me those three ships!*"

"Positions on screen," Spock said. There they were in schematic: *Bloodwing* lying a little to one side, coming after *Enterprise* but losing speed; *Rea's Helm* closing in from port and above, *Wildfire* coming in faster yet from the starboard, *Javelin* arching around toward the rear. "Mr. Chekov, watch out for him—"

"Firing rear tubes, standard spread," Chekov said, eyes flickering back and forth from his board to the screen. "Recharging."

"Clean misses," Spock said. "*Javelin* is in evasive maneuvers. Dropping back—now closing again—*Rea's Helm* is in close approach—"

"Fire!" Jim cried at exactly the moment Chekov did so. White fire lanced away from the *Enterprise,* hitting the Romulan ship exactly in a screen overlap zone over a nacelle. There was one of those seemingly month-long pauses, and then *Rea's Helm* blew up, blazing, matter and antimatter making a small sun of her. Sulu brought *Enterprise* curving about and threw her right into the expanding cloud of debris, letting the deflectors take it.

"Steady on, Mr. Sulu," Jim said, leaning forward in the center seat. "We're leaving a trail—"

"Yes, sir, I know," Sulu said. "Warp six—" He was working on his console again, while behind them sensors showed *Wildfire* screaming in from the starboard, *Javelin* trailing somewhat, and *Bloodwing* at the rear of the pack, building speed but still far behind.

"*Wildfire* is closing," Spock said calmly. "Firing to her port—" Spock paused a moment, looking down his scanner. "Explosion, Captain. She has destroyed jamming buoy. *Wildfire*'s range now five hundred thousand kilometers—four hundred thousand—"

Sulu's eyebrows went up as his hand flickered over the console. Jim watched him with uneasy delight. He was doing something Jim had seen done in starships in warp, but always at slower speeds: deforming the warpfield itself, broadening and flattening it forward, tightening it to the rear. And the ship was responding in the only way she could— slowly, gracefully nosing downward as she flashed through the *Helm*'s remains, then nosing down faster, harder, pitching forward until she was literally flying "vertically," nacelles and the broad side of the disk forward.

It was not a position a ship could fly in for more than a few seconds, in warp. Yet if this worked . . . "Mr. Sulu—" Jim said.

"I know, Captain," Sulu said, and kept *Enterprise* rolling forward—a slow somersault through otherspace at seven hundred twenty times the speed of light, while behind her, seeing nothing but the unchanged shape of her defensive screens, *Wildfire* came charging in—right into the teeth of her forward phasers. If Sulu could get her around in time! She was flying "diagonal" now, easing out of it, flattening out—flying upside down and backward, and right into their faces, now here came *Wildfire,* firing phasers— "Hits on number one shield, number three shield," Spock said, beginning to sound a touch grim now, "number one buckling, Captain; reinforcing—"

"No! Belay that!" Jim could feel Spock glancing at him, ignored it for the moment. "Another hit on number three," Spock said, "down to twenty percent—"

"Ready, Mr. Chekov?"

"Ready, Captain—"

*Wildfire* swelled on the screen, coming right down their throats, and now that the Romulan ship could see what was happening, it was too late— *"Now!"*

Mr. Chekov pounced on his board. *Enterprise*'s deadly forward phasers lashed out where *Wildfire* had expected only the lesser rear ones, or photon torpedoes. And suddenly, *Wildfire* was gone in a bloom of light—

—*Javelin,* following behind, vanished.

"Cloaking device," Spock said.

"Defeat it, Mr. Spock—"

"The cloaking countermeasure is not functional, Captain, it's a function of subspace communication."

*Oh no!* Jim stared at the empty screen, in which there was nothing but *Bloodwing* now, soaring in toward them faster than she had been. *He'll go off in some other direction—*

He stared at *Bloodwing,* and it hit him. "Mr. Chekov, fire! Everything we've got, right at her!"

"Captain!" That was Aidoann, a child's cry for a betrayed mother.

Chekov fired, photon torpedoes and phasers both at once. "Sulu, hard about!" And at the same moment *Bloodwing*'s phasers lashed out at the *Enterprise*—

—and their combined armament hit what lay directly between them, what Jim had somehow known would be using *Bloodwing* as cover, only from in front. "Spock, the shields!" he cried, but Spock had already reinforced them. Nothing else saved *Enterprise* from the point-blank explosion of another starship right in front of her. She screamed through the wreckage and the swiftly dying fire, while *Bloodwing,* plunging toward them at warp five, angled up and over them, deforming her own warpfield in a crazed, congratulatory victory roll.

"They do that too. . . ." Jim said, slumping back in his seat.

"Local traffic, Captain," Spock said sharply, looking down his scanner. "A small ship, bearing— Too late. It's cloaked."

"Our friend the 'crawling slime,'" Jim said "LLunih."

"I would say so. Evidently he suspected *Bloodwing* of complicity with us—and sacrificed his ship to test the theory."

"A wonderful person," Jim said. "Hail *Bloodwing.*"

The screen lit up. There was that cramped little control room, and in it, Ael, sweating rivers and looking haggard. *"Captain,"* she said, *"is your ship all right?"*

"We're fine. Ael, you know more about 'the better part of valor' than anyone I've ever met."

*"Probably. Why do you think I went to dinner with LLunih the other night? I wanted to see what he had hidden in his engineering room—and I got him to show me. It was an Imperial courier: that little creature in which he just saved his skin. Some day I shall have it for a pot-scouring rag."*

"His courier ship?"

*"That too. What could I do, until you deployed your jammer and I knew it was working, save increase my efforts to hold on to you as if your escape was genuinely a surprise? He will report to the Senate in doubt now—knowing that you apparently willingly fired on me to kill—and thus keep us both clear of the suspicion of complicity. They will argue—and the ship that might have gotten here from Romulus in four hours will perhaps not come for ten, or twenty."*

"I have a question for you."

*"Ask."*

"What the devil took you so long to figure out that the damn buoy was working?!"

*"Captain, our sensors are not as good as yours, especially in the high ranges, you know that. . . . I could know nothing until my subspace communication with one of the other ships failed."*

Jim sighed and said a bad word in his head, for that was true. "All right, Commander. We'd better get started for Levaeri V. . . ."

*"I agree. I'll be over in* Hsaaja *in a few moments."*

Jim looked at her, not liking what he was thinking. "What do you need *Hsaaja* for?"

*"I don't need it,"* Ael said, *"but you will. One of your warpdrive generators is destroyed. Your second one will be needed to power its companion along the 'least expected' course out of the Levaeri system. Another will be dropped in the system itself. The last one we'll install in* Hsaaja *and send on LLunih's trail—thereby slowing down his report to the High Command a bit more. Even minutes may be precious later."*

Jim nodded. "Ael," he said regretfully, "that's a sweet little ship. . . ."

*"If I'm dead,"* she said drily, *"I won't be able to fly him anyway."*

And suddenly the light dawned, and Jim sat straight up in his chair and said, "Ael—that was *five* warpdrive generators—"

*"So it was,"* she said. *"Wasn't that how many you ordered made?"* She smiled at him wickedly, and closed the channel down.

*Damn* the woman!!

# Chapter Thirteen

"Captain, would you kindly hand me that little silver spanner there?—no, the other one."

"Commander," said the captain, "is it going to be 'Captain' all the way back *from* Levaeri, too?"

Ael looked up from the hatch in the floor of *Hsaaja*'s cockpit, pushed a strand of sweaty hair out of the eye into which it had fallen, and said, "Oh. You think we are going to *make* it back then?"

"Commander—"

"You may call me 'Ael.' The Doctor does. Even Mr. Spock does." She bowed her head again, reaching down into the guts of the autopilot and starting the last of the connections to the jamming apparatus.

"Well . . . I wasn't quite sure I'd been given permission. You 'gave' us your name. But it's not the same. And permission to the doctor, and Spock, is not necessarily permission to me."

That was perceptive of him, an insight she wouldn't have expected him to reach. "You're quite right," she said. "I was withholding it."

He started to ask why, then stopped. That, too, was something she wouldn't have expected; restraint. Just as well; she wasn't certain of the reasons herself. "As for you," she said slowly, touching a connection open, reading the charge on it, and closing it again, "I can't quite pronounce the name after 'Captain.' And it's unwise to mishandle names."

"You said that before. . . ." He looked thoughtful. "Can you say 'Jim'?"

She gasped and started to laugh, so hard that she almost dropped the spanner. And when she was sure she still had it, and looked up again, the captain looked so bewildered that it just made her laugh harder. "Oh, Elements," she finally managed to say, sitting back against the seat cushion of the pilot's chair, "is that truly your self-name?"

"James, actually. 'Jim' is a contraction. . . ."

"Oh, oh my." Ael started laughing again, still harder, so that all she could do was sag back against the seat and wave the spanner weakly at him. *Reaction,* she thought clinically, in some remote part of her. *Wouldn't t'Hrienteh look askance at this? Or even the doctor.* . . . And indeed the poor captain was looking rather askance himself. "No, no," Ael finally managed to gasp, when he showed signs of getting up and leaving. "Oh, Captain. 'Jim.' Jim, I will call you that gladly, but I beg you . . ."

He made a questioning look at her.

"Don't ask me what it means! . . ."

"Well, all right. Ael, then."

"Jim," Ael said, and studied to keep her face straight. "Well enough. Let me finish this, we don't have all day." She busied herself with the spanner again, sealing the last connections. "The other name, the long form: what does it mean?"

"Nothing embarrassing, thank heaven." He cocked an eyebrow at her, and Ael wondered fleetingly whether he had stolen the expression from Spock, or Spock from him? "I looked it up once—it means 'supplanter,' or something like that."

"The translator didn't render that word."

"Someone who takes other people's rights or positions away from them."

That made *her* put an eyebrow up. "You had best be careful with a name like that," Ael said. "It could lead you into trouble. . . . But then what other position than this one could you possibly want?"

He shook his head. There was no other, and he knew it as well as she did. "And what mighty 'enterprise' was this ship named after?" she said.

"Not one particular one. Just the spirit of enterprise in general. And there were many other ships with the same name, an old tradition. . . ."

He trailed off when he saw that she was staring at him again. "Oh, no wonder," she said softly, more to herself than to him. "All of ch'Rihan has wondered why this ship has been through so much trouble, so much glory. . . ."

"Do enlighten me."

It was sarcasm, but gentle; he genuinely didn't seem to know what she was talking about. "Ca—Jim, it's dangerous to name anything, a

person, a vessel, after an entire unmitigated virtue. The whole power of
it gets into the named one, makes it go places, do things too great for
man. . . . Glory follows; but sorrow too. . . ."

"That's usually the way with people, no matter what the ship's
named." Still, he looked thoughtful.

"Tell me your thought."

"Funny, actually . . . There were other ships called *Intrepid,* you
know. A lot of them got in trouble all the time. One of the most famous
of them, the one in mothballs in New York Harbor—"

"This translator is having problems. You have little round flying insects on Earth that are eating a ship named *Intrepid?* And *you* ask *me*
about the danger of names?"

"The ship," Jim said with careful dignity, giving Ael a dirty look that
needed no translation, "is in honorable retirement. Preserved as a museum for many, many years. But she had a reputation among her crew
for being a bad-luck ship. Gallant—but unlucky. They called her the
'Evil I.' Probably that won't translate; 'i' is both the name of the letter
*Intrepid*'s name starts with, and a sound-alike for the Anglish word for
this." He pointed at his eye.

"Evil eye, yes; I see the pun. We have a sign you make against it."

"Yes. This old ship kept getting torpedoed, running aground—it was
a wet-navy ship. All kinds of annoying things like that. Well, then
comes our *Intrepid,* the first starship by that name, and it serves hardly
more than a few years before being attacked and destroyed by a spacegoing creature, a kind of giant amoeba. And then the new *Intrepid* is
built, and this happens to it. . . ." He waved vaguely in the general direction of Levaeri.

Ael nodded. "You see the problem. Name a ship for the spirit of fear-
lessness, and it forgets to fear. A bad trait. Worse when the ship is full of
Vulcans . . ." She checked the last connection, pulled the autopilot's
door down over the opening again, and sealed it. Her glance up at Jim
showed her a face that looked rather skeptical.

"Not your belief, I see," she said, standing up carefully, both to keep
from banging her head on the canopy and because of the ache in her
back. "No matter. Let's send this poor creature on his way." She flicked

switches on the consoles, looking with sorrowful longing at the familiar arrays, the screen that made her eyes hurt, the place where she had dropped the wrench once and scratched the flawless, shiny black front panel. It was a shame to send this ship out into the cold nowhere, to run alone, finally to run out of fuel and drift alone forever. But there was nothing else for it; the *Enterprise*'s shuttlecraft, which Jim had offered, didn't have *Hsaaja*'s range or speed. And both would be needed.

"You always were good at throwing things away when you had to," Jim said from behind her. "I remember once—it was the Battle of alpha Trianguli, wasn't it?—you emptied out two whole Romulan cruisers and left them drifting there crewless in space—doubled up their crews with those of two other ships and ran away, while poor Captain Rihaul went crazy over two empty ships rigged on automatic and firing at her. You didn't even have to hurry to get away. . . ."

There was rueful admiration in the tone, and something more; compassion, consolation. It sounded as if he understood what she felt.

Bizarre idea. "Yes," she said, "I remember that. Come on, Jim, he's on the timer. Let's get out of here."

They did, and on a screen in a briefing room near the hangar deck watched the sleek black ship rise up on its thrusters and glide out into the starry night. The hangar deck's doors closed, then, and Ael, standing there watching them, felt cold enough to shudder. It might have been a piece of her going away.

*It is. Why must I love things so? They pass away, one and all. . . .*

She straightened up. "We have another meeting, don't we, Jim?"

"Preattack briefing," he said. "The chief of security, the department heads, some other people. We'll keep it short . . . everybody needs rest, and we've only got about six more hours before we hit Levaeri sensor range."

She nodded, and they left the little briefing room together, heading for the lift. "This business of names . . ." Jim said.

"It's not names specifically. Just words. Even in your world, people have died for words. Sometimes they've died *of* them. One learns to be careful what one says in such a world. And like anything so powerful, like any weapon, words cut both ways. They redeem and betray— sometimes both at once. The attribute we name as a virtue may also turn out to be our bane. So we watch what we call things—in case we should turn out to be right."

Jim looked thoughtful at that too, but this time Ael left the thought behind the look alone. "We treasure names," she said. "They're the most powerful words, and our favorites. After all, what makes you respond more immediately than your name being called? . . . As long as a Rihannsu has someone to speak his name, or even if it's written, or remembered, that person is real. Afterward . . . nothing. The shadows, some say. The place where the Elements are unmixed, more *real* than here, say others." She shrugged. "But either way, names are life. . . ."

Jim appeared to be considering that for a moment as the lift doors closed in front of them. "You never did tell me what a 'bloodwing' is," he said at last.

Ael laughed softly. "The name is hardly as noble as *Enterprise*'s, I'm afraid . . . but then it's not as perilous, either. It's a flying creature we have on ch'Rhian, and my House's sigil-beast. A big, slow, ugly scavenger, so big that it can't fly without a long takeoff run, and you can keep one captive just by putting a small fence around it. But once it's in the air, nothing can match it for speed or power of flight."

The lift opened, and they walked out together toward main briefing. Coming down the hall toward them, there were Spock and McCoy. "Gentlemen," Jim said to them as they all headed into the briefing room, "you're early."

"Spock and I wanted to take our time going over the roster for the strike force," McCoy said. He sat down at the table, Spock beside him, and began sorting through a pile of cassettes he had been carrying. Ael sat down opposite, so as to see their faces better; Jim sat beside her. *For the same reason?* she wondered briefly.

"This is the best of the group," McCoy was saying as he dropped a cassette into one of the table's readout slots. "Low stress factors, good with weapons or with hand-to-hand. A lot of security people there—"

"Bones," Jim said, "let's not be too picky. What we need here is numbers."

"Numbers will not help us," Spock said, "unless they are the right ones. There is going to be very little margin for error in this operation,

Captain; but we are nevertheless taking care not to understaff you. Go on, Doctor."

"Here's the recommended list, then. Abernathy, Ahrens, Athendë, Austin, Bischoff, Brand, Brassard, Burke, Canfield, Carver, Claremont. . . ."

It went on for quite some time, a long list of unfamiliar names, and Ael leaned one elbow on the table and rested her head on her hand, bored. Not bored, exactly. What she had just done was beginning to catch up with her, as she had known it would . . . but this was no time for reaction. Nevertheless, it claimed her. *How many more lives have I spilled to prevent those phantom billion deaths?* she thought unhappily. *How many Rihannsu went back to the Elements today, cursing my name, and Bloodwing's? Sooner or later this will be paid for. Sooner, I fear. . . .*

A horrible thought intruded itself on her slowly, and refused to go away. *Suppose something has gone wrong with the researches at Levaeri—and instead of the* Intrepid'*s disappearance being a sign of their readiness, it was instead a signal of a failure—something the Levaeri people did to cover their tracks in some manner, buy themselves time, hide the fact that there's something wrong? Suppose the mind-techniques never actually come to fruition . . . then what am I? A murderer, a traitor, many times over—and for nothing, not even in a good cause—not that the ends ever extenuate the means, at least as far as the Elements are concerned. What one does is what one does, and one answers for it. . . .*

"—Khalifa, Korren, Krejci, Langsam, Lee, Litt, London; Maass, Donald; Maass, Diane—"

"I didn't hear 'Kirk' in there," Jim said rather sharply, bringing Ael back to the moment.

Spock and McCoy looked at each other, all innocence. Ael saw that there was more teasing going on. "Mr. Spock, how did we miss that?"

Spock looked mildly surprised. "Habit, no doubt. The captain never goes anywhere. . . ."

" . . . but just this once . . ."

" . . . considering that the armed escort will be ample. . . ."

"Gentlemen!"

"Gotcha, Jim," McCoy said.

Jim's smile took awhile about appearing, but finally managed it. "All right," he said. "I consider myself warned. But if you two are going to play 'mother hen,' don't either of you be surprised if you find me holding your hand."

"Fine by me," McCoy said. "But watch it with Spock. People start the damndest rumors about this ship's crew, even without provocation. . . ."

"Doctor, how *does* one hold hands with a mother hen?" Spock asked innocently.

"Gentlemen!!"

Ael kept her laughter to herself. ". . . Malkson, Matlock—"

The door opened, and the Elements were apparently joking with them all, for in came Colin Matlock, the security chief, whom Ael remembered from the briefing on *Inaieu*. He was a tall, good-looking, dark-visaged young man, half frowning all the time, even when he smiled. At the moment he chiefly looked embarrassed. "Sorry, Captain, I'll come back later—"

"No, take a seat, Mr. Matlock. We were going over the strike group. Go on, Bones."

"Where was I?"

"Matlock," Jim said, and then paused, looking slightly surprised. He glanced at Ael.

She glanced back, keeping her face quite straight, and let him wonder. ". . . McCoy, Miñambrés, Morris, Mosley, Muller, Naraht—"

"Too young," Jim said.

"Jim, he's got to go out sometime," McCoy said. "And he's got an incredibly low anxiety level. As low as a Vulcan's, nearly."

"But not enough experience—"

Ael straightened. "Jim, is this that young Ensign Rock of yours?"

Jim stared at her, then laughed. "Yes."

"Of your courtesy, take him. I ask it."

"Reasons?"

"I have none that I can explain to you." *Knowing what you would probably think about the Elements, from how little you think about names.*

"Hunch, Commander?" Spock said.

"Yes," she said.

"Well, I had one too," McCoy said. "Jim, ride with us on this one."

Jim waved his hand. "All right. Go on."

"Norton, Oranjeboom, Paul . . ."

On and on it went. At last McCoy stopped, and he and Spock looked at Jim for his final reaction.

"That's almost all of security," Jim said, "and easily half the crew. . . ."

"Captain," Spock said, "you were quite right about needing numbers." He looked over at Ael. "And Levaeri has about a hundred and fifty staff, you said."

"Yes, Jim. But they have the advantage of the ground. They will know how to hold the place against us—how to set up ambushes, seal whole sections. The more people, and with the more expertise and fire-power, the better. Our chief advantage lies in this, that the station is far inside Rihannsu space and will not be long on armaments."

"How do they protect it, then, if the installation's such a high-security business?"

"High-intensity deflector screens," Mr. Matlock said. "The specs the commander's given us indicate shields of much higher power than any mobile facility, such as a starship, can support. We'll have our work cut out for us getting those down."

"It will have to be subterfuge again, Captain," Ael said to him. "And there's worse to come; for as I told you, this is *Battlequeen*'s patrol area. There is no telling when Lyirru t'Illialhae might turn up—all Elements preserve us from the happenstance. I much fear that LLunih will try to find *Battlequeen* and bring her here. In any case, we must not linger in this neighborhood, or stop to sample the wine."

The door hissed open again. "The Rihannsu make wine?" someone said. It was Mr. Scott; and much to Ael's surprise, the scowl with which he traditionally favored her was only about half there.

"Yes," she said, slightly puzzled. "It's not quite as ruinous to the throat as our ale is . . . but it's considerably stronger."

*"Stronger?"*

"We have some on *Bloodwing*," Ael said, still puzzled, but the look of anticipation on the man's face was impossible to miss. "Perhaps I might make you a gift of some to atone for what I did to your port nacelle. A hectoliter or so? . . ."

Scott looked at Spock incredulously. "Why, that would be . . ."

"Twenty-six point four one eight gallons," Spock said, with the slightest trace of amusement showing. "Or six thousand one hundred and two point four cubic inches at—what is your wine's specific gravity, Commander?"

"Gentlemen . . ." Jim said wearily.

"We can handle this later, Mr. Scott," said Ael.

"Oh, aye!"

More people began coming in—Sulu, Chekov, then Harb Tanzer and Uhura, until finally all the department heads were present. "Captain," said Mr. Matlock, "one thing before we start . . ."

"Certainly."

"Commander," the dark young man said to Ael, "what color are the halls in that station going to be?"

"White, mostly, or bare-metal silver."

"Captain," Matlock said to Jim, with a faintly ironic expression, "I don't think it would be wise for us to attempt a board-and-storm operation dressed in bright blue and black, or gold and black, or green and black—or especially orange and black. Everyone in the party would stand out like zebras in the snow; and as for my people, they might as well have targets painted on them."

"Noted, Mr. Matlock. Order light gray battle fatigues for everybody."

"Already done, sir," said Matlock, just a little sheepishly. "Quartermaster's working on it now."

"Colin," Jim said, "I have great hopes for you. Just be careful."

"What are these fatigues, Captain?" said Ael.

"Light-colored coveralls and overboots."

"Would you give orders that they also be provided for all of my people who will be going along?"

Spock looked up from some report-pad he had been studying. "Captain, that is an excellent idea. It could very well confuse the station's complement of Rihannsu into thinking that our allies are not Rihannsu at all, but Vulcans attached to Starfleet . . . perhaps even *Intrepid* crew, escaped from confinement, or previously concealed."

"They won't think that for long, Spock," McCoy said. "Remember,

Rihannsu and Vulcan culture have been diverging for thousands of years . . . and most of the subconscious cues buried in their respective kinesics, their 'body languages,' will also now be very different. A Rihannsu would know you weren't one, if he looked long enough, not from any physical divergence—but just from a wrong 'feel.'"

"But none of them will be getting 'long looks,' Doctor, not if this works correctly," said Spock. "They will look, be briefly confused, be surprised—thinking that they are seeing Rihannsu. They will hesitate; possibly hold their fire briefly, in many cases. That will give our people an extra second to act. We cannot afford to be so proud that we throw away the advantage of surprise. Captain, I would recommend that every one of our different striking parties have at least one or two of Ael's people with it."

"That's an excellent idea. So ordered. Ladies and gentlebeings, let's get this started, shall we? Commander, please begin."

She hunted among the switches before her on the table, made her connection to the ship's computer and brought up a three-dimensional graphic above the holography pad in the center of the table. There it hung before them all in spidery lines of light, the Levaeri V station: a big rectangular prism, about twice as long as it was wide, like a brick hanging in space. "This is the research facility," she said. "You can see that it is large and complex—about two miles long and a mile wide. Not all of it is in use at this time, to the best of my knowledge—the structure you see here is a standard Rihannsu design, purposely built larger than it needs to be, to make later additions simpler. There are potentially eighteen levels, each one much divided by corridors, as you can see. At present I believe only the 'outer' six levels to be staffed; much of the inner is empty, or occupied by computer core and therefore airless."

"Commander," Scotty said, "how'd you come by this information?"

"I was there about two years ago, your time," she said. "A VIP inspection tour, before the mind-technique research was moved there. The rest of the data comes from both the Praetorate and my family's spies in High Command. This project, for all its 'secrecy,' has been as leak-ridden as any other."

Scotty nodded.

"Most of the laboratory space where I believe the actual work is being done is on the inmost level, near the computer core and the computer control rooms. This project has been most prodigal of computer hardware, since most of the actual gene-splitting and other microsurgery used to correct the 'drifted' linkages of the DNA is performed by the computers. They are in fact all that makes it possible—for each cell of genetic and neural material must be individually corrected, and thousands of years' worth of human labor would be needed to make even a gram of the stuff. The computers are the heart of the business. Put them out of operation, and part of the danger is done."

She folded her hands, staring at the schematic as it rotated. "But only part. The surgical computers are innocent enough by themselves; but the computer banks containing the actual locations of the linkages that are corrected, and the nature of the corrections, must also be destroyed. I have reason to believe that this data is extant only here, reproduced nowhere else in the Empire—partly due to the wonderful paranoia of the Praetorate, which is terrified that some other party they don't approve of might get hold of it. Destroy this information, all this data, and then you have truly destroyed the menace. It would take them years to reproduce their results—if that's even possible, for there are literally thousands of linkages in each molecule of Vulcan DNA that are corrected in the operation. No one could remember them all."

"Pity we can't just blow the place up," Mr. Chekov said.

"I agree," Jim said. "Unfortunately, I don't think the crew of *Intrepid* would appreciate it. . . . Ael, where do you think they will be?"

"My guess would be here," she said, reaching into the hologram to indicate a large area off to one side of the labs. "It is convenient to the laboratories, large enough to hold several hundred people without too much trouble—and sealed off on three sides by structural bulkheads too strong for even the massed strength of Vulcans to damage." She looked somber. "If they are able to manage anything at this point. I would hypothesize that their captors, not wanting to take chances with such a dangerous resource, have them constantly drugged, or mind-controlled, or both."

"The mind control is likeliest," Spock said, looking grim. "It would do less harm, chemically speaking, to the brain and neural tissue that the researchers are after. Which raises another problem, Commander. Do you have any idea where the already corrected tissue would be kept?"

"None."

"Why, Spock?" Jim said.

"Because it, too, is alive," Spock said, "and we must find it. It would be not only immoral but illogical to rescue the crew of the *Intrepid* and leave other living Vulcan material behind."

Ael watched Jim open his mouth, then close it. "Spock," he said, "I want you to know I'm no happier about the killing that has happened—and may soon happen—than you are. But this is just . . . I don't know . . . just meat. . . ."

"It's alive, Jim," McCoy said, very quietly. "He's right. If there's any chance, we can't leave the stockpiled material there. Not only for ethical reasons; for tactical ones as well. Any remaining material can be used to work backward and recreate the research. If we can't take it with us, it must at least be destroyed. But it must be found."

Jim looked at McCoy and Spock, then nodded. "All right," he said. "That makes things even more complicated, but what're a few more complications among friends? Mr. Matlock, let's talk about the actual plan of attack."

"Yes, sir." Matlock stood up with a small control-pad in one hand and began setting markers, small dots of light, into the hologram. "We will be dividing our attack force into four parts, and hitting the base in four different areas. Here, in what the commander has identified as staff and crew quarters, to secure those station personnel who aren't on duty; here, in two different places near the labs, flanking the area where the most resistance is likely to occur immediately on our arrival; and here, where the commander suspects the *Intrepid*'s crew to be held prisoner."

Matlock eyed the station schematic with what looked to Ael like genuine relish. "The four groups, once the station's screens have been reduced, will beam down simultaneously and each secure its assigned area, while also sealing off the unoccupied parts of the station to prevent our being attacked from several different 'rears.' Additionally, each

of these two groups"—he pointed at the attack forces near the labs—
"will secure the transporters to prevent any of the station people from
utilizing in-station beaming. Just in case, once we leave, the *Enterprise*
will have her screens up to prevent any counterattack from the station
should our hold on the transporters be broken at any time."

"That is well thought of," Ael said. "Captain, gentlefolk, a Rihannsu
is at her most dangerous when her territory is threatened . . . we are
rather atavistic that way. Even scientists will be able to fight with terrible
ferocity; and remember that at the moment this is still partly a military
facility. Not starship personnel—but soldiers nonetheless, people with a
deadly hatred of the Federation. And a worse hatred of you, if they find
out who you are: my sister-daughter had many friends." She looked
across at Spock. "Do not hesitate to kill. They will not hesitate to kill
*you* after that first second's confusion."

Spock lowered his eyes, said nothing. "The ship will be scanning
constantly," Mr. Matlock said, "monitoring the situation on the station
and advising the attack parties via scrambled communications of developments. Once the indicated areas are secure, the computer attack
group—Mr. Spock and the people he'll name for you shortly—will assemble, locate the computers, and begin that part of the operation. Sir?"

Spock looked up. "Along with the commander, Lieutenant Kerasus,
Mr. Athendë, and several others from the commander's staff and from
security, we will tap into the computers and either remove or destroy all
pertinent information concerning the mind-technique researches. In the
case that complete removal of the information proves to be impossible, I
have with the commander's assistance developed a 'virus' program that
will infect the computers the next time they are brought into operational
mode, dumping and wiping their total memories. Once the 'infection' is
successfully accomplished, we will attempt to activate the computers
and obtain the location of the already manufactured genetic material. In
the case that either of these objectives proves unattainable, we will destroy the computer installation and rejoin the main attack group."

"Which, as soon as the transporters are secured, will be locating and
freeing the Vulcans," Mr. Matlock said. "Our sensors are sufficiently
accurate at close range to tell the difference between Vulcan and

Rihannsu life-readings—unlike the Rihannsu instruments. Once the Vulcans are freed, we will call the ship and begin beaming them back aboard the *Enterprise* via cargo transporters."

"Gonna be crowded up there," McCoy said softly. "What about *Intrepid*?"

Ael shook her head at him. "That's an unknown, Doctor. My guess would be that they will have her inside the screens, held by tractors; and it's likely they will have shut her engines down. Mr. Scott, how long does a restart cycle take?"

"That depends on how long the engines have been cold," Scott said. "Postulatin' worst case, and the *Intrepid*'s refitted engines, fifteen minutes."

"The best estimated in-and-out time for this operation is forty minutes, Mr. Scott," Matlock said.

"Well, let's hope we can get at her early, then, if her engines are down. A cold matter-antimatter mix can't be hurried."

"And if for some reason we have to get out of there before she's restarted," Jim said sadly, "we can't leave her there to be taken apart and analyzed. We'll have to blow her up."

There was silence all around the table at that, except for Scott. "Ach, the poor lass," he said.

"That's all, Captain," Mr. Matlock said. "After we beam back with the *Intrepid* crew and the genetic material, there'll be nothing to stop us from heading out of Rihannsu space with *Bloodwing* at warp eight."

McCoy was going through his cassettes again. "That's all, he says."

"Very well," Jim said. "Any questions?"

"Only one," Ael said quietly.

"Commander?"

"Why did you let me talk you into this? . . ."

Jim gave her a cockeyed look. There were chuckles around the table, but Ael noticed that he did not join in them, and neither did Spock or McCoy. "We'll go into that after we've successfully completed the operation, Commander," he said. "As for the rest of you—brief your departments, get your timings from Mr. Matlock, and get into your battle grays. We assemble in recreation in two hours. Dismissed."

Out they went, obedient and quick and looking eager. Ael turned to glance at Jim, who said, "Cold feet, Ael?"

She stared at him. "My boots are fine."

"I mean, are you—" He stopped. "What a stupid question. I beg your pardon. Come with me and I'll take you down to the quartermaster's department to be fitted and armed—"

"I have my own weaponry, Captain," she said, "and I'll do best with it, I think. But as for your uniform—I shall be proud to wear it."

"Why, thank you."

". . . Just this once."

"We wouldn't want to keep you in it a moment longer than necessary," Jim said, getting up with an utterly indecipherable expression.

Ael followed him out of the room, shaking her head in unaccustomed perplexity. She had said something wrong again. Or was it as it seemed, that this man kept his pride on the outside, waiting for someone to tear it? Why did he do that? There was no understanding him. . . .

*Curses* on the man!

Two hours later she stood on the bridge of the *Enterprise* again, feeling even stranger about it than she had; for there was Levaeri V ahead of them—within sensor range, though they had not yet hailed her. "I'll wait a bit," she said to the man who stood with his two hundred gathered crewpeople, down in the recreation room. "It would not be like me to hurry in this situation, Captain. I would let them have a long, long look and be amazed."

*"Anything so long as we catch them by surprise,"* Jim said.

"Yes. Aidoann reports that control is now completely transferred to the auxiliary bridge, and your other people left aboard ship are under 'guard' with various of my folk from *Bloodwing,* so that we will pass an inspection if necessary."

*"Is Scotty all right down there?"*

"He reports all systems operational, and the next two subspace jamming buoys dropped. Meanwhile, there are no *Enterprise* people up here at all now, and I tell you it looks strange."

*"I bet,"* said the cheerful voice. *"Is Subcommander Tafv with you?"*

"Here, Captain," Tafv said, from the communications console.

*"Take care of my ship, Subcommander,"* the voice said.

"Sir, I shall. Commander, Levaeri is hailing us. We are nearing the shield boundary—and sensors are showing a starship tethered inside the shields. No ID running—but the sensor readings match its shape to that of *Intrepid*."

*"Well,"* Jim said, *"it's showtime."* He sounded annoyed, and pleased, and terrified, all at once. *"Commander, will you join us?"*

"As soon as the screens are down. Don't wait for me, Jim. Get your people down to the cargo transporters. I have your coordinates, and my grays are in the lift."

*"Ael—good luck."*

"And the Elements with us," she said, "for we'll need Them. Out."

She turned to Tafv, seeing on his face the same mixed excitement and dread she felt. "Open a frequency for the station, son. They've looked long enough."

"Madam," he said, demonstrating that same lovely and unnecessary courtesy he had shown her on coming back aboard *Bloodwing*. Ael sat straight in the center seat, finding her control, stripping the fear out of her heart.

*"Levaeri station to* Bloodwing," said a female voice.

"This is Commander-General Ael t'Rllaillieu," said Ael, very calm, very proud, "presently aboard the captured vessel *U.S.S. Enterprise*. To whom am I speaking?"

*"Centurion Ndeian tr'Jeiai, Commander."*

*O, by my Element, no—not Ndeian——*"Ndeian," she said, merry-voiced, "what in the Names of Fire and Air are you doing all the way out here? I thought you were on ch'Havran by now, raising *fvai!*"

*"Reenlistment,"* Ndeian said. *"They're desperate, Ael; they offered to make me rich. The funny thing is that I believed them—"*

"You always were credulous." Ael's heart cried out inside her. "Ndeian, are you commanding?"

*"No, Gwiu t'Laheiin is; but we've heard of your coming, we have orders—"*

—her stomach twisted itself into a knot in a single second—

"*—to give you anything you ask for if you stop. Forgive me, Ael, but I don't think they want you to stay. Our orders were to 'expedite your arrival and departure.' '*"

"We won't be here long, Ndeian. I need some provisions for *Bloodwing,* and some of my people are in need of better medical help than we have here on the ship; we had a difficult time getting hold of this bright prize. You don't seem to be doing too badly in that department yourself, though."

"*No,*" Ndeian said, "*Battlequeen brought that one in. Ael, just settle into standard orbit and we'll drop screens for you and your technical people and the doctor.*"

"Assuming standard orbit, Nedian. See you in a bit. T'Rllaillicu out."

She waved at Tafv, heartsick. He closed down the channel, then looked at his instruments and said, "Screens are down, Commander. We're in orbit under them."

"Well done." She got up, hurried out of the bridge, looking around at the place—bizarrely open, bright, lovely for an instrument of destruction. Ndeian's destruction, and a thousand others'—"Keep her well, Tafv," she said; and it was all she could manage. The lift doors opened for her. She picked up her white coverall, that lay neatly folded on the floor, and began struggling into it—sparing a hand from the business to hit the communicator button on the lift wall. "Recreation!"

"*We heard,*" the Captain's voice came back. "*We're on our way. Out.*"

The lift stopped, opened its doors. Ael ran down the hall, into one of the cargo transporter rooms, pulled out her phaser and leapt up onto the platform, with a great group of her own people and Jim's. The young man behind the transporter console set the delay, headed for the platform himself, and they all dissolved in shimmer together.

It must have been something different about the Federation transporters, something unsettling in their engineering—or maybe just Ael's own suppressed fear, crying out in her mind—that made her think she heard, as she dematerialized, the sound of phaserwhine outside the transporter room, and a scream. . . .

# Chapter Fourteen

Montgomery Scott paced the auxiliary bridge like a caged creature. "This will be the last batch going," he said to the universe in general, and to Uhura and Chekov and Sulu, who were in there with him, along with Khiy and Nniol and Haehwe. "And I don't like it, indeed I don't."

Sulu and Chekov exchanged glances, which Scotty noticed and filed away; they didn't like it either. "It's a fool's errand, that's what it is," Scotty said, looking over Chekov's shoulder at a trim control and reaching down to uselessly check its calibration.

"You should have said something in the briefing, Mr. Scott," Uhura said softly from her station.

"Aye," Scotty said, letting out a long breath. "But what good would it ha' done, lass? You know how the captain is when his mind's made up. After that, it's the universe that'd best bend, for it won't be himself that's doing it."

He paced around the little room one more time. That was the problem with it, he decided. It was little; too much power crammed into too small a space for the people who had to handle it. Like *Bloodwing*'s poor little scrap of a bridge, if you could even dignify it with the name. A black hole, it was. And this was too. Squeezed in between the armory and the downstairs food processors, a ridiculous spot—"Are they ready?" Scotty said.

"They report ready," Uhura said. "—There they go."

"Good luck to them," Sulu said, staring down at the uncomfortable view on the little screen. Levaeri V station hung there right beneath them, an ugly great sheet of metal stuck all over with pipes and stanchions and antennae and whatnot else. It offended Scotty's sense of design, and confirmed a lot of his private thoughts about Romulan engineering. "Prefab space stations," he muttered. "Where's the sense in that? Probably fall apart if you looked at it."

"They do," said Khiy quietly from the engineering station. "They're shabby, sir."

"Aye lad, I daresay." Scotty gave one last disgusted look at the thing, then turned to Uhura. "Are they transported safe?"

"Yes, sir, they report arrival—"

"Well enough. I just wish I were down there with the Captain—"

Someone shrieked. Someone did it again, and again, and Scotty recovered from the involuntary attempted leap of his heart from his chest at the sound of his ship screaming. It was the intruder alert siren, a sound like no other. "Screens," he cried at Sulu, "screens, man!"—and leapt for the board himself. Sulu had already hit the control, and the banshee wailing of the ship cut sharply off; but Uhura had turned to the rest of them with a look of terrible alarm on her face, one hand to the transdator in her ear, the other flicking switch after switch on her station's panel. "Mr. Scott, intruders on decks four, eight, nine, twelve—"

"Where from?"

"Already transported, Mr. Scott. Not traceable—"

"*Bloodwing,*" Scotty said bitterly, and swung on Khiy.

"No!" Khiy cried. "Mr. Scott, the commander would never—"

"Not the commander, lad," Scotty said, feeling himself turning red. "But I'll bet I know who. Why didna the captain see it? Khiy, seal us off from the rest of the deck—bring down all the bulkheads south of thirty. Never mind—" and he headed over to the engineering station and did it himself; poor Khiy was out of his depth, no shame to him. "Uhura, find out what's goin' on out there."

"Confused, Mr. Scott. Fighting on six and eight. Other parts of the ship calling in and asking what the problem is—"

"Tell them. No, wait. Chekov, help Khiy. I want every door in this ship locked. Cut power reversibly if you have to, we'll worry about the details later."

Chekov jumped out of his seat and hurried over to Khiy. "No good, Mr. Scott. Several Jeffries tubes have been disabled, some major system junctions are out—"

"Bloody. Excuse me, Uhura. Pavel, disable the transporters, the whole lot o' them. The captain will be usin' the Levaeri transporters to come back anyway, and I'll not have that devil Tafv usin' mine for intraship beaming. If he wants the *Enterprise,* he can fight for every inch. Also—" Scotty took a deep breath. "Override the emergency protocols and seal off the engineering hull. Those creatures'll not get at my engines."

Chekov worked bent over at the board, pointing out controls to Khiy, explaining things under his breath. Several moments later there was another horrific screaming through the ship as she announced her own traumatic amputation—the sealing off of the lower, cylindrical engineering hull and nacelles from the upper disc. The two were able to function separately, though it had been done so infrequently and in such disastrous situations that Scotty hated to think of the results. Nevertheless, all it would take now would be an explosive-bolt sequence, and the two parts would separate, leaving the lower hull and nacelles, with the warp engines, free of Romulans and still able to escape with the captain and his party and the rescued Vulcans. If they managed to escape . . .

Till then it was his business to hold that avenue of escape open for them; and Scotty vowed that should the landing party come to grief, Levaeri V would go up in one of the biggest bangs since *the* big one. He still had the self-destruct option, after all, and that option exercised in this particular spot would take the station and *Intrepid* and *Bloodwing* with it. The thought was not comforting, but he put it aside in case he should need it later. Meanwhile there was other business. "How're you doing, lad?" he said to Chekov.

"Executing, sir. The engineering hull's secure."

"Forty people trapped down there, Mr. Scott," Uhura said. "They're all right, though. A mixed group, our people and the commander's."

"Aye. . . ." That was the whole problem. These Romulans, that went around behind one another's backs so easily . . . no telling what they were thinking—But Scotty caught himself. That was hardly fair—look at poor Khiy here, keeping the faith, and doing the best he could for them. "All right. What about the transporters?"

"Out now, Mr. Scott," Chekov said.

"Aye," Scotty said. "We may be trapped here, but so are they, with the shields up . . . and we can have good hope that some of them were transportin' when the shields reestablished. A few o' them'll have hit the shields and gone splash, at any rate. Uhura, call about and find out who's where. What's our strength without the landing party?"

"Two hundred eight, Mr. Scott. We could call the captain—"

"And he would do what, lass? Our people and Ael's doubtless have their hands full enough just now, else we'd have heard more from them than just the news that they'd arrived in the station. No, we've got to handle this ourselves . . . no use in botherin' him. Two hundred and eight . . ." Scotty made a disgusted noise. "And scattered all over the ship. . . . No matter. Call around, Uhura." He paced around the room again, scowling. "Now if I were that black-hearted traitor of a Tafv . . . where would I be heading?"

"Here, sir."

"Aye, Mr. Sulu. And here we sit all alone on this deck, and sealed away from help. He'll have to fight his way here, burn his way through bulkheads and through our people—but he'll do it, and not count the cost."

"But, Mr. Scott, what about intruder control?"

"Ah, Khiy, lad, you didn't look at that board too closely, did you? He's a clever creature, that Tafv: he took it out with those Jeffries tubes, may he roast somewhere warm. Woe's the day we ever let him near the computers. . . ."

Scotty paced. "So . . . He may have taken out the most vital systems he could learn quickly. But we still know the ship better than he does. And possibly . . ." he stopped in mid-stride. "Mr. Sulu," he said, "call up a schematic of the crawlways between here and the main bridge. While he's at it, Uhura—get into the library computer and transfer it to voiceprint operation. I don't want it working for anyone but *Enterprise* personnel. And if you can rig a program so that individual terminals'll blow their boards if a nonauthorized person uses them, so much the better. . . ."

"You don't ask much, do you, Mr. Scott?" Uhura said drily. But she bent over her board and got busy.

"Mr. Scott," Chekov said, "what about the Romulans on the main bridge, our friends?"

"Aye, what about them?" He turned to look over his shoulder. "Uhura?"

"Aidoann and Khiy and Nniol all filed voiceprints with me," Uhura said, not looking up, but smiling slightly.

"And Tafv?"

Uhura looked up in mild surprise. "Scotty, I never got one from him. He was always off on *Bloodwing*. . . ."

"Aye, indeed," Scotty said, sounding bitter. "I hate to say it, but it looks as if some of Ael's crew haven't as much of that mneh-whatever as she thought. 'Twill break the lass's heart."

"*Mnhei'sahe,*" Khiy said unhappily. "Mr. Scott . . . some of our crewmembers are newer than others. There are some who were talking about . . . about the opportunity . . ."

". . . of taking *Enterprise* for real, aye lad?" Scotty's eyes grew hard.

"Even the thought was disgraceful. Some of us told some of the others so. They stopped talking about it . . . but it seems they didn't stop thinking. And when the commander chose the people who would be working on the *Enterprise*—"

"How *did* she choose them?"

"Only volunteers were considered. Some of those she left behind—not many. But it was odd that none of the ones who had talked about taking *Enterprise* actually came here. . . ."

"Our friend Tafv, it seems, had his own ideas about what to do with this situation," Scotty said. "Well, we'll spoil a few of his guesses if we can. Mr. Sulu, Mr. Chekov, let the board be for now. You two are going for a walk."

"Sir," Sulu said, slowly getting that particular feral grin of his on his face, "the armory *is* next door. . . ."

"Aye, we're thinking in the same direction, Mr. Sulu. But this isn't going to be easy."

"What do you have in mind, sir?" Chekov said.

"Well, if Tafv and his people are going to be making their way *here*, it's to gain full control of the ship, aye?" They nodded at him. "Well, then, lads, can't you just see his face when he gets here and finds this room either sealed or destroyed—and control transferred back up to the main bridge where it belongs?"

Chekov started to smile too. "It's a very long way to the bridge, sir," he said.

"Aye, lad. So you two had best slip next door to the armory and pick up anything you think you might need for the trip. Take plenty; should you feel the urge to leave a few boobytraps in the corridors for the unwary to trip over, I think I'd be inclined to condone the extravagance. And bring all the rest of it in here too. No use letting Tafv have it, and Uhura and Khiy and I may need it for one thing or another."

"Mr. Scott," Uhura said softly as Sulu and Chekov hurried out. "Sickbay wants to talk to you. Dr. Chapel."

"Aye, put her on."

"*Scotty, what the hell is happening!*"

"Treachery and mayhem, Christine," Scotty said merrily. "Not much else. Some of Ael's people have turned coats on her, it seems, and they're thinking it would be nice to have the *Enterprise* for their own uses."

"*Oh my God.*"

"So if I were you I'd lock the sickbay doors and not open them to anyone you don't know. Area bulkheads have been sealed, but there were Romulans beamin' down all over the ship for a while there, and there's no tellin' which of them are 'theirs' and which of them are 'ours,' or even where 'ours' are—"

"*Scotty, don't be silly,*" Chapel said sharply, and the reply was so unlike her usual tone that it brought Scotty up short. "*Of course we can tell them apart.*"

"Well, for pity's sake how?"

"*Scotty,*" Chapel said with rather exaggerated patience, "*you were standing right there the other day, watching me stick intradermal translators into people, and complaining about the terrible annoyance it was, having to manufacture so many cesium-rubidium crystals for them in bulk—*"

"Selective tricorder scan," Scotty said softly. "Any Romulan with an armful of cesium-rubidium is one of ours . . ."

"—*and you can do what you like with the others,*" Christine said. "*Scotty, what I want to know is, are there any casualties? If there are, M'Benga and I have to get out there and do something. We can't just sit here and play doctor.*"

"Check with Uhura," he said, for Sulu and Chekov were just coming into the room with their first load of munitions from the armory, and Scotty's eye had just fallen on a sonic grenade; the sight had triggered a wonderful memory of how to rig one with a time delay and— "Uhura, handle it. Chekov, lad, let me show you something. . . ."

The two of them labored busily together for some minutes, while Sulu and Khiy went next door again and again, emptying the contents of the armory into the auxiliary bridge. When they finished, the walls were stacked three feet deep in phasers, phaser rifles, and disruptors, and the floor was piled with six different kinds of grenades, several semiportable fixed-mount phaser guns, and various other implements of destruction.

"All right," Scotty said finally, looking Chekov and Sulu up and down. They were hung like Christmas trees with explosive ornaments; Chekov carried an armful of phaser rifles as if they were a load of firewood. "Take the safest way you can find to the bridge. It'll have to be crawlways most of the way, with the bulkheads down—but you've got the advantage of the ground. Pick up as much help as you can along the way . . . there have to be a lot of our people holding out in little pockets all over the ship."

Uhura looked up from her station with an unhappy expression. "Six decks up," she said. "That's a long way—"

"Sir—"

They all turned. Khiy was standing there looking extremely upset. "Mr. Scott, let me go with them!" he said. "I'm not much good to you here. But I know how to fight—and it's my honor that's been debased too. We swore, the whole crew swore, to be as brothers to you . . . for a while. Now Subcommander Tafv has shamed us all, betrayed us . . . and if we don't get control of the ship back, he'll surely leave our commander here to die—or kill her himself. I can't let that happen—none of us can!"

Scotty looked at the young man, thinking how very like Chekov he looked, even with the pointed ears. "Go ahead," he said. "Take some more of the guns, Khiy. Uhura and I will hold this position down till you three call us from the bridge. Ael's people were there before everything broke loose; the locked bulkheads should have kept them safe in there, and kept Tafv's other people away. We don't dare warn them you're coming—chances are Tafv has tapped into Uhura's scrambled 'com. Just get into the bridge and signal us when you're ready."

"Mr. Scott—" Chekov looked as unhappy as Khiy. "When Tafv and his people get here and there's no one but you and Uhura to hold this place—and you transfer control—the overrides will cut in and the bulkheads will go up again."

"We'll handle it, lad," Scotty said, though he had not the slightest idea of how. "Get on with you, you're wasting time."

"Yes, sir."

Sulu went to the door. It slid open, and he peered cautiously out; no one was in the hall—the deck was so far deserted. It was eerie in a ship normally as busy as the *Enterprise*. There came a shock, and a muffled sound, and all of them looked up in surprise and unease. Explosives, somewhere not too far away, were detonating inside the ship; and they heard the wine of phasers, very remote, but sounding venomous as a swarm of bees.

"Out with you," Scotty said. "Don't do anything stupid."

Sulu and Chekov and Khiy headed out.

"And if you do," Scotty said to their backs, more softly, "—sell yourselves dearly."

They paused—then were gone. The door closed again. "Come on, Nyota darlin'," Scotty said. "The youngsters will do what they can. Let's you and I go out there real quick and leave our unexpected guests some presents in the hall."

"Sounds good," Uhura said. She got up, picked up a string of sonic grenades, and started setting them for sequential detonation.

Another shudder, much closer, and another explosion, much louder, ran through the fabric of the ship.

"This deck," Scotty said.

They worked faster.

# Chapter Fifteen

"Phasers on heavy stun," Jim whispered to the group behind him. "Stand by. . . ."

Silent, hardly breathing, his crewpeople waited. And waited, and waited. Jim pulled his head back from the corner he'd been peering around and held his breath. All four parties were beamed down, and it was still that golden period before one group or another started breaking into things, and setting off alarms. This party, of about fifty, was dedicated to securing one side of the computer areas. Right behind Jim stood Spock, and Ael, and Mr. Matlock; then more assorted crewfolk, security people, and crewfolk of *Bloodwing,* with McCoy and Lia Burke and Naraht and some more security types bringing up the rear. They were all utterly silent, as Jim had never heard such a large group be before. *Nerves,* he thought. And then, with grim humor: *They should be glad they don't have* mine.

Right behind him, Spock was scanning with a tricorder from which he had prudently removed the warble circuits. "The corridor ahead of us is nearly clear, Captain," he said softly. "Considerable computer activity ahead and for the next two levels down. We are adjacent to the core."

"And the control areas?"

"If I read this correctly, they are off the main corridor that runs at right angles to the one we're facing."

"What about the *Intrepid* crew?"

"Sir, I do not scan them . . . and the tricorder is not malfunctioning. Possibly they are in some shielded area; there are many sections of this base that incorporate forceshielding in their wall structure, purpose unknown, and tricorder scanning at a distance is therefore distorted and uncertain—"

"What the—" someone said in amazement from way behind them.

"Don't fire!" Jim would have hissed had there been time. There was none; seemingly all at once he heard the surprised voice, turned, saw a dark-clad Romulan figure staring at them from the T-intersection at the end of the hall in which Jim's party stood momentarily concealed. Then he realized, with some astonishment, that he needn't have worried. The last white shape at the rear of the group leaped away from the wall in a blur, and did something too sudden for Jim to clearly make out—except that when it was finished a blink later, the Romulan was lying on the floor with his head at an odd angle, and slender little Ensign Brand was staring down at him, looking rather shocked.

Jim nodded grim approval at Brand, and mouthed at her, "Stunned? Dead?"

She bent down beside the Romulan, then glanced up again, making a cutting motion across her throat, and a little "Sorry, Captain" shrug of her hands.

He jerked a thumb at the side corridor; Brand, and the Andorian Ensign Lihwa beside her, nodded and began to drag the man out of sight. Jim turned back to Spock. "We've got to get moving, Mr. Spock. If a group comes along and finds us here, we might not be so lucky."

"Affirmative. The corridor ahead is clear for the moment. Scan shows movement in the others, but it seems routine enough, and we couldn't wait for it all to die down anyway—"

"All right, let's go." Jim waved the hand holding his phaser at the column pressed up against the walls behind him, then headed out into the hall.

His people closed in around him from behind. Ael moved silently at his left, a tiny shape looking unusually pale in grays—or perhaps from some other cause. Spock paced to Jim's right, never taking his eyes off the tricorder. "We turn right at the next intersection," he said. "Then down to the next left, and ten meters along it to the main corridor—"

A horrible klaxon began howling through the hallways, echoing off the bare white walls. "That's torn it," Jim said out loud. There was no use for whispering anymore. "People, let's go. Close formation, watch the rear, stun first and ask questions later!"

And they were off and running. Unfortunately, at the sound of the alarms, so were the Romulans. Turning right at the next intersection, there came a crowd of Romulans in dark coverall-uniforms, ten or fifteen of them—by bad luck or fast scanning running right at Jim's party. Jim took his own advice, leaping aside to fire—then became suddenly aware of Ael pounding past him, with Spock pacing her. The Romulans at the head of the group looked at the two, saw 'Romulans,' hesitated—and from behind Jim ten or fifteen phasers screamed together. The Romulans went down in a heap.

"Armed," Jim said. It was upsetting; the Romulans' response time was too fast. "Destroy their weapons and follow," he said to Matlock, and led the rest of the party on at a run while Matlock's people attended to it and then came after. "Where now, Mr. Spock?"

"Past them, Captain, and the next left—"

They ran. And around that corner came more Romulans, not hesitating at all, firing Romulan-style blasters and disruptors. Reacting before he was sure what he was reacting to, Jim threw himself toward Spock—at the same time felt someone tackle *him* from behind and take him down, so that the three of them crashed to the floor together, out of the way of the massed beams that would have burnt them dead. The three of them rolled to the sides of the hall and came up firing, while behind them Mr. Matlock and his group fired from the hall or from cover, taking the Romulans out one by one. Jim got his feet under him, saw that Spock looked slightly shaken but otherwise all right, and then reached sideways to help up the person who had knocked him down to safety. There was Ael, scrambling to her feet with a smile on her face and a most dangerous look in her eye. "Thanks," he said as they helped each other up.

She cocked an eyebrow at him, then turned to Spock, who was leaning against the wall and looking more than just a little shaken. He was going pale. "Spock?" Ael said, a husky whisper through the howling of the sirens.

"Mr. Spock—" Jim said. "Bones!"

"No, Captain," Spock said, his voice definitely not as strong as usual. "There is something—pressing on my mind. An urge not to move, not to think—making any action pain. The effect got much stronger as we came around that last corner."

"A person?" Ael said as McCoy and Lia Burke hurried up to join them.

"No. Power of mind—without personality—" Spock actually made an expression, right out there in front of everybody: loathing. "Mindless. An abomination—"

"A machine," Ael said bitterly, "working through cloned Vulcan brain tissue."

"Too strong—" Spock said, struggling for control.

"A great mass of brain tissue," McCoy said, getting a look of loathing very much like Spock's. "A tank full of Vulcan gray matter cloned from a single brain cell. No personality—but terrible power, programmed for some single purpose, and performing it mindlessly. Just another computer—"

Jim's stomach turned. "This has to be the weapon they used on the *Intrepid*."

"Or one like it," Spock agreed, straightening, gasping. "Captain, *Intrepid*'s crew must be around here somewhere. The Romulans would hardly have set this weapon up in expectation that I would arrive."

"But the Vulcans should have been on another level," Ael protested.

"Maybe they—" The sound of shouting voices cut that conversation short. Mr. Matlock and about ten of his people leapt past Jim and Bones and Spock and Ael into the main corridor, opening fire before the approaching Romulans could. Jim shouted warning at them, and a few of the security people managed to turn and meet the second group of Romulans who were coming at them from behind. Only several of these were armed; but this second group came crashing in among them with such speed and force that suddenly phasers were useless, there was too much mixing going on, too many chances to stun or kill a friend.

Jim broke into a whirl of hand-to-hand, relishing it terribly as a release for all the anger and tension and helplessness of the past week. He knew he would pay the price later—his body always ached for days after one of these orgies of anger. Or maybe he would pay for it right now, since every one of these Romulans was about as easy to handle, one-on-one, as Spock.

But training regularly with a Vulcan had its advantages; and though the Romulans might have drifted considerably from the Vulcan norm in terms of genetics, physiologically they still had the same weaknesses. The Vulcanid head and ears were relatively vulnerable, and as for leverage, Romulans flew through the air as well as anyone else. Jim busied himself with that—a double chop to the collarbone here, a broken kneecap there, a bit of *tal-shaya* that Spock had taught him over here. Every now and then he caught a glance of something that would have made him laugh, if he'd had time to breathe: tiny Ael, for instance, slamming a Romulan man nearly twice her height into a wall, putting a foot in his gut, grabbing one of his arms, and neatly relieving the poor man of his sidearm and dislocating his shoulder, all in one quick, rather casual motion. In the middle of a chop-and-kick combination Jim saw Lia Burke come up unnoticed beside a burly Romulan woman who was firing uselessly at the angrily advancing Ensign Naraht. Phasers, at least phasers on the conventional "one" setting, don't work on Hortas, but the unfortunate Romulan woman didn't have time to readjust her phaser, even if she knew that was what needed doing. Lia simply reached up a bit—the woman was tall—and swung her slender little fist sidewise into the Romulan's trachea, like a hammer. Even over the howling alarm klaxon, Jim could hear the crunch of cartilage. *Goodness,* Jim thought mildly, while breaking a Romulan's arm backward at the elbow, *if Mr. Freeman is this good too, his yearly shots are probably going to be a very interesting event. I wonder if Bones'll be selling tickets? . . .*

—and suddenly the fight was over, except that there were still shouts coming from further down the main corridor. Jim dropped the unconscious Romulan he found himself holding and looked swiftly around at his people. They were mostly gasping, some still crouched for combat, unable to stop being ready. "Injuries?" he said.

"Lahae's got a broken arm," Ael said, jerking her head at one of her people. "But she's well otherwise."

"A few burns, Jim," said McCoy. "Harrison got it bad. I've treated him, but we need to get him back topside."

"It's going to take a while, Bones. Mr. Athendë, carry Harrison. Spock?"

"Captain," Spock said, stepping out of a pile of unconscious Romulans, and still looking very unwell, "there is some direction to this mental pressure. That way." He pointed down the corridor, toward all the noise.

"That's it, Ael," Jim said. "The Vulcans *are* on this level, after all. Evidently this is one of those operations in which everything's going to go wrong right away. . . ."

"Saves us wondering," McCoy said. "Spock, can you function?"

"Barely, Doctor. As you delight in reminding me, I am half Terran— and for once that fact is serving me somewhat. My mother's side of the family has a history of being almost relentlessly non-psi sensitive. But as we get closer to the mechanism, the mind-damper, I will surely grow weaker."

"There's no guarantee that the Vulcans will be where the damper is," Ael said.

"Of course not. But if we can put it out of commission, they'll be free to try to escape—and that would make the odds a little more even."

"Well, then," Ael said, putting her head around the corner—pulling it back quickly and getting shot at for her trouble—"time to do something. Raha, give me a spare phaser, will you?"

One of Ael's people tossed her a phaser. Ael detached it from the pistol grip, turned it over in her hands. "Where—Oh, here it is." She twisted the supercharge control on the back of it all the way, and tossed it lightly once or twice in her hand as the upscaling scream that signaled imminent overload began. "How long before it goes?" she said to Jim.

"Five seconds! Ael—"

"Three, two," she said, and put her head and her arm around the corner again, and threw the phaser right down the length of the corridor— an astonishing southpaw pitch, fastball swift and going a good four hundred feet down the corridor before it even hit the floor. And as the phaser hit, right among the Romulans massed and firing at the end of the corridor, it blew. The station shuddered slightly, and the concussion struck back down the corridor at the *Enterprise* group, a blast of hot wind and light that knocked Ael back into McCoy's arms and both of them hard against the wall of the side corridor.

"Now!" Jim shouted, and led the way down the corridor, his people pouring down after him. The corridor's end was ugly, blackened by the explosion, and spattered green with Romulan remains and Romulan blood where it wasn't. *Oh, God,* some part of Jim cried in anguish, but the rest of him was far gone in the necessities of the moment, and paid the pain little heed. There was a large door at the end of the corridor. He tried his phaser on the middle of it; no response. A quick experiment on the walls and the doorframe produced the same result. "Refractory," he said. "Too thick. Spock, can you gimmick the lock? If we burn it, it'll probably just seal this permanently shut—"

"Jim," Bones said, "forget it." He was supporting Spock from one side, and Mr. Athendë, already carrying the badly burnt Harrison in his tentacles, was holding Spock up on the other; the Vulcan slumped between them, nearly unconscious, trying to fight the mind-damping effect and failing. Little spasms of pain twisted his face as he kept fighting. Until they got this handled he would not think again, much less speak or move.

"Who's here?" Jim said desperately, for he heard more shouts back in the direction they'd come: a lot more. "Electronics—" But most of his people were security, and the others were from medicine, linguistics, defense—

"Let me try, Captain," someone said, pushing his way through the group; and there was Mr. Freeman, his usual neatness much the worse for wear. He was singed and smudged and bruised and had a black eye, and his hair was all over the place. But already he was on his knees by the door, snapping open a pouch at one side, fishing for tools. He pushed his hair back in his everyday get-neat gesture while using a decoheser to pop the flush cover off a small panel by the right side of the door. "Oh damn," he said at the sight of the panel's innards, an incomprehensible welter of circuits and chips. "It's all solids."

"Mr. Freeman," Jim said grimly. The sounds of approaching Romulans were getting much louder.

"I know, sir—" Freeman said, poking around in the circuitry and doing God only knew what.

It was taking too long. "Lay down covering fire," Jim said to the people behind him. "Ael—"

"I can't help you here, Jim," she said, giving the panel only a glance and turning away. "Not a format I'm familiar with. Hilae, Gehen, Rai, over there to the side. You—Rotsler, Eisenberg, Feder, the other side. Fisher, Remner, Paul—here with me. The rest of you, mind the captain and Mr. Spock, and fire as you like. Mr. Athendë, one of your phasers. Hate to use a trick twice—"

"Mr. Freeman!" Jim said.

"Captain, this isn't just something you can—"

"Jim," McCoy said quietly, and rather sorrowfully, "the boy can't manage it, that's all. Back off."

Jim looked up at McCoy in surprise—and so would have missed the look that settled down over Freeman's face at McCoy's words, had McCoy not been looking so fixedly at the young man's back. Jim, who could see Freeman's face from his angle, saw suddenly written on it a rage so terrible that for a second he wondered if Freeman was going to blow up like an overloading phaser himself. Then Jim wondered if he'd seen the look at all, for Jerry's face sealed over into an expression as cool as one of Spock's. Freeman did something brief and precise to the circuitry, changed tools, did something else to a particular logic solid in one quick fierce motion.

The door sprang open.

Behind Jim there were explosions, cries, shouts of anger and triumph. He ignored them and ran into the room. There was equipment of some kind, three walls' worth of it, all studded with controls and switch-lights; there was a fourth wall with a great window in it and another refractory door. And there were Romulans. One of them Jim stunned; the other, too close, he kicked right between the legs, where even Romulans are vulnerable, and Romulan females no less than the males. The third he never had a chance at, for Mr. Athendë, while still carrying the burned Harrison and supporting Spock on the side, had swept into the room right after Jim and thrown one of his major handling tentacles and various minor ones around the remaining Romulan's head and body, squeezing the man's disruptor right out of his hand so that it clattered on the floor.

"Nicely done, Mr. Athendë," Jim said to the Sulamid, panting.

The Sulamid curved several stalked eyes in Jim's direction. "Must protect wounded, Captain," he said; but even his eternal humor sounded a little grim at the moment.

"All right," Jim said to the remaining Romulan. "Which of these controls the damper?"

The Romulan, still straining against the tentacles that held him, turned an enraged look on Jim. "I'll tell you nothing!"

—and the man suddenly gasped and began to turn an astonishing shade of dusky green-bronze. "Suggest you change your mind," Athendë said sweetly, as the great handling tentacles, as thick as tree limbs, began to squeeze. "Might lose temper otherwise. Or start to feel hungry. Love it when prey struggles."

The Romulan made a sudden anguished sound for which Jim could see no reason—until he noticed a runnel of green making its way down the lower leg of the man's uniform, one of the only exposed parts of him. Jim reflected briefly that he still had no idea where a Sulamid kept its mouth, though now the question of whether the mouth had teeth in it seemed to have been resolved.

"Have tasted better," said Mr. Athendë mildly. "But shame to waste. Better say something fast or will bolt my lunch and get on with work."

The Romulan shuddered and moaned and gasped, turning darker—then cried out again. "Over there!" he said, his eyes flickering to the leftmost of the consoles.

"Ael," Jim said. She hurried into the room with several of her people, and together they went to the console and began touching controls, reading screens. "This is it, Captain. We can crash the effect itself easily enough—" and Ael reached out and tapped at a keypad, then hit several switches in rapid succession. "But I don't see any control for crashing the whole system from here."

"No matter," Jim said. "We'll find the tank with the brain material and stick a sonic grenade in it." He turned around and gave his attention to that large window. Mr. Freeman was already down on his knees by the door adjacent to the window, working on another circuit panel.

Looking through the window, Jim could see why; littered all over the floor of the great room were hundreds of bodies in Starfleet uniforms. Some of them were stirring feebly.

"Captain," said a weak voice. It was Spock, whom Athendë was still half-cradling in some spare tentacles. McCoy went to him, helping him to stand. "Jim—that mechanism is full of living material—"

"Mr. Spock, I would like nothing better than to transport it out of here and find it a nice home on Vulcan," Jim said. "But the ship's screens are up, and she's not answering anyway, and we can't do it. If we leave the living material alone, it can be used against us again."

"Not easily, Captain," Ael said. "If we destroy this board"—and she touched more switches—"this whole setup will go, and the connections to the brain tissue will fuse. In any case, it's time that we did one thing or another and got moving. It is getting noisy out there, and not even *our* people can hold that corridor forever."

"All right," Jim said. "The computers at least. Everybody out of the way."

Athendë and the others cleared away from the console side of the room, heading for the door to the large room where the Vulcans had been held. "Get in there and help them," Jim said. "Mr. Spock?"

"A great pleasure, Captain," Spock said, unholstering his phaser and aiming at the key computer board. He blew it to bits.

"'Pleasure' is an emotion, Mr. Spock," Ael said from behind them as the last few crackles and fizzes died out.

Jim turned, wondering what that meant, and found Ael looking at Spock with a rather cockeyed expression. Spock gave it right back to her. "So I hear, Commander," he said, and together they turned and headed for the room full of Vulcans.

Jim hurried after them, for the noise out in the hall *was* getting pretty loud. Many of the Vulcans were on their feet now, and more every moment. From across the room one staggered across to him. It was tall young Sehlk, the *Intrepid's* first officer, and Jim reached out and steadied Sehlk as he almost fell over upon reaching him. "Mr. Sehlk, are you all right?"

Sehlk stared at Jim, his face (in the cool Vulcan fashion) bewildered in the extreme. "Captain," Sehlk said with a brief, most unVulcan access of emotion, "it is most illogical for you to be here!"

"Is it really?" Jim said, suspecting that he was going to have to get used to hearing that from every Fleet officer he met for a while. "I'm not doing anything for you and your captain that he wouldn't probably do for my people, were our places reversed. . . . Meanwhile, I would rather beg the question—"

"As you wish, sir."

"Very good. Where's Captain Suvuk?"

"Not here, Captain," the young Vulcan said. "The Romulans took him from us shortly after we were brought here. Logic would seem to indicate that they are attempting to force classified information from him—most likely the *Intrepid*'s control codes and command ciphers, that being the only information he would have and we would not that would be of use to them."

Useful indeed. With those codes and ciphers the Romulans could drain *Intrepid*'s computers dry of all kinds of useful classified data— Federation starship patrol corridors, troop strengths and distributions— "Mr. Sehlk, they didn't harm him, did they?"

"They tortured him, Captain," Sehlk said with terrible equanimity. "But that did them no good; mere torture will not break Command conditioning, as you know. The Romulans then attempted to bring their mind-techniques to bear on him. We tried to defend him at a distance, by taking the brunt on our own minds—and for a short while we succeeded in standing the Romulans off. Their techniques so far work better for large groups than for single persons. But the techniques they are using are apparently mechanically augmented in some way; once our interference was discovered, they put us all under the damper at such intensity that some of us, the more psionically sensitive, died of it." Sehlk's eyes grew cold. "Can you imagine what it is like, Captain, to lie paralyzed for hour after hour, with a mind forcibly emptied of thought, of volition—though not of the knowledge of what has happened to you, or probably will?"

"Mr. Sehlk," Jim said, "may those of us who have not be preserved from it."

"We will see to that," Sehlk said. "Captain, when Suvuk realized that they were going to use such artificial augmentation to force his mind, he drove himself purposely into *kan-sorn*—a mental state similar to coma, but with this difference, that any attempts on the integrity of a mind in *kan-sorn* will destroy both mind and body. He made himself useless to them—and so he lies, somewhere in here, comatose. Captain," Sehlk said, "we must find him." And though the statement was certainly based in logic, there was more to it than that: there was the ferocious, unconditional Vulcan loyalty that Jim had come to know very well indeed.

"We will," Jim said. "First we have to get you people out of here. Our position at the moment isn't the best—"

"Acknowledged," Sehlk said, and detached himself coolly from Jim's grip, heading off a little unsteadily to see to his own people. They were recovering rapidly, more than half of them on their feet now, going about the room as swiftly and efficiently as they could. Jim spent about half a second simply being astonished at how many different kinds of Vulcans there were. On some level he had become conditioned to their being dark, and usually tall. But here were gigantic seven-foot Vulcans and little delicate ones, Vulcans slimmer even than Spock and Vulcans much burlier—none of them actually being overweight; Starfleet regulations to one side, Jim suspected nonglandular fat of being, as far as Vulcans were concerned, "illogical." And there were fair Vulcans, blond and ash blond and very light brunette, and, good Lord, several redheads—

Most important, there were four hundred and eight of them. Jim could think of a lot of worse things than having four hundred Vulcans, all coolly furious over the loss of their captain, at his back in a charge down that corridor.

Ael came up beside him. "Well, Captain," she said, "that's half our job done."

"A third," he said. "Their captain's not here, Ael—we have to find Suvuk yet. Then the research computers and the genetic-material stockpile."

"And how are we going to find one Vulcan in this place full of Romulans?" she said, looking askance. "Jim, we've already been here more than thirty minutes! The whole population of this station is going to come down on us shortly—"

"Let them," Jim said. "The numbers are a little better right now."

"Yes, but these Vulcans aren't armed! And what about your ship? Why haven't we heard from Mr. Scott?"

"That," Jim said, his guts clenching inside him, "is something I intend to find out as soon as possible. In the meantime, your first question—"

Jim turned around to call for Mr. Selhk, but he was already heading toward Ael and Jim, with T'Leiar and the calm round Sobek in tow. "Captain," he said, "we're ready to move. What are your orders?"

"Well, first of all we're going to have to locate Suvuk."

"Captain," said willowy T'Leiar, "leave that to us. Several of us have had occasion to mindmeld with the captain before, so we are quite familiar with his basic personality pattern. And now that the mind damper is no longer operational—"

"You can track him," Jim said. "What do you have to do?"

"Sehlk and T'Leiar will hold the pattern," Sobek said. "The rest of us, even those not trained in the disciplines, will also be of use; we will lend them—I think the most precise word would be 'intention.' We will require several minutes' concentration to set up and implement the state."

"Very well, gentlemen, ladies; carry on. I'm only sorry I can't offer you some peace and quiet for what you're doing. . . ."

"Quiet is not necessary," Sehlk said, for a moment looking very like Spock did while he discussed matters Vulcan and private; reserved, intense, and hiding (not well) a great weight of feeling. "And as for the peace, it is inside us, else no outward peace would be of any use."

Jim looked up. All around, slowly surrounding him and Ael and Spock and McCoy and Athendë and the rest of their party, the Vulcans moved in close. There was nothing mysterious about it, no outward sign as in the personal mindmeld. Sehlk closed his eyes; T'Leiar simply folded her arms and looked down at the floor. But Jim suddenly began to become aware of a frightening sense of oneness settling in around him, as seemingly palpable as the Vulcan's bodies, as invasive and inescapable as the air. He told himself that it was frightening only because he had not been brought up to it—to this certainty, seemingly common in Vulcans, that any given group was far more than the sum of its parts, and the parts all infinitely less for the loss of one of them.

*Or is it so strange?* he thought, as all around him the many parts reached for the one in whom their wholeness best rested, and ever so slightly, mind-blind as Jim usually was, he found himself caught up in the search. *Ael's crew has certainly done the same kind of thing for her. And how many times has mine done it for me? Always, always we're more alike than we dare to admit—*

The air was singing with tension and resolve, though physically no one moved. Outside, the sound of the explosions, the cries and the phaser fire, all sounded very far away. The battle was inward now, one great mind swiftly turning over the thoughts of many smaller ones— some inimical, some desperate, some valiant or preoccupied or blood-mad, all frightened in one way or another. Very few parts of the great searching mind knew anything just now but a terrible, cool, controlled anger they would have rather not admitted to. One part knew that brand of anger, and other emotions as well, and accepted them all together. Two other parts knew mostly rage, and fear for their crews and their ships. All together the power of their emotions, admitted or not, and the power of their intention, wound together, reached outward, pierced—

"There!" cried T'Leiar, and as suddenly as it had coalesced, the great mind fell apart. But the memory and direction of what it had found—a single unconscious Vulcan mind—lingered still. Jim opened his eyes— amazed to find they had been closed—and felt as if he were attached to a rope, with the other end of it fastened to Suvuk. He could have found the man with his eyes closed. Involuntarily he looked up at the ceiling.

"Two levels up," he said. "Next door to the master research computers. Ladies and gentlemen and others, let's go!"

# Chapter Sixteen

Mostly Ael knew about Vulcans what she had been taught as a child. Their remote ancestors had also been the remote ancestors of the Rihannsu; they were a Federation people now; and like all Federation peoples, they were hopelessly spoiled—rich, soft, and unable to take care of themselves. The inability was a matter of ancient history. There had come a time, long ago, when they could no longer cope with the constant fighting that was the inevitable heritage of a warrior people. Those who could cope had been "invited" to leave the planet. Leave it they had—supposedly without much regret. And those who remained had embraced a frightening, demeaning, bizarre discipline of nonemotionality—bottling inside them emotions that they began pretending not to have, as if that would make them go away. The Rihannsu, hearing about this after all the thousands of years, found it a choice irony. The meek had, after all, inherited Vulcan; the Rihannsu had gone out and conquered the stars.

There was nothing wrong with logic per se; it could be as uplifting as song, as intoxicating as wine, under the proper conditions. But it was hardly bread or meat—there was no living a whole life on it. To throw out love, hate, pain, desire, ambition, hunger and hunger's satisfaction, that was asking too much. That was to turn life into a thin, etiolated shadow, lived like one long, dry, joyless mathematical equation.

Or so Ael had always thought. After first meeting Spock, she had begun to wonder whether her preconceptions had anything to do with reality at all. But then Spock was half Terran, and Terrans, though nearly as soft as Vulcans, still had virtues; courage and joy and wit and many other useful or delightful attributes. Spock, she had thought, would probably not be truly representative of a Vulcan. His inner divisions, his lights and shadows, and the reconciliations he had made among them, had turned him into far too complex and powerful a character.

Now, though—as she raced up a hall surrounded by living, breathing Vulcans, and not by her ideas about them, Ael wondered with some shame whether her brain (as her father had repeatedly insisted) was in fact good only for keeping her skull bones apart. The people around her spoke and moved and fought with a frightful cold precision that spoke more of the computer than of the arena; yet at the same time their ferocity matched that of the angriest Rihannsu she had ever seen. Their courage, as they charged unstoppable down hallways full of Rihannsu firing at them, was indomitable. And as for skill, phaser beams seemed to simply miss them, and if the station personnel threw grenades at them, the Vulcans simply managed somehow to be elsewhere. Some of it might be the mind-disciplines that seemed so much like magic to a Rihannsu. She wondered if their embrace of peace might somehow, paradoxically, have made their fierceness more accessible to them. But in any case Ael began to suspect that her belated perception of the Vulcans' virtues was like that of a child who grows up and finds, abruptly, that her parents aren't so stupid as they used to be when she was younger.

It was an annoying realization, but it was the truth; and as such, she wouldn't have given it up for anything.

She stopped at the head of one more endless corridor, leaned up against the corner, and put her hand back. This had been something of a ritual for the past four corridors, and was proving a great success. Into the hand Ael reached out, someone—perhaps Jim, or Spock, or one of her own people—slapped a phaser or other small disposable object. Ael tossed it out into the corridor. If nothing happened—well, that step would be handled as it came.

Nothing happened.

She put her hand back again. Another object: a Rihannsu disruptor, this time.

She threw it out there. And white light and heat blew up practically in her face as a disruptor blast from down the hall exploded the disruptor she'd thrown.

"There they are," she said to the people behind her. "Jim?"

"Right," he said. And out they went into the corridor, as they had the last three times: diving, rolling, shooting, throwing overloaded phasers and whatever else seemed useful. There was a limit, though, to how many overloaded phasers they could use. Ael was praying for an armory somewhere around here. In the meantime, the Elements did for those who did for themselves, and who stayed alive to keep doing it. She concentrated on staying alive.

It took about ten minutes before this particular knot of station personnel was reduced to unconsciousness or death. It had been some time now since the subject of the ethicality of killing had even crossed Ael's mind. She ached all over; she wanted to be back in her own bed on *Bloodwing* so badly that she could taste it; and it would be hours, maybe weary days, before there would be time for that, she knew. The only satisfaction that would come anytime soon was their arrival at the spot where the Vulcan captain was being held. Ael could feel the line inside her, stretched tight toward the man, around this corner and to the left.

"Clear, Captain," one of Jim's people out in the hall was saying. Jim grunted softly, pushed himself away from the wall. He had taken a wicked phaser burn along one arm in the intersection before last, and when he knew no one was looking, his face showed the same kind of weary misery that Ael felt. But let someone look at him, and there was suddenly energy in the eyes, erectness about the carriage, power and stern command. *Fire and Air,* Ael thought. *The Fire will burn bright until there is suddenly nothing left. . . .*

"We're close," Jim said.

Spock was right behind him, looking at Jim with concern, but saying nothing about that; his face was locked in a controlled fierceness much like the other Vulcans'. "Very close," he said. "On the close order of fifty yards."

"Tricorder scan—"

"Ineffective, Captain. All these walls are force-shielded."

"Wonderful. Let's go."

The leading part of the group headed around the corner of the

T-intersection, going left. Down at the end of the hall was something that surprised them all: nothing. The hall was empty. That was bizarre, for all the way up here, practically every foot of the way had had to be viciously contended. Now nothing—

"A trap," Ael said. "Jim, have a care."

"I don't think so," Jim said, eyeing the great door at the hall's end. "Spock, scan it."

The Vulcan did, and his face grew dim as he did so. "Captain, we have a problem," he said. "That door and the walls around it are solid hyponeutronium."

Ael looked up in despair. "Collapsed metal? We have nothing that can possibly break that—"

"Ship's phasers, perhaps," Sehlk said from behind them. "Nothing else."

Ael turned and walked away from the door, reduced to simple annoyance. "There are no guards here because they know they don't need any," she said bitterly. "And Suvuk is on the other side of that door somewhere."

All the Vulcans who had managed to fit into the hallway stood staring at the door as if sheer loyalty or logic would be enough to break it, phasers lacking. Spock and Jim and Sehlk were talking desperately at one another, hypothesizing hurriedly. *It will do them no good,* Ael thought. *We have at last come up against a problem all our fellowship and resourcefulness and cleanness of heart can't solve. . . .*

She walked right up to a wall and thumped it angrily with one fist. *It isn't fair!* And as usual, the old cry brought her father's old reply up: *The Elements aren't fair either. . . .*

Elements . . . it was a silly time to get religious. But what was the old saying? Meet a problem with another problem to make a solution. Meet Fire with Fire, and Earth with Earth, and Water with Water. . . .

*Earth!*

She ran back down the hall where the many Vulcans and *Enterprise* people and her own crewfolk leaned against the walls, silent or whispering, waiting for orders. One of them would not be leaning. He would be flat down on the floor, glittering, answering everyone with the same solid, cheerful, gravelly voice. . . .

She had to trip over him to find him, finally, which was all right, for that was how Ael usually came by her solutions. "Mr. Naraht," she said, catching herself on the wall with both hands, "come quick, we need you!"

"Yes, ma'am!" the rock said, and Ael hurried down the hall with him coming after in a hurry. People got out of Naraht's way when they saw him coming, knowing by experience (or hearsay, in the Vulcans' case) how fast a Horta could move when it was excited.

She led him back around the corner and up to the captain and Spock and Sehlk. "Gentlemen," she said, "I have a question for you."

They turned to her, and their eyes fell on Ensign Naraht, and Jim looked up at Ael in astonishment. "No," he said, "I think you've got an answer for us!"

He got down with some care on one knee—one of his own people has misaimed a kick, in one of the countless fights behind them, and had nearly crippled Jim as a result. "Mr. Naraht," he said, "would you see if you can eat through this door in front of us?"

"It is hyponeutronium," Spock said.

Naraht rumbled and shuffled his fringes about on the floor. "Sirs," he said, sounding pained, "I don't know if I can. I've rarely eaten anything denser than lead. But I'll do what I can."

The Horta shuffled over to the doorway, reared up a little way against it. There was a hissing and a sharp smell of acid in the air; the deckplates under Naraht began to smoke.

"Careful, Mr. Naraht," someone said from beside Ael. It was McCoy, watching the whole process with tired amusement. "Don't go through the floor."

Naraht didn't answer—just held his position for several seconds more, then slid down. There was a great ragged patch of the dark hyponeutronium metal missing, about an inch thick and shaped like Naraht's underside.

"Go on, Ensign, you're doing fine," Jim said.

"In a moment, Captain," Naraht said, sounding distressed. "It's awfully rich. . . ."

Both McCoy's eyebrows went up. Ael watched Jim get up and turn most carefully away from the door, hiding a terrible smile. "Proceed, Ensign, if you please," Spock said very gently. "We are quite short of time, and the success of the entire operation may now lie with you. . . ."

Naraht said not a word. He reared up again and laid himself against the door. The hissing and fuming of acid in the air became terrible, so that people had to retreat from the corridor, and McCoy went hurriedly about spraying something into everyone's eyes to protect them from damage. Long minutes, it went on. Ael got herself sprayed and went out into the corridor again . . . just in time to see Naraht, with a strangled little cry, flop forward through a two-meter-wide hole in the door. From inside, disruptor fire hit him, ineffective as usual . . . which was as well, for Naraht didn't move.

"*Now!*" Jim shouted, as if all the lost energy had suddenly returned. "*Don't touch the edges!*"

And immediately after the captain dove through the door, the sound of phaser fire broke out on its far side; and Spock and McCoy and many another dove through that door after Jim and Ael, none of them being too careful about the edges, and none of them caring. This room was rather like the large control room near which the Vulcans had been kept; full of consoles, control areas and data pads—and only slightly full of Romulans, several of whom lay stunned on the floor. Ael stood with Jim, turning in the smoky room to pick up the directional line again—and found herself looking at a simple, blastable door and being powerfully drawn toward it. She didn't wait. She blasted it.

She was halfway through the door already by the time the smoke cleared, Jim and Spock and McCoy coming after her. The room was set up as a wretched little barracks—a 'fresher, a food dispenser, and several cots; and on one of the cots lay Suvuk, in fetal position—still unconscious, but alive.

"Bones, take care of him," Jim said. "Spock, the computers. Ael, please go with him, assist him if you can—we've got to get that virus program running. Send Sehlk in here when you have a moment."

They did not have to; Sehlk pushed in past them as Ael and Spock were heading out. "I will need an input station," Spock said quietly. "This looks like one—"

"Here's the initializer," Ael said, and began touching switches. The computer was not unlike the library computer on *Bloodwing,* a later model of a brand she knew well. "Astonishing that these things run at all," she said, as she brought the main operating system up.

"Lowest bidder?" Spock said.

She grinned and kept working. "There you are. Can you access from this command level?"

"Easily. Now then—" His hands flickered over the keyboard with almost insulting ease. Ael turned from him to see one of the stunned Romulans slowly recovering, looking around him at the incredible wreckage, and (with considerable trepidation) at a roomful of angry Vulcans.

One of them was giving him her particular attention. T'Leiar, with two or three of her security people about her, was holding the man by the front of his coverall and conversing with him in no amiable tone. "You will introduce us," she said, "to the head of this research project."

The man glared at her. "I am its head. And it will be my pleasure to see you all executed for the damage you have been doing it—"

"We have not done nearly any damage to the heart of it as yet," T'Leiar said, "but we shall. And as for the pleasures you expect to enjoy, I suggest you reckon them up quickly. We have business with you after which the probability is high that you will no longer understand pleasure—or anything else."

The man laughed at them, such a scornful sound that Ael had to admire his courage, while at the same time wanting very much to step over there, relieve T'Leiar of him, and strangle him with one hand. "You think you can force information from me?" he said. "Do your worst. I was one of the first Rihannsu to obtain the Vulcan mind-techniques directly from your genetic material. It was I who assisted in the capture of your ship by the cruiser *Battlequeen.* Your minds hold no terror for me—"

"Oh, indeed," T'Leiar said, very softly. "But you were using an enhancer, were you not?—several thousand cubic inches of brain matter added to your own, endowing you with much more reach and scope than you have in your own mind. No," said T'Leiar, as from outside the room more and more Vulcans slipped in through the hole in the door, "I can feel you striving for control of my mind; but even my own self alone is too much for you. Now you begin to feel the weight, do you not? So we felt under your damper; and worse is to come."

The air in the room was becoming strained again, full of that awful tightness. There was no affection about this, though, no affinity, no searching, as there had been for Suvuk. This was an inimical pressure, the weight of many minds leaning together, bearing in and down, harder, sharper, their attack narrowing down to a crushing spearhead of thought. "You may tell us the location of the stockpiled genetic material," T'Leiar said in that light, passionless voice of hers. "Or you may try to withhold it."

The Rihannsu researcher lay there, his face straining into awful shapes, and twitched like a palsied thing. "No, I—" he said, in a voice more suited to groaning than to speech; and then more loudly, "No!" and again, "No!" almost a scream. And then the screaming began in earnest. No one touched him, no one moved; T'Leiar sat back on her heels beside him, motionless as a carving, her eyes hooded; and still the man screamed and screamed. Ael watched, approving on some levels, but on others horrified beyond words. The screaming went on—

—and then broke. The Rihannsu research chief gasped, and his head thumped down to the floor with that particular hollow, wet sound that Ael recognized as a dead man's head falling. His eyes stared at the ceiling, wide and terrified, and the Vulcans around him got up, or straightened, and went away, leaving him there.

Ael found herself staring at T'Leiar as she got up. The young woman caught Ael's glance and said, with utter calm, "He fought us."

"You didn't get the information, then?"

"We obtained it." She started toward the door of the little room where Suvuk had lain, but McCoy came out of it then, with Sehlk carrying Suvuk, and Jim following them.

Jim went straight to T'Leiar. "Well, Commander?"

"We have the locations of the stockpiles," she said, "and all the basic research data, both hard and soft copy, is here in this shielded part of the installation. However, there is too much of it to be handled by our group. Transporters will handle it—but the *Enterprise* is still not answering hails."

"Well," Jim said, "this station has transporters of its own, Commander."

T'Leiar looked at him with cool approval. "You are suggesting we secure those, then beam up to *Intrepid* with all our people—transferring you to *Enterprise* when it becomes clear what the problem is. If there is a problem."

"Correct. Mr. Spock, what's the status of the computer?"

"It is in a sorry state, Captain," Spock said with satisfaction. "The commander's parameters for a whole-system virus program were most effective; the system is being subverted even as we speak. Within fifteen minutes there will not be a bit of data left in it. It will make someone an excellent adding machine."

"Mr. Spock, Commander," Jim said, bright-eyed and alert again, "my compliments. Bones," he said to McCoy, who was passing by, "one question. How's Naraht?"

McCoy scowled genially at the Captain. "Boy's got the worst case of indigestion I've ever seen," he said, "but he'll be all right."

"Good. Mr. Spock, let's find those transporters and get the hell out of here. I want to know what's the matter with my ship!"

They headed for the melted door together. As they went a look of doubt crossed Jim's face—for out in the hall, he could hear their rear-guard shooting at something again.

"More company," Ael said.

"And our phaser charges are running low," Jim sighed, then grinned again—that fierce, defiant look. "Well, let's just get out there, do what we can, and hope for the best. . . ."

"Hope, Captain?" Ael said in a soft imitation of T'Leiar's voice. "Hope is illogical."

"So it is. Then let's just go out there and fight like crazy people to shame the devil."

At that Ael laughed. "Now I understand you very well. Let us shame her by all means. . . ."

They went out together into the phaser fire and the smoke.

# Chapter Seventeen

In the tight hot dark of the 'tween-decks crawlway, three shadowy forms lay one behind the other, holding very still. One of them had his ear pressed to the duct's plating. His open eye, moving as he listened, gleamed momentarily in the dull glow of a circuit-conduit's telltale.

"What do you hear?" Chekov said softly behind him.

"Disruptor fire," Khiy said. "But it sounds to be some ways off."

"Thank God for that," Sulu said from the rear. "That last little episode was a bit too close for my taste."

"Easy for you to say," Chekov muttered. "They missed *you*."

"How is it?" Khiy said, starting to inch forward again.

Chekov started to move too, and involuntarily gave Khiy his answer in a word that hadn't been taught him at Starfleet Academy.

"Hang on, Pavel," Sulu said. "We'll get you to sickbay as soon as we find some more people."

"And retake the bridge," Chekov said dismally. But he hitched himself along at a good rate. "Where next?"

Sulu had been considering that for a good half hour now, as they wormed their way along between decks, heading toward the turbolift core of the *Enterprise*'s primary hull. The access to the bridge would be fairly simple from the lift core—always granting that the lifts didn't come on again at the wrong moment and kill them all. But besides that sticky question, he didn't care for the odds. Three of them might not be enough to break through the resistance they would surely meet when they had to come out into the real corridors and access the core. Tafv would not be fool enough to leave that route unguarded. *Hikaru my boy,* he had said to himself some ways back in this seemingly infinite tunnel, *there has to be another way. There's always a loophole, a shortcut, if you can just see it. . . .*

"Pavel," he said, "I lost count. Where the hell are we?"

"Between three and four," Chekov said. "Somewhere between administrative and library science, if you're looking up at three."

Hikaru closed his eyes to look at the ship in his head, going around the circle of the disk on his mental diagram. "Then below us on four, nacelleward, are the chapel, and dining three and four, and the rec deck. . . ."

Chekov pushed himself up on his elbows a little, an alert movement. "I will bet you there are a lot of people down there—" He shook his head. "Hikaru, if we take the duct from here, that's a three-story drop to the deck!"

"Sure is. But even if we can't jump down that far, we can throw them some guns so that they can break out of there. . . . And I bet we'd get down somehow."

"Is this wise?" Khiy said softly from up ahead. "Mr. Scott did tell us not to do anything stupid. . . ."

"It's not *too* stupid," Chekov said. "And numbers would be a help. We can't afford to screw up an attempt on the bridge."

" 'Screw up'?"

Chekov said another word not usually considered part of the language of officers and gentlemen, one that the translator would nevertheless render more accurately than idiom. "Oh," Khiy said, and laughed, though so softly as not to be heard by any listener. "Yes, I agree. So where shall we go?"

"Back the way we came, and to the right."

"You are jesting," Khiy said. "In *this* space?"

"It's no joke, brother," Sulu said. "Let's move it."

It took them fifteen minutes, and besides becoming acutely aware of every bruise and aching joint he already owned, and of new ones that the painful process of turning was adding to the collection, Hikaru was acutely aware of the minutes crawling over and past him like bugs. Time, time, there was too little of it for anything: who knew what was going on down at the station, whether the captain and the landing party and the crew of the *Intrepid* were still even alive? There was no news from them—and until the situation aboard *Enterprise* was resolved, no way to get news to them either. *Damn, damn,* Hikaru thought, bending himself once more into an impossible shape, *we've got to do something, and fast, and everything's taking too much time.* . . .

He finished turning first. Chekov was having even more trouble, being bigger than Hikaru, and poor Khiy, the largest of them, was in torment; but there was nothing Hikaru could do for either one. "Pavel," he said, "the clock's running. I've got to take some of those guns and go ahead."

"Go on," Pavel said. "Hurry. We'll catch up. Khiy, try it again, you're close, but this time don't put your boot in my eye!"

Hikaru headed back the way they had come, crawling on raw hands and elbows, pushing four or five phaser rifles ahead of him and trying to ignore the renewed pain of all the phasers and grenades hung about them as they dug into his ribs and belly. He had never been fond of tight enclosed spaces; they were becoming positively hateful to him now, and he suspected he was going to have to have a long talk with Dr. McCoy at the end of all this. If there was an end to it that would leave any of them talking.

He bit his lip, watching for the turning he wanted as he went. The prospect of death had faced him often enough before; but it had always seemed oddly tolerable with his helm console in front of him and his friends and superior officers around. *Suppose something should hit us right now,* he thought miserably. *For all our trying, we die right here, crawling through a hole in the dark—or in a hundred other stupid ways, all over the ship. No battle, no valor, everything wasted, and no one will ever know what happened.* . . .

There was a peculiar horror in the thought. Theoretically Hikaru knew perfectly well that courage was courage whether anyone saw it or not; it was of value, and the universe lived a little longer because of it. Well, there was no proof of that last part, though it was still what he *knew.* But theory and that calmer knowledge, so often his in meditation, were a long way from him now. What he mostly felt could have been summed up in a single thought: *If I have to die, let me do it with my friends, and in the light!*

*That turning*—Hikaru wriggled around the corner, pushing hard, hurrying. He was close. There was sound here, too; not disruptor fire, but rather the low murmur and rumor of many voices, reflecting vaguely through the ducts. *A lot of people,* he thought, and at the prospect of being about to do something besides crawl, he forgot his horror. He hurried faster.

The voices had a sound he had never heard aboard *Enterprise* before—the sharp rasp of many, many people being angry all at once, at the same thing. It infected him; grinning, he practically shot the last twenty or thirty meters down the duct and came up hard against the grille at its end. Oh, the lovely light, the pale gray walls of the rec room, seen from right by its ceiling; and the big windows of the observation deck above, and through them, the stars. . . .

He pounded on the grille. It wouldn't give, and he didn't think any of the hundred or so people milling around down there could hear him. *Oh well,* he thought with nearly cheerful desperation. He backed away down the duct, picked up one of the phaser rifles, and blasted the grille away.

He didn't bother waiting for the smoke to clear, or the floor and walls of the duct to cool down—just scrambled forward again. And nearly got shot for his pains; just before he reached the spot where the grille had been, phaser fire came lancing up at him and hit the roof of the duct. He convulsively covered his head and eyes, but there was nothing to be done about the burns he took on the back of his scalp and the backs of his hands. *"No, you idiots, don't shoot,"* he yelled, for the moment forgetting courtesy and discipline and everything else, *"it's me, it's Hikaru Sulu!!"*

There was a moment's silence from outside. "Move forward very, very slowly," said a stern voice, "and let's see."

Very slowly indeed he poked his head out and looked down. There stood Harb Tanzer, at the head of those hundred people, aiming a phaser at the duct. He was the only one of them armed with anything deadlier than a pool cue or a bowling ball; but Romulans and *Enterprise* people alike, they all looked quite ready to do murder. Until the *Enterprise* folk recognized him. Then there was cheering.

"Oh God, I could have killed you!" Harb said, tossing someone else the phaser. "Come down from there, man. Hwavirë, how long are those tentacles of yours? If you stand on something, can you reach? Get that table over here and put that other one on top of it—"

It turned out to be rather more difficult than that. At the end Hikaru was simply glad that he knew how to fall properly. He added several bruises to his collection, but even so couldn't care much about them when he found himself lying on a heap of his friends, and still hugged tight in the tentacles of one of his Sulamid junior navigators, Ensign Hwavirë. "Didn't know you cared, Hwa," he said. "Thought we were just good friends."

"Don't tempt," Hwavirë said, with a bubbling laugh, as he put Hikaru back on his feet. "Not bad looking for hominid." And then they got to repeat the performance twice more, once each for Chekov and Khiy, with mad cheers from the Romulans for the latter.

"Get them coffee," Harb said. "What's your name—Khiy? Khiy, do you drink coffee? Never mind, we'll find out. Satha, get the first-aid kit for Hikaru's burns. You three, tell us what's happening. Hurry."

They did, interrupting one another constantly. "Scotty and Uhura can't hold down the auxiliary bridge forever," Hikaru said at last. "If we can make it to the bridge, they can transfer control to us there before Tafv and his people get at it. The Romulans stuck on the bridge are with us, they'll lend a hand from inside if they can. But we have to get there first. . . ."

"They're all around us, Hikaru," said Roz Bates, a tall broad lady from engineering. "Trying to break out seemed a little dumb before, when none of us were armed. Now, of course, the odds are a little more in our favor. But still—"

"Crawlways," Mr. Tanzer muttered. "Incredible waste of time. If only we had the transporters—"

Chekov shook his head. "They're all shut down, sir. . . ."

Harb sat there, staring into the distance for a few seconds. "Yes, they are." And then suddenly his eyes widened. "No, they're *not*. . . ."

"Sir?"

"They're not!" He got up and left the group, heading across the room and stopping to stare down at the 4D chessboard. "Roz, get the tools out of my office, would you? Moira!"

*"What's the problem, Harb?"* the games department computer said from out of the middle of the air.

"Moira, what's the present maximum range for piece control in the chesscubic?"

*"Ten meters, Harb. But no transits so large are needed."*

"I know," Mr. Tanzer said. "We traded off distance for small-scale precision when we programmed the system. I want to arrange a different tradeoff."

"Mr. Tanzer," Hikaru said, caught between dismay and delight, "are you suggesting that one of us beam out of here via the *table* transporter? There's not enough power—"

"Maybe so, maybe not. Let's find out. Moira, think about it. Maximum transportable mass, over maximum distance, after *in situ* alteration, no new parts. All possible solutions."

*"Thinking, Harb."*

Harb bent over the games table, shutting down various of its circuits. "Besides, even if the table can't handle a whole person's mass—thanks, Roz, pop that other cover off, will you?—even so, there's nothing to stop us from beaming smaller masses out."

Chekov, beside Sulu, began to smile. "Take a grenade," he said, "prime it, and beam it out into the middle of a crowd of Rom—I mean, a crowd of Tafv's people—"

"Mr. Chekov," Harb said, "I always knew you were a bright fellow. Not that solid, Roz, the next one. Don't joggle that dilithium crystal, either. Moira, what's taking you so long?"

*"You always yell at me when I interrupt. Maximum mass with maximum distance, fifty kilos, eighteen feet. Maximum mass with minimum distance, eighty kilos, two feet. Minimum mass with maximum distance, zero to fifty grams, five hundred meters."*

"Try something a little heavier."

*"One kilogram, two hundred meters."*

"That's more like it. Who's got a tricorder? Harry? Good man. Start scanning. We won't be able to tell which Romulans are ours, but—"

"Yes you will, Mr. Tanzer," Khiy said between gulps of coffee, and held out his arm.

"My stars and garters," Harb said. "Mr. Sulu, your assessment of my idiocy is accepted with thanks. Harry, scan for cesium-rubidium in the Romulans in the area. Pinpoint groups without it and note the bearings for me. Decimal places on those bearings, too! I don't want to hurt the ship more than necessary; the captain'll have my hide when he gets back, and Dr. McCoy'll rub salt where it used to be. Who're the best shots in here? Who's got a good arm? Don't give me that, Loni, I saw you with those darts last week. Have a grenade. Have several. Get off it, people; we've got work to do!"

Maybe five minutes later, Harry Matshushita had every one of Tafv's parties on the nacelleward half of the primary hull pinpointed—most particularly two parties moving along deck seven, converging on the auxiliary bridge in a pincers movement. "They're first," Harb said, looking rather sorrowfully at the sonic grenade he held in one hand. "Ready, Roz?"

"Just about."

"Good. Ladies and gentlemen and others—one word before we start."

Hikaru looked up, with the others, from the readying of weapons.

"Don't get to liking this too much," he said. "Any other way of freeing this ship would be preferable—and should we find ourselves able within the scope of our oaths to allow our enemies mercy, I will expect it of you. Otherwise—protect the ship and your shipmates. And our guests." His eyes flicked from place to place in the crowd, picking out the Romulans. Hikaru noticed that there was suddenly no more clumping of type with type—just people defending the same ship, and all wearing the same rather frightened expression of resolve.

"Good," Harb said. "Roz, we'll take care of those deck seven groups first, and then clear our own path to the lift core, and anything else this transporter can reach. I don't care to use the 'com system as yet, but I bet our shipmates will look out to see what's happening when they hear all the noise. Harry, give Roz new bearings for the auxiliary bridge, and project them a bit forward to allow for movement."

"Done, sir."

"Here, then," Harb said, and pulled the patch on the sonic grenade, and laid it on the game table.

It sparkled with transporter effect, while all around Hikaru people were counting softly. He couldn't remember a time when dematerialization had seemed to take longer—

—and then it was gone. And was that the slightest shudder in the ship, a booming of the air in the ducts?

"Bearings for the second group," Harb said. "Roz, Harry, don't give them time to react—"

"Ready—"

Harb laid down another grenade. It beamed out. Another shudder—

Harry paused to check his tricorder. "There's nothing alive in that corridor now, sir," he said softly. "Nothing *very* alive, anyway. A few weak life readings; no movement at all."

"Next," Harb said. Sulu noticed that he did not say "good," though Harb *always* said "good." "The bunch on deck four—"

All told, it took them about twenty minutes to decimate three-fourths of the force of seventy-three that had invaded the *Enterprise*. Some of the Romulans were out of the table transporter's reach, in the forward half of the primary hull; but very few, enough for them to handle.

Their own corridor came last. Hikaru watched Harb keep checking, hoping that the Romulans besieging them would go away. But they didn't. Harb put the last grenade down, took the controls from Roz, got a bearing from Harry, and beamed the shiny little egg out himself. All over the rec deck, things bounced and fell off tables and broke, and people grabbed one another for support.

"That's done it," Harb said, deadly quiet. "Weapons at the ready. Let's go."

They went to the main doors all together. Harb released the emergency lock and led them out into the hallway.

There was very little left out there to offer mercy to.

"We'll separate," Harb said. "Mr. Sulu, Mr. Chekov, you'll be needed on the bridge; take about ten people with you for security's sake. About twenty of you, come with me down to auxiliary, we'll see what the story is down there and have them release the lifts. Ten of you to the main transporters on six; ten of you to sickbay—make yourselves available to Doctors Chapel and M'Benga. The rest of you head out and see what's to be done about the forward half of the hull. Go."

"Yes, sir," they all said, and headed off in their various directions. Hikaru and Chekov and Khiy headed off toward the lift together. It took about ten minutes, but at that point Khiy cocked his head. "I hear something—"

Sulu and Chekov listened for all they were worth, but didn't hear a thing, at least not until the lift was about two seconds from arriving. The doors whooshed open for them, the obedient, wonderful doors that Hikaru had wondered whether he would ever see working again. They stepped in together, turned to look back the way they'd come—and wished they hadn't.

"Bridge," Hikaru said softly, and the doors shut.

The three of them pressed up hard against the walls of the lift before it reached the bridge, just in case anyone should fire at them from inside. It was a good thing that they had taken the precaution; several disruptor bolts hit the back of the lift as its doors opened. "No, no, Eriufv, it's us!" Khiy yelled at the bridge's occupants.

Moments later they were all being pounded and hugged. Hikaru found himself being hugged by Eriufv—who was very pretty—and considered that there were certainly worse things that could happen to him. He hugged her back, but made it very quick. "We don't have time," he said to the group on the bridge as he stepped down to the center seat, and thought simultaneously (as always) how marvelous this was, and that he'd rather be anywhere else. "Eri, you held the fort real well—and now we have to get busy attacking. First, though, we need to talk to Mr. Scott." She nodded, sat down at Uhura's station and started flicking switches as if she had been there all her life. "Auxiliary control, this is the bridge—"

*"Auxiliary,"* said that wonderful Highland voice. *"Scott here."*

"We made it, Mr. Scott."

*"Aye, so Mr. Tanzer tells me. Transferring control now."*

"Noted," Hikaru said, as all around, the "executive" lights came on at the various stations. "Transfer complete."

*"Good lad. Uhura and I are on the way up. Call the captain and find out what the devil's goin' on down there. Oh, and Mr. Sulu—tell him we found Tafv down here. Just barely alive. He's on his way to sickbay."*

Eriufv started up out of Uhura's seat, her eyes glittering with rage. "I will go down there and kill him myself—"

"As you were, Eri," Hikaru said, and said it so forcefully that Eriufv sat back down in the chair as if she had been pushed there.

"He'll have to die anyway," Eri said, more quietly, though her eyes were still angry. "There's no punishment but death for treachery."

"That's the commander's prerogative, and maybe the captain's," Hikaru said, "but not ours. I need you here. Anything else, Mr. Scott?"

*"No, lad. Call the captain, and prepare me a damage control report; I want to see it when Uhura and I get up there. Out."*

"Pavel, take care of the report," Hikaru said. "And while you're at it, activate intruder control and flood the sections where there are still Romulans. Some of our people will take a nap, but it can't be helped. Then get somebody from security and have them go in with masks and get the Romulans out."

"Right, Mr. Sulu."

"Eriufv, ship to surface. *Enterprise* to landing party, please respond!"

*"Spock here,"* said another very welcome voice. *"Report, Mr. Sulu."*

"There was an armed uprising aboard ship, Mr. Spock. Subcommander Tafv led some seventy Romulans from *Bloodwing* over here in an attempt on the auxiliary bridge and other key portions of the ship: motivation presently unknown. He seems to have timed his incursion simultaneously with your beam-out, when the shields were down."

*"Logical,"* Spock said. *"That was the only time we were vulnerable. Continue."*

"There was sabotage to systems, now under repair, and there have been numerous casualties. But elapsed time from first incursion to ship secure"—he glanced at the chrono and could not believe his eyes. The ten years he had aged had only taken—"seventy-eight minutes, Mr. Spock."

*"Understood."* There was the slightest grim humor to that. *"We also have been busy, Mr. Sulu. Drop the shields and beam us all up; we have a great deal of large-scale transporting to do and our position here is untenable to say the least."*

"Acknow—" And Sulu looked at the forward screen, and stopped at the sight of something Chekov, now staring in horror down Spock's hooded viewer, had transferred there. "Mr. Spock," Hikaru said, "I'm afraid I can't do that. Scan shows three more Romulan ships coming in fast; firing at us now. IDs read ChR *Lahai,* ChR *Helve*—and ChR *Battle-queen.*"

# Chapter Eighteen

*"Tafv did what!"*

Ael stared at Jim and Spock, and her heart hammered in her gut as if she had been wounded again. Suddenly the phaserfire all around, the sound of explosions, meant nothing to her at all. "But, but he—"

"They don't know exactly why he did it," Jim said, looking as angry as Ael did. "He's in sickbay, unconscious from injuries. The people he brought with him are almost all dead. But Ael, we don't have time for it now! We've got other problems."

"*Battlequeen* is up there, Commander," Spock said, "with two other ships, and they are firing at *Enterprise*. Your friend LLunih may have found the help he was looking for despite our best efforts."

It was easy for them to say that they had no time for other problems. Ael's rage at her own blindness and folly was terrible. The one spot she had reckoned her strongest, the one person she could trust above all others, suddenly betraying her— And her honor was truly in rags now, she was disgraced before her own heart and the Elements forever— Bitter pragmatism reasserted itself, though, the old habit ingrained by so many other defeats. "How close are we to the transporters?"

"About a hundred meters," Spock said. But they might as well have been a hundred light-years away, for this corridor was the most fiercely held of any they had come down yet. The Rihannsu at the far end of it doubtless knew that if they could only hang on a little longer, *Battlequeen*'s people would arrive in force—and there would be an end to fighting, and a beginning to an interesting evening of tortures.

"Captain," she said, "we cannot hope to break out of here! We are almost out of weapons, those few we still have are almost out of charge, we are almost all wounded, even the poor rock can barely move—"

"Hope," Jim said, still looking around him for possible options, "*is* illogical. . . . Still, it has its uses. Spock?"

"The commander's summation, while emotionally delivered, is quite correct," Spock said. "We are pinned, and scan shows another group of Rihannsu working around to join those presently attacking our rear. They do not have to do much to us, Captain. They can easily contain any attempt we might make to break out of this area."

"Noted. However, Mr. Spock—if it becomes plain that this is a non-survival situation—we will not be taken without a fight."

"Yes, sir."

And having decided that, they began to look around them for ways out again. Ael shook her head slowly, feeling shamed by their courage and privileged to have seen it. "Gentlemen—"

Jim's communicator beeped. "Kirk here."

"*Captain,*" Mr. Scott's voice said, "*we've got a problem. . . .*"

"The shields, I would imagine."

"*They're holding, sir. Barely.* Helve *and* Lahai *are whittling away at them—* Battlequeen's *not in range yet. Sir, that ship looks like one of the new model Klingon destroyers. We're going to be in deep trouble if it gets here . . . and I don't see any way to stop it.*"

"Mr. Scott," Jim said, "under no circumstances are you to allow my ship to be taken." His eyes flickered to Ael, asking her silently about her crew. She simply nodded. "The commander concurs as regards *Blood-wing* personnel aboard the *Enterprise;* you had better let them know. And should things come to that pass, blow *Intrepid,* and the station too."

"*Understood,*" Scotty said. "*What the devil—*"

"What's wrong, Scotty? That hasn't gone wrong already, anyway."

"*Ach,*" Scotty said, sounding disgusted, "*it's that* Bloodwing, *Captain; she's firin' at us now, pointblank!*"

Ael shook her head miserably and leaned it against the fire-blackened wall, sick at heart. "*Something odd about that, Mr. Scott,*" she heard Mr. Chekov say in the background.

"*What then, lad?*"

"*Her phasers are firing at minimum intensity, Mr. Scott,*" Chekov said, his voice sounding very odd—almost jubilant. "*No effect on our screens—*"

*"Give me a power consumption curve on her."*

*"Normal, Mr. Scott! No damage to* Bloodwing, *no engine trouble and she doesn't have her shields up—"*

"Scotty," Jim said urgently, "hail her!"

"Uhura—"

In the background they could hear Uhura opening a frequency, challenging *Bloodwing.* "On screen, Mr. Scott—"

*"Enterprise,"* came a familiar voice—Aidoann, frantic, but thinking as usual. The sickness about Ael's heart came undone, and she sat up straight. *"Mr. Scott, where's the commander?"*

"Scotty," Jim said, "patch me through! Aidoann, this is Kirk, the commander's with us and well—"

*"Captain,"* Aidoann said, *"you must get out of there! We can't keep up this pretense much longer, the other ships will be within range to read our status on sensors—"*

"Energize, wide scan!" Ael cried. "You can take us in three groups, four at the most! Beam us over to *Intrepid!* Captain, where? Their rec room?"

"Yes—! Spock, warn everybody—Scotty, give *Bloodwing* our coordinates, take everybody with a translator installed, the Vulcans have them too! Hurry it—"

The phaser fire broke out close behind them. People threw themselves in all directions, firing back—

—and the world dissolved in a storm of crimson dazzle, the form of fire that Ael decided right then she would always like best—

*O, by my Element!!* she thought, as *Bloodwing*'s transporter let go of her and dropped her six feet to the carpeted floor. The carpet was no help; she heard various *Enterprise* people complaining about the drop, though the Vulcans all somehow seemed to come down on their feet. "Move it," Jim was shouting, "get off the coordinates, there're two more groups coming—!"

People scrambled desperately for the walls. Ael ran with the rest, pausing only long enough to scoop up Dr. McCoy in the process and drag him along with her; he had been trying to stand and failing. Now he was testing his left leg for breaks and saying a great many things that her translator flatly refused to render. She dropped him more or less against the wall, looking frantically around her to see how her people were doing. In midair another great group of people materialized and, *slam!,* fell to the floor. "Never complain about our transporters again," McCoy was growling behind her, *"yours* are even worse!"

"Physician," Jim said, kindly but hastily, as he came up behind Ael, "stuff thyself. Better still, get down to the sickbay with Dr. Seiak and start healing some of these people." He paused, watching the third group materialize and go *slam!;* then lifted his communicator again. "Scotty, is that it?"

*"It is, Captain,"* Aidoann said. *"We've got to put our screens up; and they're getting close enough to hear our 'com.* Enterprise, *we're with you!"*—and she closed her channel down.

Ael began holding her breath.

"We've got a hole card, Mr. Scott," Jim said, as jubilant as Chekov had been. "We're going to get this creature going—"

*"But she's cold! It'll take fifteen minutes, Captain—"*

"Hold as you can, Scotty. If the situation becomes unsaveable, my earlier orders stand. No more communication, or you'll give away the fact that there's someone on this ship."

*"Aye. Good luck, sir—"*

"Same to you, Scotty. Out."

Sehlk and T'Leiar had found Jim. "Sir, we have a problem—"

"Where's Captain Suvuk?"

"Still out, in sickbay. Captain—"

"I know. Cold engines."

"It would not be a problem," Spock said from behind Jim, "if we had some 'hot' antimatter to seed the reaction."

"Too late for a jumpstart," Jim said. *"Enterprise* and *Bloodwing* both have their screens up, and they can't drop them—"

—and Ael let out the breath she had been holding at the sound and sight of a final shimmer of *Bloodwing* transporter effect in the middle of the room. The forms solidified: Tr'Keirianh and t'Viaen from her engine room, and between them a magnetic bottle in an antigrav mount.

Her two crewfolk fell and got up again, complaining softly. The bottle in the mount just hovered there.

"Captain," Ael said, "you were saying you needed some antimatter?"

He stared at her.

"I ordered it readied after the question of cold engines came up in the briefing," she said. "Unfortunately things got so busy—"

"Lady," he said, once again with that peculiar courtesy—and then stopped, and shook his head. "Never mind. Mr. Spock, Mr. Sehlk, come along. Sehlk, we're going to do something illogical and very effective to T'Leiar's engines. . . ."

The bridge of the *Intrepid* was if possible even lovelier than that of the *Enterprise*—bigger, more open and modern. And at the moment it was rather livelier, with T'Leiar holding down the center seat, and people and communications crackling in all directions. It amused Ael that while down in the station, under the worst possible circumstances, the Vulcans had seemed so very marvelous—and now, back on their own ship and theoretically in worse danger than before, they were all immersing themselves in an (apparent) calm that was utterly prosaic by comparison. *Territoriality,* Ael thought, *as strong as a Rihannsu's. They are a lot more fun when they're in trouble. Look at T'Leiar, she was like a mad* thrai *when she was fighting; now there's nothing left but a businesswoman—*

"Transporter room?" T'Leiar was saying, "report! Is the transportation of the genetic material complete?"

*"The last load is coming aboard now, Commander."*

"Are you quite certain everything's there?"

*"Commander,"* said the serene Vulcan woman on the other end of the conversation, *"we have beamed up every piece of archival copy, of any sort, in the entire station. Tapes, paper, film, metal—nothing was missed. Number four cargo hold was filled entirely with the papers and tapes alone. The genetic material took up six and nearly all of seven. . . ."*

"Very well. Engineering," T'Leiar said. "Captain Kirk?"

*"Kirk here. Five more minutes, T'Leiar—the warp engines are in restart cycle now, and Spock and Sehlk are in decontamination. Sihek says you can have impulse, though, if you want it."*

"Excellent. Si'jsk, take us out at maximum impulse. Advise *Enterprise* and *Bloodwing*."

"*T'Leiar,*" said Jim from engineering, "*have them lay in courses for eta Trianguli—but have them depart this area in three different directions.*"

"Sir," T'Leiar said politely, "there are only two of them."

"*Noted, Commander, but I want you to do it too. . . .*"

"That is what I thought you meant, Captain. But ambiguity might—"

"*Yes, I suppose it might. Is Commander t'Rllaillieu there?*"

"Here, Jim," Ael said.

"*I forgot to say thank you.*"

"For what?"

"*The antimatter.*"

"No matter," Ael said. "Perhaps I'll borrow a cup of it from *you* some day."

Jim chuckled. "*Oh, oh. Sorry, T'Leiar, Terran error creeps into calculation again. No warp engines in five minutes.*"

"No, Captain?"

"*No, warp capacity* now. *And here come Spock and Sehlk early.*"

"Noted, sir. Lieutenant T'Kiha, how far are we from this system's primary?"

"Three hundred million kilometers, madam. Well outside the warp-flight boundary."

"That's well. Warp two immediately, accelerate to warp six as soon as feasible. Advise *Enterprise* and *Bloodwing*. Mr. Setek, arm photon torpedoes and report when phasers are ready."

"Photon torpedoes charging now. Phasers ready—"

"Good. Pursuit, T'Kiha?"

"*Lahai* and *Helve* are in pursuit, but not keeping pace," said the helm officer. "Slipping behind. Also, *Enterprise* reports dropping its last jamming buoy."

"Excellent. What is *Battlequeen*'s status?"

"Gaining on us, madam. Warp six and accelerating rapidly."

T'Leiar's face, for all its immobility, indicated that she did not consider *that* excellent. "Evasive."

"Commencing."

Ael sat down at a side station. It was good evasive action, but not as inspired as Mr. Sulu's—and *Battlequeen* was still chasing them. "Commander T'Leiar, may I suggest something?"

The bridge doors hissed open. "You snake," Jim said, "what have you got in mind this time?"

"Why, only this—" She saw Jim wince, and laughed, considering that they were still living with the results of the last time she had said those words—and might yet die of them. "Jim, there's *Battlequeen* coming—"

"So I see," Jim said, annoyed. It was hard to miss that ship. "Even with *Intrepid*'s new engine refit, I don't think we can outrun one of those things. And I know *Enterprise* can't. So?"

"Well." Ael reached into her pocket and pulled out a logic solid.

"You want us to fake a Romulan ID?" Jim said, half teasing, half annoyed. "Ael, this is no time—"

"Of course it isn't, you fool." Heads turned around the bridge, and Ael ignored them. "Before Spock started infecting the Levaeri computers, I was looking through the system and stumbled on something interesting." She juggled the solid lightly in one hand. "The Sunseed program."

He stared at her blankly.

"Sunseed!" Ael said. "They had to have it to catch all those little Vulcan ships, Jim." She held it up in front of his face. "Wouldn't you like to start your very own ion storm—and leave those three ships to founder in it? Here's the program."

"Oh my *God*," Jim said. "Sehlk!"

The doors hissed open. "Will I do, Captain?" said a mellow voice—and Captain Suvuk walked in. He looked wasted and tired, and the plast that McCoy and Sihek had put on him did little more than cover the worst of his facial wounds; the thought of what injuries lay hidden under the uniform was terrifying. But the man was all power and certainty, though he staggered, and had to support himself on the back of his center seat as he stepped down to them.

"Sir—" Jim said.

"I heard," Suvuk said. "I have been listening from sickbay. Commander," he said to Ael, "there would be a certain irony in turning against

our pursuers the weapon they used on us. Am I correct in hypothesizing that we are going to need a star to make this work?"

"Yes, sir." She and Jim followed Suvuk up to the communications
station. "We would be stimulating the star's corona not only with
phasers and photon torpedoes, but our own warpfield. I understand
that though it works well enough with one ship, it would do better yet
with two, or three—"

"Two, I think, Commander," said Suvuk. "I doubt *Bloodwing* could
match the"—he paused to put the solid down on the comm station's
reading plate—"the warp eleven speeds that this requires. And we have
little time to implement; the fewer ships we must coordinate in this
maneuver, the better. I see that the parameters and frequencies for the
phasers are adaptable to our standards. T'Leiar, pass this information on
to *Enterprise*—"

"Already done, sir."

Ael blinked. "Intrepid," Scotty's voice said, "*this is* Enterprise—"

"I'm here, Scotty," Jim said. "Don't stop for discussion. Do it!"

"*Aye, sir.*" And Scotty switched off.

"Timings, sir—"

"I am adding them now," Suvuk said. The bridge doors opened and
Spock came hurriedly in, followed by Sehlk. "Sir, what we are—" they
both said, practically in unison, to Jim and Suvuk respectively.

"What a fascinating program," Suvuk said mildly. "Mr. Sehlk, pass
these phaser settings and photon torpedo dispersal patterns on to the
weapons officer at once. Do you see the ingenuity of it, madam, gentlemen? The ionization effect propagates from the star's coronal dis-
charges, but in a spiral pattern like a pulsar's series of 'rotating'
wavefronts. Of course we shall have to get quite close to that star, inside
the warp boundary in fact; but paradoxically the stimulation of the corona will keep the stellar chromosphere from being overstimulated, a
most elegant—"

"Sir," Sehlk said, in a voice that sounded much more like Jim's than
like Spock's; and Suvuk turned, looking calmly at his first officer with
an expression more like Spock's than like Jim's. Ael raised one hand to
hide her mouth. "*Enterprise* reports ready."

"Mr. Sehlk, a word with my ship, if I may?"

Sehlk nodded at the 'com console, and the Vulcan communications officer looked up at Jim. *"Scott here,"* said that oddly-accented voice.

"Just this, Scotty. Be careful not to set up a backlash effect—this is *not* the time to go back in time twenty-four hours!"

*"Aye, indeed, Captain,"* Scotty said, as close to laughter as Ael had heard him in some time. *"Good luck to you. And to* Intrepid.*"*

"The same from them," Jim said, looking at Suvuk's calm face. "Out."

*"Battlequeen* is closing in on us, Captain," said Sehlk. "One light-minute and closing."

"Implement the ion-storm maneuver, then," said Suvuk.

The ship's great warp engines began to roar. Ael, glancing at Jim, noticed that he had found himself an empty station and had closed the anti-roll arms down over his thighs: Spock was doing so on the other side of the room. Ael sat down at one of the security stations and did the same. Suvuk, hanging on to things all the way down, found his way to the center seat.

"Computer lock on the star," Suvuk said. "Shut down ship's sensors for the closest part of the pass. Screen off."

It was just as well, for they were already closer to the Levaeri primary than Ael had ever wanted to be to any star; she could see its corona already beginning to flare and twist wildly at their approach. Unfortunately, there was now no telling except by report how *Bloodwing* was doing, or how close *Battlequeen* was getting. . . .

Ael began to sweat. The thought of Lyirru blowing them all up was bad, but the thought of him getting hold of them and taking them back to ch'Rihan was worse still. *O, Elements,* she thought, *if it has to be one or the other, let him blow us up!* Then she rebuked herself; perhaps the *Enterprise* people would prefer to survive, on the grounds that while there was life there was hope. *They may have something there,* she thought. *I have never seen such a lot of survivors. . . .*

The bridge doors hissed open again, and there was McCoy hobbling in, with his left leg in a light pressure cast. He walked slowly over to where Jim was sitting, braced himself firmly against the rail, and said, "Broken fibula. I told you this'd happen some day."

"Doctor," Ael said, laughing at him, "if you have been predicting such an occurrence for so long, why are you surprised that it happened?"

"As for *you*," McCoy said, "with this damn fool idea of yours, let me tell you, young lady. . . ."

Ael said nothing, but the look Jim traded with her told her that she had been admitted to a very exclusive group: those people McCoy would rant at. She let him rant, and nodded contritely in all the right places, and otherwise concentrated on what was going on.

"One hundred million kilometers from the star," Sehlk said. "Ninety million . . . sixty . . . thirty . . ." *At this speed,* Ael thought, amazed, *if I blink I'll miss it. . . .* And indeed, a second later, everything seemed to happen at once. *Enterprise* and *Intrepid* dove into the star's corona together; *Intrepid* shook hugely as she first hit the star's bowshock at multiples of the speed of light, then created another of her own, trailing jointly behind her and *Enterprise.* The ship lurched again, and again, as photon torpedoes and phasers fired. Then a third terrible lurch of heaviness, and stomach-turning lightness, and normal weight again, as the artificial gravity wavered, the ship malfunctioned in trying to compensate for the star's terrible mass, and slowly went back to normal again.

"Report," Suvuk said, as calmly as if he did this every day.

"*Enterprise* reports intact, Captain," said Sehlk. "Maneuver complete. *Helve* and *Lahai* are far behind, not even in the area. *Battlequeen* is hitting the bowshock of the ion storm now—"

"Force reading, please."

"Force twelve and escalating."

"Evidently you were right, Commander," Suvuk said to Ael. "It is more effective with two starships. They are getting rather worse than they gave us as a distraction."

"Communication from *Bloodwing,* Commander t'Rllaillieu," said the comm officer. "They report they are cutting across our hyperbola to meet us, ahead of the ion storm. Rendezvous in approximately four minutes—"

"Thank you," Ael said.

"*Battlequeen* is slowing somewhat, Captain," said Sehlk. "Possibility that her navigations are going out on her due to the extreme intensity of the storm—"

"Intrepid, *this is* Enterprise," said Scotty's voice.

"This is *Intrepid,*" Jim said, at a nod from the Vulcan comm officer. "How's she riding, Scotty?"

"*Smooth enough so far,*" Scotty said, "*but we'd best pour it on a bit. That lad behind us isn't taking no for an answer; he's come through the far side of the bow-shock and he's accelerating again. Maintaining warp eleven cruise speed on the eta Trianguli course.*"

"Noted, *Enterprise,* we will match you," Suvuk said. "Screen on, Sehlk. Deflector shields up; phasers ready. Commander, can *Bloodwing* maintain a warp eleven cruise?"

"Not for more than a few minutes, Captain," she said. Her hands had been sweating now for several minutes over just that issue.

"Very well. *Enterprise, Bloodwing* cannot match warp eleven. I suggest we maneuver close enough together to allow a joint warpfield, and take her into it."

"*Captain Suvuk,*" Scotty said, sounding very distressed, "*with all due respect, that's extraordinarily dangerous for two ships of the same model, let alone ones with different engine specs—*"

"—which we now have," Suvuk said. "Granted, Mr. Scott, but we cannot leave *Bloodwing* behind, either. Do you wish to speak to your captain?"

"*Not now,*" Scotty said, "*but I will later. . . . Implementing, sir. Scott out.*"

Suvuk looked at Jim with calm approval. "Sir, have you ever noticed that while we run our ships, our engineers own them? . . ."

Ael watched the slow smile cross Jim's face. He said nothing, only turned back to the screen.

"Rear view," Sehlk said. And there was *Enterprise,* great and shining, all white fire and stark black shadows from the Levaeri primary, and growing dimmer as they fled the system. She was getting quite close . . . pulling up alongside the *Intrepid* now, the two of them streaking along much closer together than any two ships traveling at warpspeed had any right to be. "Coming up on *Bloodwing*'s position." Sehlk said. "She is accelerating to warp eleven to meet us. —Warpfield match with *Enterprise*—"

*Intrepid* lurched again, a violent motion that made the earlier shaking seem very mild. "Warpfield match with *Bloodwing*," Sehlk said—and this time even a few of the Vulcans went flying about the bridge.

Not Suvuk; he might as well have been glued into his center seat. "Match complete," he said. "Lieutenant T'Khia, head for the Zone, eta Trianguli course—"

"*Battlequeen* gaining on us again, Captain," Sehlk said. "Warp twelve . . . warp thirteen . . ."

"We cannot long maintain our lead," Suvuk said, looking over at Jim and Ael, "not while they pursue at warp thirteen."

"Fourteen now," said Sehlk. Spock looked across the bridge at Jim and shook his head, ever so slightly.

"Recommendations, Captain? Commander?" Suvuk said.

"Not to be taken, sir." Jim said.

"Commander?"

"I agree."

"My ship has such orders already," Jim said.

Suvuk nodded.

"*Battlequeen* is once more at one light-minute," Sehlk said. "One-half light-minute—"

"Captain," Suvuk said, "by the way—though thanks are said by some to be illogical—thank you for another three hours of life."

Jim bowed where he sat, straightened again. "My only regret is that I could not return you to your ship before this," Suvuk said quietly. "Or you to yours, Commander."

"The fortunes of war, sir," she said.

"If fortune exists," Suvuk said. "And if this is war. At any rate, I thank you also, Commander. It has been an unexpected—gratification—to discover that our cousins may also be our brothers."

Ael bowed her head too.

"One-tenth light-minute," Sehlk said into the great quiet of the bridge.

"*Enterprise,*" Jim said.

"*Aye,*" Scotty's voice came back—and that was all he said.

"*Bloodwing,*" Ael said.

"*Commander—*"

"Wait for it," Ael said softly. "We shall meet shortly."

"Four light-seconds," said Sehlk.

Ael saw Jim look across the bridge at Spock, a long glance, then another one, up at McCoy. And then at the screen, toward the empty space ahead of them, toward the border of the Zone, that they would never reach.

"One light-second," Sehlk said. "She's firing—"

The ship rocked. And rocked again, but not with the same sort of response. Someone was firing phasers near their warpfield, distorting it from the leading side.

"Contacts—" Sehlk cried. "ID's—"

But Ael sat up in her seat with a cry. There was no identifying them by shape, those white streaks that fled past them, lancing the starry night with fire; but she knew what they were. "*Constellation,*" Mr. Sehlk said, "and behind it, *Inaieu*—"

Ael turned and stared at Jim in astonishment. He was still staring at the screen, as if turning might change what had been. "They're firing," said Sehlk. "*Battlequeen* is turning to engage *Constellation*. Firing at her—"

He flicked a switch, reversed the screen. Behind them a sudden great flare and violence of light appeared, spreading outward and outward. Very slowly, Sehlk sat down at his station.

"*Inaieu* fired at *Battlequeen* point blank *en passant,*" he said, "*Battlequeen* is destroyed."

"What about *Inaieu?*" Jim said, not looking away from the screen.

"Intrepid," said the 'com. "*This is* Inaieu. *Suvuk, you old villain, where have you been? Shirking again?*"

"Without a doubt, Nhauris," said Suvuk. "Just as at Organia."

"Nhauris," Jim said, "nice job."

"*I keep my appointments,*" the Denebian said, and laughed her bubbly laugh. "*Let's get across the Zone, gentlemen, before more of the Romulans notice that the silver is missing. Inaieu out.*"

"Reduce speed, T'Khia" said Suvuk, "and set a course."

"Aye, sir."

Ael got free of her seat and went over to Jim, unable to stand it anymore. He looked away from the screen and regarded her with a truly insufferable smile.

"How did you do that?" she cried. "You called it to the minute, to the second, in all these light-years of space? How?"

He did not answer her but McCoy, who was looking at him in an astonishment as great as hers, but quieter. "You did tell me," Jim said mildly, "that I should have more confidence in my game. . . ."

# Chapter Nineteen

**CAPTAIN'S LOG, Stardate 7516.3:**

*"According to our patrol orders, we are continuing Neutral Zone patrol until such time as the starships* Potemkin *and* Hood *arrive to relieve the task force.*

*"The Zone has been unusually quiet since we left Romulan space. Captain Rihaul has speculated that this had to do with our possession not only of the pirated Vulcan genetic material (which the Romulans may fear we will use against them) but the Sunseed ion-storm generation program, very obviously worked out in their own programming languages and protocols, on their media, and with much documentation concerning the Romulan High Command's complicity with the Senate and Praetorate in the alteration of the weather hereabouts. We suspect we will not be hearing much out of the Zone for a while, as the Empire becomes busy shaking itself up.*

*"I am entering requests for special commendations for the following personnel: First Officer Spock, Montgomery Scott, Lieutenant Commander Harb Tanzer, Lieutenant Commander Nyota Uhura, Lieutenant Commander Hikaru Sulu, Lieutenant Pavel Chekov. There are many, many others on the general commendations list (see attached).*

*"Meanwhile, the crew of* Bloodwing *(formerly ChR* Bloodwing*) are preparing to depart. If it were possible to request a commendation for their commander, Ael t'Rllaillieu, I would do so. She has at all times exhibited an integrity and courage which give the lie to many of our cherished old myths about Romulans."*

. . . And there he stopped, apparently unsure what to say next, or whether to say anything. He clicked the viewer off. "Ael," Jim said, "where *are* you headed?"

She turned to him from studying the medical scanner over one of the beds in sickbay, where they had been taking care of the worst injured of her people with McCoy. "There is a lot of space," she said, "that neither Federation nor Empire owns; a lot of planets where a trim ship can make its own way, hiring out as a mercenary ship, a free trader . . . perhaps a pirate. . . ."

"Ael! . . ."

"Oh come," she said. "You know me better than that by now. Or you should."

He swung back and forth gently in the chair. "Space hereabouts will not be safe for us," Ael said, looking up at the scanner again. "We have exposed the mind-researches and Sunseed, and destroyed a great deal of supposedly indestructible Romulan material. Very embarrassing. They will not dare to strike at you in revenge—even if they find themselves able to get at you. Rihannsu have no luck with *Enterprise*, that's certain. . . ."

"The Vulcans would be glad to have you," Jim said. "If Spock's and Suvuk's word weren't enough—and I assure you they are—you've done more for that species—"

"I did not do it for them," Ael said. "I did it for my Empire, and my oaths. I will not take coincidental thanks, or gratitude that is offered me for the wrong reasons."

Her eyes rested on the door to the other room, where McCoy was working. "What about him?" Jim said quietly.

"He will not live," Ael said, her back turned. "My doing."

Jim looked at the table. "You can't blame yourself—"

"It is not a question of blame." Her voice was calm enough, but oh, the bitterness buried in it. "It's merely the way the universe is, the way the Elements are. Become careless with Fire, and sure enough, Fire will burn you. Do treachery, and treachery will be done you. Kill, and be punished with death. All these I've done. Now I pay the price, in my own flesh and blood. And more: for I'll die far from home, unless I dare the ban in my old age, and walk on ch'Rihan again, to be killed by the first person who recognizes me. And there will be no child or friend to hang up the name-flag for me before I die; no family, no one but my faithful crew who go into exile with me. Family . . . but not the same.

Never the same." She looked at him, almost in pity now. "And I would do it again, all of it. You still don't understand. . . ."

Jim looked up at her sorrowfully, again unable to find anything useful to say. "When will you be leaving?" he said at last.

"Ten or fifteen minutes."

"I'll meet you in the transporter room."

Jim went out.

It was a relief, like a weight lifted, when he was gone. But the worse weight came right down on her as McCoy came out of the next room, and looked at her, and shook his head slightly.

"His brainstem and spine were severely damaged," McCoy said. "Nonregenerable. He'll die if he's taken off support."

"And if he is not?"

"A few days of pain. A few hours, if he's lucky."

"But the same result."

"Yes." McCoy's voice was quiet, and very sad.

Ael bowed her head and went in.

There he lay, looking waxen already; and the pulled-up blanket only accentuated the place where his right arm had been. She stood by the bed a long time before speaking.

She could not see him as he was, close to death. All she could see was ten years ago, twenty years, forty: a child waving a toy sword and saying he would be like his mother. So he had been; and this was where the likeness had led him.

"You saw my writings," Tafv said, a thread of voice, thinned to breaking.

Ael nodded. His room's computer had been full of them. Years he had been planning this revenge for his beloved cousin. Oaths did not stand in his way when his opportunity arose, any more than they had stood in Ael's way when she saw her chance to betray Levaeri V, and *Cuirass,* and all the others. He had been preparing for that opportunity for a long time, suborning the newer members of her crew with money and the promise of power; and the delivery of *Enterprise* into his hands had seemed to Tafv to be a gift from the Elements. What he would have done with it, and with her, that Ael knew from his writings too. He would have become rich, and famous, and powerful in Command. She would have been swiftly a prisoner, and then a corpse. He had never forgiven her for falling silent before the Senate, for ceasing to try to save his cousin, the young commander, though the attempt might have killed her, and Ael too.

"I did what I had to do," he said. "I would do it again. It was *mnhei'sahe*."

"I understand," she said.

"Now you must also do what *mnhei'sahe* requires," he said. And the effort exhausted him, so that he lay gasping.

She stood a long time before she could agree. And then she did what she had to; for treachery had no payment but death.

When she went out again, McCoy stood aside for her, not moving, not speaking. She paused long enough to trade a long glance with him.

"Thank you," she said, and left.

And then there was only one more barrier: the transporter room, where Jim waited. At least there was no one else there.

"Spock asked me to make his farewells for him," Jim said.

"He is a prize, that one," she said. "All the Elements walk beside you in him. Take all care of him—and thank him well for me."

"I will."

She turned toward the platform. Jim made a small abortive motion that somehow made Ael stop.

"You never did tell me what 'Jim' meant," he said.

Ael looked at the closed door, and at the intercom to see that it was off, and she told him.

He started to laugh—very hard, as might have been expected—and to her own great surprise, Ael started to laugh with him. "Oh," Jim said after several minutes, "Oh, oh, no wonder. . . ."

"Yes."

He stood there with his arms folded—a gesture left over from the way he had been hugging himself while he laughed; seemingly to keep from hurting his stomach, or because it already hurt. This man . . .

"Now let me tell you what 'Ael' means," she said, glancing again at the closed door. She told him. She told him what the second name meant, and the third. And then—very quietly—the fourth.

He looked at her and said nothing at all. It seemed to be his day for it.

Ael stepped up onto the transporter platform, and waited for him to step around to the controls. The singing whine scaled up and up in the little room. And bright fire began to dissolve them; the overdone little room in the great white ship, and the man who had no fourth name to give her in return.

*But no,* she thought. *He* has *a fourth. And he gave me not just the name— but what it names.* Her . . . *whole and entire.*

To her relief, and her anguish, the transporter effect took her away before she could move to match him, daring for daring, with an equal gift.

# Chapter Twenty

Jim stood there quietly for a good fifteen minutes, considering the words he had been told, especially the fourth one—considering the nature of the sword that had cut him. *Entirely appropriate,* he thought, remembering Ael in Spock's quarters. After all, a sword was a thing of air and fire; and it was almost universally true that, with the best swords, you might not even know you'd been cut until you began to bleed. . . .

He left the transporter room, heading for the bridge: something familiar, something his, something he could control.

Something he had not lost.

It was two months' work, getting back to Earth this time, and then several days of dull and depressing debriefing on the Levaeri incident.

He put up with it all; it was part of the price of captaincy, after all. But his mind was elsewhere, especially on the last day.

By luck, or something else, the debriefing that day was at Fleet San Francisco, and the *Enterprise* was right overhead in synchronous orbit. He got out of the offices around five, went out into the fog, and called Spock; then once aboard, went down to his quarters to pick up the small object he was after, and take it right back to the transporter room.

The transporter chief had left—which suited Jim well. He paused only long enough to bring up a visual of Earth on the screen and note with satisfaction that the terminator had crept barely past the California coast; Seattle and San Francisco and Los Angeles were tiny golden spatters against a velvet darkness ever so faintly silvered with moonlight. *Perfect,* he thought, killing the screen. Jim set the transporter for the coordinates he wanted, checked his belt for his communicator, and set the console for delayed-energize.

When the shimmer died he looked around him a bit warily—he

hadn't been to these coordinates in years, and there was no telling how much the place might have changed. But he was pleasantly surprised to see that it was no different at all. Jim was surrounded by high hills, soft rounded shapes covered with scrub oak and manzanita, wild olive and piñon pine, and here and there a palm. The cooling air was sweet with sage and with the wet green smell of the creek in the gully to his right. It ran where it had run, where it should run, whispering around what seemed the same old stones. Jim smiled. Sometimes, just sometimes, things stayed the way they were supposed to.

He began to walk along the top of the gully, upstream, toward the creek's source. A long time it was since he had last been here at Sespe. Once it had been a condor preserve, hundreds of years ago when the great birds were in danger of becoming extinct. Now that they flourished, Sespe was just another part of the North American Departmental Wilderness that surrounded it—a trackless, houseless place, accessible only on foot, or by transporter. Indeed Jim could have beamed directly to the place where he was headed but he wouldn't have had time to get in the mood for what he had in mind. He started off into the great silence, moving as softly as he could; for there was no sound anywhere but the bare breathing of the wind, and his footsteps seemed too loud for the twilit sanctity of this place.

He passed other streambeds in the gathering dusk. They were dry, as well they might have been this time of year. But the watercourse Jim followed as he trudged up the hill was not affected by the weather. Breathing a bit harder than usual with the steady exertion, Jim kept climbing, making his way around the shoulder of one hill, crossing the stream with a splash and a shock of cold when he found this side blocked with an old rockfall. Another twist in the watercourse, and then one more—

Jim stopped. It was exactly the same, *exactly*. From the side of a high, dark hill, water sprang, slowing down as if from a smitten rock; and above the spring-source, growing straight out of the sheer hillside and then curving upward, there was the tree. It had apparently known some hard times since Jim had seen it last. It was lightning-blasted, this old twisted olive, so that branches were missing at the top; and the claw-

marks of black bears, their calling cards for one another, were scored
deep and ragged down its trunk. But the tree survived. Its roots were
still sunk deep in the heart of the hill, and the sharp aromatic scent of
its ripening fruit hung on the still air. Jim looked up at the tree with
silent approval and began to climb toward it.

Reaching it took some doing—the stones of the hillside were
loose—but Jim persevered. Finally he reached the great horizontal
trunk, swung himself up onto it and stepped out to where the tree's
branches began to curve outward. One strong branch thick with olives
reached out over the spring; the smell of splashing water and of new
fruit mingled, a cool spicy scent of life. *Here,* Jim thought, *right here.* He
took out the small bundle he had brought with him from the ship, un-
tied the cord around it, and shook out the little pennon—a strip of sup-
ple woven polymer that would hang here and last through years of
wind and rain, unchanged. Fasteners—Jim felt in his pocket for them,
threaded the polymer strips through the eyelets in the pennon, then
reached out to hold them shut around the tree branch one at a time,
melting them shut with bursts from his phaser on its lowest notch.

Then down the tree again, and back to his vantage point by the
streambed. The pennon hung down, swinging very slightly in a breath
of breeze that came down over the hillside—the pennon's scarlet
muted in this darkness to an ember-gray, the black characters on it
hardly visible except as blurs of shadow. Jim looked up at the sky. Not
much of it was visible, hemmed about as he was by hills; but the
brightest stars were out already, and others followed. The summer Triangle, Deneb and Vega and Altair, lay westering low. Jim smiled slightly
at Deneb, then let his eyes drift on northward through the base of the
Triangle, following the faint band of the Milky Way and the Galactic
Equator through Cygnus into Lacerta, Cassiopeia, Andromeda. There
was beta Andromedae; then a bit southward . . . Jim stood and waited
for his eyes to get used to the gathering darkness. He knew he wouldn't
be able to see the star he was looking toward, anyway. But right now,
sight, or eyesight anyway, wasn't an issue. He waited.

And when he felt the moment was right, he drew himself straight
and spoke her name the necessary five times—the fourth name by

which only one closer than kin might know her, the name by which one was known to the Elements and Their rulers. One time each he spoke that name for the Earth, the Air, the Fire, the Water; and once for the Archelement which encompassed them all, that It might hear and grant the weary soul a home in this place when at last that soul flew. The fifth time he said that name, the wind died. A listening stillness fell over everything. Jim didn't move.

That was when the great dark shape came sailing over the hill-top, low; planing down over the stream on twelve-foot pinions, black-feathered, showing the wide white coverts under the wings; a dark visitation of silence, grace, freedom, flight, indifference. Riding its thermal, the condor swept over Jim's head, a shadow between him and the stars. It tilted its head as it passed—a glance, no more, a silhouette motion and a look from invisible eyes. Then it leaned to its port side, banked away on the thermal, was over the next hill, was gone.

*The sigil-beast of my House,* she had said.

*A big, ugly scavenger . . . but nothing can match it when it flies. . . .*

Jim stared after it, and let out a small breath of bemusement, uncertainty, wonder. *How about that,* he thought. The night breeze began to blow again; bound to the olive branch, the name-flag stirred.

Jim pulled out his communicator. "Kirk to *Enterprise.*"

*"Spock here."*

"Mr. Spock, have someone get down to the transporter room and beam me up."

*"Yes, Captain."* There was a pause. Jim got the feeling that Spock was glancing around the bridge to make sure no one was listening, for when he spoke again, his voice was private and low. *"Jim—are you all right?"*

"I'm fine." Jim looked down at the watercourse, the way the dark apparition had gone, and for the first time in days, actually felt relieved. The feeling was very belated. He didn't care; he embraced it. "Mr. Spock . . . you don't suppose there might be some spot in the galaxy where we're needed right now, do you?"

*"Captain,"* the calm voice came back, *"our new patrol-information dispatches just received from Starfleet this past hour include news of two armed rebellions, a plague, and a mail strike; various natural disasters attributed to acts of*

*deity, and unnatural ones attributed to inflation, accident and the breakdown of diplomacy; seventeen mysterious disappearances of persons, places or things, both with and without associated distress calls; eight newly discovered species of humanity, three of which have declared their intention to annex Starfleet and the Federation, and one of which has announced that it will let us alone if we pay it tribute. And probably most serious of all, a tribble predator has gotten loose from the zoo in a major city on Arcturus VI, and for lack of its natural prey has started eating peoples' cats."*

Jim paused. "Well, Mr. Spock," he said, very seriously, "it's going to take us at least a week to get all that cleared up. I think we'd better get out there and get started, don't you?"

*"Undoubtedly, Captain. Energizing."*

The world faded into the golden shimmering of the transporter effect.

The pennon stirred again, saying one dark word, a name, to the wind, in the strong Rihannsu calligraphy.

Starlight glinted on the swift water. And one small star slowly subtracted itself from that light, soaring more and more swiftly outward, past the setting sickle moon and into the ancient night.

PART TWO

# The Romulan Way

For the collaborator . . .

. . . isn't it *great?*

# NOTE

The document following is a print-medium transcription of the "subjective-conceptual history" work *The Romulan Way*, copyright © Terise Haleakala-LoBrutto. The material originally appeared in substantially different form in *The Journal of the Federation Institute for the Study of Xenosociology*, Vol. LXII, Numbers 88–109.

# FOREWORD

Among many issues we are still unsure of, one fact makes itself super-evident: they were *never* "Romulans."

But one hundred years after our first tragic encounters with them, that is what we still call them. The Rihannsu find this a choice irony. Among the people of the Two Worlds, words, and particularly names, have an importance we have trouble taking seriously. A Rihanha asked about this would say that we have been interacting, not with them and their own name as it really is, but with a twisted word/name, an *aehallh* or monster-ghost, far from any true image. And how can one hope to prosper in one's relationships if they are spent talking to false images in the belief that they are real?

Over eight years of life among the Rihannsu has dispelled some of the ghosts for me, but not all. Even thinking in their language is not enough to completely subsume the observer into that fierce, swift, incredibly alien mindset, born of a species bred to war, seemingly destined to peace, and then self-exiled to develop a bizarre synthesis of the two. It may be that only our children, exchanged with theirs in their old custom of *rrh-thanai,* hostage-fostering, will come home to us knowing not only their foster families' minds, but their hearts. And we will of course be shocked, after the fashion of parents everywhere, to find that our children are not wholly our own anymore. But if we can overcome that terror and truly listen to what those children say and do in our councils afterward, the wars between our peoples may be over at last.

Meanwhile, they continue, and this work is one of their by-products. It was begun as a mere piece of intelligence—newsgathering for a Federation frightened of a strange enemy and wanting weapons to turn against it from the inside. What became of the work, and the one who did it, makes a curious tale that will smack of expediency, opportunism, and treason to some that read it . . . mostly those unfamiliar with the exigencies of deep-cover work in hostile territory. Others may think they see that greatest and most irrationally feared of occupational hazards for sociologists—the scientist "going native." By way of dismissal, let me say that the presumption that one mindset is superior to another—an old one to a new one, a familiar one to a strange—is a value judgment of the rankest sort, one in which any sociologist would normally be ashamed to be caught . . . if his wits were about him. But for some reason this single loophole has been exempted from the rule, and the sociologist-observer's mindset is somehow supposed to remain unaltered by what goes on around him. Of this dangerous logical fallacy, let the reasoner beware.

The raw data that the observer was sent to gather is detailed in separate sections from those which tell how she gathered it. This way, those minded to skip the incidental history of the gathering may do so. But for those interested not only in the why of research among the Rihannsu but in the how as well, there is as much information about the culmination of those eight years as the Federation will allow to be released at this time. I hope that this writing may do something to hasten the day when our children will come home from summer on ch'Rihan and ch'Havran and tell us much more, including the important things, the heartmatters that cause Federations and Empires to blush and turn away, muttering that it's not their business.

About that, they will be right. It is not their business, but ours; for there are no governments, only people. May the day when they will fully be true come swiftly.

                                          Terise Haleakala-LoBrutto

# Chapter One

Arrhae ir-Mnaeha t'Khellian yawned, losing her sleep's last dream in the tawny light that lay warm across her face, bright on her eyelids. She was reluctant to open her eyes, both because of the golden-orange brightness outside them, and because Eisn's rising past her windowsill meant she had overslept and was late starting her duties. But there was no avoiding the light, and no avoiding the work. She rubbed her eyes to the point where she could open them, and sat up on her couch.

It was courtesy and euphemism to call anything so hard and plain a couch: but then, it could hardly be expected to be better. Being set in authority over the other servants and slaves did not entitle her to such luxuries as stuffed cushions and woven couch fittings. It was the stone pillow for Arrhae, and a couch of triple-thickness leather and white-wood, and a balding fur or two in far-sun weather: nothing more. And to be truthful, anything more would have sorted ill with the austerity of her room. It was no more than a place to wash and to sleep, preferably without dreams.

Arrhae sighed. She was much better off than most other servants in the household: but even for the sake of the chief servant, the House could not in honor afford to make toward the *hfehan* any gesture that might be construed as indulgence. *Or comfort,* Arrhae thought, rubbing at the kinks in her spine and looking with loathing toward the 'fresher—which as often as not ran only with cold water. Still, she did at least *have* one. And there was even a mirror, though that had been purchased with her own meager store of money. It wasn't so much a luxury as a necessity, for House Khellian had rigid standards of dress for its servants. Those who supervised them were expected to set a good example.

And the one who supervised everything was *not* supposed to be last to appear in the morning. Arrhae went looking hurriedly for the scraping-stone. Granted that this morning's lateness was her first significant fall from grace; but having achieved a position of trust, Arrhae was reluctant to lose it by provoking the always-uncertain temper of her employer.

H'daen tr'Khellian was one of those middle-aged, embittered Praetors whose inherited rank and wealth had placed him where he was, but whose inability to make powerful friends—or more correctly, from what she had seen, to make friends at all—had prevented him from rising any further. In the Empire there were various means by which elevation could be attained through merit, or through . . . well, "pressure" was the polite term for it. But H'daen had no military honors in his past that he could use as influence, and no political or personal secrets to employ as leverage when influence failed. Even his wealth, though sufficient to keep this fine house in an appropriate style, fell far short of that necessary to buy Senatorial support and patronage. His home was a popular place to visit, much frequented by "acquaintances" who were always on the brink of tendering support for one Khellian project or another. But somehow the promised support never materialized, and Arrhae had too often overheard chance comments that told her it never would.

She stood there outside the 'fresher door with the scraping-stone and the oil bottle clutched in one hand, while she waved the other hopelessly around in the spray zone, waiting for a change in temperature. There was no use waiting: the 'fresher was running cold again, and Arrhae clambered in and made some of the fastest ablutions of her life. When she got out, her teeth were clattering together, and her skin had been blanched by the cold to several shades paler than its usual dusky olive. She scrubbed at herself with the rough bathfelt, and finally managed to stop her teeth chattering, then was almost sorry she had. The sounds of a frightful argument, violent already and escalating, were floating in from the kitchen, two halls and an anteroom away. She started struggling hurriedly into her clothes: she was still damp, and they clung to her and fought her and wrinkled. The uproar increased. She thought of how horrible it would be if the Head of House should stumble into the *fhaihuhhru* going on out there, and not find her there stopping it, or, more properly, keeping it from happening. *O Elements, avert it!*

"Stupid *hlai*-brained drunken wastrel!" someone shrieked from two halls and an anteroom away, and the sound made the paper panes in the window buzz. Arrhae winced, then gave up and clenched her fists and squeezed her eyes shut and swore.

This naturally made no difference to the shouting voices, but the momentary blasphemy left Arrhae with a sort of crooked satisfaction. As servants' manager, *hru'hfe,* she monitored not only performance but propriety, the small and large matters of honor that for slave or master were the lifeblood of a House. It was a small, wicked pleasure to commit the occasional impropriety herself: it always discharged more tension than it had a right to. Arrhae was calmer as she peeled herself out of her kilt and singlet and then, much more neatly, slipped back into them. Pleats fell as they should, her chiton's draping draped properly. She checked her braid, found it intact—at least *something* was behaving from the very start this morning. Then she stepped outside to face whatever briefly interesting enterprise the world held in store.

The argument escalated as she got closer to it. Bemused, then tickled by the noise, Arrhae discarded fear. If tr'Khellian himself were there, she would sweep into the scene and command it. If not—she considered choice wordings, possible shadings of voice and manner calculated to raise blisters. She smiled. She killed the smile, lest she meet someone in the hall while in such unseemly mirth. Then, *"Eneh hwai'kllhwnia na imirrhlhhse!"* shouted a voice, Thue's voice, and the obscenity stung the blood into Arrhae's cheeks and all the humor out of her. The door was in front of her. She seized the latch and pulled it sideways, hard.

The force of the pull overrode the door's friction-slides dramatically: it shot back in its runners as if about to fly out of them, and fetched up against its stops with a very satisfying crash. Heads snapped around to stare, and a dropped utensil rang loudly in the sudden silence. Arrhae stood in the doorway, returning the stares with interest.

"His father never did *that,*" she said, gentle-voiced. "Certainly not with a *kllhe:* it would never have stood for it." She moved smoothly past Thue and watched with satisfaction as her narrow face colored to dark emerald, as well it should have. "Pick up the spoon, Thue," she said without looking back, "and be glad I don't have one of the ostlers use it on your back. See that you come talk to me later about language fit for a great House, where a guest might hear you, or the Lord." She felt the angry, frightened eyes fixed on her back, and ignored them as she walked into the big room.

Arrhae left them standing there with their mouths open, and started prowling around the great ochre-tiled kitchen. It was in a mess, as she had well suspected. House breakfast was not for an hour yet, and it was just as well, because the coals weren't even in the grill, nor the earthenware pot fired or even scoured for the Lord's fowl porridge. *I must get up earlier. Another morning like this will be the ruin of the whole domestic staff. Still, something can be saved*—"I have had about enough," she said, running an idle hand over the broad clay tiles where meat was cut, "of this business with your daughter, Thue, and your son, HHirl. Settle it. Or I will have it settled for you. Surely they would be happier staying here than sold halfway around the planet. And they're not so bad for each other, truly. Think about it."

The silence in the kitchen got deeper. Arrhae peered up the chimney at the puddings and meatrolls hung there for smoking, counted them, noticed two missing, thought a minute about who in the kitchen was pregnant, decided that she could cover the loss, and said nothing. She wiped the firing-tiles with three fingers and picked up a smear of soot that should never have been allowed to collect, then cleaned her fingers absently on the whitest of the hanging polishing cloths, one that should have been much cleaner. The smear faced rather obviously toward the kitchen staff, all gathered together now by the big spit roaster and looking like they thought they were about to be threaded on it. "The baked goods only half started," said Arrhae gently, "and the roast ones not yet started, and the strong and the sweet still in the coldroom, and fastbreak only an hour from now. But there must have been other work in hand. Very busy at it, you must have been. So busy that you could spend the most important part of the working morning in discussion. I'm sure the Lord will understand, though, when his meal is half an hour late. *You* may explain it to him, Thue."

The terrified rustle gratified Arrhae—not for its own sake, but because she could hear silent mental resolutions being made to get work done in the future. Arrhae suppressed her smile again. She had seen many Rihannsu officers among the people who came to H'daen's house, and had profitably taken note of their methods. Some of them shouted, some of them purred: she had learned to use either method, and occasionally both. She dropped the lid back onto a pot of overboiled porridge with an ostentatious shudder that was only half feigned, and turned to narrow her eyes at Thue, the second cook, and tr'Aimne, the first one. "Or if you would prefer to bypass the explanations," she said, "I would start another firepot for the gruel, and use that fowl from yesterday, the batch we didn't cook, it's still good enough; the Lord won't notice, if you don't overcook it. If you do—" She fell silent, and peered into the dish processor: it, for a miracle, was empty—there were at least enough clean plates.

"I've heard you this morning," she said, shutting the processor's door. "Now you hear me. Put your minds to your work. Your Lord's honor rests as much with you as with his family. His honor rests as much in little things, scouring and cooking, as in great matters. Mind it—lest you find yourself caring for the honor of some hedge-lord in Iuruth with a hall that leaks rain and a byre for your bedroom."

The silence held. Arrhae looked at them all, not singling any one person out for eye contact, and went out through the great arched main doors that led to the halls and living quarters of the House. She didn't bother listening for the cursing and backbiting that would follow her exit: she had other things to worry about. For one, she should have reported to H'daen long before now. Arrhae made her way across the center court and into the wing reserved for tr'Khellian's private apartments, noting absently as she did so that two of the firepots in the lower corridor were failing and needed replacement, and that one of the tame *fvai* had evidently been indoors too long. . . . At least the busyness kept her from fretting too much.

The Lord's anteroom was empty, his bodyservants elsewhere on errands. Arrhae knocked on the couching-room door, heard the usual curt *"Ie,"* and stepped in.

"Fair morning, Lord," she said.

H'daen acknowledged her with no more than an abstracted grunt and a nod of the head that could have signified anything. He was absorbed in whatever was displayed on his reader; so absorbed that Arrhae felt immediately surplus to all requirements and would have faded decorously from the room had he not pointed at her and then rapped his finger on the table.

H'daen tr'Khellian was a man given to twitches, tics, and little gestures. This one meant simply "stay where you are," and Arrhae did just that, settling her stance so that she would not have to shift her weight to stay comfortable. She was mildly curious about what was on the reader screen, but she wasn't quite close enough to see its contents. At least there were no recriminations for lateness. Not yet, anyway.

"Wine," said H'daen, not looking up from the screen. Its glow was carving gullies of shadow into the wrinkled skin of his face, and though she had known it for long enough, as if for the first time Arrhae realized that he was old. Very old. It was affectation that he still wore his iron-gray hair in the fringed military crop, and dressed in boots and breeches more reminiscent of Fleet uniform than of any civilian wear. The affectation, and maybe the lost dream, of one who had never been anything worthy of note in the Imperial military and now, his hopes defeated by advancing years as they had been defeated by every other circumstance, never would. Arrhae looked at him as if through different eyes, and felt a stab of pity.

"Must I die of thirst?" H'daen snapped testily. "Give me the wine I asked for."

"At once, Lord." She went through the dim, worn tidiness of the couching room to the wine cabinet, and brought out a small urn good enough for morning but not so good as to provoke comment about waste. She brought down the Lord's white clay cup, noted with relief that it was scoured, brought it and the urn back to the table, and poured carefully, observing the proprieties of wine-drinking regardless of how parched H'daen might be. There were certain stylized ritual movements in the serving of the ancient drink, and if they were ignored, notice would be taken and ill luck surely follow. That was the story, anyway; whether there was any truth in something whose origins were lost in the confusion of legend and history that followed the Sundering was another matter entirely. Perhaps better to be safe; perhaps, equally, as well to honor the old ways in a time when the new ways had little of honor in them. She drew back the flask with that small, careful jerk and twist which prevented unsightly droplets of wine from staining her hands or the furnishings, set it down and stoppered it, and only then brought the cup to H'daen's desk.

He had been watching her, and as she approached he touched a control so that the reader's screen went dark and folded down out of sight. Arrhae didn't follow its movement with her eyes; it would have been most impolite, and besides, all her concentration was needed for the brimming winecup.

"You're a good girl, Arrhae," said H'daen suddenly. "I like you."

Arrhae set down the wine most carefully, not spilling any, and made the little half bow of courteous acceptance customary when presenting food or drink, to acknowledge the thanks of the recipient. It might also have acknowledged H'daen's compliment—or then again, it might not have. It was always safer to be equivocal.

"You run my household well, Arrhae," H'daen continued eventually, "and I trust you."

He touched the shuttered reader with one fingertip, unaware of the worried look that had crept into her eyes. A plainly confidential communication, and unexpected talk of trust and liking, made up an uneasy conjunction of which she would as soon have no part. It had the poisonous taint of intrigue about it, of meddling in the affairs of the great and powerful; of hazard, and danger, and death. Arrhae began to feel afraid.

H'daen tr'Khellian tapped out a code on the reader's touchpad, and its screen rose once more from the desk's recess. He read again what glowed there in amber on black, shifted so that he could give Arrhae his full attention, and smiled at her. She kept the roil of emotion off her face with a great effort, and succeeded in looking only intent and eager as a good head-of-servants should. H'daen's smile seemed to promise so many things that she wanted no part of that when he finally spoke, the truth was anticlimactic.

"It appears that this house will have important guests before nightfall. There is much requiring my attention before I"—the smile crossed his face again—"have to play the host, so I leave all the arrangements for their reception in your hands. It is most important to me, to this House, and to everyone in it. Don't fail me, Arrhae. Don't fail us."

H'daen turned away to scan the reader-screen one last time, and so didn't notice the undisguised relief on Arrhae's face.

Ch'Rihan was a perilous place; it had always been so—plotting and subtlety was almost an integral part of both private and political life— but now with the new, youthful aggressiveness in the Senate and the High Command, suicide, execution, and simple, plain natural causes were far more frequent than they had ever been before, and neither lowly rank nor lofty were any defense. With what she already knew about H'daen's ambition, it would have horrified but not really surprised her had she been asked to slip poison into someone's food or drink. . . .

Some vestige of concern must have manifested itself in her face, because H'daen was staring at her strangely when her attention returned to him. "Uh, yes, my Lord," she ventured as noncommittally as she dared, trying not to sound as if she had missed anything else he had said to her.

"Then 'yes' let it be!" The acerbic edge was back in his voice, a tone far more familiar to her—to any in House Khellian—than the almost-friendly fashion in which he had spoken before. "I told you to do it, not think about it, and certainly not on my time or in my private rooms. Go!"

Arrhae went.

There had been guests at the house many times before, and both intimate dinners for a few and banquets for many; but this was the first time that Arrhae had been given so little notice of the event. At least she had complete control of organization and—more important—purchase of produce. Armed with an estimate of numbers of attending, quantities required, and a list of possible dishes that she had taken care to have approved, she set out with the chastened chief cook to do a little shopping.

The expedition involved more and harder work in a shorter time than Arrhae had experienced in a very long while—but it did have certain advantages. Foremost among those was the flitter. H'daen's authorization to use his personal vehicle was waiting for Arrhae when she emerged from the stores and pantries with a sheaf of notes in her hand and tr'Aimne in tow, and that authorization did as much to instill respect for her in the chief cook as any amount of severity and harsh language. None of the household staff were overly fond of H'daen tr'Khellian—but his temper had earned him wide respect.

Arrhae checked the usage-clearance documents several times before going closer than arm's length to the vehicle. Oh, she knew how to drive one—who didn't?—but given the present mood of the inner-city constables, she would sooner find an error or an oversight in the authorizations herself than let it be found by one of the traffic-control troopers. She listened to gossip, of course—again, who didn't?—but she gave small credence to the stories she had overheard from other high-house servants of strange goings-on in Command. Though there was always the possibility that Lhaesl tr'Khev had just been trying to impress her.

Arrhae smiled at *that* particular memory as she went through the vehicle-status sections of the documentation. Lhaesl was a good-looking young man, very good-looking indeed if one's tastes ran to floppy, clumsily endearing baby animals. He tried so very hard to be grown-up, and always failed—by not having lived long enough. On the last occasion that they met, he had managed to talk like a more or less sensible person in the intervals of fetching her a cup of ale and that plate of sticky little sweetmeats that had taken her so long to scrub from her fingers. She hadn't even liked the ale much, its harshness always left her throat feeling abraded, but to refuse the youngster's attentions with the brutality needed to make him notice would have been on the same level as kicking a puppy. So Arrhae had sat, sipping and coughing slightly, nibbling and adhering to things, and being a good listener as working for H'daen had taught her how. It was all nonsense, of course, a garble of starships and secrets, with important names scattered grandly through the narrative that would have meant much more to Arrhae had she known who these doubtless-worthy people were.

But gossip apart, there was an unspecified something wrong in i'Ramnau. Arrhae had visited the city twice in recent months, not then to buy and carry, but merely to supervise purchases that would later be delivered. Because of that she had traveled by *yhfiss'ue,* the less-than-loved public transport tubes. They always smelled—not bad, exactly, but odd; musty, as if they were overdue for a thorough washing inside and out. There had been times, especially when Eisn burned hot and close in the summer sky, when Arrhae would have dearly loved the supervising of the sanitary staff. That, however, was by the way. What had remained with her about those last journeys to the inner city was the difference between them. The first had been like all the others, boring, occasionally bumpy, and completely unremarkable. But the second . . .

That had been when the three tubecars had stopped, and settled, and been invaded by both city constables and military personnel, all with drawn sidearms. Arrhae had been very frightened. Her previous encounters with the Rihannsu military had been decorous meetings with officers of moderately high rank in House Khellian, where they were guests and she was responsible for their comfort. Then, looking down the bore of an issue blaster, the realization had been hammered home that not all soldiers were officers, and indeed that not all officers were gentlemen. What such uniformed brutes would do if they found her in a private flitter without complete and correct documentation didn't bear considering. . . .

She carded the papers at last and slipped them securely into her travel-tunic's pocket, then glanced at tr'Aimne, the cook. "Well, what are you waiting for?" she said in a fair imitation of H'daen tr'Khellian at his most irritable. "Get in!"

Without waiting for him, she popped the canopy and slipped sideways into the flitter's prime-chair, mentally reviewing the warmup protocols as she made herself comfortable. Once learned, never forgotten; while tr'Aimne was securing himself in the next seat—and being, she thought, as ostentatious as he dared about fastening his restraint harness—her fingers were already entering the clearance codes that would release the flitter's controls. Instrumentation lit up; all of it touch-pad operated systems rather than the modern voice-activators. H'daen's flitter might have been beautifully appointed inside, and fitted with a great many luxuries, but it was still, unmistakably, several years out-of-date. No matter, for today, old or not, it was hers.

Arrhae shifted the driver into first and felt a tiny lurch as A/G linears came on line to lift the flitter from its cradle. Ahead and above, the doors at the top of the ramp slid open, accompanying their movement with a dignified chime of warning gongs rather than the raucous hooting of sirens. H'daen was a man of taste, or considered himself as such, anyway. Out of the corner of her eye, Arrhae caught sight of tr'Aimne tightening his straps, and his lips moving silently. Tr'Aimne was not fond of driving, and little good at being driven. "You could get in the back if you really wanted to," Arrhae said. "That way you wouldn't have to watch. . . ."

Tr'Aimne said nothing, and didn't even look at her, but his knuckles went very pale where they gripped the harness-straps while his face flushed dark bronze-green. Arrhae shrugged, willing to let him brazen it out, and took the flitter out of the garage.

She didn't even do it as fast as she might have, but nonetheless tr'Aimne changed complexion again, for the worse. "Sorry," she said. It was of course too late to change the speed parameters—the master system had them, and in accordance with local speed laws, wouldn't let them be changed without groundbased countermand. "It won't be long," she said, but tr'Aimne made no reply. He was too busy holding on to the restraint straps and the grab-handles inside the flitter. Arrhae for her own part shrugged and kept her hands on the controls, just in case manual override might be needed. The system was fairly reliable, but sometimes it overloaded: and this was, after all, a holiday. . . .

With this in mind she had let the i'Ramnau traffic-control net have them from the very start of the trip rather than free-driving it: people did forget to file driveplans, and there had been some ugly accidents in the recent past on the city's high-level accessways. One of them had in fact resulted in her appointment as *hru'hfe s'Khellian,* and she would as soon not provide someone else with advancement by the same means.

The flitter brought them to i'Ramnau far faster than *yhfiss'ue* would have, and too fast for Arrhae's liking; she was enjoying herself as she had rarely since she began working for House Khellian. Both lifter and driver of the Varrhan-series flitters were more powerful than warranted by their size, and they were less vehicles to drive than to fly. Arrhae flew it, with great enthusiasm and considerable skill. When they grounded in the flitpark, and the far door popped, followed by tr'Aimne leaning out and making most unfortunate noises, she busied herself with her own straps and lists, and carefully didn't "notice."

Finally he was straightening his clothes and had most of his color back. "Are you all right?" she said.

"I . . . yes, *hru'hfe.* I think so." He coughed again, and then spat—close enough to her feet for insult's sake, and yet not close enough to let her make an issue of it.

Well, there it was, he certainly *had* taken it personally; and she didn't need a quarrel with the chief cook, not today of all days. Arrhae glanced at the spittle briefly, just long enough to make it clear she had noticed that its placing was no accident, and then looked at him wryly. "If I had *wanted* to make you unwell," she said, "I wouldn't have done so poor a job of it—you wouldn't be able to stand. Come, chief cook, pardon my eagerness. I so love to drive."

He nodded rather curtly, and together they gathered up the netbags for the few things they would be needing and headed for the market. Arrhae pushed the pace. They were already later than she would have preferred to be.

It was annoying that she had to be in such a Powers-driven hurry on Eitreih'hveinn, one of the nine major religious festivals of the Rihannsu year. No matter that the Farmers' Festival was one of her favorites: she had no time to enjoy it today. There was only one good thing about it, and Arrhae took full advantage—the produce for sale was going to be superb.

Tr'Aimne, to her mild annoyance, refused to enjoy the shopping trip. One would have thought the sight of so much gorgeous food would have filled any decent cook with joy, but he generally dragged along behind Arrhae rather like a wet cloak trailed on the ground. *Maybe he's still not well,* she thought, and slowed down a little for his sake. But it made no difference, tr'Aimne was incivility itself at the merchants' and farmers' booths, and his manners began to improve only as they got

closer to the expensive, exclusive stores near the city center. By that
time they had acquired most of the staples they needed, in one form or
another, and had begun to shop for the luxuries that made H'daen
tr'Khellian's formal dinners the well-attended functions they were.

Rare delicacies, fine vintages, fragrant blossoms for the tables and the
dining chamber. Some were easy to find—Arrhae enjoyed the simple
pleasure of being able to point at anything that took her fancy regardless
of its price, and striking the Khellian house-sigil nonchalantly onto
whatever bills were pushed toward her—but others proved much more
difficult. And one or two were quite impossible.

"What do you mean, out of stock? You always had *hlai'vnau* before,
so why not now?"

The shopkeeper went through all the appropriate expressions and
movements of regret—none of which, of course, put any cuts of meat
in the empty cool-trays or did anything to calm Arrhae down. She had
all but promised that the traditional holiday foods would be served at
H'daen's table, and now here was this bucolic idiot telling her that he
had sold every last scrap of wild *hlai* in the city. She was sure enough of
that sweeping statement, because it could be bought nowhere else, at
least nowhere else on this particular day. Only merchants approved by
priestly mandate and subjected each year to the most stringent examinations were permitted to sell wild game on the day set aside to honor
domestic produce and the people who provided it, and this man held
the single such approval in i'Ramnau.

"Very well." Arrhae unclenched her fists, annoyed that she had let so
much irritation be so obvious; tr'Aimne would doubtless delight in reporting it to his cronies. "Plain *hlai'hwy,* then." She leaned closer, smiling
a carefully neutral smile that wasn't meant to reassure, and didn't. "But
do make sure they're properly cleaned. If any of Lord tr'Khellian's guests
break their teeth on a stray scale, your reputation would certainly suffer."

*If only H'daen's mansion was closer to a large city instead of this mudhole. If
only it weren't so fashionable to have a home in open country. If only . . .* Arrhae
dismissed the thoughts as not worth wasting brainspace on; H'daen
lived where he lived, and that was all. *But why here?* the stubborn voice
in her head persisted. *Nothing ever happens here. . . .*

The sound began as a rumble so low it was beyond the edge of hearing; Arrhae felt it more as a vibration in her bones and teeth. It persisted there for long enough to be dismissed to the unconscious, like computer hum or the white-noise song from an active viewscreen—and then it raced up through the scale to peak at an earsplitting atonal screech that chased its source across the sky as a military suborbital shuttle dropped vertically through the scattered clouds.

*Nothing . . . ? Well, almost nothing,* Arrhae thought. The shuttle snapped out of its descent pattern and made a leisurely curve out of sight; probably on approach to the Fleet landing field that lay halfway between i'Ramnau and H'daen's mansion. The echoes of its passage slapped between the city's buildings for many minutes afterward, but long before they died away completely Arrhae had finished the last of her purchases and made enough amiably threatening noises to insure that they would be delivered in good time, and was making her way back to the holding-bay where her flitter waited. *Another night,* she thought, *another dinner, probably another of H'daen's deals, struck but never completed. And with whom?*

*Oh, well. A fully belly at least . . .*

Turning away from the dining chamber for perhaps the tenth time since she had told him everything was in readiness, H'daen tr'Khellian made his tenth gesture of approval toward his *hru'hfe.* Arrhae acknowledged—again—and tried to keep the good-humored appreciation on her face when it seemed determined to slip off and reveal the boredom beneath. H'daen's guests were late, very late indeed, and without even the courtesy of advising their host of the reason why. The lateness was unusual, the lateness combined with the rudeness nearly unheard of. H'daen knew it; the original enthusiasm when he saw how well his instructions had been followed had long since eroded into an automatic wave of the hand, and these past few times Arrhae was prepared to hear herself ordered to clear the place and dump all the food. She privately gave him five more minutes before the command was given. . . .

And then the door chime sounded loudly through the silent house. Arrhae could not have said who moved first or faster, H'daen or herself, but after the first three steps he remembered his dignity and let her attend to the guests, if guests they were, while he returned to his study for what was probably a well-deserved swift drink.

The callers were indeed the long-awaited dinner companions: a man and a woman, both Fleet officers in full uniform of scarlet and black. Looking past them out into the darkness, Arrhae could see their transport sitting in one of the mansion's parking bays, and for some reason felt sure that it wasn't empty. The officers' aides, or their driver, or a guard, or—Arrhae stamped down on her curiosity before it went any further; the transport wasn't her business.

"*Llhei u'Rekkhai,*" she said in her best voice and most mannered phase of language. "*Aefvadh; rheh-Hwael l'oenn-uoira.*" She stepped to one side so that they could walk inside and straight to the laving-bowl and fair cloths set out for refreshment after their "arduous journey"; no more arduous than a stroll from the military flitter, and no more for refreshment that the token dabbing of face and fingertips, but a traditional courtesy to guests nonetheless.

"*Sthea'hwill au-khia oal'lhlih mnei i H'daen hru'fihrh Khellian . . . ?*" said the woman.

*Announce whom?* thought Arrhae. *I don't know any names yet!* "*Nahi 'lai, llhei?*"

One of the officers hesitated, a soft towel still in his hands, fingers clenching momentarily at the interrogative lift of Arrhae's voice, then glanced swiftly at his companion.

"*U'rreki tae-hna,*" she said absently, not especially interested. "*Hfivann h'rau.*"

"*Hra'vae?*" he said slowly. There was wariness and suspicion in that voice, and Arrhae wondered why. Then the officer turned full around, staring at her with cold, secretive eyes as if trying to read more than what he saw in her face. "*Hsei vah-udt?*" The demand came out like a whipstroke.

"*Arrhae i-Mnaeha t'Khellian, daise hru'hfe, Rekk—*"

"*Rhe've . . . ?*" The man didn't sound convinced. "*Khru va—*"

"Ah, Subcommander, it's enough . . ." Though his companion spoke in a less formal mode, there was no mistaking the tacit warning in her voice. "This one is only doing her job, as are we all. And well she does it." She dipped her fingers into the bowl of scented water once more, then dried them off and waved their newly-acquired perfume apprecia- tively under her nose. "Very well indeed. Tell H'daen that Commander t'Radaik and Subcommander tr'Annhwi are here."

"Madam, sir, at once. There is drink here in the anteroom, and small foods for you." Arrhae opened a door off the hallway. "And servants to attend you." *There had better be,* she thought. Neither of H'daen's house- guests were the languid desk-captains she was used to; there was a quick and haughty anger about the man tr'Annhwi, but the lazy, con- trolled power of Commander t'Radaik was more disturbing still. The woman's every word, every gesture, bespoke a confidence in her strength or her rank that suggested both were far beyond what first sight might suggest. Arrhae bowed them through the doorway, saw that at least three of the other house servants were waiting with trays and cups and flagons, and slipped the door shut on her own silent sigh of relief.

She had cause, once or twice in the next hour, to enter or pass through the dining chamber, a place of dimmed lights and muted voices, where H'daen and his guests discussed what seemed matters of impor- tance. Like any good servant, Arrhae could be selectively deaf when nec- essary, and moreover had little enough time to eavesdrop even had she more inclination to do so. The unexpected work created by her shop- ping trip meant that everything else was running hours behind—an in- spection of the guestrooms, completion of her half-finished audit of the domestic purchase ledgers, and even getting herself something to eat. . . .

A successful raid on the kitchen produced a glare from tr'Aimne— also meat, bread, and a jug of ale, watered down until it was almost palatable. After making a swift reverence, Arrhae fell to with a will. She hadn't realized just how hungry she had become until the savor of the baked *hlai* reached her nostrils. She made short work of everything on her platter.

Not that it took long, because even the dinner which the three up- stairs had eaten was no many-coursed banquet, for all its elegant presentation, and Arrhae's stolen meal was only a degree or so above left-over scraps. Yet set against the standards of everyday fare it was a feast indeed, if not in quantity, then at least by virtue of its quality and flavor. The Rihannsu were not—with few exceptions—a wealthy people, reckoning riches more by honors won and past House glories than in cash and precious things. She ate off one such precious/not precious article tonight: a dish that was part of the set made by H'daen's ancestor nine generations back from the remnants of her warbird, after the vessel had safely returned to ch'Rihan after a nacelle accident that should have killed everyone aboard. It had been decommissioned and scrapped after that, but its memory as something that continued useful when all reason and logic said otherwise was contained, with a sardonic humor that Arrhae liked, in the dining-service made of its breached hull.

She was debating whether or not to venture down to the kitchen again for any more of whatever was left, when the summoning-bell went off, loudly enough to make her jump. Its normally decorous sound had been turned up to an earpiercing clangor like that of a warship's tocsin, and that, Arrhae knew, was something H'daen would not normally tolerate. Even as she scrambled to her feet, wiping her mouth and straightening her tunic, she was wondering *who, and how, and why . . ?*

She found out.

Commander t'Radaik met her at the head of the stairs. No longer benevolent and defensive, the woman looked every inch what Arrhae had come to suspect she was: someone whose actual rank or status was far, far higher than that claimed or indicated by insignia. One of the guests at a dinner-party two years past had given her the same feeling—and it had been vindicated when the man, ostensibly a Senior Centurion, had announced his true rank of *khre'Riov* and his position in Imperial Intelligence, and had arrested Vaebn tr'Lhoell, another of the guests, on charges of espionage and treason. Arrhae and all the other house servants had been interrogated to learn if they had seen anything suspicious during the party, and since tr'Lhoell had negotiated her present post in House Khellian, she had been terrified lest some ulterior motive should come to light and indicate that she was somehow implicated in whatever crime he had intended.

T'Radaik had that same look of a mask having been removed, and Arrhae thought abruptly and horribly of H'daen's enigmatic offer to take her into his confidence. Once again the small worm of fear twisted into life within her belly, and she fought with all her strength to keep any expression that might be construed as guilt from becoming visible on her face.

There was more introspection than anything else on the commander's face; she had the air of a person deep in thought, and at first didn't see Arrhae five steps below. Then she focused on Arrhae as coldly as a surveillance camera, and her eyes burned right through Arrhae's to the brain behind, seeming to read whatever secrets were hidden there—and disapprove of them all. *"Hru'hfe,"* she said, all business now, "which guest-chamber in this house has a lock that can be overridden from outside?"

Arrhae paused, wondering why such a place was required, needing to think about her answer and feeling foolish because of it. Commander t'Radaik watched her impatiently. "Come along, hurry up! H'daen tr'Khellian seems to think that you're reasonably intelligent. . . ."

"The commander's pardon," Arrhae said, embarrassed, "but this house is such that none of the guestrooms ever needed to be locked from outside. The storerooms, however, all—"

"Show me."

"I. . . . Of course. As the commander wishes."

The store was very definitely a store; there was no way in which it could possibly be redefined as anything approaching *guest* quarters, and even terming it *living* quarters was questionable. But t'Radaik liked it. She inspected the barred and shuttered windows, the thickness of the door and how well it fitted to its jamb, and the all-important lock, pronouncing herself well-pleased with everything. "Have this place cleared, aired, warmed, and furnished," she said, sliding the heavy door shut and seeming most satisfied with the ponderous sound of its closure.

Arrhae tried not to stare, but decided at last that to swallow all her curiosity would be worse than to let a little out. "If the commander permits—what purpose is there in all of this? It looks like a"—realization

struck her and she wished suddenly that she hadn't begun to speak—
"like a prison cell. . . ."

"*Hru'hfe* Arrhae t'Khellian." Commander t'Radaik spoke softly. She
didn't look at Arrhae, but she had the chill air of one fixing a face and a
name securely in the memory. "Ask no questions, girl, and hear no lies."
And the commander looked at her a little sidelong. "H'daen makes
much of your intelligence; he also says you can be trusted. Don't make a
liar of him. Matters afoot in this house are no concern of servants, even
trustworthy ones; if you love life, keep your questions to yourself."

She unclipped a communicator from her belt and said several words
into it; they made no coherent sentence and were plainly a coded command, but the mere use of the device brought home to Arrhae the jolt-
ing realization that concealed by the uniform's half-cloak, t'Radaik was
wearing a full equipment-harness. Including a holstered sidearm whose
red primer-diodes glowed up at her like the hot eyes of some small, vicious animal.

Arrhae walked very quietly behind the commander after that; well
behind, avoiding notice as best she could but quite sure that she had
drawn too much notice already. She replied to t'Radaik's occasional
questions with unobtrusive monosyllables, ventured no opinions of her
own, and heartily wished that she had kept her mouth shut earlier on.
T'Radaik said nothing more regarding excessive curiosity, and seemed
content to let Arrhae sweat over the possible consequences of her own
error, or was once more engrossed in her own private thoughts and had
dismissed the matter from her mind. Arrhae sent out a small, fervent
prayer to the Elements that such was the case, but she didn't dare believe it. Not yet, anyway.

Subcommander tr'Annhwi was waiting for t'Radaik, and the house
door was open at his back. It was very dark outside; they were far
enough from i'Ramnau for the city glow to be only a pallid thread on
the horizon, and sometimes, if she had leisure after her work for the
day was done, Arrhae liked to go outside on a clear night and look up
toward the myriad stars and think very private thoughts to herself. But
not tonight. Ariennye alone knew what was out there, or what would
happen to any who tried to see without the authority of the two officers

who now stalked past her with blasters drawn. The weapons' charge-
tones sang an evil two-chord melody in Arrhae's ears, making her skin
crawl and pushing any inclination toward curiosity very far down inside
her mind. Feeling superfluous and, standing in a well-lit hallway looking out into the ominous dark, very exposed, she began to back away.

"H'ta-fvau!" snapped tr'Annhwi. He didn't turn around, much less
level his blaster at her, but Arrhae knew without being told that it
would be his immediate next move. She ventured a weak smile, and
came back as bidden.

H'daen appeared from the dining chamber with traces of wine on
his lips and chin. Arrhae glanced at him, and could see his hands trembling slightly; she wondered what he had been told to bring on such a
fit of the shakes, and then decided that she really didn't want to know.
There was already movement outside, the sound of approaching military boots, and Arrhae remembered her first suspicion that the military
flitter was carrying more than just H'daen's two dinner guests. It
seemed that she was to be proven right—but the reason for the other
personnel and their secrecy was not something that she wanted to dwell
upon. There was too much similarity between tr'Lhoell's arrest and
now. Arrhae's fears had never truly died away, and now they returned
full force to haunt her.

The metalwork of weapons and helmets glittered as six troopers filed
into the front hall of H'daen tr'Khellian's house, but it was not the in-
congruous presence of soldiers that made Arrhae catch her breath. It
was the figure in the midst of them, staring from side to side at his surroundings; a man whose craggy features and angry eyes could not conceal the apprehension that he held so well in check. A man who wore
civilian clothing, out of place in so martial a company, and more out of
place than any form of dress might make him . . .

Because he was not Rihannsu hominid, but Terran human.

If Arrhae stared, her staring was no more apparent than that of the
rest of the household, most of whom had never seen an Earther before.
Heard of them, yes; lost kin to them in one Fleet skirmish or another,
quite probably. But never yet seen any face-to-face until now, when one
stood in their own front hall and looked with faint disdain at the Fleet

troopers who surrounded him. He looked at them all in turn: at H'daen, wiping the blue winestains from his face, at the house servants who had abandoned their duties cleaning up the dining chamber and who now stood gaping like so many fools, and at Arrhae.

She flinched from his direct gaze, so startlingly blue after the dark eyes of Rihannsu, and something about the way she flinched made him stare still harder. In the background of her confusion Arrhae could hear Commander t'Radaik's voice: ". . . a most important guest of the Imperium. Treat him well until the time for treating harshly comes around. . . ."

While in plain sight of all present, the man's hands moved together in a gesture that might have been and certainly appeared to be simple nervousness. Except that it wasn't. It was one of the Command Conditioning gestures by which one Federation Starfleet officer might know another when more straightforward means of identification were impossible. Such as when one or both were acting under cover in a hostile environment.

Such as now.

Arrhae remained quite still for a long moment, not daring to move even an eyelid for fear it should compound her self-betrayal. It had been so long since she had looked on faces that were other than alien. So long that she had almost forgotten who she really was, or what her purpose had originally been. Almost—but not quite. Her hands began to move almost of their own accord in the standard gesture of reply; and then she stopped short while a wave of trembling passed through her entire body. What if this were some trap and the presence of Commander t'Radaik no more than a means to insure that she betray herself? Arrhae dropped her hands and was still, or as still as her shuddering would let her be. She looked to H'daen.

"The commander has bidden me prepare one of the locked stores as a secure guest accommodation," she heard her own voice saying as calmly as if the house were invaded daily by military people with prisoners in tow. "With your permission, I shall attend to it at once."

H'daen waved her away, not really listening to what she said. He was hanging on every word spoken by t'Radaik, seeing the chance of importance at long last for his house—and more immediately, for himself.

"Who is *this?*" Arrhae heard him ask. She continued her steady walk away, not turning around no matter what was said, or who said it.

"*I* can tell you who I am, sir," the man said angrily . . . and Arrhae broke out all over in cold sweat at the sound of him. She was not wearing a translator, and he spoke Federation Standard, and she *understood* him. Not that this should have been strange, of course. Arrhae's composure began to shatter, and she kept walking, steadily, to be well out of sight before it should do so completely.

"I'm Dr. Leonard E. McCoy," he said, and, O Elements, it was a native Terran accent, from somewhere in the South of EnnAy, probably Florida or Georgia. Arrhae made herself keep walking without reaction, without the slightest reaction to the language she had not heard from another being for eight years, and had stopped hearing even in her dreams. "I'm a commander in the United Federation of Planets' Starfleet—and what your people have done is a damned act of war!"

# Chapter Two

## PASTS

"I am a Vulcan, bred to peace," said S'task long ago to the alien captor who asked him for his name and rank; and many a Vulcan has quoted him over the years since, ignoring both the fierce irony inherent in what S'task did to his captors while escaping them, and the pun on the poet's name. Or perhaps they are not ignoring either. The Vulcans are not so much a taciturn race as they have been painted, but a reserved one; their rich mindlife demands a privacy that less espertalented species find suspect, and their altruism is based on that firmest of foundations, necessity. The declaration is not just a statement of preference, but a description of what has become necessary for them to survive as a species and as individuals.

It was not always this way. So much scholarship, drama, and fiction has been written about pre-Reformation Vulcan society that it is unnecessary and perhaps useless to say much more about it. The images of a brutal and savage splendor spreading over a desert world, a fierce and lavish culture full of bizarre and secretive ceremony, wonders and horrors wrought by the unleashed and uncontrolled power of mind—of blood sacrifices, massive battles, single and multiple combats on which kingdoms were staked, and (most often) of wild passions and doomed loves destroyed by mindlock, clan jealousies or mere ambition—all these have sunk as deep into mass-culture consciousness as the semi-mythical Ten Lordships of the Andorian Thaha Dynasty, or the cowboys-and-Indians Old West of Earth. And this Vulcan has approximately the same relationship as those to historical reality: being careful, here, to mean history as "what truly came to pass" rather than history as "what historians believe probably occurred."

We do know that Vulcan was on the brink of economic, political, and perhaps moral disaster before the Reformation: and that within three generations after it the planet was almost completely recovered and stable and at peace with itself as few worlds have been before or since. Something plainly happened that mere history can barely account for. On other worlds, where aggression seems to have a much lighter grip or never quite took hold—Duiya, for example, or Lahain—one could easily accept the appearance and swift appeal of a Surak. In Vulcan's case, if we knew nothing of the truth, we might be tempted to take his story for a fiction as wild as any yet written. But there is Surak, and there is the Reformation, and ready to hand before us is the world that resulted. What happened?

Some writers have looked at the man's history—of inflexible peace, utter compassion, a man who laid down his life for what he believed in, and died horribly, slain by the enemies he had been offering peace— and have seen in it parallels to situations on other worlds, where powers from outside have seemed to come and redeem the hopelessly fallen. On this subject and this outlook, the Vulcans are absolutely silent. They refuse to deal with anything but the facts: that Surak arose and taught peace, died for it, and was followed by hundreds and thousands who did the same, until the whole world renounced unmastered passion and gave itself over to that which English scholars of Vulcan (and the Vulcans themselves) translate as "logic" but which is more accurately defined as "reality-truth." But Hirad and other commentators point out that "reality-truth" in pre-Reformation times also meant the presence of God, immanent in the real things of the world and therefore also in the workings of the reasoning mind. The only response the Vulcans have made on this has been T'Leia's rather dry observation that "reality-truth" by either definition also includes error—a thing all too real—and all those who commit it.

What the Vulcans also often decline to comment on is that the cool proud man who declared himself "bred to peace" is the same man who turned his back on Surak, his teacher, and on the world that had become Surak's: the man who led more than eighty thousand Vulcans out into the interstellar night in search of a place where they could practice their beliefs in what passed for peace among them. In a most unusual inversion, it was the old beliefs that went out hunting the new world: not persecuted, but gladly, angrily self-exiled. The Eighty Thousand and S'task were the first Rihannsu.

Less than eighteen thousand of them finally made planetfall on ch'Rihan: and their pride was sorely tested in the two thousand years between the Worldfall and the days when they arose again in their reinvented spacecraft to trouble both the fledgling Federation and its enemies. But arise they did: and since that time the Vulcans have looked in their direction with a terrible calm that some find most interesting. It may be true, as the doomed T'thusaih said, that neither race will be whole until they are reunited, and heal one another's wounds. But on this, too, the Vulcans have no comment, and the Rihannsu smile in scornful silence and sharpen their swords.

There are some historians who say that the great rift that divided Vulcans into Vulcans and Romulans grew, not from any influence within the planetary societies, but from xenophobia following their first contact with other intelligent species. This is one of those theories that must be approached from both sides. On the one hand, why should Vulcans show xenic reaction to intelligent species? After all, Vulcan falls among the twenty percent of all known worlds that are inhabited by more than one intelligence. Contact from prehistoric times with the *sehlat*s, and with the various intelligences of the deep sand, should have adequately prepared the Vulcans for the shock of sentience in nonhominid form.

And their technology, that most elegant and effective combination of the physical and nonphysical sciences, was already turning toward starflight. By the time of Surak, the first landing on Vulcan's closest planetary neighbor was several centuries in the past, and mining expeditions to the other inner worlds of 40 Eridani were becoming, if not commonplace, at least not unusual. The thoughts of the whole planet were beginning to turn outward as philosophers and engineers postulated the likelihood of intelligent life-forms living on other worlds. Vulcan science fiction of that period—couched in those favorite Vulcan literary forms, the epic poem and the serial syllogism—is some of the best literature to be found on any world, and it fanned to a blaze a whole world's smoldering interest in the stars. By the time one small group of Terrans was building the pyramids, serious research was going on among Vulcans of all nations in the physics and the psi technologies that would support generation ships on their journeys to the nearest stars, sixteen and thirty light-years away. Taken as a whole, this does not look much like xenophobia.

But there is more than one kind of xenophobia. Vulcan historians naturally do not admit to shame or embarrassment about anything, but their relative reticence about the times before the unification of the planet makes their attitude toward those times quite plain. In the oldest Vulcan societies, where all life was a struggle for survival against a terrible desert ecology, one had no need to fear the stranger who came suddenly out of nowhere. It was your neighbor who continually competed with you for water, food, and shelter. It was your neighbor who was your enemy.

Vulcan hospitality was (and still is) legendary. Vulcan enmity toward neighboring tribes, states, and nations passed out of legend into epic; their wars escalated with time and technology to astonishing proportions. Between the dawn of Earth's Bronze Age at Catal Huyuk, around 10,000 B.C., and the fall of the Spartans at Thermopylae, there was only one period of ten standard years during which as much as ten percent of Vulcan was *not* at war. Without Surak the planet would probably not exist today except as a ragged band of radioactive asteroids in the second orbit out from 40 Eri. Even with him it did not survive whole.

To do justice to another side of the xenophobia argument, it might be safe to say that the universe awaiting the Vulcans was not one they had ever imagined. It was ironic that the sudden beacon in their sky, the da'Nikhirch, or Eye of Fire, which stirred many Vulcans to even more intense interest in neighboring interstellar space, and which (some said) heralded the birth of Surak, was also to be the cause of such terrible anguish for the planet. No one has ever proved that it was a sunkiller bomb that made sigma-1014 Orionis go nova, but the destruction of the hearthworld of the Inshai Compact planets certainly suited the expansionist aims of their old enemies in trade, the "nonaligned" planets of the southern Orion Congeries.

With the great power and restraining influence of Inshai suddenly gone, a reign of terror began in those spaces. Wars, and economic and societal collapse, decimated planetary populations in waves of starvation and plague while the decentralized interstellar corporations, their fleets armed with planetcracker weapons, fought over trade routes and sources of raw materials—blackmailing worlds into submission, destroying those that would not submit. In the power vacuum the surviving Compact worlds could not maintain their influence, or their technology, much of which derived from Inshai. They, too, turned to extortion and conquest to survive. Formerly peaceful worlds like Etosha and depopulated ones like Duthul became the home bases of the companies and guilds who degenerated over centuries into the Orion pirates. And Vulcan looked out into the darkness, where these dangerous next-door neighbors were stirring, not realizing that they had already turned on the houselights for them. It was around the time of Surak's birth, when the FireEye's light reached Vulcan, that the first electromagnetic signals from Vulcan reached Etosha in their turn, and notice was taken.

Their first contacts with the Orion pirates, forty-five years later, would have been enough to disillusion even a Terran steeped in all old Earth's legends of bug-eyed monsters intent on stealing their women and subjugating their planet. The Vulcans had no such legends: they expected to deal with strangers hospitably, and courteously, though always from strength. They had no idea that their strengths were in areas that would mean nothing to the Duthulhiv pirates who first reached them.

The subterfuge used by the raiders had worked on many another world. They surveyed Vulcan for months, monitoring communications, learning the languages, and assessing the world's resources for marketability. Then initial contacts began, properly stumbling ones made by conventional radio from pirate scout craft transmitting from several light-weeks outside the system. The pirates used a simple series of trinary signal-pulses expressing atomic ratios and so forth. Their own records, preserved on Last Etosha, make it plain that no one ever cracked this code as swiftly as the Vulcans did. "It was almost as if they had been expecting it," one pirate scientist was reported to have said. Messages began to flow back and forth immediately.

When communication was established, the pirates offered peaceful trade and cultural opportunities; the first messages were debated for several standard months in councils around the planet. Several wars or declarations of wars were in fact put on hold, or postponed, while the officials conducting them were recalled to their capitals to assist in the discussions. Finally the Vulcans decided to receive the strangers as a united front. On this at least they were agreed, that their own position of strength would be stronger yet if they acted all together. If a more pressing reason for this lay in the minds of various parties—the idea that this way, no one faction would be allowed to get a jump on the others—then no one voiced it out loud.

The date for the first physical meeting was set: nine Irhheen of the Vulcan old-date 139954, equivalent in Terran dating to January 18–19, 22 B.C. There at the agreed landing place at ShiKahr—then a tiny village of a ritually neutral tribe—five hundred twenty-three of the great ones of Vulcan gathered: clan and tribal chieftains, priestesses and clerics, merchants, scientists and philosophers, who went out in all their splendor to meet the strangers in courtesy and bring them home in honor. What met them in turn, when the strangers' landing craft settled, were phasers that stunned those who were to be held for ransom or sold into slavery, and particle-beam weapons that blew to bloody rags those who tried to fight or escape.

By the merest accident, Surak was not there: an aircar malfunction had detained him at the port facility at ta'Valsh. When the news reached him, he immediately offered to go to the aliens and to "deal peace" with them. No government would support him in this, most specifically since half the nations on the planet that day were mourning their leaders: the other half were staring in rage at ransom demands radioed to them from the slaver ships in orbit.

Thus war broke out—'Ahkh, "the" War, Vulcans called it, thereby demoting all other wars before it to the rank of mere tribal feuds. No ransoms were paid—and indeed if they had been, they would have beggared the planet. But the Vulcans knew from their own bitter experience with one another that once one paid Danegeld, one never got rid of the Dane. The space fleets of the planet were then no more than unarmed trading ships: in one of those lacunae that puzzle historians, the Vulcans had never even thought of carrying their warfare into space. But the ships did not stay unarmed long, and some of the armaments were of the kind that would not show on any enemy's sensors. The chief psi-talents of the planet, great builders and architects, and technicians who had long mastered the subtleties of the undermind, went out in the ships and taught the Duthulhiv pirates that weapons weren't everything. Metal came unraveled in ships' hulls; pilots calmly locked their ships into suicidal courses, unheeding of the screams of the crews: and the Vulcans beamed images of the destruction back to Etosha, lest there should be any confusion about the cause. The message was meant to be plain: kill us, and die.

That meeting was to prove the rock on which Vulcan pacifism first and most violently ran aground. S'task's handling of it differed terribly from his master's, as they differed at that part of their lives on everything else. S'task was at the meeting at ShiKahr, one of those who was taken hostage. He it was who organized the in-ship rebellion that cost so many of the slavers their lives: he was the one who broke the back of the torturer left alone with him, broke into and sabotaged the ship's databanks, and then—after releasing the other hostages safely on Vulcan—crashed the luckless vessel into the pirate mothership at the cost of thousands of pirates' lives, and almost his own. Only his astonishing talent for calculation saved him, so that weeks later, after much anguished searching, he was picked up drifting in a lifepod in an L5 orbit, half starved, half dead of dehydration, but clinging to life through sheer rage. They brought him home, and Surak hurried to his couchside—to rebuke him. The words "I have lost my best student to madness" are the beginning of the breaking of the Vulcan species.

No writer has recorded those anguished conversations between Surak and S'task. From contemporaries we know only that they went on for days as the master tried to reason with the pupil, and increasingly discovered that the pupil had found reasons of his own which he was not willing to let go. Peace, S'task said, was not the way to deal with the universe that now awaited Vulcan. The only way to meet other species, obviously barbaric, was in power to match their own—power blatantly exhibited, and violently, if necessary. Over the next few months, through the information networks and "mindtrees" of the time, S'task spread his views, and his views began to spread without him. Surak's coalition and support base far outnumbered that of those holding S'task's opinion, but mere majorities have never much influenced Vulcans: and no one was really surprised when the riots began in late 139955. Several small cities were burned or wrecked, and Surak himself was almost killed in the disturbances in Nekhie, trying to deal peace with those who did not want it.

It was at this point that S'task went into seclusion, hunting solutions. He loved his master, though he had come to hate his reasoning: and he well saw that their disagreement would destroy any chance Vulcan would ever have of facing as a unified entity the powers watching it from outside. (This surveillance had been confirmed toward the end of 139954, when another ship from Etosha arrived—cloaked, it thought, against Vulcan detection. The ship's wreckage, preserved by the desert dryness through thousands of years, is still visible outside Te'Rikh, carefully kept clear of sand by the Vulcan planetary park authorities.)

The problem was a thorny one. S'task was no fool: though he was sure he was right, he knew that Surak felt that way, too, and one side or the other was bound to be tragically right rather than triumphantly so. One side or the other would eventually win the argument, but the price of the victory would be centuries of bloodshed, and a planet never wholly at one with itself. Once again the ancient pattern would reassert itself, and S'task's vision of Vulcan as one proud, strong world among many would degenerate into just one more thing to have a war over: the goal itself would be forgotten in the grudges that its partisans would spawn in others and nurture in themselves for hundreds of years. For this reason alone S'task was unwilling to push the issue to its logical conclusion, civil war. But another question, that of ethic, concerned him: he was still Surak's pupil, and as such acknowledged that no cause or goal, however good, could bear good fruit of so evil a beginning. "The structure of spacetime," Surak had said to him at their first meeting, "is more concerned with means than ends: beginnings must be clean to be of profit." S'task had taken this deeply to heart.

So he proposed a clean beginning, and the proposition made its way through the mindtrees and the nets like lightning. If the world was not working, S'task said, then those Vulcans dissatisfied with it should make another. Let them take the technology that the aliens had inadvertently brought them, and add their own science to it, and go hunting another world, where what they loved would be preserved in the way they thought it should be. Let there be another Vulcan: or rather, the *true* Vulcan, Vulcan as it *ought* to be.

The arguments went on for fifty years, while the fartravel ships were being built, while more pirate attacks were beaten back and the first radio signals from other species farther out were decoded. Slowly the Eighty Thousand rallied around S'task, and on 12 Ahhahr 140005 the first ship, *Rea's Helm,* left orbit and drove outward into a great silence that was not to be broken for two millennia. The last message from *Helm,* sent as it cut in its subdrivers, provoked much confusion. It was a single stave in the *steheht* mode. Like all other Vulcan poetry, its translation is never certain, but more translations of it have been attempted than of any verse except T'sahen's Stricture, and so the sense is fairly certain:

> Enthrone your pasts:
>     this done, fire and old blood
>     will find you again:
> better hearts' breaking
> than worlds'.

It was the Last Song, S'task's farewell to Vulcan, and the last poem he ever made: after it he cut the strings of his *ryill* and spoke no other song till he died. Some on Vulcan consider that a greater loss than the departure of the Eighty Thousand, or all the death that befell as they returned to the counsels of the Worlds two thousand years later.

In their absence, under Surak's tutelage, Vulcan became one. The irony has been much commented on, that the aliens who presented the threat that almost destroyed Vulcan were eventually the instrument of its unification, and the world which had never *not* been at war became the exemplar of peace. It has been said that evil frequently triumphs over good unless good is very, very careful. This is true: but it should be added that good frequently has help that looks evil on the surface of it, and that "even God's enemies are some way his own." Surak spent his life, and eventually gave his life, for an idea whose time had come—an idea the accomplishment of which would fill other planets, in future times, with envy or longing. But the other side of the idea, the lost side, the incomplete, the failed side, was never out of his mind, or Vulcan's. Among his writings after he died was found this stave:

> Dethrone the past:
>     this done, day comes up new
>     though empty-hearted:
> O the long silence,
> my son!

# Chapter Three

His present cabin was one of the most comfortable berths that Leonard McCoy had enjoyed for a long while. The ship was a civilian liner, not subject to Starfleet regulations, and as an honored guest—and first-class passenger—he was getting the full treatment. At a guess he'd put on half a kilo in the past three weeks. Life on the *U.S.S. Enterprise* might not be so luxurious, but it certainly kept a man in trim; well, there'd be reassignment when this was over and he'd finished all he had to do. Back with Jim Kirk and the rest, "hopping galaxies" as somebody had once put it. McCoy smiled a little at that. With *Vega* running in other-space at warp three, what else was he doing but hopping galaxies right now? Or star systems, anyway. . . .

He pushed back from his desk and from the datapad still keyed for comparative xenobiology, knuckling a yawn to extinction as he watched information flick across the screens on their way to hardcopy dump. To all intents and purposes this was no more than a busman's holiday. The zeta Reticuli orbital research facility didn't need *him* for its setup inspection; any senior medic from Starfleet Academy would have been quite sufficient. But they wanted the famous Dr. McCoy from the famous *Enterprise*—and Command had agreed he should go.

So here he was, Leonard E. McCoy, fifty-year-old medical whiz kid, traveling first class on a luxury starliner, working on the learned dissertation he was expected to present, getting no exercise, getting bored, and wishing he were somewhere else. There was such a thing as getting too much R & R, and he was getting it right now. . . .

The electronics squeaked politely at him as they finished transcribing, and produced a bound copy of his dissertation notes with the slightly self-deprecatory air of a chicken laying an egg. McCoy picked it up and thumbed through the pages, looking halfheartedly for typos so that he would have something worthwhile to grumble about. There weren't any. That was the whole point of textsetting onscreen, but it was always worth a look anyway. He hadn't forgotten the time when a glitch in the *Enterprise* sickbay processors had overprinted every fifth word of Jim Kirk's monthly health report with a random selection of the most favored obscenities in seven Federation languages. Jim had laughed, and even Spock had been observed to raise one eyebrow. McCoy, however, had been audibly, indeed volubly, embarrassed, and had made a private promise that such errors wouldn't get past him again. Hence his almost obsessive care over this particular piece of work. After presentation to the Facility's medical board it was going straight into the *I.C.Xmed. Journal,* and that august publication would find mistakes neither ironic nor amusing. He set the checked script down and looked at it thoughtfully. *Always the same. Four submissions accepted, printed, and praised to the stars—and I'm still like a cat on eggs about whether I've got it right or not. Oh, well, maybe the fifth will feel diff—*

Then the desk kicked down at his thighs and the whole ship jerked as viciously as a bone shaken by a dog.

*That's impossible,* a rational voice said at the back of his mind. *No it's not,* said the same voice an instant later as his stomach supplied more data. Something had flickered the *Vega's* artificial gravity net, slapping him—and presumably everyone else aboard—from null-G to maybe 4 G's, and then back to 1-G standard all in the space of half a second. And that something had to be either a collision, or—

Proximity alarms began yelping as the liner shuddered out of warp and back to realspace.

Somebody had just fired on them!

*Here we go,* he thought. It was almost a relief, in a peculiar way. Maybe the trip was going to be worthwhile after all. . . .

McCoy hit two tabs simultaneously: one lit up the courtesy you-are-here starfield map on the back wall of his cabin, and the second unshuttered clearsteel ports set in the outer hull. Those he kept shut while the *Vega* was running at warpspeed; nobody—apart, of course, from Spock, who was the exception to so many rules—actually *chose* to look out at unfiltered otherspace. But he opened it up anyway, no matter how pointless that might seem in the interstellar void, because he wanted if at all possible to see whatever the hell was happening.

And he did.

For just a second there was only velvety dark pinpricked by the light of distant stars. The swirl of motion came from nowhere, a wavering haze that first set those stars to dancing and then swallowed them as it condensed into a ship hanging less than five hundred meters away. Criminally close—although that would concern this vessel's captain not at all, if McCoy's memory of ship-silhouettes was accurate.

The Federation's five-klick traffic limit was not observed by Klingons.

At least (*at least?*) it wasn't the familiar brutal hunchbacked-vulture shape of an *Akif-* or *K't'inga*-class battlecruiser. This was smaller and more rakish, one of the *K'hanakh* class frigates—still with firepower capable of blowing a target into a cloud of free electrons if the word was given. But what in the name of all things holy was a Klingon raider doing this deep into Federation space? They were much closer to the Romulan Neutral Zone . . . and the Romulans often used Klingon ships. He would *much* rather that the ship was Romulan.

As if responding to his thought, the warship pivoted gently on its maneuvering thrusters and slid toward the *Vega* and McCoy. Already its outline was fading again. He got no more than a glimpse of the insignia painted across its underbelly—an abstract spread-winged bird of prey—before ship and painted bird alike were gone from sight. McCoy stared out at the emptiness of space for several minutes even though there was no longer anything much to see, then turned and lifted the bound dissertation with a reluctant feeling of relief. *Cloaking device,* he thought. *Well, that's that. We're rolling . . . it's just as well. . . . I hate public speaking anyway!*

McCoy grabbed his jacket from where he had thrown it and left the cabin at a dead run, almost too fast for the automatic door. He didn't know his way around the *Vega*, but right now he wanted to get to the bridge, and he wanted it fast. The ship's corridors were chaotic, full of panicky people, most of whom didn't know what was going on; McCoy had a feeling that if they *did* know, the situation would get rapidly worse. He managed to stop one of the liner's stewards—a Sulamid—as it whirled past him, and was dismayed to see the alternating blue-green patterns of its tentacles. This particular Sulamid was so scared that reflex was overriding the good manners which usually kept its emotional-display pigmentation under control.

"Sir sir not restrain, urgency prime/paramount thistime," it said hurriedly, trying to squirm past him.

"Just hold on there, mister," said McCoy, blocking as best he could. "Get me to the bridge; I've gotta speak to the captain."

"Prohibited passenger bridge access alltime, doublemost prohibited thistime absolute."

*I'd hoped I wouldn't need this, but . . .* McCoy reached inside his jacket and pulled out the flat case containing his Starfleet ID, flipping it up in front of the Sulamid's five nearest eye-stalks. "Passenger yes—civilian not." He tried to keep the impatient growl out of his voice and used holophrastic speech for quicker understanding. "Authority override: rank, position, knowledge previous situations same ongoing. Please immediate bridge/captain contact *now!*"

The Sulamid stared with all eight of its eyes first at the ID card and then at him. "Knowledge previous situations/situation thistime?" it said hopefully.

*Too damn many for comfort, son.* "Knowledge yes. See presence alive/healthy; confirm situations survived yes? To captain speaking important hurry please."

Again the rustle, and a nervous writhing of three big handling tentacles. Then the Sulamid came to a decision and flipped two of the tentacle-tips at the floor. McCoy knew enough of this particular non-hominid species' kinesics to recognize a despairing shrug when he saw one. Starfleet or no Starfleet, it plainly expected trouble from the captain. "Sir to bridge guide follow," it said, and made off without waiting for an answer.

*"—mind the damned procedures! Just get an all-band distress squawk out on subspace before that's jammed too—"*

*"—taken out all the drive systems! Impulse? You gotta be joking—I said* all, *didn't I . . . ?"*

*"—our ID was running, I tell you! They knew we weren't military traffic!"*

"—which is why they attacked in the first place—d'you think if we'd been a Starfleet cruiser they'd have dared to—"

"—who are they anyway . . . ?"

The bridge was in a state of lively turmoil when McCoy and the reluctant Sulamid reached it, and they went unnoticed for several seconds while the chaos boiled around them. Then someone with executive officer's stripes and a ferocious mustache swiveled his chair and began to hammer data into a terminal-pad, saw something he didn't expect, and did a double-take to confirm it. "What the—! You! Who the hell are you? No—just get off the blasted bridge, mister! And I mean *right now!*"

"I know who they are," said McCoy, unperturbed by the yelling. "I saw them, and they're—"

"Captain Reaves! They're Orion pirates, sir!" shouted somebody at the comm board. "I caught an ID-transmission leak before they shut it down and—"

"Any visual contact?" The *Vega*'s captain kicked his command chair around, saw McCoy, and favored him with a blistering glare, then dismissed the presence of intruders on his bridge in favor of more immediately important matters.

McCoy was not so easily ignored. "You'll not get a fix on that ship, Captain," he said, cutting through whatever reply the liner's flight crew might have made. "It's cloaked." He took advantage of the sudden silence to continue in a more restrained fashion. "Captain Reaves, it was pure luck that I looked through my viewport at where I did, when I did. I saw the ship drop out of warp and raise its cloaking device; we're under its phasers right now. . . ." His voice trailed off at the expression on the captain's face. "You don't believe me."

"Mister, I—"

"—that's Doctor, Captain. Of medicine."

"All right. Doctor. So you *saw* this raider come out of warp and then you *saw* it disappear again. If you're a medical man"—and from his tone Reaves was doubtful—"you'll know how that sounds. Agreed?"

"Here." For the second time in five minutes McCoy flipped out his Starfleet authority and held it up in front of the captain's eyes. "Doctor, also Commander. I know what I'm talking about. I don't care if they ID as Orions, Gorn, or my old Aunt Matilda! There's a Klingon-built, Romulan-owned Bird of Prey frigate right outside your damned front door, so you'd better start listening. If they're jamming on wide-band subspace frequencies, then try a narrow-focus tachyon squirt—"

"A man of parts, Doctor." Reaves glanced toward two screens, swore softly, and looked quickly away from them. "Do you *really* know what you're talking about?"

McCoy bristled just a bit. "Enough for your comm officer to understand. Let me finish before you interr—"

*"Terran Starliner* Vega, *phasers are locked on target. Do not attempt to raise your shields. Prepare to receive a boarding party."*

The new interruption had nothing to do with the captain, or with anyone else on the liner's bridge. Battered almost to incoherence by the energy-sleet of an activated cloaking device, it crackled from a speaker module on the comm station's translator board. In the shocked stillness after the speaker cut out, *Vega*'s people looked at one another and then, helplessly, at McCoy and Reaves.

The young officer manning the liner's external scanners didn't look. He hit a bank of activator-toggles with a sweep of his hand and said, "Visual, sir." Then he audibly caught his breath as the image he had tracked sprang to high-magnification life on the main screen.

The outline was vague at first, but rapidly became hard-edged reality. The warship decloaked—and they stared straight down the glowing maws of activated phaser conduits. That hailing transmission had been no idle threat; but then, neither Romulans nor Klingons were known for bluffing if superior firepower could be used instead.

"Oh, God," said someone very softly. Four columns of glittering crimson fire swirled to life on the bridge, and nobody needed to hear the reports that abruptly began spilling from *Vega*'s internal communicators to know that the same thing was happening all over the liner. Each firespout collapsed into itself in a storm of glowing motes and became human.

No. Romulan.

Each trooper wore a helmet with his uniform and carried an ugly businesslike disruptor rifle, but the officer who accompanied them was bare-headed and held a phaser pistol nonchalantly in one hand. He looked about the bridge with that cool, neutral expression worn most commonly by Vulcans, then smiled at the man in the command chair. "I am Subcommander tr'Annhwi, set in authority over Imperial Vessel *Avenger*," he said in good if heavily accented Federation Standard Anglish. "All aboard this ship are my prisoners."

"Reaves, J. Michael, captain of civilian starliner *Vega*, out of Sigma Pavonis IV." The words were spoken calmly enough, but his fingers were clenched too tightly on the arms of his command chair. "Subcommander, has there been a formal declaration of war between our governments? If not, then explain what you're doing aboard my ship."

"Your restraint does you credit, Captain h'Reeviss. It is a most wise attitude to adopt. I wish to see this vessel's crew roster, cargo manifests, and passenger listing."

"I'll see you in hell first, you bloody pirate!" Reaves wasn't even halfway out of his seat when a phaser-bolt melted the deck-plating between his feet.

"Carefully, Captain. Sit down." Subcommander tr'Annhwi's voice still carried its tone of cold amusement, but his smile was gone and the anger in his narrow eyes had killed whatever similarity he might have had to a calm, logic-governed Vulcan. "If you insult me again, you will die. If you try to attack me again, you will die. If you do anything other than by my order again, you will die. Is all of this quite clear, h'Reeviss, J. Maik'ell?" The captain didn't reply, but tr'Annhwi nodded anyway. "Good. Run the information to this screen here; my antecenturion will do the rest."

McCoy watched, saying nothing, as columns of data began to scroll past tr'Annhwi's interested gaze. He turned an empty station-seat around and settled into it with the serenity of a man coming to terms with his own fate. *It must have felt like this back in the twentieth century when the doctor told you it was cancer,* he thought. *We've beaten the disease, but not the feeling.*

"These names: crew, or passengers?" tr'Annhwi asked. There was no reply until he touched his fingertips ominously to the firing-grip of his phaser, and even then Captain Reaves left the answer to one of his junior officers.

"The data is presented as you asked for it, Subcommander. Crew, then cargo, and passengers last of all." The young man contrived to be subtly insolent in his brief explanation, but tr'Annhwi either missed it or chose to let it pass.

"Very well," he said. "Proceed on my order. *Erein t'Hwaehrai, h'tah-fveinn lh'hde hnhaudr tlhei.* Commence, please." Every few seconds tr'Annhwi stopped the flow of data and waited while the antecenturion flickered her fingers across the keypads and took note of one item or another of interest to her commander. "The accuracy of these manifests will be checked, of course," he said over his shoulder. "No comments, Captain?"

"They're accurate," said Reaves sullenly.

"So you say." Tr'Annhwi tapped at the screen, which had completed its scrolling and gone dark. "Finished? Then screen off, and print it all." The antecenturion glanced at him quizzically. *"Lloann'na ta'khoi; t'Hwaehrai, haudet's s'tivh quinn aedn'voi."*

*"Ie, erei'Riov."*

A printer sat humming to itself in the silence of the liner's bridge, and then dropped a sheaf of hard copy into Antecenturion t'Hwaehrai's waiting hands. She leafed quickly through the flimsy pages to make sure that tr'Annhwi's remarks had been emphasized properly, then handed them over to him.

"An eclectic assortment, is it not?" he muttered. It would have sounded more like a voiced private observation had he not spoken in Anglish. "Let me see. Hold *A.* Alcohol, beverage, one hundred fifty-seven hektoliters." He tapped his teeth thoughtfully with a scriber, considering, then marked the page and read on. "Textiles—silk, wool, synthetics. Foodstuffs—basic, luxury, gourmet, stasis-secured. Salt and spices, total weight sixty-three kilos.

"Hold *B.* Pharmaceutical supplies." Another mark, different this time by the way the scriber moved. McCoy stiffened. "A rock sample, weight one and one-half tonnes. Grain and associated phosphates, two thousand four hundred forty-one tonnes. Machine parts." This time as he scribbled something down, tr'Annhwi was smiling to himself, a grim look. "Of course machine parts."

McCoy relaxed a little. He was actually beginning to believe that this was going to work.

"And finally, Hold *C*. Art treasures—paintings, twenty; sculptures, three: helmeted head of a goddess, in marble, Terran Hellenic period; convolutions representing thought, in extruded crystal, Hamalket second T'r'lkt era; unfinished portrait, in several substances, Deirr modern. Mail, one thousand eighteen items. Alcohol, industrial, seven hundred ninety-five hektoliters."

Tr'Annhwi's smile was still there as he flicked a disdainful finger at the cargo manifest and stared at Captain Reaves. "Intoxicants *and* drugs. These goods are subject to confiscation, Captain, and you to a fine."

Reaves wasn't about to take that sitting down, but with the barrel of a disruptor rifle resting none too lightly on either shoulder he had little choice but to stay right where he was. Tr'Annhwi watched the impotent fury on the Earther's face and grinned with pleasure. "You keep forgetting what I told you, Captain. Remember please, or you will surely die. Also, these 'machine parts'; come now, not even the Klingons bother using that label for gunrunning anymore. And by the way, no matter what your Federation Starfleet may think of us, the Imperium regards the unauthorized transportation of weapons in just the same way as all other civilized persons. Illegal. There will be another fine."

"This ship," said Reaves, speaking slowly and carefully as if reasoning with a clever two-year-old, "isn't carrying any form of illegal cargo. No drugs other than those requested by the new zeta Reticuli medical facility; no alcohol other than that intended for the Malory-Lynne-Stephens mineral processing plant on Sisyphos—and no weapons, concealed or otherwise, Subcommander tr'Annhwi. Run a physical check of the cargo holds if you like."

"Oh, I will, Captain. But my thanks for your permission anyway. Of the four ships I have searched this past standard day, this one interests me most of all."

*"What?"*

"Singular as the honor may appear, you aren't my paramount reason for entering Federation space. Although this ship might well be. After reading your passenger list, who knows . . . ?"

"We've upward of four thousand passengers aboard this vessel, Subcommander. I trust that you've plenty of time."

"Enough to find the names I want. Afterward we shall determine if more time is necessary, perhaps to blow your ship apart. Run sections *K, M,* and *S.*"

*Finally,* McCoy thought, and regardless of his relief, began to sweat again. *Took the boy long enough. Thought I'd come all this way for nothing.*

Sensing the increase of tension, even though they didn't understand its source, the bridge crew of the *Vega* watched Subcommander tr'Annhwi as he read through the three subsections of their vessel's passenger listing without comment or even drawing so much as an unnecessary breath. And then speed-scanned the entire list of four thousand two hundred and seventy-three names from beginning to end.

"What is the meaning of this question-symbol?" he said at last.

"That refers to a 'no-show' passenger," explained the junior officer who had been so delicately insulting at first. Uncomprehending eyebrows were raised, and he elaborated. "It's a passenger whose place has been booked in advance, and who then doesn't arrive to claim it."

"Ah." Tr'Annhwi uttered the sound in great satisfaction, as though many things were suddenly clear. "There are only twenty-one out of all the names shown here." He reached out for the single sheet that Antecenturion t'Hwaehrai had prepared in anticipation, and ran his fingertip down the single column of print. "Brickner, G.; Bryant, E.; B'tey'nn; Farey, K.; Farey, N.; Ferguson, B.; Friedman, D.; Gamble, C.; Gamble, D.; H'rewiss. . . . All of these persons were expected, but did not appear?"

"Yes."

"So. H'rewiss, yes; Johnson, T.; Kh'Avn-Araht; King, T.; Meacham, B.; Meier, W. *and* Meier, W. . . . Most interesting. Sadek; Sepulveda, R.; Siegel, K.; Talv'Lin; T'Pehr." The Romulan shuffled both sets of hardcopy data together, and there was a look of faint loathing on his face. "I can comprehend why Vulcans and a Tellarite might travel on a Terran-registered vessel, Captain. But some of these others are not"—everyone saw how he looked at the Sulamid steward—"not even *shaped* like you!"

"That isn't an issue under question, Subcommander," said Reaves, staring at tr'Annhwi, "and I recommend you not to start."

There was a brief silence, and then tr'Annhwi shrugged, apparently not understanding Reaves's reaction, and not caring that he didn't. "No matter. As you say, Captain. It is not under question."

He turned back to t'Hwaehrai at the computer terminal. "So," he said. "To work. I would think—would you not, Captain?—that some most interesting conclusions might be discovered if one correlated each passenger with his, her, or its supposed ports of embarkation and added on the cargo-loading manifests."

Reaves blinked, not making sense of the Romulan's words for a moment. Then realization dawned and he glanced from t'Hwaehrai, whose fingers were already pattering briskly at the terminal's access console, to the satisfied little smile that tr'Annhwi was wearing. "Whatever you're thinking, Subcommander," he said, "you're wrong."

"Am I? Perhaps. Or perhaps not."

"*Ta-hrenn, erei'Riov!*" Antecenturion t'Hwaehrai looked decidedly pleased with herself. "*Eh't ierra-tai rh'oiin hviur ihhaeth.*"

"*Hnafirh 'rau.*" Tr'Annhwi leaned over to read what was on the screen and his smile became a wide grin. "*Ie. Au'e rha. Khnai'ra rhissiuy, Erein.* Much as I expected to find, Captain," he said, "despite your protestations. You still insist that nobody on this ship has seen the passengers Sadek, T'Pehr, Kh'Avn-Araht, or the coincidentally identical Meiers?"

"Of course not. You saw the list yourself—all of those passengers failed to board before departure."

"Yet items of cargo were loaded at each port of embarkation, yes?"
"Yes."

"And the cargo holds of this starliner are maintained to the same pressure-temperature-gravity parameters as the life shell, yes?"
"Yes. . . ."

"So conceivably, if aware of this, any 'no-show' passenger might be snugly ensconced within a cargo space, yes?"

*"No!"*

"You sound very sure of your facts, Captain h'Reeviss. Most decisive. And since you are so certain, you will scarcely mind opening the holds to space for fifteen standard minutes."

"I will not!" Reaves thumped his clenched fist against the arm of his Command chair as violently as he dared while surrounded by armed and wary Romulan soldiers. "Maybe you don't realize," he said, forcing himself to behave more calmly, "that my contracts specify safe delivery of cargo."

"And perhaps *you* do not realize, Captain, that if you do not vent the holds, I shall. My weapons officer on *Avenger* is very skilled. You have five standard minutes in which to make your choice." Tr'Annhwi glanced at the image of his warship which filled *Vega*'s main screen and unclipped a communicator from his belt. "Ra'kholh, *hwaveyiir 'rhae: aihr erei'Riov tr'Annhwi.*"

"Ra'kholh, *erei'Riov. Enarrain tr'Hheinia hrrau Oira. Aeuthn qiu oaii mnek'nra?*"

McCoy listened, and began to sweat. Perhaps Captain Reaves might have suspected, but nobody else on the bridge could know about the translator nestling snugly against the brachial nerve in his forearm. Certainly even the captain wasn't aware of how well it was working. After the Levaeri V incident, Starfleet's intradermal translators had been reprogrammed with augmented details of the Romulan/Rihanha language, even down to the then-current military slang. There was no slang being used here, on either side of the conversation, and even the bridge centurion's "all-well?" inquiry had been formally phrased. He guessed that Subcommander tr'Annhwi wasn't an officer who encouraged familiarity—or who made idle threats.

"*Ie, ie. Oiuu'n mnekha. Vaed'rae, Enarrain: rhi siuren, dha, iehyyak 'haerh s'* Vega *rhudhe dvaer. Ssuej-d'ifv?*"

*Only* the cargo spaces? McCoy shivered, and rubbed a film of moisture from his palms. No matter how good the Romulan gunnery officer was, he was far too close for that sort of precision fire with shipboard batteries. At less than five hundred meters, the weapon systems on the *Avenger* were more likely to crack *Vega* open like an eggshell than just puncture her holds.

*Even so,* McCoy thought to himself, *don't jump the gun. You have to give this a chance to look right . . . and give the boy a chance to chicken out.*

"*Ie, ssuaj-ha', erei'Riov. Hn'haerht dvahr.* Ra'kholh *'khoi.*" The frigate shifted slightly, bringing its main phasers to bear, and then faded from the screen in a flicker of static as someone on its bridge transmitted an override. It wasn't a view to inspire confidence—*Vega* as seen by the Romulan targeting computers, a schematic outline whose lower hull was marked in three places by the glowing orange diamonds of image-enhanced phaser locks.

"Five minutes and counting, Captain," said tr'Annhwi, looking with unnecessary emphasis at the elapsed-time display onscreen. No matter that all the visible symbology was Romulan; this was easy enough to follow. And time was running out.

"Subcommander . . . !" There was an edge of desperation in Reaves's voice now, and he turned hurriedly to his own crew. "Number One, activate the loading-monitors at full and free mobility—cut in full internal lighting. Exec, patch the signals through to the main screen. Insert mode—over *that.* And for God's sake, hurry!"

It was common practice for a vessel's cargo spaces to have track-mounted surveillance cameras, and there was one in each of *Vega*'s holds. The pictures they transmitted were high-definition, good enough to read the labels on the bulk flasks of Saurian brandy in hold *A* or the stenciled THIS WAY UP instruction on crated medicinal drugs. Certainly good enough to show if anything was amiss—or if anyone was there.

"Look, Subcommander! Can't you see? There's nothing that shouldn't be there!"

Tr'Annhwi looked, not especially interested, and began to turn away. "Three minutes," he said. And then his head snapped back toward the screen. "There! Something moved!"

"You're imagining—" Reaves started to say, but shut his teeth on the words as tr'Annhwi leveled a phaser at his face.

"Close your mouth or I'll burn another one in your head to keep it company," the Romulan snapped. And to the still-active communicator in his left hand: *"Ie'yyak-Hnah!"*

The screen went blank for an instant, then flicked back to a tactical sketch of a Federation liner with computer-graphic splatters of blue fire raking all across its belly.

And at the same instant, *Vega*'s substructure howled in protest as she was gutted. The vessel wrenched out of line in three dimensions at once, flinging both crew and intruders into bulkheads or onto the shuddering deck. Alarms and people alike were screaming. The bridge consoles overloaded in a convulsion of sparks and choking smoke, the screen was flashing HULL INTEGRITY VIOLATED and nobody was paying any attention. . . .

Leonard McCoy clambered stiffly to his feet, coughing the stink of seared insulation from his lungs. He was bruised and shaken, his spine hurt from the three-way whiplash, and he was appalled that the Romulans had actually made good their threat. In that one instant, in the warship of one state firing on the unarmed civilian vessel of another, it had gone beyond piracy to war. And he was right in the middle of it.

Or was he . . . ? The bridge extractors cut in and began to clear the smoke, and the first thing he saw was tr'Annhwi on hands and knees on the deck. The second was the expression on the subcommander's face. It was a mingling of rage and terror such as McCoy had seldom seen on any face; terror at the consequences of a panicked action, and at the consequences yet to come, and fury at being placed in such a situation by all the circumstances which had led him there. Worst of all, the quickest way tr'Annhwi could cover his blunder would be by blowing *Vega* to subatomic particles. Maybe he might not be as ruthless as that, but his last overreaction and the way that he looked now made him more dangerous than the coldest, most efficient starship captain would ever be. Because tr'Annhwi had already shown that he might act without thinking, and he was scared enough to do it again—except that this time people were going to die. . . .

Unless he was distracted.

McCoy stood up, the first man on the bridge to do so, straightened his rumpled, smoke-stained jacket, and met the stares and the leveled weapons with as much equanimity as he could summon. "Subcommander tr'Annhwi, I'm on your list. The name's McCoy—of the *Enterprise.*"

He had gone beyond butterflies in the stomach; it felt like three heavy cruisers on maneuvers in there, but it was still worth it just to see the way tr'Annhwi's face changed. At first the Romulan plainly didn't believe him, then wanted to believe and didn't dare, and finally decided to make quite sure.

The making-sure was brief, and fortunately painless. No matter that *Vega* bridge was smashed, the Romulan frigate's computers were still in perfect working order—and their intelligence data on a trio of much-sought Federation officers, there by no coincidence at all, made short work of providing a tri-D likeness. It arrived in a flicker and hum of transporter effect: a fat dossier with squat blocks of Rihanha charactery on its cover.

Tr'Annhwi looked at it; then at McCoy, then back at the dossier. McCoy already knew that Romulans frowned when deep in thought. If he hadn't, one look at the subcommander would have made him sure of it, because the crease between tr'Annhwi's brows was indented deep enough to put his brain at risk.

The pictures under study weren't at first familiar, and seeing them only by inverted glimpses didn't help. *Where did they get . . . ?* McCoy started to wonder, then recognized the background details and guessed right. They had been taken from the deck-monitor system of the only—so far—Romulan vessel he had ever boarded (and even that had been a Klingon-built *Akif*-class D7 battlecruiser). *Hers. . . .* Ael's sister's-daughter's ship, *Talon.* "She's your *niece?*" He could remember his own voice quite clearly, and its near-squeak of astonishment. Somehow one never thought of enemies with families; brothers or sisters, fathers or daughters. It made keeping them distanced, keeping them enemies that much easier.

And then all of a sudden there was one enemy who was commander of a warbird and at the same time an aunt—and a mother. *A mother who killed her own son in the name of honor and justice.* Mnhei'sahe, *they call it. I call it murder. And yet I stood by, knowing what she was about and pretending not to know, and not wanting to know. And I took her thanks afterward and said nothing.*

"Close enough," said tr'Annhwi grudgingly. There was a cheated air about him, as if having started violence he would as soon have gained his answers after more of it. "Take him." Two disruptors nudged McCoy, in chest and spine.

He looked down at the weapons with disdain—there was no longer any point in being scared, or at least obviously so—and glanced in the subcommander's direction. "Are you expecting me to pull a phaser out of somewhere, sir? Or run? I've had ample time for both—yet here I am." He pushed the nearer, more aggressive rifle to one side and smiled just a bit at the helmeted young trooper who carried it. "Put that away, son, before somebody gets hurt. Subcommander tr'Annhwi, now that you've got what you came for, let these people"—his wave took in the bridge crew and by inference everyone else aboard *Vega*—"be about their business."

"No." The Romulan shook his head in a very Terran gesture of denial. "Dr. Mak'khoi, even without you I find this ship fascinating. Worth a closer look, especially—" His communicator squawked a summons, and when he opened a channel, the voice on the other end sounded very urgent.

*"Subcommander, we have a long-range contact. ID is NCC-2252, Federation light cruiser* Valiant. *Closing speed is warp seven. May I recommend immediate—"*

Tr'Annhwi made an irritable noise and his officer went silent. "Yes, another look indeed," he muttered, "but not here." The orders he snapped back at Centurion tr'Hheinha were too fast for McCoy's translator to make sense of all the words, but "rig for high-speed towing" came through quite plainly. As did "battle stations."

"This is an active shipping lane, Captain." Tr'Annhwi turned to Reaves, using Anglish again and plainly proud of his ability to speak it. "*Avenger* has made her presence known to three other vessels, but yours has taken up more time than my schedule allowed." He smiled, that thin and far from pleasant smile of a man with all the aces in his pocket. "Mine, and that of the Starfleet local-patrol ship. Normally we would have had some hours in hand, but our earlier acquaintances seem to have cried wolf-in-the-fold. We are therefore returning to more friendly space. With you and your ship as our guests."

"I won't let you—"

"By doing *what?*" This time tr'Annhwi didn't bother with anything so overt as pointing his phaser at the outraged captain. He just let the situation speak for itself; and it did so, very clearly.

Reaves tugged in a halfhearted way at his uniform tunic, more for something to do with his hands than through any hope of making the ripped and filthy garment anything like presentable. It was obvious that those hands wanted to reach out and take the smile clean off tr'Annhwi's face, together with his more prominent features. The Romulan could see it as clearly as everyone else on the bridge. But he—all of them—knew that it stopped at wanting. With holes already blown in his ship, Reaves wasn't about to take any further chances.

"Not to worry, Captain h'Reeviss." Tr'Annhwi made the placatory gesture of holstering his phaser, although he didn't order the other Romulans to follow suit. "Your crew and passengers have nothing to fear. After our experts on ch'Rihan have checked your ship properly, it will be repaired and all of you released to go your way." He looked a little sideways, at the only person on the bridge still held at ostentatious gunpoint. "All but the war criminal Mak'khoi." The communicator, still activated and in his hand, squeaked several worried noises involving approach vectors. Tr'Annhwi raised one eyebrow. "And he comes with me now. *Aihr erei'Riov.* Ra'kholh, *hteij 'rhae.*"

"*Hteij 'rhae. Lhhwoi-sdei.*"

"*Hna'h. . . .*"

As the *Avenger*'s transporter beam engulfed him in scarlet shimmer, the last thing that McCoy saw was tr'Annhwi's smile—

—an unpleasant smile, that survived quite unscathed and if anything had grown wider during the transition.

"Welcome aboard, Doctor." The courtesy was decidedly mocking now, delivered by someone in an even greater position of strength than before. "This is *Avenger.* Neither so large nor so impressive as *Enterprise,* but bearer of a worthy name. And an apt name, Dr. Mak'khoi"—the smile was fading fast—"because it is best you know that I had close kin serving on both *Rea's Helm* and *Battlequeen,* which your *Enterprise* destroyed. It would be joy and *mnhei'sahe* for me to take their death-vengeance upon you. Take him out of my sight."

McCoy doubted that it would do him any good to tell the Romulan that *Battlequeen* had been destroyed by Captain Rihaul's *Inaieu* and not by the *Enterprise* at all. Whatever was said would be the wrong thing to say, and in tr'Annhwi's present mercurial mood, saying anything at all was downright dangerous. He let two helmeted security troopers hustle him off toward what he presumed would be the brig, and was silently grateful that tr'Annhwi's orders required him alive, unharmed, and in one piece. McCoy had a feeling that without such orders, his time aboard the *Avenger* would be notably unpleasant. . . .

As he lay back on the thin, hard bunk, he could feel jolts running through the Romulan frigate as it engaged tractor beams and locked them on *Vega,* but the lurch as its warpfield was extended around the damaged vessel knocked him off the bunk and onto the deck beneath it. McCoy swore viciously, rubbed at two fresh and three renewed bruises, considered lying down again, and did. But until the warship was well under way and the subharmonic drone of her main drive was making his teeth shake in their sockets, he lay on the floor.

They entered Rihannsu homespace in ship's night. McCoy hadn't been asleep, just leaning back with his crossed arms behind his head, looking up into the darkness and thinking the sort of convoluted thoughts men think when they can't sleep. And then the darkness became bright, and tr'Annhwi stepped through the afterimage glow that was all that remained of the force-shielded door, and he was smiling again. McCoy was growing very tired of that smile.

"Well, here you are," the Romulan said.

There was something nauseating about an enemy commander trying to be avuncular, and McCoy's glare and nonStandard suggestion both escaped before he thought of what effect they might have on his continued health.

Tr'Annhwi's smile only widened even further. "Oh, not me, Doctor," he said. "Not for some while yet. But you, quite possibly—and certainly quite soon. They are capital charges, after all. Now get up. You *do* want to see your ultimate destination, don't you?"

McCoy did; he wanted to see anything, anywhere, just so long as it was different from the four walls of the cell where he had been for almost three days. "Which is?" he said, swinging his feet to the deck.

"Ch'Rihan," said tr'Annhwi. He said it again as the planet rotated slowly on the *Avenger*'s main screen, while he lounged in his center seat and McCoy stood uncomfortably flanked by armed guards right behind it. "We are now in a geosynchronous parking orbit above the city of i'Ramnau. The place where you will spend your last few days before going to Ariennye—the hell you wished on me with such feeling, Dr. Mak'khoi—by whatever painful route your judges decide. After they have done with you and the news is known, perhaps the Federation will be more respectful of Rihannsu space, and lives, and secrets."

"Subcommander"—one of the crewmen on the cramped little bridge swung his seat around and took a translator from his ear—"Fleet Intelligence personnel and a scanning team are en route from the surface. Commander t'Radaik requests that the prisoner be made ready for immediate transfer to her shuttle. You are invited to accompany him. I have readied Hangar Bay Three for immediate turnaround and—*what in the Elements' name!*"

The whole ship vibrated and alarms warbled briefly, but died as damage control reported in. "External visual—there." The *Vega*, locked into the same orbit as her captor, was wreathed in a swirling mist of liquid and letters that billowed from the rip in her belly and danced a Brownian-motion polka around the liner's hull.

"Captain h'Reeviss, what happened?" Tr'Annhwi sounded more embarrassed that an intelligence officer should have seen this mess than concerned for the safety of his prize.

*"You blew a hole in my bloody ship and then dragged her half across the galaxy, that's what happened!"* crackled Reaves's voice. *"I'm only surprised the alcohol-cargo tanks lasted this long before—"*

"What losses, Captain? Was anyone hurt?"

*"No—but no thanks to you, you—"*

"Then what else? I see papers and liquid vapor—was that all?"

*"Some of the artwork blew out—explosive decompression sent it into atmosphere—lost items worth more than you'll earn in a—"*

"Good. No harm done." Tr'Annhwi didn't bother hiding his relief. "Now, Dr. Mak'khoi, if you would follow me . . . ?"

McCoy felt that the politeness of the request was rather offset by the vigor with which someone prodded a phaser into his back, but he followed anyway. It was better than being pushed the whole way to ch'Rihan.

None of them had said anything after tr'Annhwi's brief introduction, neither the subcommander nor the cool-eyed female commander who was uncomfortably like two other Romulan women officers in her quiet self-assurance, and certainly not the six soldiers who had accompanied her up to *Avenger* and back down, and who had sat stolidly gazing at McCoy the whole day long. Though to tell the truth, he hadn't felt inclined to open a conversation himself. Odds were that the soldiers didn't wear translators, and there wasn't much to talk about. He hadn't seen a great deal of ch'Rihan after landing, and before that—well, one M-class planet seen from orbit looked very much like another.

They had been sitting in the back of an armored military flitter for what felt like hours now, and McCoy had become very glad of the little 'freshbooth built into the vehicle's tail-section. Once in a while he wondered simple things: *Is it day or night outside? Will there be food soon? What does a Romulan city look like . . . ?* because his mind wouldn't go blank no matter how he tried to force it, and unless he thought of ordinary needs, the doubts and terrors kept creeping back to harry him. Of course, that was what they wanted, and why they had left him like this, but knowing it and being able to do something about it were two entirely different things.

The mouse-squeak of a Romulan communicator was so sudden and unusual that for a moment McCoy couldn't place it. But the guards stood up, and two opened the rear hatch of the flitter to admit a blessed breath of nonrecirculated air, while the remaining four escorted him out. If "escorting" actually described being seized by the upper arms and manhandled like a parcel.

It was night outside indeed, and alien constellations burned above him in a clear, clean sky. The dwelling toward which he was being "escorted," for the two larger guards had not yet released their grip on him, was a low, rambling place that was itself star-spotted with light, some harsh and artificial but the rest a warm amber glow of live-flame torchères.

The soldiers let him go at the foot of a short flight of stairs, and shifted to a parade march-step as they advanced up the steps alongside him. McCoy looked up at the building's open doorway and smiled briefly despite the untidy mixture of emotions that were filling him. *Wonderful,* he thought wryly, *a familiar, friendly face to welcome me.*

Tr'Annhwi was standing in the doorway wearing an expression fit to curdle milk, and the tall shape of Commander t'Radaik was right beside him. They were both armed, and not with phasers but with brutal-looking issue blasters. McCoy was simultaneously angry and amused. *Are they expecting trouble at* this *stage?* he thought. *Not from me, no sir!*

The hall inside was full of people, all Rihannsu, all staring hard, and McCoy felt uncomfortably like an animal put on show. He felt quite within his rights to stare back, at the soldiers and the officers, at the old man with wine on his chin, and at what had to be servants—

And suddenly, intently, at one in particular. A woman in servant's clothing, but with an elaborate garment over it that made him think of a fleet officer's half-cloak. But it wasn't her clothing. She had moved . . . *strangely* was the only way to describe it, and McCoy wondered something that was far from simple. *Is this the one? Am I in the right House after all?* His hands moved together in a recognition gesture, one that any Federation agent would spot immediately; its response was simple enough that she could reply at once, in plain sight. . . .

Except that she didn't. Oh, there was a fluttering of sorts as her fingers moved, but it wasn't the right movement. It wasn't any sort of gesture, just a twitch of nervousness. McCoy felt his guts give a little acid heave as the realization came home to him. Worst scenario. Very worst. Either this agent had gone the way Starfleet Command suspected, spent so long in deep cover that she'd gone native and literally forgotten who and what she really was, or—or maybe there'd been some horrible mistake and he'd been brought to the wrong House, wishful thinking had misread her body kinesics, and she wasn't an agent at all.

His mouth moved as he spoke bold words, bolder than he'd dared to utter yet, because there was a feeling that he had nothing to lose by them anymore. Maybe he was alone there after all.

Maybe he *was* going to die.

# Chapter Four

## PREFLIGHT

Naturally one does not just say good-bye to one's planet, build a fleet of starships, and take off in them . . . though this is often the image of what happened on Vulcan during the Reformation.

S'task showed some canniness about handling Vulcan psychology when he slipped the concept of a massive off-planet migration quietly into the Vulcan communications nets and mindtrees rather than making an open, hard declaration right off the bat. "When people think an idea is theirs," he said later in his writings aboard *Rea's Helm,* "they take it so much the more to heart than if they think they got it from someone else, or worse, followed a great public trend. There is nothing people want to do more than to follow great trends, and nothing they want less to *seem* to be doing."

The declaration itself, the document to be known much later as the Statement of Intention of Flight, appeared first in the journal of the Vulcan Academy of Sciences—then an infant body of the Universities—under a title that translates approximately into Terran academic-journalistic idiom as "A Study of Socioeconomic Influences on Vulcan Space Exploration." It was a sober and scholarly investigation into the economic trends that had moved the various Vulcan space programs over a thousand years, and it discussed in depth one recurring trend with disquieting correlations to the aggressiveness taking place on the planet at a specific place and time. When a given part of the planet grew too crowded to adequately support its population with water, food, and shelter, said this theory, then wars broke out there as the neighboring tribes or nations fought for resources. When wars broke out, technology, both physical and nonphysical, flourished during the "war efforts" of the various sides. And after the war in question was over, the technology was spun off into the private sector, with a subsequent substantial increase in the ability of a given part of the planet to support its population . . . until the next peak in the cycle.

S'task was therefore the first Vulcan to manage to introduce into Vulcan mass consciousness a statement of what on Earth has come to be known as Heinlein's Law. The idea had, of course, occurred to many people at many times over Vulcan's history, but S'task was the first to spread the concept so widely, into that "threshold number" of minds necessary for a culture to begin working change on itself. And, whether on purpose or accidentally, S'task framed the concept as the conclusion of an exercise in logic—asking, at the end of the article, whether it would not be more logical simply to have the increase in technology and subsequent spinoff and omit the war.

Many who read this saw in the article a potential reconciliation between S'task and Surak, but the old teacher knew better. He is said to have wept after he first saw the presentation of it, knowing that his student, whether in spite or cunning, was using logic, Surak's great love and tool, as a weapon against him.

It is sometimes hard for humans to understand that logic as a way of life did not instantly descend upon the whole Vulcan people immediately after Surak announced that it would be a good thing. Very quickly, by historical standards, yes: but not overnight. There were many false starts, renunciations, debunkings, persecutions, and periods of what seemed massive inertia; and the idea of the logical life went through many of the stages that other, less sweeping popular phenomena do. Around the time of the Statement of Intent, "reality-truth" was still truly only a fad among Vulcans, an "up-and-coming trend." This is something else that people, particularly humans, find hard to grasp. The difficulty is understandable, susceptible as we are to our own blindnesses to fads like the scientific method, and the various ways in which each new generation tends to twist the sciences to fit its own *zeitgeist*. Surak could see the time when reason would be truly internalized in the behavior of a whole population, and would guide the whole planet. But despite its validity as a tool, at the moment logic was only an easy gateway into people's minds because of its novelty status—and S'task was not ashamed to use it as such.

S'task also used the article to suggest something slightly radical: the idea that a largish planetary migration might be the tool necessary to curtail the planet's violence. If the whole planet's population were lessened, then the whole place would better be able to support the people who remained, and wars might be fewer. He never even mentioned the question of any philosophical disagreement, which was the root of the matter, and in truth it would have been inappropriate, in the context of the journal in question, to do so. As it was, the argument he used smacked of *a priori* reasoning, but its end product was something that too many people wanted to hear. This, too, is difficult to explain to humans—that despite their violent history, the Vulcans did not *like* violence, war, terror, or death. They simply had it . . . rather like the populations of many other planets that did not seem able to stop fighting. They wanted it to stop, or at least to slow down . . . and anything that seemed likely to do that seemed very good to them.

In any case, the article served to found the context for the flight: the idea that not only *could* many thousands of people leave Vulcan, but they *should*. Rather than having people trying to stop them from going, the travelers found pressure on them to go. There were, of course, some factions pressured into going against their will, and they made their belated displeasure known in the counsels of ch'Rihan and ch'Havran much later, to the intense annoyance of the majority of the Rihannsu. Several of these "forgotten" factions are the reason that there sometimes seem to be numerous different versions of the "Romulan Empire," all espousing different aims and behaving in different ways. More of this later.

So the context was established in the popular mind that a sort of "New Vulcan" should be established somewhere far from the decadent excesses and "liberalism" of the old. Support for this viewpoint grew across the board during the fifteen years or so that the argument officially lasted.

But the part of the "board" hardest to convince was, of course, industry, and S'task had to concentrate his efforts on them for some years before achieving the results he needed.

S'task knew quite well that finding venture capital to build fifteen ships of a kind that had never been seen before—generation ships—was not going to be possible. So, as usual, he went around the problem to an unexpected solution.

The mindtrees and networks had for some years been discussing the question of who should go. By 139970 the number of the *seheik,* the "declared," was approaching twelve thousand. Into this context S'task inserted the suggestion that perhaps only those should go who were willing to give nearly everything they had in support of it. The suggestion was a risky one, but also wise: it began functioning to "shake out" those who were not completely committed to the move because of the philosophy behind it. Subscriptions began to pile up in the escrow accounts established by S'task's followers, and as they did so, concern built in the Vulcan financial community.

It was at the point where about eight thousand people had made contributions varying from ten percent to a hundred percent of their estates, and construction had begun on *Rea's Helm* and *Farseeker,* that the community first began to seriously discuss what should be done about the flight. Their concern was understandable . . . since the travelers' movement was growing with a speed unprecedented until then. It had seemed only a fad until the 139980s, but by the end of that decade something like five percent of the population had committed to the journey. Within the close order of eighteen years, as much as twenty to thirty percent of the total capital wealth on Vulcan might be completely removed from the banking and credit systems. The Vulcan financial ecology could not withstand such a blow: any withdrawal of funds and labor potential greater than eighteen percent would cause a depression too deep for the planet to ever recover from. Yet such a withdrawal was certainly coming, unless something was done to halt or slow the spread of the traveler movement. At that time the question of financing enough ships to carry everyone was constantly in the nets, and attracting a great deal of attention to the issues of the traveler cause itself, which in turn was causing more and more Vulcans to contribute their time and money to the cause.

The major banking cartels conferred over this problem for nearly a year, and then took the only action possible to them: one that cost them the equivalent of billions of credits, but both saved Vulcan from a depression and made them a great deal of money later. They financed the building of the starships themselves, as well as much necessary research and development. Crookedly, in a way S'task himself had not expected, his twist on the Heinlein principle began to prove itself. The technologies born in the shipbuilding paid for themselves many times over, since all the major patents were owned by the banking cartels. It is true that the banks gained a measure of control over the journey by limiting the number of ships, and therefore of travelers, and with the problem of transport solved, some of the attractiveness of the journey as a "desperate cause" was lost, and the number of new subscribers to the journey dropped off. But S'task was willing to accept this, and to grant the banks their small measure of control. He had what he wanted from them. Also, he, too, had been worrying about the economic impact of the journey on Vulcan: he was angry at his homeworld, but not so much so as to want to reduce it to poverty.

Some have pointed out an unforeseen and unfortunate side effect of starting an interstellar colonization effort by subscription. Many fortunes large and small, many "nest eggs" and hoards of family money, went into the building fund even after the banks began financing the journey. Many a family was bitterly divided over the issue, and much Vulcan fiction of this period revolves around the Sundering. Among those making the journey, a peculiar mindset began to form, born of the poverty and scarcity that many of the travelers had to suffer while waiting to leave Vulcan. Many of the travelers came to feel that possession of more than one's daily needs was an evil, that one should share as necessary with those others also making the journey and otherwise eschew personal possessions and wealth. Some cultural sociologists have stated the opinion that this "foundation context" of privation and scarcity as a thing somehow good and noble came to affect the Rihannsu later in their development. These sociologists suggest that had the journey not started this way, the Rihannsu would not have had the problems with poverty and scarcity that they had later. But then again, neither would they have been Rihannsu as we now know them.

With design and construction, funding finally available for the ships, serious consideration of where they should go could begin, had to, since this would influence the ships' design at every level. Mass interferometry and spectrometry of neighboring stars had been fairly encouraging. The area around 40 Eri contains several large congeries of stars, one a group of Population II blue and blue-white giants, and the two others both large collections of Pop I stars ranging through types G through M, with the occasional N, R, and S "carbon stars." There were at least twenty stars within five light-years of Vulcan, another eighty within fifteen light-years, and of both these groups, the mass interferometer indicated that some twenty had planets. The astronomers involved in the journey had a merry time arguing over the optimum course, but finally agreement was reached on an initial twelve-year tour of the most likely close stars, with an optional fifty-year tour of the less well-scanned outer ones. There were five very likely candidates in the first sequence, three of them type M stars like Vulcan, the others a type K and a G9, rather more orange than yellow. All five had planets, several of them large ones Vulcan's size or larger, and the Vulcan version of Bode's Law indicated that each system had at least one planet at what (for Vulcans) was the right distance from its sun.

To help (or some said hinder) them, they also had some information salvaged from the computers of the crashed or captured Etoshan pirate ships, concerning the locations of populated planets. This data the Vulcans were generally inclined to mistrust, since the Etoshans had already lied to them. However, they did use the information in a negative way: they kept far away from any star mentioned in it. The travelers did not want to be found by aliens again. All the courses plotted were to take them far from space known to the Etoshans.

With all this in mind, the ships built were designed as fairly short-term interstellar shuttle ships, with an option for use as generation vessels should both the first and second tours prove barren. Each ship was meant to carry about five thousand people in an arrangement of six cylinders clustered and bound together by accessways and major "thor-oughfares." The design of these craft closely approximates those used for some of the L5 colonies around Terra, except that gravity was pro-vided artificially rather than by spin. Drive for the vessels was conven-tional iondrive with the Vulcan version of a Bussard ramjet (a piece of design they did not mind stealing from the Etoshans). Later on, when they discovered it during the journey, the psi-assisted "bootstrap" method was also occasionally used, by which an adept instantly acceler-ated the whole vessel to .99999c, and then allowed the ship to coast "downhill" to the next star. This method was used only when there was an extreme emergency threatening the vessel; it tended to kill the adept performing it, and only a jump-trained adept could train others in the technique. Whichever method was used, the ship could use a given star's gravity well to slow it down, and then move on subdrive to the primary's planets: or if the star's planets looked unpromising, it could pick up momentum again by using the gravity well for the acceleration phase of a "slingshot" maneuver.

Ships were not the only thing being built, however. Many of the travelers had realized that if they were going to truly become their own world rather than a sort of retread of the failed Vulcan, they would have to discard a great deal of their culture, and invent new institutions as re-placements. The matter of choices took the whole fifteen years between the Statement of Intent and the launching of *Rea's Helm,* and to this day the controversy about some choices has not died down.

The records of the arguments on the nets, and transcriptions or paraphrasings of the discussions on the mindtrees, fill some six hun-dred rooms in the archive on ch'Havran, and some hundreds of ter-abytes in the Vulcan Science Academy's history storage. Vulcan foods, literature, clothing styles, weapons, poetry, religions, social customs, furniture designs, fairy tales, art, science, and philosophy all were end-lessly examined in a fifteen-year game of "lifeboat." Only the best, or the ideologically correct, were to be taken along on the journey. No one person or committee was ever set up as the arbiter of taste: the roughly eighty thousand minds participating in the nets and the travelers' mindtrees would argue themselves to a rough consensus, or to silence, and in either case each traveler would decide for himself what to do about a given issue. Mostly they agreed, and it may be astonishing to Terrans how often these people did so. They were possibly more like-minded than we, or they, would like to admit, or else they were terrified by how closely their previous disagreement had brought their planet to disaster.

One thing they agreed on quickly was that they could not stop being Vulcan while they still spoke the language. A team of semanticists and poets, S'task among them, began building the travelers' new language just after the ships' keels were flown. They did not, of course, try to divorce it completely from Vulcan, but they went back to the original Old High Vulcan roots and "aged" the words in another direction, as it were—producing a language as different from its ancient parent and the other "fullgrown" tongue as Basque is different from Spanish and their parent, Latin. The new tongue was a softer one, with fewer fricatives than Vulcan, and many aspirants; long broad vowels and liquid consonant combinations, both fairly rare in Vulcan, were made commonplace in the new language. To Terran ears it frequently sounds like a combination of Latin and Welsh. The language came strangely to Vulcan tongues at first, but its grammar and syntax were grossly similar, and over the years of flight, the travelers spoke it with increasing pleasure and pride. From it they took what was to be their new name, which by attachment became the language's also. *Seheik,* "the declared," became *rihanh* in the new language. This, in the adjective form, became *rihannsu*. The building of the language is often overlooked in studies of Rihannsu culture. It deserves more attention than there is room to give it here—the only "made" language ever to be successfully adopted by an entire planetary population.

But though this and many other good things were added to the Rihannsu culture, many things were also lost. The matriarchal cast of the civilization remained, though power would come to distribute itself rather differently from the council-of-tribes structure under which Vulcan had been operating for thousands of years. Much literature was condemned as "decadent" or "liberal" and left behind. A considerable amount of science scavenged from the Etoshans was relabeled as Vulcan. The encounter with the Etoshans itself, the trigger of all this, was retold as the foundation of the persecutions that caused the travelers to leave the planet, and the "straw that broke the camel's back." When one looks at this bit of revisionist history, the xenophobia of "Romulans" becomes entirely understandable. Fifty generations of Rihannsu were taught that anything alien was probably bad, and vice versa. Earthmen saying "we come in peace" were not likely to be believed. The Etoshans had said the same thing.

For good or ill (though meaning good), the travelers decided to rewrite history for their children and teach them all the same thing. Mostly it came to the idea, as stated above, that aliens were dangerous, that even their own people had once made a dangerous choice, but that they (the fortunate children) had been saved from it; they must take care not to let the same thing happen to them, or *their* children. And indeed to this day there are two words in Rihannsu for fact: "truth" and "told-truth."

There were, of course, cultural and artistic "smugglings." Not even the Vulcan-trained can police the thoughts of eighty thousand fiercely committed revolutionaries (or counterrevolutionaries). Bits of non-approved culture, science, and law sneaked in here and there. Some of them were the source of endless anguish. Some were afterward cherished as treasures.

One of these was S'task's own, and not even his own people could much blame him for it. As poets often are, he was a swordsman as well, and besides his wife and daughter and the clothes on his back, the only things he brought with him on the journey were three swords by the smith S'harien.

S'harien was the greatest of all the smiths working by the edge of the desert that other species call Vulcan's Forge, and he was also something of an embarrassment to everyone who knew him. He lived for metal: beside it, nothing mattered to him, not his wife, not his children, not eating or drinking. He was usually rude and almost always unkempt (in Vulcan culture, the most unforgivable of bad habits), one of those people who is always being taken places twice . . . the second time to apologize. He was almost always forgiven, for this cranky, perpetually angry creature could create such beauty in steel as had never been seen before. "He works it as a god works flesh," said another smith, one of his contemporaries. Petty kings and tribal chieftains had often come offering everything they had to purchase his swords. He insulted them like beggars, and they took it. They had to: he was S'harien.

He was also a diehard reactionary. In a time when so many other Vulcan men were taking the five-letter names beginning with S and ending in K in token of their acceptance (or at least honoring) of "reality-truth" and its chief proponent, S'harien purposely took a pre-Reformation name, and an ill-omened one, "pierceblood." S'harien loved the old wars and the honorable bloodshed, and hated Surak's name, and would spit on his shadow if he saw it—so he told everyone. On his hundred and ninetieth birthday, hearing that Surak was nearby, he went to do so. And everyone became very confused when, a tenday later, S'harien very suddenly started buying up all his swords and melting them down, in ongoing renunciation of violence. Even Surak tried to stop him from doing this: a S'harien sword was a treasure of gorgeous and dangerous workmanship that even the most nonviolent heart could rest in without guilt. But S'harien was not to be dissuaded.

There was consternation late one night when a flitter docked outside S'task's quarters in the orbital shipyards, and the short, dark, fierce shape in the pressure suit stepped through the airlock with a long bundle in his arms. The security people stared in astonishment. It was in fact Surak. They took him to S'task and made to leave, though very much desiring to stay: master and pupil had at that point not seen each other for six standard years. But Surak bade them stay, and handed the bundle to S'task. "Keep these safe, I pray you," he said in the Old High Vulcan of ceremony. And S'task, stricken by the formality of the language—or perhaps by the worn look of his old master—took the bundle, bowed deeply, and made no other answer. When he straightened, Surak was already on his way out.

The bundle contained three of the most priceless S'hariens on the planet, two of which had been thought to belong to kings, and one to the High Councillor, himself a bitter enemy of Surak's. How Surak had come by the swords no one ever found out, though various Vulcan families have (conflicting) tales of a shadowy shape who came to them around that time and begged them for "their sword's life." There was argument about keeping the swords, at first—they had after all come from Surak, and there were sore hearts who wanted no gifts from him: gifts, they said, bind. But S'task said a few quiet words in the swords' behalf in meeting, some nights before the ships left, and put the issue to rest. In time the travelers came to treasure the S'hariens greatly, as a gift from their most worthy adversary, and as beautiful things in their own right, but most of all as a symbol for the ancient glory they were leaving behind.

The S'hariens were, after all, "swords of the twilight," made in the style of the swords of the ancient Vulcan empires, by methods that no one but S'harien had been able to reconstruct. But those empires were long gone, and the planet was even now a far calmer place than it had been in those times of enormous ferocity and splendor. If Surak's teachings took hold, as all the travelers now felt sure they would, then Vulcan would become quieter still. They would take the swords with them to remember the old Vulcan by—the energetic, angry, beautiful, whole Vulcan, all blood-green passion and joy that dared death, laughing. They took the swords though it was their enemy who gave them, and though the man who made them would sooner have seen them destroyed than in Rihannsu hands (or indeed any other). The sword became both the cause and the symbol of the Sundering. It was the sword that parted Vulcan. It was the sword that would eventually draw the two sundered parts together over the years, though neither side was to know that as *Rea's Helm* glided away from Vulcan and Charis, leaving its one stave behind it in the dark.

Perhaps those angry hearts in meeting were right. Perhaps gifts do bind. Or perhaps, despite millennia, blood is enough.

# Chapter Five

Arrhae had never before been so happy to be dismissed. Her thoughts were still in a whirl as she pattered downstairs more quickly than was proper, wondering, *What to do? What to do?* in a sort of frantic litany. Her hands were shaking and she couldn't make them stop, her heart was pounding far too fast, and for one horrible moment she thought that she was going to be sick right there and then.

The nausea passed without shaming her, and Arrhae leaned against the wall, pressing her head to the cool stone and feeling a droplet of sweat ooze clammily from her hairline. "Calm," she said. "Control." Then whimpered in sudden terror and clapped one of those shaking hands to her mouth, for the words had come out in Anglish.

This time she *was* sick, making it to the Elements-be-thanked 'fresher just in time. Arrhae sat for some minutes on the floor, shuddering and feeling wretched, before she felt capable of even turning on the disposal-sluices. *Poor tr'Aimne. If this is what he felt like in the flitter . . .*

That memory of ordinary everyday things, which seen now were neither, and never truly had been, helped to get her shocked mind back into some sort of coherent working order. Rinsing her face and her mouth with cold water, and feeling much better for it, Arrhae started to think of what had to be done. Not about McCoy the Federation officer—if that was truly what he was—but about Mak'khoi the prisoner, and where she was going to put him.

The storeroom, obviously—but had it been cleaned yet? Aired? Heated? She had a sneaking suspicion that none of those things had been done, and why? Because she, *hru'hfe* of House Khellian, had preferred to gape at visitors like the lowliest scullery-slave rather than be about her proper business.

*There, that feels more like it.*

Arrhae's mouth quirked with annoyance. Half an hour ago she wouldn't have needed to consciously review her thoughts like that—and wouldn't have been thinking in Terran Anglish either! All of her acclimatization was ruined, and she had a feeling that she had already given herself away to the Terran—

—*No, his name's McCoy, and he's not a "Terran," he's one of my people . . . !*

—*But I'm Arrhae ir-Mnaeha t'Khellian, and he's one of the* enemies *of my people!*

"O Fire and Air and Earth," she moaned softly, sitting down again and wrapping her arms around the legs that were suddenly too weak to hold her up. Arrhae closed her eyes and rested her head on her knees, rocking backward and forward, backward and forward, no longer even sure of how to make her prayers. "Ohhh, God help me. . . ."

When it came, as come it must, the brief storm of weeping was shocking in its intensity and for a time left her drained of all emotion. That at least was good, for it meant that she could be cold and rational for a while, before her mind began to churn again and the terrors came flooding back. Arrhae washed her face a second time, straightened her rumpled clothing, and eyed herself critically in the burnished metal mirror.

"*Ihlla'hn, hru'hfe,*" she told the reflection. *You'll do. For now, anyway.*

She channeled all of that pent-up nervous energy into organizing a scouring-squad for the new "secure quarters." The next half hour did nothing for Arrhae's popularity among the servants, but a great deal for her reputation as a maniacally efficient slave driver. Not that she shouted, or struck anyone. There was no need for such crude methods when her tongue and vocabulary seemed to acquire fresh cutting edges, new depths of subtlety, and new heights of eloquence. Even while they cursed her name and ancestry under their breath, more than one of the house-folk laboring with mops and cleaning rags were making mental note of some superbly original insult for their own later use. . . .

Arrhae had at first hoped she wouldn't be able to think of private matters if she allowed the fine fury of cleaning-supervision take her over, but she was wrong. There was always a voice tickling at the back of her mind, demanding that she attend to everything it had to say. Finally she switched over to automatic, at least where the cleanup was concerned, and began to listen in the hope that once heard, the words from her subconscious would go away.

"*. . . Please sit down, Lieutenant Commander Haleakala . . .*"

"*. . .* fed in the program parameters, and yours was one of the first names to come out."

Commodore Perry had been more than courteous in the hour or so since she'd been ushered into his office at Starfleet Intelligence Headquarters; the big man had been downright kindly, taking pains to disarm her nervousness—which had been more obvious than she liked to think—before starting to explain why she'd been pulled out of xenosociology aboard *Excalibur* at such short notice.

"Romulans," she said. Just that. It was more than enough.

Perry nodded, touching the molecular fiche on the desk in front of him with one fingertip. It was tabbed with a data scrambler and the yellow/black/yellow-on-red of MOST SECRET, EYES ONLY information, almost the highest security level in Starfleet and certainly the highest that she'd ever shared a room with. "They call themselves *Rihannsu*. And that's just about the only reliable information that we have. Everything else"—he flipped one hand dismissively at the air—"is educated speculation at best and wild guesses at worst. We need to know more. Much more."

"'Know your enemy.' Is that it, sir?" *Oh, very bold, Terise. Tell him you disapprove of the word "enemy" now, why don't you?*

"In one way, yes. But not in such simplistic terms as you seem to be implying, Commander."

*Ouch . . . !* "Noted, sir."

"There are a few agents already planted in the Romulan Empire; ninety-plus percent are Romulans themselves, and what information we glean from them is military—which would be all very well if we were planning war. If we were, say, Klingons. But what we want, and what the Federation needs, is a basis for *understanding* these people."

Perry glanced at something that flickered across the readout at one side of his desk, punched a couple of buttons to acknowledge it, and lifted one of the data chips that sat in an impeccably straight line beside their scanning-slot. "Vaebn tr'Lhoell," he said. "One of our Romulans, and a good, reliable agent. There's just one problem. The Romulan agents are too—too Romulan. They were born to and brought up with aspects of their culture that we can't begin to comprehend, and they can't explain them to an outsider any more than a bird could explain the sky. Only a deep-cover agent can do it, and physiology restricts us to either Terran or Vulcan. Even then, Romulan physiology is Vulcan rather than Terran; that much has been learned already. So where necessary, there'll have to be . . ." Perry's voice trailed off as he hunted for an appropriate term.

"'Cosmetic changes'?" Terise suggested. "And that's why"—with a sudden flash of brilliance—"my name came up in the personnel scan." Terise had a full name that sometimes felt yards long, a dusky complexion inherited from a Polynesian mother and an Italian father, and a facial bone-structure all her own that was sharp enough to split kindling. Several of her less lovable schoolfellows had called her "the Vulcan" because of it, although that had stopped once she graduated to Starfleet Academy and there were real Vulcans in the classes with her—as well as Andorians, Tellarites, and weirder species who departed from the bipedal hominid norm. Xenopathic screening of the student body also had something to do with it. Small use crewing a starship with half-a-dozen races and not making sure they wouldn't be at what passed for one another's throats before their first mission was a week old.

"Quite so. And you require fewer, er, changes than most. The ears, obviously, will need slight remodeling"—Perry cleared his throat noisily, now more ill at ease than she was, and Terise came very close to patting his hands in reassurance. "Hemoplasmic pigmentation tagging, primary craniofacial restructure . . . ? Who the hell wrote this? We're talking about people, not refitting a starship!"

"Commodore, I don't mind; truly I don't. If I'd been that thin-skinned, I'd never have survived high school. And sir, you've got at least one volunteer." All the words came out in a rush, the comforting inconsequential ones and the ones that might end up killing her. When it was done, Terise sat up very straight in her chair and swallowed, hard. That was such a cliché, but there came a time in everyone's life when only the tried and trusted gestures felt sufficiently adequate, and this was such a time right now.

"You do understand what you're letting yourself in for, Ms. Haleakala? Or is that Ms. LoBrutto? I've been presuming you don't use the hyphen, either. Excuse me. . . ."

"Yes and no, Commodore. Yes, I know what I'll be going into, and the prospect terrifies me—but I'm a sociologist by profession and nobody trained in that discipline would ever pass up an opportunity like this." Terise hesitated over that sweeping statement, wondering if she should add *except the ones who want to live* and decided not to bother. Instead, she smiled wryly. "And no, it is hyphenated. You got it right first time."

"Thank you. For that and other matters. But I'm not logging your acceptance until after you've been briefed on the setup." Terise's eyebrows must have shot up involuntarily, because the Commodore looked at the security-blazoned fiche and then grinned at her. "Don't worry, Commander. What I'll tell you isn't anything like as confidential. Not at all. You won't be asked to sign anything in blood." He grinned again. "Not yet; not until it's green."

Terise made the sort of hollow laugh that would have sounded more genuine had she simply said "ha-ha" and been done with it.

"Quite so," said Perry. "But keep your sense of humor—you're going to need it." He dropped one of the data chips into its slot and keyed a string of characters. There was a momentary mosquito-whine, and sparkles of color sleeted across his desk readout as the monomolecular scanner kicked in.

*"Authorization?"* it said.

"Perry, Stephen C., Commodore, UFP Starfleet Intelligence Corps, CEG-0703-1960MS."

*"Accepted. Data up and running."*

"Good." Perry caught the "was that all?" look on Terise's face and nodded. "Yes, Commander, that's all—for this information at least. Getting at the other . . . Not so simple. Anyway, this is the game plan for this particular play, and I warn you right now, you won't like it. . . ."

*". . . like it?"*

"Eh?" Arrhae jolted back to the bad dream that was real life, wondering who had been saying what. The *who* was S'anra, one of the scullery servants, and the *what?* had been repeated for Elements alone knew how many times.

"*Hru'hfe,* all here is finished—do you like it?"

She came back to awareness quickly enough after that, and glared around with the expression of someone expecting to find the work done poorly if at all. Instead, and to her unvoiced surprise, it had been done well. The floor, first brushed then scrubbed, had finally been polished brightly enough for Arrhae to see her quizzical face reflecting back from its tiled surface.

"Excellent," she said, genuinely pleased. "All of you have done well—and by that, done honor to our lord. My word as *hru'hfe* on it, I shall name all your names to him, and speak highly of them. S'anra, Ekkhae, Hanaj, you three attend to the furnishings—and, by my order, commandeer as many strong backs as you need to carry things. The colors and the patterns"—Arrhae hesitated, and made her hesitation plain. Only her decision was made plainer—"I leave to you." She smiled thinly at them, a lesser servant and two slaves entrusted with something she should attend to herself. "I may have to change things—but I would think well of you if I could leave all as I find it."

She looked around the storeroom while the servants filed past, confused by the warmth of her words but giving her profound reverences because of them, and she thought of how soon it would be a prison cell, and suppressed a shudder. Hangings of fur and textile relieved the starkness of the room's plain walls and gave a certain primitive splendor to the rough-hewn stones. Only the high-tech look of thermotropic heaters and incantube lighting made the place seem any different from the dungeons in the old tales of T'Eleijha and the Raven. Stories that Arrhae had loved to watch or hear, whenever she had the free time for either.

Stories that were no more than alien folklore to Lieutenant Commander Terise Haleakala-LoBrutto.

Commodore Perry had been right. She didn't like it. Neither the plan, nor the execution of it. Had she not made a promise to herself before she volunteered that she wouldn't back out no matter what, Terise would have put in for an immediate transfer back to the *Excalibur* right after Perry told her what would be expected of her. No matter that the M-5 combat exercise didn't sound much fun, it didn't sound dangerous either.

This did.

Starfleet's basic plan was that she learn as much Romulan data and language as they had on file and then be seeded on one of their Romulan double agents as a sleeper, for fine-tuning before becoming an active deep-cover operative.

The realities behind the plan were less simple: for one thing, the language-tutoring would have to be a form of chemical-cnhanced speed learning, and while that was highly efficient in its own small way, it was also the means to a three-day migraine headache that matched the Big Bang for intensity. Terise knew all about *that,* because to her lasting shame she had used it for illicit revision at college. Once . . . On all the other occasions she had done her assignments the way they were supposed to be done, and been thankful that any headaches earned had just been little ones.

But it was the prospect of sleeper-time that she really didn't like. Starfleet's knowledge of the Romulan language was restricted to what clipped military communications the Neutral Zone spy-satellites were able to monitor—and that wasn't anything like enough.

So she was going to be a slave. The ancient sold-into-bondage, chain-on-the-neck—"I gather it's been refined down to a sort of dog collar with the owner's name and address on it," Perry had told her in an attempt at comfort—sort of slave who was one degree up from the domestic animals because slaves *usually* didn't need to be told things more than once. . . .

Granted that her master was to be Vaebn tr'Lhoell or one of the other Romulans who would only pretend to treat her as property, the whole notion still made Terise feel twitchy. *What if anything goes wrong?* had been her first thought. After she had heard how she was to be "sold as unsatisfactory" to a more highly placed household once tr'Lhoell was certain that she could conduct herself as a native-born Rihanha, it had been her final thought as well.

How final that thought might turn out to be, Terise didn't like to consider. Certainly matters had proceeded apace once she had insisted that her acceptance of the mission be placed on record; almost as if somewhere high up in Starfleet there was a fear that she would back out if given enough peace to reconsider what she had done.

Terise was just a little bit uneasy at the speed with which she assimilated Romulan. She knew of the dangers confronting deep-cover operatives in hostile territory, and those dangers were not always a result of being caught. Sometimes the greatest hazards lay in *not* being detected, and in adapting too well to the role of an alternate personality. There was the standard cautionary tale of the longterm prisoner who tried to escape from jail by simulating madness, and who succeeded so completely that when he was released, it was into the care of an insane asylum. Such risks were not usual during an ordinary tour of duty in the lab of a starship, but this was no tour, and *nothing* about it was ordinary.

The name they gave her soon replaced her own—for the simple reason that no one at the Intelligence facility ever called her anything other than Arrhae ir-Mnaeha. Terise/Arrhae found the supposedly cumbersome Romulan names easy enough to manage, because only a few of them seemed to have more syllables than her own . . . or the name which had *been* her own and which was now fading away like a dream after waking. And they all had a meaning, which made the actual understanding of them a relatively simple thing once the language structure was shoehorned into her brain. But the shift in mindset necessary for that understanding, and for the many, many other things that intelligence people had spent so long briefing her about?

That was something which she was certain that she would never accomplish. . . .

. . . Until she did.

"Madame, sirs, all is in readiness." Arrhae made the announcement from just inside the doorway, and was careful not to look directly at the man Mak'khoi. *McCoy,* her mind corrected. She ignored the correction. He was Federation—and that meant he was an enemy until the time when he could be proven otherwise. It made matters easier if she thought of him only as an abstract danger, like a venomous *nei'rrh* loose in an empty room. The sort of thing that she could walk softly around, in the knowledge that if she didn't disturb it, then she was safe. Always assuming, of course, that the *nei'rrh* in question wasn't feeling irritable, or pugnacious, or had had its feathers ruffled.

This one was suffering from all three. He knew not only what she had said, but all the substrata of meaning behind her simple declaration. That he was to be imprisoned; that a special place had been prepared for him; and that she was not going to reply to his signal. That, most of all, burned in his eyes as he stood up and Arrhae at last glanced toward him, knowing that not to do so would appear unnatural. Not a *nei'rrh* at all, she thought. A *thrai,* with all the memory for wrongs done him that *thraiin* were supposed to have. She tried to visualize Mak'khoi bearing such a grudge for years until the time was ripe for vengeance, like that old Klingon proverb people were so fond of quoting with a sneer, and found that she could not. There was a gentleness about the man that ran so deep it accorded ill with the hot rage he wore like a garment. As if he knew himself justified in his anger, but would as soon find reason to put it aside, even here, among his enemies.

"Soon enough, Doctor," she heard tr'Annhwi say. "When your trial is concluded and the sentence is in progress, think of my kinfolk as you howl."

Arrhae had heard threats uttered before; now and again, when in their cups, officers and other persons of sufficient rank to have had more sense would go so far as to make dueling challenges over H'daen tr'Khellian's dinner table, but what tr'Annhwi said, and the coarse, brutal way in which he said it to a prisoner with no means to respond, made Arrhae's hackles rise and her dislike of the subcommander increase to detestation. She had many reasons, of which his behavior toward her in the hallway of her master's house was only the most personal. Arrhae ir-Mnaeha might have begun as a slave, but as her career advanced, so she associated with persons of good character and learned to comport herself in similar fashion. Such folk did not threaten the helpless, even when they were enemies; *mnhei'sahe* forbade it. Rather, they treated all, and especially their dearest enemies, as companions and equals worthy of respect and honor; *mnhei'sahe* required it.

Except that *mnhei'sahe* seemed to have become an outmoded concept. . . .

Except among people like her master and Commander t'Radaik, both of whom glared at tr'Annhwi in a way that wished him ill. "You will stay here, Subcommander," t'Radaik said. "And later, I think, we might discuss and clarify certain matters. The courtesy once considered part of Fleet rank, perhaps—or which rank is more appropriate to a lack of it? Sit down, and await me."

Tr'Annhwi stared at his superior for a few seconds, with the expression of a man not believing his own ears. Not that he had never been disciplined before—very few in the Romulan military could make that claim—but to have it happen before civilians and an enemy . . .

He sat down with a jolt, mouth hanging open and eyes that had momentarily been wide with shock now narrowing with affront and fury. T'Radaik ignored his little performance, ignored *him,* as if he had ceased to exist. She turned instead, and pointedly, to Dr. McCoy, and gestured—Terranwise, with a crooking of all her fingers—that he should accompany her.

"Not all the Empire is so lacking in manners, Doctor," the commander said, speaking Standard and choosing the correctness of her words with care. "Only most of it."

That was a perilous statement, and one which she dared not make in Rihannsu before so many witnesses. Only tr'Annhwi understood and might have proven dangerous—except that after his justly corrected rudeness, heard by all, any accusation that he could make would be seen only as spite.

Arrhae also understood, but was not so foolish as to make it known. She had very properly lowered her eyes while those of higher rank exchanged hard words; except in certain notorious Houses, servants were neither deaf nor expected to be, but they were expected to remain attentive while not *obviously* listening. At such times, her facial muscles relaxed to an almost-Vulcan impassivity so that no matter what was said,

she would not react to it. But for all her control and all her training in
the hard school of slave to manager-of-servants, Arrhae's mouth still
went dry at t'Radaik's next words. She tried to watch the commander
from under her brows while keeping her head bowed far enough to
hide the expression which was surely plastered all over her face.

"Arrhae t'Khellian is *hru'hfe* to this House, Dr. Mak'khoi. She will
attend you here, with"—a swift and winning smile was directed at
H'daen—"her master's permission, of course."

H'daen gave his approval in the manner that he preferred over more
modern things—such as saying *yes* and leaving it at that—with the elegant salute and half-bow that was so many years out-of-date. Even in
the throes of early panic Arrhae wondered why the commander had
made a request instead of issuing the direct order which was more right
and proper. And McCoy gazed at her, seeming no more than mildly curious. Then he merely nodded and walked past her without another
glance, smiling thinly as captives do when hope recedes.

A gallows smile, like that which Vaebn tr'Lhoell had worn when they
dragged him away with the food and the wine and the blood all
smeared across his face and clothing. Arrhae shuddered and began to
issue orders for the dining chamber to be cleared and cleaned.

*Vaebn,* she thought somberly. *Oh, Vaebn, what did you do wrong? And
how do I avoid the same mistake . . . ?*

". . . if matters are well with you, Arrhae, then they are well with me
also."

Though his verbal greeting was traditional, the handshake that followed it was not. Vaebn tr'Lhoell looked less like the Romulans of
Terise's enhanced imagination than did several Vulcans of her immediate acquaintance. He was of only medium height, around her own
meter and a half, and very slender, with that cool serenity which so
many people associated with pure Vulcans and which she had encountered in so few at intelligence center. Oh, they had been calm and logical enough, but there was always an underlying tension about them
when she was present, especially after the hemochromic tagging and
the augmentation surgery. This man, this Rihanha who was to be her

protector and her mentor and her master—*O-sensei,* suggested the part of her mind that came up with an appropriate word or phrase now and then, usually too late for it to be witty and worth saying anymore—was more in control of himself than all of them together.

*Has to be, I guess,* she thought in that garble of Romulan and Standard Anglish that her mind had been using of late, *because one false move and he's dead. And* I'm *dead with him! I wonder why he does it? Why any of them do it? Even me . . . ?*

The start of the mission was as dangerous as the rest seemed likely to be. A cloaked scoutship had seemed like a good idea while Commodore Perry had been bandying it about like an ace up his sleeve, but Terise had learned later that the cloaking device had been "acquired" from the Romulans themselves, and so recently that it was still throwing the occasional tantrum when fitted to Federation vessels. The three small ships run by Starfleet Intelligence for their clandestine missions were prototypes; laden with new technology, each had several untraced bugs to make their flights more interesting.

This particular scout had developed a small, irregularly recurring fault in—typically—its cloaking circuitry at a stage in the mission—also typically—where turnabout was out of the question. They had flipped out of cloak for two seconds while crossing the Neutral Zone perimeter, barely twenty thousand kilometers from the close-cordon patrol cruiser NCC-1843 *Nelson,* and those had been the longest two seconds of Terise's life. Because they hadn't been running an ID and had behaved—thanks to the malfunctioning cloaking device—like a Romulan vessel, they had been fired on, and had barely escaped with hull or hides intact.

It had given Terise an interesting demonstration of just how the ostensibly peaceful Federation military regarded Romulans, and never mind what Perry had said about cross-cultural education. She required no effort at all to guess how a notoriously belligerent warrior people might feel about the Federation, its personnel . . . and its spies.

She had been a "slave" in House Lhoell for fourteen standard months, and her "master" had tutored his stupidest possession exhaustively in the language, etiquette, and customs of the elevated society in which he moved. What the other slaves saw, and snickered over, was the new arrival spending a great deal of time in her lord's private chambers and seeming excessively tired as a consequence. Terise/Arrhae didn't let the coarse teasing worry her; some of her school "friends" had been just as cruel to a child far less able to cope than the Command-conditioned adult she had become.

She learned all the things that a native-born Rihanha was supposed to know, but the revelation of language came as she had been told it might: suddenly. Between one of Vaebn's sentences and the next, familiar things went strange and then snapped back to being more familiar than they had ever been before. Only their names had changed. Or not changed, been remembered correctly for the first time. After that, everything seemed to happen faster and faster, like a ball rolling down a hill.

A short time later Vaebn tr'Lhoell purchased himself a new slave. She was young and startlingly beautiful, and within days of her appearance—and nightly disappearances into Vaebn's private chambers—wagers were being laid among the other servants concerning how long Arrhae ir-Mnaeha would tolerate the situation. The staged fight when her patience "broke at last" surely provided gossip for months thereafter. Arrhae heard none of it. Her name, three-view image, listed abilities, and price were in the area computer's database before nightfall, and she was away from House Lhoell by late afternoon of the next day, as if Vaebn had sold her to the first bidder of a reasonable sum.

She knew differently. House Khellian had no connections to Starfleet Intelligence, Vaebn had warned her of that much, or indeed any connections to anywhere much. But it was an ideal base for an operative on such a mission as hers. Arrhae wondered, sometimes, just how the sale had been arranged. . . .

A House of good lineage fallen on hard times, Khellian was poorly served for the simple reason that its lord could afford to buy or employ no better than the dull slaves and sullen servants who misran the place. But Arrhae was aware of what Vaebn had told H'daen tr'Khellian about her capabilities and the true reason for her sudden sale. She had heard them laughing about it in H'daen's meeting room while she knelt on the floor outside in the proper submissive posture. Coarse masculine laughter at first, and then a softer, more thoughtful chuckling. H'daen had bidden his guest farewell, brought her to his study, struck a key on his personal computerpad, and then shown her what was on the screen. Her manumission, and her right to use his House-style as her own third name.

She had earned that freedom a hundred times over in the years that she had served House Khellian, scrabbling her way up the ladder of service until only Nnerhin tr'Hwersuil, *hru'hfe* of the household, held a higher rank. Nnerhin's death in that appalling traffic accident had left the way clear, and she was the obvious, indeed only, choice. But sometimes, lying awake in the darkness, Arrhae had wondered: *was that arranged as well . . . ?*

If there was an answer, she didn't want to know.

For a man who had just been verbally chastised by a senior officer, Subcommander tr'Annhwi looked improbably cheerful. He watched her as she bustled about, supervising the other servants and trying to keep herself so busy that she wouldn't have to think. She had labeled him as the sort of touchy, prideful man who balanced perpetually on the edge of anger, and who wouldn't tolerate any slight to his honor, and yet here he was, quite self-contained, sipping wine and smiling slightly at her every time their eyes met. That, most of all, made Arrhae uneasy.

He drained the winecup and waved away the servant who would have refilled it, pushed himself upright with only the slightest hint of sway in his posture, and made a quick military salute in her direction. "Too much wine already, *hru'hfe*. I should have drunk less at dinner. Then I wouldn't have . . . said what I did." He tugged at his uniform, straightening its half-cloak at his shoulder. "I shall make my apologies, and leave this house."

*If a* hnoiyika *looked contrite after it killed something,* thought Arrhae, *it would look something like you do now.*

"You think badly of me, too, don't you?"

"I . . . no, sir. Of course not. A gentleman may take wine with his fellows and—"

"That makes me glad." His smile widened and grew warmer. "Then I *can* visit you again?"

Arrhae felt as though someone had dropped a pound of ice into her guts. She had an overwhelming sense of having been maneuvered into a corner, because no matter what she said now would be either a self-contradiction or an insult—and she had no wish to insult *this* man. "You want to . . . visit me?" she managed at last, wondering what had prompted this and hoping that it was the wine.

"I do, and it would please me if you said yes. I was rude to you at first, but that was before I saw you properly."

*Small excuse! And he talks like someone from a cheap play!* There was only one problem; she had heard front-line Fleet officers, tough military men with only the merest veneer of culture, use exactly that sort of second-hand romantic speech to their ladies. It scared her. First Mak'khoi on her hands, with all that meant, and now this. She wasn't even sure what scared her most about it, that tr'Annhwi might need an ulterior motive to bring him back—or that he might be sincere.

"Uh, sir," she said, hunting for a way out that wouldn't sound like one, "I can make no such agreement without my lord's word on it."

"Then have no fear, lady, for I shall speak at once to H'daen tr'Khellian on this matter."

*Lady . . . ?* she thought wildly.

"And make"—for just an instant his smile became predatory—"suitably contrite apologies. Until we meet again, my lady." He bowed low with an easy play-actor's grace and left Arrhae to her work and her confusion.

*Oh, Elements, let H'daen be as angry as he seemed. . . .* She blinked several times, and glared at the other servants who were staring at her and plainly on the point of tittering behind their hands. "This place," she said softly, "had better be clean when I come back. Or we'll see who'll be laughing then."

# Chapter Six

## FLIGHT

*Rea's Helm* was the first ship to leave Vulcan, on 12 Ahhahr 140005. She spent three leisurely months accelerating out of Vulcan's solar system at nonrelativistic speeds, sending back close-flyby data from the nearby planets as she passed them. Behind her, in twos and threes, came the names still preserved in the Rihannsu fleets, both merchant and military, and never allowed to lie idle: *Warbird, Starcatcher, T'Hie, Pennon, Bloodwing* and *Corona, Lance* and *Gorget, Sunheart, Forge* and *Lost Road* and *Blacklight, Firestorm* and *Vengeance* and *Memory* and *Shield*. The ships stayed in communication via tightbeam laser and psilink. At first they tended not to stay too close to one another, in case some disaster might take several ships out at once. But the first ten years of the journey broke them of this habit, as the sixteen ships forged outward and found interstellar space singularly uneventful, and close company a necessity.

There were numerous minor malfunctions aboard all the ships, as might be expected when technology has been custom-built for the first time and tested only as far as logic requires by a people both cautious and extremely impatient. But for those first ten years very few lives were lost: mostly results of maintenance-people's accidents while in vacuum, falls in high-gravity areas while ships were in acceleration phase, and so forth. There were several crop failures, mostly of non-survival-required crops like flatroot. When the wiltleaf blight struck the graminiformes on *Vengeance* and *Gorget*, the other ships were still able to supply them with surpluses of their own root production. (It is amusing to note that to this day, Rihannsu hailing from the south-continent areas settled from the populations of *Gorget* and *Vengeance* will tend to refuse to eat flatroot: those unfamiliar with finer points of their history will put this down to "religious tradition." But diary entries of that time are full of condemnation of "the wretched root," which was about all the two ships' people had to eat for nearly two years.) The travelers were encouraged—if such minor problems were the worst they would have to contend with, they would do well indeed. It only remained to see what the universe itself had waiting for them in the way of planets.

The first star the ships reached, 88 Eri, was as we presently know it: a type K star with fifteen planets, all barren and too hot for even a Vulcan to appreciate them—there were lakes of molten lead on the closest planets. The ones farther out had long had their atmospheres burned off, and the travelers had neither the equipment nor the patience for extended Vulcaniforming. They looped around 88 Eri and headed for 198 Eri, another of the K-type stars that had looked equally promising.

The cost of relativistic travel first began to be felt here, though the travelers had long been anticipating it. Their exploration of this first of many stars—acceleration, deceleration, in-system exploration, and assessment of planet viability—had taken them three years by ship time: on Vulcan, thirty years had passed.

The reestablishment of communication came as a shock for everyone involved. To begin with, while the travelers were accelerating, and for most of the deceleration stage, psilink communication had naturally been disabled. To a sending mind on Vulcan, the thoughts of a mind moving at relativistic speeds were an unintelligibly slow growl; a receiving mind on one of the ships, when listening to a Vulcan mind, would hear nothing but another person living (it seemed) impossibly fast, too fast to make sense of. And even when the travelers were nonrelativistic, there were other problems. Some of the linking groups, specially trained to be attuned to one another, had had deaths; some planetside teams had lost interest in the travelers, being more concerned with occurrences on Vulcan. And indeed there was reason. Surak's teachings were spreading swiftly: there was some (carefully masked) dissatisfaction, even discontent, that energy should be wasted communicating with people who had disagreed violently enough with them to leave the planet. And Surak was no longer there to speak on their behalf in the planet's councils. He was dead, murdered by the Yhri faction with whom he had been dealing peace on behalf of those already united.

The news hit hard, though the travelers had disowned him; there was mourning in the ships, and S'task was not seen for many days. There was a ship's council meeting scheduled during the period when he was missing, and the other councillors, S'task's neighbors, were too abashed by what they had heard about the depth of his grief to inquire of him whether he planned to attend. When they came together into the council chambers of *Rea's Helm,* they found S'task's chair empty, but laid across it was a sword, one of the S'hariens that Surak had brought him. The councillors looked at it in silence and left it where it was. When S'task returned to council a month or so later, he would not comment, he simply found himself another chair to sit in. For many years thereafter, the sword remained in that chair, unmoved. After *Rea's Helm* made planetfall, and new chambers of government were established on ch'Rihan, the chair sat in them in the place of honor, behind senators and praetors and an abortive Emperor or two, reminding all lookers of the missing element in the Rihannsu equation: the silent force that had caused the Sundering, and still moved on the planet of their people's birth, though the man who gave it birth was gone. To touch the sword in the Empty Chair was nothing less than a man's death. Even naming it was dangerous—oaths sworn on it were kept, or the swearer died, sometimes with assistance.

The journey went on, and had no need to turn homeward for its griefs: it found others. The second starfall, around 198 Eri, was disastrous. It was not quite as bad as it might have been, since numerous of the ships' councils had elected to have the ships accelerate at different rates, thereby stringing the ships out somewhat along their course. With psilinked communications, ships farther along the course could alert others of whether a star was viable or not, and the other accompanying ships could change course more quickly. The tactic was a sort of interstellar leapfrog, one that many other species working at relativistic speeds have found useful.

This might have worked out well enough, except that communications with Vulcan were again impossible. There was therefore no way that the travelers could be warned of what Vulcan astronomers had detected in the neighborhood of 198 Eri with equipment newly augmented by improvements obtained from the Hamalki. Seven of eighteen ships were lost over the event horizon of a newly collapsed black hole. *Pennon, Starcatcher, Bloodwing, Forge, Lost Road, Lance,* and *Blacklight* all came out of the boost phase of the psi-based "bootstrap" acceleration to find themselves falling down a "hole" through space in which time dilated and contracted wildly, and physical reality itself came undone around them. Even those ships that had warning were unable to pull out of the gravitational field of the singularity, though every jump-trained adept aboard the ships died trying to bootstrap them out again. The inhabitants of those ships spent long days looking through madness at the death that was inexorably sucking them in. No one knows to this day what the final fate of the people aboard the ships was—whether they died from the antithetical nature of "denatured" space itself, or whether the ships mercifully blew up first due to gravitational stress. Those from the surviving ships unlucky enough to be in mindlink with them succumbed to psychoses and died quickly, possibly in empathy, or slowly, raving to the end of their lives.

The tragedy slowed down the journey immensely, as the ships approached 198 Eri and found its planets as hopeless as 88s had been. Every argument that could come up about the conduct of the journey did so almost immediately, and the arguing continued for several years while the ships orbited 198 Eri and stored what stellar power they could. Should the travelers turn back? Little use in that, some said. Vulcan might not want them back, and besides, what friends and families had been left behind were all old or dead now: relativity had taken its toll. Or keep going? Unwise, said others, when even empty-looking space turned out to be mined with deadly dangers you could not see until they were already in the process of killing you. Should they keep all the ships together (and risk having them all destroyed together)? Or should they spread them out (and risk not being able to come to one another's aid)? Should they stop using the bootstrap acceleration method, despite the fact that it used no fuel and conserved the ships' resources more completely than any other method? And the question was complicated by the fact that there was no more help available from Vulcan, even if any would have been offered them. The ships had recently passed the nine-point-five light-year limit on unboosted telepathy. Even at nonrelativistic speeds, no adept heard anything but the mental analogue of four-centimeter noise, the sound of life in the universe breathing quietly to itself.

Three and a half years went by while the ships grieved, argued, and looked for answers. They found none, but once again will drove them outward: S'task had not come so far to turn back. Many in the ships were unwilling, but S'task carried the council of *Rea's Helm* and declared that his ship at least was going on: and the others would not let him go alone. Under conventional ramscoop drive at first, then using bootstrapping again as the memory of pain dulled a little, the ships headed for 4408A/B Trianguli, a promising "wide" binary with two possible stars.

4408B Tri is, of course, the star around which orbits the planet Iruh, and the travelers could not have made a worse choice of a world to examine for colonization. If they had analyzed the Etoshan data more thoroughly, they might have avoided another disaster, but they did not. At one time the Inshai had cordoned off the system, but they were now long gone from those spaces, and all their warning buoys had been destroyed by the Etoshan pirates during their own ill-fated attempt to subdue the planet. So it was that the travelers' ships came in cautiously, by ones and twos, and found 4408A surrounded by worlds covered in molten rock or liquid methane, and 4408B orbited by six planets, one of which registered on their instruments as a ninety-nine percent climatic match for Vulcan . . . and rich in metals, which Vulcan at its best had never been. The first two ships in, *T'Hie* and *Corona,* slipped into parking orbits and sent shuttles down to take more readings and assess the planet's climate and biochemistry. The shuttles did not come back, but long before there was alarm about the issue, it was too late for the travelers in orbit.

The Iruhe were doing as they had done with so many other travelers: they had sensed their minds from a distance and insinuated into their minds an image of Iruh as the perfect world, the one they were looking for. What use is an accurate instrument reading when the mind reading it is being influenced to inaccuracy? And not even Vulcans were capable of holding out against the influence of a species rated one of the most mentally powerful of the whole galaxy, with a reconstructed psi rating of nearly 160 (the most highly trained Vulcans rate about 30: most Terrans about 10). The crews of the shuttles served as an hors d'oeuvre for the Iruhe, and confirmed what had fallen into their toils, a phenomenal number of fiercely motivated, intelligent, mentally vigorous people. With false "reports" from the shuttles that seemed absolutely true, because the crewpeople seeing them were supplying familiar faces and details from their own minds, the Iruhe lured *Corona* and *T'Hie* into optimum range—close synchronous orbit—and proceeded to suck the life force out of the entire complement of both ships, over twelve thousand men, women, and children. Then they crashed the ships full of mindless, still-breathing husks into Iruh's methane seas, and waited eagerly for the rest of the feast, the other travelers.

The torpor of a whole species of intellivores after a massive and unprecedented gorge was the only thing that saved the other ships. *Sunheart* coasted in next, and her navigations crew noticed with instant alarm that the ion trails of *T'Hie* and *Corona* stopped suddenly around Iruh, and did not head out into space again. *Sunheart*'s command crew immediately made the wisest decisions possible under the circumstances: they ran. They veered off from the paradisial planet they saw, and warned off the other ships. In the hurry there were several mistakes made in navigations, and *Firestorm* and *Vengeance* fell out of contact with the other ships and only much later made the course corrections to find them again. But the hurry was necessary: there was no telling how long or short a grace period they would have had before the Iruhe "woke up" and noticed the rest of their dinner arriving.

The travelers were, in any case, very fortunate. Few species had gotten off so lightly from encounters with Iruh: many more ships and several planets (after the Iruhe got in the habit of moving theirs around that arm of the galaxy) were to fall victim to the insatiable mind-predators. Not until some seventeen hundred years later, when the Organians were asked to intervene, could anything effective be done about the Iruhe. And the irony is that no one knows to this day just what was "done." The planet is empty and quiet now, and there is a Federation research team there, sifting the ruined landmasses for what artifacts remain.

The courses of the traveler ships still remaining become harder to trace from this point onward. *Firestorm* and *Vengeance* wandered for a long time, hunting the other ships, hearing the occasional psi-contact and using the vague directional sense from these to try to course-correct. The other ships meanwhile went through much the same experience— years and years of wandering among stars that turned out barren of planets, or among stars that had planets that were useless to them. The travelers had thought that the odds of finding a habitable world, away from the aliens that troubled them so, were well in their favor. They found out otherwise, painfully. Here again, paying attention to the data from the Etoshans might have helped them. The Etoshans knew how poor in habitable worlds the Eridani-Trianguli spaces had been. It was one of the reasons they had been so surprised to find the Vulcans in the first place.

But might-have-beens were no use to the travelers. They spent the next eighty-five standard years of relative time—nearly four hundred and fifty, out in the nonrelativistic universe—hunting desperately for a world, any world, that might suit them. Now they would be glad to Vulcaniform a planet, if they could only find one at all suitable, but most of the stars in deep Trianguli space were older Population I stars that had long before lost their planets, or were too unstable to have any to begin with. The planets they did find were uniformly gas giants or airless rocks that nothing could be done with in less than a couple of centuries.

The desperation was even worse because the ships had been built with hundred-year "viability envelopes." No one had expected the search for a new world to take much longer than fifty years, and their supplies, systems, and facilities had been designed with this timing in mind. Food was beginning to be scarce in some of the ships, systems were breaking down, and almost all the replacement parts were used up. *Warbird* was lost to a massive drive system malfunction; she had no adept left who could bootstrap her, and she fell into 114 Trianguli trying to slingshot around the star to pick up more boost. *Memory* went the same way, trying to use a black dwarf. The pulses from the small X-ray star produced after the collision are still reaching Earth.

The remaining ships—*Rea's Helm, Gorget, Sunheart, Vengeance,* and *Firestorm*—kept going as best they could. It was never easy. Odd diseases began to spring up in all the crews. There was speculation that radiation exposure was causing new mutagenic forms of diseases to which Vulcans were normally immune . . . since the symptoms for some of the "space fevers" resembled already-identified Vulcan diseases like lunglock fever, though they were more severe. The medical staff of all the ships had been attenuated by deaths from old age as well as from the diseases. They were able to do little, and before the epidemics began to taper off, from fifty to seventy percent of each ship's complement had died.

These diseases only aggravated—or, one might also say, "ended"—a problem that had been worsening with the decay of the ship's viability envelopes. There were no more psitechs. Those that did not die boot-strapping the ships now died of disease, and there were no completely trained techs to replace them—partly because much of the oldstyle Vulcan psi-training required "circles" or groups of adepts to bring a psi-talented person to viability. There were no longer enough adepts to make up the necessary groups.

The documentation available—though quite complete—was also too objective: people who tried to teach themselves the mind techniques "by the book" never became more than talented amateurs. The direct "laying on of hands" was necessary to properly teach telepathy, mind-meld, and the other allied arts. So they died out as the ships voyaged, and the sciences of the mind became the matter of legend. The Vulcans believe that present-day Rihannsu possess the raw ability to be trained in the mind sciences, but the actual experiment will doubtless not happen for quite a long while.

Meanwhile, the diseases took their toll everywhere. S'task's wife and children all perished within days of one another during *Rea's* epidemic of mutagenic infectious pericarditis. S'task himself came very close to dying, and lay ill for months, not speaking, hardly eating. It was a very gaunt and shaky man who got up from his bed on the day *Rea's* chief astronomer came to him to tell him that they thought they had found yet another star with planets.

The star they had found was 128 Trianguli, one of the group 123–128 Tri: a little rosette of dwarf K-type stars so far out in the arm as not to have been noticed by even the Etoshans. It would require *Rea* some ten years of acceleration—all their bootstrap adepts were now dead of old age or jump syndrome—and another ten to decelerate. This was the worst possible news: the period was well outside of *Rea*'s viability envelope.

"We may all be dead when we get there," said the chief astronomer to S'task.

"But we will have gotten there," said S'task. Still, he took the question to Council, and the surviving population of *Rea* agreed that they should take the chance and try to reach the star. The other surviving ships concurred.

They began the long acceleration. Other authors have covered in far more detail the crazed courage and dogged determination of these people as they bent their whole will to survival in ancient, cranky spacecraft that had no reason to be running any longer. But the spacecraft had, after all, been built by craftsmen, by Vulcans who loved their work and would rather have died than misplace a rivet out of laziness, and the workmanship, by and large, held. Nine years into deceleration they came within sensor range of 128 Tri and confirmed the astronomers' suspicions: the star had six planets, of which two were a "double planet" system like Earth and Earth's Moon . . . and both of the two were habitable within broad Vulcan parameters.

There were, of course, major differences to be dealt with. The two worlds had more water than Vulcan did, and their climates were respectively cooler. In fact, both planets had those things that the Vulcans had heard of from the Etoshan data but never seen, "oceans." Some people were nervous about the prospect of settling on worlds where water was such a commonplace. Others entertained the idea that in a place where water was so plentiful, one of the major causes of war might be eliminated. S'task, looking for the first time at the early telescopic images of the two green-golden worlds, and hearing one of his people mention this possibility, was silent for a few moments, then said, "Those who want war will find causes, no matter how many of them you take away." This proved to be true enough, later. With survival needs handled, the Rihannsu moved on to other concerns, matters of honor, and fought cheerfully about them for centuries. But that time was still far ahead of them. Right now they were merely desperately glad to find a world, two worlds, in fact, that looked like they would serve them as homes instead of the tired metal worlds that were rapidly losing their viability.

The year immediately following starfall was spent in cautious analysis of the worlds and how they should be best used by the travelers. The larger of the two worlds had the biggest oceans, and three large land-masses, two with extensive "young" mountain ranges. The third was ninety percent desert, though its coastlines were fertile. The other planet, the one "frozen" in orbit around the larger body, again like Earth's moon, had five continents, all mountainous and heavily forested. Both worlds revealed thousands of species of wildlife, a fact that astonished the travelers: Vulcan has comparatively few, only three or four phyla with a spread of several hundred species, mostly plants.

The ships' scientists were fascinated by the fact that the species on both planets were quite similar, and there were several near-duplications. Arguments immediately began as to whether these planets had been colonized or visited by some other species in the past, or whether this astonishing parallel evolution had happened by itself. No artifacts suggestive of any other species' intervention or presence, however, were ever found. The question has never been satisfactorily answered, though there are possibilities: the 128 Tri system lies in the migratory path of the species known to Federation research as "the Builders," who played at "seeding" various planets with carbon-based life, predominantly hominid, some two million years ago. There is no ignoring the fact that ninety percent of the wildlife on the Two Worlds is compatible with Vulcan biochemistry, even if only by virtue of being carbohydrate. Levorotatory protein forms, common on almost every "nonseeded" planet, were almost completely absent in the ch'Rihan/ch'Havran biosystems.

Research went on, while the travelers, eager to stop traveling, decided the questions of who should live where. No logical method could be approved by everyone, especially since there were several pieces of especially choice real estate that one or more groups had their eyes on. There was also concern that people should be sufficiently spread out so as not to overtax the resources of any one area in the long term. After several months of extremely acrimonious argument in ships' Meetings, S'task wearied of it all and suggested that the ships merely choose areas to live in by lottery. To his extreme surprise, the complements of the other ships agreed. Some ships preferred to go into the lottery as entire units, others divided up along family or clan lines, so that septs of clans scattered among the four surviving ships would all go to one area together.

The two planets were duly named ch'Rihan ("of the Declared") and ch'Havran ("of the Travelers"). It was rather odd that the results of the lottery left many of the more "reactionary," Vulcan-oriented houses living on ch'Havran, since the name more recalled the journey than its end, as ch'Rihan did, and ch'Rihan became the home of the more "forward-looking," secessionist, revolutionary houses (S'task's own house was placed on ch'Rihan by the lottery). Notice was taken of this, perhaps more notice than was warranted, perhaps not. A people who have come to speak an artificial language will naturally be preoccupied with the meanings of words and names. The results of the lottery were taken as a sort of good omen, that the language fit the people, and vice versa, that this was indeed the place where they were supposed to be, the place to which they had been meant to come. Who the Rihannsu thought was doing the "meaning" is uncertain. Vulcan religion had changed considerably over the years of the journey, and would change further.

It is also interesting to note that the "troublemaker" groups, those clans and tribes who had been pressured by one faction or another to make the journey, almost all ended up on ch'Havran, and on its east continent—remote, rugged, and poorer in resources than the others. There have been suggestions among both Rihannsu and Federation historians that the lottery was rigged. There is no way to tell at this remote period in time. The computers in which the lottery data was stored and handled are long since dust.

If the lottery was, in fact, rigged to this effect, then evil would come of it later. The cultures that grew up unchecked on the east continent, mostly out of contact with those on ch'Rihan and the other parts of ch'Havran, grew up savage, exploitative, and cruel, even by Rihannsu standards. Those east continent factions would later instigate and finally openly provoke the Rihannsu's first war with the Federation, and the crews of ships from the Kihai and LLunih nations would commit atrocities that would adorn Federation propaganda tapes for years to come. It is mostly these nations that the Rihannsu have to thank for horrors like the abandonment and "evacuation" of Thieurrull (tr: "Hellguard") and the capture and rape of innocent Vulcans—atrocities that the Senate and Praetorate would have severely punished if they had known they were being planned and carried out by eastern-based and easterner-commanded ships, and secretly backed and funded by eastern praetors. Punishments there were, indeed, but much too late. The whole business was later taken, by people who believed that the lottery was rigged, as more evidence of the desperate correctness of Surak's statement that beginnings must be clean.

Other peculiarities set in as a result of the scattering of the populations of the many ships across two planets. Vulcan society has always had a distinctly matriarchal cast: this tendency came out strongly in several of the nations on ch'Havran, and most strongly in the Nn'verian nation on the north continent of ch'Rihan. It was the nation in which S'task came to live (the short while that he did), and by virtue of that the seat of government and the seat of the first and only Ruling Queen of the Two Worlds. T'Rehu (later Vriha t'Rehu) seized power and set her throne in the newly built Council Chambers, in front of the Empty Chair; she spilled the first blood in those chambers—regrettably, the first of much—and declared the rule of women (or at least woman) over men returned again. The Vulcans had tried this some thousands of years before, and had only indifferent success with it: women were generally not interested enough in war for the Vulcan nations of that time to support such rule for long. T'Rehu was cast down, and the council returned to power after ch'Rihan's first war. But from then until now women have held more than seventy percent of all positions in the government, and about sixty percent of those in the armed forces.

Another interesting thing happened over which sociologists are still arguing: Rihannsu women began to get interested in war. Many of the high-ranking east continent officers responsible for the Hellguard atrocities were women. The etiology of this change, and the question of why it should happen so soon after the end of the journey, is still a puzzle. Of the other "matriarchal" or female-oriented species in the galaxy (some seventy-five percent), only one other, the Bhvui, has done anything similar, and the histories of the two species are too different to make comparisons meaningful. But in any case, Rihannsu women warriors have become almost as much of a legend as pre-Reformation Vulcan, and there are countless gossipy stories of "Romulan"-dominated worlds ruled by suave and sophisticated warrior princesses with harems full of good-looking men. The only thing to be said about these stories is, if they were true, the Rihannsu would not have had to enter into so many destructive deals with the Klingons to keep their economy afloat. They could have done quite nicely from the female tourist trade.

But again, these developments were in the future. The eighteen thousand remaining travelers slowly left the ships over some three years, cautiously establishing support bases for themselves, until there were very few people still living in the ships. Some did choose to remain, mostly those people who had become agoraphobic over the long journey, or had been born in the ships and wanted nothing to do with open skies and planets. The Ship-Clans, as they came to be known, lived quite happily aboard their great echoing homes, looking down on the Two Worlds around which they coasted in asynchronous orbits.

The ships were resupplied and repaired over some years from planetary resources: people would return to the ships for holidays, out of nostalgia or curiosity. Over many more years this sort of thing came to an end, as the population turned over and there was no one left who had been born on Vulcan, or on shipboard during the journey. The long run through interstellar night became something sung about, but not a thing anyone wanted to have experienced. Ch'Rihan and ch'Havran were the real worlds now, not those ancient ones with metal walls and skies that echoed.

Though they slowly dwindled, the Ship-Clans maintained the four ships of the journey, and evening and morning they could be seen low above the planets' horizons, bright points in the sky. They did not stay there forever. Some hundreds of years later, due to neglect, government squabbles, economic troubles, and war, one at a time the stars fell: and the Two Worlds orbited Eisn, their "Homesun," cut off from the rest of the universe in the beginning of their long isolation. It was an unfortunate paradigm for the loss of sciences and technologies that began during that time and would continue for a thousand years to come. But the songs of the Rihannsu still recall the evening stars at sunset, and the breath of wind in trees, and the love of starlight seen through evening rather than through the hard black of space. "The journey is noble," said one bard's song, "and adventure and danger is sweet, but the wine by the fireside is sweeter, and knowing one's place."

# Chapter Seven

H'daen tr'Khellian was gazing out of the antechamber window when Arrhae came in to answer his summons. He didn't turn around, merely twisted somewhat and watched over his shoulder as she gave him the customary obeisance. He looked thoughtful and somewhat ill at ease.

"Fair day, *hru'hfirh*," she said as usual, straightening.

"After a poor night." H'daen looked her full in the face, as if searching for something that might give him an answer before he had to ask any questions aloud. Apparently he saw nothing, and shrugged. "Arrhae, is there truth in what I hear of you and Maiek tr'Annhwi?"

"My lord?" Arrhae had no need to pretend surprise. She knew that one of H'daen's body-servants was on intimate terms with Ekkhae, who had been among those cleaning the dining-chamber last night, but she hadn't expected the gossip to travel quite so fast as this. Nor had she expected anyone to give credence to it.

"The subcommander sought me out before he left, and apologized at some length for his behavior. Then he asked if he was forgiven, if he would be permitted to enter my house again—and if I granted him the right to visit you. He told me that you wanted him to speak on this matter." H'daen crossed the room and sat down at his desk, pouring himself a cup of wine rather than asking her to do it. He had been drinking more of late, and earlier in the day, but with Eisn not yet clear of the horizon this cupful was more a continuation of last night's drinking than a new day's start. He swallowed perhaps half the cupful and refilled it before saying any more, and when he turned to face her again, his face was troubled. "It was my impression that you already visited with Lhaesl tr'Khev. Was I mistaken?"

Arrhae lowered her eyes uncomfortably. Lhaesl hadn't yet been officially snubbed, and was either too enamored or too dense to realize of his own accord that she had no interest in him. Granted that they were physically of an age, the differing metabolism of Rihannsu and Terran—no matter how accurately the Terran might be disguised—still meant that his twenty-eight and hers left him at a behavioral equivalent of fifteen. A pretty child, but a child for all that. "Tr'Khev visits me, lord. I do not encourage him; and though I should, I have not yet discouraged him in whatever way it needs for him to understand."

"Oh. Thank you. The situation becomes clearer, Arrhae. Then I was right in what I told tr'Annhwi."

"Told him . . . ?"

"That he could visit with you, that you were a free woman and one with a mind of your own, and that he would learn soon enough if he wasn't welcome."

Arrhae barely kept the strangulated squeak of horror in her throat, when what it really wanted to do was leap out as a full-fledged yell of *You old fool!!* Two days ago she wouldn't even have considered addressing the Head of House in any such fashion, but then, two days ago, she had almost forgotten who she was and what had brought her here. "And if I choose not to make him welcome, lord?" she wondered tentatively.

"I would prefer that you did, Arrhae."

*"Prefer" indeed! That was an order. I wonder why?* She watched him, but said nothing.

"House Annhwi is strong, wealthy, and well-placed—"

*Question answered.*

"—and the subcommander's friendship would prove an asset to House Khellian. Arrhae, sit down. Fill my cup again and . . . and pour a cup for yourself."

The invitation was so out of place that Arrhae felt her face burn hot. "Lord, I am *hru'hfe* only, and—"

H'daen raised one finger and she was silent. "You are *hru'hfe* indeed, and a worthy ornament to this house, honored by its guests. Why wonder, then, that I bid you drink with me out of respect for that honor which reflects so well on me and on my House? Sit, Arrhae, and drink deep."

She sat down straight-backed, most uncomfortable with the situation but aware of being closely watched, and determinedly did as she was told. Expecting something rough as ale, Arrhae found the wine so much smoother and of better flavor that she put her mouthful down in a single gulp, then grimaced and felt tears prickle at her eyes as the liquid revealed itself correspondingly stronger—when the swallow had passed the point of no return.

H'daen smiled thinly but without any malice. "It takes everyone that way the first time they drink it. Even me. Now, again. It won't be such a shock; you might even start to like it."

He was right. Arrhae managed to down her second mouthful without spluttering, and actually enjoyed the small fusion furnace that came to life in the pit of her stomach. As for the rest of it, she set the cup down carefully and began to turn it around and around, watching the pretty sparkling of the reflec glaze. She would have watched moisture condense on glass, or paint dry—just so long as she didn't have to watch H'daen's eyes on her. At the back of her mind there was a suspicion, no matter how unfounded it might be, that H'daen might be trying to make her drunk in order to pry secrets from her. Only great caution would avoid that; she would appear to drink as she was expected to do, without absorbing any of the powerful toxins in the wine.

Yet H'daen himself was drinking without restraint, and the first and last rule of making someone drunk to loosen their tongue was not to get drunk first. He was on his third cupful now, and no matter how accustomed one might be to the potent liquor, immunity was a different matter. It wasn't as if he were drinking from another jug, either. Each pouring, his and hers, came from the same vessel. Arrhae caught him glancing in her direction once or twice, and the glances weren't furtive—she was used to those by now, and knew how to recognize them—but nervous. As if he were drinking to summon up enough courage to raise some delicate subject.

"McCoy," he said at last, and gave it Federation rather than Rihannsu inflection.

"He still sleeps, *hru'hfirh*,'" she said. "Or so I presume. I answered your summons before visiting his quarters." She made pretense of sipping more wine, barely allowing it to moisten her lips, even though she "swallowed" and made the appropriate small sigh of enjoyment.

"You grow accustomed faster than I did." H'daen swerved off on another tack as if frightened by the two syllables he had previously uttered, and he sounded almost envious.

"After drinking ale, lord, even coolant fluid becomes palatable." A dangerous thing to say, with its possible insult of his preferences in wine, but a joke if it were seen as such. It was; H'daen laughed quietly, forcing it so that it sounded more than it was, but genuinely amused for all that.

"Indeed so—especially if you drink it without water." There was a swift, small silence before he pushed both cup and jug aside halfway through yet another refill. "Enough of this. The Terrans call it *small talk*. Around and around like a bloodwing gathering its courage to settle on a dying *hlai*. Always around, and never to the point."

"And the point, lord, is Mak'khoi?"

"Yes. I . . . I have told you in the past that I trust you both with private words and with the honor of my House. That trust has not yet been misplaced." H'daen's stare was undisguised now, and he was trying to read her face as he might read charactery on a viewscreen. She met the stare for as long as seemed suitable, saying nothing, then demurely lowered her head in a bow of gratitude. "Now this Starfleet officer is given into my hands for safekeeping until the Senate brings him to trial." He pushed back from the desk, stood up, and began to pace.

"That Fleet Intelligence entrusted him to you is surely a great sign of favor in high places, lord."

"If it was widely known among my 'friends,'" H'daen said bitterly. "More probable that he was left here as the least likely place any rescuer would begin to look. You know how House Khellian fared when you came here. I owe you thanks, not as master to servant, but as one who appreciates the effort and effect of hard labor."

For all his dismissal of small talk, he was using it again, deferring the evil moment when he would have to say something that Arrhae was coming to expect might be treasonous. If it was, she didn't want to hear it; if it was spoken aloud under this roof, she wanted away from the house; and if it was spoken by H'daen, she would as soon be out of his employ and a beggar on the road before he said it. Surely he didn't think that Intelligence would leave so important a prize here and not leave some means of watching him . . . ?

Perhaps he did.

And perhaps this disdained old *thrai* was wilier than any gave him credit for, because he closed relays on his reader's keypad so that when the thing's viewscreen unfolded from the desk, it was already emitting a white-noise hum that set Arrhae's teeth on edge. And which would almost certainly make nonsense of any audio pickup hidden in the room. If a visual scan had been installed, H'daen played for its lenses by starting to work, in a most realistic fashion, with various electronic probes and fault-finders on the reader which had plainly "gone wrong." After a few minutes passed, he "gave up," sat down, and began to ponder about the problem—and his pondering seemed lost without at least two fingers and more usually a whole hand near or over his mouth. Only then did H'daen dare start to speak.

"There are those on ch'Rihan," he said, "who would pay more than a chain or two of cash to lay their hands on an officer of the Federation vessel *Enterprise*. And there are those who would look most highly on the man and the House who made such an acquisition possible."

"My lord . . . !" said Arrhae, shocked. "Commander t'Radaik—"

"Jaeih t'Radaik is of an ancient and noble House. To one like that, hardship and dishonor are words without meaning. Whereas to me . . ." He let the sentence hang, not needing to finish it.

"I—I understand, my lord."

"Yes, and disapprove. Good."

"My lord . . . ?"

"Do you think, Arrhae, that I would have taken you into my confidence where this plan is concerned if I suspected you were other than honorable? You're shocked, of course—but since mention of this would bring me, you, and the House you serve into still more disrepute, you'll say nothing and disapprove of me in private."

"But if Intelligence learned of what you have just told me, *hru'hfirh?*" It struck Arrhae even as she said it that the question was unnecessary, one with an obvious answer. She was even more right than she guessed.

"Then they could have learned from only one source, and would also learn—from a similarly anonymous source—that my so-trusted *hru'hfe* is a spy for the Federation, suborned by her late last master tr'Lhoell," said H'daen silkily. "Tell me, whom would they believe?" Then he swore and scrambled to his feet with his hands reaching for her shoulders, for Arrhae's face had drained of color so fast and so completely that he thought she was about to faint. "Powers and Elements, Arrhae, it was a brutal answer to the question, but I didn't mean it!"

"No . . ." she whispered, waving him away, not wanting to be touched, not wanting him anywhere near her. In the single instant between H'daen's words and his realization that he had gone too far, all the suppressed horrors of her years undercover had run gibbering through her mind. Even now, knowing that he had threatened without knowledge of the truth made her feel no better. It was a reminder of too many things: of the Rihannsu paranoid fear of espionage, of her own delicately balanced position, of how the confession had been twisted out of Vaebn tr'Lhoell and what had been done to him afterward. Of the shattering of that which she had thought of as her life.

H'daen pushed her cup, refilled, across the desk and she drank eagerly, holding the cup in both hands but almost spilling it even so. "That was cruel, *hru'hfe* Arrhae. I ask pardon for it." She heard his voice as though from a great distance, saying unlikely things that no *hru'hfirh* ever said to a servant, no matter how senior or how favored. He was blaming himself and asking forgiveness. Wrong words, impossible words, that made her feel uncomfortable and wish that he would stop. But she knew what had provoked them, and it hadn't been the wine.

"You were frightened of what you had said, lord," she told him, coming straight out with it rather than trying to find some more acceptable substitute. He stared at her, unused to such plain speaking, and then shrugged. Arrhae took the shrug as approval, or at least as permission to continue. "And that made you say things that I know my own good lord would not have said. Yes, I disapprove of what you plan for Mak'khoi. Not only because Commander t'Radaik entrusted him to your keeping—but because you intend to sell him. I know what being sold is like, my lord, and *I* was sold only to work. He . . . would be going into the hands of those whose sole delight would be to prolong his death. Better to kill him now yourself. It would be a cleaner and more honorable thing to do."

"It seems that my *hru'hfe* is more than simply an efficient household manager," said H'daen, speaking in a flat, neutral tone that gave Arrhae nothing but the words it carried. She waited, her stomach fluttering, to learn if she had overreacted and said too much. He watched her for what felt like a long time, his face unreadable, then nodded. "It seems she is my conscience. Very well, Arrhae, carry my guilt if you must. But whatever happens, know this: if I or my House can benefit from this unlooked-for gift, then whatever must be done will be done—and the moral scruples of a servant will not get in my way. Do you understand?"

Arrhae pushed her winecup away with the tip of one index finger, knowing that the brief while when she and H'daen might drink together as equals was gone beyond recall. "Yes, lord," she said, standing up and making him an obeisance. "I understand perfectly. With my lord's permission, I will be about my duties now."

"Go—it's already late into the morning, and you have yet to attend Mak'khoi. By my word, treat him as a guest. How could he pass unnoticed if he tried to run, and where on ch'Rihan would he go?" H'daen shut down the whining viewscreen and folded it into his desk once more, remembering to play his role to its logical conclusion by slapping the monitor pettishly and muttering something about inadequate maintenance. But there was nothing pettish about the look he flicked at Arrhae; it was both a promise and a veiled threat.

"Remember," he said, and turned away.

So he was locked up again. So what? Leonard McCoy's only concern right now was about the woman he had seen. And about the way she moved. That first flinch when he came in had been all wrong, and he would stake—

McCoy recognized the bland comment that had been forming inside his head in the way that he could sometimes spot tired old medical phrases like "finish the course" and "not to be taken internally." Except that there was no longer anything bland about it. Staking his life on it was exactly what he was doing. If his briefing had been wrong, if planetfall had been wrong, if information had been wrong . . .

Then he was a dead man.

The door opened and his jailer came in. *Think of the devil . . .* McCoy suppressed a humorless smile and watched the young Romulan woman as she moved about his cramped quarters, straightening the recently vacated bed and unlocking the heavy window shutters. His intradermal had translated her title of *hru'hfe* as "servants'-manager," and it struck him that if she was doing the work that she would more normally have overseen, then she was probably the most trusted member of staff in the whole household. *Which might be a bad thing—or a very good one.*

"You're Arrhae," he said in Federation Standard.

She moved his pillow, a cylinder of stuffed leather as concession to Terran weakness instead of the smooth stone that a Rihanha used, and punched it to shape with unnecessary vigor before looking at him disdainfully down her hawk nose, rather as Spock might do. McCoy was half-expecting an eyebrow to go up. *"Ie,"* she replied. *"Arrhae. Hru'hfe i daise hfai s'Khellian. Hwiiy na th'ann Mak'khoi."*

"Is that my title: 'the prisoner McCoy'? I'd prefer something else. Try 'Doctor'—though my friends call me 'Bones.' "

*"Hwiij th'ann-a—haei'n neth 'Mak'khoi,' neth 'D'okht'r,' neth 'Bohw'nns' nah'lai?"*

"No, it doesn't matter what you call me. But I'd prefer something other than a label, thank you very much. And try speaking Anglish!" He pitched her that one out of left field, watching for a reaction. Actually *hearing* one came as a surprise.

"If it would content you," she said. The Romulan accent was very thick and her intonation was heavy and oddly placed, making it hard for him to understand, but the words were Federation Standard. McCoy's eyebrows lifted and he was momentarily at a loss for anything to say, having considered every response that she might make—except this one. "But there is small need," the woman continued, and unless his ears deceived him, her accent was improving with every word. "You

have a translit—trans*lator* and so understand Rihannsu. I am not a prisoner and have not need to understand *you*, Dr. Bones."

"Either Doctor or Bones, not both."

"Which? Choose."

"All right, Bones then. At least it'll *sound* as if there's a friend in the
room." *And that, Dr. McCoy, was excessively waspish even for you.*

"So. Bones. Have you eaten firstmeal today, Bones?"

He shook his head. "Nor lastmeal yesterday. I haven't seen a hum—
er, a soul since I was locked in here last night. Your Subcommander
tr'Annhwi wasn't too keen on granting me any home comforts, and
t'Radaik assumed and didn't think to ask."

Arrhae scowled and sucked in a sharp breath through her teeth.
"Tr'Annhwi is not 'my' subcommander, and never will be. No matter
what he thinks. Doctor, you are already found guilty before your trial is
convened, but for all that, do not judge all Rihannsu by that one's measure. This house is honorable, at least. You are a prisoner of the Imperium, but a guest under the roof of Khellian. Take comfort from that,
at least."

"Your Anglish improves with practice, *hru'hfe*," said McCoy carefully.
"Yet you didn't tell Commander t'Radaik that you spoke it. . . ."

Arrhae gave him what amounted to the Romulan version of an "old-
fashioned look." "So that you have no cause to puzzle the matter,
Bones, I shall explain. Privately, for your ears alone. My first master
taught me the art, for his amusement, as one might teach *fvaiin* tricks."
She turned away from him and busied herself with other things, talking
all the while. "But he was a spy and a foul traitor, and met the fate that
he deserved two farsuns past, and since that time I have had no cause to
use the speech of my people's enemies. Nor would I—to learn one
thing from a traitor might be to learn others, or so my present master
might believe." Arrhae swung on him, doing nothing now but stare. "I
advise you to forget. I shall not speak this speech to you otherwise, nor
will I speak it either out of this room or in the company of any other
person. Do you understand me?"

"Quite clearly." McCoy understood more clearly even than that; he knew the sound of something that had been carefully composed and then learned by heart. He stood up and glanced at the door that Arrhae had locked behind her. "Do you bring my food in here, or do you slide it under the door?"

"I have told you—you are a guest in House Khellian. My master H'daen has said it. Thus at night you will be here, and the door locked. By day you may walk freely in the house, and in the gardens around the house." She glanced out of the window, then back at McCoy. "Betray this trust and you spend all your time here. Try to run and you will go to a military detention cell—if someone with kin lost to the Federation Starfleet does not take out your entrails first. On ch'Rihan, you are not difficult to identify."

"And who was—"

Arrhae, on her way to the door, stopped and looked at him with a mixture of amusement and impatience. "Doctor, do you wish to eat, or to talk? If talk, then stay here and do it yourself. *I* am hungry."

Nothing was said during their brief meal, eaten under the curious gaze of many eyes. Arrhae conducted herself with the same faultless manners and distant courtesy that she had seen H'daen employ when he disapproved of one person or another, making it plain to those watching eyes—any pair of which could be reporting directly back to Intelligence—that she resented being made to feel like the keeper of some performing animal. From the look of him, McCoy knew what she was thinking. And didn't like it.

"You wear a translator, Mak'khoi?" Arrhae said as the dishes were being cleared away, using Rihannsu and speaking for the benefit of whatever ears went with spying eyes. The man nodded, still far from pleased with her if his face was anything to go by. "So know this, Lord H'daen tr'Khellian grants you guestright to walk as you please. . . ."

The brief lecture and its veiled warning done, she pushed back from the table and stood up, turning in time to see three heads peering in from the kitchen. They jerked back out of sight, but Arrhae compressed her lips into a thin line and stalked toward the door, working out something suitably irritable to say. McCoy was still in his chair, watching her.

The man wasn't smiling—they both knew he was in too dangerous a position for that—but her renewed acquaintance with Terran facial expressions told Arrhae that the glint in his eye had something to do with sardonic humor. He understood exactly what she was about, and approved of it.

"I'm for taking a stroll in the gardens, Arrhae," he said.

She looked back at the sound of his voice. "Ridiculous," she said, annoyed. Then to him, more loudly, "Don't waste time making noises that I can't understand, Mak'khoi. Can you show me by signs?" He snorted at that, then gestured at the open window, tapped his chest, and made walking movements with two fingers on the table. "Oh. I see. Yes, go. But this could so easily become an embarrassment. I shall ask the lord for some kind of translating unit, Mak'khoi. Until then, keep your needs simple. Go *on,* I said. I have my work to do. . . ."

That work was much as it had always been, despite the secret upheaval in Arrhae's life. Making her disapproval of eavesdroppers quite plain to the kitchen staff was a break in the routine, but the rest of it was mostly another attempt to get the accounts sorted out when documents and receipts said one thing but the expenditure tally in the household computer said something else entirely.

Once in a while she wondered what McCoy was doing with his time. There was no point in trying to escape on foot from the Khellian estate, because it was quite simply too big. For all H'daen's straitened circumstances, that was only where money was concerned; his true wealth was in land, and if he would only sell some of it to the developer-contractors in i'Ramnau. . . . Arrhae had once, very diffidently, made the suggestion, and had sparked a tirade of startling intensity for daring to presume that "a few dirty chains of cash" could buy the property that his ancestors had enriched with their blood. It had been the only time that Arrhae had ever seen her lord lose his composure and shout at her. Strange that pride and honor would keep him poor in the midst of potential plenty and that same honor-created poverty would make him contemplate something so dishonorable—and so dangerous—as betraying Commander t'Radaik's trust. Imperial Fleet Intelligence was not likely to forgive what he had in mind for McCoy if he went through with it. Whatever H'daen was paid, he wouldn't have much time to enjoy being rich before he became dead. . . .

Arrhae tapped another string of figures into the computer and stared at the screen without really seeing it, her brain so dulled by the boredom of the repetitious task and the confusion of the past day that it was several seconds before the meaning of the readout sank in. And she began to laugh.

Chief Cook tr'Aimne, heading for the coolroom with a basket of prepared meatrolls, paused in her office doorway to look at her as if she had lost her mind. "I got it right," Arrhae told him, fighting to get coherence through her giggles. "Five days at this damned-to-Ariennye keyboard, and I got it right at last!"

Tr'Aimne stared, and Arrhae guessed that this frantic laughter had little to do with her successful computing and a great deal to do with what she had been going through. Concealing this, pretending not to know that, being controlled and calm at all times . . .

"Well done, *hru'hfe,*" said tr'Aimne in a deadly monotone. He plainly still hadn't forgiven her for that flitter ride into i'Ramnau, and he wasn't getting excited over any of *her* successes, no indeed. At least his undisguised dislike helped Arrhae get some sort of leash on what was too near hysteria for her liking.

"Thank you, Chief Cook," she said, equally flat. "I'm so very glad you're pleased. Now—get those to the coolroom and stop wasting time." He glared at her as the status quo restored itself with a thud, then whisked disdainfully away with his nose in the air.

"'Find a man who's a good cook, learn what he knows—then lose him,'" Arrhae quoted softly to herself. She glanced sidelong at the computer-screen and grinned a bit, hit SAVE and PRINT with a finger-fork in one quick motion, and caught the sheets as they emerged, then stood up, flexing her shoulders luxuriously. "Time off for good behavior," she said. *Time off spent doing your extra duties. Take a walk and find out what he's up to.*

She had walked almost around the mansion before she saw McCoy. He was sitting on top of one of the ornamental rock arrangements in the greater garden, and Arrhae was pleased to see that he had taken care not to disturb the mosses that surrounded and enhanced the pattern of the rocks. His back was toward her and he was hunched forward so that his elbows rested on his knees. She hesitated; every line of his body indicated gloom and depression and—by the sound of it—he was muttering to himself. *Hardly surprising,* Arrhae thought, wondering if she should leave him to be miserable in peace.

Then, even though she had made no noise, he straightened and snapped around at the waist, suddenly enough to make Arrhae jump. "Yes?" he said, staring at her.

"I wondered where you were."

"Not far away. Where could I go? You said that much yourself." He sounded bitter, and that wasn't surprising either. "And should we be talking anyway, since you 'don't understand me'? Or have you suddenly remembered again?"

*Stubborn, prideful . . . !* "Doctor, what I said inside—about a translator—I meant it. Then we *can* talk, without needing one eye in our backs for every word." Arrhae saw his brows go up. "For my back, anyway. If they thought I was a spy . . ."

"I understand," said McCoy, and all the anger had left his voice. "At least, I begin to understand."

Arrhae turned away, studying the mosses with apparent interest while she tried to decide what *that* might mean. Nothing much, most likely. It was merely proof of what she had thought at the very beginning; McCoy would sooner be amiable than angry, and his gruffness was no more than a mannerism, like H'daen's preference for gestures over words. "Thank you for making the attempt anyway," she said in an effort to be graceful over the business and restore something of her own crumpled honor. "Your translator: could you read a Rihanha book, perhaps?"

*Small talk, Arrhae, small talk. Do you want to hear a Terran voice so much that you'll indulge in pointless chatter with a Fleet prisoner?* The answer to that, despite the danger, was an unequivocal *yes.*

McCoy looked at her strangely, and shook his head. "It only operates on received speech. But thanks for asking, anyway." He tapped the heel of one boot thoughtfully against the surface of the rocks and glanced first toward the house and then back to her. "I was wondering—which is my room? That one?"

"No, that." She pointed Romulan-fashion with a jerk of her chin. "At the corner. You can see the storage-access doors; inside, they're behind an embroid—" Arrhae broke off short. "You're not a fool, Dr. Bones McCoy. Neither am I. You knew which room it was all the time. Why ask me?"

"Curiosity, nothing more. I wasn't sure. And I don't have an escape planned, if that's what's wrong. Everyone keeps telling me what a waste of time it is."

"You should come in."

"I'd as soon stay here for—"

"Doctor, I was not asking you, I was *telling* you."

McCoy got to his feet and brushed a little dust off the seat of his pants, then shrugged ostentatiously at her and sauntered back to the house.

# Chapter Eight

## FORCE AND POWER

The ch'Rihan of the four morning and evening stars, the ch'Rihan of song, is a fair place. Wetter than Vulcan ever was, rich with seasons whose change could be perceived, full of game and food, full of noble land on which noble houses were built, green under a green-golden sky, wide-horizoned, soft-breezed, altogether a paradise. Looking back at those songs, it is sobering to consider that of the eighteen thousand surviving travelers, perhaps six thousand died in the first ten years of their settlement.

Relatively few of these died from privation, lack of supplies, or any of the other problems common to pioneer planets far from their colonizing worlds. Most of them died from war: civil wars, international, intertribal, and interclan wars. They died in small skirmishes, epic battles, ritual murders, massacres, ambushes, pogroms, purges, and dynastic feuds. So many people died that the gene pool was almost unable to sufficiently establish itself. When the mutated lunglock virus spread around the planet and to ch'Havran fifty years after the settlement, the population dropped to a nearly unviable nine thousand. Only through the vigorous, almost obsessive increase of the population over the following several hundred years—through multiple-birth "forcing," creche techniques, and some cloning—did the Rihannsu manage to survive at all.

The later Rihannsu historians have almost unanimously joined in condemning Lai i-Ramnau tr'Ehhelih for suggesting that the Rihannsu brought this devastating result on themselves by leaving Vulcan in the first place, and thus "running away from the problem" that should have been solved as a whole planet before they left. "They brought their wars with them in the ships," he said in Vehe'rrIhlan, the "Non-Apology." "Their aggression, which they fought so hard to keep, was their silent passenger, their smuggled-on stowaway, the one voice not raised at meeting. But for all its silence, they knew it was there. They brought their problem with them when they fled it, as all do who part company with a trouble before it is completely resolved. Change of place is not solution of problem, change of persons is not solution of problem, but they threw even this shred of logic away when they left Vulcan. They attempted to become a new culture, but they went about this mostly by turning their backs on the old one. One who follows such a course is still following nothing but the old programming in reverse, or twisted— as if a computer programmer turned over a punch card and ran it backward. The results may look new, but the card is the same, and the program is the same, and sooner or later terribly familiar results will follow. The travelers fought for the freedom to fight. They won the freedom, but they also won the fighting. . . ."

They killed Lai tr'Ehhelih some years after he wrote those words, and his works were expunged in many kingdoms and councillories. In others, mostly eastern strongholds on ch'Havran, they were carefully hidden and preserved, which is fortunate. Otherwise we should know nothing of this hated, feared, angry little man, who told the truth as he saw it, and was so universally condemned. In retrospect, there may have been something to the truth he told. The Two Worlds have never been at peace with each other or themselves, and the first thousand years of their settlement were a broil of violence. The warfare led finally to unity and a sort of power, but the union was uneasy, and the power passed frequently from one hand to another, and never rested easy in any.

The government of ch'Rihan and ch'Havran, as mentioned before, began as extensions both of the civil structure of the ships and the governmental structure on Vulcan. Unfortunately, the first of these proved more divisive than inclusive, and the settlement scheme for the Two Worlds began to interfere almost immediately with the second.

Originally there was supposed to be in the Two Worlds: one Councillory—consisting of the Grand Council of the planet (to which each local clan, tribe, or city sent one or more representatives) and the High Council (consisting of the thirty most senior councillors from the Grand Council, and ten of the most junior). By choice, people had been widely scattered in settlement, so as not to overtax natural resources. But not every family had its flitter anymore. The Rihannsu had brought maybe a thousand small vehicles with them among the surviving ships, and every trip in every one of them was grudged. Most of them were solar-powered, true, but there was the matter of spare parts, wear and tear, and so forth. For those first years, status was often reckoned not in land (of which many people had a great deal) but transportation.

With mobility so decreased, it was no longer a matter of simply calling a Grand Council meeting and having people flit in casually from all over the planet, every week or so. There had to be fewer meetings. It was a logistical problem getting everyone together, especially in the years before the communications networks were completely settled in place. With fewer meetings, more problems piled up to be handled, and the meetings had to be long—a problem, since pre-Reformation Vulcans were no fonder than the post-Reformation ones of spending endless hours in pursuit of bureaucracy. Less got done in council meetings, both the Grand Council and the High one. The High Council in particular suffered from quick turnover in the early years, as many of the oldest councillors were in extreme old age, and there was less continuity of experience than was usual. More misunderstandings and mismanagements cropped up than had done at home on Vulcan, and people at home were often dissatisfied with the results.

In addition, there were more things to fight about than there had been in the old days . . . both more concrete problems and more abstract ones. Not only were there the familiar divisions, but blocs that voted with what ship they had been in. These "ship-blocs" often disastrously divided votes on important matters. Land—its boundaries and use of its resources—often became an issue, and there could be as many as fifteen or twenty factions—subdivisions of clans, tribes, or ship-blocs—fighting over who would get what. Here again, tr'Ehhelih may have told the right truth: even in the midst of plenty the Rihannsu could not get the context of the ancient scarcity of good land out of their minds, or their hearts. The squabbles, raids, and annexations were endless.

Government was slowed down by both these sets of problems at times when it could hardly afford to be, during the first half-century of the Settlement. Its ill function caused its collapse, an abrupt one, and the Ruling Queen's rise.

The most obvious trigger of the bloody events was the terrible famine in the south continent on ch'Havran, during which almost half of the fifteen hundred people scattered across it died of starvation in the seventy-eighth year after the settlement. But it could be said that the system had already been staggering under a burden of distances increased beyond management, and reduced logistical and technological support. It was bound to fall soon, and perhaps the sooner the better. However, the Councils fell badly, and the toll in lives and resources— and honor—was high.

The Ruling Queen's rise is paradoxical to this day, even among Rihannsu. She was one of those people with that inexplicable quality that Terrans call "charisma" and Rihannsu *"nuhirrien,"* "look-toward." People would listen to her, gladly give her things they could hardly spare, forgive her terrible deeds. Her power was astonishing, and unaccountable. She was not a great physical beauty, or a very mighty warrior, or marvelously persuasive, or any of the other things people normally find attractive. She simply had that quality, like Earth's Hitler, like (at the other end of the spectrum) Surak, of being followed. Some have used the word "sociopath" to describe her, but the term loses some of its meaning in Rihannsu culture, where one is expected to reach out one's hand and take what one wants . . . as the travelers did.

T'Rehu was a north continent Grand Councillor's daughter who succeeded her father in office after his death. (Rihannsu political offices to this day change hands by birth succession rather than election, except when relatives are lacking or there is dishonor involved. A Senator whom his district considers substandard cannot be voted out of office, but his senatoriate can send him their swords by way of suggestion that he use them on himself. Very rarely is the suggestion ignored.)

At first there seemed nothing special about her. She was capable enough, and her councillory (Elheu district, in the ship-bloc nation called Nn'Verih) prospered, and its clans with it. As time went on, however, others looked at their prosperity and became suspicious of it, noticing that the neighbors of Elheu were dying off, or being killed in inexplicable feuds, and ceding their lands—choice ones—to Elheu. No one quite had the nerve to suggest treachery, but all the same, puppets of T'Rehu's house or members of her family were soon sitting in the council chairs of more and more Nn'Verih districts. And there were disturbing reports of armed raids, House-burnings, forced marriages, and mind-betrothals, forced conceptions and births so that children related to T'Rehu's House would inherit councillories and (after suitable training in her house) dance to her lyre.

Not all of these reports were true, of course. But it seems true enough that T'Rehu was vastly dissatisfied with the way the council system worked. Numerous families of her district had, in her youth, suffered from terrible lack of the basic needs: food in that part of the continent was scarce, there were famines and plagues, good medical help was hard to come by. No one knows whether the story is true that T'Rehu lost a lover to lunglock fever because the council "could not afford" to send a healer out with the vaccine, newly developed and very expensive. It may be propaganda generated by one of T'Rehu's people. But even if it is, the story was probably truth somewhere else, painfully indicative of the kind of suffering that went on in the Two Worlds during their early days.

Time passed and the problem grew too slowly, perhaps, for either the Grand Council or High Council to perceive it clearly in their busy and infrequent meetings. The population increased in Nn'Verih, and most especially in Elheu, increased almost fifty percent over twenty years. Scientists were welcome in Nn'Verih, especially if they specialized in fertility or cloning. The place got a great name for research, though where the money for it was coming from, and the facilities, was often in question. The usual explanation was that Elheu had political connections with the Ship-Clans. People who looked too closely into the question tended to stop abruptly, either out of seeming choice or because they were suddenly nowhere to be found.

And rather suddenly, about sixty years after the settlement, Elheu had an army. Oddly enough, this came as a surprise. For all its warfare, Vulcan was never very good at organizing it: there had been no standing armies. A leader with a cause would raise what force he could by spreading the news around as to why one should fight: if you convinced people well enough, you would have a larger army than your enemy, and you would have a chance to beat them. Then after your victory (Elements granting you won), everyone would do what looting and spoiling they felt was necessary, and take the booty home to their own clans and tribes. For these reasons, alliances were never considered to have any more permanence than a pattern of dust on a windy day: you could not keep the force that had made you worth allying with. A standing army would have been considered an outrageous expense. Where would you keep them? And more important, where would they get food and water?

This situation was probably fortunate: if Vulcan had supported the standing-army concept, there would probably be nothing there now but sand, burying the tallest spires of the last-standing cities. What was unfortunate was that ch'Rihan did have enough resources of local food and water to support large organized groups of people. T'Rehu had made the conceptual jump, and invented the standing army. She did not sit around thinking of things to do with it for more time than was absolutely necessary.

She did wait a while, however. She waited until it was perfectly obvious to both the Grand Council and High Council what she was likely to do if anyone crossed her. Between the years 60 and 72 A.S. she made pointed examples of a few small territories not far from Elheu. She massed troops on their border (only a matter of a couple of thousand, but in those days, those were numbers to be reckoned with) and then had them sent false intelligence that, for political purposes, she was bluffing them. Predictably, to look bold before the other Houses, they defied her. T'Rehu then came down on them—little pieces of the world, county-sized by Earth standards, full of gentleman farmers busy scratching their livings out of a still-protesting planet—and she burned their crops and houses and killed those who resisted, and captured those who did not. If they entered her service willingly, well. If they did not, she turned her adepts loose on the captives and had them mind-changed, so that they went into her service anyway. If the mindchange didn't work, the captives in question were never seen again.

The Grand Council immediately convened and went into uproar. T'Rehu went among them, utterly cool—as well she might have been, with her bodyguard about her. Very nearly she swept the Sword off the Empty Chair and took it for herself, but at the last moment prudence or fear prevented her. She had her guards overturn the Master Councillor's chair, with him in it, and sat down there herself with her S'harien across her lap, unsheathed—one of the few of the great swords that Surak did not put aboard the ships himself. There she stayed for a noisy half hour, and let them rave about honor and outrage. "Say what you like, and do what you like," she said at last, "I am your mistress now. Idiots and old men shall not run my land anymore, nor any other I can get my hands on."

This panicked the council, as well it might have. Perhaps a hundred of the three hundred twelve of them had lands that bordered on T'Rehu's . . . or might later, at the rate she was going. Councillors from the other continents were scornful. Granted that the woman had outstepped her bounds on the north continent, and should be punished, but how could she hope to transport an army across the seas, or to ch'Havran?

She merely smiled and reminded them of her friendship with the Ship-Clans. Many hearts went cold in their owners' sides as they remembered the mass transports lying in hangar-bays in the four ships, each transport capable of handling five hundred people at a time. There were more than enough transports to manage a smallish army . . . or a largish one.

They did the only thing they could think of, they offered her the Master Councillory, the lordship of the Grand Council, if she would hold her hand. S'task stood up at that and walked out of council, which he had been attending by courtesy (High Councillors might, though they had to ask permission of the Grandees). "I did not give you leave to go," the imperious voice rang out behind him.

"I have no need to ask it, of you especially," said S'task. His voice was not so firm as it had been once: he was very old, even by Vulcan standards, and troubled with circulatory and bone-marrow problems that may have been caused by cumulative radiation exposure on the journey. But he was as fierce as he had ever been, and few dared to cross his mild voice when it was raised in either Council.

"I shall kill you if you do not ask leave," said T'Rehu, standing up with the S'harien in her hand.

He turned to her, and the carefully preserved council tape records, for all that they have been copied hundreds of times, still clearly show the cool scorn in his eyes. It might have been Surak dealing with some childish flaw in logic. "You may do so," he said. "That is the prerogative of force. But I give no honor to force. Power, yes. But you have no power, none that I recognize. I ask no leave of you." And he walked out of chambers, while T'Rehu stood behind him with the sword shaking in her hand.

"You will not do that twice!" she cried, and then found her composure again, and was seated, while the chamber stirred and murmured in fear at the terrible audacity of the woman who would challenge the authority of the father of the Two Worlds, the leader of the journey. Their fear became too much for them. Possibly had they united against her then, they might have stopped her. There might have been a war, but it would have been a small one.

They did not unite against her. They gave T'Rehu the Grand Councillorship, and for a while it held her quiet as she played with the politics of the "lower house" and amused herself. But it did not hold her long, and the thought of her rebuff in front of the Grandees still rankled. She waited for an excuse, and one presented itself.

There are several theories for the cause of the famine in the south continent in 78 A.S. The accusation that T'Rehu started it herself is probably baseless: Rihannsu biotechnology was not far enough along to make germ warfare at all likely. As far as anyone can tell from the records remaining, the weather was quite enough to do it—one of those paradoxical years that happens in many a temperate climate, when winter simply refuses to let go, and temperatures remain subnormal all year long. Freak weather killed most of the imported cultivated graminiformes, and the south continent people were short of other staples. They would not plant "the wretched root," and so had none when it might have saved their lives. Help was marshaled and sent from other continents and nations, but not quickly enough to save a thousand lives. Part of this (though T'Rehu did all she could to conceal the fact) was the sheer stubbornness of the southerners: they had a tradition of bearing suffering without complaint as they had in *Gorget* and *Vengeance*. And without complaint they died, by hundreds. The help arrived too late.

To T'Rehu, it was a gift from the Elements. She swept into the Grand Council and delivered them a long diatribe, berating them for not doing better for the people in their care. (Carefully she avoided any line of reasoning that might have indicated she, as Master Councillor, was at all responsible for "her" governing body's failures.) "It will not be allowed to happen again," she said, and the next day she informed the High Council that the Master Councillor required them to meet.

They sent back to say that the "request" was incorrectly made, but nonetheless they would accommodate her. What the forty had not been expecting was to find her waiting in chambers for them the next morning, with five cohorts of a hundred warriors each standing outside (and many of them inside that crowded little room as well). T'Rehu told them that their rule was ineffective. Others better suited to handling the affairs of two great worlds would now assume it.

The forty, to their credit, did not freeze as completely as the Grand Council had. They had suspected something of T'Rehu's intent, and had come armed; they defied her. But her eye was not on them. She was watching S'task. He rose up, and slowly and carefully turned his back on her, and headed toward the chamber doors.

"I have not given you leave," she said, and this time her voice was heard to be shaking in the hush that had fallen on the room.

S'task said never a word.

She signed to her guard, and one of them threw a dart-spear at S'task, and it pierced his side and his heart, and that was the end of him. Only he lifted up his head as he lay there bleeding out his life in the uproar and the massacre that followed, and he said to T'Rehu, "The beginning is contaminated, and force will not avail you, or it."

So he died there, two hundred forty-eight years old, in the building whose cornerstone he had laid, as he had laid the cornerstone of the journey itself. Not many missed the irony that it was the old "Vulcan," the way of kings and queens and unbridled passions and wars, for which he had fought, that had killed S'task at last.

It killed the High Council, too, and some members of the Grand Council as well fell victim to T'Rehu as she purged the "corrupt" government of ch'Rihan and ch'Havran and set herself as Ruling Queen in its place, taking as her model the Ruling Queens of Kh'reitekh in northern Vulcan in the ancient days. Her accession was a gaudy affair, and well attended, though it might seem strange from our end of time that people would turn out peaceably to see the murderess of S'task take up the spear of royalty. The truth was that most of the attendees were local people, some of whom had been ordered to attend or their families would suffer, and S'task's popularity had been quietly waning for some years, as if now that the journey was done, most people had no more need for him. Perhaps the citizenry had been looking, as the governed sometimes will, for something, anything, to replace a government that bores them. For eighteen years the Rihannsu got one that was not at all boring . . . and that was about all that could be said for it.

Eighteen years is a short term in any office by Vulcan or Rihannsu reckoning. T'Rehu took the title-name *Vriha,* "highest," and conducted her court in the old high-handed fashion, handing out life and death as it pleased her. She did not have time to do much harm to the Two Worlds, she was by and large too busy gratifying her own desires, mostly for bigger palaces, more luxuries for her favorites, and more money to pay her soldiers. She had the vigorous love of pleasure of a Terran Elizabeth I, without either the sense of responsibility or the high intelligence that drove that monarch. At first she made a great show of being a "just ruler," sending help to the famine-struck south continent (and the help did no more good than that previously sent by the councils—most of the people were already dead). But eventually "her people" came to concern her only insofar as they gave her money or bowed before her.

T'Rehu had the old council chambers razed and built new ones, bigger and grander, with a throne for her, one ostentatiously blocking the Empty Chair from view . . . though she did not quite dare to get rid of it or the sword. She chose new councillors, one of them from each continent, totaling twelve in all, mostly women. She made each of them responsible for their whole landmass, and if things went ill there, there was no use pleading for mercy. The floors were marble, and easily washed clean. She went through a fair number of councillors this way, and no one dared chide her for it. They might be next.

She was not mad enough to let all her political connections lapse when she came into power. She enriched the Ship-Clans considerably, delaying for a little the beginning of their decline. In return she demanded a great deal of application of shipside technology to the problems of ch'Rihan and ch'Havran, particularly the transportation and communication problems. Naturally these were for the benefit of her throne—it being difficult to control two worlds properly without quick communication and widespread swift transportation—but accidentally these measures did the Rihannsu people some good as well. The first factories for communications hardware and small transport were set up under her aegis, and by 96 A.S. a tolerable videotelephone system was in operation, and at least one House in every five had its own flitter, or could afford one.

But her rule could not last long, simply because it would occur to other people to do what she had done as well. The east-continent factions on ch'Havran smarted under her rule—since their continent was poor, she paid little notice to them—and they decided to do something about it. By themselves, without assistance from the fertility experts, without cloning, they doubled their continental population during T'Rehu's reign and they quietly raised and trained their own young army in philosophies that the Spartans would have recognized instantly. Ruthless hatred of the enemy, self-sacrifice, instant obedience, and the nation above all—not the state. In this case, that was T'Rehu. They made their own arrangements with the Ship-Clans as well, for one thing their rugged hills had that T'Rehu did not know about—mines with some of the largest optical-grade rubies ever seen on any world, perfect for generating large-scale laser light.

The easterners descended on T'Rehu in the eighteenth year of her reign, brought her (unwillingly) to battle with twice her forces' numbers, and killed her on the plains of Aihai outside the capital city of Ra'tleihfi, which she was still completing. There was not so much rejoicing at this in the Two Worlds as confusion. The easterners might have moved into the power vacuum and set themselves up as kings, but to their credit, they did not. They wanted a return to a quieter sort of government, one in which tyranny would have difficulty going for such a long time uncorrected.

From this victory in ch'Rihan's first war, after some squabbling among various continents for supremacy, came the Praetorial and Senatorial structure that we know today, a resurrection of the councillories crossed with the Queen's Twelve. Our Federation Standard terms are, of course, worn-down Latin cognates: "Praetor" for the Rihannsu *Fvillha,* "landmaster," and "Senator" for *deihu,* "elder." The Rihannsu functions are fairly close in some ways to the Roman ones: the Senate passing and vetoing legislation (in the Rihannsu version, one half of the Senate being assigned the business of doing nothing but veto, probably as a reaction to T'Rehu's tyranny), the Praetorate wielding judicial and executive power for whole continents, implementing the laws passed . . . and sometimes getting laws passed for which they feel the need. The Senate is counted as two houses, so that all the governing bodies taken together are *seiHehllirh,* the "Tricameron." Together the Three (or Two) Houses have weathered many troubles, and even the occasional Emperor or Empress . . . very occasional. History has shown the Rihannsu to have little trust in "single rulers." They have long seemed to prefer them in groups, feeling perhaps that there is safety in numbers. If one gets out of hand, the others will pull him or her down. And indeed the doings of the Praetorate sometimes look, to an outsider, like nothing so much as the minute-to-minute business of a bucket of crabs—each trying to climb out on the others' backs, the ones underneath unfailingly pulling off balance the ones climbing on them.

It proved to be a form of government not very stable in the short term: a never-ending swirl of alliances, betrayals, whisperings, veiled allusions, matters of honor shadowy and open, machinations, string-pulling, and arguments forever. Yet despite this, the Rihannsu governmental system proved perfect for the people they were in the process of becoming, and stable in the long run, for people wanted no more T'Rehus. The Tricameron survived through the loss of the ships and the loss of spaceflight technology, through the rediscovery of the sciences and the flowering of the Rihannsu arts, through several more wars and several surprisingly long periods of peace, through the first Rihannsu contact with an alien species and the intertwining of the Two Worlds' affairs, willy-nilly, with those of the Klingons and the Federation. It survives yet, the crabs climbing up and pulling down as of old. And if the Rihannsu have their way, it will go on for as long as their worlds have people on them. "Certain it is and sure," says the song, "love burns, ale burns, fire burns, politics burns. But cold were life without them."

# Chapter Nine

There were fewer people in i'Ramnau than at the same time last week. Fewer people, and poorer produce. Arrhae was grateful for the one, but annoyed about the other. And wary all the time. Nobody *looked* unfriendly; but then, that was the problem. Any of the other shoppers who passed her by could be—and probably were—intelligence operatives watching the person responsible for their latest and most important catch.

There was no way in which she could forget about McCoy, not with the translator device belted around her waist that bumped her hipbone most uncomfortably every time she moved. H'daen had presented it to her only yesterday, with some ceremony and an interminable list of do's and don'ts. *Be careful with it, it's expensive Fleet property; don't lose it; don't play with the control settings; and above all, keep it out of McCoy's hands.* H'daen was simply passing on instructions that he didn't understand, and that one most of all. Arrhae ir-Mnaeha wouldn't have understood it either—but Lieutenant Commander Haleakala-LoBrutto did. Unless Romulan translators were vastly different from the Federation handtrans units that she was used to, the internal duotronic translator circuitry could be converted, with a lot of knowledge and a little work, into a small, crude, but very nasty form of primitive blaster.

Terise thought about that, and about what would become of her otherself if anything of the sort should happen, and strapped it on at once. It hadn't been farther than an arm's length away ever since.

McCoy was the principal reason for her being here anyway. After the translator had arrived, and she had been able to talk to him for the "first time"—without a lengthy explanation of her sudden linguistic ability—she had tried to find out what an unenhanced Terran metabolism could, and more important, couldn't digest. Not only was it important for his jailer to keep her prisoner well and healthy, but more personal reasons could see that the man had enough trouble already without a dose of *llhrei'sian*. "The Titanian two-step," McCoy had called it, and at the old, old Starfleet slang Arrhae/Terise had laughed out loud for the first time since he came into the house.

Most of the goods for the house were being delivered, and that left only McCoy's own provisions to be bought and carried about the town. Shopping for what were largely unusual items, Arrhae managed to forget her troubles, at least for a while. Most especially when she was bargaining stallholders up from their excessively honorable—and excessively low— first prices toward something that the honor and status of House Khellian required her to pay. It amused her that a people who had attained warpflight and who had learned how to cloak something the size of a battlecruiser still couldn't buy meat and vegetables without haggling like the feudal societies she had studied in college.

And then she saw him again.

It was the fourth time now that he had been standing off to one side, watching her. A small man, darkly good-looking—and not really paying attention to the goods he was about to buy. Arrhae was unaccustomed to being looked at by young men on Earth, but here—well, Lhaesl tr'Khev, bless him, had been far from subtle in his compliments, and though she had never dared admit it, even to herself, the small, sharp, high-boned features that hadn't drawn a second glance at home went beyond pretty into what Romulans regarded as classic beauty. Except that this man didn't have the speculative, appraising, or just plain appreciative expression that she was used to. Instead, he was looking at her with the intensity of someone trying to remember a name or where they had last seen a face. On an arrest-sheet, perhaps . . .

Arrhae felt her mouth become dry and metallic-tasting. She turned away quickly, as if not looking at the man could banish him to some distant place, and began to scoop parceled *hlai*-filets from the countertop. At least this meat was the final item on her list of purchases; everything else—another quick glance sideways confirmed that her shadow was still where she had last seen him—was going to wait until another day, and she was ready, willing, and able to face down anybody, including H'daen himself, in defense of her decision. Or Chief Cook tr'Aimne, who for a blessing wasn't with her today even though—or perhaps because—H'daen, pleased that she had brought the Varrhan flitter back undamaged, had given her the use of it again. At least there was a quick way out of the city and back home. Bidding the meat-vendor a fair day in a voice that trembled only very slightly, she made off with as much haste as dignity and a full load of groceries permitted, leaving the man holding uncollected change from five full chains of cash and wondering what had happened to so suddenly increase House Khellian's opinion of its own honor.

Two armored constables sauntered past her, local men, exchanging cheerful comments with shoppers and salespeople alike, and Arrhae wondered if she dared. . . . A swift look behind gave her the answer to that, because her pursuer was no longer in sight and without him what could she say? *Nothing,* she thought savagely, and hurried past them in the general direction of the flitpark.

She didn't go straight there, but followed a twisty, convoluted course through the greater and lesser streets of i'Ramnau, with much doubling back and breathless pausing in doorways. No sign. . . . Even the park was almost deserted, flitters in less than a quarter of its bays on a day when it was usually filled to capacity, and she began to smile at her own fears. Lhaesl tr'Khev wasn't the only young man who needed a lesson in manners when it came to the admiring of ladies. Dropping her packs beside the Varrhan, she leaned one hand on its warm hull and reached out with the other to pop its cargo-bay—then jumped backward and almost screamed aloud when a hand came from the vehicle's interior and grabbed her firmly by the wrist.

"*Hru'hfe s'Khellian?*"

Arrhae tugged once, uselessly. "*Ie,*" she said in a defeated voice.

"Good."

The young man who had followed her—probably from her first arrival in the flitpark if she but knew the whole of it—eased himself out of the prime-chair and straightened up with a little sigh of relief. "Hot in there without the 'cyclers running," he said. "Then your name would be Arrhae ir-Mnaeha?" He still hadn't let go of her arm.

"Yes."

"Good." And this time he let her go.

Arrhae rubbed at her wrist more for something to do than because it pained her; the man hadn't been brutal, just most decisive. She glanced around the park for a potential rescuer if one should become necessary, and then back at him. "Why good?" she said, while inside her otherself Terise speculated on how she could take him out with a minimum of noise and disturbance. "Why were you following me?"

*"Mnhei'sahe,"* he said quietly.

Arrhae shivered at the word, and Terise went far, far away into her subconscious. *Mnhei'sahe* was controlled more by circumstances than by definition. It could mean lifelong friendship or unremitting hatred, but the friendship did not always mean long life or the hatred sudden death. The word was as slippery as a *nei'rrh,* and often as deadly, and the Rihanha that was Arrhae wondered what its meaning might be this time. She tried to remember who she might have offended in the past; who might have decided that this was a good time to take revenge for real or imagined slights. She looked nervously at the young man and wondered if, concealed somewhere, he carried the edged steel that was considered appropriate for honorable murder.

As far as she could see, he was unarmed; and he was smiling. It was one of the weakest smiles that she had seen in her life, a poor somber apology of a thing, but at least the grimness was turned inward rather than directed at her.

"Nveid tr'AAnikh," he said with a little bow of introduction. The name meant nothing to Arrhae, and it seemed likely that her expression told Nveid as much. He looked around, then gestured at the flitter. "Could we get inside please, and drive?"

"Where?" Arrhae said coldly. She had recovered from her fright, and anger was starting to replace it, because if this was an arrest, it was the strangest she had ever heard of; and such a recovery was inevitable anyway, she was getting so much practice at being scared and hiding the fact from various people. Either that or just give up and take refuge in madness.

"Wherever you like. I'm afraid they might have had me watched."

"Who?" Another irritable monosyllable from Arrhae, who once again was smelling the unpleasant aroma of intrigue and wanted nothing more to do with it.

"My family," he said. "They don't approve of my attitude."

Arrhae managed a very good hollow laugh. This man was neither her master nor anyone of such importance as Commander t'Radaik. For the first time in long enough, she was confronted by someone whose requests she could refuse. "Because you accost other people's servants about their lawful business? Are you surprised, tr'AAnikh?"

"It isn't that. It's because of my brother."

She brushed past him and dropped her parcels into the Varrhan's cargo-space, then made to get inside. His arm was braced across the doorway, and Arrhae looked at it with disapproval while Terise Haleakala-LoBrutto gazed calmly through the same eyes and noted wrong-way striking angles directed against the locked elbow joint. "Are you fond of using that arm, Nveid tr'AAnikh," she said gently.

He looked right back at her, paler now than he had been, and said, "McCoy."

Arrhae took a single step backward, her facial muscles already frozen and expressionless. "Get in," she snapped. "You know how, invited or not."

Nveid scrambled inside with the quick, economical movements of someone who had spent time in the cramped confines of a Fleet warbird. "You should lock the doors," he said, smiling.

"Why bother? Without the drive codes you wouldn't have gone anywhere." She slid into the prime-seat, strapped herself in, and punched in the activator program, noticing absently as she fed in a manual override to her logged routeplans that he was right, it *was* hot without the 'cyclers running. They cut in even as she thought about them, as the flitter's systems came to life and she lifted it clear of the parkbay in a smooth, tight 3-G arc that squashed tr'AAnikh back into the padded seat.

"You drive like Nniol used to," he said when he had the breath to do it.

Arrhae glanced at him, confirmed that the overrides were up and running, and took the flitter out toward open country at a speed just below city-traffic limits. "What about McCoy?" she said, not interested in who or how she drove like. "And what does *mnhei'sahe* have to do with all this?"

"Return to auto," said Nveid.

Arrhae laughed scornfully. "Can't take the thought of a woman at the controls, eh?"

"I've seen how you react to a shock, and I don't intend to die because of it."

That stopped her laughing, and an instant later persuaded her to let the flitter's onboards take over. "Very amusing, tr'AAnikh," she said quietly. "Why shouldn't I be proud and haughty and throw you out right now?"

"Because you want to hear me."

"Then talk to me, man, and hope I don't throw you out anyway. . . ."

"I doubt it." Nveid looked confident enough, almost too confident for Arrhae's liking, though she pushed that thought back until it became important again. "I told you before: it concerns my brother Nniol, and *mnhei'sahe,* and Dr. McCoy of the Federation vessel *Enterprise.*" He paused as a thought struck him. "That *is* the man held at H'daen tr'Khellian's mansion? Not some other of the same name?"

"McCoy of the *Enterprise,*" Arrhae confirmed. "So?"

"My brother Nniol served aboard Ael t'Rllaillieu's *Bloodwing,* and my sister aboard *Javelin* under LLunih tr'Raedheol. I don't know all the details—nobody does outside High Command—but there was some treason involving *Bloodwing* and *Enterprise* and . . . *Javelin* was destroyed."

"Your brother killed his own sister . . . ?"

"Who knows? *Bloodwing* will never return to ch'Rihan, and *Javelin*'s dust can tell no tale. But my family decided. They formally disowned Nniol. His name was written and burned. . . . I displease them because I speak about him still and because I say that *mnhei'sahe* required him to do what . . . what he did."

"Oh. That one. All duty and obligation goes to your commander, not to your family?"

"Always. We are an honorable house, and my sister would have done the same. As would I. On board ship the commander becomes *hru'hfirh,* although some are more deserving of the courtesy than others. Ael t'Rllaillieu may be a traitor now, but in her time she was the best captain that my brother had the honor to obey."

"And McCoy? Where does he fit in? Do you want to kill him in requital for your brother and sister . . . ?" Nveid stared at her, shocked. "Isn't that what your honor requires?" Arrhae was beginning to doubt it somehow; this man wasn't like tr'Annhwi, or, if he was, he hid it well.

"No, it isn't." He sat back in the seat, relaxing a little. "*Hru'hfe,* there are entire Houses who think that way—but there are also entire Houses who think as I do, that their bloodkin acted with *mnhei'sahe* in this sad business. One of them would have spoken with you—maybe s'Khnialmnae—except that every one of them is under close observation by Fleet Intelligence. I need only worry about my immediate family. . . ."

"Then what do you and these other Houses want to do with McCoy?" The impatient edge in Arrhae's voice—adopted from one of the Fleet officers who visited House Khellian—cut through Nveid's reminiscing and brought him bolt upright. He blinked and stared at her with the injured air of a man who'd heard that tone from his superiors and hadn't thought to get it here as well.

"We want to help him escape."

Arrhae knew that this youngster had been quite right to insist she put the flitter back on automatics before surprising her like that—otherwise she would probably have crashed it into the side of a hill right here and now. At least she managed not to show it this time. Practice, probably. Why did people keep saying things like this to her? Why couldn't she just go back to being a full-time servants' manager and a very part-time deep-cover spy? What had gone wrong with her life? "Oh, is that all?" she said, very controlled. "Nothing else? Why not the Sword from the Empty Chair as a parting gift, perhaps?"

Nveid laughed softly. "You're as cool as a Vulcan," he said. "I hadn't expected it—but then, that's why Fleet put McCoy in your hands, I suppose. We'll make it worthwhile, of course, and nobody will know you were ever involved."

"You do know the Senate punishment for treason?"

"Of course." Nveid's voice went harsh. "The Justiciary Praetor read sentence on Nniol's name. If he's ever caught, they'll carry it out. All of it. The penalty for espionage is much the same, except they start with eyes and ears instead of tongue and hands. And *that* they've planned for McCoy, sometime in the next tenday. The Houses I represent aren't going to allow it. There is still such a thing as—"

"—honor on ch'Rihan, yes. How did I guess you'd say something like that? And Nveid, I don't know what value you and your friends put on 'worthwhile,' but there isn't enough money on ch'Rihan to match the value I put on my skin."

"But I told you, nobody will know—"

"Until somebody does, and where would that leave me? Being slowly shredded on the public-broadcast channel, like they did to Vaebn tr'Lhoell. I'm sure he thought nobody would ever know about him, either."

"You could consider our proposal, at least."

Arrhae brought the flitter onto a course back to i'Ramnau and locked into the traffic-grid before she turned to look at Nveid. "You heard me consider. You heard my conclusion. Listen to me. You found out where McCoy was being held, and I—doubtless to my regret, if it ever comes out—confirmed that the man in House Khellian was indeed the one that you and your friends suspected. I want nothing more to do with it. You will get out of this flitter when I get back to the park, and you will go away, and you will leave me alone or I swear that I'll report the lot of you just to make sure that I'm safe!"

Her voice had risen to a near-shriek during the tirade, so that Nveid was watching her now with wide, shocked eyes and a plainly visible doubt that this woman would have been of any use at all. That was as Arrhae wished. She had no desire to be made use of again; it was already happening far too much for her liking. The flitter settled into its recently vacated bay with a jarring thump that almost certainly took paint off the A-G housings, but she was past caring about such details, and past worrying whether H'daen saw the damage and forbade her to go anywhere near i'Ramnau ever again. The way she felt now, that wouldn't be a punishment.

She hit the canopy control-tab and watched as Nveid tr'AAnikh climbed out. He moved more slowly than she had seen him do before, and the look he directed back at her was more regretful than anything else. "Reconsider," he said.

"No. What do you expect from a servant, man? We leave the concerns of honor to those with free time to worry about them."

"Then that's your last—"

"I said, *yes!*" Arrhae snapped the canopy shut on whatever else he was trying to say, and lifted the flitter clear with enough violence to trigger a stress-warning alarm. *Last time you'll get clearance for this,* she thought grimly. *And I think it's time I had another talk with the good doctor. Otherwise things are going to get right out of hand. If they haven't already . . .*

Outside, it began to rain.

Arrhae disabled the autos and took the flitter into its garage on manual. It was a simple test; either she was back in control of herself and could handle the vehicle safely, or she would crash it and kill herself. Sometimes that seemed preferable. Certainly it would be less complicated. She sat for a long while in the quiet, after the engine noise had died away, and listened to the pattering of rain on the roof, wondering what to do next. *Unload the shopping,* she thought. *And then go see McCoy.*

S'anra met her in the corridor as she left the garage area, summoned most likely by the door-chime as the flitter came in. "You're back!" she began excitedly. "There's someone here to see you, and—"

"Take these to the kitchen and store them." Arrhae pushed the parcels into S'anra's arms. They were caught by no more than automatic reflex, and a bundle of vegetable tubers fell off the unstable pile. She picked it off the floor and slapped it emphatically back on top of the heap of packages. "And tell whoever it is that I'm busy."

"But Arrhae . . ."

*That* drew a disapproving glare. Junior servants and slaves were not permitted to call their superiors by name, only by rank or title. "Mind your manners—and don't contradict me. I have work to do, so I'll be along in a while. Go say so."

S'anra gaped like a landed fish for a second or two—because of her mistake maybe, or because Arrhae was being unusually tetchy, or for some other reason restricted to scullery slaves—then scurried away with the groceries. Arrhae watched her go, thinking back to when she had been no more than a slave herself, with a slave's small concerns and worries. And with only the problems of learning several thousand years of cultural history hanging overhead. She smiled thinly, and went to find McCoy.

He wasn't in his room, and Arrhae had a momentary fit of the horrors while she imagined all the things that might have happened while she was away. *While you were away—as if your being here would have made any difference if a squad of Fleet troopers came for him. . . .* Then she began thinking, more sensibly again, of all the places that McCoy had grown fond of during the past tenday.

First and foremost was the garden. *In* this *downpour?* Arrhae thought dubiously, looking out at the lowering gray sky. *Well, why not. The quicker you go out to see, the quicker you can get back indoors. . . .*

And, of course, that was where he was. She found McCoy as she had seen him so many times before, sitting on top of the rocks in the garden, talking to himself. Arrhae could hear the soft mumble of his voice as she approached, and he most certainly heard her splashy footfalls, for he climbed down and came to meet her. "Do you really like this weather so much?" she demanded, feeling a rivulet of chilly water starting to wander down inside her supposedly rainproof overrobe. "Look at you, man; why didn't you ask for a coat! You're soaked to the skin!"

McCoy shook raindrops from his hair. "Yes, in fact I do like it. I can't see the house through the rain, and that way I don't have to think about being locked up all night. And I couldn't ask for a coat because nobody here speaks Anglish and the only translator in the area had been taken shopping. But I wanted some fresh air, so I came out anyway. I knew you wouldn't mind."

"Dammit, McCoy, you're impossible!" she yelled. And then realized that the words were idiomatic Anglish and had come out in a voice untainted by any trace of a Rihannsu accent.

*Oh, no. O Elements. I am betrayed. And by myself . . .*

"Good," McCoy said, exactly as Nveid tr'AAnikh had done. Then he smiled the small smile of someone whose theories have been conclu-

sively proven. "But you're right. I am impossible. And it's getting wetter out here than even I like, so shouldn't we go indoors now?" Since
McCoy's clothing was already so waterlogged that it had stopped soak-
ing up the rain, his remark was more to give her an out than because he
was concerned.

Arrhae took it as gracefully as she could, though she pointedly refused
to say anything to him either in Anglish or translated Rihannsu. She had
an unpleasant feeling, justified or not, that he had laid a trap for her—
and the even more unpleasant feeling of having walked right into it.
After eight years of cautiously avoiding the attention of Imperial Intelligence, it irked her to realize that this drowned rat of a medical officer
had maneuvered her into a position that would mean unpleasant death if
anyone else had overheard her words. All her intentions of talking to
him were evaporating fast, and yet there were things he had to be told.

"Be more careful in future," she said at last, speaking low and letting
her accent do whatever it wanted to—which in this instance was to slur
and jump most alarmingly. "Not that you have much of it. Your trial's
been set for sometime soon, and the sentence has already been agreed."

"Death, of course."

"Of course. But it seems, Doctor, that you're very popular among . . .
certain groups. That popularity spread to me, briefly, and I didn't like
it—but I think you can expect visitors after dark."

"Oh, wonderful." McCoy didn't sound impressed. "It should relieve
the boredom of being locked in all night." He passed her, squelching,
rather, on the wet ground, and looked back briefly. This time he wasn't
smiling. "And Arrhae, I think we should have some sort of talk soon,
about languages, and history, and people who aren't what they seem."
McCoy waited for a reaction, saw none, shrugged, and walked back
toward the house, leaving Arrhae to the rain and to her own thoughts.

"Where were you, *hru'hfe?*" Ekkhae pounced on her as she stamped irri-
tably into the house, quailed from the glower that the question provoked, but continued determinedly for all that. "Mister H'daen has
been waiting for you since you came back from the city. In the antechamber. He has a guest. . . ."

"Another one? Who is it this time?"

"A visitor." Ekkhae came down hard on the word, as if it had some special significance, and smiled oddly as she said it.

Arrhae took off the sopping overrobe and tossed it at the little slave. Despite being suddenly encumbered by a swathe of clammy fabric, Ekkhae's smile grew wider and more peculiar. "What's wrong with you?" Arrhae snapped. "Your teeth hurt?"

"No, *hru'hfe.*"

"Then put that away—and drape it properly; I don't want creases."

"No, *hru'hfe.* I mean yes, *hru'hfe.* That is, I—"

"Just do it," said Arrhae wearily, thinking *yes, hru'hfe,* and saying it under her breath as Ekkhae bustled away. She wasn't ready for an afternoon of fending off Lhaesl tr'Khev, and by the sound of it, that was who awaited her. She could almost feel sorry for H'daen, being forced to play the host until she arrived to rescue him. Lhaesl was an amiable fool—with the emphasis on *fool.*

Except that it was tr'Annhwi instead.

The subcommander set his winecup down and stood up as she came into the room, smiling as pleasantly as he was able—which wasn't very. "I told you that I would come to visit you," he said, making his usual theatrical bow.

Arrhae groaned inwardly. There was only one way out of this, and with H'daen sitting on the other side of the table, that way would make a fool out of him and a liar out of her. "I . . . I hadn't thought my lord H'daen would have granted permission after—"

"After what happened? Your lord forgave me. He is a generous man." Again the smile. "You will find me generous too."

"But Lhaesl . . ."

*"What?"* H'daen's winecup thumped against the surface of the table and, overfull as usual, immediately spilled. Elements alone knew what he had said about their conversation of last week, but by the sound of it he had said enough to wish that Arrhae had kept her mouth tight shut. It was too late now; the damage had plainly been done and all H'daen could do was try to extricate himself with as much dignity—and as much speed—as he could muster. The look on his face boded ill for the

next conversation with his *hru'hfe,* but Arrhae felt that she could weather that storm more easily than spending an evening with tr'Annhwi.

Who was looking remarkably unconcerned. "I regret this misunderstanding, *hru'hfirh,*" he said without the anger Arrhae might have expected from a man whose passions seemed to run so high. When he looked at her, there was no longer any more interest in his face than when anyone looked at a servant. "Your lord's wine is spilled, woman." Tr'Annhwi's voice was cold now, drained of the warmth that she guessed had been false all along. "Clean up this mess and refill his cup."

H'daen said nothing to confirm or deny that she should obey. He didn't even look in her direction. Instead, he inclined his head to tr'Annhwi, as if inviting him to continue with something he had been saying before Arrhae came in. "You mentioned something about Mak'khoi, Subcommander," he said, ignoring Arrhae's efforts to tidy his desk as he might ignore a piece of furniture, and thus not seeing the brief glance of shock she directed at him. "About handing him over to you. You said that you would make it worth my while. Tell me: what amount of money are we talking about . . . ?"

# Chapter Ten

## FLOWERING

"Rihannsu are conservatives," Lai tr'Ehhelih said once in another of his more unpopular books, "though they would die rather than admit it. No revolutionary who has come many light-years through terrible privation and suffering would want to admit in public that he secretly misses the conditions he left behind. It makes fascinating viewing, from the sociological standpoint, to watch them decrying the 'corrupt customs' of the Old World, and then settling into just slightly different versions of those customs, with the greatest self-congratulation and smugness. When change happens on ch'Rihan, it happens by chance, or the boredom of the Elements. No one here ever set out to change anything, not on purpose."

Tr'Ehhelih was being bitter, as usual, but also as usual there were elements of truth in his words. There were areas in which the Rihannsu were truly innovative—some sciences and arts—but somehow the energy always seemed to start seeping out of those areas after a while. Innovation would slowly drop off, the whole matter would fall gradually into tradition, and a generation later no one would ever know that there had been invention or different ways of doing something. There would be one way, and that way "the way it's always been done."

Spaceflight was one of these areas of accomplishment, and perhaps the most tragic. The body of engineering talent that built the ships was one of the most astonishing collections of determined genius ever gathered on Vulcan, and the travelers tried hard to preserve the fruits of that genius. All the ships' libraries were crammed full of technical information in every field known to the Vulcans. The ships' librarians were

aware that they were stocking "time capsules." Each of the ships dupli-
cated information found in all the others, and no one grudged the redundancy, which, considering the history of the journey, was wise.

But the one thing they could not stock the ships with, with any certainty, was talent and incentive to use the information preserved there.
The brilliant minds that designed the ships' systems, for the most part,
went along on the journey. But many of them died, in the various
tragedies that befell the travelers, or later on of old age. More specialists
in navigations, space science, and astronautical engineering were
trained in the process of the journey, of course, but there is no forcing a
person to be brilliant at a science—especially one that the children of
the time tended to think of (in the early years) as something of a nuisance. They either remembered Vulcan, and were ambivalent about
having been forced to leave it, or they were born on the journey and
were full of stories about the wonders of living on a planet, in the open
air. Some of them were understandably bored or annoyed with the
whole issue of ships.

This, unfortunately, was the generation that finally landed on ch'Rihan,
and knowingly or unknowingly went about setting the course of the
planet's civilization for the next thousand years or so. The government
that came into power after the accession of the Ruling Queen acted, by
inaction, for the whole generation. Their general feeling was that they
were still getting the world on its feet, and had no time to start designing
new starships, or (worse yet) devoting the then-scarce cash or venture
capital of the planet to large building efforts. That they *did* find fairly
large amounts sometime later to spend on wars in the south continent
and in the east on ch'Havran was a fact pointed out to the Senate on several occasions. But very few voices made this complaint, and little notice
was taken. The majority of people in the Two Worlds felt that they had
thought enough about space for a while. The past two hundred years
had been devoted to it. It was time to settle down, get some crops yield-
ing properly, and find out who their neighbors were, and their enemies.
If anyone needed to worry about it, let it be the Ship-Clans.

Unfortunately, the Ship-Clans had problems of their own. They
were dwindling. The travelers in general had little interest in keeping

up the populations of the ships, with a new world underfoot to live in, and there were defections from the Ship-Clans as time went on— people who saw no particular reason to stay inship, among metal walls, while there was green grass to walk on and green-gold sky to walk under for the first time in almost a hundred years.

There were other problems. At first funding and material support from ch'Rihan were fairly munificent: but after the reorganization of the Praetorate and Senate, the assistance began to taper off slowly as the loyal voices in the government became preoccupied with other concerns, or died out and were replaced by people who cared less. The hydroponics gardens on the ships were the first to go, then data storage and processing, as valuable spare parts were shipped on-planet, and no replacements made. There had been agreements that a priority of manufacture, once it got going, would be semiconductor and transtator technology to support both the ships' needs and those of the telecommunication and defense networks that would have to be built. But for the first century and a half these needs were almost completely ignored in favor of farm manufactures—agricultural machinery, fertilizer, and food-processing equipment. It was ironic that the gardens of ch'Rihan and ch'Havran flourished as never before, while the vast shipborne flats that had kept so many Vulcan plants alive to see the new world now lay barren, and the computers that had so successfully calculated what species could fit in where in the new ecosystem were down now half the time and uncertain of operation the rest of it.

What it all added up to was a slow slide in space technology, so that by around 250 A.S. the Rihannsu would not have had the ability to get quickly off-planet if they had needed to. True, there seemed to be no need. By accident (if there are such things, which Rihannsu religion generally doubts), they had found the one good spot in a backwater, an area of the galaxy ignored as a "desert" by most of the spacefaring species in the area. It would be some seventeen hundred years before the Klingons and the Federation found them, which was just as well, for they were woefully unprepared. Other than the ships, only a few heavy transports were built to handle food shipments from ch'Havran (whose drier climate proved more conducive to the Vulcan grains they had brought with them; the north and northwest continents of ch'Havran became the "breadbasket" of the Two Worlds). Once the transports were built, there was very little further interest in space, and one by one the ships were allowed to fall. They were obsolete, it was said. Something better and newer could be built. There was no need for them anymore—there were no signs of alien presence out this far. The few voices lifted in protest, the people who said the ships should be kept at least for history's sake, were ignored. Never has the classical Rihannsu character flaw, that of deadly practicality, proved more fatal. The Ship-Clans slowly left the ships as their engines were shut down and their orbits began to decay. Between 300 and 400 A.S. they all fell.

The Rihannsu at least decided to build a planetary "defense" system—though critics pointed out that if the system noticed anything coming at the planet, it would not be able to carry the battle to it. What kind of defense was that? But this, too, fell on deaf ears, especially since several key Praetors of this period had significant political and financial involvements with the guilds building the defense systems.

To do them justice, the network they prepared to build to warn them of incoming alien craft was an ambitious and forward-looking design, and would have been an effective one had it not been scaled down to almost nothing over later years by Praetors filching the funds dedicated to it for "more important" pet projects. When it was finished in 508 A.S., it consisted of a network of chemically fueled and solar-powered defense satellite/platforms armed with particle-beam weapons and solar-output lasers connected to an outer "warning network" of twelve satellites in long hyperbolic orbits around the Eisn system. The coverage of the warning satellites was incomplete—by rights there should have been about fifty of them—and because not enough money was spent on the code for the computers running the inner defense satellites, they had a nasty habit of firing at the few friendly craft that used local space. The original outer satellites are still there, their atomic batteries and cesium clocks ticking faithfully away though their computers have long since crashed. The close orbital platforms have fallen into ch'Rihan's atmosphere and burned up, except for the one preserved as a museum. For the next fifteen hundred years or so, no one would much

care. Later, they would care a great deal indeed, and Houses would rise
and fall because of money "reappropriated" into private pockets for
hunting lodges, banquets, and the occasional murder. But in the meantime, the Rihannsu, rich and poor alike, settled down each after his or
her own manner to cultivate their fields, their families, and the arts.

War was counted as an art, perhaps the chief of them. The mindset
of the Rihannsu at that point regarding war was that it (and, in its turn,
peace) should be practiced *in extremis*. The simple delights of home and
household, and the greatest luxury available according to one's means,
should be shared with friends and enemies alike in time of peace. War,
when it was needed, should be brutal, swift, fierce, and *enjoyable*. Noble
pleasures should accompany the army into the field. There should be
fine food and excellent wine and discussions of epic poetry the night
before the battle. In the morning there should be blood in green rivers,
and single combats of note between both champions and the lesser
knights: no pity or quarter granted save to the properly prostrated foe—
to him or her, courtesy, honor, and the extraction of a fat ransom after
the victory dinner.

Honor was the heart of it all, and grew more to the heart of Rihannsu culture as time went by. In war was often its best example, since
there more than elsewhere the Rihannsu (as other species) had an "excuse" to forget about it in the heat of the moment. To their credit, they
did not often forget. The given word was kept. They still sing of besieged Ihhliae, that great city, ringed around with the troops from
neighboring Rhehiv'je, and how the Senator from the city came out
and begged the Rhehiv'jen to have mercy on her starving people. The
answer was no surprise, especially since the Rhehiv'jen had been there
since the beginning of the year, in the foulest weather in memory, and it
was now high summer, and their crops not in. The Ihhliae were told
that there was no help for it—all their men were going to be put to the
sword. But as a courtesy to the ladies of the city (it was one of the very
few regions where women did not fight), they would be allowed to
come out the next morning, and to leave with whatever they could
carry that was of value to them. There was chagrin and considerable
surprise when the women came out the next morning, each carrying

her husband on her back. But the word had been given, and when the men came back and besieged Rhehiv'je the next year, it was all taken in good part.

Arts of other sorts were also practiced. Few species have been so fond of the pleasures of the table, without turning entirely into gluttons or food critics, than the Rihannsu. Ch'Rihan in particular was rich in foods that they could adapt. There were several hundred species of fowl, numerous flightless lizards, and several flying ones that made very tasty roasts, as well as various large herd beasts that could feed whole Houses for days, and endless fruits and grains.

There was also ale, and wine. Vulcans knew about wine—the pre-Reform joke was that it was discovered just before the very first war, and caused it when the first man pointed at the second, drunk, and laughed at him. But the poor dry fruits of Vulcan were no match for the *lehe'jhme* of ch'Rihan, that grew in rich rose-colored clusters on trees three hundred feet high, in unbelievable abundance. The first Rihannsu saw the herds of wild *hlai* staggering and croaking their way across the southern veldts like a mass migration of sozzled giant ostriches, and they knew they were onto a good thing. They followed the herds in the deeps of summer, through the blue and emerald grass, and found that they had been drinking from waterholes into which the *lehe'jhme* had fallen in great numbers and fermented. From the drinking-holes, courtesy of the inebriated *hlai* of past centuries, come the more than five thousand Rihannsu wines that are coddled, blended, and smiled over around the planet today.

Ale was another story, a "poor man's drink" (or northern Havranha's drink—most fruits do not grow there) coerced out of roasted Vulcan *kheh* grain and "malted" native Havranssu breadmake, the whole first brewed and fermented for a month or so, then distilled and recarbonated. People drink Rihannsu ale for the same reason they drink Saurian brandy—to prove they *can*.

There were other arts than eating and drinking. The "plastic arts" were always highly developed on Vulcan. Their abstract sculpture and painting were particularly fine. During the journey (with its scarcity of materials to work in), the pictorial and sculptorial arts became more concrete, not less—an unexpected development. Or perhaps not, in a situation where people in general and artists in particular were looking most definitely forward into a future they hoped would be better than the past they had—and looking with equal intensity at a present which they had created themselves and which they were, to put it mildly, stuck with.

The stark, clean, conceptually advanced, mathematically derived concepts and images formerly reserved for "high art" in the old days began to turn up everywhere—on clothing, in furniture and hangings, personal effects, sprayed or painted on walls of the ships. Later, on ch'Rihan and ch'Havran, they expanded to cover whole mountainsides (e.g. the Mural Chain in west-continent ch'Rihan). No home, however poor, was complete without "pictures" of one kind or another. Everybody made them, and most of them were stunning, and the tradition has continued unchanged for fifteen hundred years. Rihannsu art, especially the painted, sculpted, and woven, is treasured all over the worlds for its vitality, tenderness, ferocity, clarity, and sheer style—often imitated, but the spirit of it rarely if ever caught, and only approached in a cool manner by the Vulcans. The Rihannsu culture has the highest artist-per-capita ratio in the known galaxy. No one knows why. "Perhaps," tr'Ehhelih said, "giving up your world enables you to *see* the one you finally wind up with."

The nonphysical arts and humanities did as well. They had fifteen hundred long and comfortable years to mold themselves, and the changes in philosophy, religion, literature, and poetry were greater than tr'Ehhelih would have liked to admit.

Vulcan religion before the flight was, to put it mildly, haphazard. Most worlds have two or three or five major religions, sometimes mutually exclusive, sometimes not, which arise over a millennium or so and then contend genteely (or not so genteelly) with one another for almost the rest of the planet's existence. Vulcan had about six hundred religions pre-Reformation: a vivid, noisy, energetic, violent sprawl and squabble of gods, demigods, *animae,* geniuses, demons, angels, golems, powers, principalities, forces, *noeses,* and other hypersomatic beings of types too difficult to explain to Earth people, who, by and large, are spoiled by the ridiculous simplicity of their own beliefs. The phrase "the one God" would have brought the average Vulcan-in-the-street to a standstill and caused him to ask, "*Which* 'One'?" since there were about ninety deities, protodeities, holy creatures, and other contenders for the title. Some planets never discover Immanence: Vulcan was littered with it.

The travelers came of a wild assortment of religions, but one "major" professed faith began slowly to sort itself out among them as the journey progressed. Perhaps at first it was not so much a religion as a fad or a joke. "Matter as God," that was where the idea started, with some nameless traveler in *Gorget* who left a dissertation on the subject in the message section of the ship's computer net.

"Things," she said, "notice." It did, in fact, begin as a joke, one that other species share. Have you noticed, she said, that when you really need something—the key to your quarters, a favorite piece of clothing—you can't find it? You search everywhere, and there's no result. But any other time, when there's no need, the thing in question is always under your hand. This, said the nameless contributor, is a proof that the universe is sentient, or at least borderline-sentient: it craves attention, like a small child, and responds to it depending on how *you* treat it—with affection, or annoyance. For further proof, she suggested that a person looking for something under these circumstances should walk around their quarters, calling the thing in question by its name. It always turns up. (Before the reader laughs, by the way, s/he is advised to try this on the next thing s/he loses. The technique has its moments.)

The initial letters in the contribution were naturally humorous ones, but the tone grew increasingly serious (though never somber: jokes were always part of it). There was something about this philosophy that seemed to work peculiarly well for the travelers, who had "made" their own worlds and their own language, and had come to exercise a measure of control over their own lives that few planetbound people do, or ever become conscious of. The "selfness" of matter became an issue for these people: the (to us) seemingly mundane observation that the physical universe had *existence,* had weight, hard edges, "the dignity of existence," as one contributor called it. Things *existed* and so had a right to nobility, a right to be honored and appreciated, as much as more sentient things that walked around and demanded the honor themselves. Things had a right to names: when named, and called by those names, of course they would respond positively—for the universe wants to be ordered, wants to be cared for, and has nothing to fulfill this function (said another contributor) but us. Or (said a third person) if there are indeed gods, we're *their* tool toward this purpose. This is our chance to be gods, on the physical level, the caretakers and orderers of the "less sentient" kinds of life.

More than nine thousand people, from *Gorget* and other ships, added to this written tradition as time went by: they wrote letters, dissertations, essays, critiques, poems, songs, prose, satire. It was the longest-running conversation on one subject in the history of that net. The contribution started two years after the departure from Vulcan, and continued without a missed day until seventy-eight years thereafter, the day the core of the computer in question crashed fatally, killing the database. However, numerous people among the remaining ships had hardcopy, and over a thousand of the travelers contributed to restoring the database. It was as if it were something that mattered profoundly enough to them that their precious private time—for everyone worked on the ships—was still worth contributing to the preservation of the thread.

Names became a great issue for these people. Many of them already had *rehei,* "nicknames" (like the "handles" of Earth's early nets) in the computer network. Many of them adopted these as "fourth names," thus identifying themselves as people participating in the contributors' net. Over several hundred more years, fourth names became commonplace, then slowly began to be kept private, shared only with one's family or most intimate friends. A fourth name was not given you by someone else: you found it in yourself—it was inherent in you, as a "proper" name was inherent in a well-named physical object. You just had to look for it, and if you looked carefully enough, you would find the "right" name. It is perhaps because of this tradition, exercised on things as well as people, that the names given places, animals, vegetables, and minerals on ch'Rihan when the travelers arrived have rarely been surpassed for vigor, humor, appropriateness, and a sort of affectionate quality. It was if the travelers were naming children. And by and large, the Two Worlds were kind enough to their colonists.

In addition, the types of matter themselves became an issue. This part of the discussion was at the start more clearly a joke than any other. There was a long and cheerful side-thread on how many "elemental" kinds of matter there were, some people holding out for four—earth, air, fire, and water, as on many another planet—others opting for five (add "plasma") or six (add "collapsed matter"). But the reckoning finally settled down to four, and people would converse learnedly (though only about half-seriously) about the "attributes" and "tendencies" of different kinds of matter: the impetuosity, ravenousness, and light-contributing nature of Fire, the malleability and passiveness of Water, and so forth. Slowly, in this tradition, the Elements became as it were embodiments of themselves, personifications (for want of a better word) of "arch-matter," which when invoked might aid the invoker, but only if the aid flowed both ways. "Be kind to the world, and the world will be kind to you," seems to have been the philosophy. People, too, were judged by their temperaments as to which Element they had most affinity to. In later years such sayings became very commonplace: "She has too much Fire in her, she'll eat you alive." "He's all Earth and no Air: he'll never move an inch." Almost certainly people sometimes perceive themselves as "having the traits" of certain Elements, and so the joke came full circle and began to be taken seriously.

S'task knew perfectly well about this growing tradition, for he himself was one of the contributors, though a rare one. He watched with some amusement, during the late part of his life, as these traditions settled into "the way things have always been," and other older religions and beliefs slipped away, gently, without alarums or excursions. For his own part he was what an Earth person would consider an agnostic. "I am unsure of everything," he remarked in one message, "except of the fact that I am certain to remain unsure." But to the "Elemental" school of thought—especially the part about treating the universe kindly—he gave a certain grudging acceptance. He would not admit publicly, of course, that this had anything to do with Surak, and the voice saying to him long ago, "The universe is concerned with means, not ends. . . ."

"Surely there is no harm in taking care of the universe," wrote S'task in the contribution, "for parts of it certainly seem to need it. If it craves order, so do human beings, and we have common cause; if (as it appears) it delights in diversity, we should cast out fear and help it be diverse, and learn to do so ourselves. If we must move through the worlds and change things, let us then be kindly caretakers: let us be toward matter as we would have the forces that move our own lives be toward us. It is no guarantee of preferential treatment by Things. But we will at least know we acted with magnanimity and honor, and if the universe sometimes seems insensible to this, let us keep acting that way until it notices."

Some people listened to him, some did not. Ch'Rihan and ch'Havran were never united about anything, and they would have been bored with life, one suspects, if they had been. The Two Worlds spent a relatively happy fifteen hundred years taming their worlds, living in them, enjoying them, untroubled by anything but their own wars and (sometimes) their own peace. But the end of the Golden Age came at last, too soon, the day the failing defense net woke up and reported something approaching the system, decelerating rapidly from the speed of light. All that happened after that, in the past hundred years, makes a terrible tale, but most terrible to the Rihannsu, who feel that their tranquil "childhood" as a people was stolen from them when two of the most driven species in the galaxy stumbled over their paradise. "Perhaps," said one rueful commentator of the time, "we have not been as kind to the Elements as we thought. . . ."

# Chapter Eleven

McCoy sat down on the hard bed and cursed under his breath. The business in the garden had been a near-perfect chance to open proper communications with Terise Haleakala-LoBrutto, and like a fool he had let it slip. Well, maybe not quite so badly as all that; they had reached a certain understanding now. At least he was certain that this "Arrhae"—damn Starfleet Intelligence for picking such a common name!—was the deep-cover operative who was at the center of this clandestine mission. The beginning of the mission, just as he was the end of it. How final that end might be depended on so many variables that his head began to pound just in anticipation, and he had to lie back with his eyes shut for some minutes until the throbbing receded back to its usual dull ache in his temples.

"All right," he muttered, "tomorrow. Like it or not." Despite all his experience in medical and psychiatric practice, he had never been comfortable with this sort of thing. How do you tell a woman who's spent eight years doing a job you couldn't handle for a week that Starfleet isn't sure about her mental health anymore? Come straight out and ask her? "Excuse the question, Lieutenant Commander, but we haven't had a report from you in two years. So tell us—are you still a Terran agent, or would you prefer to be a Romulan . . . ?" Not the sort of subtle approach that might be expected from a man who was "the best we've got."

That was what Steve Perry had called him, anyway. Except that if being bait for a Romulan frigate and its rabidly xenophobic subcommander was what compliments from Starfleet's chief of intelligence led to, then he'd stick to Spock's insults and be glad of them, thanks very much. Except that chief medical officers—even when they were "the best"—didn't talk that way to admirals. They took what was said to them with the best grace that they could muster, and when they were asked to jump, their only question was supposed to be "how high?"

Or "where to . . . ?"

He had sat on the far side of Perry's desk, flanked by Jim Kirk and Spock, listening while the admiral outlined a plan as complex and dangerous as the cloaking-device theft of eight years ago. There were only two advantages: he knew more about Romulans now than he had done then, and—most important of all—he was being told about it in advance. That was where being "the best" came in.

Specializations in xenopsychology and -psychiatry, and longterm experience as CMO of the *Enterprise*—thus an acquaintance with what amounted to a gestalt life-form, for that defined the multi-racial, multi-species environment aboard the starship more accurately than simply crew. All of it added up to why he had been selected and then approached for this mission over the heads of other, perhaps equally talented, officers. It had been an unnerving hour for McCoy, sitting there watching his future being measured out in very small doses. For although the intricacies of the plot had been laid long and deep, using sleepers and double agents on both sides of the Neutral Zone, still, when it came to the crunch, his life or death was going to depend on timing.

And he had volunteered for it. Not at first, but after several refusals that nobody, particularly Kirk and Spock, had seen for other than his habitual grumbling. There had never been any question of conscription, not for him, not for anybody—not for a mission like this one. As soon conscript a spy and then expect the reports to be other than cautious, shallow, and lacking in any form of detail, if any reports ever came back at all. That was another thing: the spy—Perry preferred the term "deep-cover agent" to the older, more traditional word, but McCoy knew a spy when one was described to him—who had provided such excellent data for six years and then fallen silent in the past two. Last reports had shown her as a high-ranked servant in a poor but respectable Romulan noble house, and there had been nothing to indicate her activities—acquiring sociological background information rather than military or governmental secrets—had attracted anyone's attention.

McCoy had been given a chance to read through the nonclassified sections of her dossier, and after what amounted to a high-level intercession at Command level—Admiral Perry looked after his own, even when they only worked for him part-time—he was cleared to see all of it. The MOST SECRET stuff made fascinating reading. . . .

But that was all by the way; he had already made his feelings known on various matters, including the leaking of his (prearranged, naturally) traveling plans to Romulan agents, both those who were already known and, as a form of test, to several suspects. That same data, accurately provided by Federation double agents in the Empire, would serve to improve the reputation of any whose past reports had been of dubious quality, and hopefully make their future survival more secure.

Except for one problem: that the Romulans might not fall in with the theory behind all the other machinations, that if opportunity arose, they would want to capture a member of the *Enterprise* command crew—notorious war criminals all—and bring them back to ch'Rihan for trial. Their outrage over the Levaeri V debacle might run so high, even after the passage of a standard year, that instead of taking the offered bait as a prisoner, they might send a hunter-killer ship to blow the proposed captive into plasma. . . .

That was a risk they had all debated, and finally set aside as unlikely. So many highly placed Romulans had grudges to settle with the *U.S.S. Enterprise* that an anonymous, impersonal photon torpedo wouldn't satisfy them. The Romulan psyche was such that any punishment would have to be protracted, degrading, and painful—and administered after due process of their elaborate legal codes.

Listening to that particular part of the discussion had given McCoy a nasty crawling feeling at the nape of his neck, but at least the plan had worked. So far.

The storage-access doors at the back of his room rattled a bit, and he sat up. There was a small click as one door opened, revealing a vertical slice of the rainy Romulan night, and a vague, low outline entered the room, closing the door neatly—if a little awkwardly—behind it.

McCoy put his eyebrows up . . . and smiled

★    ★    ★

"If mere money is all you want for him, then name your price." Sub-commander tr'Annhwi gazed equably at the man across the table, reading him like an open book. He knew avarice when he saw it; but he could also recognize hope, and in this instance that was something he could play on to even better effect. "As I told that"—his narrow eyes flicked briefly toward Arrhae and then away again—"I am a generous man. But I can offer you much more than that: privileges, and the recognition of your House as a power in the Senate. I can offer you the restoration of everything that you have seen slip away from s'Khellian in these past years. H'daen, I can give you back your honor."

"In exchange for this one man?" Tr'Khellian plainly couldn't believe what he was hearing, and equally, wanted to believe it as much as anything he had ever heard in his life. "But why so much for so little—for a single Federation prisoner?"

"I told you before." Impatience and a hint of what lay beneath his bland exterior lent an ugly edge to tr'Annhwi's words before he recovered himself and twisted his mouth into an expression that approximated a smile. "There are too many factors, but most concern *mnhei'sahe,* my personal honor and that of my own House. That one represents a tiny portion of the blood-debt owed the Imperium by the Federation, which policy"—tr'Annhwi sneered the word—"forbids us to collect. But *mnhei'sahe* transcends policy, as you well know, and McCoy is a Command officer of the ship which owes blood-debt to many Houses. All will gain a morsel of contentment when sentence is executed on him, but I want all of it, for the honor of House Annhwi—and for my own satisfaction."

"What will you . . . ?" H'daen didn't complete his question. There was no need for it, or an answer, and he was a squeamish man at best.

"Cause him pain in whatever fashion pleases me," said tr'Annhwi. "For as long as pleases me. And then—eventually—I shall kill him."

"But Commander t'Radaik left him with me," H'daen said, as if reminding himself rather than the uncaring man across the table. "How will you explain the"—he swallowed, looking unwell—"the state of his body?"

"What body?" Tr'Annhwi drew the sidearm he wore as part of his uniform and laid it with a dull metallic clank beside his winecup. "A phaser set to disrupt doesn't leave one. At least"—he favored H'daen with an ugly, feral grin—"not one with enough molecular integrity to show what it looked like before it died. And you need have no worries about t'Radaik blaming you; prisoners are always being shot while escaping, and she'll never know it didn't happen this time. . . ." He picked up the phaser again and bounced it once or twice on the palm of his hand as if it were a toy, smiling indulgently.

H'daen stared at it with the horrified fascination of a man unfamiliar with weapons and uneasy in their presence. He was visibly relieved when tr'Annhwi tucked the phaser back into its holster and instead withdrew a small rectangle of plastic from the pouch on his belt. It wasn't quite so noisy as the phaser when he flipped it onto the table, but it carried just as much impact in H'daen's eyes.

"Prime-transfer authority," tr'Annhwi said—unnecessarily, because H'daen knew perfectly well what it was.

And what it meant. His guest might have come to the house with some romantic notion in the back of his mind, but the appearance of this thing made it clear that romance was not the subcommander's first concern. Nobody carried transfer authorities for any longer than their business required, because each card represented enormous wealth in cash or securities, deposited somewhere for exchange once the card itself was exchanged and a deal completed. Even upside down, H'daen could see the amount of data with which it was imprinted. This one small card could buy half the city of i'Ramnau—and the half worth buying, at that.

He sat quite still for a moment, just looking at it, then held out the winecup in his hand toward the empty air. Arrhae, commanded to clean the anteroom and not daring to stop until the order was countermanded, darted immediately to fill it, met her lord's eyes, and saw not the greed that tr'Annhwi had read there, but a terrible confused indecision. It was as if all that H'daen had thought was right and proper about his world had suddenly been dashed to fragments about his feet. Arrhae recognized that expression more readily than most, for something much the same had stared out of her mirror on several mornings since McCoy arrived to complicate the house.

"My lord," she said, "there is a matter from i'Ramnau that needs your attention."

"Not now, Arrhae. . . ."

There was no certainty in the way he said it, or she would never have dared to persist; not with tr'Annhwi's suspicious eyes on her. "It would be best dealt with at once, *hru'hfirh;* then you can return to your other business without further interruptions."

"Get about your duties, servant!" snapped tr'Annhwi, and his glare should have killed her on the spot.

*He knows—or at least guesses—what I might say,* she thought, flinching from the promise of pain in the subcommander's cold face. *O Elements, let H'daen hear me!*

He heard something at least, the same thing that had caused no reaction less than a quarter-hour before. Before certain things about his guest had come to light. But now . . .

"Subcommander, Arrhae ir-Mnaeha is *hru'hfe* to this house, and no mere servant for all and any to command." There was a strength and dignity about H'daen's voice that Arrhae had not heard for many months; it came from an awareness of the Naming of his House, which if it had fallen into poverty and insignificance was at least decent and worthy of the fair-speaking that many higher Houses had forfeited these past few years.

Tr'Annhwi opened his mouth to say something—insulting, by the twist of his lips—then remembered where he was and shut it again without uttering a sound. No matter how wealthy or how powerful he might be elsewhere, right now he was only a Fleet subcommander guesting under the roof of an Imperial Praetor, and not merely courtesy but caution dictated his behavior.

"Arrhae," said H'daen, getting to his feet, "come with me." He turned from the table, not without a long, thoughtful look at the prime-transfer card, and walked out of the room with Arrhae at his heels. Once the door was shut behind them, with tr'Annhwi on the far side of it, he turned on her. "You had best have a fine explanation for this, girl, or I shall—"

"My lord, your worst punishment would be better than the kindnesses of that one," she said, and looked him in the eye as she said it. "I am *hru'hfe* to the house, and you were pleased to call me your conscience. These are not moral scruples now, but my own fears for your honor. You know me. You know I speak what I perceive as truth," Arrhae paused, watching him, and smiled quickly, "so far as manners permit."

"This also is truth. Speak more of it, Arrhae. I will hear you."

"There is little more, lord, and I speak as a servant ignorant of the policies within a noble House—but how can the Elements favor any House, when honor is set aside and the brief regard of men can be only attained by breaking trust and selling a helpless man as though he were a beast? There is guest-right on Mak'khoi, and your word on that right. Only your word can betray it. . . ."

H'daen stood where he was for a brief time, very still, looking with blank eyes at something only he could see. Then that dull gaze focused on Arrhae. "Have you no duties of your own, that you must interfere in my private affairs? Go—do something of use to earn your keep, and leave me be!" He turned away from her and went back inside the antechamber, and the sound of its door closing was like the lid of a coffin coming down. She took three slow steps in the direction of McCoy's room, hoping against hope that H'daen would summon her back with a change of mind, but there was no other sound.

On her fourth step, Arrhae began to run.

McCoy heard the footsteps pattering along the corridor a bare two seconds before someone began to fumble with the lock. He glanced around his room and at the companion who had slipped into it half an hour before, and realized that there was nowhere and no time to hide.

No time at all. The door burst open, slammed shut as quickly—and Arrhae, his jailer, went sprawling as she tripped over something that hadn't been there before. He picked her up, brushed her down, muttered softly when he saw the grazes running from knee to ankle along both shins, and waited for the questions to start.

He didn't have to wait long, only enough for the woman to recover the breath that the fall had knocked out of her. There was a very brief wince as skinned legs made their presence felt, and then a mental hiccup that reflected clearly in her eyes, as everything she had been intending to say when she came through the door was suddenly replaced by a lot of things she hadn't expected to say at all. The first one was fairly obvious.

"What's this rock doing in here?"

Less obvious, at least to Arrhae, was the possibility of an answer from the rock itself. She got one all the same.

"I was speaking to Dr. McCoy, ma'am," it said in a courteous if rather grating voice that came from an unmistakable Starfleet voder on its back, marked with equally unmistakable lieutenant's stripes. "I hope you didn't hurt yourself."

Arrhae gave a startled squeak and took a hasty step backward, this time almost tripping over the low table that was one of McCoy's few pieces of furniture. Though she caught herself from falling, she sat down on it hard enough to jolt the wind out of her yet again. She stared, wide-eyed and gasping, while the rock shuffled around to "face" her with the sound of one large slab of granite dragging over another. At least, so she presumed, because the rank insignia on the voder was now right side up and she had the definite feeling of being looked at—except that there was nothing that corresponded to eyes on the crusted, sparkling surface.

McCoy had eyes, though, and they were glittering with wicked amusement at Arrhae's discomfiture. He was grinning at her, and she didn't like it. "What goes on here?" she demanded. Shock, confusion, fear, and now more shock hadn't made for a particularly good evening so far, and she had the nasty feeling that it would start to go downhill rapidly once her questions were answered. Always assuming that it hadn't happened already.

"Commander Haleakala," said McCoy, "allow me to introduce Lieutenant Naraht, *U.S.S. Enterprise,* on temporary assignment to Starfleet Intelligence. He's acting as my backup."

"He . . . ? But it's a rock—isn't it?"

"No. A Horta." McCoy grinned quickly as he realized something important. "Of course, you were landed on ch'Rihan before they— Commander, the Hortas are native to Janus VI; silicon-based life-forms that live in rock, burrow through it, and eat it."

"You're joking. . . ."

"They're also highly intelligent, and good-humored to a fault—which is just as well, otherwise Naraht would be very tired of hearing comments like that. Why say I'm joking when the proof's right there in front of you."

"I'm sorry. Excuse me, Lieutenant, I didn't know people like you existed."

"My mother thought the same about"—Naraht shuffled the shaggy sensory fringe that edged his body, seeming slightly embarrassed—"about carbon-based people. Like you and the doctor. No offense taken, Commander."

"Um, quite so." Terise looked at Naraht somewhat oddly. "What I don't understand is why you're not on fire." McCoy looked up at her quizzically. "Well, I mean," she said, "an oxygen atmosphere is the equivalent of a reducing atmosphere to a silicon-based creature. Or they always told us in xenobiology that it would be, if silicon-based life was ever discovered. How is he able to walk around without doing the equivalent of burning, or rusting?"

McCoy smiled, and if it was a look of pure triumph, then it was justified. The solution to the problem was his, and had indirectly made the introduction of Hortas into Starfleet possible. "He's been sprayed with Teflon on his top layers and his tentacular fringe," he said. "It seals the oxygen in our atmosphere away from his silicon, and doesn't react itself to either the silicon or his ambient acids—since Teflon is less chemically reactive than even glass. His bottom layer doesn't need it: it's made of a natural Teflon analogue anyway, to protect it from the acid he secretes."

"He sometimes secretes," said Naraht gently. "I'm not such a glutton that I need to eat every time I move."

"Well, I'm not sure you eat enough as it is," McCoy said. "Boy your age should be half again your size. I've never been sure that starship food agrees with you. Wretched synthesized rock, it's not the same as the real thing. Not enough minerals."

Arrhae shook her head, still bemused. "But Mr. Naraht, how did you get planetside without being captured?"

"Meteorite-style." Naraht might have had no face, but his voice smiled. "My carapace has a higher ablative rating than tempered ceramic or glasteel. Once we were in orbit over ch'Rihan, I arranged an explosion in the *Vega*'s hold and bailed out . . . and went down in free fall."

McCoy nodded. "He's a good navigator—could have worked out the accelerations and ephemera himself, the boy's got a calculator in his head, like most of his people. But the Romulans obliged by putting us in a holding pattern up there." He jerked a thumb a couple of times at the ceiling, then let the hand drop and grinned some more. "Congratulations," he said.

"Why?"

"On the way you're taking all this."

"Dr. McCoy—"

"Bones, please."

"Bones, there's a saying here: 'If the sword shatters, take its fragments to a forge.' I've had a long time to put a lot of pieces back together, and I'm getting good at it."

"'If life hands you a lemon, make lemonade.'"

"I prefer the Romulan version."

"Do you now?" McCoy looked at her very thoughtfully, but didn't enlarge on his comment.

"It has more dignity. . . ."

"Of course."

"Now, why do you keep calling me Commander? What sort of ship is *Vega,* and how were you captured? What brought you to this house? And don't deny that you were expecting to find me here! And tr'Annhwi's back, trying to buy you from H'daen. . . ."

McCoy had been smiling a bit indulgently at the stream of questions, but that last took the last traces of smile right off his face. "Perry didn't reckon on that," he muttered, knowing that he should have realized the possibility himself, after seeing at close range what Romulans were capable of doing when it came to honor-based grudges.

"Perry?"

"The Service," McCoy said with some asperity, "takes care of its own. . . . Look, Commander—oh, you were promoted, don't look at me like that—look, never mind the personal aspect, but I can't be the subject of a personal vendetta just now. I'm supposed to appear before the Senate and . . ."

"I tried, Bones. I really tried. I thought that what I said, and the way I said it, would have made H'daen throw the whole dirty notion out, but he—well, it's his only chance to do something for the reputation of his House, to lift it out of the gutter, and I think—" She stopped, and cocked her head to one side, listening. "Get Naraht out of here! We're going to have company. . . ."

Her ears were more attuned to sounds in the house, but after the noise of Naraht's departure had faded—and McCoy was still amazed at how fast the Horta could move when he was in a hurry—the angry voices were distant but distinct. And the heavy slam of the frontmost door was completely audible. Silence fell briefly, and was broken after a little while by footsteps in the corridor outside. McCoy stayed where he was, sitting on the single low chair that was all his room could boast, but Arrhae rose from the table and took up a wary position in front of the storage door with its neatly, almost invisibly snapped lock.

And H'daen tr'Khellian came in. There was the print of an open hand across one side of his face, already greening into a bruise, and he looked crumpled, but not crushed. "I thought that I would find you here," he said to Arrhae, and bowed greeting to McCoy with a stiffness that looked more a consequence of pain than of reserve.

"Yes, my lord," she said, carefully noncommittal.

"I considered tr'Annhwi's offer. And refused it, to his displeasure— as you might surmise from my appearance. But I decided that if his was an example of the honor of young and wealthy Rihannsu, then I would rather remain part of the old and poor. Here. A keepsake for you. The price of one alien, soon to die—or half the city of i'Ramnau." He extended one hand and poured the snapped quarters of the prime-transfer card from his palm to hers, smiling as thinly and ironically as the indignity of a fast-puffing lip would let him. "It still isn't enough to buy honor, not the old-fashioned kind."

Arrhae closed her fist on the broken card and felt a sudden, ridiculous sting of tears fill her eyes. It had nothing to do with the small pain as sharp corners pricked her skin and drew small beads of emerald blood, nothing to do with that at all. She glanced at McCoy, wondering if he understood, or would ever understand, just what had been done for him. "Lord," she said then, and doubled over to give H'daen the deep, deep bow that was his due as Head of House, and that she gave him now for the first time because she wanted to and because he deserved such respect rather than because it was something that went with her role.

McCoy did understand, and was annoyed that there was no way he could show some form of respectful thanks without giving too many secrets away. He had to sit unconcernedly, "not knowing" what was being said until Arrhae thought to activate her translator, and hoping that H'daen didn't notice they had already been talking without it.

"Since you seem likely to tell Mak'khoi what has happened whether I give permission or not," H'daen said quietly, "I allow it. Tell him also . . . Tell him that he will be tried before the Senate in six days. That the sentence has already been agreed upon. And that it is not the way I would interpret our ancient laws. And Arrhae . . . ?"

"My lord?"

"I intend to sleep late tomorrow. Very late indeed. This has been a tiring day." He smiled crookedly. "But educational. Very." He closed the door behind him as he left.

"Now, that," said McCoy, "is a Romulan gentleman of the old school. Like a lady I once knew. Here. Wipe your eyes."

Arrhae took the proffered handkerchief, only a big layered sheet of soft paper from the supply she had instructed should be put in here, but very welcome for all that. She hadn't expected to cry into them herself. She hadn't expected to cry about anything much, least of all H'daen. After a little while she felt better, apart from an inclination to sniffle, and managed a damp smile for McCoy's benefit.

"You're bearing up well, Terise," he said. "I'm glad of that. We were worried about you. Seriously worried. No reports from you for two years, even though other operatives were able to tell us where you were and what you were doing."

"You thought I'd gone over. Turned Romulan."

"It was a possibility. One of the chances that were taken when you went out in the first place. I'm glad we were wrong. Now, Terise, I'm authorized to ask you this: when I'm pulled out, do you want to be pulled as well?"

"Pulled out? Taken out, you mean. In case you didn't understand H'daen, or the meaning wasn't clear, you're going for trial in six days. But you've been sentenced already. Bones, you're dead!"

To her astonishment he smiled. "I've been pronounced dead by people far more qualified to do it than you, Terise, and people far more certain of what they were saying. Yet here I am."

"You thought that I might have gone native, or gone schizophrenic, or gone mad—have you ever thought of looking at yourself that way?"

He looked at her with ironic astonishment, and a little wickedness. "Don't be silly," he said. "I'm the psychiatrist here. I have paperwork that says I'm sane."

From her expression it was plain that Terise had her doubts. "Doctor," she said very slowly, as if speaking to someone with a hearing impairment, or an impairment somewhere more vital, "don't you understand it? Your trial is nothing but a formality. They're going to pull you to pieces, and they're going to make an entertainment of it!—if you even make it that far. If someone else doesn't come in here and make H'daen an offer he can't refuse . . . or just come in and take you by force. You have to get out while you can!"

McCoy shook his head slowly. He was beginning to feel sorrier for this woman than he felt for himself, at this stage of the game, no mean accomplishment. "I have things to do," he said. "Anyway, I'm not going to leave this planet without seeing the sights. The Senate Chambers. The Council of Praetors."

"The scenic execution pits!!"

McCoy put one eyebrow up at her and grinned, a wicked look. "Think I'll just give that last spot a miss. Don't you worry about it. Meantime, I've got things to take care of, and I'd guess you do too. Why don't you go take care of them."

She looked at him rather helplessly. "Do you always hedge like this with your friends? What are you planning? How am I supposed to help you if you won't tell me?!"

He sighed, and smiled again, a little ruefully. "You're not supposed to help me . . . yet. You go on, Terise. Take care of things. You won't be able to be any help to me if they fire you or something."

She nodded, looking at him with extreme irritation that nonetheless had a sort of edge of affection and grudging admiration on it. It was a look he had seen from many a patient in his time, the "you won't let me run things my way, dammit!" expression. McCoy was pleased. There was hope for her after all, and he could relax a little, as much as anyone can relax who has most of two planets out for his blood.

"All right," she said. "Good night to you, Bones."

"Good night," he said. Then he remembered something. "Oh, and Arrhae?" he said to her back as she headed toward the door.

"Yes?"

"I'm told the soil in the back garden needs lime."

He leaned back on his couch and smiled, hearing the sound of laughter go down the hall, laughter that was not hysterical at all.

# Chapter Twelve

## EMPIRES

"We were excited," said the captain of the Federation vessel *U.S.S. Carrizal* during the postmission debriefing following its return from the Trianguli stars, a little more than a hundred years ago. "It was the first hit we'd had in nine months of scouring that sector. A hominid culture, obviously highly developed, a large population, it was everything we had hoped for. Better yet, the same people were on *two* worlds . . . an Earth-Moon configuration. Mike Maliani, our astrogator, suggested Romus and Remus as nicknames for the planets until we found out their real names from the people who lived there. After the twin brothers in an ancient Italian myth." On the debriefing tape, Captain Dini smiles rather ruefully. "I was never a specialist in the classics: I wish I were. Mike's misspelling of 'Romulus' is going to haunt me to the grave. But at that point I thought he knew what he was talking about."

A pause. "Anyway, we were really excited. You know how few spacefaring species there are: the standing orders are to closely examine any we find. But we weren't so excited that we went in without the proper protocols. We gave them everything we had: the classic first-contact series—atomic ratios, binary counting, pictures. You name it. There was never any answer, even though we're sure they knew we were there. They had an outer cordon of defense satellites that noticed us, and after the messages from the satellites were received on the planets, the message traffic on the bigger planet increased by about a thousand percent. But there was nothing we could do with it by way of translation—after that first message there was silence, and everything that came later was encoded—some kind of closed-satchel code, very sophisticated, and no way to break it in anything short of a decade, without a supercomp or the code key."

There is a long silence on the tape as Captain Dini shakes his head and looks puzzled. "We never came any closer to their planet than two orbits out," he says, "right beyond the fifth planet in the system. We never came near them. We just observed, and took readings, and went away quietly. I'll never understand what happened."

What happened was the First Romulan War, as the Federation later called it. What it looked like, from the Federation side, was a long, bloody conflict started without provocation by the Romulans. From the other side it wore a different aspect.

The appearance of *Carrizal* caused such a panic as the Rihannsu had never known since they became Rihannsu. In terms of a Rihanha's lifetime, it was thirty generations and more since the settlement, and the actual records of the appearance of aliens on Vulcan, all those many years ago, were not so much lost as largely ignored. People *knew* through the history they were taught in the academies what had happened on Vulcan in the old days . . . and the history had bent and changed, what with telling and retelling, and neglecting to go back to the original source material. Not that that would have helped much. The source material itself had been altered in the journey, but very few—scholars and historians—knew this, or cared. What the Rihannsu knew about this incursion into their space was that it closely matched the pattern followed by the Etoshans so long ago: quiet observation coupled with or followed by proffers of peaceful contact. They were not going to be had *that* way again.

Ch'Rihan and ch'Havran had, over sixteen hundred years, become superbly industrialized. The Rihannsu have always had a way with machines: and this, coupled with their great concern for taking care of the worlds they found after such journey and suffering, produced two planets that were technologically most advanced at manufacture, without looking that way. Few factories were visible from the atmosphere, let alone from space. Aesthetics required that they be either pleasant to look at, or completely concealed. Many factories were underground. Release of waste products into the ambient environment, even waste so seemingly innocuous as steam or hot water, was forbidden by Praetorial indict, and a capital crime. A starship passing through, even one looking carefully, as *Carrizal* did, would see two pastoral-looking worlds, unspoiled, quiet. One would hardly suspect the frenetic manufacture that was to start after *Carrizal*'s departure.

There was frantic action elsewhere as well. In the Praetorate and the Senate some heads rolled, and the survivors scrambled to start working on the defense of the planet—or to otherwise take advantage of the situation. The defense satellites had not been approached closely enough by the invading ship to trigger their weaponry. Cannily, it had stayed out of range. There was no way to tell if the Two Worlds could be defended against the ship that had appeared there, no telling what kind of weaponry it had. But from their experience in air combat (almost every nation of each planet had its own air force, which they used liberally for both friendly and unfriendly skirmishes), the Rihannsu military specialists knew that even a heavily armed ship should not be able to do much against overwhelming numbers.

They got busy, digging frantically through ancient computer memories and printouts and film and metal media for the forgotten space technology they needed. Had the ships been spared, even one of them—had their data been preserved in one place rather than scattered all over two worlds—the Federation's boundaries might be much different now. But even what remained was useful, and the Rihannsu were frightened. It is unwise to frighten a Rihanha. Within a year after *Carrizal*'s visit, ch'Rihan's numerous nations had built, among them, some three *thousand* spacecraft armed with particle-beam weapons and the beginnings of defensive shields. Ch'Havran had built four thousand. They were crude little craft, and their cylindrical shapes recalled those of the ships, though there was no need for them to spin for gravity: artificial gravity had been mastered a century or so earlier.

It was three more years before the next ship came. The unlucky *Balboa* came in broadcasting messages of peace and friendship, and was blown to bits by the massed particle beams of a squadron of fifty. After that the Rihannsu grew a little bolder, and went hunting: a task force caught *Stone Mountain,* to which *Balboa* had sent a distress call, and captured her by carefully using high-powered lasers to explosively decompress the crew compartments. They towed *Stone Mountain* home, took her apart, and shortly thereafter added warp drive to their little cruisers.

The Federation considers the war to have begun with the destruction of *Balboa*. In the twenty-five years of warfare that followed, no less than forty-six Federation task forces of ever-increasing size and firepower went into Rihannsu space to deal with the aggression against them, and even with vastly superior firepower, most of them suffered heavy damage if not annihilation. "I can't understand it," says one fleet admiral in a debriefing. "Their ships are junk. We should be able to shoot them down like clay pigeons." But the huge numbers of the Rihannsu craft made them impossible to profitably engage; even "smart" photon torpedoes could target only one vessel at a time. When there were twelve more climbing up your tail, the situation became impossible. Starfleet kept trying with bigger and better weapons—until two things happened at once: there was a change of administration, and the Vulcans joined the Federation.

The only indication of what the Rihannsu looked like had come from a very few burned and decompressed bodies picked up in space. When Vulcan was discovered, and after negotiation entered the Federation, their High Council was pointedly asked whether it knew anything about these people. The Vulcans, all logic—and selective truth—told the Federation that they were not sure who these people were. There had indeed been some attempts to colonize other worlds, they admitted, but those ships had been out of touch with Vulcan for some seventeen hundred years. The first Vulcan ambassador, a grimly handsome gentleman who had just been posted to Earth, made this statement to the admirals of Starfleet in such a way that they immediately found it politic to drop the subject. But through the ambassador, the Vulcan High Council gave the Federation a piece of good advice. "Make peace with them," Sarek told the admirals, "and close the door. Stop fighting. You will probably never beat them. But you can stop your ships being destroyed."

The advice went down hard, and Starfleet tried to do it their own way for several years more. But finally, as Vulcan's increasing displeasure became plainer, Fleet acquiesced. The war ended with the Treaty of Alpha Trianguli, probably the first treaty in Federation history to have been negotiated entirely by data upload. No representatives of the two sides ever met. The Rihannsu had no interest in letting their enemies find out any more about them than could be revealed by autopsy. They might be back someday.

The treaty established what came to be called the Romulan Neutral Zone, an egg-shaped area of space about ninety light-years long and forty wide, with 128 Trianguli at its center. The Zone itself was the "shell" of the egg, a buffer area all the way around, one light-year thick, marked and guarded by defense/monitoring satellites of both sides. Everything inside the Zone was considered "the Romulan Star Empire," even though there was as yet no such thing. The Federation was not exactly hurt by this treaty: as far as they were concerned, there were no strategically promising planets in the area. Perhaps they were not looking hard enough. Later some Federation officials would kick themselves when finding out about Rhei'llhne, a planet just barely inside the Neutral Zone in Rihannsu space, and almost richer in dilithium than Direidi.

So the war ended, and as far as the Federation was concerned, for fifty years nothing came out of the Zone, not a signal, not a ship. Perhaps, some thought, the people in there had gotten sick of fighting. Wiser heads, or those who thought they knew what stock the "Romulans" had sprung from, suspected otherwise.

The Rihannsu had stopped fighting indeed, but as for being tired of it, this was unlikely. There was a matter of honor, *mnhei'sahe*, still to be resolved. So much of the Two Worlds' economies were poured into starship weapons research that they still have not recovered entirely from the austerity it caused the contributing nations. They rebuilt the defense satellite system to hundreds of times its former strength, and trained some of the best star pilots ever seen in any species anywhere.

They also decided not to make the mistake their forefathers had made with the Etoshans. The Rihannsu scientists spent literally years translating the complete contents of the reference computers of the Federation ships they had so far managed to capture. They realized from what they found that they were one small pair of planets caught between two Empires, and that to survive, they were going to have to have an Empire themselves.

So began the "expansionist" period of Rihannsu history, in which they tackled planetary colonization with the same ferocious desperation they had used to build a fleet out of nothing. They needed better ships to do this, of course. They wound up reconstructing numerous large people-carriers along the ship model, though, of course, with warp drive these craft did not need generation capability. Twenty planets were settled in eighteen years, and population-increase technology was used of the sort that had made ch'Rihan and ch'Havran themselves so rapidly viable. Not all the settlements were successful, nor are they now: Hellguard was one glaring example.

During this period the Rihannsu also developed the warbird-class starship, acknowledged by everyone, including the Klingons and the Federation, to be one of the finest, solidest, most maneuverable warp-capable craft ever designed. If it had a flaw, it was that it was small; but its weaponry was redoubtable, and the plasma-based molecular implosion field that warbirds carried had problems only with ships that could outrun the field. Another allied invention was the cloaking device, which tantalized everyone who saw it, particularly the Klingons.

The Klingons didn't get it until much later than the Federation did. The Klingons got other things, mostly defense contracts.

The relationship was a strange one from the first. The Rihannsu economy began to be in serious trouble, despite the beginning inflow of goods and capital from the tributary worlds, because of all the funds being diverted to military research. There was also a question as to whether the research was, in fact, doing any good: a warbird out on a mission to test the security of the Neutral Zone ran into a starship called *Enterprise* and never came back again. At the same time, the Klingon Empire was beginning to encroach on the far side of the Neutral Zone, and the first two or three interstellar engagements left both sides looking at each other and wishing there were some way to forestall the all-out war that was certainly coming. Rather cleverly, the Klingons made overtures to the Rihannsu based on their own enmity with the Federation, and offered to sell them ships and "more advanced technology," some of it

Federation. Everyone, they claimed, stood to benefit from this arrangement. The Neutral Zone border on their side would be "secure," and the Klingon economy (also in trouble) would benefit from the extra capital and goods.

The deal turned out to be of dubious worth. For one thing, the Rihannsu buying ships from the Klingons was comparable to Rolls-Royce buying parts from Ford. The Klingon ships were built by the lowest bidder, and performed as such. Also, most of the Federation technology the Klingons had to offer was obsolete. But the treaty suited the aims of the expansionist lobbies in Praetorate and Senate, and so was ratified, much to the Rihannsu's eventual regret. In the meantime, the Rihannsu shipwrights (and some of the ship captains) muttered over the needlessly high cost of Klingon replacement parts, and did their best to tinker the ships into something better than nominal performance. Mostly it was a losing battle. Klingons build good weaponry, but their greatest interest in spacecraft tends to be in blowing them up.

Meanwhile other forces were stirring. The Federation sent the only ship that had been successful with Romulans to see if it could get its hands on the cloaking device. It did, and *Enterprise,* merely an annoying name before, became a matter for curses and vengeance. How some of those curses turned out, and what form the vengeance took, other chroniclers have recently covered more completely in the press.

In terms of policy, matters have changed little from that point, some few years ago, to the present day. The Rihannsu lie inside their protected Zone, while their Praetorate and Senate hatch plots, count the incoming funds from the tributary worlds, and look for ways to regain an honor which they never truly lost. Some people in the computer nets (still cherished as a quaint but much-loved relic of the ship days) have ventured the opinion that some kind of overture toward peace should be made. The Federation at least builds decent starships. And, some have said, if the Federation truly wanted to destroy the Rihannsu, why haven't they come and done it in force? Their resources are presently huge enough to crush the Two Worlds as the little ships swarmed over *Balboa,* by sheer strength of numbers.

But so many only reply to this line of thought with ridicule. "Cowardice," they say. Others point out that the Rihannsu, however hostile they may be to the United Federation of Planets, also serve as the Federation's buffer between them and the Klingons. Annex the Rihannsu spaces (even if they could) and suddenly Federation and Klingon policies come into direct conflict. It makes more sense to let the Rihannsu take the brunt. This argument generates more bitterness among Rihannsu than even the first. Fear of the Rihannsu—that a Rihanha can understand, though he loathes it. But being ignored, or taken for granted, that is the unforgivable. For those who ignore the power of the Two Worlds, no hate will ever be sufficient.

The voices still speak quietly of the old ways here and there: of peace, and nobility, and perhaps even *rapprochement* with the Vulcans. But that turn of mind has a long way to wait before it comes into vogue in the Praetorate. The Rihannsu in power now are the children of the twenty-five years of blood: their memories are long, and the fear that awoke when *Carrizal* arrived is still cold in their stomachs at night. Perhaps a hundred years from now, perhaps two hundred, children will be born who will sleep sounder, and think more wisely by day. Until then, the Two Worlds are alone in the long night. Nothing has changed since the ships: the worlds still have walls.

Hope is not dead, of course. Every now and then some one hand reaches out—not necessarily the hand of a great general or statesman—and hits the wall, and a bit of stonework falls down. Perhaps the hands of the little do less than the hands of the great. But there are many more of them, and they tend not to squabble among themselves as much as the great do, nor are they terminally embarrassed by statements like the one heard for so many years on both sides of the Zone, "I don't understand. . . ." They are the ones likely to work to understand: to find answers, and to share them. As long as this goes on, there is always a chance: and if the small ever manage to teach this art to the great, the Elements Themselves will not contain all the unfolding possibilities, as the walls come down at last.

# Chapter Thirteen

McCoy pushed the reader-screen aside and rubbed both hands over his face. Romulan law was one of the most stultifying subjects that he had ever studied, and despite the amount of persuasion he had employed to get a logic-solid reader with an onboard visual translator, there were times—usually deep into the pontifications of some long-dead Senator—when he had the feeling that he would be better employed doing something else, like watching the grass grow. It was intricate, and the older legal terms sometimes refused to translate into even the stilted Federation Standard that the reader produced. There was no such thing as an out, anyway; even the Right of Statement, a standard clause in capital crimes—of which there were an excessive number—was no more than an opportunity to explain or defend the offense for which the speaker would afterward be executed.

At least the implant was giving him no problems other than those anticipated. McCoy had expected a headache, had almost hoped for one, just a little one, something that he could grouse about to intelligence and say *I told you so* when he got back. Turning a man into a living data recorder—it wasn't proper. But at least it worked. When the microsolid buried in his cortex memory centers was in operation, his normally excellent memory was enhanced out to auditory and visual eidesis. He remembered *everything*. And until he mastered the neural impulses that switched the blasted thing on and off, he had to leaf through a mass of data equivalent to the *Index XenoMedicalis* to find the scribbled margin note that said "socks are in boots, under bed."

There was information locked into it already, supplied by *Bloodwing*'s surgeon, t'Hrienteh. Names and faces, the workings of the Senate— t'Hrienteh's family were highly placed—medical background on Romulan psychiatry and body kinesics. All the things that would make his task on ch'Rihan easier, or at least more straightforward. That was why he had to stay on-planet for long enough to be taken before the Senate and the Praetorate, so that he could interpret what he saw and heard in the light of what he knew. A delicate business at best, and already very dangerous.

McCoy's chief interest in the Romulan law books was an attempt to find out how long espionage trials might be expected to last, how much time he had to play with before the legal system began to play with him. Using knives . . .

Arrhae took a step backward from the door, and stared at the two men who had evidently rung the chime a few seconds before. After their parting in i'Ramnau, Nveid tr'AAnikh was the last person on ch'Rihan that she expected to see. "What are *you* doing here?" she wanted to know. "And who is this?"

Nveid's companion was a little taller and a little fairer, but the most obvious difference was that while Nveid wore civilian clothing, the other man was in Fleet uniform. "Llhran tr'Khnialmnae," he said, saluting her. His gaze shifted from her face to the hall behind her, checking that it was empty. "Nveid has spoken to you already about—certain matters. My sister Aidoann was third-in-command of *Bloodwing*."

"Llhran is taking a great risk in coming here," Nveid said. "I told you of the families who supported the action of their kinfolk aboard *Bloodwing;* House Khnialmnae is one of the more outspoken. Their respect for honor is very high."

"And what," Arrhae said through her teeth, "of their respect for the peace and the lives of those who want no part of this madness? I want you to let me alone. And alone is not standing two by two with a surveillance subject on the steps of my master's house. Go away."

"*Hru'hfe,* we should like to speak with H'daen tr'Khellian." Llhran spoke now in a more formal phase of language, one that made quite clear the difference between a Senior Centurion and a senior servant. "It is a matter concerning the prisoner Mak'khoi."

"And how much do you two want to offer me . . . ?" H'daen looked down at them from the balcony above the door, his face weary and his voice totally disinterested. "Or are you just taking him away at long last?"

"My lord . . . ?" Nveid was confused, and it showed. Whatever had brought him here, it was nothing to do with helping McCoy to escape. Not yet, anyway. "We wanted to speak to the Federation officer held captive here."

"Do it. Do whatever you want. Just don't ask me to get involved again." He touched his cheekbone just beneath the right eye, where a blue-brown bruise mottled the skin. "Involvement hurts too much."

"My lord, you are a Praetor, and we—"

"I am a make-weight," H'daen responded with all the savagery of a man who had too recently discovered that his place in the scheme of things was far lower than he had believed. "The only Praetors you need ask permission of are the young *hnoiyikar* who believe that wealth and the freedom to employ brutality are all that honor means." He turned away from them and went indoors.

"So . . . ?" Nveid was watching Arrhae closely, more closely than she liked, and she shrugged dismissively.

"I'll take you to him and leave you a translator. After that, say what you want out of my hearing. And leave quickly."

Llhran looked at her, then at Nveid. "Servants have better manners where I come from," he said pointedly, and Arrhae blushed.

"Sir, I doubt that servants are so frightened where you come from," she said, and ushered the pair indoors before either man could think of a suitably cutting response. "If you would follow me, I shall take you to Mak'khoi. And then I have work of my own that needs attention. Evidently"—and she watched Nveid carefully—"the Senatorial Judiciary have decided that their prisoner would feel more comfortable with a familiar face beside him—so before we go to the trial in Ra'tleihfi I must deal with everything that won't be done while I'm away. . . ."

"*You* are going to the capital?" Llhran clearly didn't believe what he was hearing. "A servant?"

"*Hru'hfe* of an old House, Llhe'," Nveid said. "Different places, different customs. She's rather more than just 'a servant.'"

"Oh." He didn't sound convinced.

Not that Arrhae was concerned; she was past worrying about anybody's opinions other than McCoy's and her own. "In here," she said. "That is, if he isn't in the garden"—and she smiled—"communing with nature. . . ."

McCoy wasn't, although he probably wished that he were. Instead, he was sitting with his head in his hands, mumbling legal phrases and looking very like a man with a sore head. Which was entirely accurate. Right now, never mind all his other troubles, what Leonard McCoy wanted in all the world was a twenty-mil ampule of Aerosal and a spray hypo. Dammit, he'd settle for three aspirin and a glass of water. He looked at his visitors without much interest, automatically registering their body language—both of them were extremely apprehensive about something or other, and trying not to show it, and the man in uniform had the air of someone whose opinions had been gently but firmly squelched—before turning his attention to their faces. Young faces, closed and wary, but inquisitive for all that. He summoned up a smile and nodded to them, began to shut down the reader's input-output systems, shutting down his own "onboard" circuitry as he did so. At least that was getting easier. McCoy added the last data-solid to the stack that already filled his little table to overflowing, and wondered if the two Romulans had ever seen a Terran face before. He doubted it.

Arrhae introduced them to him as if to her lord, then made herself scarce and closed the door as she went out. McCoy wondered who had been giving her a hard time, and put his money on the centurion. That young man didn't have the hardness of another tr'Annhwi, but there was a determination about him that suggested he wasn't open for any sort of nonsense from his subordinates. The sort of mindset that would have put a lad who looked about eighteen into a senior centurion's uniform. Or maybe he was just somebody's sister's kid. . . .

"I recognize your House-names," McCoy said, switching on the boxy Romulan-issue translator and trying to find somewhere to set it down. It balanced rather precariously on top of the smallest heap of computer junk, and he cocked a wary eye at it before he let it go. "Your kin on *Bloodwing* were in good health last time I saw them. Take a seat, both of you—if you can find one."

"Thank you, Doctor," said Nveid, offering him the ghost of a bow. Llhran began to salute, thought better of it in the presence of an enemy officer, and nodded his head fractionally instead. Once they were both seated side by side on the bed, very straight-backed and looking far from comfortable, Nveid cleared his throat significantly. It amused McCoy to find that sound used in exactly the same way it was back home. "Sir," the Romulan began, "did the *hru'hfe* tell you that I spoke with her in i'Ramnau yesterday?"

McCoy shook his head. "The *hru'hfe* regards me as an unnecessary disturbance of the peace in this household. She'll be glad to see me gone."

Nveid frowned and muttered something to Llhran. Though he spoke too softly for either the translator or McCoy's ears to catch the words, his tone sounded irritable. *Good,* McCoy thought with a touch of satisfaction, *that should give Terise a bit more cover.*

"What was the subject of the conversation?" asked McCoy, wondering if this was what Arrhae meant about him becoming overly popular, and whether that was a good or a bad thing. Nveid cleared his throat again, a mannerism that McCoy decided was mostly nervousness, mixed with just a bit of affectation.

"You were."

"Oh? In what sense? Good, bad, or indifferent?"

"You may find it good, I trust." Nveid took a long breath and glanced at Llhran tr'Khnialmnae, who nodded quickly. "Sir, there are many Houses on ch'Rihan who . . ."

". . . and both duty and the obligations of honor therefore require that we do other than stand by while you are condemned and killed."

"And what form would this 'other' take, Nveid tr'AAnikh?"

"We would endeavor to help you escape from ch'Rihan and from Imperial space, and return you across the Neutral Zone to your own people. The starliner *Vega* was released yesterday, after repairs to her hull were completed, and . . . well, we have supporters everywhere, those of us who have no love for the pirates who would try to run this Empire as the accursed Klingons run theirs. Several of our people are seeded among the traffic-control nets." McCoy grinned suddenly. "They 'acquired' all of this tenday's access codes for the inner-system approaches."

"Even through the planetary defenses?" said McCoy, grinning even harder.

"Of course—all of the weapon-platforms run by automatics anyway."

"Then bear it in mind for later."

"Later . . . ?"

"Yes. After I've been to the Senate Chambers and had a chance to study how the Praetorate runs this particular show."

"*Study* them?" Llhran was halfway to his feet, shocked out of his military composure by McCoy's declaration. "Doctor, they want you dead. Get out while you can!"

"Calmly, son, calmly. I know what I'm doing, and I've got my orders to back them up. Standard procedure: if a suitably qualified officer is in a position to obtain new social understanding of another intelligent people, it is incumbent upon him to gather such information as he deems useful to that end. Failing to comply, Centurion tr'Khnialmnae, would place my honor as a Starfleet officer in jeopardy, instead of just my life."

"Ah." Llhran subsided, understanding that particular argument as he might not have understood something with no parallel among the Rihannsu. Personal honor, especially among military personnel from the noble Houses, was a currency more widely used than any other.

"So what *can* we do to help you, Doctor?"

McCoy smiled a little to himself at Nveid's eagerness to do anything at all, and do it at once. There was something about the young Romulan's earnest enthusiasm that reminded him of Naraht when the Horta was a newly graduated ensign. When he had referred to the youngster as a "space cadet" he hadn't been making fun. Nveid tr'AAnikh was a little like that except that he was a Romulan and therefore most likely susceptible to the use of violence in discussion. Any people that used suicide, whether genuine or enforced, as an instrument of political policy could aspire only to benevolence on their better days, and on most of the other days needed watching.

"Try this," he said, choosing his words with care. "If your traffic-control system is anything like ours, there'll be regular tests of the communications network—so have one of your people transmit a test signal of a standard geometric progression based on the first three prime numbers." McCoy closed his eyes briefly and when they opened again they were staring intently at something only he could see. "Exactly one standard Romulan day after that, send a tight-beam tachyon squirt on a decohesive packet frequency of 5-18-54 to coordinates GalLat 177D 48.210M, GalLong +6D 14.335M, DistArbGalCore 24015 L.Y. No repetition, no acknowledgment. That should do it."

When his eyes slid back into focus, they met the suspicious stares of two Romulans who were plainly beginning to wonder whether the requirements of honor weren't getting them into something more than they had bargained for. "Doctor," said Llhran, speaking, McCoy guessed, with the full weight of his centurionate training behind him, "what will receive that signal?"

"Not an invasion force, Centurion. A single ship, and not even a Federation warship at that."

"But cloaked with the device stolen from us by your Captain Kirk."

"Ah, well. That's history, isn't it? Anyway, the ship'll come in, pluck me from the very jaws of imminent dissolution, and whisk me away before the Imperial fleet is any the wiser."

"So you say. Can we trust you?"

"Or I you?" McCoy's shoulders lifted in a dismissive shrug. "'Trust' isn't a word much used between the Federation and the Imperium. I think starting to use it is long overdue. Instead of taking the chance you offer me now, I'll do what honor dictates and trust that when I'm on trial, you'll have done your part to get me safely away. If you don't trust me after I trust you, then I'll die—I presume unpleasantly—and where does that leave the *mnhei'sahe* you mentioned so often?"

He sat back while the two Romulans muttered softly to each other, not trying to overhear what they said since he would be told their verdict soon enough. His hands were sweating. Not unusual. They sweated before he undertook any sort of surgery, and this excision of mistrust was one of the hardest operations he had ever performed.

Nveid and Llhran came out of their huddle, and McCoy was startled to see how much color both men had lost. Putting their own lives on the line was evidently one thing, but making a decision that might well be laying their homeworld open to attack was another matter entirely. "Very well, Dr. McCoy," said Nveid. "Trust it shall be. If anything goes wrong, then Elements all witness that we acted as we thought best for all, now and in the future."

"Come along, Doctor," said Commander t'Radaik. "You have had quite enough time to set your affairs here in order." She stood in the doorway of his room with armed and helmeted guards at her back and watched as McCoy bundled the few possessions he had accumulated into a grab-bag.

*Enough time?* he thought, nervous even though he hoped it wouldn't show. *No. There's never anything like enough, not when there's a trial and an execution in the offing.* He was determined, however, not to resort to the black humor that was such a cliché on occasions like this. Granted that few of his psych patients had ever been in the gallows situation for real, but—

"Doctor . . ."

Now, that was the voice of a Romulan Intelligence officer whose patience was finally at an end. McCoy glanced quickly around the room, hoping that he had overlooked nothing of importance, then lifted his small bagful of property and took the first step of the last mile.

It was rather farther than a mile, and he wasn't going to be walking it. The Senate Chambers in Ra'tleihfi were more than three hundred kilometers due north of H'daen's mansion, an hour's ride in an ordinary flitter, rather longer in the heavy military vehicle squatting like a gray-armored toad in front of the house.

Arrhae was standing beside it, looking ill at ease in the company of so many soldiers, and McCoy managed to summon up a smile for her especial benefit. The expression she gave back might have been a smile—it might equally have been the facial spasm of someone with indigestion.

"In," ordered t'Radaik. They got in, surrounded by disruptor-armed guards; there wasn't a lot of choice in the matter. McCoy looked back toward the house and saw H'daen tr'Khellian watching them. The man looked as uneasy as both of them, and McCoy thought about what H'daen had said five nights before. Something about this not being the way Romulan law should be interpreted. Well, just recently he had read enough of that same law to know that H'daen was being optimistic. Trials weren't a nice, civilized judge and jury, with mannered arguments and reasoning from defense and prosecution, even in cases where the verdict and sentence hadn't already been settled well in advance. The onus of proof was on the accused rather than on the accuser. "Guilty until proven innocent," and God help you if the court decided that all they needed was a confession. Romulan judiciary inquisitors were supposedly so skillful that they could not only get blood out of the proverbial stone, they could also force the stone to admit that it was spying for the Federation.

McCoy thought of Naraht, young Lieutenant Rock, and put that line of reasoning as far out of his mind as it would go. . . .

The flitter's rearmost hatch rose with a hiss and whine of heavy-gauge hydraulics, settling into its hermetic slots and shutting off all light until the vehicle's internal systems were switched on from the control compartment. After that it was only a matter of minutes before the flitter rumbled into the air and whisked off north toward Ra'tleihfi. Toward the Senate, and the Praetorate, and those scenic execution pits that Arrhae had mentioned.

Arrhae leaned over him, offering a small flask that by the scent contained good-quality wine. "Naraht?" With an appropriate lifting of the flask, she made the word sound like an invitation to take a drink.

McCoy accepted, taking a single careful swig of the liquor before handing it back. "Later," he said. "In the city. When I really need it." He hoped that the Horta could burrow to Ra'tleihfi as fast as Naraht had claimed he could, homing on the logic-solid buried in McCoy's brain. Between Naraht and the as yet unconfirmed rescue ship all using him as a beacon, and Intelligence using him as an ambulatory information-gathering system, what McCoy most looked forward to about completing this mission and getting home safe was to lie down on a nice friendly neurosurgery table and let Johnny Russell take the hardware out of his head. Of course, if things went wrong, some Romulan would take it out—but McCoy doubted he would appreciate that surgery quite as much.

The four Romulan guards glanced at their charges, shrugged expressively, and since nobody was offering wine their way, they resorted instead to the ale-and-water mixture in their issue canteens.

The flitter reached Ra'tleihfi before noon, traveling through the high-level zones reserved for priority traffic. Even with the starships back on maneuvers in his stomach, McCoy had enough curiosity to open the shielding on one of the armored viewports and peer out at the Rihannsu capital city nearly a mile below. It was smaller than he had imagined; at the back of his mind had been an image of something like L.A.Plex, a sprawling metropolis that went on for miles. Instead, he saw a place that was more like New York Old City: clustered spikes of tall buildings crammed together into the smallest groundspace possible, all steel and glass and plastic, a strangely pleasing hybrid that was hi-tech out of Art Deco and a style of classic severity like that of the antique Doric order.

Scattered here and there among the towering crystalline columns were buildings antique in their own right, rather than through any similarity to an Old-Earth school of architecture. McCoy knew, because Arrhae had told him, that the Senate Chamber and the Praetorate building had both been dedicated directly following the tyranny of the Ruling Queen. That meant they had been standing in the same place, and had been in continuous turbulent use for more than a millennium. No building now standing on Earth could boast such a history.

The flitter settled ponderously into a reinforced bay at the rear of the Senate Chamber, crouched buglike on its landers for a few seconds, then slid underground. If the procedure was meant to unsettle prisoners, it worked. For prisoners who were unsettled already, it worked even better.

"Leonard Edward McCoy." The Judiciary Praetor read his name with a passable Anglish pronunciation. McCoy watched her and wondered why every courtroom charge-sheet across the galaxy managed to look like every other charge-sheet, no matter how much they differed in form and style and material. The Praetor was reciting biographical information about the soon-to-be-accused, in considerable—and accurate—detail. McCoy wondered how many of the personnel at Starfleet Command were Romulan and Klingon equivalents of Arrhae/Terise.

He looked down at his wrists, snugged close together by a fine silk ribbon. It looked like no more than a token binder, more symbolic of his position in this court than of any practical use. Except that he had seen how it had been heat-sealed, not the band of gray silk, but the monofilament running through the center of its weave. Token binding indeed. *Honorable if honorably worn,* the security chief had said as it was put on. *Don't test it and it won't hurt you. Pull, and . . .* He hadn't bothered to say, but McCoy knew quite well enough without explanations. Any pressure on a strand one molecule thick—far too fine for the naked eye to see—would insinuate it between any other molecules it came in contact with. Pull, and both your hands fall off.

"Charges," said the Praetor, her voice echoing through the marble chamber that had heard the same word God—or the Elements—alone knew how many times since it was built. With the marble floor that was so easily washed clean . . . McCoy began to pay attention, more through curiosity than real interest.

"Espionage. Sabotage. Conspiracy. Aiding and abetting the theft of military secrets. Damage to Imperial installations. Complicity in the impersonation of a Rihannsu officer. Actions prejudicial to the security of the Imperium and the public good. The sentence of this tribunal, duly considering all evidence laid before it, is that the prisoner is guilty of all charges and shall die by the penalty prescribed. . . ."

# Chapter Fourteen

McCoy swallowed. Anticipating something like this, no matter how accurate that anticipation might have been, hadn't really prepared him for hearing his own sentence of death read out in open court. For maybe fifteen seconds he sat there sweating, with his guts in an upheaval that reminded him with acidic immediacy that he hadn't eaten so far today. And then the feeling went away as a twinge of discomfort shot through a very certain filling in his rearmost right molar.

Phantom pain was one thing, tracking-sensor feedback was quite another. His equanimity reasserted itself somewhat. *You're the one with the stacked deck,* he thought, *don't panic now. Besides, we all die sooner or later.* . . . Not that he would not rather put off the "evil day." He wiped his hands briskly on his pants legs, squelched the highly inappropriate smug smile that was threatening to take over his face, and got to his feet. Immediately he was the focus of attention, and the aiming-point for the phasers which by rights his guards were not supposed to carry within the Senate Chamber lest they dishonor the Sword in the Empty Chair. McCoy looked at them, and at the leveled weapons, then dismissed them all with a lift of disdainful eyebrows, and turned his attention to other matters. "Ladies and gentlemen—"

The Judiciary Praetor glared at him. "The condemned will sit down and be silent!"

"Why should I?" McCoy snapped back, then took a deep breath. "When I demand the Right of Statement."

There was immediate and noisy uproar in the house, and McCoy smiled thinly as he observed that for the first time in several years, the Tricameron was unanimous in a proposal—that he, Leonard E. McCoy, be suppressed severely and at once. He reviewed the mental-neural protocols that cut in on the analysis-solid, felt reality waver for an instant, and then with his enhanced awareness of the situation, realized just what a large splash his demand had made in the otherwise-tranquil pool of poison that was the Rihannsu executive. He wondered what "suppression" meant, and had a sudden vision of being put into a bag and sat on, like an Alice-in-Wonderland guinea pig. Except, of course, that someone was far more likely to yell "Off with his head!" in the comforting knowledge that it would be done.

Indeed, the Judiciary Praetor would be more than willing to do the deed herself, and was entirely capable of it. One of the most important pieces of acquired information in the logic-solid was a names-and-faces list of the Praetors and the most notable Senators, and while he hadn't been aware of her rank, he knew—uncomfortably—that this hawk-faced woman was Hloal t'Illialhlae, wife of *Battlequeen*'s late Commander and a most appropriate consort for that vicious gentleman. The information in the solid was that this woman had turned into a regular harpy since her husband's death in the Levaeri V incident. Understandable. But McCoy wasn't going to let it move him at the moment.

"Well?" he said stubbornly. "What about it? If you're subjecting me to the full rigors of the law, you'd better realize that it cuts both ways. Otherwise, why bother with this farce at all?"

The Praetor ignored him for a moment. "Disable those monitor cameras," she commanded, "and black out all transmissions on the public channel!" Once it was done and confirmed, Hloal turned her attention back to McCoy. Her smile was predatory. "Yes, indeed, Doctor. Why bother?"

"Let him talk, t'Illialhlae," called someone from the Senate benches. "It might be fun."

McCoy glanced at the woman who spoke. She was in uniform, her hair worn up in a braid and her face marred by a scar running from one ear to the corner of her mouth so that she smiled constantly on that side. *Eviess t'Tei*, the memory told him. *Senator, regional governor, noted duelist.* And someone whose suggestions aren't ignored more than once. For a few seconds Hloal matched stares with Eviess, while McCoy watched in fascination; then Eviess traced the length of that shocking scar with one fingertip and smiled sweetly, as if she remembered the original wound and reveled in the memory.

"If the house so desires . . . ?" asked Hloal abruptly. It was most interesting to see her back down in front of the entire assembly, trying all the while not to seem ruffled by her defeat. "All those in favor of the Right of Statement, so indicate." Most of the men and women in this chamber came to their feet, paused to check their number, and sat down again with an air of collective satisfaction. "Against?" Many fewer this time; McCoy spotted more "familiar" faces, most of them people he had been warned about.

"The proposal is carried by majority vote," said Hloal, speaking as if the admission tasted bad. "The Right of Statement is granted. Unbind him." She gazed at McCoy and he saw calm return slowly to her as she remembered that he was the loser no matter what small victory he won right now. "There is no time limit to the Right of Statement, Dr. McCoy; you may talk for as long as you like." Equanimity became amusement. "Indeed, you may talk for as long as you can. And when you are no longer able to talk, sentence will be carried out. It would be more dignified if you accepted the inevitable."

"I requested the Right," said McCoy stubbornly. "I stand by it."

"As you wish. The honorable members of the house may come and go as they please," she said clearly enough for the Praetors and Senators to hear, "but so far as you are concerned, there will be no recesses or meal breaks in this particular Senate session. And no, ah, relief breaks either. There you are, and there you stay. No matter what." Hloal smiled faintly. "So I suggest you make yourself comfortable. It will be a long, long, day."

McCoy knew what Hloal and the rest thought that they were seeing: a coward trying to hold on to his life for just a little longer. Maybe, their faces said, when the torturers came for him at last, they would have to drag him to the execution pits, pausing now and then to humorously pry his fingers free of whatever he had clung to in an attempt to slow his progress.

He smiled, and saw her eyebrows lift, for despite its grimness the smile had nothing of the usual false bravado about it. *The day's going to be longer than you think, dear. You've never heard a good ol' southern filibuster before. I hope your seat cushion's a soft one. . . .*

"Mak'khoi!" Eviess t'Tei was on her feet, looking disturbingly enthusiastic. "With or without the option?"

"Option?" he echoed, not understanding her.

"Of single combat. To give you the chance of an honorable death."

"You presume, madam. What if *I* win?"

Eviess didn't actually laugh in his face, but there was a twitchy smile on her lips that suggested she was humoring him by even considering the possibility. "If you win, then you fight another representative of the court. And, if necessary, another. The end will be the same, sooner or later. But cleaner and less protracted."

"That," said a voice McCoy remembered without resorting to the data-solid, "depends on who your opponent is. Eviess t'Tei, I claim first fight."

"Subcommander Maiek tr'Annhwi," said t'Tei. "But then, who else? Your manners still need mending. . . ."

Of course tr'Annhwi was here. He wouldn't miss this trial—or the execution afterward—for all the wealth of the Two Worlds, and if there was any way in which he could make his presence more personally felt, he would do it. If McCoy let him. Except that playing d'Artagnan to the subcommander's Jussac wasn't high on his list of Important Things to Do.

Instead, he smiled at tr'Annhwi and all the others, put one forearm across his stomach and the other across his back, and offered them a ludicrous dancing-school bow that impressed nobody and—as intended—affronted many. But at least they quieted down. It took a moment for the silence to suit him.

"Praetors, and ladies and gentlemen of the jury—wherever they are—unaccustomed as I am to public speaking, I should like to take this opportunity to thank all of you for your consideration in not wearying me with such unnecessary details as a fair trial. No matter that this is a common practice amongst civilized peoples—like the Klingons—" As the first uproar of the session echoed through the Senate Chamber, McCoy's smile got even wider. He always had loved a good audience. . . .

\* \* \*

Arrhae listened first with disbelief at his audacity, and then with slowly mounting admiration for the man's stamina and invention.

He had talked about everything, beginning relevantly enough with a discussion of the Romulan legal system as it pertained to espionage and the preservation of fleeting military secrets, and then progressed outward as though in concentric circles, touching briefly on war as an exercise in honor and then dwelling for a considerable time on treachery as an entertainment, a hobby, and an art form. Names were named, and members of the Senate could be seen blushing and shifting uncomfortably on their benches as certain of their ancestors were used as examples of notably shady behavior.

After that, McCoy's subjects had grown steadily more diverse, and he had given each the attention it deserved no matter how little it might have had to do with the Right of Statement as laid down in legislation. There had been the monologue—there was no other word to describe it—on the correct preparation of "Tex-Mex chili" ("whatever that is," Arrhae heard from the Praetorate benches behind her), together with a vituperative diatribe against those heretics ("ah, religious schism . . .") who recommended the use of beans ("whatever *they* are . . .") in the pot instead of as fixin's on the side. ("'Fix' means to repair," said someone sagely, "therefore this *t'shllei* is without doubt a medication." "Why?" There was a pause for near-audible thought while Arrhae fought down her giggles. "Well"—conclusively—"he *is* a doctor—though Federation medical practice sounds a little primitive to me. . . .")

Although none present could make the connection between crude medicines and food, he then proceeded to recall in impassioned detail the eating-houses of New York Old City and the dishes served there. Shortly afterward a technician was summoned to adjust and retune the translator circuitry, but without success. At one stage it was throwing out three words in five as untranslatable or meaningless: neither *pii'tsa*, *blo'hnii*, or *t'su-hshi* had any comparable term in Rihannsu, and *fvhonn'du*, rather than a food, seemed an analogue of a torture technique—now fallen from favor—in which parts of the subject's body were immersed in heated oil. . . .

He was playing for time, of course—although what Naraht could do all by himself, she didn't know. McCoy probably did, but he hadn't had an opportunity to tell her yet, and by the sound of things, wouldn't have the time for hours yet. Then he coughed, cleared his throat, and coughed again, a harsh racking noise that sounded to Arrhae like a death rattle. She saw many of the Praetors and Senators who had been half-asleep with boredom jerk suddenly awake and lean forward like a pack of *thraiin* whose prey has faltered at long last. And as if in a dream she felt herself rise from the bench she had been assigned, lift water, ale, and a cup from the nearest of the many refreshment trays set about the chamber, and, greatly daring, take them to McCoy. . . .

Holding forth on the War Between the States—or the Late Great Unpleasantness, depending on the company—was difficult enough when the listener was another southern gentleman, and downright awkward in the vicinity of a damn Yankee, but during a Rihannsu Right of Statement it became well-nigh impossible. McCoy's throat was parched and gritty, and his entire jawbone hummed with feedback subharmonics. He had seldom been so glad to see a drink as when Arrhae held out the cup of neat ale to him, and didn't give her time to cut the vivid blue liquid with water before he gulped it down.

And spent the next few seconds wondering if the brain implant had gone into overload. After the first fine flurry of spluttering, gasping, and wiping his eyes, McCoy hem-hemmed experimentally to make sure that his gullet was still where he had felt it last—and then held out the cup for a refill.

"If you people ferried some of this across the Neutral Zone, you'd all be rich," he said. "Though personally I'd use it only for medicinal purposes. Rubbing on sprained joints, sterilizing instruments, taking the enamel off teeth. . . . That sort of thing. I can tell you, it wouldn't make a mint julep. For that you need Kentucky bourbon, and you need fresh mint—and you can't grow proper mint unless . . ."

And he was off again. Arrhae looked at him without smiling, wondering how long this could last before the voice tired.

*What's he waiting for?* she wondered. It all made no sense, not as a mere exhibition of bravado. Sooner or later his invention would run out. True, he was waiting for Naraht—but McCoy acted as if—

—*as if he really thought he was going to get out of here*—Off the planet. Out of the system. Home. To the Federation . . .

She heard his voice twice: once, here and now, raspy, saying something about bourbon and the size to which ice should be shaved, and how a glass should be properly chilled: once, clear, calm and a little tired, in her head. *I'm authorized to ask you this: when I'm pulled out, do you want to be pulled as well?*

Home?

Arrhae paled. Terise was staggered. Home . . .

*But this is home!* part of her cried . . . and the worst of it was, she couldn't tell which part.

Eight years here. Working, learning Rihannsu in all its subtlety, learning customs, reading, learning a people, its troubles and joys. She knew the Rihannsu now better than she had known any Earth people, and understood life here far better than she had understood life on Earth. *Who comes to their own life, after all,* she thought, *and studies it as if it were a strange thing, something completely alien to them? Perhaps more people should—*

But her problem wasn't what other people should do. McCoy's question hung fire in her mind, tantalizing her. She had never given him an answer.

Starfleet again. To give up constant fear, and drudgery—being *hru'hfe* was never easy—and to go back to freedom, the stars, other worlds, other people. To see how her old friends on Earth and Mars were doing. To bleed *red.*

She shuddered. Abruptly it seemed an odd color to bleed.

McCoy might be doing it right here, very shortly, if whatever he was planning didn't work out. And she didn't know how to help him.

*You don't have to help me. Not yet.*

She shuddered again.

*I'm authorized to ask you this. . . .*

Arrhae wished he had not.

And she felt a little tremor in the floor, as if someone had dropped something.

Arrhae looked around. No sound. No one had dropped anything, it had to have been her imagination. McCoy was going on at length about cocktail shakers.

The tremor repeated itself, more strongly this time. Arrhae glanced quickly from side to side, wondering if anyone else had noticed or if it was indeed just a trick of her overwrought mind. It had to be; all the members of the Senate and the Praetorate were settling back into their attitudes of boredom and McCoy was preaching the virtues of first melting the sugar for a julep in a little hot water.

But just as he began to describe how some of the mint leaves should be bruised and others left intact, he stopped talking. Hloal t'Illialhlae and Subcommander tr'Annhwi were on their feet almost simultaneously, grinning. And then the grins were wiped from both their faces as a crack appeared in the middle of the floor, right before the Empty Chair itself.

The crack widened with a small, crisp *snap* that echoed astonishingly in the silence that had filled the Senate Chamber. Then it exploded wide open with a hiss as of strong reagents and a nostril-tingling scent of acid, and a *thing* reared up out of the Earth to begin rumbling across the floor, leaving a track in its wake that was eroded into the very marble slabs themselves.

*What happened to him?* she thought, for Lieutenant Naraht was twice the size that he had been when Arrhae tripped over him only six days ago, and his rank-marked voder now looked like a badge rather than a piece of electronics. Whether Hortas had some sort of silicon-based late-adolescent growth spurt, or whether he'd just followed doctor's orders and indulged in a bit of feeding-up between H'daen's house and here, she didn't know. It was enough that he had arrived, and arrived in such a way as to create the maximum amount of confusion. There was plenty of it, what with normally staid persons of rank running about like *hlai* with their heads cut off, and screaming, and the air sharp with acid fumes, and the shouting of orders that no one heeded. . . .

Terise began to suspect that McCoy just might manage to pull this off after all.

For McCoy, it all made a most satisfying parallel to the scene on *Vega*'s bridge after her holds were blown open. A phaser whined shrilly, almost at his elbow, as one of the four guards drew his illegally carried sidearm and sent a bolt of disruptor-level energy crackling into Naraht's side. The Horta didn't even notice, but the Rihannsu guard did briefly, before McCoy shifted his stance on the podium and jabbed that so-convenient elbow backward into the man's throat. *One thing about being a medic,* he thought as he dived to scoop up the fallen phaser, *you know which parts to aim for.* Then thoughts of anything other than survival got pushed aside as more phaser fire ionized the acid-heavy air and blew the podium to jagged fragments. . . .

He was lucky; apart from that one attempt to dust him, they kept stubbornly shooting at Naraht despite the fact that it was clear they were wasting their time and ammunition-charges. But when a living Representative of the Elements moved among mortals, those mortals could scarcely be blamed for throwing rational behavior to the winds. Naraht wasn't being damaged, but he was angry, confronted with ludicrously imbalanced odds and doing whatever had to be done moment by moment, whether that meant barging about like a sentient tank, breaking things and people with the brisk efficiency he brought to everything. "Took you long enough to get here!" McCoy shouted at him across the room.

"Doctor," Naraht said, ramming a firing guard into the wall, "let's see *you* burrow through two hundred fifty-three miles of rock that fast."

"And another thing," McCoy shouted, "what happened to you? You're twice your size!"

Naraht laughed, a sound so bizarre that several Rihannsu who had been about to concentrate their fire on him broke and ran away. "You're the one who's always twitting me about needing to put on some weight! So I snacked on the way. Besides"—and the artificial voice got unusually cheerful—"the granite here is *very* good."

Several other people concentrated phaser fire on Naraht, three beams together. It must have stung: Naraht charged them. One of them did not get out of the way fast enough, holding his stance and firing. Then the man tried to scream and didn't finish it before Naraht lunged over him and left a shriveled, flattened, acid-eaten lump behind. Very few corpses looked as dead as those left by a Horta. . . .

McCoy took a chance to do some pouncing of his own, out from behind a sheltering bench that was neither high enough nor thick enough for his liking, to grab Arrhae by the arm and drag her under cover. She tried to wrench free, and lashed out at him before realizing who it was, which was just as well since it made her look just as he wanted, a hostage seized by an armed and desperate man. A hostage, moreover, who was *hru'hfe* of a House presently riding high in the favor of Imperial Intelligence. With his captured phaser pressed to the side of her head, it looked as though McCoy was uttering warnings and threats, and thanks to Naraht's rampage, no one was close enough to know any different.

"The ship's on its way down, Terise," he said, using her real name quietly despite the noise and violence only a score of feet away. "Not long now—then we can go home."

She twisted away from him, far enough to turn and see his face, almost far enough—McCoy dragged her back a bit—to put herself at risk again, and took a quick breath of the smoky, smelly air, and said, "You go. I'm staying."

He looked at her carefully. "You must have expected it, Bones," she said. "Surely you must. If I go home, I'm just another sociologist with her nose buried in a stack of books, more memories than some, but that's all. No family, no ties, nothing. Here—here I'm unique. I'm of some use. And I've grown used to ch'Rihan, used to the people and the customs, I . . . Oh, Elements, Bones, I *love* this place!"

He glanced away from her for several seconds. When he looked back, he was smiling slightly. "Do the job, Terise. Do the job and do it well." He took a moment to stick his head up and snap off two quick shots, then ducked behind the bench again, staring expectantly at the Senate Chamber ceiling. "We'll have to find another outside contact," he said. "There's no one to pass your reports through anymore."

"I'll work something out. A *hru'hfe* has a *little* pull." And she evidently had a thought, for her eyebrows went up in the Rihannsu version of a suppressed smile. "Maybe in goods shipments," she said. "There *is* some clandestine trade across the Neutral Zone. You could order some ale. . . ."

"I already have," McCoy said, and laughed under his breath. "Listen. You take the phaser and make a break for it, I'll go after you and grab you. You throw me and go for Naraht. I have a confession to make—" He cocked an eye at her, feeling slightly sheepish. "I second-guessed you and told Naraht you'd probably want to stay. He won't hurt you too much. Keep your eyes closed. The acid is pretty strong up close when he's busy. Your people'll be convinced whose side you're on."

She took his hand, neither squeezing nor shaking it but simply holding it. "Leaving my adopted family would hurt more," she said softly.

"Prosper, then," McCoy said as quietly. "Stick with them. And if you can, if they'll listen . . . tell them that the rest of the family is waiting for them to come home and join the rest of us."

Arrhae nodded. Then her grip tightened and the balance of her crouch changed, and McCoy yelped as she bit him in the hand he was trying to keep over her mouth. The phaser was ripped out of his hand, and he was slammed sideways into the bench so hard his head spun. . . .

Arrhae ir-Mnaeha tr'Khellian broke free of her captor in the sight of many present, stole the phaser right out of his fingers, and fled before he could seize her again. If there had been more phasers in the chamber, or if she hadn't been so frightened that she forgot to use it, he could have easily been killed or struck down by a stun-charge so that the various penalties could have been executed after all. Instead, she ran from him and was attacked at once by the Earth-monster that had ravaged the Senate, injuring or killing many. Senators and Praetors, people of note and substance, saw Arrhae stand her ground as many of military Houses had not, and shoot her phaser at the monster while it bore down on her and brushed her aside as if she did not exist. . . .

Arrhae sprawled on the ground, gasping with the pain of a collarbone that had snapped like a stick when Naraht's fast-moving bulk had slammed into her braced shooting-arm. Her entire left side throbbed and tingled both with the impact and the heavy-sunburn sensation of mild acid burns. McCoy had been right, it did hurt. But she had been right too . . . and sometimes that fact could make a marvelous painkiller.

*Home. Home by choice. At last.*

Arrhae took that thought with her to the shadows. . . .

Someone was yelling for more guards—none of whom had yet answered the summons—and was adding demands for heavy weapons. *Come on, what are you waiting for?* he thought . . . and as if on cue, a fine plume of dust started spiraling down out of nowhere, adding its powdery texture to the cocktail of suspended solids in the air. Other plumes joined it quickly, and a wedge of stucco popped out of the frieze that ran between walls and ceiling proper.

Then the whole roof and ceiling structure shuddered as some vast weight settled on them, and moaned with intolerable anguish at the strain. It was a horrifying thing to hear a stone building seem to groan with pain, and inside the Senate Chamber all had become as quiet as when they saw the first crack in the floor. Someone went to the great double doors and pulled them open, looked out—and refused to cross the threshold. He turned very slowly and walked back to his place on the veto side of the house with his face the color of new cheese and his eyes seeming sunk back into his head. Only when he was seated again did he look his fellows in the face. "The building is ringed with soldiers," he said to all and none of them. "They are not Rihannsu. And there is a starship on the roof."

Nobody laughed.

A column of crimson sparkle came alive in the middle of the floor as somebody beamed in from the "starship on the roof," and still nobody spoke or moved. As the transporter-dazzle faded, McCoy got off the floor, dusted himself down, and endeavored without much success to put right the ravages of the past few minutes' activity. *The cavalry's arrived,* he thought. But he didn't say it aloud.

Ael i-Mhiessan t'Rllaillieu stood there surveying the Senate Chamber of Ra'tleihfi on ch'Rihan, and said nothing. She looked much as she had when McCoy had seen her last: a little, straight, slender woman who came about up to his collarbone, with long dark hair neatly braided and coiled around her head—a woman whose face looked fierce even when it was quiet, a lady whose eyes were always alert and intelligent, sometimes wicked, often merry.

Right now the eyes were very alert indeed, but not so merry. To McCoy she had the look of a woman briefly possessed by memories. She had a right to be. From what she had told him, the last time she had stood here she had seen her niece, the young "Romulan" commander whom McCoy and Kirk had known, formally stripped of House-name and exiled. It had been a little death for everyone involved, McCoy thought. *And Rihannsu rarely leave death unavenged. She not only has them where she wants them, she has you there, too, Leonard, my boy. What if she decided on a whim to get rid of you as well? In her eyes, way back when, when we first met, you were as culpable for the commander's trial and exile as Jim Kirk was. . . .*

He brushed the thought aside as a result of all this physical exertion. The tension of it made him a little paranoid sometimes. Ael was simply standing and looking around the place, not so much at people but at the building itself. Many of the ancient sigils hanging here and there now had blastholes in them, and the white marble of the place was all burnscorched and spattered with the viridian of blood.

She moved at last. Her boots crunched on broken stone and other, grimmer remnants as she walked slowly forward, her eyes moving, always moving, from face to face, from floor to walls to ceiling. Their gaze rested a moment on the smashed body of one of McCoy's guards, a phaser still clutched in one hand even though the arm lay feet from where it should have been. "Weapons," she said softly. "Indeed." The silence in the room became profound. The holster at her own belt was conspicuously empty.

Ael picked her way carefully across the torn paving. "*Bloodwing* roosts on the roof," she said conversationally, "and her phasers have stunned all for a kilometer around this building. No use in waiting for your guards. Or for any small patrol-craft foolish enough to try anything. The phasers are no longer set to merely stun."

She came to stand beside the Empty Chair, looking thoughtfully at what lay in it. "Poor thing," she said to the Sword. "For a millennium and a half no other weapon less noble has been permitted under this roof for any cause, not even for blood feud. Now they bring in blasters wholesale to guard one poor weak Terran. Or simply to terrify him for their pleasure."

People shifted where they stood. She ignored them, smiling a terrible smile at the Sword. "It seems nobility is gone from this place . . . among other things. The kept word . . . the paid debt. Honor."

"Traitress!" someone shouted. "You, to speak of honor!"

She turned slowly, and McCoy was glad the look in her eyes was not turned on him. "When I helped the Federation attack and destroy Levaeri V," she said clearly, "the only thing I betrayed was a government that would have used the technology being developed there to destroy the last nobilities and freedoms of the people it was sworn to guard. I would do the same again. Beware, for if you give me reason, I *shall* do so again. Only respect for this old place that S'task built keeps me from putting a photon torpedo into it to keep you all company." She grinned, and that wicked look was back. "I have always wondered how one of those would go off in atmosphere."

She turned again to the Chair. "This is no place for you," she said. The Sword lay there, a long silent curve of black metal sheath, black jade hilt, so perfectly made that there was no telling where one began and the other left off except for the slight difference in the quality of their sheen. Ael put out her hand and picked up the Sword by its sheath.

The silence that fell was profound. "You have sold honor for power," she said to the Senate and the Praetors. "You have sold what a Rihannsu used to be, to what a Klingon thinks a Rihannsu *ought* to. You have sold your names, you have sold everything that mattered about this world— the nobility, the striving to be something *right*—for the sake of being feared in nearby spaces. You have sold the open dealing of your noble ancestors for plots and intrigues that cannot stand the light of day, and sold your courage for expediency. Your foremothers would put their burned bones back together and come haunting you if they could. But they cannot. So I have."

She hefted the Sword in her hand. "I have come paying a debt, to show you how it is done . . . in case you have forgotten. And meanwhile, my worthies, I shall take the Sword, and if you want it back, well, perhaps you might ask your friends the Klingons to send a fleet to find me. Or perhaps they would laugh and show you how to truly run this Empire as they run theirs, by sending that fleet here instead. They half-own you as it is. You might still change that . . . but I see little chance of it. Cowardice is a habit hard to break. Still, I wish that you might . . . and I will gladly serve the Empire again, when it *is* an Empire again . . . the one our fathers and mothers of long ago crossed the night to build."

And Ael turned her back disdainfully on the entire Tricameron of the Romulan Empire, and looked at McCoy.

"Doctor," she said very calmly, as if they had met under more peaceful circumstances, "my business here is done. Are there other matters needing your attention, or shall we take our leave?"

"I'm done here," he said. "And so's Naraht."

"Ensign Rock—or Lieutenant now, I see." McCoy had a definite feeling that Ael was deliberately "not noticing" things unless they were of some importance to her at a given moment. Passing Naraht by unnoticed was all very well in a garden rock arrangement, but on what had been a flat, bare floor—and which was still reasonably clean, so far as skirmish sites went—he was hard to miss. "You've grown, sir."

Naraht shuffled and rumbled a bit before replying, the Hortan equivalent of a blush. "Madam," he said, "you are more beautiful than I remembered."

McCoy put an eyebrow up in mild surprise, then smiled slightly. "Must be the ears," he said to Ael. "His mother always did have a soft spot for them."

"Soft spot?" said Naraht. "*My* mother?"

Ael smiled, and bowed slightly to Naraht. "I make no judgment as to that," she said. "But as regards beauty, if that is your perception, may I remain so. May we all." She glanced back at the others in the chamber, and her amusement diluted somewhat as she flipped open a communicator. "In any case, I would as soon not overstay my welcome here, and I suspect I did that within the first second of my standing on the floor. *Bloodwing,* three to beam up. These coordinates. Energize. . . ."

Arrhae drifted in and out of consciousness as she lay on the floor, aching. She had seen moments of Ael t'Rllailleu's visit to the Senate Chamber, but each of those moments had faded to black before anything of interest happened. She opened her eyes again just as Ael, McCoy, and Naraht dissolved in a whirl of transporter effect, and heard Ael's final words before the beam whisked words and speaker both away. "*Bloodwing* is the only ship of any size here, so we—"

As the darkness rose around her mind again, Arrhae thought she heard the chirp of another communicator opening, unless it was just a memory of the first. The voice that spoke into it was no more than a susurrant mumble, like waves on the seashore, and she wasn't able to concentrate on who it was or what they said. Her arm hurt, and she was so tired.

"*Avenger,* this is tr'Annhwi . . ."

So tired . . .

"Beam me up! Emergency alert . . . !"

So . . .

"Go to battle stations. . . ."

. . . tired . . .

# Chapter Fifteen

McCoy had been aboard a Rihannsu warship before, but that had been a Klingon-built *Akif*-class battlecruiser, and it had at least been roomy. *Bloodwing* was nothing of the sort. None of his kinesic-analysis studies of viewscreen recordings that showed warbird bridges had prepared him for the reality of just how *cramped* the rest of the ship might be. Not that it caused him to stoop or anything so obvious; there was just a lot less free space than he was used to on the *Enterprise,* and if Naraht had indulged his appetite any further, the Horta would have been in real trouble.

He recognized familiar faces among the small group waiting for them in the transporter room. With the implant running, they would have been as well known to him as the crew of the *Enterprise,* and even now their names came back like those of old friends: Khoal and Ejiul and T'maekh, big Dhiemn and little N'alae, and his fellow protoplaser-wielder, Chief Surgeon t'Hrienteh. She at least looked pleased to see him there, but the rest had eyes only for their commander, and for what she carried cradled like a child in the crook of one arm. Not a one of them spoke as Ael stepped down from the transporter platform, looking for all the world like a queen—or the Ruling Queen herself.

"Now *there* is a tale for the evenings," said someone softly and reverently.

Ael smiled a bit and reversed the Sword so that its scabbard-chape grounded with a small, neat click against the deck. "A long tale for many evenings, my children. But not just now. Are the landing party up and safe?"

"All up, Commander," Ejiul said, checking a readout for confirmation. "They came up by cargo elevator through the rear hangar-bay. Since we had landed, more or less, it was quicker than using the transporter."

"Excellent." Ael toggled the wall-mounted intercom and said, "Bridge, all secure. Lift ship."

*"Vectors on line, up and running."*

McCoy recognized the voice as that of Aidoann t'Khnialmnae, and wondered with a little shudder whether Nniol tr'AAnikh was aboard as well. There were thanks he had to make at second hand, and not waste too much time about doing it.

Then Aidoann's voice came back sounding more concerned than before. *"Commander, we have detected another beam-up from the Senate Chambers. This wasn't anything to do with us."*

"Tr'Annhwi," said McCoy to the air. He suddenly remembered that despite not wearing a weapon with his uniform—tr'Annhwi respected that tradition at least—the subcommander had been wearing an equipment belt. That meant a communicator. And *that* meant he could get back to *Avenger,* which if its captain was on-planet, had to be in orbit waiting for him.

"You know one of House s'Annhwi, Doctor?" asked Ael as she made for the door and the turbolift beyond. "Then my compliments on the quality of your enemies."

If he had thought the transporter room was cramped, that was nothing to being inside a turbolift with a Rihannsu commander and a noticeably oversized Horta. Getting out onto *Bloodwing*'s little bridge was almost a relief—though once Naraht rumbled after them, the situation became much as before. Nobody looked up to stare, even though the news of their arrival with the Sword had probably run through the ship in the few seconds that they were in the lift, and nobody moved from their seat while their commander was on the bridge. Or almost nobody.

None of Ael's people wore Rihannsu Fleet uniform now, even though they were still dressed in a distinctly military style, but the young man who kick-swiveled his station chair around and then left it in a single springy bounce wore neither Romulan nor makeshift. He was Terran-human, in a Federation Starfleet command uniform, and he was grinning as he reached out to shake the doctor's hand.

"Well, Dr. McCoy!" he said, shaking as vigorously as someone priming an old-style water pump, "I'm glad to see you're not dead yet!" And grinned even wider as McCoy gaped in confusion. This was an elaboration he hadn't expected. "Luks, sir. Ensign Ron Luks, of Starfleet Intelligence."

"Ah." Everything became suddenly clear. "So Admiral Perry sent you to hold the old man's hand. On the wrist, or off it?"

Luks stopping shaking hands and went a little pink. Then he grinned again. "I acted as courier for the access codes on our side of the Neutral Zone, sir—and I *was* hoping to see some action," he said, "but so far it's just been a flitter-ride."

"A very long flitter-ride," said Ael, sitting down in her Command chair. "Or perhaps it only seemed that way. Starfleet's ensigns, Doctor, seem to vie with one another in the display of enthusiasm. But I think we've found the action that you wanted so badly. Tactical." Schematics came up on the main screen, showing their position near the surface of ch'Rihan and that of *Avenger* in a high geosynchronous orbit.

"This is more like it," said Ensign Luks, pointing at the screen. The blue triangle representing the frigate was underscored by a rapidly scrolling column of data, and McCoy suspected he knew what it meant.

Aidoann confirmed it. "*Avenger* was in orbital shutdown until a matter of seconds ago, Commander," she said, enhancing the image so that more information filled it. "They've just gone over to active status, while we are lifting clear . . . *now.*"

The ship jolted somewhat under McCoy's feet and the viewer image reformatted, putting the schematic display up into a screen window overlaid on an exterior scan of Ra'tleihfi as the city dropped away beneath them. There were several columns of smoke crawling skyward, last traces presumably of those patrol-craft Ael had mentioned so scornfully. For all that he had to admire the courage of anybody who would attack something the size of a warbird with no more than a lightly armed atmosphere shuttle. It was very much more the traditional image of Romulan behavior than that which he had learned in the past days, and he wondered if it was typical because of the tradition, or traditional because it was a typical character trait. Whichever, it seemed entirely in accordance with the old custom of honorable suicide. . . .

*Bloodwing*'s people began bustling about in the way that McCoy had seen so many times on the *Enterprise,* with the same quiet determination—and the same pre-combat nerves that were more or less well hidden.

"This could be fun," said Luks, grinning again. McCoy snorted. He sat down at an empty station, closed the antiroll arms across his thighs in anticipation of a rough ride, and waited for the "fun" to start. Luks watched him for a second or two, then decided that there might be something to the precaution after all and followed suit.

"Power availability?" Ael said quietly.

"Minimal, Commander. Maneuvering on thrusters, no more. We can't use impulse power in atmosphere, and the lift tubes—"

"Noted—but hurry it up. Photon torpedoes?"

*"Armed. All tubes charged and ready."*

"Phaser banks . . . ?"

*"Locked on target. Standing by."*

"Shields?"

*"Raised."*

"Screens?"

*"Maximum deflection."*

*"Bloodwing,* this is Ael. Battle stations, battle stations. Secure for combat maneuvers. Success to you, and *mnhei'sahe.* Ael out." She turned around and gazed with dry amusement at Ensign Luks, who had followed everything with the expression of someone whose dreams were coming true. "This is the 'fun' part, Ensign," she said, lecturing him gently. "We are down here. *Avenger,* a more modern and more powerful ship, is up there, blocking our escape route. We must therefore dodge and feint until an opening presents itself, without getting blown up in the process, and without taking too long about it in case somebody recodes or overrides the defensive-satellite chain so that they'll be waiting for us too. Enough fun for you?"

Luks had gone a little pale during Ael's recitation, but he recovered fast. "You'll run?" he said, plainly not expecting such behavior from Rihannsu, even renegade ones.

"Of course. Starting now." Ael returned her attention to the tactical display, where *Avenger* was running at nominal capability. McCoy watched her, and saw irritation in every line of her body as she sat bolt-upright in her command chair, refusing to make use of its comfortably padded back.

The two ships were engaged in a slow-motion race for viable in-atmosphere power, and the first to get it would win. Normally starships with a landing capability could ascend from or descend to their landing fields only out of parking orbit, but the maneuvering thrusters for attitude control in zero-G dock could be adapted from normal configuration. Ael seemed to be silently cursing herself for not having it done earlier—or perhaps for not firing on *Avenger* when she first had the chance.

Except that doing so was not the Romulan way. Or, at least, not Ael's way . . .

*"Master Engineer tr'Keirianh, Commander: We have power . . . !"*

McCoy saw Ael's left hand relax from its fist as *Bloodwing*'s engineer made his jubilant report, then saw it clench tight an instant later as she looked at the screen and realized that *Avenger*'s engineer was probably saying exactly the same words. The schematic flipped out to fill the screen again, and more figures began to flicker across it in pursuit of the tiny ship-silhouettes. Then *Bloodwing* jolted as if she had hit something—or something had hit her.

"Phaser fire, atmosphere attenuated." Aidoann, at the helm station, transferred the screen to visual again; below was a gray-green-brown blur of land, and above, in the gray sky, were the fading bluestreak traces of hard radiation sleeting from the track of *Avenger*'s phaser beams. "Returning fire—"

*"No!"* Ael was most decisive, and although a lesser captain might in very truth have struck fist against seat arm, she allowed her voice to do that work. "Not until we reach space," she said. "I will not take that responsibility—"

This time *Bloodwing* bucked like a high-spirited horse with spurs struck into its flanks, and McCoy felt the familiar sensation of being pitched in three dimensions at once. For just one instant he thought that he could hear the thunderclap roar of some huge explosion, although that might have been the tinnitus brought on by the implant in his brain. Or he might indeed have heard the sound of a photon torpedo detonating in sound-bearing atmosphere.

"Tr'Annhwi's mad," said Ael flatly. "O Elements, to use a torpedo so close to ch'Rihan . . ." She glanced back at McCoy and Ensign Luks, spared a smile for Naraht, and tightened the smile to a ferocious grin. "Enough. If he was obeying the rules of war, it might be worthwhile to keep running, but he's thrown out the rules of common sense as well. Take us up!"

*Bloodwing* leaped for space with Aidoann and Hvaid performing a two-part chant of countdown before cutting in the impulse drive. It was a fine-spun line they traveled, for using impulse power in atmosphere would not only shatter windows over hundreds of hectares, it would probably cause widespread molecular disruption of the planet's ozone layer. That was the sort of thing which tr'Annhwi's casual use of heavy weapons might have caused already—there was no way to be certain, and only one sure way to stop it from happening again.

"Confirming: phasers locked. Firing."

Needles of fire spat from the warbird as *Avenger*'s vulture shape swelled ever larger on the screen—superimposed now with gunnery and targeting data—and the long, lean, wide-winged shape vanished behind expanding globes of incandescent energy before slashing through them with her shields barely affected and delivering not one but a salvo of photon torpedoes straight at *Bloodwing*.

"Evasive," snapped Ael. It was already engaged, if speed of response was anything to go by, and McCoy felt the gravity grids flutter along a 3-G variant curve during the maneuver stresses, and then cut out completely for a long half-second when the volley of proximity-fused torpedoes exploded beneath and behind them, flinging out enough wild energy for the screen to black out completely as it filtered the glare. *Bloodwing*'s phasers opened up again as *Avenger* twisted past at .25c less than eight klicks away, an impossible point-blank full-deflection shot that still succeeded in bracketing the other ship.

*Avenger* flipped over, belly-up like a dead shark, and for an instant it seemed that she was beginning the long tumble that would end only when a scratch of brilliant light flared and faded across the Romulan night sky. Then she completed the roll and corrected the plunge planetward, skipping across the outer envelope of atmosphere with a flare of friction-heated particles dragging in her wake, opened momentarily to full impulse power, and came back at *Bloodwing* yet again.

"These damned Klingon gunnery augmentation circuits should be—" Ael said fiercely, and didn't bother completing the curse.

McCoy watched from his seat, listening and trying to remain as detached about this as he had been about the death sentence in the Senate Chamber. It was difficult; space battles, even this unfamiliar dogfighting at low impulse speeds, were situations in which familiarity did not breed contempt so much as terror. Evidently some Klingon-built improvement to *Bloodwing*'s phasers was proving ineffective against *Avenger*, a latest-generation warship built by those same Klingons.

For an instant the high-mag image of tr'Annhwi's ship ran head-on toward *Bloodwing*, wingtip phaser conduits glaring intolerably bright as they spat destructive energy. The screen became a Bosch vision of Hell seen through a stained-glass window in the nanosecond before it filtered down to impenetrable black, and *Bloodwing* shuddered under the flail of sequential direct hits.

"Commander," said Aidoann calmly, "shields four and five are now reduced to sixty-five percent efficiency, and the progression curve indicates failure after three more strikes."

Ael nodded. "What about *Avenger*'s present status?"

"Sensors indicate a shift in energy consumption; they're channeling more power through the weapons systems. Shields are holding at . . . eighty percent of standard."

"Oh. I see. Typical of him. And in that Klingon scow too. Well, let's see it catch us when we go into warp and—"

A communicator whistle interrupted her. *"Engineering, this is tr'Keirianh. Can you give me seven standard minutes to put this mess back together?"*

Ael looked at the speaker/mike with an offended, betrayed expression, and McCoy looked at her. She was not a lady who liked her words suddenly made hollow before they were fully spoken, even by a chief engineer whose problems and requests sounded very familiar.

"Do what you can, Giellun," she said after a glance at the tactical repeaters, "but I can't promise you so much as seven seconds. . . ." And then she turned right around, as did McCoy, to stare at movement where right now no movement should have been.

Ensign Luks was standing by his chair, looking confident, eager, determined—and scared stiff. *Oh, God,* thought McCoy, *another space cadet!* "Sit down, son," he said aloud. "This isn't your affair any more than it's mine." Luks stayed where he was, and gave no sign of even having heard McCoy. All his attention was directed at Ael.

"If you need seven minutes, then you also need a diversion," he said. "Clear the cutter for takeoff."

There might have been surprise in Ael's mind, or confusion, or disbelief, or scorn. "You're going to die," she said matter-of-factly.

Luks shrugged at that, then grinned broadly. "Maybe—most everyone I know will too. But not right now. Not me. I'm the best you've got."

"Son," said McCoy, "did you take the *Kobayashi Maru* test?"

"Yeah, I did, sir." Another grin. "Tried it once, and didn't like it. It's such a downer."

"But worth remembering."

"Not for me—I like something a bit more cheerful. Catch you in ten minutes or so, Doc. You can buy me a drink." Luks grinned some more, until McCoy wondered whether some muscle rictus was at work. "But don't leave without me on that account."

He headed off with Hvaid, whistling some catchy tune or other that McCoy couldn't place. *Bloodwing* shuddered again, and orange warning lights began to flash on the ship's-schematic board. Evidently tr'Annhwi's scanner officer, that overly keen Subcenturion tr'Hwaehrai, had noticed the weakness in *Bloodwing*'s shields, because those last shots had hit fair and square on the damaged sectors and reduced them to barely forty percent effective.

"He's away!"

*Bloodwing*'s screen flickered to a new image as Luks's cutter shot from the rearmost hangar-bay and darted straight at *Avenger* like a mouse attacking a lion. *Avenger* sheered off with enough violence to threaten her nacelle integrity, though whether it was because of the incongruity, or the unexpectedness, or the ferocious salvo of fire from the cutter's single phaser mounting—or because it was so very definitely a Federation cutter—nobody on *Bloodwing* knew.

Luks *was* the best, McCoy decided—or if he wasn't, he would do until the best arrived. He flung his little vessel about the combat area, raking *Avenger* with insignificant but probably infuriating blasts, and then disobligingly evading the response. And he was having fun, which was more than McCoy could say about his own part of the mission. *Well, that's what he wanted, isn't it?*

"Engineering, report. How go the repairs?" Despite her coolness while he was here, Ael watched Luks's gadfly attacks on the screen and nipped the tip of one finger between her teeth. Since the cutter was launched, *Bloodwing* had gone unscathed as her opponent concentrated planet-cracking firepower against a ship no bigger than one of its warp-drive nacelles. "Engineering . . . ?"

*"Two more minutes—maybe less."*

"One. That's all. This . . . performance . . . can't last much longer."

There was a silence at the other end of the channel, but it still had the unmistakable hiss of an open carrier. Ael stared at it, her finger poised over the recall button on her personal comm board. Then tr'Keirianh came back, coughing and breathless but sounding very pleased with himself.

*"The mains are back on line, Commander. Up to warp four at your discretion."*

"Not enough—but it'll have to do. Bring that young fool back in here and—" Her words stopped short when a phaser beam as thick as the cutter's hull clipped Luks's ship and split it open. "Oh, *no!*"

McCoy was on his feet, fingers gripping the padded arms of the station chair so tightly that they had sunk through the skinning and into the foam beneath, watching fragments of metal and plastic sparkle in the light of Eisn. *Avenger* cruised disdainfully through the cloud of glittering slivers, and swung with ominous deliberation back on *Bloodwing*'s trail. *He knew the risks.* That was the only coherent thought his mind could form right now, and it was totally inadequate for—

"Bloodwing . . . ?" Luks's voice was weak, and not just because of a poor transmission signal. McCoy had heard too many mortally injured men not to recognize one now. "Bloodwing, *you still there . . . ?*"

"This is Ael, Ensign. Yes, we're still here. We shall use a tractor beam and—"

"—*and nothing! Get out of here before that . . .*" His voice trailed off and there was silence for so long that Ael leaned forward to cut the connection. *Avenger* was forgotten just for these few seconds. By *Bloodwing*'s people, anyway. Not by Luks. "*I'd as soon not . . . be their guest,*" he managed to say. "*And you folks deserve some peace. . . .*"

There was a click as he cut the connection, and everyone's eyes went to the main viewscreen, dominated by the predatory outline of tr'Annhwi's *Avenger.* The brief flash of an attitude thruster was noticeable only because it took place in the warship's shadow, but the consequence of Ensign Luks's decision was going to be enough to cast shadows of its own as far away as ch'Rihan.

His crippled cutter drove like a piloted torpedo straight into the nearest of *Avenger*'s nacelle pods and cracked it wide open, letting in space. The matter and antimatter of two warp-capable ships combined, uncontrolled. A blink later there was nothing but a single globular spasm of destruction as furiously radiant as a nova. It expanded, pure white light, impossible to look at. It would not fade for hours.

On board *Bloodwing* the main viewscreen swung away from the blinding light to the cool starfields that surrounded 128 Trianguli. Nobody said a word to McCoy for what felt to him like a very long time, until Ael touched her communicator gently. "Damage reports?" she said.

"*The shields took all of it—whatever it was, Commander.*"

"Good. Prepare for warpspeed. Aidoann, you know the course, through the Federation Neutral Zone, and . . . and he left his codes programmed into the navigator's station. Implement warp four on my command." Ael sat back and closed her eyes, looking very tired. When she opened them again, it was to gaze steadily at McCoy, who gazed as steadily back.

"Well," he said.

"Or ill. But his choice. Our peoples have more in common than either of them choose to see. You're the doctor. Tell me, how long to cure the blindness?"

"I don't have that answer for you, Ael," he said softly.

"I thought not. Too long for my lifetime, at least. Or if they listen to your little Arrhae, maybe not so long after all. Aidoann, Hvaid, warp four. Take us away home."

# Epilogue

"They will be convinced, Doctor," said Ael. "Rest assured of that. I saw what Lieutenant Rock left of two or three who stood up to him"—Naraht shuffled and rumbled, plainly not proud of himself—"and any who faced him with that knowledge in mind would surely be either heroic or insane. From what you say, Arrhae ir-Mnaeha is a most self-possessed young woman. She will have them dueling for the privilege of lacing up her sandals."

"Um." McCoy rolled neat ale around in a chunky crystal glass, staring at its color and feeling pretty blue himself. "I keep thinking about her. And about Luks . . ."

The postmortem on the day's events had run on long into ship's night, without really getting anywhere but back to the beginning again. Food had been prepared, toyed with, and nibbled at, but for the most part ignored in favor of wine and ale. Lots of both.

"He was all fire, that one," Ael said quietly, "they burn bright, and burn out. He knew what he did, and he did well. Leave him his brightness. The Elements did not mind doing so."

The Sword lay on Ael's side of the wardroom table, a reminder of events past and events yet to come, but more cutting even than the Sword's edge was another empty chair where Ensign Luks was meant to sit. "Turn down an empty glass," McCoy said, drained his, and did.

"Knowing *that* one, he would rather you filled it and drank," she said, "but you've done enough of that for any three Terrans. I think"—and she pulled the ale bottle and the winejug across the table and out of his reach—"that *these* belong where you can't get at them. This is not medical advice. This is the owner of the drinks-cabinet speaking."

Very, very slowly he began to smile. "You sound like my ex-wife," he said.

Ael considered that. "I'll assume you meant that as a compliment. Don't correct me if I'm wrong."

"Correct a lady? Never."

"At least not on her own ship. Come, then, enough of you, all Earth and tears . . . a walking mud puddle. We are all heroes here, and deserve to make ourselves better cheer. Tell me about Arrhae. Why did she stay behind? I confess to fascination, because given the chance to go home myself . . ."

He looked at her speculatively. "She wanted to stay with her family."

Ael made a Spock-eyebrow at him. "Indeed. How strange it is: we feel closer to the kin we adopt than to the ones we're born to. A perceptive young woman, I would say."

She sat back and looked at the Sword. "And you?" McCoy said. "Whom have *you* adopted lately?"

"Ah," Ael said. "The paid debt. I wondered when that would come up to be handled."

"But, Ael, you don't owe me anything. Or the Federation, or even Jim."

A slight smile tugged at her lips. "Jim. No, of course not. So much the more reason to pay the debt back. Or forward."

McCoy scowled. "Bloody *mnhei'sahe* again. Not even the implant does anything about that word."

Ael smiled. "Only people can do anything about it. And the day you understand it," she said, "that day our wars are done. Meantime . . . we must still translate for others. By actions, not words. I have an Empire to rehabilitate. You have your own worlds to save, I shouldn't wonder."

He looked at her and saw no mockery. He had none for her either. "All of them," he said.

She stood up and stretched. "A heroic goal, befitting a hero. But even heroes must start small. And for me, that means a ship to run. For you, a liter of ale to sleep off. Drink less next time . . . but dream well now. We're going home."

"Not to yours."

"Someday," she said from outside the door.

★   ★   ★

Arrhae i-Khellian t'Llhweiir stood in the dark silence of the garden and looked up at the aurora curtain hanging in the night sky. It was fading now—which was to say that it was no longer bright enough to be seen during daylight hours—but it still rippled and crackled wonderfully as it ran through its random color-shifts. Arrhae watched as the blue-green background glow became suffused with an astonishing chrome yellow shot with incandescent red, and the whole fragile structure seemed to billow like a drapery of finest silk. Scores of cameras had been pointed skyward and hundreds upon hundreds of recreational tapes had been made, regardless of what had been the cause of the phenomenon.

The public channels had claimed that brave and noble Fleet warships had brought the "pirate" vessel to battle just beyond ch'Rihan's atmosphere, demonstrating with many and various models, diagrams, and computer-simulated animations the manner in which it had been englobed and blown apart as it tried frantically to flee from the engagement. . . .

However, Senators knew differently.

It was probably unheard of in the long history of the Rihannsu for any House, no matter how noble, to be served both willingly and well by a *hru'hfe* with her own entirely independent House-name, much less one who held a seat in the Senate Chambers, though that was a nominal matter for the present, since the actual building was still closed for extensive reconstruction and, until another had been built, Arrhae could have held her assigned seat—or its fragments—in her two cupped hands.

The image of what that august body would have said and done had they known the true provenance of their latest member was one over which Arrhae preferred to draw a veil. . . .

Once the dust had settled and various outraged persons had been mollified by the execution, suicide, or banishment of various others, Arrhae had found herself a hero. And after her collarbone had been set, regenerated, and, most important, had stopped hurting, she began to enjoy herself. It was rare behavior nowadays, but in the past the elevation of a trusted servant to a position of nobility had been a common reward for services beyond that normally expected. In her case, someone had spent a long time rummaging through the records to find sufficient authority for her promotion to the Senate.

Then there had been the interview with Commander t'Radaik's replacement, which had become a sort of drunken picnic in the garden after the intelligence officer had arrived at House Khellian with enough food and alcohol for the entire household and had begged time off for everyone. Arrhae remembered that quite fondly, because the man had been *very* handsome—and, more to the point, had gone away entirely satisfied that nobody here had known anything about the shocking debacle at the last espionage trial but one.

*Khre'Riov* or not, intelligence or not, he hadn't found it easy to get by H'daen tr'Khellian, who had promoted himself to honorary uncle, father figure, and, for all Arrhae knew, representative agent. The reprehensible behavior of the late Subcommander tr'Annhwi had soured him against his old practice of cultivating any and all who seemed likely to be of use; and with a Senator working under his own roof, he no longer needed such doubtful patronage anyway.

When that Senator was also a hero who had the good fortune to be a beautiful young woman and unmarried besides, what H'daen was finding he did need was a stick to beat the suitors away from his front door. . . .

She looked up at the sky, at the aurora and at the stars beyond. . . . *If they'll listen . . . tell them that the rest of the family is waiting.* . . . "They're not ready to listen to *me,* Bones," Arrhae said softly to the night and the darkness. "Not just yet. But they'll be ready sooner than they think, and when they are, I'll be ready too. I . . . or my children."

She smiled at the notion, and because she had dared to say it aloud even to herself; then she turned from the stars and walked back into her House: her home.

# PART THREE

# Swordhunt

## (ORIGINALLY PUBLISHED IN TWO VOLUMES AS *SWORDHUNT* AND *HONOR BLADE*)

For Wilma, T.R. and Sara,
who saw all this begin
in the House of the Dangerously Single Women
. . . and for Wes, Lee, Gene and Peter,
who left us all much less Single
(though no less Dangerous)

# Prologue

The shadows of Eilhaunn's little yellow sun Ahadi were slanting low, now, over the pale green fields all around the flitter port, as the work crews ran the harvesting machinery up and down the newly cut rows to bind the reeds into the big circular bales that Hwiamna's family favored. Hwiamna i-Del t'Ehweia stood there off at the margin of the field, watching the two machines that her son and daughter were driving, and she sighed. They were racing again. They loved to race, each challenging the other every morning to do the work better, faster; and whichever one was the victor, on a given day, chaffed the other mercilessly about it until the next daymeal, when there might be another victor, or the same one. Hwiamna routinely prayed to the Elements that the victories should alternate; otherwise home life became rather strained.

Hwiamna smiled, took off her sun hat, and wiped her brow, while taking a moment to beat some accumulated windblown reed-seed off the hat's thin felt, against her long breeches. Since the twins were born, Kul clutching at Niysa's heel, this kind of thing had been going on; and it would doubtless go on well past the end of the year, when their acceptances came through. Naturally as soon as they were both old enough, they had both applied to the Colleges of the Great Art on ch'Rihan; there being no higher possible goal, to their way of thinking, for anyone born on a colony world so far from the heart of the Empire, with so little else to recommend it. Hwiamna was not sure about their assessment—her foremothers on one side of the family had willingly come here three generations ago from the crowded city life of Theijhoi on ch'Havran—and once they had paid off their relocation loan, won their land grant, and tamed the earth to the bearing of regular crops of stol-reed, they had found life good here. But farm life, and even the prospect of managing the family flitter port, was not good enough for the new generation. Their eyes were on the stars—which should possibly have been expected, for Hwiamna's father was of Ship-Clan blood, native to Eilhaunn for two generations—where Hwiamna's eyes were on the ground. She had no doubt whatever that both of the twins would be accepted. Then this rivalry would go on as always, but within the structure of the colleges, and later on, with appointments to Grand Fleet. Perhaps they would go further, into diplomatic service or the uppermost reaches of Fleet. Knowing her children, Hwiamna had little doubt of that, either. But right now all she could wish was that they would fail to destroy the farm machinery, which had to last for at least a couple of seasons more before it went back to the cooperative for recycling or replacement.

She put her hat back on and walked back over to what she had been inspecting—the piles of firewood carefully stacked up in hand-built racks twenty *rai* from the edges of the flitter port's landing aprons. Hwiamna knew, for she had seen pictures of them, that on the Hearthworlds the ports did not have such, but the images always looked bare to her, and somehow underutilized, as if an opportunity was being missed. Here, out among the Edgeworlds, resources could be scarce enough that no possible energy source could afford to be ignored. The resinous dense wood of ealy, a tree native to Eilhaunn, burnt hot and long; it was excellent for controlled combustion in power stations, and also for the small hearthfires of the householders in the area. They all helped to cut it—thus keeping the surrounds of the landing aprons clear—and they all helped to stack it in the racks; and each winter season, when the first snows began, all the householders gathered to take away bundles of the dried, cured wood, carefully divided according to how much time they had spent in the work of coppicing and stacking. *The trouble is,* Hwiamna thought, looking with some resignation at the racks, *that time alone should not be the only criterion by which we judge the division. . . .*

The comm button clipped to her pocket squeaked. "Mother?"

She reached in and touched it. "Kul dear," Hwiamna said, "pray, don't pass so close to your brother in the middle of the rows. You're going to make life harder for whoever has to pick up the bales."

"That will be him," Kul said, cheerful, "and it's right that life should be harder for him, if I have anything to do with it. But, Mother, we're almost done now; is there anything else needs doing out here before lastmeal?"

"I don't think so, daughter," Hwiamna said. "Though I may have some words for the two of you about the way this wood's been stacked. Your supervision last cutting-day leaves a little to be desired, I think." She turned away from the rack she had been regarding critically.

"Mother," Niysa said, "that wasn't her fault; it was the Droalls. Those people couldn't be troubled to cut their own wood straight, leave alone anyone else's. And they can't be made to do it, either, stand over them how you like. I think you should cut them out of the coppicing rotations in future; they're more trouble than they're worth."

Hwiamna sighed, amused. As usual, there was no upbraiding one of the twins for anything whatsoever without the other coming straight in to his or her defense. "We'll talk about it later," she said; though privately Hwiamna was inclined to agree with her son. "Get yourselves finished, get yourselves in . . ."

"Should I come fetch you, Mother?"

"No, *bhun,* you go on ahead; the walk will do me good. . . ."

She watched one of the machines half an *irai* away finish its row; then both machines made for the unplanted strip at the edge of the field and began racing down it over the slight rise in the ground there and back toward the apron, where their house was built a little ways back from the old road leading to the two low prefabricated cast-stone buildings which the government had installed as the flitter port's administrative center.

Hwiamna gave the wood racks one last look and then began walking back around the edge of the apron toward the house. It had been a good year for the reed, for once; a welcome change from last year, when the growing season had been blighted by endless wet weather and what seemed equally endless uncertainty over what was going on in their region of space. They were a long way out in the Empire. That was one of the reasons it had been so easy for the family to move out all this way, in her grandfather's time. New uncrowded worlds had been as plentiful as birds in the sky, it had seemed then, and the government had been easygoing about relocation finance and support for new colonists. Now, though, people were beginning to realize what the real price for such worlds might be. The government was not so forthcoming with aid anymore, a stance which was starting to cause complaints as the inhabitants of worlds like Eilhaunn began to realize that interplanetary trade and defense were matters they were increasingly expected to manage themselves—though there was notably no talk whatever of excusing them from taxes. It all made for nerve-racking times, as last year, when there had been talk of the government beginning a program of granting the farther-flung outworlds "autonomy"—code, Hwiamna strongly suspected, for leaving them completely to their own devices.

But that kind of talk seemed to have quieted down since, much to Hwiamna's relief. And the weather had settled itself, too. This last season had been nothing but the dry fair weather that was normal for north-continent Eilhaunn-uwe this time of year, and there would be no lack of grain—a relief, for reed was Eilhaunn's great staple, of all the plant foodstuffs the one that grew most readily here. But as usual, the growing was not the end of the business: nothing was guaranteed until the grain was out of the pod and into dry storage.

Hwiamna glanced up one more time as she ambled across the landing apron—the habitual gesture this time of year. No one wanted to see cloud moving in when the reed was being cut, since it needed at least a day on the ground in the sun before it could be threshed—otherwise the enzymes in the seed pods would not activate to let the grain loose. Hwiamna scanned the turquoise sky, and breathed out. No cloud.

Yet she squinted into the brightness for a little longer, her curiosity aroused. High up there, very high up, were some thin pale lines of white . . .

Getting less pale, more white.

Not cloud. Contrails.

Hwiamna looked at them and swallowed. The contrails were growing steadily broader toward their arrowy approaching ends. Dropping into atmosphere . . .

Her heart went cold in her side. *The children,* she thought, *where are the children?* For everyone knew what contrails like those meant. The news services had been full of the pictures of them, in the last few months.

Hwiamna started running across the apron. As she ran she missed her footing once, and under her the ground shuddered, faintly at first, then harder. *O Elements,* Hwiamna thought as she ran, *no, not here, why here?!*

And then there was no more time for questions, for over the hills at the edge of the valley came a terrible rumbling, and Hwiamna saw the cruisers come up low and fast over the hills, five of them, firing as they came. She knew the shapes all too well, those long bodies and down-thrust wings and nacelles, like *oiswuh* diving, their long necks thrust forward, the terrible claws out. They too had been in the news services . . . but far away, at what had seemed at the time like a safe distance.

The ships came screaming down and over, and the ground all around the port shuddered as the phaser bolts and photon torpedoes slammed into the fields. Great blooming black-shot clouds of orange fire came boiling up from the impact sites as dirt and rocks shot out from them in all directions, and the biggest one of all from the torpedo that the foremost ship fired into the airport buildings.

Charred and burning wreckage flew, and Hwiamna flung herself down on the shaking ground, the air knocked out of her lungs by the force of the explosion. When she struggled up to her knees again, she peered desperately through the smoke and fire to try to make out what was happening. Wind whipped up by the passage of the second and third Klingon cruisers blasted across the apron, pushing the smoke aside for long enough that Hwiamna could see someone moving out on the edge of the flitter port, well away from the buildings—Kul, running for one of the flitters.

"*Kul!*" Hwiamna screamed. Then she slapped at the comm button. "Kul! Daughter, *no—!*"

But her daughter would not listen to her in this, as in most else. She had already slapped the side of the flitter, and the canopy was levering itself up, and Kul was climbing in—

That was when the phaser blast from the next cruiser hit it. Hwiamna knelt there frozen as shreds of glittering and burning metal and flesh blasted out from the site. Billowing smoke then veiled the spot where the flitter had stood, but not before Hwiamna had seen too much of what preceded the smoke. Her hands clenched together. There was nothing she could do. "Kul . . ." she whispered.

Motion from elsewhere on the apron distracted Hwiamna. The other flitter, rising, its engines screaming. "Niysa," she whispered. She would not call him now. If she did, he might be distracted. "Fly, my son, fly for it, get away—!"

It was the last thing on his mind, for he had seen them kill his sister. The flitter was in the air now, and came wrenching around in a high-grav turn that should have pushed the blood right out of his brains; but Niysa was a pilot born, with *neirrh* in his blood, as his instructor had said, and he flew like one of those deadly little birds, racing after the closest of the Klingon cruisers. *He's mad,* Hwiamna thought in anguish, *it hasn't enough weaponry to do anything at all.*

But her Niysa did not care, and flung his craft at the cruiser, firing its pitiful little phasers. "No," Hwiamna whimpered, for he was actually gaining on the cruiser as it plunged over. Niysa fired, fired again, poured on thrust—

Almost absently the phaser bolt lanced out from the back of the Klingon vessel and touched his ship. It bloomed into fire, vanished in smoke. Lazily the cruiser arced around; and the cloud behind it began to rain splinters and fragments of metal, and lumps of scorched burnt stuff.

Hwiamna screamed then, wordlessly, a cry of total horror and grief. The world, all her world, was over, finished, destroyed. Her face streaked with tears of rage and loss, Hwiamna stared up into the turquoise sky, now hazed and blackened by the smoke of burning reed, and raised her clenched fists to the heavens, and screamed to the pitiless Elements, *"Why?!"*

Her only answer was the disruptor bolt that killed her.

# Chapter One

Deep in the longest night, in a ship passing through the empty space thirteen light-years from 33 Trianguli, a Rihannsu woman sat in a hard-cushioned chair behind a desk and looked out through a small viewport at the stars, waiting.

Her surroundings were blessedly familiar; her own small cabin, in her own ship. It was everything outside, now, which was strange to her—the spaces in which she was a barely tolerated guest, the stars that filled them, either unheeding of her presence or subtly inimical to it. . . .

She raised her eyebrows briefly at her own fancy. *I grow whimsical,* she thought, and her gaze slid sideways from the surface of her tidy desk to the chair which now sat by itself against the far wall. *But perhaps, having* you *around, there is reason.*

In the present dim nighttime lighting of the cabin, what lay across the arms of the chair seemed barely more than a sliver of shadow; pure unrevealing darkness, absorbing whatever light fell upon it. Not quite straight, but very faintly curved, the sheath and the hilt seeming to fade seamlessly into one another by the skill of the ancient swordsmith, the Sword occupied another empty chair much different from its former one, and the thoughts of the woman whose cabin it now shared.

*Occupation . . .* She smiled faintly. It was as good a word as any for the hold which this object had had over her since she put her hand out in the Senate chamber, two months and a lifetime ago, to take it. In her people's traditions there had always been tales of creatures or objects which expressed the Elements unusually perfectly. These tended to bend the universe out of shape around them, as intense gravity fields bend light, and equally they bent awry the intentions of those mortals who had close dealings with them.

She had little thought to find herself, ever, so used. It had simply come to her, in that moment's impulse in the Senate chambers, that she would willingly take possible disaster on herself in order to save the most sacred part of her people's heritage from further dishonor. Now she wondered, sometimes, exactly whose impulse that had been; exactly who was the Sword, and whose were the hand and will wielding it.

In the weeks following that day, when she and her crew had returned to these spaces where the Federation had allowed them to take refuge, she had spent a number of hours in what was little better than shock—amazement at her own temerity, worry over what would follow it, fear for her crew. Then pragmatism set in, as always, which was as well; for within only a few days more, the messages began to arrive. Her act had swiftly begun to bear fruit in the form of consequences, and the fruit was ripening fast, faster than even she could have imagined.

And soon, now, if she was any judge of events, the first fruit would fall.

The comm signal sounded, and the suddenness of it made her start. She had to laugh at herself, then, though there was no one here to hear except that dark and silent listener lying across the arms of the chair, it wearing its eternal slight uncommunicative smile.

She reached out and touched the control on her desk. *"Ie?"*

*"T'Hrienteh says a message has arrived for you in the last comm packet, llhei. . . ."*

Aidoann's voice had a slight tinge of eagerness to it, and Ael knew whence that eagerness came. All her crew had been infected by it since she came back to *Bloodwing* carrying what now lay on the chair across from her.

"Send it along to my computer," Ael said. "I will read it here. And Aidoann, for the Elements' sake there is little point in *you* 'madam'ing me. The crew will think we have fallen out."

A pause, then a chuckle. *"Very well, ll—Ael."*

"Not in private, anyway," Ael said, hearing her antecenturion's old slight discomfort with amusement, and wondering idly how many years yet it would take her to lose it. "We can afford a little ease among ourselves these days, as long as our performance in action is not impaired. Which I think unlikely to happen. In any case, it is not as if some superior officer is going to come along and reprimand us for a breakdown in discipline."

*That* image made Aidoann laugh outright. "So," Ael said. "What has tr'Keirianh had to say about the engine tests this morning?"

*"He said little, madam, but smiled a great deal."*

Ael's mouth quirked up a little at that. Her chief engineer might be sparse of speech, but he had no skill at concealing his feelings. "Dangerous to make assumptions," she said, "but that would seem to bode well. *Ta'khoi* . . ."

As she cut the voice connection, her terminal showed her the herald for an incoming message, encrypted. "Decrypt," she said, and sat back, watching the terminal go black, then fill with amber characters that shimmered into meaning from meaninglessness.

About half the screenful was comm routing information, interesting only insofar as one chose to be endlessly fascinated by the means her correspondents found to evade the ever-increasing interest of the security services on ch'Rihan and ch'Havran. Some of the messages were relayed numerous times among the subject worlds of the Empire and right out to the fringes of Rihannsu-dominated space before making their way out into the spaces beyond. This one, she saw, had gone clear out into the Klingon communications networks—which in itself was amusing, considering what one of these messages might eventually mean to the Klingon Empire if things went the way she thought they might— and from there had passed to one of the commercial subspace relay networks in the "nonaligned" worlds buffering between the Klingons and the Federation, before making its way to her ship. *The long way around . . .* she thought, and touched the screen, stroking the routing information away and bringing up the message.

Under the origin and destination fields, both forged, the message itself was brief. The body of it said only:

THE PART YOU HAVE REQUESTED (NTCS 55726935–7745–9267–93677) IS PRESENTLY UNAVAILABLE. NEAREST ESTIMATE OF AVAILABILITY IS BETWEEN THREE TO FIVE

MONTHS. IT IS SUGGESTED YOU SUBSTITUTE PART
NTCS 55726935–7456–8344–86009 AS AN INTERIM SOLU-
TION. CONTACT US AGAIN IN THREE STANDARD
MONTHS REGARDING ORIGINAL PART.

There was, of course, no signature. She sat back and looked thoughtfully at the two long "parts numbers," carefully rearranging their digits
in her mind according to the usual method . . . then held very still for a
few moments, digesting what those two sets of numbers together
meant. *So quickly . . .*

She folded her hands again, leaned her chin on them once more, calculating. *They are furious, indeed, for their innate inertia to be so quickly overcome. Yet I cannot believe their consensus is genuine. I have merely given them
cause for a show of unity. Beneath that, no question but that their divisions remain.*

*Yet will those still run deep enough to serve my turn?*

She shifted her eyes back toward the dark, slight curve of the Sword,
and felt it looking at her. *Impossible, of course . . .* But the feeling persisted, and others had reported it as well. How something so inanimate
could yet seem to have awareness of its surroundings, and an intent that
looked out at the world through that awareness, Ael could not tell. Yet
for many long years this potent artifact had lain in that chair in the Senate, untouched, unmolested by even the most violent and powerful of
the personalities who passed through—and that fact argued some in-
dwelling power of the Sword's more dangerous, in its way, than Ael
much liked to think of.

She got up, then, came around her desk, and stood before that chair,
looking down at the slice of darkness that lay there defeating the dim
light of her cabin. "Well," she said softly. "Now is the time, if ever. Shall
we serve each other's turn? I am willing . . ."

She reached out slowly, hesitant; her fingers dropped to the hilt,
brushed it. . . . Nothing happened; no jolt of power, no arcane or silent
voice shouting agreement down her bones. She expected none, well
knowing the difference between a symbol and the powers it stood for.
Nonetheless, the answer to her question was plain.

She turned away and waved the cabin lights up, then went back to the desk, reached down for the comm control again. "Bridge."

It was young antecenturion Khiy's voice. *"Yes, khre'Riov—?"*

She had to smile that so many of her people still called her that, though none of them belonged to the service any longer, and the service indeed would be the instrument of all their deaths were they ever caught. "The message which has just come in tells me what I thought it would," she said. "They are finally coming for us . . ." She could not hold back a somewhat feral smile. "We have much to do to prepare."

"Khre'Riov—" Khiy's voice held a most unaccustomed nervousness. *"Are we going back with them?"*

Ael laughed softly. "Did you truly think it?" she said. "Aye, going back . . . but never in the way they think, or the company. Is Aidoann still there?"

*"Here,* llhei."

"Shortly I will have some more messages to send, and we must take care with the routing of some of them, lest they come too soon where they are wanted. T'Hrienteh and I will confer about this at length. But first you should call the crew together. There are things to be discussed in detail before we go forward."

*"Yes,* khre'Riov!" Aidoann said, and the comm went dead.

Ael t'Rllaillieu gave the Sword in the Empty Chair one last glance, and smiled briefly; then waved her cabin door open, and went out to battle.

There would be those who said she had started this war. Ael was not so sure about that. *But beyond doubt,* she thought, *I shall be the one to finish it. . . .*

In the heart of Paris, just off to one side of the Palais de Chaillot, between the great reflecting pool and the Avenue Albert de Mun, stands the tall and handsome spire of the "troisième Empire" edifice built late in the twenty-second century to house the offices on Earth of the president of the United Federation of Planets. It was November now, though, and half the spire was hidden in the chilly fog which had come down on the city the night before and shrouded all its lights. The mist had risen a hundred feet or so, but no more. Now the view from the terrace outside the room where the president was meeting privately with the chief of staff of Starfleet Command was mostly indistinct, with only a glimpse or two of distant buildings showing here and there as flitters and little ion-driven shuttles passed, and the mist swirled with their passing.

The room was very still even though the door to the terrace was open, the mist muting the sounds of the city outside; and the thin pale light fell cheerlessly on the dark-paneled walls and the Shaashin, Kandinsky, and T'Kelan oils hanging there. In the middle of the room hovered a large oval sapphire-glass desk on paired pressors, and behind it next to a matching cobalt-blue chair the president stood, his tall dark bearlike bulk slightly stooped as he looked down at the desk, reading from the display embedded in it. He had been up all night, and looked it.

"When did you receive the message, sir?" Fleet Admiral Mehkan said. He was a smaller man, considerably slenderer than the president, and very fair, as a lot of people from Centaurus are.

"It must have been about midnight," said the president, touching the display to bring the report up again. "The Strat-Tac people," he said, "are very thorough in their briefings. I'd thought this would have arrived a little sooner—but apparently her enemies back home have been making sure they have everything they need in place before they move."

"And now," said the chief of staff, "we have to start working out what to do . . ."

"Sit down, Dai, please," the president said. Mehkan sat down on a chair like the president's on the other side of the desk.

The president lowered himself into his own chair, leaning on the desk while he finished rereading the report. "She'll have received the same message, I assume," he said.

"At about the same time, yes, sir. Her sources supply us as well, rather more directly."

"And you're sure that the source of the information is completely reliable."

"It's not just *a* source, Mr. President. It's *our* source."

The president nodded slowly. "I had wondered. . . . Well, the inter-esting part of all this," he said, "is going to be anticipating what she does."

"She has to have known they would come right after her," said the chief of staff.

The president nodded. "Unquestionably. If I understand the relative importance of the artifact she took with her, to produce the same result on Earth she would have had to have stolen the Articles of Federation, or the old Constitution, or the Magna Carta. . . ."

"Combined with the Crown Jewels, the Black Stone, and the Holy Grail," said Mehkan. "The Romulan government will do anything they have to, to get that thing back . . . or to make sure it doesn't fall into un-friendly hands."

"Such as ours," said the president.

Mehkan nodded.

"But it's still just an excuse," the president said. "They've been wait-ing for a chance like this for a long time. There are elements in the Sen-ate which have been looking for a cause célèbre, something to push their relationship with the Federation out of the rut it's been stuck in for all these years. The Neutral Zone chafes them, limits their trading opportunities, annoys their expansionist and nationalist lobbies . . ."

"An excuse for them to push outward," said Fleet Admiral Mehkan, "would certainly be welcomed."

"Well, it's not as if there aren't also elements in Fleet which would welcome the resolution of a persistent tactical problem on one of our borders," the president said. "Massive resources are spent policing and patrolling the Neutral Zone every year. Everyone would find it an im-provement if suddenly that necessity went away . . . wouldn't they?"

The Fleet Admiral twitched a little. The president noticed, and said nothing about it. "Yet at the same time," the president said, "no one has wanted the situation to resolve itself in an uncontrolled manner. Some-times, unfortunately, you just don't have a choice. We've known for a while that there would be a war involving the Romulan Empire within the next five to ten years. Political tensions, economic pressures, even personal issues at high levels in the Empire have been bringing it closer and closer. Now here it comes: a little sooner than expected, maybe. But hardly unexpected."

He got up and came out from behind the desk, pausing in front of his terrace door and gazing out for a moment. Across the Seine, the lower half of the Eiffel Tower was now visible; the rest was lost in fog, producing an effect suggesting that someone had come along and sliced its top off with a knife. "That being the case . . . what matters is to protect our own people, naturally; but also to try to steer events so that they do the most people the most good over time, both on their side of the Neutral Zone and on ours."

"The altruistic approach . . ." said Fleet Admiral Mehkan.

"I know that tone of voice, Dai," said the president, beginning to pace slowly in front of that window. "I did Strat-Tac only a year after you did at the Academy, and I remember old Dickinson's lectures as well as you do. My job simply requires that I approach the problem from a slightly different angle. A wider one, maybe. War . . ." The president paused. "Any war is undesirable, Dai. A war that benefits one of your opponents at the expense of the other, and weakens both . . . that's also undesirable, but less so. However, a war that leaves you with, instead of two opponents who keep each other busy, only one opponent, now much stronger due to the defeat of the other . . . that is very undesirable indeed."

Mehkan said, "And things have been trending that way for some time, Mr. President."

"Yes. Well, events seem to be giving the forces in the Romulan Empire a different focus to 'crystallize out' around. We have two main concerns. Tactics, and readiness." He looked up at the chief of staff of Starfleet. "And two questions. If we go to war with the Romulan Empire, can we defeat them?"

Fleet Admiral Mehkan was very slow to answer. "Strat-Tac says yes," he said. "But it would be a long, bloody exercise. There would be hundreds of millions of casualties, maybe billions, on both sides. And it would take both sides decades, if not a century or more, to completely recover."

"And if the Klingons come in on their side at the beginning?"

This time there was no pause in Mehkan's answer. He shook his head immediately. "A shorter exercise. A *much* higher death toll. The modern version of what they once called 'mutual assured destruction' . . . the possible loss of starflight capability to all three cultures, if things went on long enough."

"An unacceptable outcome, obviously. But I suspect Strat-Tac thinks the Klingons would wait to see how things went . . . then come in and attack the weaker of the two combatant parties at an opportune moment."

Mehkan nodded. "Their own Empire is slightly overstretched at the moment in terms of supply lines," he said, "and I think they're sensitive to the possibility that the Romulans, once hostilities were well enough under way, might attack the further-flung Klingon worlds with an eye to cutting off the trade routes to the inner planets."

The president leaned against the terrace door, gazing out. "Well," he said, "it's going to start. So our job is to keep this war from killing any more of us, and any more of them, than is absolutely necessary; and to manage it in such a way that the powers left standing at the end of it are unlikely to go to war again for a long time."

"And if we can't?"

"We have to," said the president. "By whatever means. And one fairly straightforward means to the end is lying ready to our hand . . . if we use it intelligently."

Fleet Admiral Mehkan looked profoundly unhappy. "I wish we knew for sure that we could trust her," he said.

"We can trust her to be Romulan," said the president.

"That's what I'm afraid of."

"And we don't so much have to trust her," said the president, "as to anticipate her. In *that* regard . . . we have at least one resource who does that fairly well."

"I was afraid you were going to say that," said Mehkan. He got up and went to stand by the terrace door as well. "Mr. President . . . there are people high in Command who are going to resist this suggestion strenuously."

"You among them," said the president.

"Kirk is increasingly difficult to predict as time goes by. If he—"

"If we selected starship captains just for predictability," said the president, "most of them would be dead within the first year of their first five-year mission. Lateral thinking, creativity, the ability to outflank the dangers that face them . . . that, I would think, is the set of characteristics Fleet sorts for. Or have the criteria changed since we last did a review?"

"No, but—"

"You know what the problem is as well as I do," the president said. "It is not a question of predictability, in the case of the captain of the *Enterprise;* it is a question of loyalty . . . in this particular case."

"Only," said the chief of staff, "a question of where that loyalty lies."

"I have no doubts, in this case," said the president. "By the time things come to a head, neither will you. In the meantime, *Enterprise* herself has significant symbolic value to all sides involved in the argument which is about to break out . . . and that value would be much lessened with a change in her command."

He took one last look out the window, then turned back toward the desk. "So take care of it," said the president. "Get *Enterprise* out there. Cut Kirk orders that will protect Fleet if . . . action has to be taken." His face set grim. "But leave him the latitude he needs to get the job done. Our job, meantime, is to put together the assets she will need after the trouble starts. I want a meeting with the chiefs of services tomorrow at the latest. It'll take at least a few days, possibly as long as a week, for the Romulan force to materialize where we have to take official notice of them. We need to start putting our assets in place immediately, before it can possibly be seen as a reaction to what's about to start happening. And then . . ."

"Then we wait," said the chief of staff of Starfleet.

"The worst part," said the president, "as always. Get caught up on your sleep this week. *I* sure will, because once things start happening, we're both likely to lose plenty."

Fleet Admiral Mehkan nodded and headed toward the office door. Halfway through it, he paused and looked over his shoulder.

"There really *is* no way to avert this, is there?" he said, very softly indeed.

The president shook his head. "This time, unfortunately," he said, "we're right. We're just going to have to pray we're not as right as we're afraid we are."

Mehkan went out. The president of the Federation let out a long breath and looked out the window again at the mist lying over the city, softening and obscuring everything in a veil of increasingly radiant obscurities as the sun now tried to come out above it all. The soft view would not last long. Soon enough would come the awful clarity of phaser fire in the darkness, ships bursting in vacuum, the screams of the committed and the innocent together. At times like this, he hated his job more than anything.

Nevertheless, he turned back to his desk and set about doing it.

On ch'Rihan, in the planetary capital city Ra'tleihfi, stands an old edifice built with the elegant classical proportions of the "Ehsadai" period—that time when the Rihannsu were new to their planets from the depths of space, and just beginning the business of taming the Two Worlds to their will. The building itself was much newer than the Ehsadai era, having actually been built after the fall of that terrible woman Vriha t'Rehu, the so-called Ruling Queen. The Rihannsu who built it were, like many of their people, looking back with both relief and longing to a time when the arts of peace and war in the Two Worlds had seemed to be at their height. By building again in that style, and incorporating what remained of the older structure on the same site, the architects hoped to remind Rihannsu everywhere of what they had so nearly lost to the tyrant—freedom, honor, the rule of ch'Rihan and ch'Havran by the millions descended from those who had crossed space to live there, as opposed to rule by the whim of any one Rihanha, however well-intentioned.

But memory is such a fleeting thing. Soon enough, within ten years, twenty, fifty, the tyrant's awful depredations were happily enough forgotten by people busy rebuilding their lives and countries after the wars that Vriha t'Rehu's ambition triggered. Soon enough, as the Senate and Praetorate resumed their ancient powers, the old jockeying for power began, as the few fought for influence among the many; and the people scattered across the worlds accepted this, once again, as part of the normal conduct of life . . . some few Senators or Praetors overawing their many co-gubernals by virtue of family connections or wealth rather than drawing them into agreement by common sense. The Rihannsu forgot, and the Senate and Praetorate were content not to remind them, that the Two Worlds are rarely in such danger as when only a few hold rule; and they forgot what the building meant, except that it was old and beautiful.

Now, on this morning of the thirty-fifth of Awhn, that building was still old; but its beauty was marred. There was a great crack running right across the massive low dome that was the central chamber's ceiling, roof, and another straight across and through the mighty slab of marble which had floored the great chamber under the dome, big enough to hold the whole Tricameron in session at once. Now formal sessions of both Senate and Praetorate were being held elsewhere while workers labored among the ugly pillars and struts of emergency scaffolding inside the building; and outside, tractor beams and pressors were supplementing the normal stresses that had formerly held the dome unsupported over the chamber. The architects had planned superbly, but they had not anticipated that the chamber would ever have a starship sitting on its roof.

The three men who stood there now, under the scaffolding, looked across the blaster-scarred and acid-stained marble of the chamber and said nothing. The workers, for the time being masters of this domain, paid no attention to them. The three men in their somber dark uniforms of state, sashed in black, not gold, were themselves paying little attention to the workers. The gazes of all three were directed toward the far side of the room, where there sat an old, old chair. One of the workers had thrown a couple *ells'* length of protective sheeting over it, but this did not disguise the fact that the chair was empty.

"Come on," said one of the men, the tallest of them, a big, fair, broad-shouldered man with a long, somber face. The three turned away and walked toward the entrance, which once had been perhaps the noblest part of the building, with its great bronze doors all cast and carved with episodes from the Empire's history. But the doors had sprung out of their sills when the ship came down, and were now off being repaired, leaving nothing but protective sheeting hanging down and crackling noisily in the hot fierce wind that ran down the streets of Ra'tleihfi in this season.

They stepped out into the day, a fair green day under that windy sky, and stood a little to one side at the top of the great flight of steps leading down into the city's central plaza, all surrounded and walled about with the close-packed spires and towers of the capital. A constant stream of workers came and went past them, and also many city people, coming up the steps as far as they were allowed to see the damage done, and going away again, muttering. Tr'Anierh, the tallest of the three, looked at these casual observers coming and going, and said under his breath, "Perhaps we should seal this off."

"Why?" said the second man, the one in the middle; a short roundish man with a broad, cheerful face, bushy eyebrows, and hair beginning, perhaps prematurely, to be streaked with gray. "It's good for them to see what the damned traitress did. And what their taxes are going to have to pay to repair. Anything that brings *that* home to them is worthwhile."

Tr'Anierh looked over at the third of them—a Rihanha of medium height, medium build, medium skin tone, dark hair, a man almost resolutely ordinary-looking even to his customary bland expression—and wondered, as always, what he was thinking. "Well, Urellh?" he said. "Does Ahrm'n have the right of it here?"

Urellh tr'Maehhlie let out a breath as if he grudged it. "It doesn't matter," he said. "It's not the people whose opinion will matter when we bring her back. It's the Senate, and the Praetorate. They're the ones who have to be reminded how she slighted them, denigrated their power, took the oldest symbol of it into her own thieving hands and ran off with it. When we go fetch her back, we must make sure that no distractions from outside keep them from killing her at last. More, though: we must make sure that they do not mistake her capture, and the Sword's return, as all that's necessary to bring this episode to an end."

"There's more to revenge, then," said Ahrm'n tr'Kiell, "than just her . . ."

Tr'Anierh looked back at where the doors should have been, glanced over toward the side-flight of steps leading out and down to the plaza, and moved slowly that way. The other two came with him.

"It's time we faced the realities," tr'Anierh said. "Things have been the same now for too long. We sit trapped here between two powerful enemies . . . one which has been kept from acting against us only by weakness caused by its empire being too far-flung for its forces to hold securely; the other by weakness at its root, a chronic unwillingness to fight unless forced to it by circumstances. And the first, as we now see, is shaking off its inactivity. The other is all too likely to do the same. Time we stopped acting the *hlai* trapped between two *hnoiyikar,* afraid to move one way or another lest one of the predators turn and bite its head off." *And ideally,* tr'Anierh thought, *time we found a way to get them to turn their attention to each other and leave us alone.*

"You sound," said tr'Kiell, "like the Senate yesterday."

"And the day before," said Urellh, "and the day before that, and for many days before. Endless cries of 'Revenge!' and 'Blood or honor'— but no one willing to lead the first ship out, against either side, for fear of being blamed for the bloodshed to follow." His voice had acquired an edge of disgust.

"And would you, then, Urellh?" said tr'Anierh, trying to seem casual. But he turned away a little, not anxious to see Urellh see him holding his breath, or seeming in any way overinterested in the answer. *He has become entirely too sensitive to opposition, for whatever reason. If anything should make him realize how I detest his politics, everything I've been planning could be imperiled. . . .*

There was a long pause. "Aye, indeed I would," said Urellh. "The blow to our reputations, even eventually to our sovereignty, is a massive one. The insult grows harder to bear by the day. And others are watching. Not the Federation." His smile grew suddenly bitter here. "We see now what the Klingons think of a neighboring Empire that cannot stop one ship from coming in through our system defenses and taking the most sacred possession of our people."

"But that was treason. The defenses were taken down from the inside—"

"And what does that matter? The Klingons will say to themselves,

'Where once treachery's rank weed sprang up, it can be sown again.' No matter that it was chopped down once; they will see the ground as being favorable. They have always been willing to use such means if tactics required. And if treason does not work, they will use main force with joy. Any system that can be compromised by so few people, so quickly, has revealed a fatal flaw . . . and has revealed itself as easily broken by any who apply enough brute force to it."

"That flaw has been mended," said tr'Anierh. "Those people are dead now, or fled."

"Happy the dead," Urellh growled, "for they're beyond what will happen to those who fled, once we catch them." He looked over at Ahrm'n tr'Kiell.

Tr'Kiell shrugged. "If you expect news of new arrests, I have none. The Two Worlds are not a small place, and there are endless boltholes and empty places on both worlds where criminals and traitors can go to ground . . . especially on ch'Havran, which has never been as unified in its loyalties as it should have been. And then there are the client worlds . . ." He sighed. "Our intelligence services are doing what they can to find them, day by day. . . . But it's a live traitor's nature to come out and take up his treason again when he thinks it will be safe. And those who helped the cursed t'Rllaillieu take the Sword will find that it will never be safe for them, no matter how long they wait."

"In any case," tr'Anierh said, "the matter is now, as you say, beyond choice. The Klingons have spotted what looks like a weakness at the very heart of our empire. They are already moving to exploit it. And it's when an enemy is moving that he is at his most vulnerable."

"We hardly have the forces to strike at them directly," said tr'Kiell, "with any hope of success."

"Not if we are the only combatant," said Urellh.

The others looked at him. "Communications are always subject to misunderstanding," Urellh said, "and misdirection. Even in peacetime. Most certainly in wartime. And in the time just before a war, communications are more easily lost, misread or misconstrued than at any other time whatever. The Klingons are moving? The sooner, the better, for their movement will give the Federation pause. If word came to the

Federation that the Klingons had struck—say, one of *their* outpost worlds—that news would serve to turn their attention away from us. With the result that we are left free to act—"

"They would not be so foolish as to become involved in a two-front war," tr'Kiell said. "It would be suicidal, even for them."

"They will become involved in whatever we present them with," said Urellh, "as always. They are not a proactive people, the Federation. Indeed, they are not a people at all, but a confused mass of hundreds of bizarre species with hundreds of agendas, all conflicting; they cannot act boldly or straightforwardly, by virtue of their very structure. It is a fact we have been slow to exploit. But now we will make up for some lost time, Elements willing; we will show them what a united people can do . . . and what real boldness looks like. Information, meanwhile, can be twisted into many strange and unusual shapes in transit between worlds. We will see what can be done in this regard in the very near future."

He fell silent, gazing out into the morning as some workers moving slabs of white marble on hovercarries went by. Tr'Anierh was glad of the few moments' respite, for this unusually communicative mood of Urellh's had begun to cause him concern. *What trap does he set for us here?* tr'Anierh wondered. After a few moments, though, he put the thought away. The three of them, by virtue of long careful manipulation of the economic, dynastic, and political assets that chance and ancient House affiliations had cast in front of them, had over the past several years risen to the position of *aierh te'nuhwir,* "first among equals" in the Praetorate. Each of them, by virtue of sheer personal power, now swung behind him a considerable bloc of the votes in both Senate and Praetorate. Each of them knew too many of the others' secrets to be afraid of what the others might do. Tr'Anierh knew his fear, therefore, to be foolish, yet he knew the others had it too . . . and it kept them cautious.

"As for the Klingons," Urellh said after the workers had passed, "they may come to see that the Federation is not invulnerable, either. There are members of their own High Council who would not be averse to sending their fleets in that direction, as much for the sake of changes in their own status quo as for revenge, battle, or booty."

"An interesting concept," said tr'Anierh. "But the main problem remains. The woman, and her cursed renegade confederates aboard our stolen cruiser *Bloodwing* . . . and the Sword."

He looked closely at tr'Kiell. "The Senate is ready to act," tr'Keill said. "If you think I have been acting to delay the matter, you think wrongly."

"But you have a personal connection," said Urellh, "and who could doubt that you would have mixed feelings about the situation?"

"I think the source of my mixed feelings is better dead," tr'Kiell said, "and enough said about that. With luck, the Elements being with us, it will soon be so." He fell silent for a moment, and then added, "And our other assets on *Bloodwing,* it would seem, are still in place; that confirmation was long in coming, and there was some uncertainty, but it came at last. So now we can give our increasingly noisy Senate something to do before it so completely loses its patience or its wits that it starts attempting to press the thorny chaplet of blame onto one of *our* heads." His smile was wintry. "They may safely be turned loose to enact the legislation which we will propose them tomorrow."

"Who did the wording?" Urellh said.

"I did," said tr'Anierh. "It needed some delicacy of shading. But the meaning will be clear enough even for the Senate, and our fellow Praetors will of course ratify it without discussion. The task force to be sent out on this foray will number six ships: more than enough both to handle the business of entering Federation space on a diplomatic mission, and to be able to pursue our own interests even if they attempt to block us. Most particular attention has been paid to the newer aspects of the ships' weaponry." He smiled slightly. This was his own area of expertise. "We will go to them, seemingly with our hands open, and demand the return of a war criminal for trial on her homeworld. If they turn her and the Sword over to us, that will be well. If they merely allow us to pursue her, that also will be well. She cannot long elude pursuit, and we will track her down and bring her and the Sword home—or just the Sword. And if they do *not* assist us by allowing pursuit, or turning her over to us—"

"Then war," tr'Kiell said.

"They will have forced us to it," said Urellh, in a tone meant to simulate regret. "We will have no choice but to do what is necessary to recover our property . . . and our honor. An evil chance, but some good will yet come of it. At best we will push them some ways back from the spaces they occupy on the other side of the Neutral Zone; there are some choice planets there. At worst we will do the Federation great and memorable damage along the border—destroying as many of the monitoring stations along the Zone as we can, and forcing them to spend vast sums restoring and restaffing them and installing new infrastructure."

"Hurting not only them," said tr'Kiell, "but various others who will realize that they have misperceived our weakness."

"Oh yes," said Urellh. "And meanwhile, in the first hours or days of that war, the first-in task force will locate the woman, whether she shelters behind the Federation's kilts or not, and destroy her and the Sword both, if need be. They shall not have her, or it; and she shall not live to keep it in our despite. Better it should be destroyed than fall into alien hands . . . if indeed she is not more than half alien herself already, in heart. Likely enough, bearing in mind who bore her company at Levaeri V."

"And while we resolve the issue that started the war," said tr'Anierh, "the war itself will yield its own rewards. . . ."

"Perhaps more than anyone expects," Urellh said. "Ahrm'n, have you ever had an infestation of *ehlfa?*"

Tr'Kiell blinked. "I have little leisure to notice such things. If *ehlfa* should become a problem around my property, I would have the *hru'hfe* of my house call the exterminator."

"Ah, but if you watched the exterminator, you would see something worth your while. He puts down bait and tempts the creatures to leave their nest. Out they march in their little columns. They find the prize. They tell each other the news with their body chemistry. Wholesale they race to the bait, falling upon it, busying themselves with worrying it into little pieces to take to their home. And while they do so, the exterminator comes to their home, all empty but for the king-*ehlfa* and his courtiers, and burns it. With their home destroyed, their king murdered, nowhere to go, the *ehlfa* are left distraught and witless; they wander away in every direction, and are eaten by predators, and the infestation is shortly merely a memory. . . ."

Urellh smiled. It was not a smile that tr'Anierh would have liked to have turned on him. "You are very bold," he said softly, "to speak of this under the open sky."

"In this company the news is safe," Urellh said. "But no other. After the way Sunseed was betrayed, and the DNA acquisition project with it, some harsh lessons about the need to know have been learned. Not least by me." He got a grim look.

"Can you actually be telling us," said tr'Kiell, "that the package is ready?"

"Nearly," said Urellh.

It was this news that tr'Anierh had hoped against hope to hear . . . even though it also frightened him. "So you are now suggesting," tr'Kiell said, "that we could seriously contemplate its delivery to one of the possible recipients . . ."

"Or the other," Urellh said. "It is a matter of seeing which homeworld would be the most likely to endure such a delivery with most of its assets intact. If the answer is similar in both cases . . . well, let both systems receive such a gift. . . . But for now there is only one package. The single prototype has not been tested, but testing it would reveal its provenance, and alert our enemies to a need to protect against it. So its first test must be its first use."

Tr'Anierh actually shivered, hoping that neither of the others saw. "So many billions of lives . . ." he said. "Even against *them* . . . even if it is only used against the Federation, Urellh, there will be questions among our own people. What do we say to them, afterward, when they come to us and ask us about the billions? . . ."

Urellh gave him a bland look. "A thousand dead," he said, "are a tragedy—a thousand million, merely a statistic. And anyway . . . they are only aliens. What about our people, and *their* welfare? Think of how it could be for the Two Worlds and the client planets, to live in a universe where there was *no* Federation . . . *no* Klingon Empire . . . not anymore. No more striving to keep every *ell* of space or every Elements-forsaken dustbowl of a planet on which some few pitiful scraps of food can be grown. Freedom to be what we are, no longer fenced in, hemmed in, oppressed. Freedom to grow, to extend our boundaries and our culture right through the galaxy, taking what is ours to take . . ."

"Freedom," tr'Kiell said softly. "It is a noble dream."

"Freedom," said tr'Anierh, and for the moment said nothing else.

"What time does the Senate meet tomorrow?" said tr'Kiell.

"Eighth hour," said Urellh. "I will stand and propose the diplomatic mission at the ninth hour. All the important personnel are selected; all that remains is to have the Senate come to believe it has selected them, and then approve the assignment of ships in the usual way. They can be on their way by the threeday's end."

"Until tomorrow morning, then," said tr'Kiell, and saluted them both, and went on his way down the steps.

They watched him go, making his way down across the plaza and into the street leading to emn'Thaiven, the wide pale-paved Avenue of Processions. "There," said Urellh, "we shall lead the traitress to her death in chains, in not too long a time. And afterward we shall set about putting things right; mending the world, the Worlds, to be as they should have been long ago."

Tr'Anierh nodded, still saying nothing for the moment. The thought was in his mind: *What in the names of Fire and Air has come to this man, that he speaks so openly? As if he had nothing whatever to fear from anyone?*

He glanced over to find Urellh looking at him: a casual look on the surface, but there was no missing the assessment in it. "I must go," Urellh said then. "Honor to the Empire, confederate."

"Honor," said tr'Anierh to Urellh's back, as he swung away and went down the steps in tr'Kiell's wake. Discreetly, from off to one side, Urellh's personal secretary came down along the steps to meet his master and began to speak to him, head down, as they went.

Eveh tr'Anierh watched them out of sight. He was filled with fear, but he dared not show it. *We are all riding the* daishelt *together now,* he thought. *No choice but to hang on tight to the horns, lest we slip back to where the claws can rend us. . . .*

He turned at last and went back up into the shattered building, to meet his own secretary and arrange matters surrounding the speech in the Senate tomorrow. There were some other messages to be sent now, as well. Eveh started composing the first one as he passed through the clear sheets that hung where the bronze doors should have; and in that hot wind that ran down the streets between the tall graceful buildings of the presidium, the sheets whispered together, saying *aish,* again and again, *aish:* the word for war. . . .

James T. Kirk finished rereading the report that had been appended to his most recent orders on the viewer in his quarters, and let out a long breath. For the better part of a month and a half now, he had been wondering, as he occasionally had before: *Where is* Bloodwing? . . . Now he thought he understood why she had made herself more than usually scarce. *But that's about to change.*

"It's happening," Jim said, "at last."

He looked up from the viewer in his quarters at McCoy and Spock. Spock was wearing that look of complete calm that only a Vulcan could assume; but Jim knew what was underneath it . . . or at least he had strong suspicions. McCoy was frowning, but then he had been frowning a lot since he came home from his last leave, a "vacation trip" that had wound up taking him a good deal further away from home than many people would have initially expected.

"The orders," Spock said, "are, on the surface, routine."

"As if any orders containing the words 'Romulan Neutral Zone' are routine," McCoy said. "Now or ever, but especially now."

"But the orders contain no such phrasing, Doctor," Spock said. "They refer only to the space around 15 Trianguli . . ."

"You know as well as I do, Mr. Spock, that any space in the direction of Triangulum and further away from Earth than about fifteen hundred light-years is hotter than the insides of a warp containment vessel," McCoy said, "and about as safe, at the moment. 15 Tri is plenty close enough to the Zone to provoke interest in some quarters."

"Those 'quarters' being the Senate and the Praetorate," Jim said, leaning back in his chair. "Who it seems, after the events of the last month and a half, are ready to start some serious shin-kicking."

He looked over at Spock with some concern. "The moment we start moving at all directly toward that space," he said, "word will get to the Romulans, either via moles in Starfleet or other intelligence sources here and there. And our movement will be taken as an excuse to start things rolling."

"Your analysis is likely to be correct, Captain," said Spock. "But the orders seem clear."

"Everything about them is clear except the time frame," Jim said. "They haven't come right out and told me 'Head in that direction but take your time about it,' but that's what the instruction factors down to. So I'll take the time." He thought for a moment. "Scotty has been complaining about some adjustments he wants to make to the warp engines' matter-antimatter annihilation ratios: I intend to proceed at a leisurely enough pace to let him do that. At the same time, I know why they're sending us to the neighborhood of 15 Tri. We are intended to meet a ship, quietly, out in the system's fringes, to discuss a few things with its commander."

"And while we're doing that," McCoy said, "I have this feeling a few other ships may drop by to chat about this and that. All very informally, of course."

"Of course," Jim said. "But the Triangulum area being as lively as you say, Bones, I think we may dodge over in the direction of alpha Arietis first . . . bearing in mind that we also still have a technological problem that we haven't yet figured out what to do with."

"Sunseed," Spock said, somber.

"The trouble with technology," McCoy muttered, "is that you can't stick it back in the damn bottle once it gets out."

"Any technology that allows a ship on the fly to create ion storms on demand," Jim said, "is too damn nasty to let out into the world. But here we are, stuck sitting on the thing. The Romulans would have used it as a weapon—*did* use it—which was bad enough. We took it from them lock, stock, and barrel, which was something of an accomplishment . . . but since we're certainly not going to use it, we need to find a way to make it unusable before it leaks out somehow . . . which it is eventually bound to, no matter how closely Fleet tries to guard it." He folded his arms. "Scotty has a few ideas on the subject, but he says he could use some assistance at the theoretical end. So we'll go get him some." Jim looked at Spock. "Estimate of total time?"

"Four days and fourteen hours to alpha Arietis at warp six," Spock said, "from our present position. Then five days, twenty hours at the same speed to the neighborhood of 15 Trianguli."

Jim nodded. "See to it, Mr. Spock."

"Captain," Spock said, and went out. The door shut behind him.

McCoy paused. "There was," McCoy said, "something else."

Jim put his eyebrows up, trying to look surprised. "There was?"

"Jim," McCoy said, "this is no time to start trying to play the wide-eyed innocent with me. You should have started years ago, or not bothered at all. Now, I'm not going to ask for details about the sealed portion of these orders . . ."

Jim's mouth quirked into half a smile.

"But I wouldn't mind knowing," McCoy said, "whether I should start actively preparing myself to meet my Maker. Again."

"I'd have thought that after your little holiday on ch'Rihan," Jim said, "you'd be all caught up in that regard."

McCoy gave him a dry look. "And whether our own side is as likely to wind up shooting at us as the other one. Or other *ones*."

There it was: the same concern that had been riding Jim for the past few hours, while he digested the content of the orders he'd received— both the parts that he could disclose to his crew, and the parts that he could not—and started to game out the way he thought things might go in the next month or so. "Bones," he said, "believe me, I'm going to be doing my best to keep matters straightforward. One side shooting at us at once is more than enough for me. But things can change fast sometimes . . . so you'd better fasten down anything that's loose in sickbay. And keep a chair ready for me when I need to come to talk."

"I'll take care of it," McCoy said, and went out.

The door hissed shut behind him. Jim sat down behind his desk again and leaned back in the chair once more. He held that position for a good while, his eyes resting on nothing in particular. Then he reached out to the computer console on his desk. "Computer."

*"Working."*

"Record a message and seal under my voiceprint."

*"Recording."*

"Latest communication received here confirms our last joint discussion on strategy. Meet us as previously arranged." He thought of signing it "Jim," but encryption was such a fragile and ephemeral art these days; the security of the message could not be absolutely guaranteed, and there was too much to lose should it be broken. Besides, he could just hear the laughter at the other end when the receiving party heard the signature.

"Code and send," Jim said.

*"Working. Sent."*

He hit the comm button again. "Bridge. Lieutenant Commander Uhura."

*"Uhura here, Captain."*

"I just routed a message to your system. What's the subspace transit time?"

There was a moment's silence. *"Judging from the relay address in that message's 'capsule,' I'd say fifteen hours."*

"Thank you, Commander. Mr. Sulu?"

*"Yes, Captain?"*

"Lay in a course to alpha Arietis, warp five, and execute immediately."

*"Aye, sir."*

"And Mr. Sulu—do you have a 'tank' session scheduled in recreation this evening?"

Sulu chuckled, very low. *"Yes, Captain. We're finishing up a round of tournament play."*

"Maybe I'll stop by," Jim said. "Kirk out."

He switched his viewer to show the bridge screen's view as *Enterprise* made her change of course, a big wide swing to the galactic "southward," and added a warp factor or two, the blue-shifted stars pouring past her like so many burning arrows in the night.

*I'd hoped I was wrong when I saw this coming,* he thought. *But I was right. I just hope the trend holds. Otherwise . . .*

He killed the external image and went back to studying his orders . . . looking for the loophole that would let them all survive.

# Chapter Two

They came out of warp a scant light-week from Orundwiir, or alpha Arietis as the Federation stellar cartographers called it; a great blaze of a star, even at this distance, burning dazzlingly orange-golden in the long cold night. *Bloodwing* went sublight with all her weapons hot and her sensors stretched out to their utmost . . . and found no one there waiting for them.

Khiy looked up from his post at the steersman's console. "Should we decloak, *llhei?*"

"No, not yet," Ael said softly. "Let us wait our time."

Her people kept their eyes on their instruments, saying nothing for the moment, and Ael watched the screen, sitting in her hard straight command chair, and said nothing.

"They're late," said t'Hrienteh, in slight amusement.

Ael looked over her shoulder at the ship's chief surgeon, who had been doing part-time duty on scan and comm for some time now while training the ship's last remaining junior officer in the position. "Possibly our time-ticks are out of synchronization," Ael said. "It would not surprise me; the computers have been through so much tinkering recently, and tr'Keirianh has not had time or leisure to look over all our shoulders and supervise as he would like to . . ."

"You mean constantly," t'Hrienteh said. "Fortunately, the master engineer must sleep sometimes." Her tone was wry. "But I very much doubt anything is really wrong with the computers, *khre'Riov.*"

In reality Ael agreed with her. What she would not voice was her concern, even after so much evidence to the contrary, that something might yet go wrong with her dealings with the Federation, now that matters were becoming genuinely crucial.

Ael stretched herself a little in the command chair, gazing at the screen and admiring the giant midsequence star centered in it. Even away out here the brazen-golden fire of it was extraordinary, like Eisn but easily thirty times the hearthstar's size. No one else was paying the great burning monster much mind, though. She glanced around her at the familiar faces, all bent to their work at the moment. There were different familiar faces on her bridge than had previously been here, for *Bloodwing* had lost about a third of her crew component during the operation at Levaeri V, either in battle on the station itself or on *Enterprise* owing to her son's final treachery, and it would now be impossible to recruit replacements. *And will it indeed ever be possible?* Ael thought. For there would always be the chance that any new crew picked up in passing would actually be an agent in the service of the intelligence agencies based on ch'Rihan, intent on *Bloodwing*'s destruction, perhaps even to the point of suicide. *No,* she thought, *for the time being we must just scrape along as best we can. . . .*

"Incoming vessel," t'Hrienteh said, and Ael glanced up. "Just dropped out of warp; subluminal now and decelerating fast."

"On screen—"

The view changed, losing that burning core. Instead, a faint golden spark reflecting Orundwiir's fierce orange light came coasting in toward them, the glow growing swiftly brighter as she came. Ael sat there and mused briefly over the numerous conflicting feelings that accompanied the sight of *Enterprise,* all gilt with the system primary's fire, approaching with her screens down, graceful, massive and—in these spaces— massively unconcerned. *How many times over all the years before Levaeri V did I wish much to see this sight,* she thought, *and to be lying nearby, cloaked, with weapons ready. And now the wish comes true. But how circumstances change with time, and how little satisfaction our wishes bring us once fulfilled! Yet another of the Elements' small jokes with us . . . and if we are wise, we laugh.*

"She is hailing us," Aidoann said.

Ael smiled slightly. It would not matter to Kirk that his ship's sensors showed nothing here while *Bloodwing* was cloaked. *He knows,* she thought. "Decloak and answer the hail," she said. "Barely two *stei* late, t'Hrienteh: I think you may forgive him that."

"Bloodwing, *this is* Enterprise," said a familiar female voice. *"Welcome to Hamal . . ."*

"T'Rllaillieu here," Ael said. "Thank you kindly, Lieutenant Commander Uhura."

*"You're a shade early, Commander-General,"* said another familiar voice.

"Or you are late, Captain," she said, amused. "We have been discussing which might be the case. We really must see to it that our computers are better synchronized."

*"Mr. Spock and Aidoann can sort that out between them, I'm sure,"* Kirk said. *"Meanwhile, would you care to beam aboard? We have a lot to discuss . . . and when the first discussions are done, there are some people over here who want to greet you."*

She watched *Enterprise* dump the last of her velocity and slip up alongside *Bloodwing* with easy precision, a very neighborly kilometer away. "I will be with you in a matter of some minutes, Captain," Ael said. "I have a thing or two to make secure here first."

She waved at t'Hrienteh to kill the communication, then stood up and stretched. "Your orders, *khre'Riov?*" Aidoann said.

"There's nothing needs done," Ael said. "Stand easy. But when did I ever obey any such request immediately, as if I had nothing better to do? Always wisest to leave even one's close associates a little uncertainty; a little room to wonder what one is up to. That way, if one day you must suddenly change your course, or your mind, without warning, you will have left yourself room to maneuver." She smiled.

"Even Captain Kiurrk?" Aidoann said, with a small smile of her own.

"Even the captain," Ael said, "may someday need to change his mind . . . or may have it changed for him. For that day, which may never come or which may be hard upon us, we must yet remain prepared. Khiy, the center seat is yours. Mind you match their movements exactly. Their helmsman is watching you, and you know Mr. Sulu's sharp eye—you must do us proud. Come along, Aidoann, t'Hrienteh; we have a meeting. . . ."

Jim stood there in the transporter room in front of the console, which Scotty was presently manning. His hands were sweating.

*Ridiculous,* he thought. But at the same time, there were few guests aboard *Enterprise* about whom he had had more thoroughly mixed feelings than the one who was coming back aboard now. Here was a woman who had sat in his center seat, and had somehow managed to look like she belonged there; a woman who had not only thrown him in his own brig—*well, yes, it wasn't as if I didn't cooperate*—but had decked him out as well—*all right, I returned the favor almost immediately, but still*—

He caught himself, and smiled. "Worthy opponent" was the very least of the descriptions he might apply to Ael i-Mhiessan t'Rllaillieu; and there were others, more appropriate still, but he would not spend too much time thinking about them now. They would only make his hands sweat more.

He wiped them off against his pants and breathed out in brief annoyance. "Something holding them up over there?" he said.

Scotty shook his head. As he did, the door opened and Spock came in, closely followed by McCoy. It was just shutting when the communicator whistled. *"Captain,"* said Uhura's voice out of the air, *"we have an incoming shuttle."*

Jim leaned over the transporter console and punched the comm button. "From the starbase?" he said. Starbase 18 circled Hamal's furious amber fire a couple of hundred million kilometers out.

*"From the base, yes, but not Fleet registry,"* said Uhura. *"ID shows the shuttle as registered off Hamal III."*

"Aha," Jim said. "Very good. Clear the shuttle through into the bay. We'll be down to meet the passenger shortly."

*"Yes, Captain. Bridge out."*

The faint hum of the transporter came up. "Coming through now, sir," Scotty said.

Three faint pillars of sparkle began to form on the transporter platform; the light swirled, went solid, and the bodies it formed were held in a fractional second's immobility as they finished becoming real.

She was looking right at him, and Jim thought, almost with annoyance, *How does she do that . . . ?!* A little woman, slight, dark, slender, in the faintly red-glittering tunic of a Romulan officer, the sash across it glowing a subdued gold in the transporter room's low lighting; dark breeches and boots below, and above, long dark hair braided tight and coiled at the back of her head. She might have seemed unexceptional enough, except for those eyes—which even in this frozen moment held in them what seemed an uncomfortably assessing, knowing, look—and her carriage, even now like that something held proud and ready for a fight; a banner, a sword . . .

The shimmer of sound and light died away completely. "Commander," Jim said.

She glanced around her for a second, taking in her surroundings, and half glanced off to one side of her: then looked forward again. Jim swallowed. Big blond Aidoann t'Khialmnae, Ael's new second-in-command, was on the pad to Ael's right, as Jim had expected, and Surgeon t'Hrienteh, whom he remembered from the way he had kept finding her in McCoy's company when they were preparing the attack on Levaeri V, was on the transporter pad behind her. But Ael's brief glance had been toward someone who was not there, and Jim thought of how he had first seen her son Tafv beside her, much taller than his mother, but as erect and proud. He would not now ever stand beside her again, of course; but it was poignant that Ael still carried herself, somehow, as if there were someone standing to her left, in his accustomed place. *If I have my own ghosts,* Jim thought, *so does she. . . .*

She came down from the transporter and reached out to take his hand.

He took it, not to bow over it, having learned that the gesture, polite enough for an honored lady on Earth, was charged with meaning for a Rihannsu which he didn't desire to invoke. He simply clasped it a little above the wrist, and she returned his grip and met his eyes forthrightly. The expression, as always, had an element of challenge to it, and more calm than Jim thought he would have felt under the circumstances.

She let him go. "Well met," she said, "so far into your own spaces, and after such a time."

"You're very welcome," Jim said, "in whatever time, and whatever space."

That elicited a shadow of a smile. "Commander," Spock said, stepping forward.

Did that assured expression become just slightly haunted as she looked at him? Hard to say; the look was concealed by the slight bow of her head to him, which Spock returned. "Mr. Spock," she said, "well met indeed." Then she straightened. "And Mr. Scott: do you do well?"

"As well as possible under the circumstances, Commander," Scotty said. Jim tried to keep his grin from getting out of hand. Scotty had been sympathetic enough to Ael, but her involvement with *Enterprise* had caused the ship considerable structural damage, some of it actually planned rather than as an accident in battle, and Jim suspected Scotty was already having misgivings about what kind of trouble her presence was likely to bring this time.

"As do we all . . ." she said, possibly thinking along the same lines Jim was. She turned, then, and said, "Well, McCoy, and what of you?"

He simply smiled half a smile and reached out to squeeze her hand. "It can wait."

A few more moments were spent greeting t'Hrienteh and Aidoann; but finally Jim said, "The doctor's right, Commander. We shouldn't linger here. Someone else is arriving whom you should meet."

They all headed for the doors. "Someone from Starfleet?" Ael said.

"Occasionally," Jim said. "I believe her commission may have been reactivated for the time being; officially she's retired."

Ael raised her eyebrows. "I am sorry to trouble an elder's peace."

McCoy made an amused face. "Nothing much troubles her," he said, "and, besides, this 'elder' is somewhere between one and three years old, depending on whose years you're using."

"Doctor," Spock said, "in Hamalki reckoning, it is considered an error of reckoning to separate out new 'incarnations' from the total life span—"

Ael looked over at Jim in some bemusement as they all got into the turbolift. "Doubtless this will be made clear to me shortly."

"As clear as it gets," Jim said.

There was some small talk in the lift, inquiries about Ael's crew and *Bloodwing*'s whereabouts over the past month or so.

Then the doors opened and they all stepped out. Jim was amused to see Ael's eyes widen a little at what they met first: a rugged rounded glittering shape nearly two meters tall and three meters broad, patched in what looked like rough amethyst, tourmaline, and ruby, with dark fringes all around that sparkled in the bright hangar bay lights as it moved.

Ael strode right up to that domed figure and stood there a moment with her arms akimbo, looking him up and down. "Mr. Naraht," she said, astounded, "what in Earth's name have you been doing to yourself to *grow* so great?"

The rough scraping sound that emerged was plainly a compromise intended for those who used airborne sound in its higher frequencies; but it was also plainly laughter. "Commander," said the Horta through his own translator, "just eating. But I'm told that's enough."

"We were a little surprised too, at first," Jim said, "but it turned out we'd been laboring under a misconception about sizes. The only full-grown Horta we had seen was the lieutenant's mother . . . and after many, many years standing guard duty over her eggs, she'd worn off a lot of her bulk."

"During the pre-hatching period," said McCoy, "it turns out the momma Horta doesn't have much of an appetite, and doesn't eat much. I suspect as much because she's a natural-born worrier as because of the basic biological setup of the species. But the youngsters have started coming up to the full 'normal' size for the species real quick, once they've passed latency."

"That is a relief," Ael said. "I would not have liked to think I had caused you to become obese by all that hyponeutronium I suggested you eat at Levaeri V . . ."

Naraht's fringes rippled. "It was a little uncomfortable for a while, madam," he said, "but I burned off the excess soon enough."

"Might have brought his growth spurt on a little sooner," said McCoy, "but that's all." He patted the lieutenant's outer "mantle" idly. "You want to slow down soon, though, son, or we'll have to keep you permanently in the hangar bay, and all you'll be good for is being dropped on people we don't like."

"I should say he has done well enough at that . . ." Ael said, with a wry smile.

"More than well enough," Kirk said. "Well, carry on, Lieutenant."

"Yes, sir. A pleasure to see you again, Commander," Naraht said, and rumbled away out of the hangar bay, filling the corridor outside nearly from wall to wall as he went.

They walked out into the hangar bay, where the ship that had just landed was cycling back into launch position on the turntable. It was of unusual design, an oblong four-meter-thick spindle of glassy ropes and angular shapes woven and melded into one another, some straight and edged, some smooth and curved, some even radiating into what looked like a brush of spines at what might have been the propulsion end. Even here under the artificial lights the "glass" seemed to keep something of the color of Hamal's sunlight, a gleam of dark gold under the glitter and sheen of the brilliantly polished surfaces.

The turntable stopped. As they watched, the whole smooth side of the craft facing them seemed to lose that smoothness, going matte, then revealing a fibrous structure like something woven or spun, then finally refining itself away to a delicate-looking webwork of threads that vanished away entirely, leaving what looked like a cocoon cut in half, all sheened inside with webs and points of light.

Down out of the cocoon stepped a glass spider—if spiders had twelve legs, each a meter long, arranged evenly around a rounded central body, the top of that body furred with spines of clear glass almost too fine to see, and a raised ridge of nubbly crystal running back to front amid the "fur," with four eyes in the middle of the ridge and two clusters of four eyes each, near each end of the ridge. With every movement of the much-articulated legs came a delicate chiming, and as the entity came walking, nearly waltzing, over to them, more chimes filled the air—a brisk staccato of glass bells, running up and down the scale, and saying, "What a pleasure to see you all; it's been too long—you're very welcome to Hamal!"

Jim stole a glance at Ael. She had shown surprise at the sight of Lieutenant Naraht before, but him she knew. In this case, she was managing herself more carefully—but Jim had seen this calm expression on Ael before, too, and knew what it concealed. "Commander," he said, "allow me to present K's't'lk. She's one of the senior Hamalki physicist-engineers associated with Starbase 18. K's't'lk, this is Commander-General Ael i-Mhiessan t'Rllaillieu."

K's't'lk reached up one delicate limb and laid it in Ael's outstretched hand. "My great pleasure, Commander," K's't'lk said. "I've heard of your doings; and I hope to be of some service to you shortly." She cocked an eye up at Jim. "I hope you don't mind my bringing my own ship along, J'm."

"Seeing that we weren't going to be coming within transporter range of 18," Jim said, "what was I going to make you do? Walk?"

She chimed unconcerned laughter at him, and Jim turned back to Ael. "K's't'lk and the *Enterprise* have had some history together," he said.

"Not so much history," K's't'lk said to Ael, "but a fair amount of mathematics. Though often enough, the two have come to nearly the same thing. . . ."

"When she's not rewriting the local laws of physics," Jim said, "she also does research in various arcas of astrophysics . . . and one area which has been of particular interest to her has been the study and manipulation of stellar atmospheres."

"I see," Ael said. "That may indeed be of use to us all soon . . ."

"But what we need more first," Jim said, "is news. Let's take a break to get everyone settled . . . then we'll meet in the main briefing room and get caught up."

Hvirr tr'Asenth had thought he had known what cold was, before. Now he knew he was wrong.

Emni, behind him, was crying silently as they slowly walked. He would have dropped back to put his arm about her again as they walked, but twice now she had pushed him away, if gently enough, the second time whispering, "You already have Dis to carry: I can manage." And indeed she was carrying more than he was, at the moment, the few belongings the soldiers had let them take. But he knew the real reason that she would not bear his comfort. She was ashamed to need it. Hvirr could not see why: anyone would need it, in a situation like this. But there was no telling Emni that. She came of proud people, and was harsher to herself than anyone needed to be, especially now, when she felt she should be acting as Mother-of-House in their time of trouble, and a tower of strength. It was bitter to her that shock had derailed her strength, that she had gone along with all the others when the soldiers told her to, just like one more victim. *Maybe,* Hvirr thought unhappily, *it's just as well that she should find her pride a piece of baggage too heavy to take with her on this trip. Precious little any of us are likely to have left of it, by the end. . . .*

The snow lay all around them, in drifts and hillocks blown among the tall narrow *maithe* trees, faintly reflecting what light of the stars in the hard black sky managed to make its way down through the forest's boughs. But the starlight was too little to make the going at all easy, and the moons were both dark tonight. For a mercy, the wind had died down, and the snow here was not crusted, but light enough to kick aside as one walked. But otherwise life, if this could be called any kind of life, went on for Hvirr and Emni and their fifty companions as it had for the last two days and a night: the endless marching through bitter weather, without a rest. Ahead of them went the faint light borne by the man who had volunteered to lead them, the one who knew the way over the pass. *And how sure are we of that?* Hvirr thought, desperate, trying to swallow, finding nothing to do it with: his mouth was dry as any desert. *What if he gets us lost? We will all die out here.*

*Though I suppose it is preferable to being shot.* It was supposedly a merciful death, the death by cold: weariness, then sleep, a sleep from which there was no waking—

Hvirr grimaced in anger, shook his head. Ice crystals cracked and fell away from his coat hood and neckwrap at the gesture. Hvirr gazed down sadly at the wrapped-up bundle he held, and hoped that the wrapping was enough. Dis was only two, and had always been somewhat delicate of health. Still, he was sleeping; that was better far than him being awake in this frightening dark place, so unlike the sunny little house in the valley, where they had lived until three days ago.

The house. Odd how clear everything about it seemed now, in memory: the particular hiss the front door had when it opened, the sun across the flagstones in the front hallway, the warm clear light in the kitchen when the hearthfire was going and Emni lit the table lamp to do her late work on the family finances on her small computer. *Who has our house now?* Hvirr thought, no longer having the energy to even be bitter about it, only resigned.

Emni came trudging up beside Hvirr, then, her faced wiped as if she had not been crying. But he could see the telltale darkness in her cheeks, the chapping already starting from the cold. It was why Hvirr had stopped letting himself cry many hours ago, though desperately he wanted to. He had miseries enough already without adding chilblains to the list. "How is he?"

"Asleep, I think. Oh, I wish I were too."

He nodded, swallowing, finding it hard, with his throat so dry. "Don't think about it," Hvirr said, "it just makes it worse."

"I am so angry," Emni said, though the weary, dreamy tone of her voice made it seem a strange declaration. "And all our neighbors standing there, letting it happen. After all the years we've been there. Could none of them have said a word?"

"It's hard to find your voice sometimes," Hvirr said, "when the ones you'd try to convince are holding guns, and you have none." The memory of that first gun, on his own doorstep, was burned into his memory as if lightning had etched it there. A great misshapen ugly thing, eloquent of imminent death, with an emitter bell that seemed big enough to put his head into—it seemed to float there by itself, until Hvirr comprehended, in the clear bright light of the morning, that it had a man attached to it, that the man was wearing dark-green military armor, and that he was pointing the gun at Hvirr and saying, "You have ten minutes to get your stuff and get out." At first it had seemed like a joke, then like a misunderstanding.

"Get out? Why, what's the matter?"

"Get out," the man said, bored. "Relocation order. All the people on this list—" He flashed a padd at Hvirr, not even letting him look at it. "You're to be out of the town in an hour. Twenty *stai* away by noon tomorrow."

"But where will we go?"

The soldier had already turned his back on Hvirr, not leaving, but just dismissing Hvirr as something he didn't have to deal with anymore. Then Hvirr realized that what he and Emni had seen on the news was happening to others, on this continent of Mendaissa—the forced relocations that had seemed so unnecessary, so sad, so distant— were distant no longer. It was happening here, happening to them.

They had gathered together everything they could: some food, some spare clothes, their credit chips, Emni's little computer and the charger for it. One of the others who had been turned out, a distant neighbor whom they knew by sight, having seen him at market sometimes in the next town over, came to the little confused knot of them, maybe twenty people from six houses in Steilalvh village, "I know the way over the pass to Memmesh. Nothing's happening over there, it's safe. Come with me and we'll all get out of here together. Have you got warm clothes? Then hurry, come on—"

That was when this unreal walk had begun. Morning, through afternoon, through night, through the next morning, the next afternoon, and night again . . . It was twenty minutes in the co-op flyer, this journey to Memmesh town, over the pass. Never in Hvirr's wildest imaginings had it occurred to him that he might ever walk it. The pass was two *stai* up in the clouds, for Fire's sake! But now they had come over it, gasping for air—and filled with terror, for Dis had turned dark green as he slept—and all of them had survived, the child getting his proper color back quickly. That had been this morning. Under cover of the trees, though they had been walking for a day already, they kept going, hearing the constant scream of iondrivers and impulse engines overhead—the sky suddenly alive with cruisers and government shuttles. This too they had heard about in the news: that the space around the Mendaissa and Ysail star systems was being fortified against possible Klingon invasion, that the government would protect its people—that to help it protect them, certain unreliable elements of the population were being removed from security-sensitive areas—

*That was us, of course,* Hvirr thought. *And everyone else in this part of the country who has Ship-Clan connections.* "It's the big spaceport at Davast," he had heard one of the people farther up the line mutter to someone else, her brother, Hvirr thought. "They're worried about security, there have been attacks on some other planets . . ." Her voice dropped to a whisper. Even among themselves, those who had been driven out of the valley didn't want to be caught talking about it. Even here, who knew, there might be spies. . . .

But they were on the downhill side now. It was, their guide had come back to tell them, earlier in this second darkness, only a few more hours. The path had been getting easier, even if the snow was no less deep. "I only wish I knew where we were going."

"Memmesh, dear one."

"I don't mean that. I mean afterwards. We can't stay there, they won't have room for all of us . . ." She looked at Dis, in Hvirr's arms. "He's been sleeping so much," Emni said. "I hope he's not sick." She paused.

"But then I suppose we should count ourselves lucky," she continued. "Other people had their money taken from them too, the soldiers charged them to let them get out of villages they'd been commanded to leave on pain of being shot." The bitterness briefly showed its edge in her voice again, then sheathed itself once more in weariness. "At least we've still got a little . . ."

Hvirr did not say that he wasn't sure it was going to do them any good. Anyone who had both Ship-Clan blood and a scrap of sense would try to get off the planet now. But there was no one who could take them, legally, and those who would do it illegally would charge the sun and both moons for passage.

"This is all my fault," Emni said. "Because I am Ship-Clan."

"Don't be a silly *hlai*," said Hvirr. "As if you could choose your heredity!"

He looked up, then, for ahead of them was a rustling, a shuffling. He could see the people up ahead bunching together, hear a kind of confused murmur from them. The path through the woods flattened out, there, opened up: he could see the green-blue of sky past and through the trees.

Hvirr scuffed through the snow toward them, craned his neck to see what they were looking at. Behind him Emni came up and looked too.

Down there was Memmesh village. Landed around its scatter of houses, in the thin snow sifted over its surrounding pastures, were five or six government armored shuttles, shining their hot bright spotlights around in the dark. Another shuttle came screaming right over their heads as they stood there, heading down toward the village. Down there, tiny specks of men were standing around some of the houses, gesturing with tiny, tiny guns, and men and women and children were being driven out into the cold dark night.

All their group stood there silent. Hvirr heard someone say softly, "Where will we go now?"

And Dis woke up and began to cry.

It was not a meeting of all the ship's department heads. Jim would call for that later, when the circumstances into which they were moving were clearer to him. *And when they've become clearer to Starfleet,* he thought, hoping desperately that that hour would come soon. For the moment, all that was needed was a consultation among allies. That was likely to become thorny enough.

Ael seated herself down at one end of the table in the briefing room with her officers to either side of her; Jim took the other end of the table with Scotty and McCoy, and Spock in the angle of the table at his usual spot handy to the computer. K's't'lk stood, that being more comfortable for her than any of the seating presently in the room. "T'l," Jim said as they all got settled, "I've sent for a proper rack for you: it'll be here later."

She laughed, a brief arpeggio of bell music. "It's no issue, J'm."

Everyone finished settling themselves, and Spock finished setting up the computer to minute the meeting. "Commander?" Jim said.

She bowed to him a little from the other end of the table. "Captain, before you spell out the details of why you have sent for me—not that I do not believe I already know—I would like to ask for your assistance. Or more specifically, Mr. Spock's."

"Anything, Ael."

She produced one of those wicked smiles which had once or twice before made Jim sorry to have offered her carte blanche. But it didn't last: he was being teased. "Mr. Spock," Ael said, "I would welcome some assistance with an assessment and reorganization of *Bloodwing*'s computer systems. We are shorthanded after Levaeri V, and have been forced to automate many more of our systems than we would normally prefer. Also, both the programming and hardware we have been forced to install for this purpose are very much of the improvised sort. If you would be able to assist us, I would be in your debt."

"Commander, it would be my pleasure," Spock said.

"Thank you, sir. Tr'Keirianh, my chief engineer, will confer with you." Ael looked back down at the table at Jim. "In the meantime, Captain . . . perhaps you will tell us what *you* know of the news I have heard."

Jim nodded and glanced around the table at the others. "The Federation has received a communication from the Senate," he said. "This came as something of a surprise . . . or rather, it was allowed to seem as if it came as something of a surprise. In any case, the Senate has asked permission to send a diplomatic mission across the Zone into the space in the Triangulum area: six ships. The Senate's message said they had something to discuss with the Federation that was too important to trust to the third-party means of official communication, which are all that have been used officially for the years since the First Romulan War and the treaty that ended it. They were no more forthcoming than that, at first . . . but in the unofficial communications associated with the official one, there were some hints."

"It is, of course, me they want," Ael said. "I wonder, though, whether I should be insulted."

McCoy gave her a look. "Insulted? Why?"

"Only six ships, Doctor? They value me too lightly."

"It might begin with six ships, Commander," Spock said, "but it most certainly would not stop there."

"No," she said, "I know that, Mr. Spock. Forgive my jesting."

"Mr. Spock is right," Jim said. "Where it will all stop is very much the question. Fleet has been treating the matter—not casually, of course; no feeler from such a formerly unresponsive source would ever be treated casually. But without any overt show of alarm."

"Nevertheless," Ael said, "I would imagine forces in the Federation quietly converging on Triangulum space and this side of the arm."

"Not just Federation forces are moving," Jim said. "Your people are shifting ships around as well . . . even with our limited sources, and the only other source of hard information being the monitoring stations scattered up and down the Neutral Zone, we can tell that much. The Klingons are moving, too."

Ael nodded. "That I too had heard. I have become an excuse, then, for more than just my own people."

"I would say, though," Spock said, "an excuse that has long been sought. Am I correct?"

Ael's smile acquired a bitter edge. "It has been sought since well before *Enterprise* and *Bloodwing* visited Levaeri V together. The Rihannsu have been feeling confined and harassed for a long time . . . and now, with the Sunseed routines stolen and the mind-control project destroyed after nearly fifteen years of work, both panic and fury are running high, for once more the Praetorate and Senate feel their old enemies putting on the pressure. They will feel they must do something to defuse it. But they will not be satisfied with merely defusing it at home. Their least goal will be to take me back. But a better one will be to set you and the Klingons at one another's throats, while destabilizing the Neutral Zone as much as possible."

Ael looked very calm, but Jim knew quite well what turmoil her mind must be in. "Leading up to that goal, and after it . . ." Ael said. "There are many ways this business may go. But first I must ask you, Captain—"

"What Starfleet's intentions are toward you?"

Ael's regard was steady. Jim hoped his was too. "They haven't yet confided that information in me. I think they may not be sure yet which way to jump. I imagine we'll know within a few days. Meanwhile, *Enterprise* is one of the ships detailed to meet the diplomatic mission, most likely because Starfleet considers it to be a name that the Senate and Praetorate respect . . . and because they assume that where we are, you will feel secure in being also."

"When we eventually arrive at the scene," Ael said, "yes; for I doubt Starfleet will want me sitting under their noses while the negotiations are ongoing. My people might be tempted to some improvident action." She gave Jim a mischievous look. "Meanwhile, I must tell you that whatever Fleet decides, I have no intention of allowing the diplomatic mission to take *Bloodwing* back with them."

"It might not be *Bloodwing* per se that they're after," McCoy said.

Ael favored him with a small dry smile. "At the end of bargaining, Doctor, perhaps not," she said. "But the bargaining will certainly begin with nothing less. They will tell you they must have their property back, and the traitor crew that took it, and the woman who led them to do so, and the Sword she took with her when she left ch'Rihan last. As circumstances shift, they will allow one or another of the counters to be knocked off the table. Probably the ship first: then her crew. But they will by no means agree to settle for less than me and the Sword. And at the last, they will throw both of us away—kill me and destroy the Sword—rather than allow either of us to remain in your space or to escape their vengeance."

Spock had folded his hands together and steepled the fingers, and was looking at them in a contemplative way. Now he glanced up and said, "Commander, you have said what you will not allow to be done with *Bloodwing* and her crew. But you say nothing of what you have planned for the other two 'counters' on the table."

Her look was as controlled a one as Jim had ever seen from her. "Perhaps you would not be surprised," Ael said, "to know that I, too, have not yet made all my choices. My own options are still falling into place, and it would be premature to speak of them until I know more of where they lie." She sat straighter in the chair. "But I tell you now, I shall not go back with them willingly. Nor will I allow the Sword to go back. Flight would not be my choice, should worst befall; but I would consider it . . . except that it would help nothing. You would still be left with a war on your hands. For they will have war, now; never doubt it."

She folded her hands too, and stared at them.

"That's a certainty we will try to avert," Jim said, "and at the very least, we'll try to spoil their guesses on the way. If they get a war, it won't be the one they want."

"So long as it is not also the one *we* don't want," Ael said, "I am with you, Captain. So there let it rest awhile."

"We've still two issues which will need resolution pretty quickly," Mr. Scott said. "First, is there any chance they might resurrect the mind-control project that was housed at Levaeri?"

"The scientists originally involved in that project are nearly all deceased," Spock said, "and the research could not be reconstructed without both their notes and large amounts of Vulcan genetic and neural material. We are in possession of all the first; and, Vulcan now having been warned of the danger, they will never again be allowed to acquire the second. This reduces the threat to an extremely low level, in the short term."

"In any case," Jim said, "the main danger would be if Vulcans were going to be involved in this operation. But the word from Starfleet is that they will not."

"Possibly this is appropriate," Spock said. "For there are as many Vulcans who are sensitive about dealing with or admitting their relationship to Romulans as there would appear to be Rihannsu who prefer not to think too closely about Vulcans." He glanced over at Ael.

She bowed her head once in agreement. "Perhaps better that they should not be involved," she said, "for the sake of the ways the relationship may find room to change in the future."

She folded her hands and looked at them thoughtfully. "I should also mention," Ael said, "that while I was once able to acquire information about that particular clandestine operation through my connections to the Praetorate and my family's spies in the Senate and the government, my sources inside the Empire are now very few indeed. And while they suspect that there are more clandestine operations going on at the moment, it has proved impossible to get the slightest whiff of what they are. Alas, the government has learned its lesson after Levaeri. But it would be wise to assume that they are preparing some deadly stroke against you. You should sift all your present intelligence carefully for communications that seem to make little sense in context."

"The second problem," Scotty said, "is Sunseed."

He touched a control on the computer pad in front of him. The hologram projection field came alive over the table, suddenly full of the image of a star, its great sphere burning orange-gold. "The star's the one we seeded in the escape from Levaeri V," Scotty said. "I've used its data set, and as you asked, Captain, besides the ships that followed us, I've added a class-M planet at a distance from the star equivalent to what Earth's distance would be from Sol—"

Two tiny points of light came diving in out of the darkness that surrounded the star: two starships, *Enterprise* and *Intrepid.* The frequency of light in the hologram changed so that the color of the star's chromosphere dimmed down and the corona brightened into visibility, an even pearly shimmer, about half a diameter wide, surrounding the star. It was even, anyway, until the starships dove into the corona itself and began to swing close around the star. Their phasers lanced out in slim lines of light, and infinitesimally small bright sparks leapt out from them into the lower levels of the corona—photon torpedoes. "We were doing warp eleven at the time, so it's all much slowed down, of course," Scotty said, as the ships arced through the corona, now beginning to writhe and flare around them with horrible and unnatural energy.

The ships streaked away, out of the corona, out of view. The corona wreathed and threw out long warped streamers after them, almost like a live thing trying to catch its tormentors. The coronal streamers reached much farther out than seemed normal, on all sides now, attenuating, overextended, a rage of ionized plasma—

And then the corona simply collapsed back against the star, falling flat, vanishing. For a long horrible moment, nothing happened—

*Flash!* A blinding sphere of high-level ionization leapt away from the star and blasted outward. The pursuing Romulan vessels that dove into view and toward the star a few moments later were caught by it. The effect, powerful enough in its first flush to propagate into subspace, deranged their warp fields. In tiny flashes of light they were annihilated, blown to plasma, and the plasma swept away before the relentlessly expanding front of an ion storm a hundred thousand times more powerful than anything that nature could have produced.

The view changed, backed off hundreds of millions of kilometers to show a planet like Earth—laced about with the orbits of satellites, patched under its swirls of creamy weather with the sapphire blue of seas, the greens and browns of continents, and on the nightside, great spills and spatters of the lights of civilization. Past that planet, its innocent-looking star was visible, but so was the only faintly visible wall of furious ionization that was tearing toward the world through local space. "I've sped it up a little now," Scotty said, "and marked it, for there'd be no seeing it this far out except with instruments. Ten minutes or so, this would take. But now—"

Like a tidal wave, completely invisible but marked as a hot blue line in the reconstruction, the ion storm struck the bowshock of the planet's magnetic field. For a fraction of a second, a faint glitter of massive particle annihilations and alpha and beta emissions manifested itself along the intersection's curvature, but the bowshock could offer no slightest resistance to an event of such intensity. The ion storm blasted past and through it, stripped away the planet's Van Allen belts, and a second later swept over the world in a wavefront now some forty thousand kilometers thick.

In orbit, every satellite was either scorched out of commission or simply slagged down to a lump by the sheer intensity of the radiation. A second later the whole planet's atmosphere was a maelstrom of hectic light from top to bottom. The upper reaches and the ozone layer went wild with blue and green and white auroral fire, not just the usual small circles one saw from space when a star hiccuped a minor flare at one of its satellite worlds, but huge interlocking circles that grew and ran across and around the planet's sphere, indicators of massive imbalances of potential. Millions upon millions of massive lightning strikes five or ten or twenty miles high leapt up from the ground or down to it everywhere; cities went dark as power grids went down all over that world, overloaded or destroyed; weather systems had imparted to them huge doses of heat energy that would derange the planet's entire atmospheric ecology with days or weeks of violent windstorms and vicious torrents of rain. Shortly there was no light left on the planet's surface but that of the scourge of lightning which would take days yet to die away, and the millions of wildfires the strikes were still kindling, while the upper atmosphere convulsed and rippled, burning blue with continuing ionization, and the tattered remainder of its ozone layer evaporated away. The seeded star's storm-wavefront passed, ravening on out into the system, vanishing from view. But in its wake, the surface of a class-M planet was swiftly becoming an image of Hell. . . .

Jim nodded at Scotty. Scotty looked uneasily at the burning image, and touched a control: it vanished.

"You'll understand why Starfleet is sitting tight on the details of those routines at the moment," Jim said. "But they're not so foolish as to think they're going to be able to do so forever. The secret will get out—if not from the Romulan side, from ours. Starfleet's desire is to find an 'antidote' or countermeasure that will make the Sunseed routines essentially useless, and to disseminate that information freely to every inhabited star system. They want to teach every vulnerable system a way to make both ships and planets effectively immune to the routine, able to stop it as soon as someone starts to use it."

Ael looked doubtful. "That will be a good trick," she said, "if you can find a way to bring it about. Do not forget, either, that my people have been using this tactic defensively against the Klingons, along our shared border, for some years. They may start using it offensively against you . . . and not just your shipping. Any defense you can produce against the Sunseed routines may in itself suffice to save many millions of lives."

K's't'lk had been chiming gently where she sat. "The problem's interesting," she said. "I think for the purpose of simpler implementation, we can leave the 'creative physics' of my people out of this solution; the less elegant but perhaps more robust 'hard physics' of realspace and subspace will suffice us, since the forces we're dealing with are fairly straightforward."

Jim had to put his eyebrows up at that. He suspected that someone in Fleet might have had a word with K's't'lk regarding the effects of creative physics on species less able to deal with the idea of rewriting the basic laws of the universe on demand. *Something to ask her later* . . .

"Sc'tty has described the basic induction routines to me," K's't'lk said, "and they really are rather simple. For an ion storm sufficiently violent to propagate into subspace and disrupt the warp fields of passing traffic—not even as violent as the one we just saw—you need a star of type K or better, at least one starship of a minimum 'significant' mass, doing at least warp eleven, phasers adequately pumped to very specific energy levels, and between five and ten photon torpedoes. All these requirements fortunately put the effect out of the reach of most users except for planetary powers and large fleet-running organizations such as Starfleet and the various interplanetary empires."

"So what we need," Scotty said, "is, first of all, a mobile form of protection, for ships. But then we'll also need a way for a planetary installation, or even something ship-based, to stop the effect once it gets started."

"And from a distance," K's't'lk said, "without having to go chasing after the ships initiating the effect, and without too time-consuming a setup, either." Her chiming died away to a faint glassy tinkling for a few moments as she thought. "Well, it might be moderately easy to protect individual ships by very carefully tuning their shields to match the average wave generation frequency of the ion storm in question. Mr. Spock?"

Spock looked thoughtful. "That would require very swift and complete initial and ongoing analysis of the oncoming wavefronts of the storm. Specialist routines would have to be written for the scanning hardware, to maximize data input and minimize processing time."

Scotty was rubbing his chin. "Aye. But you want to make sure there's no degradation of shield function. Our shields are useful, but they're not meant to do too many things at once. . . ."

"I agree," K's't'lk said. "As for the 'heavy,' nonmobile implementation of a defense . . ." She chimed softly to herself for a few moments, then trailed off. "It *will* be a good trick if we can do that," she said finally, "since what you're essentially doing with the high-energy 'seeding' of the star's upper atmosphere is turning its corona temporarily into something resembling a quadrillion-terawatt cyclotron. All that energy has to go *somewhere* once it builds up; and out, in the form of one or two big bursts of ionized radiation, is the easiest place. . . ."

"Well," Jim said, "I think we can safely leave the problem with you three for the moment. Please get to work on it. Meanwhile, we have the matter of the incoming diplomatic mission to deal with. Another five Starfleet vessels will be meeting us at the preliminary rendezvous point, which is 15 Trianguli. We will then proceed to a spot not far from the borders of the Neutral Zone, and meet the diplomatic mission there. And then . . ."

"Then no one has the slightest idea what'll happen," McCoy said.

"Our only consolation," Jim said, "is that matters will take a while to unfold, and we'll have time to anticipate them. The negotiating team assembling on the Federation side apparently has instructions to attempt to solve some other outstanding issues as well."

"And will the Rihannsu embassy be empowered to deal with these as well?" K's't'lk said.

"We're not sure," Jim said. "This may prolong the proceedings somewhat. . . ."

"Possibly," Spock said, "that is a goal of the Federation negotiators . . . though one they doubtless would be unwilling to advertise more openly."

"I'd agree with you there, Mr. Spock," Jim said. "We'll depart Hamal this time tomorrow, to meet the other Starfleet vessels at 15 Tri in five days' time. Spock, will this give you enough time to have a look at *Bloodwing*'s computer installation?"

"More than ample time, Captain. I will start as soon as we are finished here, with the commander's permission."

"Granted, Mr. Spock, most willingly." She bowed to him where she sat, then straightened and looked down the table at Jim. "Meanwhile, Captain, who is this who wishes to greet us?"

"About half the crew," Jim said, "as if you don't know."

"It will be my pleasure," Ael said, and rose; the others rose with her. She caught the glance Jim threw her, and said, "Aidoann, I will speak with the captain alone for a moment. Do you go with Mr. Spock and the doctor and the others. I will follow shortly."

"Yes, madam," said Aidoann, and along with Spock and McCoy and the others, she and the surgeon went out.

The door shut, and Jim looked over at Ael and said nothing for some seconds.

"It is difficult . . ." she said.

*She has a talent for understatement,* Jim thought, *but she always did. . . .* "Ael," he said, "first, I wanted to thank you. For McCoy."

She shook her head. "But you sent me a message saying as much long ago."

"It could use saying again," Jim said. "Fleet sometimes sends us into very uncomfortable situations . . . and that particular one would have gone beyond discomfort and into the 'terminal' for Bones, had you not come through."

Ael raised her eyebrows. *"Mnhei'sahe,"* she said, "takes forms that surprise us all, sometimes. But McCoy commands loyalties of his own, as you know. It is not an intervention I regret . . . mostly."

The smile flashed out just briefly, then. Jim grinned back. "'Mostly'?"

"I have no regret at all for plucking him out of the middle of the Senate," she said, pushing her chair back and coming around the table to stand by him, near the window; they looked out at the stars together. "But I brought something else away with me as well. And *that* action . . ." She shook her head.

"It's a little late now for regrets," Jim said. "And if that hadn't happened as trigger, something else would have, eventually."

"I would like to come to believe you," Ael said. "That may take a while. But no matter. Tell me now why you were so little eager for our ships to meet where Starfleet initially desired them to, at 15 Trianguli."

He had been afraid she would ask him that. "Mr. Spock," he said, "has given me some odd looks over that. A hunch?"

"Are you asking me or telling me?" Ael said, looking bemused.

"Neither," Jim said. "I simply didn't care for *Bloodwing* to be openly advertising her unescorted whereabouts at the moment . . . even indirectly."

"And that would also be why you desire to go no further in-system."

"Yes. It's a shame, because the starbase here is an extraordinary piece of engineering and you would enjoy seeing it—the Hamalki are tremendous builders. But there are too many beings in-system who notice who goes and comes. Even out here, where there's a lot less notice taken than you'd get closer in to Hamal."

Ael nodded. "Starfleet, though, may be confused by the roundabout manner in which you are proceeding."

"Right now they won't mind a little confusion," Jim said. "They gave me some latitude; I'm using it. Later I may not have so much."

"And what will you do then?" Ael said. "When they order you to fetch me and the Sword back to where the diplomatic mission is waiting, and hand us over to them?"

He looked at her in silence. Then he said, "Maybe it won't come to that."

The look she threw him was ironic, and skeptical, in the extreme.

# Chapter Three

In the normal course of things it was not unheard of, but it was unusual enough, for a single Senator to be asked to meet privately with one of the Praetorate. When such a thing happened, the Senator in question tended to attract a great deal of attention for days, perhaps months, afterward, as other Senators and various lesser political figures, more on the margins of things, tried to work out which party had what advantage over the other. This being the case, Arrhae i-Khellian t'Llhweiir, the newest and least senior Senator in the Tricameron, could well understand at least one reason why the summons to meet with the Praetor Eveh tr'Anierh might have come to her house so late at night—late enough for almost all the household to have long since sought their couches. What was still a matter of some concern to her was why she should have received such a summons at all . . . and how it might now affect her other business.

The whole place had immediately gone into a flutter. Those of the servants who were still awake woke half the others, for they understood the unusual nature of such a summons. Now half of them were excited, and half of them were terrified, and once again Arrhae resolved to get the secure comm terminal moved into her bedroom so that the whole place would not be disrupted every time an official call came through. When the terminal had first been installed a month or so ago, she had thought it was unlikely to go off much, and had had the workmen put it on a stand out in the House's Great Hall. But the wretched thing went off constantly, five or six times a day, and the shriek that the Hall's bright acoustics made of its alert tone was becoming a trial to her temper.

It had been worse for H'daen tr'Khellian, the Old Lord of the House. Every time the device went off he had resurrected some new and more awful language from his ancient days in Fleet, until Arrhae found herself half wishing it would go off, on some of those long hot late-summer afternoons, merely for the diversion of hearing him curse it. But finally H'daen had decided that this season in i'Ramnau city was too hot for him; and (since the House's fortunes had looked up somewhat with Arrhae's accession to the Senate) he had taken himself off up northward to the Edrunra Mountains, where the House had an old *ehto,* or summer shieling-cottage. There he was busying himself bossing around the workers who were renovating the place, enjoying the cool weather under the conifers on the mountainside, and reveling in the complete lack of comm calls of any kind whatsoever. "You want me," the old gray-haired man had said, on the morning a tenday ago when he took himself away, "send a flitter, Senator."

Arrhae had found no need for that. She was busy enough, and all too many of her afternoons were spent answering the wretched terminal, so that she would have had to leave her other business until late at night even if that were not her preferred time to handle such. Arrhae was not only a new Senator, but was seen by some of her fellow legislators, she now realized, as a potential marriage-match as well. This amused her, for she was determined to remain matchless indefinitely, if not indeed permanently. She was frankly enjoying the experience of being an "independent," wooed and sought after by every faction in the Senate, and she had no intention of doing anything except hold all her wooers, political and personal, at arm's length while she spent the foreseeable future assessing the situation into which she had newly fallen. *Besides . . . marriage would interfere with "other business." No, that would not be something to think at all seriously about.*

Meanwhile Arrhae knew that half the people who called her, or called on her, were simply fascinated by the concept of a Senator who, a month and a half before, had been a servant—*hru'hfe* of House Khellian, yes, the chief steward of the house over its other servants, but hardly anyone to be reckoned with. But one day it had all changed, as an intelligence officer turned up on the House's doorstep with a Federation Starfleet officer in tow. Within what seemed no more than a matter of days, Arrhae had been threatened and intimidated by various

Rihannsu, utterly terrified by a human, and then run over, under the very dome of the Senate chamber, by a Horta. A scant half tenday later than that, she had been brought under the poor cracked dome again and given her signet. It had been a very full month.

And now everything was shifting again. Arrhae stood outside the front gates of the House, with little old Mahan, the ancient door-opener of the House, standing behind her. *"Hru'hfe,"* he said, "you be careful now."

Arrhae smiled, looking up into the dark and turning the senatorial signet around and around on her finger, a habit she hoped she would be able to break eventually. He was ancient, was Mahan, and odds were good that he would never stop calling her that, no matter how other matters changed. For him there was only one lord of the house, the Old Lord, and a Senator more or less under the same roof made no differ-ence. "I will," Arrhae said, hearing the thin whine of a flitter coming through the darkness. "You lock up when I'm gone, Mahan, and take yourself back to couch. I may not be coming back tonight."

"When, then?"

The whine of the flitter got louder; she could see its lights, now, as it homed in on the landing patch in front of the house. "Possibly in the morning," Arrhae said. "Either way, I'll call and let you know."

"What if that thing goes off?"

"Ignore it," Arrhae said, more loudly, as the flitter settled before them, and its underlights came up more brightly to illuminate her way; its hatch popped, and a uniformed figure scrambled out of the seat next to the pilot. "Go on, Mahan! Sleep well."

But he would not move, and finally Arrhae walked away from him to where the officer stood waiting. He bowed to her, and said, *"Deihu,* if you would, kindly be pleased to enter the conveyance—"

It was a courtesy, but still Arrhae wondered what he would say or do if she refused. One did not usually refuse a praetorial request, even at one removed; such were assumed (by the prudent) to have the force of an order. Not that Arrhae would have refused this one; her curiosity was aroused. *And so will everyone else's be,* she thought as she gave the officer a fraction of a gracious bow and followed him to the flitter, *when word gets out.* It was half a string of cash to twenty that someone in the house was on the normal comm channel this moment, calling one of the local-world news services to tell them about this midnight meeting. Or one of the Havrannsu ones; they were always slightly hungrier for news, for political reasons with which she was becoming all too familiar.

Arrhae stepped up into the flitter's passenger compartment. It was luxurious, but she was becoming used to this, though (she hoped) not too used to it. "Madam," said the young officer, plainly trying not to stare at her, and not doing too well at it, "there is a light collation laid on in the side cupboard. Also ale and wine, in the top one . . ."

"Thank you, *eriu,*" Arrhae said. "I'm sure I will be perfectly comfortable."

"We will be in Ra'tleihfi in three-quarters of a standard hour, madam. If there's anything you desire—"

"Getting there might be nice," Arrhae said, she hoped not too tartly. But at the same time she was not a night person, and declined to pretend to be. The young man gulped and gently shut the door.

They lifted off lightly enough, but the flitter then rocketed forward at such speed that Arrhae was hard put to restrain her smile. *I must learn not to scold,* she thought. But for so long that had been a significant part of her job here . . . besides keeping her ears and eyes open, of course, on other accounts. The difference was that if a *hru'hfe* scolded, no one suffered from it but the household's servants. If a Senator scolded, effects tended to be much more widespread.

*And if a Praetor scolds? . . .*

One would expect serious trouble indeed. And this was not just any Praetor she was going to see, not merely some one of the Twelve. Eveh tr'Anierh was what, in the language she had recently begun practicing to think in again after a brief hiatus, would have been called a triumvir. Except that triumvirates in the original context had been directly elected by the citizenry—poor, rigged examples of democracy though those ancient elections had been. These three men had acquired their de-facto position by means of manipulation of the other nine Praetors, and to a lesser extent by favors done for the various power blocs in both houses of the Senate—as many for those who expunged laws as for those who enacted them.

*And what in the names of Air and Earth does such a man want with* me?

There was, of course, always that one fear, the one that would never quite go away . . . but probably safer that it did not. The only time in Rihannsu politics that people stopped asking questions about you, normally, was when you were dead . . . and sometimes not even then, for the actions of the dead could be, and sometimes were, used to incriminate the living. Arrhae, for her own part, was both alive and, if anyone ever got wind of what her other business was, exquisitely incriminable. Even now, in her present position—honored as a hero, elevated to the Tricameron, desired as a possible strategic Housematch—there was always the question: *What if someone has found out? What if* he *has found out?* All the rest of it would matter not a straw's worth in the wind, if that ever happened. Honors bestowed could be stripped away again . . . and the revenge on the party who had allowed them to be fraudulently bestowed would be most prolonged and painful.

Arrhae let out a long breath and stretched her limbs, then opened the bottom cabinet. *Dear Elements,* she thought, *do they fear I will starve in three-quarters of an hour?* The "light collation" looked as if someone had pillaged the Ruling Queen's cold table. *Look at all this!* Kheia, *roast* lhul, *sliced cold* irriuf *mousse,* alhel *jelly.* It was just as well she had eaten lightly before bed, otherwise the sight of all this food could have left her feeling queasy. Still, she reached up for a cup from the top cupboard and poured herself a tot of ale, and then picked up a pair of tongs and smiled slightly. House Khellian was doing better than it had done in a while, but not so well as to afford *kheia* on a regular basis.

Quite shortly, it seemed, they were landing; either the pilot had made better speed than originally intended, or Arrhae had been paying more attention to the *kheia* than she realized. She put the eating things away and dusted the crumbs off, making a note to have the House's new *hru'hfe* inquire about the recipe. Then she peered out at the compound into which the flitter was settling, out of the glare of the roads and towers of Ra'tleihfi. Paths to and from the landing patch were lit, but the house at the center of it was not; that was a low long dark bulk, only faintly visible by light reflected from other sources, and in all of it Arrhae could see only one light lit in a first-floor window.

The flitter grounded most gently, and the young officer was at the door again for her when it opened, and handed her down. Outside, on the flitter patch, she found a small honor guard awaiting her. *In the middle of the night?* Arrhae thought. *For me, or is someone else more important here?* They raised their weapons across their chests in salute, and she bowed to them, another fractional superior-to-inferior bow, another of the things she was having to get used to these days—for a Senator was almost everyone's superior. There were, however, exceptions.

"This way, if you please, *deihu,*" said the foremost officer in the honor guard; and he turned. Arrhae followed him as he led the way, and the rest of the guard fell in behind.

They made their way toward the darkened house through the soft summer night. It was not a very old building, perhaps no more than a few hundred years in existence; and as they drew closer to the pillared portico that hid the main doors, the pale beige stone house showed no outward sign of the status of its occupant, which was still something that could happen even in these symbol-conscious days. But there was no missing, on the security vehicles parked outside, and on the side of the one that had brought her here, the taloned, winged sigil that gripped the Two Worlds one in each claw, and the characters scribed around it: *Fvill-haih Ellannahel t'Rihannsu,* Praetorate of the Romulan Star Empire. If the Twelve themselves sometimes disdained making a show of their power, those who served them usually did not.

The officer commanding the honor guard went up a low flight of steps into the portico. Arrhae followed, and as she came up the steps, the two great doors in the shadows opened outward, to reveal a single tall figure standing there against the light. He was fair; that by itself was a little unusual for her adopted people, but just as unusual was his height, which would have marked him out regardless of his hair. He was dressed casually, but richly, in long kilts and a long tunic, appropriate enough for the time of night, but dark enough that he might have come from some formal engagement earlier in the evening and not bothered to change.

He stepped forward to greet her as she came up to the top of the steps. "*Deihu* t'Llhweiir," said tr'Anierh, "you are very welcome to my house, and at such an hour."

His bow to her was deeper than it needed to be. She returned the compliment, giving him a breath's more time than he was strictly entitled to. "The *fvillha* honors me by asking for a consultation," Arrhae said.

"The *deihu* is being politer to the *fvillha* than necessary, given the hour," said the Praetor, "and probably wonders what in the Elements' Names causes the Praetor to call the Senator out so late."

The man's wry look was open, and invited sympathy. Arrhae simply smiled at him. She was not going to discuss business out here.

"Dismissed," tr'Anierh said to the guard. They bowed, all, and took themselves away into the silent darkness.

"Please come in," tr'Anierh said. Arrhae followed him through into the light, and behind them the House's door-opener shut the great doors and went back into his little room. The hallway through which the Praetor led Arrhae was nearly as wide as House Khellian's whole Great Hall, all done in polished viridian stone and dimly lit with only the occasional faint star of lamplight as suited the time of night; shadows moved under the high ceilings with the lamplights' flickering.

"It's a great barn of a place," said tr'Anierh as they walked. "Wonderful for entertaining, but a nuisance to heat in the winters. Fortunately I needn't pay the fuel bills; it would be my whole salary. . . . Here's my study, *deihu:* do come in."

A door slipped open as they approached one wall. This was the room Arrhae had seen from the flitter, with its light on. Here there was a wide worktable of polished blackwood under the window, and another, smaller, in the middle of the room, with two big black chairs drawn up to it and facing one another across the table, all on a carpet of a beautiful dark blood-green, very thick and soft to walk on. The walls of the room were all lined with blackwood shelves stacked with tapes and books and solids, some of the stacks tidy, some of them looking about to collapse.

"Please, *deihu,* sit and be comfortable," tr'Anierh said, going around to the chair on the other side of the table. "May I give you some draft?"

The polished clay pitcher on the tray down at one end of the table was plain reedgrain draft, Arrhae could tell by the scent, and frankly at such an hour she welcomed the prospect; the stimulant content would certainly do her no harm. "Please do."

"Spice?"

"No, I thank you. Blue, please."

He poured, handed her the tall stemmed cup. Arrhae pledged him, drank, and took a moment to look at the table. It was not plain black-wood, as might have seemed the case on first glance, but was inlaid right around its perimeter with one long sentence in dark *heimnhu* wire. She traced the middle of the passage with one finger. "T'Liemha's *Song of the Sun,*" she said. "What a lovely piece of work. . . ."

"They told me you were a cultured woman," tr'Anierh said, "and I see they were right."

Arrhae simply smiled slightly at this. Some of her new senatorial confederates had, on meeting her, made remarks to her of this sort. They varied between gracious and subtle to extremely silly, and mostly they factored down to meaning *I'm surprised you haven't come to the Senate carrying a mop.* She raised her eyes from the exquisitely inlaid wood, and met his look. "I will not start polishing it, *fvillha,*" Arrhae said, "if that was your concern."

His eyes widened slightly. Then he grinned at her. "Well enough," said tr'Anierh. "Doubtless I deserved that."

She lifted the cup to him and drank again. "How can I assist you, *fvillha?*" she said. "It is surely late for both of us."

"It is that," he said, and rubbed his face briefly before picking up his own cup and drinking. When he put it down again, tr'Anierh looked slightly more composed. *"Deihu,"* he said, "you will have heard just now of the mission which the Tricameron sends to the Federation."

She would have had to be deaf not to have heard of it; the racket in the session yesterday had been extraordinary. "Indeed so," Arrhae said. "A most historic time is upon us."

"Yes," tr'Anierh said. "And we have . . . some concerns."

She gave him a questioning look as she drank. "That would be understandable," she said. "But about what, exactly?"

"Do you know the names of the party who are going?"

"A great list of them was read out in session," Arrhae said, "which the Senate approved by acclamation. I confess I only recognized about twenty of them; but things were happening rather quickly then."

"The names of the chief negotiators, though, you may have recognized."

"Oh yes," she said. Several of the names had figured prominently in the trial of a Federation Starfleet officer here recently, all people who had been profoundly annoyed at having been cheated of the sight of his execution. Others Arrhae knew as jurists, or Senators of considerable seniority; if they shared one characteristic that she knew of, it was a near-hysterical hatred of the Federation. When the Senators in question spoke on the subject in session, they did not so much speak as froth at the mouth.

"How do you like them?"

Arrhae started to have a suspicion where this was leading. She wondered how most safely to proceed. "They are very . . . emphatic," she said, "in their opinions."

Tr'Anierh gave her another of those wry looks. "So they are," he said. "I would like to add a name to the list of those who will go." He let the remark hang in the air until she grasped its meaning.

"*My* name?" Arrhae said. "*Fvillha,* I beg pardon: but why me?"

He sat back in his chair. "For one thing," he said, "you are an independent; and genuinely so, for you have had no time to be coopted— not that I think that would come soon, anyway. Even your casual conversations have already made your stance fairly plain." Once again Arrhae drank, meanwhile reminding herself never to forget how closely she was listened to. "Nearly every other member of the party that will go with this mission is already chained down tight to one or another of the five great blocs. It would, I think, be in the Praetorate's interest to see that there are at least a few Senators on hand whose perceptions of our enemies, and whose reactions to what they may say, have not already been dictated by someone else."

Arrhae nodded. "But you have another thought as well."

"You have had dealings with humans recently," tr'Anierh said.

It was hard not to freeze. Arrhae put her cup down on the tray, and said, "It is not an easy business at the best of times."

"I think you may be in a position to understand them better than many of us might," said tr'Anierh. "And that position might enable you to perceive something, or discover something, about the Federation negotiating position, or their situation, that others of us might miss . . . and which might make a very great difference to the Empire in the long run."

The only thing Arrhae could do was laugh. "Praetor," she said, "a few conversations in a storeroom are all the experience I can bring to this exercise. You honor me very greatly, but I think maybe it would be a skilled translator you would find best fitted to this work."

He gave her a thoughtful look. "If there are personal reasons you would not choose to travel at this time—"

"Not at all," Arrhae said. "But I am very uncertain how much good I could do. I would serve gladly, but—"

"But will you go?"

There was something odd about his intensity. Arrhae did not know what to make of it. It came to her, then: *I must go. I must find out what is behind this. And I certainly will not find out if I stay here.*

"*Fvillha,* I will go," Arrhae said, "and I will try to do my Empire honor."

"*Deihu,* I think you cannot fail to do so," tr'Anierh said. "The mission will be leaving tomorrow evening. Can you be ready by then?"

There would have been a thousand things to do first if she were just a *hru'hfe;* but if she were, she would hardly be being asked to go on a diplomatic mission. Some formal clothes would be what she needed to pack; not a great deal more. "*Fvillha,* I can."

"That is good news," tr'Anierh said. "I will arrange for you to be billeted aboard *Gorget,* where the most senior members of the mission will also be. There are people attached to the mission, administrative staff and so forth, who will make themselves known to you over the first couple of days in warp; they will have leisure to explain to you the kind of concerns we have at the moment about the conduct of the mission . . . and I would urge you to do all you can to help them. Other details I will message to you at your House tomorrow, before you depart."

*You have had no time to be coopted,* Arrhae thought with some irony. *Well,* now *you have . . . no matter that it is happening at so high a level.* She wondered what she would be called upon to do with the data she would be acquiring . . . and how she was going to get out of this one, after they were finished with her. It was occurring to Arrhae at the moment that, as the most junior possible member of the Senate, she was probably also the most expendable member possible—no matter who she had been talking to, in what storeroom.

Nevertheless, she finished her cup of draft like a good guest, and stood, knowing a dismissal even if it was being much more politely handled than it would have been for a *hru'hfe*. *"Fvillha,"* she said, and bowed to him, "I am at your disposal in all ways."

"Until tomorrow then, *deihu.*"

"Until tomorrow," Arrhae said. The door opened; a servant was standing there to see her out. On the steps under the portico, once more the honor guard was awaiting her, and its officer handed her into the waiting flitter and closed the door. A few moments later the flitter lifted itself up into the darkness, and the night took it.

So it was that *deihu* Arrhae i-Khellian was sent off to spy on the Federation; and at the back of her mind, Terise Haleakala-LoBrutto, sent off years ago by the Federation to spy on the Romulans, found the jest very choice.

She could only hope, now, that it would not be the death of her.


15 Trianguli was one of those stars that had no particular interest for anyone except because of its position. It was a little type-K8 star, not quite small enough to qualify as a dwarf, orange-red, and planetless. There might have been an asteroid belt around it once, but if there had, long attrition had almost completely destroyed it. All this part of the Empire, on the far side of the Zone, shared the same dearth of re-

sources; an unlucky chance for Ael's people, but one which circumstance and lack of resources elsewhere had forced them to ignore. They had once come a long way out through this region, looking toward space which they could see had more stars, younger ones, stars big enough to have planets that could support hominid life. Unfortunately, it was Federation space they were looking at, those Rihannsu of nearly a century ago. Now this part of space was generally unintruded upon by either side, with the Zone not so far away . . . a desert again, untroubled, with nothing to attract anyone.

Except for now, as *Enterprise* and *Bloodwing* approached 15 Trianguli at warp five, preparing to drop out of warp well away from the star itself.

"T'Hrienteh?" Ael said, standing behind her center seat and studying the viewscreen, which showed stars and nothing else.

"Scan is flat," t'Hrienteh said, and t'Lamieh, her trainee, nodded agreement over her shoulder.

"But it would be," Ael said softly. She felt naked, for *Bloodwing* was not cloaked; in *Enterprise*'s company, it was for the moment unnecessary.

"*Commander?*" Jim's voice said.

"All seems clear, Captain," Ael said. "No sign of the Federation vessels as yet."

"*They may be running a little behind,*" Jim said. "*It wouldn't be unusual, especially if our clocks really are out of synch. I've got to mention that to Starfleet. Mr. Sulu, drop us out of warp. Decelerate to half impulse.*"

"The same," Ael said to Khiy, gripping the back of her chair.

The two ships dropped out of warp together, braking to dump down quickly out of the relativistic speeds. Ael swallowed . . .

. . . and saw, on the screen, at least one great twin-nacelled form shimmering out of cloak practically in front of them.

"*Evasive!*" Ael said to Khiy: but he had seen it before she did, and was already doing it. "Captain, ships decloaking—!"

"*I see them,*" Jim said. "*Company. Lots of company—*"

The sweat broke out all over Ael to match what was already dampening her hands. Two or three ships, four or five, that she could have understood. But this flock of them, suddenly surrounding her, an open globe, tightening—it put her quite out of countenance.

Nevertheless she stood taller, put her shoulders back, gripped the back of the chair, and grinned. There were still options. She thought gratefully now of how Khiy and Mr. Sulu had spent all that first night of meeting, before *Bloodwing* and *Enterprise* departed for these spaces, standing in one corner and making strange motions at one another in the air with their hands, so that they had to repeatedly put down their drinks to continue the conversation. Their crewmates from both sides had teased them about this at the time—all but Aidoann, who had been nearby, listening and watching them closely, and sent her a report on the exchange. It had all seemed quite farfetched at the time, and she had hoped it would not be necessary. Now, though, she would find out how farfetched it was. And as for the rest—

"IDs, *khre'Riov*," Aidoann said. "ChR 18, ChR 330, ChR 49, ChR 98, ChR 66, ChR 24, ChR 103—"

*Amie, Neirrh, Hmenna, Llemni, Orudain:* all cruisers of *Bloodwing*'s own class. And the big ones, the old supercruisers, *Uhtta* and *Madail*. None of them commanded by friends of hers, only the supercruisers better armed than *Bloodwing*, and the difference not so great considering the Klingon-sourced phaser conduits that had been clandestinely installed in her. But there were seven of them. *"Not taking any chances, are they?"* said Jim's voice, remarkably calmly, from *Enterprise*, still outside the globe. *"One of them leaving globe now, coming for us. Are any of these ships anybody you know, Commander?"*

"Not personally," Ael said. "And at the moment, I fear we shall only meet in some other life."

*"Still feeling insulted?"*

"I will consult with you afterward as to that."

Jim laughed. *"Understood. Implementing."*

She swallowed. "Khiy," Ael said, "show us your mettle now—"

*"Ie, khre'Riov,"* Khiy said.

The whole ship lurched sideways as he pulled *Bloodwing* around in a turn that made her structural field groan, and flung her straight at *Hmenna,* accelerating again toward warp, and firing like a mad thing, as if none of the rest of those ships closing in around them existed. They were basic enough tactics: to prevent englobement, pick a hole in the globe and escape. Sometimes it worked with one ship, sometimes it did not. *Hmenna* fired back, swelling in the screens—

—and then suddenly let loose a couple of hurried photon torpedoes and swung hastily away to port and "downward," as *Enterprise* came hurtling straight in at *Hmenna* from behind, as if planning to engage in a game of stones-crack-egg with *Bloodwing,* using *Hmenna* as the egg. The two of them passed at nearly the same moment through the gap left by *Hmenna's* frantic movement with barely a third of a kilometer between them. *Bloodwing* went out of the globe through the gap: *Enterprise* went in and plunged straight across the inside of it, straight for *Madail,* pushing up through .9c and making for warp, though not firing, since using phasers at such transitional speeds can have unfortunate results.

*Mad, he is mad!* Ael thought. Maybe *Madail* thought so too, for after a couple of ineffective phaser blasts at her shields she quickly moved sideways to let *Enterprise* out, rather than be rammed. Out *Enterprise* went, curving up high "over" the globe and down again, righting herself, making for the star.

*Hmenna* was after them now, and the globe was breaking up to follow. "Pay them no mind, Khiy," Ael said. "Do your business as it was agreed. Tr'Keirianh! Shields?"

"Holding, *khre'Riov,* but—"

"No buts," Ael said softly. "Do what you must, but hold them for your life, or that will prove short."

They headed straight for 15 Trianguli.

Jim sat watching *Bloodwing* as both ships broke into warp, and swallowed hard. "Mr. Sulu—"

"Well outside the critical warp radius, Captain," Sulu said. "Warp ingress went safely. No complications."

"*Yet.*"

"I'm on it, Captain," Sulu said. "Warp two now. Khiy, you know the drill—"

"*Will this work, Hikaru?*" said Khiy's voice from *Bloodwing.*

"K8," Chekov said under his breath. "The star is marginal for the routine. Checking the spectroscopy—"

"No time for that now," Sulu said, and dove for it.

"There may not be enough mass," Chekov said. "It's borderline dwarf—"

"Captain?" Sulu said.

Jim breathed in, breathed out, clenched his hands on the arms of the center seat. "Seven of them. Two of us. Better find out," he said.

*Enterprise* and *Bloodwing* dove together for the star. Chekov was backing the bridge viewscreen's image intensity down as they went, but the glare was filling the bridge more unbearably every moment. Dwarf the star might be, "just a little K8," but this close to it, it started to look like Hell itself, and Jim found himself sweating and hoping he was not about to be in a position to make a much more detailed comparison. "Spock, what about the shields?"

"Holding," Spock said, peering down his viewer. "No degradation. Tuning." There was a pause, and then Spock said, "Shield tuning is showing some slide."

Jim hit his comm switch. "Scotty," Jim said, "the shields are losing their tuning."

There was a jangling from somewhere else in engineering as the ship began to shake, a bone-rattling vibration that combined very uncomfortably with the howl of the warp engines through *Enterprise*'s frame as she accelerated into the higher levels of warp. *"Compensating,"* Scotty said, sounding tense. *"The star's marginal, Captain! The corona's not as hot as it ought to be, it's changing the way the field-tuning equations affect the shields—!"*

"The paired iron lines are there," Chekov said suddenly. "Fe IX imaging is good. Working out the torpedo drop pattern now, *Bloodwing*—"

*"Mr. Chekov, kindly hurry,"* Ael's voice said. *"We seem to be having some difficulty with the tuning of our shields. If the ion wavefront hits us and we are not adequately protected—"*

"Recompensating," Spock said. "Commander, here are better frequency-prediction algorithms for you. Transmitting. Use them to retune."

"Got it," Chekov said softly. "Aidoann, here they come."

A pause. *"Evaluating,"* Aidoann's voice said, over an increasing engine roar from the other side. *"Retuning shields now. Mr. Chekov, this means eight photon torpedoes for us at one per one-point-four Federation seconds. Coordinates plotting now."*

"Sounds right," Chekov said, eyeing the targeting viewer as it came up on his side of the helm. "Here comes the reception committee."

"Fire aft, Mr. Chekov," Jim said. "Don't let them singe our tails!"

The pursuing ships were firing already, but with less and less effect as *Enterprise* and *Bloodwing* both dived closer to the sun; light-based weapons, even pumped to compensate for use in warp, are just as subject as any other kind of light to being bent out of true by the gravity well of a star. "Clean misses," Sulu said, sparing a moment from his piloting. "Ours too. Dropping out of warp to sublight. Coming down to ten thousand kilometers for the firing run—"

The ships chasing them were dropping out of warp and dropping back too, both unwilling to overshoot their prey and also unwilling to singe their own tails—possibly reasoning that *Bloodwing* and *Enterprise* could not keep this madness up forever. *And they're right,* Jim thought; for though the ships' shields were being tailored to cope with high-speed ionic discharge, there was little they could do about simple radiant heat . . . and it was getting hot already. "Scotty, how much time can we spend here?" Jim said.

*"Twenty-four seconds total,"* Scotty said. *"Plus or minus two. After that the hull will start to buckle—"*

Jim held on to the arms of his seat, while the front viewscreen, turned down as low as it could go without actually being turned off, was still blazing with the furious dark orange fire of 15 Tri. Ahead of them, a scarcely seen black blot against the roiling "rice-grain" plasma structure of the star's low atmosphere, *Bloodwing* was skimming even lower than they were over the photosphere, firing photon torpedoes off to both sides, into the "base" of the star's corona. "Phaser program starts now," Chekov said, and hit his controls.

The *Enterprise*'s phasers stitched through the star's corona, flickering, the fire looking almost continuous, but not quite, like the flicker in old-fashioned neon tubes that Jim had seen. Chains of sunspots abruptly began to bubble blackly up all over the star's surface, responding to the changes being induced in the uppermost part of the star's magnetic field. "Dark sprite effect," Chekov said. "Base percentage reached—"

"Uhura," Jim said, hanging on as the ship began to shudder more violently, and sparing a hand from holding on to wipe the sweat off his forehead, "elapsed time?"

"Eighteen seconds, Captain."

It felt like eighteen years. "Preparing for warp eleven," Sulu said. "Accelerating out of the gravity well now."

"Back in a moment, *Bloodwing*," Jim said. The ship was cooling again, but that would not last. Out they went into the dark, and three of the seven ships came after them.

"Warp two. Warp three. Pursuit is in warp and accelerating."

"Ready on the aft phaser banks, Mr. Chekov. Prepare a spread of torpedoes."

"Ready, Captain."

"Warp five," Sulu said. "Warp six. Turning." Everything slewed sideways. The ship was groaning softly now, the skinfield complaining about the stresses being applied to it . . . and worse was to come.

"Aft view," Jim said. The screen flickered. Jim saw two of the pursuing Romulan vessels trying to turn to match, but not doing as well, turning wide, losing ground. The third one, the biggest of them, was turning and gaining on them, and firing.

"Clean misses. Warp eight," Sulu said. Suddenly 15 Trianguli was swelling to fill the screen, flashing toward them. "Warp nine."

"Mind that helm, mister," Jim said softly.

"Warp ten. She's steady, Captain," Sulu said, while the ship began to shake and her structural members to howl in a way that suggested Sulu's definition of *steady* was a novel one.

"*Captain—*" Scotty's voice called out from the comm.

"Duly noted, Mr. Scott," Jim answered calmly, never taking his eyes off Sulu at the helm.

"High photosphere. Warp eleven!"

*Enterprise*'s engines roared; the ship lurched as it hit the star's "near" bowshock, lurched again, and then began to accelerate powerfully around the tight end of a "cometary" hyperbolic curve with the star at its focus. The sun's corona, already irritated by the photon torpedoes and tuned phaser fire, was now pierced straight through by the carefully deformed warp field of a starship doing warp eleven . . .

. . . and nothing happened. 15 Trianguli's corona lashed furiously at them as they whipped around and flashed away, but there was no burst of sudden ionization. The ship following them most closely, *Madail,* began to fire again. *Enterprise* shuddered.

"A hit on the port nacelle," Spock said. "Shields down fifteen percent."

*"They won't take that kind of thing for long!"* Scotty's voice came from the engine room. *"All those laddies have to do is keep firing at us, eventually they'll get lucky."*

"The stellar atmosphere is insufficiently stimulated," Spock said. "Another pass—"

*"Mr. Spock, we* can't—"

"The warp-field incursion effect has not yet attenuated," Spock said. "It will last another eight point six seconds. *Bloodwing*—"

*"Mr. Spock!"* Ael said. *"We seem somewhat short of results here!"*

"If you will make one more sweep at ten thousand kilometers, with phasers tuned a third higher than ours—"

*"Do it, Khiy!"* Jim heard Ael say.

*"Implementing."*

They plunged outward and away from the star. "View aft!" Jim said. The Romulan ship that had been chasing them was still doing so, firing still. They were keeping ahead of it, but it was starting to catch up as they watched *Bloodwing* dive low toward the chromosphere one more time. Overstimulated ions trailed behind her in a million-degree contrail from which *Bloodwing* was preserved only by its tenuousness. "For God's sake be careful," Jim said softly. The last thing any of them needed right this moment was for *Bloodwing* to be thrown back in time. Her phasers lanced out into the corona, flickering nearly as steadily as *Enterprise*'s had—

The star's corona wavered around her, went sickly and pallid, and collapsed.

Jim swallowed. *"Bloodwing,* get out of there!"

She angled around and upward, arrowed away from the star. They all saw it start to come, then: a secondary curve of faint light over the surface of 15 Trianguli, not orange but bizarrely blue, rearing up right across the body of the star, like a bubble blowing—but a bubble nearly as big as the star was, easily two-thirds of its diameter. "Here it comes!" Sulu cried, and hit the ship's impact alarms.

The screech of them went through everything. "All hands, brace for impact!!" Jim shouted, and braced himself as best he could, knowing that his odds of staying where he was were no better than fifty-fifty. "Maximum warp, Mr. Sulu, now or never!"

The bubble continued to bend itself up and up from the star's chromosphere, arching, inflating, its "surface" swirling like that of a soap bubble with that virulent blue glow—getting taller all the time, impossibly tall, compared to the star. Any spicule, any prominence, would long since have either fallen back into the chromosphere, or blown away entirely . . . but not this thing. It *grew*. From engineering, over the roar of the engines, he heard a voice like a very nervous xylophone saying, *"Dear Architectrix, Sc'tty, look at it, it's not supposed to do that—!"*

*Oh, wonderful,* Jim thought. *"Bloodwing—!"*

*"Right behind you, Captain,"* Ael's voice said. But they were *not* right behind *Enterprise,* they were well behind. *If their shields aren't tuned properly—*

The other Rihannsu ships had seen that upward-straining shape too. They turned, in a welter of different speeds and in seven different directions, and fled.

Blue, bulging, awful, the bubble strained outward . . . and then the bubble burst.

The Sunseed effect, as K's't'lk had said, released so much energy into such a small volume of space at such a speed and intensity that much of it had no choice but to propagate into subspace as a sleet of stripped ions, cyclotron radiation, and other subatomic particles. Once there, the newly created ion storm did not go faster than light itself, but it affected anything in subspace that did, such as ships with warp fields. The effect, so close to its source, was as if a great hand had grabbed *Enterprise* and was trying to use it for a saltshaker. Jim hung on tight, grimly determined that even if he died right now, he was going to do it in his command chair and not rolling around on the floor.

But dying was apparently not in the cards. The shaking began to ease off. Jim stared into the screen and saw eight sparks of light scattered over a great area of space behind him, all of them brilliantly backlit by an orange star, suddenly abnormally bright, with an equally sudden, swiftly expanding spherical halo of dimming but deadly blue-white fire. That halo expanded to meet them, surrounded them, rushed past them—

Seven of them flowered into fire themselves, one after another, as their shields failed, and in both realspace and subspace a billion tons of plasma struck them at a temperature of nearly two million degrees. The little spheres of pure white fire produced by the instantaneous annihilation of all the matter and antimatter in what remained of their warp engines was briefly hotter: but not by much, and not for long.

And one spark burned bright for a moment, its tuned shields shrieking light . . . then dull again, and duller still as the star behind it began to recover from its very brief solar flare.

"*Bloodwing,*" Jim said.

Silence.

"*Enterprise,*" Ael said, after a moment.

Jim breathed out. "Is everyone all right over there?"

"*My nerves are a casualty, I would say,*" Ael said. "*But the shields held, for which I praise Fire's name . . . having seen It so close to hand, and lived. We have some minor structural problems, I believe.*"

"We too will need to examine the hull, Captain," Spock said. "But initial indicators seem to suggest only minor damage."

"Good. Let's get it taken care of," Jim said, and stood up, now that it was safe to do so. "Scotty, K's't'lk, nice work."

"*Thank you, Captain,*" Scotty said.

"*I must apologize, Captain,*" K's't'lk said. "*I had hoped for better.*"

Jim paused. "Sorry?"

"*There was supposed to be a lovely evenly generated ionization effect that propagated right around the corona,*" K's't'lk said, sounding mournful. "*Not just a coronal mass ejection like that, all lumpy and asymmetrical.*"

"*I thought it worked rather well,*" Ael said, sounding dubious.

"*But not the way it was supposed to,*" K's't'lk said. "*Captain, Commander, I am mortified. We were very nearly all roast.*"

"You mean toast," Sulu said.

*"Toast, thank you."*

*"Nonetheless,"* Ael said, *"we are all alive . . . a situation on which I would have been unwilling to suggest odds when I first saw what was waiting for us. If a few adjustments in your version of the process need to be made, well, that is the history of science. But meantime, the effectiveness of the tuned-shield approach against the Sunseed routines is very neatly proven."*

"Assuming one knows the frequencies to which the shields must be tuned ahead of time," Spock said. "Assessing and tuning them when the star cannot be analyzed ahead of time, but must be assessed at the *same* time, will be a considerable challenge."

"I leave that to the three of you," Jim said. "Meanwhile, we have another problem. There were seven Romulan ships in Federation space when they had no business to be there. I don't suppose that was the diplomatic mission. . . ."

*"If it was, we have committed nearly as serious a breach of protocol as they did,"* Ael said dryly. *"But I very much doubt they had anything to do with the ships we are still expecting."*

"So do I." Jim sighed and rubbed his face. "Commander Uhura, prepare a message with a record of what just happened here and prepare to send it off to Starfleet, suitably encrypted." For the moment he was willing to put his concerns about possibly broken encryption aside. If the Romulans could decode this message, let them. It would give them something to think about. "No technical details for the moment, though; keep it dry. Let me see it when it's done. I'll be in my quarters for a little while."

*"Bridge?"*

Jim punched the comm button again. "Problems, Bones?"

*"Nothing serious, but I'm glad you told me to fasten things down, down here. What the devil was that?"*

"I'll have Uhura send you down a recording to view at your leisure," Jim said, and grinned. Now that it was over, grinning was possible again.

*"Thanks loads. Out."*

Jim turned to Spock. "Mr. Spock, when is the task force due?"

"Twenty-eight hours and eighteen minutes from now, Captain."

"Very well. Let's get whatever repairs need to be done out of the way, and take the evening off. Keep the shields up, though, except as necessary. Commander, perhaps some of your crew would join us for dinner, and afterward."

*"Our pleasure, Captain."*

"Excellent. Maybe you would call me in my quarters in a few minutes? There are some things we should discuss."

*"Certainly, Captain. Out."*

Jim got up, went into the lift, and tried to order his thoughts. After a pell-mell encounter like the one of the last few minutes, sometimes this took a while. But he busied himself with one of the breathing exercises Bones had taught him, and shut his eyes while the lift hummed along, concentrating on seeing space as a calm place again, full of cold and silence and the fierce pale light of the stars. By the time the lift doors slid open again, things were better . . . except in one regard.

The call was waiting on his viewer when he came in and sat down in front of it. At the sound of his movement, Ael looked up. She had moved down to her own cabin from *Bloodwing*'s bridge.

*"So you were right,"* she said, *"about the ambush."*

"And so were you."

*"I? I did nothing but agree with you."*

"True." Jim leaned his elbows on the desk, laced his fingers together, and put his chin on them. "And without discussion. Which suggests to me that you had previously had your suspicions as well . . . which you did not exactly spell out to me."

She went quiet at that. *"I dislike being thought merely paranoid,"* Ael said.

"You also dislike being wrong," said Jim.

*"Yes,"* Ael said, *"but more lives than mine, or mine and* Bloodwing's, *are on the line here. Various people's actions in the Empire will be powerfully influenced by ours . . . and many innocents may live or die according to what those people do, when news of what has happened to us will make it back to the Two Worlds."*

"It won't be brought back by *those* ships."

*"No."* There was a brief pause. *"Even now, Jim, even after what we went through at Levaeri, when my son, my own son, turned traitor and tried to take your ship, and he and all the people who turned with him suffered the penalty for such betrayal—even after that, I still believe there are still most likely agents of the Empire aboard my ship; crew who did not reveal their affinities then, but conceal them still, passing messages back to ch'Rihan when they can. I did not dare generally reveal my thoughts about what might be waiting for* Bloodwing *at 15 Trianguli if we had kept to the original schedule; and I did not tell my crew at large that we were going to divert to Hamal first, or that we would leave it accompanied, instead of going alone to 15 Tri. Now behold what has happened . . . for* Bloodwing *comes to the spot where it was intended to wait alone, and finds seven Rihannsu ships waiting. And now no ship will go home to ch'Rihan to tell what happened; which is a good thing."*

"Commander," Jim said.

Her eyes widened a little at his tone.

"How the *hell* am I supposed to trust you," Jim said, "if you won't trust *me?*"

She made no answer to that right away. After a moment, Ael glanced down at her desk. *"I see that I have done you an injustice,"* she said. *"Habit . . . can be very difficult to break."*

"Something for you to talk to your chief surgeon about, maybe," Jim said. He was angry, but he wasn't going to let that affect him any more than necessary. "God forbid I should criticize you for calculating . . . your calculation has saved both our lives, once or twice. But there's no reason for you to do it *alone*. Especially when it's my crew's lives on the line, as well."

She was silent.

"In the meantime, I was right, and you were right, to take the course of action we did. And you're right about this too: regardless of how many spies may still be aboard *Bloodwing,* we now have enough evidence for my own purposes that there are intelligence leaks fairly high up in Starfleet, and those leaks are reaching straight back to ch'Rihan. Very few people at our end of things knew when you were supposed to be at 15 Tri, alone, to meet the task force that will shortly be arriving. My problem is that, after what's happened, they'll know that *I* have reason to suspect those leaks. This may translate into a loss of advantage for me, depending on how high up the leaks go . . . and I'm damned if I know what to do about it."

*"They will not know that,"* Ael said, *"if I tell them that I convinced you to accompany* Bloodwing *there."* Jim opened his mouth. *"They will half believe that anyway, Jim; for Starfleet cannot at the best of times be very sanguine about our association. Certainly they must look at it and see all manner of things that are not there."*

Jim closed his mouth again. After a moment he said, "Interesting idea."

*"And this I will be glad to do when the task force arrives,"* Ael said. *"It seems like the least I can do . . . by way of apology."*

Their eyes met. After a second, Jim let out a breath. "Let's see if it's genuinely necessary," he said.

*"Very well."*

"Meanwhile," Jim said, "the presence of those ships themselves is evidence that you were right in more than one way. There *will* be a war, now. Their presence in Federation space, without permission given beforehand for the transit, was itself an act of war according to the terms of the treaty that established the Zone . . . which tells me that someone in your government is getting ready to throw that treaty right out the window, no matter *what* Starfleet decides to do about you and *Bloodwing* and the Sword. From our two points of view, that certainly is going to change things."

*"Yes,"* Ael said softly. *"It will."*

"I want to discuss this with you further," Jim said. "But let's leave that for this evening, when your crew are here as well. That way there'll be a little less notice taken when you spend a good while talking to me . . . in places where we can't be overheard, by your crew *or* mine."

She briefly gave him a rather wicked look. Jim flushed. "Not like *that*," he said crossly.

*"Indeed not,"* Ael said. *"The thought was furthest from my mind."*

Jim raised his eyebrows. "Why, thank you. I think."

*"You are very welcome. What time shall I begin the leaves, Jim?"*

"A couple of hours." She reached out for the control for her viewer.

"Ael," he said.

She paused, looking at him thoughtfully.

". . . It's all right."

Ael's eyes dwelt on him for a moment more. *"That must yet be seen,"* she said, and she bowed her head, and cut the connection.

Jim sat there for a while, frowning, thinking. *She may not be alone in the doing-an-injustice department,* he thought. *Think of the shock of being betrayed, not just by a co-officer, but by your own son.* The thought was profoundly uncomfortable. He wanted to turn away from it, but forced himself to face it regardless. The loyalty of his officers and crew, not unquestioning but utterly reliable, was something Jim had come to take for granted, like air to breathe. He could not conceive of life on *Enterprise* without it. Ael, though, having had something very like that with her own crew, had now seen that seemingly solid ground fall away from under her feet. And across that suddenly shifting, crumbling landscape, she was now walking into what would be, if Jim was right in his guesses, the greatest challenge of her career: if indeed she considered that she had a "career" left as such. At any rate, it was a situation from which she would emerge alive and triumphant—or dead. He could still hear that proud, cool voice saying, "Flight would not be my choice . . . it will solve nothing." One way or another, unresolved details aside . . . she was still resolved to fight. And all this without knowing, any longer, if she could completely trust her own crew.

*Once burned . . .* Jim thought. *But it all still comes down to trust. If this situation is to be survivable—she's got to learn to trust me.*

*And can she ever?*

He sighed, then got up and went off to have a shower, and see about a meal.

# Chapter Four

Many light-years away from 15 Trianguli, two men sat in a dim-lit room, awaiting the arrival of a third. The two scowling around them at the high-ceilinged, tapestried, weapon-hung surroundings, which were unusually rich and splendid even as high-caste Klingons reckoned such things, a twilight of crimson and dully gleaming gold. The two Klingons were also scowling at one another, for normally, had they met in the street, they would have attacked one another.

There was blood feud between Kelg's House and Kurvad's, a feud that both Houses had cultivated with pleasure for a decade. Unfortunately, the House in which the two enemies now sat was senior to both of theirs by centuries, and the man whom they awaited was so high-caste that any feud must needs be set aside until they had discharged whatever errand he might set the two of them. The necessity did not make the waiting any easier, though, and the silence between them was broken by the occasional snarl. That, at least, propriety permitted. Kelg entertained himself with thoughts of what else he would do, some time soon, when circumstances brought him and Kurvad together in some less ritually restrictive environment.

For nearly half an hour they had to sit in the dimness, waiting. Somewhere nearby the noon meal had been served, and Kelg's gut growled at the smell of choice viands, the smoky hint of *saltha* on the air, the scent of bloodwine. But nothing was offered them. Kelg sat there fuming at the insult until the great black carved doors swung open, and K'hemren walked in. Kelg and Kurvad stood to greet him, then sat down again.

"I will hear your report," said K'hemren, reaching behind his tall chair. The scent of the feast to which they had not been invited swirled in the air around them as the doors to K'hemren's counseling chamber closed.

"They are finally moving," said Kelg, determined to speak the first word at this meeting in Kurvad's despite, and as much intent on drowning any sound his gut might make. "And doing it with surprising openness. No hiding it . . . no cover stories."

"Beware the *targ* without a bone in his mouth," said Kurvad, sneering, "and the Romulan without a lie in his."

"The cliché is true enough," said Kelg. "And what are we to make of what they are doing? Not what they *want* us to, surely?"

K'hemren had brought out from behind the tall chair a long, curved, extremely handsome *bat'leth*. This he now laid in his lap. "It is toward the Federation that they move," he said, glancing up. "And some interesting pieces of news have come to us, through their own news services, and even via messages routed through our own message networks."

Kelg and Kurvad looked at him curiously, but he did not elaborate. Finally Kurvad said, "The arch-traitress whom they've all been yelping about the last couple of months apparently has gone to ground in Federation space. Seems that she may either be about to ask them for asylum, or else she has done so already . . . I am none too clear on the details."

Kelg, laughing at him, got up and began to pace. "They will never give it to her! She would become an occasion of war, and if there is one thing they never want, it is a war!"

"She has already become such an occasion," said K'hemren, thoughtfully stroking the *bat'leth,* "and she is indeed now in their hands. Yet they have not sent her back across the Zone, which would have been the most straightforward response." He smiled slightly. "But there is a reason for that, it seems."

Kelg paused. He and Kurvad looked at K'hemren curiously.

"She has been with Kirk," K'hemren said, "in *Enterprise.*"

Kurvad spat on the floor and leaped to his feet, beginning to pace as well, though at the mandated safe distance from Kelg. "I thought ill enough of human manners," he growled, "but the man mates with aliens, with animals, as well? It is intolerable—"

". . . that one who behaves so, nonetheless also beats every ship of ours he meets?" K'hemren looked down at the *bat'leth* in amusement. "Maybe so. But his victories cannot be denied him—may the last Dark only devour him soon."

"That the two of them should be conniving together—" said Kelg. "It bodes ill for someone."

"The Romulans, I think," said K'hemren. "That one does not love her people. She has betrayed them before. So she meets with Kirk, as before, to hatch out some new betrayal." He smiled slightly. "But then she is a madwoman. Her niece was betrayed by Kirk and his half-breed first officer, and yet the woman blames her own people for what happened to the niece. Irrational."

Kelg stood still for a moment, thinking about that irrationality and what might be made of it, if the circumstances were right. The woman had been deadly enough in her way; the thought of somehow pushing Kurvad into her path was amusing. "One could wish she would only turn on Kirk some fine morning and tear his throat out," said Kurvad.

"It would be too much to ask of the universe," said K'hemren. "Meanwhile, these ship movements . . ."

"They concern me," said Kelg, beginning to pace again, though more slowly now. "The Romulans would not dare move toward battle unless they had acquired something which made them completely fearless."

"You underestimate them," said Kurvad. "They have the strength to conduct a little border war, surely. . . ."

Kelg sneered at the idea, typical of Kurvad's witlessness and cowardice, and was amused by Kurvad's outraged look. "Have they indeed! They didn't react to our attack on Khashah IV—what is it they call it? Eilhaunn? They withdrew their forces, they *let* us take it!"

"A trick. While they do that on the one hand, on the other they move directly into Federation space—"

"With all of seven ships!"

"Do you think me a complete fool? There have been many more ship movements than that in Romulan space near where the Zone meets Federation space, over the past two weeks. And similar movements where the Zone comes close to our own space! Once again they use the Zone to cloak their own movements. And their new cloaking device is in use as well; who knows what they are letting us see just to distract us from what we can't see elsewhere?"

Kelg laughed again. "There are no great strategists among them . . ."

"There do not have to be!" K'hemren roared. Kelg stopped, shocked still for the moment. "They are afraid—which makes them dangerous. And more, they have no hope!"

K'hemren's vehemence silenced both Kelg and Kurvad for a moment. "We have closed down our relations with them much too tightly in recent months," he said. "Now they have no hope in dealing with us . . . and one should never leave one's enemy without hope. First of all because it is a weapon in one's own hand, sunk in their guts, which one can twist when one needs to. But secondly because an enemy without hope swiftly becomes an enemy with nothing to lose!"

It was good sense in its way, but Kelg was reluctant to admit this. "The chancellor," he muttered, "is not going to have much patience for these philosophical discussions. He is going to want to know how many more planets we have taken since we spoke to him last. It does not take a thought admiral to see that the present answer will not please him."

K'hemren shrugged, studying the *bat'leth*'s steel, and turned it over in his lap. "Even the chancellor cannot have everything his own way," he said. "It would be a fool's act to attack any more worlds before hostilities break out. Let the fog of war descend first. Under its cover, many attacks can take place, and no one will know whose responsibility they are."

"No one who does not bother analyzing the ion trails and residues," said Kurvad.

"Kurvad, are you *entirely* without a spleen?" Kelg cried, taking a few steps toward the other, but not so many as to come close enough to him to entitle him to retaliate physically. "There will be no time for forensics when this war breaks out in earnest! Our business now is to designate targets for when it *does* break. We need metals, heavy and light; and we need slave labor. Those we will be able to get in plenty from the worlds around our bridgehead at Eilhaunn." He did not add what use his House, involved in the attack on that planet, would be able to make of those resources; they would shortly be rich, and the riches would buy them the influence with the chancellor's advisers that they had never been able to afford before. After that, the Romulans could go to whatever hell they preferred. Kelg's House would have more important things to think about. *Maybe even, someday, the seat of Empire itself*— "The damned Romulans will have their hands full with the Federation, anyway. They are concentrating most of their forces on that side of the Zone."

"Not all of them—"

"All the ones that would cause us trouble! And the Federation is taking the bait, moving their own ships into that sector as well. Now at last comes our chance to take back much of what was left in the Federation's hands when the curst Organians interfered. The Federation has left their flank too unguarded. Only a little while more of ship movements like this, in which they seek to overawe their enemy and keep him from fighting, and they will have unbalanced themselves enough so that the enemy which *does* want to fight will be able to move in and start a real war, not this pitiful little border skirmish!" He spat on the floor again and turned away; seen only as a shadow, a slave crept in to mop up the spittle.

Somewhere distant in the great house, voices were lifted in song. Cups could be heard clanking, at that feast to which Kelg had not been invited. *But that will change. Soon the feasts of triumph will begin, and I shall be foremost at them all—and Kurvad's skull will be bound in steel and used as a spittoon.* "What else have you to report, then?" said K'hemren.

"Nothing else," said Kelg. "When must we return?"

"I don't know," said K'hemren. "I must first speak with the chancellor. Go back to your fleets and get them ready for battle. I will contact you when he has orders for you."

"Will it be war?"

"I think that will probably be unavoidable," said K'hemren, with a smile.

Kelg and Kurvad did the only thing they could conceivably have done together: they leapt up from their chairs and shouted for victory. K'hemren stayed seated, stroking the *bat'leth*'s pattern-welded steel. "Yes," he said, "you will have your chance at both the Romulans and the Federation, I make no doubt. But beware lest some unhappy fate throws you in the path of Kirk and that bitch-traitress of his."

"It would be no unhappy fate for me," said Kelg. "My brother served with Kang, and came to grief at Kirk's hands." The images of what revenge he might take if the man ever crossed his path had long been the delight of his idle moments. Now, there was at least a chance that they might come true.

"And my cousin," said Kurvad, "when he served with Koloth: the same."

K'hemren said nothing. "Go back to your ships," he said, "and wait."

Kelg glared at K'hemren for just a second or so, for he had not declared their errand complete: they could not try to kill each other, as they had been longing to do. *But there'll be another day,* Kelg thought. *Is not war full of unfortunate accidents?* He headed out of the room with only a single angry glance at Kurvad.

Behind him, as the door shut, he caught a last glimpse of K'hemren, not hurrying out to his interrupted feast, but sitting quietly in the chair, in the dimness, stroking the *bat'leth,* thinking.

That evening there were a lot of people in the rec deck. There was no special event arranged—nothing but the usual scatter of games, conversation, occasional music or song, and people moving around and eating and drinking casually. Still, Jim could, after long experience, feel the tension in the air—the sense of there having been a very close call—and could also feel it discharging itself. But this was what rec was for, at its best; this was one of the reasons why the recreation department was classified as part of medicine, and reported directly to McCoy. McCoy was in fact here as well, as much for his own discharge of tension as to keep an eye on everyone else—though which reason was more important to him, Jim thought he knew.

There were, as Jim had intended, a fair number of Rihannsu in attendance—though for Starfleet's peace of mind, and indeed Jim's, they were all in here, and not wandering around his ship without supervision. The food processors were proving extremely popular, and when Jim came down from the balcony where he had been keeping an eye on things to greet Ael shortly after she entered, he found her standing with a disappointed look next to one of them. To K's't'lk, beside her, Ael was saying, "It is rather unfortunate. I have something of a savory tooth, and *kheia* is very choice . . . and something we could not normally afford to have on *Bloodwing,* I can tell you that."

"Problems?" Jim said.

"My crew, the greedy *hlai,* have eaten all the *kheia,*" Ael said. She glanced over at Aidoann, who was standing nearby with a pair of tongs and a plate that was very nearly empty. "Is this *mnhei'sahe,* then? To starve your commander?"

Aidoann shot Jim an amused look, and then held out her plate, and her tongs, handles first, to Ael. "We exist to serve," she said. Laughter came from the various other crew around her, Khiy and tr'Keirianh the master engineer, who were eating just as fast as they could and seemed in no rush to make gestures of self-sacrifice.

"Oh, away with you," Ael said, laughing. "There are more than enough other dainties. Just look here; see the size of this *llsathis!* Here, I will have a slice of that, and just a cup of ale, and leave the *kheia* to my poor starving children." Her people laughed at her lofty tone, apparently not at all fooled by it.

"Allow me," Jim said, and cut her a slice of what appeared to be a giant blue gelatin ring. "Ael, why is so much of your food blue?"

She blinked as she took the plate and a spoon. They strolled away from the table, K's't'lk coming with them with a plate held up on two of her back legs. "Why should it not be?"

"It's not a very usual color for us."

"Perhaps. But one person's usual is another man's odd, I should think. Surely it would not be usual for you to eat . . . Forgive me, madam, but what *is* that?"

"Graphite," K's't'lk said, picking up another chunk of it as they walked, and bringing it close to her body. Jim didn't see where it went—he never had, where solid foods were concerned—and he had given up staring to try to find out. "I am off duty now, and may permit myself to indulge a little."

"It is an intoxicant?"

"For us, yes." She gave Jim a look out of what was currently the frontmost cluster of eyes. "And all too often present company has encouraged me to indulge, when we were in private."

"You're interesting when you start getting atonal," Jim said, "that's all."

K's't'lk chimed at him in major ninths, a sarcastic but still goodnatured sound. "You two are old intimates, then," Ael said, "and do not merely work together."

"Oh yes. Many a long quiet talk the captain and I have had in his quarters," K's't'lk said, "about life and the universe. But that cabin is famous across the quadrant, Commander. Beware how you go!"

"Why," Ael said calmly, "what should happen to me there?"

Jim looked at K's't'lk with mock outrage. "You're a fine one to talk," he said, "after what *you* did in my quarters!"

"What did she do?" Ael said.

Jim opened his mouth, shut it again, then laughed. "I'm not sure exactly how to describe it," he said.

"*H't'r'tk'tv'mtk,*" K's't'lk said, or sang. "The term has no close equivalent among hominid species, Commander. I reproduced myself."

"What," Ael said, "right *there?*"

Those blue-burning eyes, full of their shifting fires, dwelt on Jim again with some amusement. "Certainly it's not something one would do just *anyplace,*" K's't'lk said. "It needs a secure environment. A certain amount of intellectual and emotional engagement. . . . And shelves."

"Oh, well, thank you very much," Jim said, nonplussed. " 'Shelves.' " Then he laughed. "You two really should get together sometime and discuss it further. Meanwhile, T'l—what about 15 Trianguli?"

"I was hoping you wouldn't mention that."

"Somebody has to," Jim said. "That star didn't behave as advertised."

"In a manner of speaking it did," K's't'lk said, sounding even more embarrassed. "The only reason the technique didn't work correctly was that, as Mr. Chekov mentioned at the time, the star is only marginally a candidate for being seeded. If it had been just a very little more massive, or a touch hotter, say a K6, we would have gotten a smooth propagation of the ion-storm effect into subspace, instead of a coronal mass ejection, which was not what I had in mind. A thing like that could kill you."

Jim and Ael exchanged a look over her back. "But certainly," Ael said, "this experience will have provided you with valuable data for more accurately establishing your baselines in the future."

"Commander," K's't'lk said, "you are a gracious lady, and I thank you for trying to make me feel better. But, J'm, I apologize to you. Once more I have put your ship in danger by not adequately predicting all the variables in a situation."

"Oh, come on, T'l . . ." Jim said. "You did what you could with what you had; it wasn't as if you could have sent that star back and got a better one. And we all came out of it well enough; consider this a minor setback. What *did* work brilliantly was the shields."

"Yes, they did function nicely, didn't they?" K's't'lk said. She sounded slightly more cheerful. "The only problem was the way we had to keep retuning them separately on both ships."

Ael's expression became puzzled. "I am not sure how that could be avoided. The ships are after all discrete entities, each with its own warp signature and structure, requiring different tuning for each warp field's shape."

"Oh, of course," K's't'lk said, "but for joint operations like this it would be more elegant to have only one mechanism handling both sets of tuning." She chimed softly for a moment. "You know," she said then, "if you . . . No."

"No?" Ael said.

"No, it would just bring in the equivalence heresy," K's't'lk said, "and hard on the heels of *that* come all kinds of quantum uncertainties as well. Unresolved energy-state phyla, subspace phase-shift intransigences. There are enough of those already." She sighed, a sound like minor-chord windchimes.

"T'l," Jim said, "you were supposed to be enjoying yourself a little, here. And look, you've run out of graphite."

"Don't tempt me. Now, *intransigences . . .*" K's't'lk said, in a rather different tone of voice. "Now *there's* an interesting thought. I should go talk to Sc'tty. Captain, Commander, if you'd excuse me—"

K's't'lk went jangling off across the room at speed. "Now you've done it," Jim said, watching her go.

"*I* have done it?"

Jim chuckled as they walked away. "I take it," Ael said, "you are well used to not being clear about what she is discussing."

"You have no idea. The things she's done to my ship—" He smiled. "Well, I'll forgive her a great deal; the results have sometimes been spectacular. Come on, Ael, let's sit down and relax."

He led her up to the balcony at the top of the recreation deck, nearest the great windows, where a few chairs and tables had been set out. *Bloodwing* had little in the way of ports, Jim knew; and he knew the impulse to bring her up here had been the correct one as she stood there and looked out the huge clearsteel windows, silently, her food momentarily forgotten.

"There's an observation deck above this one," Jim said. "Quieter, if you prefer it—"

"No," Ael said, "this suits me well enough. I have had enough quiet and solitude over the last couple of months; this makes a pleasant change . . . even if the voices breaking the silence, some of them, are strange."

They sat down and watched the mingling crews beneath them for a while, during which time Ael demolished the blue gelatin-stuff on her plate, and Jim sat cradling the old port which McCoy, now down there talking to tr'Hrienteh, had handed him on his way over to greet Ael. Finally the two of them were left sipping their respective drinks, while beneath them people chatted and sang and laughed and played quiet games, and the evening slipped by.

Jim wasn't sure how long they had been up there, discussing this and that, before Harb Tanzer was coming up the steps toward them. "Captain," he said, "Commander, can I get you anything?"

"Ael?" Jim said.

She shook her head. "I am in comfort," she said. "It has been a pleasure to be here, for a change, when hostilities were not in progress." Her voice was a touch sad. Jim could practically hear her thinking, *As they are about to be again.*

Harb only nodded. "Yes," he said. "The last time you were here, there wasn't much time for recreation as such. This place . . ." He looked around, plainly seeing it as it had been once when the corridors outside had been full of Romulans suddenly turned treacherous, and the inside was full of *Enterprise* crew and Romulans friendly to them, but unarmed. "This place," Harb said finally, "got to be a mess." He looked around it now, gazing at the crewpeople, human and Rihannsu and many others, who were milling around eating and drinking and talking. "It's much improved now."

There was a faint rumbling through the floor, and Harb looked up as Mr. Naraht came in. "Aha," Harb said. "Captain, Commander, would you excuse me? I want to go see what he thinks of the new batch of granite."

"Go on, Mr. Tanzer," Jim said. "I'll be pleased to hear."

He went on down into the crowd on the main floor, which was thinning somewhat now as the evening went on. The day had taken its toll on everyone. "Ael," Jim said after a few moments. "We can't leave it much longer. They're going to be here tomorrow."

"I know," she said softly.

"So tell me now. What are you going to do?"

Ael sighed, a heavy sound; and it came to Jim that he had never heard her sigh before, or at least couldn't remember it. "Only this," she said. "I think I must lead a force of ships and ground troops back to ch'Rihan and ch'Havran, and meet the forces of my homeworlds in battle . . . with an eye to unseating the government."

"Oh," Jim said.

She gave him a look. "Aye, I hear you thinking: 'Where is she keeping this force? I have not seen it.' Well, nor have I. But it is there, and growing . . . if my sources tell me true. And I believe they do."

"If they don't," Jim said, "you're going to be in for a very interesting time."

"I am in for that regardless," Ael said.

"Your government's been in place a long while," Jim said. "I doubt it's just going to let you walk in and topple it." *And what if she thinks it will? . . . We may be in big trouble. . . .*

She sat back and folded her arms. "In the older days," Ael said, "what you say would unquestionably have been true. Its strength was better distributed, then. But now it grows top-heavy, and therein lies both the source of some of our troubles as a people, and their solution."

She got a brooding look. "It is not so much the Senate with which I quarrel," Ael said. "It works well enough. But the Praetorate has acquired far more power than it used to have in the days when it was mostly our high judiciary, ruling on finer points of the law which the Senate had passed and the Expunging Body could not muster enough of a majority to remove. Now, for various reasons of expediency and habit, the Praetorate has begun to sway the Senate itself, pushing the power blocs which compose it into what directions they please. In some cases I suspect it—as do others—of encouraging the formation of those blocs itself, to make the Senate as a whole easier to manipulate. 'Independent' Senators are few and far between, these days, and those who choose to remain so for long are either blind to the forces moving around them, or stubborn enough not to care. A Senator unaligned with one of the major power blocs is all too likely to become suspect, attracting the attention of intelligence or other unfriendly organizations subject to the Praetorate's dictates. All too soon Senators who realize this tend to fall into line."

Jim turned that over in his mind. *What a mess. . . .* But he had not missed her annoyed tone. This was plainly something Ael would very much like to do something about. "I get the sense from what you're saying that the Praetorate itself has its own blocs."

Ael nodded. "And therein lies the problem. There are only twelve Praetors, and when so much power is concentrated in so few hands, trouble inevitably starts. Once upon a time all Praetors came of houses of great power and wealth, so much so—it was thought—that they would not need to strive one against another in the political realm. But too little of Rihannsu nature the lawmakers knew who believed that. Over time a tendency has manifested itself for two or three or four of the Twelve to dominate the others, either by straightforward means such as kinship-alliance, or by secret guile or the threat of force." That brooding look got darker. "We are not at our best, as a people, when rule is concentrated in the hands of just a few . . . and just one would be far worse. The memory of Vriha t'Rehu, that bloody and terrible woman, the Ruling Queen as she called herself, is too much with us still. Close enough she came to destroying both our worlds."

Ael shuddered. "For our people, as regards government, safety lies in numbers . . . the more, the better. But at present, though the outer forms of a representative democracy, as you would call it, may yet remain, the reality is otherwise. Our Empire has become a tyranny. There have been times when luck or the Elements have sent us tyrants who were benevolent, as there were such times in your own world. But such times are rare, and this is not one of them. The Three who rule the Twelve, right now, are a force under whom *mnhei'sahe* as we used to understand it has become a scarcity, too precious either to spend on ourselves or to waste on our enemies. For them, expediency has become all. And the Empire, in their hands, has become a tool used not as originally intended, to feed its people and further their lives and aspirations, but to keep power concentrated as it is now, in the hands of those who have long possessed it, and prefer to keep it that way."

She took a long drink of her ale, then sat for a few moments turning and turning the cup around in her hands. "The Three have ascended relatively young to power, and delight in using it; indeed their use of it has molded all the doings of Federation and Empire, one with the other, for the last half decade. They it was who started to send our ships across the Neutral Zone, spending the lives of brave officers to test the peace which had held so long and which so irked them. Theirs was the force behind the vote of the Senate which stripped my sister-daughter of her ship and her title and her name, after you stole the cloaking device from her, and sent her into exile, the Elements only know where. They it was who, when I began to speak out openly against them, sent me away to the Outmarches on *Cuirass* for that tour of duty intended at the least to punish me, and at best to bring about my death. And they were the ones who, before they ascended to power, started the researches that terminated in the work done at Levaeri V; the ones who ordered *Intrepid* captured and all its Vulcan crew to be put to death for the sake of the power which chemical mastery of Vulcan mind-control and mind-reading disciplines would give them and their creatures on ch'Rihan and ch'Havran."

She fell silent a moment. Jim watched with some admiration for the coolness with which she spoke of these people who had tried to destroy her. His own frustration at how badly she had been treated by the Empire she served was severe enough. *Would I be able to be that levelheaded about them, I wonder? And will she be able to stay this way . . . ?* "If I am bitter against them in my own regard," Ael said, "perhaps you will agree I have reason. But all my trouble began with an attempt to see the Three moved out of power by working within our own system. That attempt, and those that followed it, failed. That being the case, I came to you—for as I said at the time, when one's friends are helpless to make a difference, one turns even to one's enemies; especially the honorable ones. But it has not been enough, Jim. The work we have done together, while useful, yet falls short of what will cure the illness of which Levaeri V was only the symptom. Now I must raise what forces will answer me when I call, and move against my own world and people, though they call me traitor for it, and burn my name while I am still living, and curse it when I am dead."

Ael bowed her head.

Jim sat and considered, for the details of his sealed orders were on his mind. There had been a time when his own ancestors had been involved in a revolution like this, and he was proud now of that involvement. But five centuries' distance and the settled verdict of history now lent an aspect of comfortable respectability to that old war. Seen up close, as contemporaries, coups were not such comfortable companions. *At this end of time it's easy to say, yes, I would have been a patriot, I would have helped! But hindsight inevitably contaminates the vision. And being involved in a coup at its beginning, helping to hold the match to the fuse . . .* For that was the kind of help Ael was seeking from him.

He looked out at the stars. *On the other hand . . . sealed orders aside, if you see an injustice, and don't move to right it when you have a chance, history won't forget that, either.*

Jim turned back to her. "All right," he said. "So let's assume that your supporting force materializes as scheduled, and you sweep into the Eisn system, fight your way down to the surfaces of both planets, against whatever odds, put a significant number of troops on the ground, and carry the day. Then what?"

She leaned back and gave him a droll look. "Why, then that very day we have the Three and their minions dragged in chains down the Avenue of Processions in Ra'tleihfi, and put to the sword: and then from the ranks of the Senate, where here and there some old praetorial blood yet remains, we cause the elevation of twelve new Praetors . . . and then we go to our noonmeal."

Jim snorted. "Yes," Ael said, "it would be rather less simple than that, and I make no doubt there will be complications that neither of us could foresee. But one must start somewhere. Right now the Praetorate is too united under the Three's domination, and the Senate is too divided, for them to bring about a change in the status quo by the normal method. A credible threat to the Empire—or at the very least to the power structure at the top of it, and the armed forces which support that structure—will give them reason to change their thinking, especially when I make my cause known, and when it becomes obvious that I have power to back it."

"It may also give them reason to unite," Jim said, "and try to crush you."

"If the forces brought against them are sufficiently strong," Ael said, "I do not look for that. And additionally . . ."

She got that brooding look again. "Things are shifting," Ael said. "Increasingly there are signs that people around the Empire, not just on ch'Rihan and ch'Havran where the government's grip is tightest, are beginning to recall times when honor meant something—when we were content with what we had; when our people's history, painful and tragic as it has sometimes been, was a part of us, and not something we had to forget, or get over." Ael's look grew fierce. "If I must lead a force against my own world to rouse my people to take back their heritage, the power rightfully theirs, the thing worth fighting for . . . then so be it. There are, it seems, many who will follow me. For one thing, news of Levaeri V got out, and many people could see for themselves what that technology would make of our worlds if widely used. For another thing, the outworlds in particular, the colony planets and client systems in those spaces which march with the Klingon side of the Empire, have been suffering terribly of late. They are not all unarmed; indeed some of our oldest and most honored families, the great old Ship-Clans descended from the generation-ship captains, pilots, and engineers who brought us to the Two Worlds, are settled out there in force. Once they were proud, and their voices were great in the Empire. But in recent years the government has sought to reduce their power, either by oppressing them directly, or by ignoring them, refusing to support their worlds. And now they are growing weary of this treatment . . . and growing restive."

"Restiveness is useful as an indicator," Jim said, "and early indications are always nice. But what happens if you raise the banner . . . and no one falls in behind you?"

Ael lifted her eyes to his. "Then I go over the hill by myself," she said, "and take the consequences. I have done it before. If I die in so doing . . ." She raised her eyebrows. "Is it so bad a way to die? Even if no one answers the call to arms, if all the Empire from Eisn outward ignores me, and I must go down into ch'Rihan's gravity well alone . . . then alone I shall go."

The two of them sat quiet for some moments. Around them and behind them the lights of the rec deck were dimming as it slipped into gamma-shift mode, ship's night. The stars outside did not move, but hung there, still as watching eyes.

Then, very softly, Jim said:

"Like hell you will."

It was late again in Eveh tr'Anierh's study, and he had taken a moment away from the desk to try to stabilize some of the least stable of the piles of books on one of the shelves. With his arms full of books, he paused for a moment as he heard the front door open. *Now at this hour,* he thought, *who*—

He knew within two guesses. Not many people dare to come uninvited to a Praetor's house after couch-time but another Praetor; and of the other eleven of those—

The study door swung open. There was Urellh, and behind him, there was also poor Firh the door-opener, scandalized because he had been unable to stop this guest from interrupting his master, and terrified because of who the guest was. "Urellh," said tr'Anierh immediately, "come in; make yourself welcome. Firh, why are you yet up so late? Where is Serinn?" He was the night door-opener.

"He was away, Lord—"

"Well, no matter. To your couch, man. We have an early day tomorrow, you and I."

Firh bowed and closed the door, looking vaguely relieved. Urellh had already seated himself in the chair opposite the one that tr'Anierh had left pulled out. He was already pouring himself herbdraft from the pitcher waiting there on the tray, and the spicy scent of it wafted to tr'Anierh's nostrils as he turned his back on Urellh and went back to restacking the books on the shelves. "Well," he said, "you did not come here just to drink my draft, however fine the imported herbs might be."

"You have been too busy in your little glade of knowledge here, then," Urellh said, "to see the news tonight."

"I saw the sunset news," tr'Anierh said. "Once a day is enough for me. We normally get what else we need to see in session during the day. Or plenty enough of it for me, at any rate. What's amiss?"

"Ch'Havran," Urellh said, and said it as a curse. "The damned insurrectionists are out in the streets. Who would have thought they would have dared, so soon after the lesson they were taught three months ago? Or that we thought they had been taught. And whose damned name do you think they were shouting?"

Tr'Anierh could guess this, too, within a half a guess; but he said nothing for the moment, finishing with one stack of books and beginning to dismantle the next. Outside the windows in one of the trees, a *dalwhin* tried a single piping note, then another, with the uncertainty of summer, when nesting was done and the immediacy had gone out of the defense of its territory. "If it is who I think," tr'Anierh said, "what matter? She is light-years away, soon to be a prisoner . . . or dead in battle."

"Oh indeed," Urellh said, "so you think, do you." He drank his cup of draft and slammed the cup down on the inlaid table. "What I want to know is what the news service thinks it's playing at, showing such things at all. If they'd just let well enough alone, such little local ructions would pass off without comment. But no, both worlds have to see it, and half the Empire, in a day or three. Out there where there's no control anymore, such ideas start to achieve common currency—"

"Which ideas?"

"Aah, the usual idiocy about our high history and how we've squandered it, and how our honor is in shreds and our Empire's wealth all bought with treachery—" He snorted. "Take the bread and the meat off their plates and the ale from their cups, and we'd see how soon they'd care a scrap for honor. But her name always gets worked into it somehow. As if any of them would shed a drop of green for her if it came to fighting." His look was sour. "Before this they did not dare put their heads up over the wall, for fear the intelligence services would deal with them. And their agendas were always so different, anyway, that their own divisions and squabbling did for us what the intelligence people failed to do. But now all of a sudden they've found a new name to cry. I wouldn't have thought them capable."

The *dalwhin* outside sang a long sweet phrase, about a breath's worth, in a minor key, then fell silent. Tr'Anierh raised his eyebrows at Urellh. "You know as well as I do," he said, "that the harder you try to keep these little groups' demonstrations from happening, the more attention they draw. Ignore them and they do pass off, eventually. People's memories are short. And as for the news services—" He shrugged, turned away from the shelf. "Let such things be shown commonly, and soon people stop paying attention to them; they become background noise."

Urellh did not answer him immediately. "There has been more news than only that," Urellh said after a few moments, softly. "Not on the news services, but it has been coming through, this past halfmonth, anyway. Ainleith. Mahalast. Orinwen. Taish. Relhinder." Tr'Anierh raised his eyebrows. They were all colony worlds of the so-called second class, worlds founded directly on emigration from the Two Worlds instead of by "second intention," not conquered client worlds, or "overspill" colonies of colonies.

"There have been demonstrations there as well," Urellh said. "All very proper, very polite. Petitions passed in to the local governments, with thousands of names." He paused for a few long moments. "Treason," he said.

"For what do these petitions ask?" tr'Anierh said, though he knew.

"Treason," Urellh said again. "'Freedom.'" It was a growl. "Why, what else have we given them all these years but freedom to be safe, to be provided for, to have safe trade with the Hearthworlds and defense against those whom we know to be their enemies. Now let there be a slight change in policy, strictly temporary of course, but necessary, and you see quickly enough where their loyalties lie—" He broke off. "Damned Ship-Clan families," Urellh said softly, after a pause. "They have never really been one with us, not when we were in the ships, and not afterward when our people came down out of the wretched things to live on real worlds again. There is no getting the steel out of their blood, or the vacuum out of their brains. Their time is done, you would think they would have the sense to see it by now. The ships are fallen, the computers are dust, their time as the great 'guardians of our destiny' is over! But no, they cling to this 'nobility' that no one can see but them. History, heritage . . ." He snorted. "Anachronism! Time to look forward now, not back. The future is waiting for us, and all they can think of is division and backsliding when we should be united, looking to the future—"

"I would think," said tr'Anierh carefully, glancing over at the table where Urellh had slammed his cup down and then reaching for a dusting cloth from the bottom shelf of one of the bookshelves, "that they too are a passing force, nearly spent. There are few enough of those old families left anymore. And were they ever so numerous, the thing that gave them their power base is now gone. Without the great ships, what are they?"

Once again Urellh was silent for some moments. As tr'Anierh came around toward his desk, pausing by the table to mop up the spilled herbdraft, the other Praetor looked up at tr'Anierh from under those dark eyebrows of his. In the subdued lighting of the room, tr'Anierh was suddenly stricken by how very dark and fierce the man looked.

"Everything is a light thing to you, is it not?" Urellh said. "At least, when one asks you about it to your face."

Tr'Anierh was opening his mouth to answer, but Urellh did not wait for him. "You have tried to forestall me," Urellh whispered, and the whisper was very cold. *"Why did you try to forestall me?"*

Tr'Anierh flushed first hot, then cold, and prayed that in this lighting, neither of them showed. For the moment he concentrated on folding up the dusting cloth.

"You have no taste for war," said Urellh. *"That* is your problem. Do you not see, are you too stupid to see, that our people do have one, if you do not? . . . and if you do *not* give them a war, every now and then, they will have one in your despite? You may play the fool with your own hide, tr'Anierh, and those of your creatures in Fleet that see fit to obey your orders. But not with *my* hide, and not with the lives of the people I rule."

The turn of phrase was one that tr'Anierh filed away carefully for future study . . . but right now he had little time to waste on it. "Our people," he said, putting the cloth aside, "would be better served if all this were finished quickly, rather than dragged out into war over one woman—"

*"It is not merely over one woman!* There is much more at stake, and the act was idiocy! Now we will go to this meeting, and the cursed Federation will say, 'Why should we believe anything you say? Here we have evidence of you crossing the Zone illegally after the woman and attacking her in our space.' Besides losing us seven ships—*seven ships!*—you have forfeited the moral high ground to the Federation! What can you have been thinking of!"

Tr'Anierh swallowed. In the quiet, the *dalwhin* in the tree outside sang another timid little phrase, a few piped notes, and fell silent again. "Rogue elements can easily enough be blamed," he said. "The Federation know as well as we do that there are divisions among our people, Urellh. They have as many spies among us as we have among them; do you think I do not know?"

"I know that your heart is going cold in your side," said Urellh, "and I don't intend to permit that to ruin our plans. You are growing too like the indecisive ones in the Senate: you put out your hand to the sword and then snatch it back when you smell the blood on the blade." His eyes narrowed. "There are some, even in the Praetorate, who so fear a just war that they would even leak information to the enemy to prevent it. Just how," Urellh said, much more softly, "did the Federation get word about the mind-control project, for example? And do not tell me the despicable t'Rllaillieu told them. She got that information from somewhere. And it would not have been from one of the sottish wind-talkers in the Senate; the information was not disseminated that widely. It would have been from among the Twelve, from one of the very *Prae-torate,* tr'Anierh! Some one of us, maybe even more than one of us, is a traitor."

He looked long and hard at tr'Anierh. "You will not lay that at *my* House's gate, Urellh," said tr'Anierh, as steadily as he could. "And certainly not publicly; not unless you wish to find out exactly how quickly I 'snatch my hand back' when accused with such a calumny, and how 'lightly' I take everything. I would not trouble to take the matter to the judiciars. I would have you meet me in the Park."

Urellh's face stilled a little at that. "And as for this latest matter," said tr'Anierh, "if I knew of it, what of it? If it had succeeded, the Sword would either be safely destroyed, forever out of the hands of our enemies, or else it would now be on the way back to where it belongs. Our people's pride would to a great extent have been restored, and we would not now need to put our head into the *thrai*'s mouth to find out whether it has any teeth left or not. Has it ever occurred to you that it might have grown new ones faster than the old ones were pulled, and might bite indeed? What if the Federation suspects the diplomatic mission for exactly what it is, the prelude to war, and decides to strike first? And on the other hand, our own sources in Starfleet tell us how divided that organization has been of late. Very nearly they did not agree to meet the mission at all. What would we have done then? We would have been left with no t'Rllaillieu, no Sword, and no recourse except to invade in the routine manner, with the result being a full mobilization on Starfleet's side instead of the partial, uncertain, halfhearted one we see now. The Klingons would fall on our outworlds in force, in numbers, without a second thought. It is we who would be forced into a two-front war, not they. And what remained of the Empire after that—after the Klingons' brutality and the Federation's cruel mercy—would be a pitiful thing indeed, not worthy of the name. You are to count yourself most fortunate that they accepted, and that matters stand even now as well as they do."

Another brief silence, but the *dalwhin* outside sang no more. "You said nothing of these misgivings before we stood up before the Senate and proposed the mission," Urellh said. "I question whether they are not rather recently assumed . . . possibly in the wake of the failure of this 'rogue element.' The actions of which are themselves an act of war, in contravention of the treaty—so that any protection we might have had from that tattered rag of a document is lost to us now. I think it only right that *your* creatures in the diplomatic mission should be allowed to assume the responsibility for explaining it to the Federation negotiators. You are to count yourself fortunate that the fools will most likely accept the explanation, since they know so little of what passes among our worlds . . . the Elements be praised. Equally it will be fortunate for you, in the long run, that they know nothing of the package that will soon be on its way to them; for this nasty little business has at last decided *that* destination. That only will save your skin, when all the reckoning is done after the battle is complete. And meanwhile—" He got up, walked around the table, and put his face quite close to tr'Anierh's, nearly close enough to be an insult—though not quite. "It was an act of the most utter folly, meant to make me look a fool," said Urellh, "and I will not forget it."

He stormed out, and slammed the door behind him.

Tr'Anierh stood there until he heard the outer door close again. Then he breathed out a long breath, and went back over to the bookshelf and chose another pile of bound codices to reorganize.

*Honor,* tr'Anierh thought. Urellh had not said *mnhei'sahe;* he had used the lesser word, *omien.* Tr'Anierh considered that. It came to him that very few people seemed to say *mnhei'sahe* anymore. It was as if the word hurt them somehow. Even he himself avoided using it; perhaps not to be seen distinguishing himself too obviously from others, as one championing virtue—that was a sure way to cause your enemies to go tunneling like *kllhei* for proof that your virtue was a sham.

*But then the word always did have edges. And held incorrectly . . . it cuts. . . .*

He started making, in his mind, a list of the people he would need to call in the morning. Urellh was a bad and sore-tempered enemy when he had been crossed. Sometimes these moods passed off him quickly; sometimes they did not do so at all, or took long months to abate. At the moment, that could be a problem. Tr'Anierh thought about what to do . . .

. . . and about the seven ships.

Jim sat up in one of the briefing rooms for a long while, late that night, after leaving the rec deck and seeing Ael down to the transporters and back to *Bloodwing.* He was looking at the maps of the Federation, the Klingon Empire, and the Romulan Empire, and he was thinking hard.

The room was one of those with a big holographic display in the middle of the table. There Jim had sketched out for himself in the display, in red, a five-parsec sphere around the spot where the Rihannsu were scheduled to cross the border tomorrow. The larger portion of the task force that had been sent to do escort duty would meet them there and bring them into Federation space, to the spot selected for the rendezvous. Then the extra ships would depart, leaving the numbers equal at the rendezvous point, and talks would begin.

Jim looked at that red sphere now and thought, *Why here?* The Romulans had specified where they intended to cross the Zone for these talks. The Federation had made no counteroffer.

*And why not?* Jim thought. That by itself struck him as a failure. *Your opponent wants to do something—you force him to do something else. Partly to see how he reacts. Partly to make sure you stay in control of the game.* But for some reason, Starfleet had not reacted to that particular move. It was as if they had conceded something early, something they didn't see as particularly valuable, in a larger strategy.

For his own part, Jim had played too much chess with Spock—2D, 3D, and 4D—to much like the idea of conceding moves to anyone, especially first moves. They were strategically as important to him as later ones. And any move that did not advance your game, push you into your opponent's territory and threaten him somehow, was a wasted move. Wasting moves was criminal.

There was nothing terribly interesting about this part of space. It was largely barren. *But a lot of Triangulum space is like that,* Jim thought, *until you get in further.* There were richer spaces, better provided with planets with suns, and developed planets at that, in the Aries direction. But that whole area was also much better provided with Federation infrastructure. There were two starbases there, 18 at Hamal and 20 at gamma Arietis / Mesarthim; each was well provided with weaponry of its own and a large complement of starships, and Starbase 20 and its starship complement had the additional advantage of being staffed by the Mesarth, probably one of the most aggressive species in the Federation ("except for humans," Spock had once commented rather ruefully). *If I were a Romulan,* Jim thought, *I wouldn't waste my time going that way. Too much resistance. . . .*

But it still left him with the question: Why *here?*

Jim looked at the map for a while more. Leaving aside the issue of the "diplomatic mission," which he thought was as likely to be the spearhead of an invasion force as anything else, Jim was also thinking about the seven ships that *Enterprise* and *Bloodwing* had met at 15 Trianguli. *Someone was willing to take the chance of throwing away seven capital ships,* he thought, *for something. And not just for Ael.* Redoubtable as her reputation was, seven ships just for *Bloodwing* made no sense. They were even too much for *Bloodwing* and *Enterprise* together.

*Someone wanted to test our preparedness,* he thought. *If they got her, too . . . fine. But something else is going on. They wanted to test* this *area, not just the area over by the rendezvous point.*

Jim leaned his chin on his fist and looked at the hologram, telling it to rotate so that he could see the way the Klingon and Romulan Empires interpenetrated one another. The only "regular" boundary in the area was the Neutral Zone, which was a one-light-year-thick section of an ovoid "shell" with Federation space on one side and Romulan space on the other. Elsewhere, bumps and warts of Klingon and Romulan territory stuck into and out of the main volumes of the two Empires with great irregularity where they bounded one another. The contact surfaces suggested many years of the two players playing put-and-take in that part of space.

Jim stopped the hologram and instructed the viewing program to zoom in on the Neutral Zone. As he did, the monitoring satellites became visible, scattered fairly evenly along and across the Zone's curvature. *Now, were those ships* detected *coming across the Zone?* Jim thought. *And if not, why not? What's the matter with the monitoring satellites and stations?*

*Is it possible one or more of them have been knocked out, or sabotaged? By whom? And why wouldn't we have heard?*

He pulled his padd over and made a note on it, one of many he had made while studying the map. *And if the ships* were *detected crossing,* he thought, *why weren't we alerted by Starfleet?*

Jim tossed the stylus to the table and looked at the map again. The satellites were much on his mind. *If we have here some program of sabotage that has been in preparation for a while and is now ready to be tested . . . was this possibly the first test?*

*If it was . . . what will their reaction be when their seven ships don't come home again?*

He kept looking at the map. *Could it be that what we're looking at here,* Jim thought, *is an intended breakout in two different places? One in the area where the "diplomatic mission" will be—and one over here by 15 Tri? It will, after all, have the "New Battle" cachet. . . .* One of his Strat-Tac instructors, years ago, had mentioned to him some strategists' tendency to overlook a possible location for conflict because there had just been one there, the idea apparently being that an enemy was as unlikely to immediately fight twice on the same battlefield as lightning was to strike twice. This was, of course, a fallacy. A smart enemy, if he had the resources to waste and the brains to pull it off, might stage an unsuccessful battle on likely ground in order to tempt an unwary adversary onto it for a second and more murderous passage at arms. *You'd have to wonder why they were bothering with this one spot, though,* Jim thought. *Either because they've been assembling matériel close to it, or because it's convenient to something else.*

*The Klingons, maybe?* 15 Tri was convenient enough to the area where the Neutral Zone, the Klingon Empire, and the un-Zoned part of the

Romulan Empire drew close together. *A lot of scope for confusion there,* Jim thought. *Suppose the Romulans break out there—and instead of coming for us, swing around and attack the Klingons from our direction. Then duck back into the Zone in the confusion of the war that's already going on elsewhere, near the rendezvous point, say, and maybe somewhere else along the Zone as well.*

The hair stood up on the back of Jim's neck. *Two-front war,* he thought. *Bad. Very bad.*

*So that's one possibility,* he thought, sitting back in his chair. *And there's another. One of these two breakouts is a feint, to distract us from something more important happening somewhere else.*

He sat looking up at the map. *You must assume that they are preparing some great stroke against you,* Ael had said. *Revenge . . .*

*And they'll have more reason for it than ever, now,* Jim thought. *Seven more of their ships, we've written off . . . with their own weapon, too.* He touched the tabletop and started the map rotating again, more slowly this time. *I need information we probably aren't going to be able to get,* he thought. *I need to know what Rihannsu resources are sited over here at the moment.* He looked over at the area where the two Empires ran together near the Neutral Zone. *And what's been moved into that area recently . . .*

Again, information he probably wasn't going to get, certainly not over an open channel from Starfleet. Not that he didn't want to talk to them anyway about the status of the monitoring satellites, and those seven ships.

*Those ships . . .*

The idea that there should be a leak to the Rihannsu from Starfleet upset him profoundly. But at the same time, such leaks could be used to the advantage of a commander in the field . . . if you fed the correct information into them. You might be able to track the leak by where the information came out, in what shape. And even if you couldn't, your opponent would be misled . . . with results that you could turn to your own advantage.

Jim sat there a long while. *Ael will be back in the morning,* he thought, *to look in on that conference with Scotty and K's't'lk. This is the last chance we're going to have to confab before we have half of Starfleet looking over our shoulders.*

*Time to make our plans. . . .*

"Jim," said McCoy's voice behind him.

"I thought you'd turned in," Jim said.

"No," McCoy said. "Just off having a talk with Spock."

Jim raised his eyebrows. "Anything I need to know about?"

"Ael."

"What else," Jim said, and yawned, and rubbed his eyes.

McCoy came to sit down by him, and looked up at the map. "Yes," he said. "I thought so."

"And what's your tactical assessment, Doctor?"

"That you're about to head straight up the creek without a paddle."

Jim would have phrased it a little more strongly. "Bones," he said, "thank you. I'll call the Strat-Tac department at Starfleet and tell them you said so."

McCoy's look was unusually gentle. "Jim, listen to me. The way you're heading, you are shortly going to be caught in between *Bloodwing* and Starfleet again. It's not like you to make the same mistake twice."

"Well," Jim said, "you can put your mind at rest on that account, Bones, because this time I wasn't the one who made it." He looked up at the map. "*They* did."

"Starfleet?"

"They did not send *Enterprise* to meet *Bloodwing* here just because they know she and I are . . ." He was about to say "friends," but the word suddenly seemed both likely to be completely misunderstood, even by Bones, and completely inaccurate, for reasons he could barely describe to himself. He looked up to find McCoy looking closely at him. "Associates," Jim said.

"And in some ways," Bones said, "very much alike."

"That may be so," Jim said. "But they expect me to find out what she's going to do—or worse still, to anticipate it—and to act on what I discover, in Starfleet's best interests."

"And can you do that?" McCoy said.

"It's not a 'can,'" Jim said, "as you know very well. It's a 'must.' My oaths to Starfleet are intact, Bones, and I intend to keep them that way."

"But at the same time . . ."

"She has her own priorities, Bones," Jim said, settling back in the chair. "She wants peace . . . but she knows the only way that's going to happen, on the Romulan side of things, is war, and sooner, rather than later." He was quiet for a few moments. "I'm short of less slanted data at the moment, and I'd welcome some. But right now there isn't any."

"There may be some," McCoy said, "when the Romulans arrive."

Jim raised his eyebrows at that. "Oh?"

"Just a guess," McCoy said, "but I would be very surprised if at least one of the sources Starfleet's been gettin' its data from was not on that mission when it turns up."

Jim eyed McCoy thoughtfully. "Medicine is a creative art," Bones said, "just like command . . . and doctors get hunches the same way starship captains do."

"I hope you're right," Jim said. "Anyway . . ." He looked up at the map again. "Ael is a realist, if nothing else. I think she knows as well as I do that the situation, as it's presently shaping up, will result in war, no matter what she does. Equally from the realist's point of view, she has decided to play the active role, not the passive; to take control of the forces that are looking toward her now, as a catalyst, and to use them."

Jim slumped in the chair and rubbed his eyes again. "Yup. She's a catalyst, all right," he said.

"*Nuhirrien* . . ." McCoy, very softly.

"What?"

"You said people there were looking toward her. That's *nuhirrien,* almost literally," Bones said. "It's Rihannsu. Charisma, we would say . . . the quality of attracting people, of being followed by them." He let out a long breath.

"I keep forgetting, you did that chemical-learning course for the language."

"Sometimes I still wish I hadn't. I can't even *look* at a bowl of soup anymore."

Jim thought about that, and resolved firmly not to ask why. "Anyway," Bones said, "*nuhirrien* is a dangerous characteristic, for Rihannsu. Dangerous for Ael, too, if it seems she's got it."

"Why?"

"It's more associational than anything else," McCoy said. "The Ruling Queen had *nuhirrien,* they say. People would follow her, the way they once followed Hitler, centuries ago."

"Into tremendous evil," Jim said softly.

"Sometimes. It can blind people to the realities."

"We'd better hope it doesn't come to that," he said. "Bones, was there anything else? I'm about done here."

"Just so you know," McCoy said, "that, despite the imponderables . . . we're with you."

Jim stood up. "It's worth knowing," he said.

He killed the display and made for the door, with McCoy in tow. "You know," Jim said, "you're the one who should be talking to her. You've got the language, now."

"She's been avoiding me," McCoy said as they went down the corridor, "or so it seems."

*There* was data, and a piece that Jim wasn't sure what to do with. "Well," he said, "see what you can do about it. Choices are going to have to be made thick and fast around here in a couple of days, and I don't have all the information I need as yet."

"I'll do what I can," Bones said as Jim paused outside the turbolift, and its doors opened for him. "Meanwhile, you should get some sleep. Early meeting in the morning."

"Yes. Good night, Bones."

"Night, Jim," McCoy said, and the turbolift doors shut on him.

"Deck twelve," Jim said. The lift hummed upward.

*The big end of a court-martial,* Jim thought, and shivered.

# Chapter Five

If there was one thing Arrhae had not been expecting about going to space, it was having very much room to do it in. Long long ago, in another life (or so it felt), she had been used to fairly cramped quarters on starships; not unpleasantly so, but you wouldn't have room in your quarters for a game of *nha'rei,* either. Since then, in all her life as *hru'hfe* in House Khellian, the sense of her personal life as something lived in a fairly tight, small space had been reinforced to the point where she simply forgot about the possibility of things being any other way. On becoming Senator, and more senior in House Khellian than any servant, things had changed . . . though again, not to extremes, the house was richer in honor than in space.

But once again everything had shifted. She had climbed into the flitter that had been sent for her the evening after she talked to Eveh tr'Anierh—having spent the whole day, it seemed to her, not packing, but reassuring the household that she would be all right—and realized that her life had become peculiar again. The flitter had not taken her to the spaceport, but straight up and out of atmosphere, to the new heavy cruiser *Gorget.* She had stepped from the comfort of the flitter out onto a great shining floor in the cruiser's shuttle bay, with yet another honor guard waiting, this time of Fleet personnel; and these had brought small arms up to honor poise and walked her through the corridors of *Gorget,* Arrhae thought, like a queen. At a door high up in the deck structure of the cruiser they had halted, and one had opened the door for her; and Arrhae had walked into a space in which she could have had that *nha'rei* game, if she had chosen.

Huge windows on space, and carpeting, and antique furniture, and artwork, and a table off to one side, laden with food, and looking so good that Arrhae had to remind herself to treat it with disdain at the moment—the place was palatial. *If all Fleet lived like this, I could see why young Rihannsu would fight for commissions,* Arrhae thought. But she had a strong feeling that most crewmen didn't live like this; she knew that *Gorget* had recently been refitted, probably with an eye to the transport of notables and government figures. *If a small fish like me gets rooms like these,* she wondered, *what do the more senior Senators and the diplomats get?*

The honor guard had presently taken itself away, and Arrhae had discovered that the suite came with a small service staff of its own— maidservant and steward, the more senior of whom, Ffairrl the steward, bowed and scraped to Arrhae in a most unseemly way, one that suggested that he was either a spy (possible) or used to being mistreated by the high-ranking guests (equally possible). She allowed him to show her around the suite—a master bedroom with a bath suite that must have been most extravagant in water use, even aboard a starship where water could be manufactured at will from ramscoop "scrapings"; a bedroom and sitting room which together were nearly a quarter the size of House Khellian's Great Hall; and the outer meeting room and sitting room, with a buffet sideboard loaded with piles of food and pitchers of drink, and a small ancillary workroom and study, equipped with a state-of-the-art computer and communications suite. The tour over, Ffairrl begged to be allowed to give Arrhae food and drink. This she allowed him to do, and then sent him away, over his protests, while she wandered through the place, getting the feel of it and wondering where the listening and scanning devices were.

In the little office Arrhae had found a tidy printout of information concerning the mission. This went well enough with the "solid" information which she had received by courier that morning, and had read between fits of dealing with her own panicky household staff. The solid had contained copies of the legislation that had empowered the mission to leave, the mission statement, the document with which the mission would present the Federation on arrival, and a much fatter document containing speculation by intel staff on the Federation's possible reactions to the presentation document. The printout sitting on the desk included names and some limited personal information on each of the Rihannsu delegates empowered to actually negotiate on the Empire's behalf, the Senators assisting them, and the so-called observer group, of which Arrhae was one. She flipped along to her own description and was amused to see its brevity. *Signeted 20.10.02156,* it said. *Senator for i'Ramnau-Hwaimmen. House: Khellian. Decorations: none.* Many of the other biographies had a category that said "Service," but not hers. Arrhae wondered if someone had been embarrassed by the prospect of the jokes it might enable.

She had looked up from her examination of her biography that evening at the slight shudder that had gone through the ship. *Gorget* was moving out on impulse, heading past the golden glare of Eisn; when there was enough distance between her and the star, she went into warp. Arrhae had breathed out when that happened, and then realized how she had been holding her breath. *Anything could happen to me now,* she had thought. *What if I never see that star again?*

The thought had left her peculiarly cold. Arrhae had pushed it aside, taking her reading out into the main room, where she could keep the buffet sideboard company.

The next day, and the day after that and the day after that, she had been kept busy with meetings with the other delegates, other members of the observing group, and with more reading. Arrhae knew that she had very much been tossed in at the deep end of Rihannsu politics, but she was moderately well prepared for that. Her years on ch'Rihan had not been spent only telling people where to dust and mop. Part of the job Starfleet had assigned her was to be as perfect in understanding of the language as she could, and this had meant doing all the listening and reading, of all kinds, for which her position allowed her time. By virtue of that—time stolen late at night, reading and watching the news services, days spent in judicious eavesdropping—she had learned as much about the politics of the Two Worlds as most Rihannsu ever did, and more than many ever bothered to. Now, of course, the game had moved up to a higher level, and she started meeting the faces who belonged to names which until now she had only read or heard of.

Noonmeal on the first day had been another lavishly catered affair— Arrhae made a note to herself to find out whether the ship had a gymnasium, or even a steambath where she might try to melt some of the carbohydrates off her between "briefings." It had ostensibly been informal, a "meet and greet" gathering of the delegates, negotiators, and observers. The way people carried themselves, and the groups into which they gathered, soon enough told Arrhae that, despite the polite introductions, everyone knew what everyone else's job was, and what their status was, and anyone who stepped out of position would soon enough be reminded. The negotiators kept to themselves, talking in a jovial and important way, and looked down on the delegates: the delegates did the same and looked down on the observers. The observers, having no one to look down on but the officers and staff of *Gorget,* did so, and Arrhae watched with considerable annoyance as they ordered the poor underlings around.

Arrhae for her own part tried to be social with her fellow observers as she met them over the second and third days. They were mostly jurists and tribunes—sober, sometimes somber people who seemed rather taken aback by the position into which they had suddenly been elevated—and a couple of other Senators whom Arrhae knew slightly. One of these, a round, blunt, balding little man named Imin tr'Phalltei, had plainly expected her to carry the drinks tray around out of habit when he met her first in the Senate, and was openly surprised to see her here. The other, a handsome, tall, broad-shouldered woman named Odirne t'Melanth, a Havrannsu with a name like that, had greeted her kindly when they met at that noonmeal, and Arrhae had realized that she found all this as disconcerting, and as absurd, as Arrhae did. "That lot over there," Odirne said, signing with her chin at the negotiating group which had ostentatiously seated itself, as if of right, up at the top of the table, "do they even want to breathe the same air as we do? Great swaths of observing we'll be able to do, indeed, once they get down to their work. As if they'll let us near them when they're making their alleged minds up about what to do!"

At first glimpse Arrhae was inclined to agree with her. Some of the negotiators were not exactly congenial types. And two of them were Praetors, though not on the level of the Three, of course—none of the Triumvirate would go out on a mission like this: their job was to sit home and rule on the information the underlings, even the very high-class underlings, sent to them. One of the two Praetors wore a face Arrhae recognized slightly from McCoy's trial: Hloal t'Illialhlae, the tall, dark, hawk-faced woman who had been wife to the commander of *Battlequeen,* one of the ships lost to the Federation attack on Levaeri V. His death had made a martyr of him, and a harpy of her—if anyone would be pushing for the last drop of blood from the Federation in this negotiation, it would be she. The other Praetor was Gurrhim tr'Siedhri, a great name on ch'Havran. He was a big, bluff, growling *mirhwen* of a man, a fire-breathing warrior and former Senator, one of the stranger and more individual figures in the Praetorate, and very much a nobleman in the old mold—as proud of being a farmer (if on a spectacular scale, for his family's lands spread around a quarter of the planet) as a poet. He was one of very few exceptions to the rule that the negotiators and general delegates on the mission were inimical to the Federation. Tr'Siedhri did not like the Federation much, but he did not hate it either; and he emphatically did not fear it—which, Arrhae thought, was possibly a contributing cause to his lack of hatred. Either way, his presence here was something of a puzzle to Arrhae, for he was ill liked by most of the other Praetors, who had to put up with him whether they liked it or not because of the vast wealth and power his family had amassed over the past three centuries. *Unless,* Arrhae thought, *someone has sent him here to embarrass him somehow—which will happen if he tries to treat the Federation fairly, and all the others side against him.*

*Or possibly someone wants to try to get rid of him,* said some small suspicious voice in the back of Arrhae's head.

There might always be suspicion . . . but Rihannsu life was full of unproven suspicion and paranoia, and eventually it would fade.

Arrhae thought about that as the second and third days went by, and she went to meetings and firstmeals and lastmeals with her fellow observers, making sure that she was available for the contacts she had been told would come. The one that did come, finally, on the morning of the third day, was as unwelcome as it could have been.

Her steward was bustling around trying to feed her, and Arrhae had been trying to resist him, while attempting to put right the formal clothes that she had packed—they had all looked good in the clothes-press, all these kilts and flowing dark tunics, but now they seemed to require endless belting and pinning to drape as they were meant to. And the doorchime had gone, and Arrhae had breathed out in annoy-ance; it would be the "door-opener"—not that *Gorget*'s doors did not open automatically by themselves, but this particular Fleet officer was doing the same office as a ground-bound opener, arriving to escort guests around the corridors of the ship, which was all too easy to be-come lost in, and making sure they got where they were needed with-out putting their noses in anywhere they didn't belong, or stealing the silver. "Of your courtesy, get that," Arrhae had said to the steward, turn-ing away to try to straighten out one more wayward pin, and then very carefully sitting down to her dinner. She was ravenous; the good dark smell of the *osilh* stew that Ffairrl had laid out on the little table beside the most comfortable chair had been making her stomach rumble, and Arrhae was determined to do something about that quickly, before she embarrassed herself in the day's first meeting.

The door slipped open and the steward said not a word. Arrhae sighed, looked up . . . and found herself looking at Commander t'Radaik of the Rihannsu Intelligence Service.

*What have I done to deserve this,* Arrhae thought, trying to ignore the shiver that ran down her spine. The woman stood there, with those oblique eyes and sharp cheekbones of hers, tall and cool and good-looking in her dark, green-sashed uniform of tunic and breeches and too-shiny boots, and gazed down from her considerable height at Ar-rhae with an expression that suggested it took more than clothes and a signet to make the Senator. Still, *"Deihu,"* she said, and bowed, and Ar-rhae gave about her two-thirds of a breath's bow from where she sat, not an overly committal gesture, one way or the other.

Arrhae looked over at the steward. "Out," she said, so that t'Radaik would be deprived of the opportunity to say it first. Ffairrl took himself away at speed.

"Well, *deihu,*" said t'Radaik, looking around her with incompletely concealed amusement, "you seem to have settled in nicely."

"Except for interruptions," Arrhae said, "which not the Elements Themselves could prevent, it seems. What can I do for you, Commander?" She lifted the ale cup standing beside her plate, and drank.

T'Radaik bent that cool, arrogant regard on her again. "You have spoken in the past with the Terran, Mak'khoi," she said.

"With no great pleasure," Arrhae said, and at the time it had been true. She picked up a small round flatbread that was still warm, tore it in two, and turned her attention to the plate of dark, spicy *osilh* stew that Ffairrl had laid out for her.

"You were . . . close to him." She was watching Arrhae very closely.

"Only in terms of seeing to his needs," Arrhae said, "as one might see to the needs of a guest of one's House." And irked by the intensity of t'Radaik's regard, she scooped up a little of the *osilh* with the flat-bread, and ate. It was a calculated insult, to eat in front of someone and not offer them anything, especially if they fancied themselves your equal . . . but right now, Arrhae didn't care.

T'Radaik's eyes narrowed. "And he treated you in a friendly manner."

"In that he did not kill me when last we met," Arrhae said, becoming increasingly annoyed as she began to suspect where this was leading, "if you regard that as 'friendly', yes."

"You might then have reason to be grateful to him," said t'Radaik, "and to wish him well."

"I might also feel like killing him should we meet again," Arrhae said, tearing off another bit of bread and scooping up more stew with it, "but somehow I doubt that such an action would suit your intentions at the moment."

T'Radaik gave Arrhae a lofty look. "It would not. The service requires your assistance. You will be given a package which will be—"

T'Radaik stopped suddenly as Arrhae put down the piece of bread and fixed her with an angry stare. Arrhae lifted her right hand, turning its back to the Intelligence officer so that her signet was in plain view.

"The service may indeed desire the *deihu*'s assistance," Arrhae said, keeping her voice level, "but the service is the *Senate*'s servant. Does it not say so, in great handsome letters, right around the seal emblazoned across your main building in Ra'tleihfi?"

T'Radaik simply looked at her. "I have been charged by the Praetor Eveh tr'Anierh to assist you," Arrhae said, "and to *his* wishes, I am obedient. But I would advise you to mend your manners, Commander, and mind your tone, or the Praetor will hear of both. There is rarely such a galling sight, or one so likely to provoke the great to action, as an ill-behaved servant stepping out of its place."

T'Radaik opened her mouth. "And you are thinking that you knew me when I was only a *hru'hfe*," Arrhae said softly. "Think more quietly, Commander. Things change, in this world. 'Half the Elements are mutable; nothing stays the same,' the song says. And no matter what I was three months ago, the office of Senator still commands some respect. Now tell me about this package, and whatever else you need me to know, and then begone. I have no intention of allowing you to make me late for my next meeting."

T'Radaik swallowed, a woman choking down anger, but not dismissing it. It would be saved carefully for another time. "The service has a small package which it asks you to deliver," she said. "It will be left here in your rooms later today. Should the Terran Mak'khoi be present at the negotiations, you are requested to see that it comes to him."

"Not without knowing what is in it," Arrhae said, picking up the rolled-up morsel of flatbread and popping it into her mouth.

T'Radaik frowned. "That is no affair of yours."

"Indeed it is," Arrhae said after a moment, "for a Senator's *mnhei'sahe* rides on such knowledge, and on acting correctly upon it. I know enough of how the service works to desire to be sure of what passes through my hands."

"A data chip," said t'Radaik. "Nothing more."

"Oh? Well, I shall open it first, and read every word."

Arrhae thought as she tore off one more bit of flatbread that taking on quite so assertive a shade of green did not improve t'Radaik's otherwise highbred looks. "I am not such a fool as to think it is love poetry," Arrhae said. "It will either be something that does us good, or does McCoy or the Federation some harm. I will know which before I assist you."

T'Radaik looked at her darkly. Then she said, "Disinformation."

Arrhae waited.

"There are Federation spies among us," t'Radaik said, "and you more than most people here should know it."

This stroke Arrhae had been expecting, and now she raised her eyebrows and gave t'Radaik an ironic look. The thought of what had happened to her old master Vaebn tr'Lhoell after he "sold" her away into the safety of House Khellian was much with Arrhae, but if t'Radaik expected her to react to the painful memory with terror, she had misjudged her. "Such is inevitable," Arrhae said, "as inevitable as our having spies in the Federation, I would suppose. So?" She used the bread to eat one last bit of stew.

"We catch them, sometimes," said t'Radaik, and this time she actually smiled. "Usually we manage to get at least some useful information out of them before we kill them. In this case, we managed to get quite a lot."

"I am delighted for you," Arrhae said. "Again: so?"

"We desire that the information the spy sought, along with other data of our own providing, should come to the Federation by quicker means than usual," t'Radaik said. "Seeing that you have had contact with the criminal and spy Mak'khoi in the recent past, you are the perfect one to pass it to him. If you must justify your actions, you will pretend concern for him, and feign that this information comes from someone who was trying to contact him when he was on ch'Rihan last—for we have learned that his capture by our forces was not an accident. It was planned by the Federation itself, to allow him to check on some of their agents here."

Arrhae allowed herself to look astonished while she took another drink of ale, relishing the burning fruit of it as much as t'Radaik's annoyed look. "They must have little concern whether he lives or dies," she said.

"Little enough, though they make such a great noise about his value as a starship officer. But there are indications that some in Starfleet are becoming weary of *Enterprise*'s officers in general, not just her captain, and wish they could be rid of them." T'Radaik smiled. "Possibly the only goal we share. Mak'khoi's being sent on this mission of espionage may have been a way to reduce the number of those officers by one. In any case, at least one of the Federation spies on ch'Rihan was instructed to try to make contact with Mak'khoi while he was here, passing him certain information about the Empire. He failed to make that contact. But he also failed to sufficiently cover the tracks of his attempt to make it. We caught him, and he gave us the information he had been preparing for Mak'khoi. Now, having examined it, we desire the data to reach Mak'khoi . . . suitably altered. That information will come by him to *Bloodwing* . . . and once there, will do its best work." Her smile was that of a woman enjoying this prospect entirely too much.

"For all this trouble," Arrhae said, "I hope you may be sure of that."

"Oh, we will be informed promptly enough when the information has come where it needs to be."

*Will you really?* "Well," Arrhae said, trying to sound offhanded about it as she put down the cup, "this sounds as if it will not unduly affect my honor. I will find a way to pass the chip to Mak'khoi, should he present himself."

"We are sure he will," t'Radaik said. "The first night of the meeting with the Federation starships, tomorrow night, there will be a social occasion—" Her look was sardonic. "As if one can be social with such vile creatures, half aliens, half animals. Nonetheless, we will go along with the charade, and at this meeting you will certainly have the opportunity to speak with Mak'khoi, and to pass him the material in question."

A soft chime came from the office: the alarm that Arrhae had set in her computer. She reached for the lap-cloth by her plate, dusted her hands with it, and stood up. "Very well," she said, and very rudely turned her back on t'Radaik, going off to fetch her carryall for the meeting she was about to attend. "See to the package's delivery, then. You may go."

The door hissed open. Arrhae turned and just caught sight of t'Radaik's back going out. As the door closed again, Arrhae permitted herself just the slightest smile. She detested that woman, and she suspected t'Radaik had known as much before Arrhae ever opened her mouth. *No harm in letting her know she is right,* Arrhae thought.

At least, she hoped there would be none. . . .

★   ★   ★

It was summer in that hemisphere of Samnethe, and the weather had been holding fair for some while: hot and sunny, the sky piled high with good-weather cloud. In and out of that cloud, the rakish and deadly shapes of Grand Fleet shuttles could be seen all day, ferrying troops and equipment up to the birds-of-prey, the great starships presently in orbit. Now it was sunset, the heat of the day cooling. Mijne t'Ethien leaned against the fiberplas surface next to the door of the group shelter where she and fifty others, men and women, slept together since the government warnings of imminent attack had gone out, and the ingathering to the secure site at the planet's main spaceport, Tharawe. The hum of the place that one heard all day, from the habitués of the other five thousand houses of fifty, always began to hush down as dusk crept in. Now, in that peace, with her washing done and the daymeal inside her, Mijne leaned there and looked past the security fence toward the spaceport field, and was filled with wonder. Early that morning the sky had been full of the ugly swooping shapes of Klingon vessels, of phaserfire and the shriek of impulse engines. Now it was empty and peaceful again, and only the occasional shuttle going about its business broke the silence.

"They beat them," Mijne said to herself. "It is a miracle."

Behind her, a rough old voice said, "It is the dawn of a disaster; one which will start tomorrow."

Mijne turned to look at her grandfather with a mixture of annoyance and fondness. He had been predicting disasters since the two of them had been brought here. "Resettlement," the government had called it, "due to a state of emergency." "Internment," Amyn tr'Ethien had muttered when the message came down the terminal on that rainy morning, "as a matter of expediency."

"Don't be silly, Grandsire," Mijne had said then, and she said it again now. She had been annoyed at having to shut up the summerhouse just after it had been opened, but it seemed foolish to rail against the government's attempts to keep them all safe, and there was no protecting a population scattered as thinly across a planet as Samnethe's was. The growing Grand Fleet presence stationed at the planet would have had to fly all over the place, patrolling living area and wasting its resources and manpower. It made much more sense to gather them all together where some security could be found. "The Klingons, it seems, hit our defenses as hard as they could, and couldn't break through except to destroy a few hangars and small ships on the ground, not even anything important."

"You believe that, do you," her grandsire said. Mijne rolled her eyes. She did not mind being the last member of her family alive to take care of him; one had, after all, a duty to one's House. But he could be annoying sometimes, and since they came here he had embarrassed Mijne with his outspoken opinions and his doomsaying a goodly number of times.

"Why shouldn't I believe it?" Mijne said, walking away from the common house.

He walked away with her, linking his arm through hers, plainly knowing her intention—to get him away from there before he embarrassed her further in front of those with whom they were currently rooming—and clearly amused by it. "Granddaughter," he said, "when was the last time you were near a news terminal? Not that those are to be entirely trusted, either."

She laughed. "Grandsire, you're so paranoid."

He laughed at her too, shaking that head of shaggy silver-shot hair. "Consider it one of the side effects of venerable old age. But what have you to base the statement on, except rumor?"

She rolled her eyes again. He was in one of his pedantic moods tonight. "It's all we've got, at the moment."

"But not necessarily better than nothing," he said. "I have lived a long time, Granddaughter, and I—"

"—have seen many things," she said in unison with him: mockery, though not entirely unkind. "All right, then, you old fortune-teller, you old stargazer. Tell me how the Elements have decreed that events shall fall for the next day or so."

They had walked a short distance away from the common houses over the beaten-down, dusty ground; he looked at her, smiling slightly, and wouldn't answer. They kept walking into the cool of the growing dusk, in the general direction of the security fence.

He stopped, and she did too, and together they looked toward the low, dimly seen line of the hills twenty miles away. "What a lovely evening," she said, "even down here in the heat."

"Yes, it is," he said. His eyes were raised higher, to where a bright-burning point of light hung over the hills: Erivin, the only other planet in the system besides Samnethe, closer to the primary than Samnethe was, and its evening star at this time of year. "The last evening, for me."

She looked at him, wondering what he meant. "Oh, Grandfather! Don't tell me your heart has been paining you again."

"Not at all."

"And the Klingons aren't going to come back! They've been beaten. Everything is going to be all right now."

"Is it."

She looked into his face, confused.

"Granddaughter," he said, "tomorrow everything changes. Tomorrow is the day our status shifts. And I do not know if I will survive it."

"What?"

He patted the hand which lay over his, and walked her on a little ways. "When I was in Grand Fleet, on outworld patrol, in the ancient days," Mijne's grandfather said, "I saw how our ground ancillaries behaved when things needed to be repaired in a hurry. I grant you, it's hard to see the port well from here, especially the way they keep opaquing the fence during the day. But they have the fence on automatic timing now, and they've misjudged the time of twilight, which is why we can see *that* as well as we can. Just look at it."

They gazed out toward the port facilities. The landing surface was all pockmarked with holes and craters and huge long gashes gouged out by phaser blasts.

"Tomorrow," Mijne's grandsire said, "we'll be told to go out there and start repairing that. Or else we'll wind up as 'replacements' for other automatics around the base that were damaged and cannot be repaired. We will prove our loyalty by faithfully serving those who have oppressed us."

He grinned. The grin was feral. Mijne thought she had never seen such a ferocious look on anyone, and she was certainly at a loss to see it on her old grandsire, who had spent her childhood spoiling her and giving her treats, and whose voice she had never heard raised.

"Oppressed us?" she said. "Grandfather, you're—" She wouldn't quite say "mad."

"Oh, come, Granddaughter, surely you don't believe they rounded us all up and brought us here to *protect* us!"

"But they said—"

"Of course they did. Free, though, and in our homes, we can't be controlled. With the planet going about its business as usual, there are too many ways we threaten this base's security. For we're mostly Ship-Clan folk, aren't we?—not really to be trusted, different from other Rihannsu, as they like to think, another breed, possibly disloyal. So they distrust us from the start. But also, our world's in a bad spot. We are a long way from the hearth of the Empire, and the Empire would hate to see Samnethe's privately owned shipbuilding facilities falling into the Klingons' hands, while the employees are running around free in the neighborhood, available to be simply swept up and put to work for the Empire's enemies. So instead, the government rounds us all up, the whole workforce of this planet which really has no other industry worth speaking of, and puts us where it can keep an eye on us, while this attack is handled, and the government thinks about what it wants us to build for them . . . never mind what our industry cooperative thinks. Should it look as if the Klingons might somehow get the upper hand here, well . . . someone can make sure that this particular highly skilled workforce is never taken by them as slave labor."

"And a good thing, too! I would die rather than be a Klingon's slave, or any being's!"

"Quite right," her grandfather said. "Quite right. But wouldn't you rather be free to make that choice for yourself, Granddaughter . . . rather than have it made for you?"

She stared at him.

He kept walking gently along. "Well, if we are lucky, it may not come to that. The military may be telling the truth for once, or some of it. Though I doubt it. Sooner or later, though, we'll come to the real reason they've put us here. We will be forced to start work at the base.

After that, they will find other work for us to do—either shipbuilding again, on their terms and pay—if any pay at all—or something less pleasant, maybe not even on this planet. And our durance will not end until this not-yet-declared war ends . . . and maybe not even then." He raised his eyebrows.

He was so calm and matter-of-fact about all this that, to Mijne's horror, she was beginning to believe him. "But—I don't see what we can do," she said at last. "They are the government."

"We are Rihannsu," her grandfather said. "We can refuse!"

She stared at him, fearful. "But our duty—"

"Is not to follow stupid orders blindly," her grandfather said fiercely. "Or orders that blithely destroy the freedom our long-ago ancestors brought us here to enjoy at such cost to themselves, after they in turn refused to be other than they were. How should we have become so craven as to acquiesce to our own enslavement? Our government has no such rights over us, of internment, of forced labor. And yes, they will say, now and afterward, it was an emergency, we are fighting for our lives, we will make it up to you later, all your rights will be restored to you!" He gave her an ironic look. "Do you believe that?"

To her horror, Mijne found she didn't. In the last few years she had become troubled by some of the things she saw on the news channels, reports from the outworlds of mass arrests, "security problems," purges of local governments. Then, over the last year, she had seen few such reports, almost none. At first she had thought, *Good, things are quieting down.* But then a small voice had started to say, in the back of her mind, *Are they really? Or are the news services simply not telling these stories anymore? And if not, why not?*

"This system and others like it will shortly be the front line of a war," her grandfather said softly. "And we can only hope that those in the other colony worlds have not yet forgotten how to die for what they believe in." He let out a long breath. "For that is what we will have to do now."

"'We'—"

"I am a grandson and a twice- and three-times great-grandson of engineers," her grandfather said, stopping now, looking up at that evening star as it slid toward its setting. "Our ancestors and their families left safety, in the ancient days, to bring the rest of our people here. We risked our lives to do it. We died with the ships that died, and in some of the ships that didn't. Now it looks like some of us will have to die again."

His voice was curiously calm. Now it even began to sound amused. "But not in vain, I think, for the Empire's own greed has sown the seeds of what will now begin to happen. It wasn't enough for them to tax us for the privilege, when we desired to spread out into the new worlds discovered after ch'Rihan and ch'Havran were settled. They sited the shipbuilding facilities on the new outworlds, and made us pay for those too. They made us staff them locally, and pay the staff ourselves." He smiled. "And then, when the exploration ships our more recent ancestors built in turn found new, livable worlds, they taxed us for landing and living on those as well, and those colonists in turn had to pay for and run the new shipbuilding facilities established on the second- and third-generation worlds. Did they never think what they were doing?"

"Grandsire—"

"Mijne, listen, just this once. Greed blinded them—or else the Elements did. The Empire forced the tools of our future independence into our hands . . . and then made them all the more precious to us by forcing us to pay for them, yet withholding true ownership." That feral grin appeared again. "What people need to see at all costs is that we are not powerless . . . *for we are still holding the tools.*"

"To do what?"

"We will have to ask our people, and find out," her grandfather said. "Meanwhile . . ."

He stood still and silent for a few moments more, while Mijne shook in the growing cold.

"One can always say no," he said, as the evening star winked out behind the hills, and the fence went opaque again.

The next morning they were all called together for the usual morning mass meeting in which duties and details were announced. The base commander himself was there. "Considerable damage has been done by yesterday's Klingon attack to base facilities," the commander said. "Immediate repairs must be begun on the landing pans, repair cradles, and cranes if we are to carry the attack to them effectively, or repulse the next one." People looked at each other dubiously. *"Next one"?* The word had gone out that this had been a victory, that the invaders had been driven off, and the rumors had gone on to add that within a few days everyone would be able to go home and pick up their lives where they had left off. "To facilitate this goal, by order of the Empire, work crews will now be formed from the camp's population, consisting of everyone between ages sixteen and one hundred fifty. You are required to form up in groups of one hundred, by registration numbers. Officers will be detailed to each group to describe your duties and work hours. When a project is finished, your officer will inform you of the next project to be begun. Starting with these numbers—"

There was some muttering among the great crowd, but it was muted. The officer seemed not to pay any attention to it, merely kept reading his numbers. The crowd, like a live thing, hesitated, then started to drift apart, fragmenting itself.

One fragment, though, moved through it, in a straightforward direction very unlike the uncertain motion of everyone else. He made his way out of the crowd, clear of the other people, and stepped out onto the bare concrete, stepped out of it, toward the officer. The officer, looking up and seeing him, stopped, puzzled.

The old man drew himself up quite straight, quite tall. In a voice sharp and carrying as the report of a disruptor bolt, he said:

"I will not serve!"

The crowd fell deadly silent.

Mijne blanched as the officer lowered his padd and stared at her grandsire. *He's a hundred and ninety, he doesn't have to serve, Grandsire, what are you—* "Grandsire!"

The officer looked at her grandfather in apparent bemusement. "I beg your pardon?"

"I said," her grandsire said courteously, as if anyone within a half mile could have failed to hear him, *"I will not serve!"*

The officer looked at him. Then he looked at one of the security people off to one side, and muttered something.

The security man lifted his disruptor and fired.

The scream of sound hit Mijne's grandsire, and he went down like a felled tree.

She ran to him, fell to her knees beside him. Between neck and knees he was one great welter of blood and blasted flesh. Her grandsire looked at her with eyes clear with shock. "Did he hear me?" he said.

"He heard you," she said, weeping.

Her grandsire stopped breathing. Unbelieving, Mijne looked up, looked around. All that great crowd looked at what had happened . . . then slowly, slowly began to drift apart again, into groups.

Mijne got up and walked back among them, only very slowly getting control of the sobs that were tearing at her. After a while she managed it. She went to the group she was supposed to be with, and did the work they were given, filling blast craters with rubble; and that night they all went back to their common houses, and a great silence fell with the dark.

But in it, here and there, very faintly, in the depths of night, in Mijne's mind and in many another, a whisper stirred, slowly beginning to look for ways to speak itself in action:

*I will not serve . . . !*

Arrhae's meeting turned out to consist of three dreary hours of procedural wrangling among the negotiators, during which the observers' and delegates' opinions were neither solicited nor (clearly) desired. On one level, Arrhae didn't mind; she was glad enough to have time to turn over in her mind this new turn of events and what to do about it, though it was a pain to have to appear, at the same time, as if she were paying attention to the mind-numbing arguments of the negotiators about how the parts of the demand to the Federation should be rephrased. When midmeal break came round, it came not a second too soon for Arrhae, and she was all too glad to slip back to her suite for a bite to eat by herself.

Ffairrl appeared and began to fuss over her, and Arrhae suffered it for a few minutes, letting him bring her a cup of ale and a small plate of savory biscuits, but nothing more. "Lady," Ffairrl said, sounding rather desperate, "*deihu,* they will think I am not serving you well!"

"If you give me another midmeal like yesterday," Arrhae said, "you will have to serve me by rolling me down the hall on a handtruck!" Though now she would be wondering who *his* "they" were. Did the intelligence people browbeat even the poor servants? *Well, and why would they not? They tried it with* me. But to what purpose? One more question to which she was not likely to get an answer any time soon. . . .

And then the door signal went off.

Arrhae looked up at the clock on the nearby table with some indignation. It was nowhere near the end of the midmeal break yet. "*Now* what?" she said, and then thought, *Ah, the package. . . .* Ffairrl, with a nervous look, headed for the door.

It opened . . . and Arrhae saw who stood there, and slowly got up.

A slim, slight young man, a handsome dark-visaged young man hardly much taller than she was, in Fleet uniform, with a cheerful and anticipatory look on his face: Nveid. Nveid tr'AAnikh. The last time Arrhae had seen him, he had been following her while she did her shopping. Initially she'd thought he might have been following her for her looks. That did happen occasionally, for she was unusually good-looking by Rihannsu standards, that having been one element of her cover—her old double-agent master having been widely assumed to have originally bought her for other purposes than household work. But that had not been the reason, and Arrhae had begun to suspect that tr'AAnikh was possibly with one of the intelligence services . . . until she found out how wrong she had been about that, too.

Now Nveid stepped into her suite and bowed to her . . . a breath's worth, then up again, jaunty, like a suitor who thinks his suit is going to go well and doesn't see the need to be overly formal. "Noble *deihu*," Nveid said, "I had to see you."

"I am not at all sure the need is reciprocal," Arrhae said, in as hard a voice as she could manage. "Tr'AAnikh, how *dare* you come here? I thought you would have understood after our last encounter that I do not welcome your attentions." This was true, though not for the reasons any listener might suspect. *What is he doing here?* she thought. The brief conversation they'd had in i'Ramnau some weeks ago—though it felt more like half a lifetime now—had suggested that his family might have been under suspicion because they had kin on *Bloodwing*. *Gorget* was the last place she would have expected to see him.

"I am in attendance on my mother's sister-cousin, *Deihu* Odirne t'Melanth," he said. "I was seconded to her service a tenday ago, when the mission began to be assembled." Nveid stepped closer to Arrhae, and smiled. "She has found my services invaluable, she says . . ."

The verb *mmhain'he* had the same possibilities for double entendre attached to it that the word *service* had in Anglish, and many more, and Arrhae was not amused by the implications. "Insolence!" Arrhae said. "You are not welcome, I tell you. Go away!"

He stepped still closer. "I did not believe you when you told me that the last time," Nveid said. "And when I heard you were here, I knew it was the Elements Themselves that had ordained it so. Fire will have its way, Arrhae, the Fire of hearts. . . ."

He was moving closer. Arrhae was slightly alarmed, but more bemused by the poor-quality romantic rhetoric, like something off of the less well subsidized public entertainment channels . . . and more bemused still because there was no reasonable justification for it on his side, not after a total of ten minutes' conversation two tendays ago, and no justification whatsoever on hers. "We burn in the same conflagration," Nveid said, right in front of her now, reaching out to her, taking her by the upper arms. "You denied it then because you were but a poor servant, and could not follow your heart. But now you are noble, now you can avouch your true desires without fear. . . ."

*Oh, come on now,* Arrhae thought. *What is he at . . . ?!*

He pulled her to him. For a second she was too amazed to struggle, and he put his lips down by her ear and actually nuzzled her.

"The Ship-Clans are rising," he quickly whispered, so softly that even she could hardly hear it. "Bear the winged one the news."

And then he pulled away a little, looked her in the astonished eyes . . . and leaning in, he kissed her, quite, quite hard.

Arrhae's eyes widened at what she felt. What happened after that was sheer reflex. Nveid went flying through the air and fetched up hard, *bang,* against the wall near the door, more or less sitting on the floor and looking dazed, with reason. Arrhae stood there, breathing hard, and staring at him . . . and thinking, *Did I see him wink at me? Did he actually wink??* Rihannsu had that gesture in common with Terrans, but Arrhae wasn't entirely sure that he hadn't simply had something in his eye.

She turned around to find the steward standing there with a disruptor in his hand. *Now where did he get that?* Arrhae thought. *Is he some kind of undercover security guard?* But whether he was or not, she was in no mood for any more surprises. "You're a little late with that, aren't you, Ffairrl?" Arrhae said. "Not that it matters. Put it away, you idiot; he's no threat."

Ffairrl stuck the weapon in his apron pocket, and the haste and clumsiness with which he did it suggested to Arrhae that he had nothing to do with any security contingent—or was acting superbly. *Either way, I hope he put the safety back on . . . !* "Noble lady, shouldn't I call the guards?" Ffairrl said.

"For *this?*" Arrhae said, turning to regard Nveid again. "Hardly."

She stepped over to the buffet sideboard, picked up the pitcher that was always there, went straight back to Nveid and upended the pitcher over him. "There's water for your 'fire,' " she said, and chucked the pitcher over her shoulder. There was a crash as it broke on something, possibly that expensive glass-slab table in the middle of the room. She didn't bother to look. "Beware how you invoke an Element in someone else's name when it's not there, you young fool. I intend to have words with your lady about this. We'll see how she likes it that her staff are running around in the corridors like *hieth* in heat, accosting their betters!"

He got up, and made a rather pitiful attempt to put himself right, dripping as he was. "Noble lady—"

"Not another word," Arrhae said. *"Out!"*

He went. The door closed, and Arrhae stood there and breathed out, wondering what in the names of Earth and, yes, Fire, was going to happen next.

*Doubtless I'll find out,* she thought. *Meanwhile I have other problems. . . .*

"I must go wash my mouth out," Arrhae said, in a tone of voice she hoped was rich with disgust. "As for you, Ffairrl, not a word of this to anyone, otherwise it'll be all over the mission in a *stai* . . . and if I hear about it so, it'll be *your* hide I take the strips off, no one else's."

"No, noble *deihu,* of course not, great lady . . ."

Arrhae paid him no more mind. She took herself off to the great bathroom, ran a great deal of water in the highbasin, found a toothscrub, and went to work.

She spent a good while at it—long enough, she thought, to bore anyone who might be watching. And when Arrhae finally turned away from the sink, having run a finger once over her gums in front as if afraid they might have been hurt by the violence and intrusiveness of Nveid's kiss, she was quite sure that no one had seen her remove the tiny square of silicon which she had squirreled away between gum and cheek just after she threw Nveid at the wall.

*What a lot of reading I will have to do this evening,* Arrhae thought.

The first part of it she did after the day's sessions were over. The "package" t'Radaik had promised her, the data chip, was waiting for her in a little slipskin envelope on the somewhat-scratched glass table when Arrhae came back from the afternoon session. She ate in, that evening, rather than going to the inevitable buffet with the rest of the senior members of the mission, and munched her wafers and *tlheir* at the desk in the luxurious little office, sipping berry wine the while.

The data from t'Radaik's chip was all dry stuff on the surface, seeming to have to do with ship movements and materiel movements on ch'Rihan and ch'Havran. It suggested a great reshuffling of resources in the part of the Empire nearest the Neutral Zone. *True or false?* Arrhae wondered. Surface meanings could be deceptive; there was probably coded content buried in this text, and if it genuinely was sourced from a Federation deep-cover agent like herself, the people who would accompany the Starfleet forces to the negotiations would be equipped to extract it. There was no use her trying her own ciphers on it. Even if they had been brand new, which they weren't, they would not be the same as another agent's.

*All I can do is pass this on to McCoy as instructed,* Arrhae thought. *But not without warning him that the information in it's been compromised . . . or fabricated. It's as I told t'Radaik; there is likely enough a bombshell hidden in this somewhere.*

*And as for the rest of my reading . . .*

She would have to wait for that, but not too much longer . . . it was late. Ffairrl came in from his little butler's-cupboard room, looked at the empty plate and cup, and said, "*Llhei deihu,* can I get you anything else?"

No answer to this question ever suited this man but yes. "O Elements, have pity on me," Arrhae said. "Ffairrl, all right, give me some bread and some ale, and for something hot, a bowl of *hehfan* broth. Without the dumplings, thank you. And then do go; there's nothing more to be done tonight, as I flatly refuse to eat anything further."

He went away to make the broth. *What I would like to know is why they're so sure McCoy will be here,* Arrhae thought. *Unless they have somehow discovered that he had that chemical Rihannsu-comprehension procedure, and will be brought along as an extra, "covert" translator—for besides the usual Universal Translator links, there will almost certainly be a live language specialist with them as well.*

And there was always the possibility that, as t'Radaik had implied, they might have someone on *Bloodwing* who had been in touch with McCoy, or someone else on *Enterprise,* and knew where he was going to be. That too was something she was going to have to warn McCoy of. *At least I have the opportunity . . . which intelligence itself has given me.*

*And which they may be hoping to use to find some evidence that I am a double agent. . . .*

Ffairrl came in with the bread and soup and ale, and Arrhae thanked him and bade him good night. "Lady," Ffairrl said somewhat nervously, "should that gentleman return . . ."

She raised her eyebrows at him. "Did you replace that pitcher?" she said.

He gave her the slightest smile. "Yes, noble *deihu.*"

"Then that's all I'm likely to need. Go you now, and sleep well."

"Yes, lady," Ffairrl said, and went out; and Arrhae heard the door lock behind him as it shut.

She drank her soup, and drank her ale, and nibbled at the bread while she finished her reading. Then Arrhae shut the computer down, with a yawn not entirely feigned, went to the clothespress in the main room, and pulled out her carrybag. She went through it until she came up with a bottle of the *dheiain*-wood bath oil she favored; and casually she also took out of it her own rather old and crude little pad-scriber, which she had brought from i'Ramnau with her, and had already taken along to one or two of the daily meetings. The excuse was that she was used to it, and liked it, and did not need newer equipment—at least, that would be the excuse if anyone queried her about it. Like Gurrhim tr'Siedhri, Arrhae also had the potential excuse of eccentricity, which others would expect from her, and mock her for behind her back as they mocked tr'Siedhri for holding forth endlessly about the virtues of life on the land, calling him "farmer Gurri" behind his back. *They'll call me* hru'hfe, Arrhae thought, *and laugh . . . until I catch one of them at it. That* was a slightly chilling thought, for *mnhei'sahe* dictated a certain kind of response should that happen.

For the time being, though, Arrhae wasn't going to worry about it. She hoped the eccentricity would be enough to disguise the important thing about having this scriber with her: that she knew it was not bugged.

She straightened up, yawned and stretched again, and headed for the bathroom, dropping the scriber on the table by the bathroom's door, within sight of the big bath. Then Arrhae began testing the plumbing most thoroughly.

The scriber was not out of her sight all during the bath, though Arrhae hoped that fact would pass unremarked by any watcher. When she got out at last, rather wrinkled but very clean indeed, Arrhae left it where it was while she went off to make herself a final cup of herbdraft. With it she sat down in one of the biggest of the big comfortable chairs, watching the stars pour silently by the huge windows. A long while she sat, composing in her mind, sipping the draft until long after it was cold.

At last she got up, put the cup on the sideboard, and started preparing to retire. Arrhae moved gently about the suite, shutting off the lights, picking up the scriber absently and dropping it on the table near the couch.

Then she slipped in under the sleeping silks and waved the last light off. A good while, Arrhae lay there, listening hard, though she knew she would hear nothing; those who listened to her were most unlikely to betray themselves.

*It must be long enough now,* she thought. Very softly, in the dark, Arrhae reached out and pulled the scriber under the covers . . . then pulled the covers up over her head. As she had done many a night when she was still a *hru'hfe,* she activated the scriber by feel alone, her knowledgeable fingers easily managing the keying of its silent pads in the dark. When the light of its tiny strip of faint-lit screen began to glow, Arrhae slipped Nveid's little scrap of a chip onto the reader pad, and started to read.

Much later, in the blackness, Arrhae put another chip onto the pad, and began to type . . . smiling all the while.

Jim came into main briefing the next morning to find that Ael was there early, watching Scotty and K's't'lk put the final touches on the bones of their scheduled briefing to the science staff on their progress with the "safing" of the Sunseed routines. "Did you rest well, Commander?" Jim said, standing behind her and looking at the hologram she was examining.

"Not too well," said Ael. "But any rest which does not involve being shot at is a good one, I suppose." She turned her attention back to the image currently playing itself out over the center of the table. It was a holographic display of an eclipse of Earth's sun, a particularly splendid one, the primary's corona licking and writhing away from the obscured disk of the photosphere like the wind-rippled mane of some furious and glorious beast.

Jim had seen this particular image before, at the Academy, and afterward occasionally elsewhere. "2218?" he said to Scotty.

"Aye, that's the one," Scotty said, not looking up from his work at the table computer for the moment.

Ael glanced from it to Jim. "It is a great wonder," she said.

"We're more or less used to it now," Jim said. "It happens with some frequency."

Ael laughed, one of those small nearly inaudible breaths of humor that Jim had nearly forgotten the sound of. "Certainly, though, you have considered how astronomically unlikely such an exact fit of the apparent size of star and moon, as seen from Earth, must be." She gazed at the image again. "I thought, when I saw it for the first time, that the image had been taken by some space vessel or satellite specifically positioned for the purpose."

"No," Jim said. "It just came that way."

She gave him an amused and extremely skeptical look. "You truly believe that this is a coincidence?"

"The universe has seen stranger ones," Jim said.

Ael raised her eyebrows at him, leaning back in the seat. "Perhaps. Though I should like to discuss the statistical realities of the situation with Spock someday. Doubtless even in his dry way he might cast light on the provenance of this miracle which he might not otherwise intend."

Jim wasn't sure what to make of that idea. "But there are those of my people who would have taken such an apparition in our own skies as an explicit message from the Elements," Ael said. "An invitation to venture out and discover what it was that had engineered such a spectacular and transient terror. Or simply a message that so colossal a coincidence could not have simply happened: that it was indeed *made,* and that there were makers."

Jim nodded. "Oh, we have our own people who think that the Preservers or some other of the 'seeding' species passed through fifty thousand years or so ago, and nudged the moon just enough in its orbit to produce the effect." He shrugged. "There's no proof of it, naturally. The moon does have some microscopic orbital 'wobbles' that can't be accounted for by its interactions with the Earth and the sun; but as for what causes them—" He shrugged.

"But meanwhile," Ael said, "the wonder remains. And may yet do us good, for worlds used to eclipses even without such a perfect fit tend to be further ahead in research on coronal science than others. Earth being one of them."

Scotty smiled. "Flattery will get you everywhere, lass," he said, not looking up.

Jim looked back at the eclipse, still caught in the repeating loop of the few minutes of totality as seen from the northern Pacific. The so-called Great Eclipse or Fireball Eclipse of 2218 had not only had an unusually long totality, but had coincided with a sunspot maximum, and the solar storm ongoing during the umbra's track across the Earth had produced coronal behavior like nothing ever seen before during an eclipse—outrageous, frightening, enough to give the impression to a viewer that the sun was actually angry, and might do something terminal to its subject worlds. Ael reached out and touched the control to let the image continue through its normal cycle. ". . . It's temporary, at any rate," Jim said. "The moon's getting slowly further away from us. Thirty or thirty-five thousand years from now, and the fit won't be perfect anymore. Nothing but annular eclipses for us, then, until the oscillation stops and the moon's orbit begins closing in again."

"And then what?"

"Then it starts to fall," Jim said, "and tidal forces pull it apart. If we're lucky, Earth ends up with rings. If we're not lucky . . . rings, and most likely a 'cometary winter.'"

Ael looked rueful. "Much later, though, I assume."

"Five or six hundred thousand of our years, give or take a few."

Ael smiled slightly. "Not something we need worry about overmuch, then. Our own concerns lie closer in time."

Jim nodded. The corona licked and lashed in apparent fury; then there came a tremor at the trailing limb, the solar brilliance piercing through the lunar valleys, and the "diamond ring" effect flashed out in full glory, blinding. Ael stood up, gazing at it with the expression of someone faced with an insoluble riddle. "The Elements clearly do have a sense of humor," she said at last, as the sun showed a full blazing crescent of its limb and the corona faded to invisibility. "Unwise of us to ignore it when we see it being displayed. Few are angrier, the poet says, than those who tell a joke and hear no laughter. . . ."

"I don't like to step on anyone's punch lines either," Jim said.

McCoy came in and paused, looking at the eclipse with a somewhat jaundiced eye. Jim noticed the look. "Problems, Bones?"

"After I saw the recording of the bridge view from yesterday," McCoy said, folding his arms, "I don't much like the look of *that*."

"If you like, Doctor," Spock said as he came in the door, "I will send down to catering for a pot for you to bang on, to frighten away the wolf."

"'Wolf'?"

"The one you no doubt feel sure is eating the sun."

McCoy's look got slightly sourer as he sat down at the table. "No need to get cute, Mr. Spock. I was merely suggesting that the sun here looks like it was about to pull the same kind of trick 15 Trianguli tried yesterday."

Spock sat down with a slight expression of weariness. "Earth's primary has been known to produce the occasional coronal mass ejection," Spock said, "but normally it does so unassisted."

"Yes, well, 15 isn't likely to try anything like that unassisted *now,* is it, as a result of being tampered with?"

"I would estimate the odds for that as being—"

"Minuscule," Scotty said, and "Vanishingly small," K's't'lk said, and "Statistically insignificant," Spock said, all of them together.

Jim and Ael exchanged a glance. "So much agreement," Jim said, sitting down at the head of the table, "frightens me more than usual. I would move out of the area immediately, except that people are meeting us here. How long till the task force turns up now, Spock?"

"Twelve hours and thirty-three minutes, Captain."

"Thank you."

Other crew began coming in: more science department staff, especially several of the more senior astrophysics specialists; and a couple more department heads, including Uhura; and some of Ael's people from *Bloodwing,* among them tr'Keirianh the master engineer and Aidoann t'Khialmnae, who was doubling as science officer until another more junior crewman should be elevated to that position from the ranks. *Or what they have left of ranks,* Jim thought as the rest of the group filtered in. *I wish I could help her out somehow. Spock's had a look at their automation by now, but there's no substitute for people you can trust. . . .*

"Are we all here?" Jim said. "All right. Anything we need to handle before we get started?"

"One thing, Captain," Uhura said. "Just before I left the bridge, we received a message from the *Sempach.* There have been some schedule changes, it seems. At least a couple of the other ships will be joining us en route to the meeting point at RV Tri, and *Sempach* is now scheduled to rendezvous with us much earlier than the other starships meeting us here, perhaps within the hour. Commodore Danilov sends his compliments, and would like to see you at your earliest convenience."

"Very well." Uhura would have repeated the commodore's phrasing word for word, which made Jim just slightly nervous. "Earliest convenience" might sound polite enough, but it was not-very-secret code for "the minute I arrive, and not a second later." Dan was either very worried about something, or his nose was out of joint, or possibly both. But at least Jim thought he might hear something from Starfleet that they hadn't seen fit to transmit to *Enterprise* on the usual channels. *Or I'm going to get a very long grilling about what happened when we got here. . . .*

"All right," Jim said. "Let's hear what you've got."

K's't'lk tapped at the reader on the table in front of her and brought up her own notes, which she started chiming her way through at speed for the benefit of the science department staff on hand. Jim, who had read her preliminary abstract over breakfast and had then immediately resolved never to do such a thing again before the caffeine took, now settled back to wait for the expanded analysis, which would mean more to him than the raw figures.

It took a while, during which he had leisure to worry about Danilov's arrival. "We had been looking for indications of what stars would definitely not be candidates for the Sunseed process," K's't'lk finally said, "so that we could concentrate on the ones that *were,* and could avoid spreading our energies into areas that didn't require them. We feel we don't really need to worry too much about stars that genuinely fall into the 'dwarf' category, because they are the most difficult candidates for induction . . . and indeed, without some genuinely inspired on-the-fly calculations by Mr. Spock, we would not have managed induction at 15 Tri at all. Our conclusion is that dwarf stars are not massive enough to produce coronae with a high enough 'ambient' energy level to induce ion storms using Sunseed. And this includes Sol, which is a genuine nonmarginal dwarf G0, so that's one less thing for the Federation to worry about."

The computer console chirped softly as Scotty worked over it, preparing another display. "However, there are plenty of other non-dwarf stars that have inhabited planets," Scotty said, "the ratio being about one dwarf to four. Based on what we've seen most recently, and on data from the induction that followed the pursuit of *Enterprise, Intrepid,* and *Bloodwing* by the Romulans on the way out of Levaeri V, we've managed to cobble together some suggestions for protecting normal main-sequence stars from such inductions. All these are very tentative, of course. . . ."

Scotty killed the eclipse hologram, and the space above the middle of the table started filling up with diagrams and bar charts and pie charts and graphs with jittering lines. "While the coronal mass ejection we produced was a 'standard' one of the halo type with helium alpha," K's't'lk said, "there were interesting variations. One of the most telling phenomena for our purposes was the way the sunspots came up all of a sudden during the induction, completely unnaturally, in a pattern that bears no resemblance whatever to the usual 'butterfly' diagram, the plot of the heliographic latitude of the sunspots versus time. *Much* too much intrusion of the spots into the polar latitudes, suggesting that Sunseed's specific effect on the solar magnetic field is to derange the field intensities not above, but *below* local average rates, a 'curdling' effect which spreads all through the lower stellar atmosphere and . . ."

Jim glanced down the table at Ael. She was making desultory notes on a clipboard-padd, though nothing like the hurried and systematic ones which were being made by tr'Keirianh beside her; and she looked up, caught Jim's glance, and smiled, very slightly, a look of complete bemusement. Jim went back to making his own notes for the moment, which were mostly about things to discuss with Danilov when he got in.

". . . this being the case, the 'best' candidates, the top of the 'bell curve' and the stars most susceptible to this kind of interference, would be Bw stars with sufficiently weak helium lines, or Be stars with the necessary 'forbidden' lines in their spectra," K's't'lk was saying. "And fortunately, few of these have planets."

Scotty looked up then. "But most other stellar classes suffer as well. Nearly *all* stars with planets around them, in both Federation and Klingon space, fall on the upper side of the bell curve—probably nearly all the Rihannsu ones as well, though data on that is less certain. We have good astrocartography on the area, but less data on which stellar systems are populated."

"I will gladly help you there," Ael said. "But some of the rumors coming out of the Empire suggest that the data may not be correct for long. Populations are moving, or being moved, or in extreme cases being wiped out, along the fringes of the Imperium. Mostly the latter."

Scotty nodded, pausing to bring up another starmap in the hologram over the table, one which filled with a map of the Neutral Zone boundary and many pulsing points of light. "At any rate, as you see here, nearly every populated star system in which the primary is *not* a dwarf is now a potential target for attacks which at best will make interstellar shipping difficult, and at worst will impair starships' ability to achieve high warp, damage many of them, destroy some of them. This weapon can be moderately easily deployed by an enemy willing to divide his forces sufficiently, going from star to star at warp speeds and leaving bigger and bigger ion storms in his wake."

"There is also a possibility that Mr. Scott and the commander have not mentioned," Spock said, "which is a theoretical one, impossible to test . . . but I would dislike seeing any test made. If too many ion storms of this sort were started at one time by a group of ships in a given area of space, the storm front could possibly gain enough energy to propagate itself for a prolonged period along a wavefront light-minutes or even light-days long. At such energy levels it could propagate into subspace as well, deranging its structure and fabric." Spock looked much more troubled than the mere unpredictability of results could account for. "Such an 'ion firestorm' might render subspace useless for communication, or even incapable of supporting speeds higher than $c$ . . . which would at best mean that there were patches or ruts in subspace where starships could not go. At worst it could mean the end of warp-speed travel in this part of the galaxy, for everyone involved."

Jim looked at Ael. "Do your people know about the possibility of this effect, do you think?"

"I cannot say," Ael said. "But if they find out about it, I make no doubt they would consider its use as a weapon of the 'doomsday' sort."

Jim nodded to Scotty, who killed the displays. "So. Recommendations?"

Scotty looked uneasy. K's't'lk jangled, an unnerved sound, the Hamalki version of nervously clearing one's throat. "Captain," Spock said, "my simplest recommendation for the moment is not under any circumstances to allow Romulans, the party most likely now to use the Sunseed routines, into Federation space in strength. But that may shortly become impossible."

"And if they *do* get in?"

The engineer and the Hamalki looked at him rather bleakly. "I'd prevent that if I could," K's't'lk said. "For the time being."

"Hope springs eternal," Scotty said, smiling at K's't'lk a little grimly. "But Captain, the next recommendation is to start building solar orbiting facilities in every inhabited star system, heavily shielded for defense, carrying complements of photon torpedoes and lasers capable of disrupting any attacking ship's attempts to 'seed' a corona."

"That would take years!" McCoy said.

"Aye," Scotty said. "Years we haven't got. And any mobile platform can be destroyed if you bring enough power to bear."

"'For the time being,' though," McCoy said, looking over at K's't'lk. "I thought you were also looking for 'remote solutions.' Ways to handle this problem without having to chase around all over space. Orbital stations aren't all that remote."

Scotty and K's't'lk threw each other a regretful glance. "No," K's't'lk said. "They'd be an interim solution at best. Remote solutions are a lot harder, because we're still trying to write equations that will adequately express the problem. Mr. Spock has had a run at this . . ."

McCoy glanced over at Spock. "And you haven't solved it already? You mean you hit a problem and *bounced?*" The look in his eye was not entirely regret.

"Doctor," Spock said, "one must have a complete question before one can find answers. Even in your slightly chaotic science, you would not treat a patient before he had been properly diagnosed. In this situation—"

"*Slightly chaotic—?!*"

"—partial solutions are worse than none at all. The only way to affect stars remotely, without directly applying energy to them via phasers, photon torpedoes, and other such mechanical methods, is to alter the structure of the medium in which they are immersed—space and subspace themselves."

"It's not easy," K's't'lk said, her chiming becoming more complex, a toccata scaling up in sixths. "Leaving out the use of supraphysical instrumentalities like elective mass to alter the shape of space—"

"You'd *better* leave them out," Jim said sharply. "No messing around with my engines this time, Commander! We've got too much trouble in this reality to go getting ourselves immersed in some other one."

K's't'lk contrived to look faintly embarrassed—a good trick for someone with no facial features to speak of, except all those hot blue eyes. "I did promise, Captain," K's't'lk said. Jim settled back and tried not to look too stern. "At any rate, Sc'tty and I have been investigating some other possibilities for ways to stop a Sunseed induction. Some of them have to do with stellar 'diagnostic' techniques which go back a ways. The most promising of these involves atomic resonance spectrometry, and evaluation of the acoustic oscillation of a given star, with an eye to bending subspace so that it alters the frequency of that oscillation, changing the solar magnetic field's influence on the corona and derailing the Sunseed effect that way—"

McCoy looked up suddenly. "Wait a minute. 'Acoustic'? As in sound? You mean the whole thing—a whole star, a sun, *vibrates?*"

"Oscillates, yes, indeed, Doctor. Like a plucked string. As for sound, naturally you could not hear it in vacuum, there being no medium to transmit it, but acoustic vibration it remains nonetheless. Possibly the 'music of the spheres' your people used to talk about."

"Now, hold on just a second—"

"But even your poets mention stars singing. I'd thought perhaps they were unusually perceptive of stellar physics in either the acoustical or nonphysical mode . . ."

"Uh," McCoy said.

"Give up while there's still time, Bones," Jim said softly, and smiled.

"You mean they weren't? Then they were inspired," K's't'lk said. "But in any case, the oscillation is a phenomenon that has been known for centuries, even among your own people. Your astrophysicists have been using it for some time to analyze the general health of your stars, and to predict their moods."

"Commander," Spock said, looking interested, "this line of inquiry was not mentioned in this morning's précis . . ."

"No. Scotty came up with it on the way here in the lift, and we've been discussing it since."

"It is a fascinating concept," Spock said, folding his hands, steepling the fingers. "A star treated in such a manner might be made to produce oscillations that would cancel out those induced by the Sunseed routines, along the 'canceling sines' principle."

Scotty looked uncertain. "I follow you, Mr. Spock, but you've still got the problem of the complexity of the waves induced in the first place. They're not so simple as sines, either in the original generation or the way they interact with one another after induction. It's not one standing wave you'd have to cancel, but ripple after ripple in the solar 'pond,' all washing through one another and altering one another's frequencies and amplitudes. And then there's the matter of how the star's chromosphere reacts to the stress. Depending on the class of the star and the balance of the various heavy metals—"

"I grant the validity of the concern," Spock said, "but more to the point is the manner in which subspace is caused to make this alteration in the star's acoustical 'body.' Again one comes up against the logistical difficulties attendant on needing to build, deploy, and defend a mobile field generator of some kind."

Scotty raised his eyebrows, and bent over the computer console again, which chirped softly as he started doing some calculations. "It's possible that such a generator might not actually have to be near the star," Scotty said, "if you were using subspace to transmit the information about how subspace was itself going to be altered elsewhere. Like throwing a rock into the water. The ripples start here, but they wind up there . . ."

"That would take quite a while," K's't'lk said, her chiming going minor-key. "Unless you feel like invoking the equivalence heresy, and I'm not sure that's appropriate with our present data. Now if, instead, you altered subspace string structure by using the Gott III hypothesis to—"

"Sorry, K's't'lk, you lost me," Jim said. "'Heresy'? Kind of an odd term to come up in a discussion of astrophysics . . ."

"Oh, it's not just astrophysics, Captain," K's't'lk said, "it's physics in general. The simplest way to explain the heresy—if indeed it is one, the tests of the theory have all been equivocal—would be as an outgrowth of those parts of quantum theory that suggest that it's possible to make a particle over *there* do something by doing something to a particle over *here* . . . the effect propagating to the distant one in some way we don't understand. Early versions of the heresy mostly appeared because of the limitations of physics in earlier times, when science hadn't yet come to understand as much as we do now about the nature of subspace and its complex relationship with some of the more exotic subatomic particles. Now we're a little better informed—"

"A wee bit," Scotty said, looking as if the information wasn't enough for *him*. He hit a control on the computer to save the calculations he had just done, and it chittered softly in response.

"But there are still large areas where we're unsure of what's going on, especially as regards the curvatures of subspace, whether those curvatures are isotropic, or permanently isotropic . . ." K's't'lk waved a couple of forelegs. "And the equivalence heresy springs from one of these. Some theoreticians have suggested that, if small-scale shifts like those of one quark affecting another at a distance can happen, then larger-scale ones happen too . . . and we should be able to *cause* them to happen. If cause is the right word, when something is done to a particle, or atom, or molecule here, and another particle does the same without it being even slightly clear *why*."

"Sounds like magic to me," said McCoy.

"But not to me, sirs and ladies," said Master Engineer tr'Keirianh suddenly, and everyone turned to look, even Ael. "The mathematics of our physics would suggest that such could happen. But our physics also has an ethical mode which suggests that the Elements are one in Their nature, straight through the universality of being . . . and there is no way such 'plenum shifts' could *not* happen: 'as at the heart of being, so at the fringes and out to the Void.'" He frowned a little, his look for the moment closely matching Scotty's. "I will agree, the mathematics involved is thorny. Finding a way to describe accurately what we think might be happening . . ." He shrugged, a purely human gesture, and Jim looked at the graying hair and the lined face and suddenly, he couldn't tell why, conceived a liking for this man. "It is challenging. And also disturbing."

K's't'lk chimed soft agreement. "Yes," she said. "It has been very controversial among my people's physicists. There have been some unplanned reembodiments over the issue."

Knowing what he knew about the Hamalki life cycle, Jim wasn't sure whether this translated exactly as "suicides." He hoped it didn't. "K's't'lk," he said, getting up and walking around the table to where she sat, "how do you mean 'controversial' exactly? Your people have been rewriting physics cheerfully for centuries, on the local scale anyway . . . something that other physicists find distressing, but that doesn't seem to bother you people in the slightest. But *this* is 'controversial'?" He shook his head. "After all, you could just do it if you wanted to."

"If," K's't'lk said, looking up at him. "Of course we could. But our physics, like that of the Rihannsu, includes an ethical mode as well as a strictly mathematical one. The math tells you how . . . and the ethics tell you whether you *should*. In this case . . ." She jangled a little, an uneasy sound. "If equivalences on this scale are indeed possible, they might break the unwritten 'first law of space.'"

"You mean there are *written* ones?" McCoy said, with his eyebrows up.

"In the form of the clearly expressed physical behavior of the universe, of course there are," K's't'lk said. "'Don't let go of a hammer above your feet while standing over a gravity well. Don't breathe vacuum.' How large does the print have to be?" She chimed laughter. "But Doctor, this is something else. The inferred, inherent right of being to be *otherwise*."

"*That* I understand," McCoy said emphatically.

"You may," Jim said, "but now *I'm* lost."

Scotty folded his arms and leaned on them. "Captain," he said, "have you ever heard the saying 'Time is God's way of keeping everything from happening at once'?" Jim nodded. "Well then," Scotty said, "there's a corollary to that law: Space is God's way of keeping every-thing from happening in the same place. God or not, space seems to vi-olently resist physical objects coinciding—say by sharing the same volume, like someone beaming into a wall—"

"Doctor," Ael said, concerned, "are you cold?"

"No, Commander," McCoy said. "Not yet, anyway. But thank you."

Jim smiled. "—or by being forced into synchronization in other ways. Some have called it a reaction against the oneness of all matter and energy or the 'ylem' of pre-time, before the Big Bang. Whatever, the general tendency of the universe is presently away from order, toward chaos. That's just entropy. But it can also be expressed in an-other way. Things don't want to be the same, or stay the same; they want to be different, and get more so."

"No *'Plus ça change, plus c'est la même chose'* . . . ?"

"In life, yes. In this area of physics, no. . . ."

The communicator went. *"Bridge to Captain Kirk,"* said Mr. Mahasë's voice from the bridge.

Jim stepped over to the table, hit the comm button. "Kirk here."

*"Sempach has just dropped out of warp, Captain, and is closing. ETA five minutes."*

"Hold that thought," Jim said. "Not the one about *Plus ça change:* the other one. I know you're still feeling your way through this, but we need solutions fast." He looked down the table at Ael. "Commander, would you walk with me briefly?"

She rose and accompanied him out the door. When it closed behind them, Jim said, "Ael, the commodore in command of *Sempach* is likely to have mixed feelings about your crew at large spending any more time aboard *Enterprise,* even as controlled as the circumstances have been. You, and your senior officers, under supervision, I can now jus-tify . . . but no one else for the time being. And things may change without warning. I hope you'll understand."

"Captain," Ael said, "I understand better than you think. And I thank you for trusting us so far . . . when I have sometimes misstepped in that regard."

Jim nodded; then said, "I should go see the commodore. Spock will assist you with anything you need in the meantime; I'll see you later."

"We will be moving out for the rendezvous point," Ael said, "after the rest of the task force arrives?"

"That's the plan as I know it. If the commodore gives me different news, I'll see that you know about it as soon as possible."

"Very well," Ael said. "I shall be on *Bloodwing* for the time being. With another Federation ship in view, and more coming, my place is with her. Until matters stabilize."

They stepped into the lift together. "Until they do . . ."

"Till then, luck and the Elements attend you," Ael said.

"Thanks," Jim said, thinking, as the lift doors shut, *I hope I don't need it, or them. . . .*

# Chapter Six

*Sempach* was one of a newer, experimental class of cruisers, the *Constellation* class, named in memory of Matt Decker's old ship that had been lost against the planet killer in the L-374 system. The class-name ship and *Sempach* had been the first out of the shipyards, with *Speedwell* close behind, and all of them were already busy performing their basic function—trying out a new four-nacelle design that was supposed to provide starships with a more streamlined and reliable warp field, capable of higher speeds. The technology, referred to as "pre-transwarp" in some of the literature Jim had seen, was extremely interesting but technically somewhat difficult to understand, and Scotty had passed it on to his captain with a single comment: "Rubbish." Nonetheless, the technology seemed so far to be working all right, and the design crews had plainly been busy elsewhere too: the ship was very handsome from the outside, with a lean and rakish look to her. As the transporter effect wore off, Jim looked around *Sempach*'s transporter room, surprised at its size and its somewhat nonutilitarian look; there was even a small lounge area off to one side, with comfortable seating. *Kind of overdone,* Jim thought as he greeted the transporter technician at the console and then raised an eyebrow at himself. *She's affecting me. Still, it'd be nice not having to stand around waiting for visiting dignitaries to arrive.*

The transporter room doors opened, and Commodore Danilov came in, looking much as he had when Jim had last seen him in San Francisco: a brawny man of medium height, dark with a combination of Polynesian and eastern European blood, the dark hair going silver-shot now above a broad, round face, surprisingly unlined for someone of his age.

"Sir," Jim said, "you hardly had to come down here to meet me . . . "

The commodore gave him a wry look out of his sharp dark eyes as they shook hands. "Captain," Danilov said, "I'm still learning to find my way around this ship. I know I could have sent a lieutenant for you, but they get lost too. Come on."

They went off down the corridors together, the commodore making his way quickly enough despite his disclaimer. Jim's feelings about his superior officers ranged from the respectful to the occasionally scandalous, but here was one man in whose case he came down hard on the respectful side: twenty-five years in Starfleet, the kind of officer who flew a ship or a desk with equal skill—though he fought them more often than he simply flew them. Danilov's experience and effectiveness in battle had become legendary; in particular, he had probably scored more points during the last big war with the Klingons than any other commander except Captain Suvuk of *Intrepid,* until the Organians blew the whistle and stopped play. Jono Danilov had that invaluable commodity for a commander, a reputation for luck. He always seemed to come out only slightly scorched from any trouble he got into, no matter how the trouble seemed to seek him out—and it did.

"She's a fine ship," he said to Jim as they turned a corner, "a little fidgety at first, but she's settled in nicely now. Fleet's pleased; they're already flying the keels for the two new ones—*Stargazer* and *Hathaway.*"

Jim nodded. "She's a real lady, Commodore. And she still has that new-ship smell."

"I want to keep it that way for a while," Danilov said, shooting Jim a look, "and avoid getting things all scorched and smoky. The question is, will I be able to."

He came to a door without a label and waved it open. Danilov's quarters were considerably bigger than Jim's on *Enterprise,* and the office was also a lot more spacious. "Palatial," Jim said. "Rank hath its privileges."

"Hardly. This is the standard captain's cabin for this model. Sit down, Jim, please. Can I offer you a brandy?"

"Thank you, Dan, yes."

He went over to a glass-doored cupboard and got it, and Jim sat looking around him for the moment at the furnishings, as spare as most field personnel's, but still individual: on the desk, a sleek, round old

Inuit soapstone sculpture of a bear; a good amateur watercolor of the Ten-Thousand-Step Stair in misty weather, hanging on the wall behind the desk along with a brace of latoun-inlaid "snapdragon" flintlocks from Altair VI; a shaggy blue tree-pelt from Castaneda draped over the back and seat of the high-backed chair behind the desk.

Danilov handed Jim the drink in a heavy-bottomed crystal glass and seated himself. *"Viva,"* he said, lifting his glass.

"Cheers," Jim said, and sipped.

They sat appreciating the drinks for a few seconds, but no more. "So," Danilov said, "tell me about this little engagement you had here."

"Little!" Jim gave him a look. "Seven ships against two, sir; not my kind of odds. And circumstances were less than ideal."

"It would have been seven against one," Danilov said, "had things gone strictly by the book."

"They didn't," Jim said, "because I used some latitude in construing the orders that Fleet had specifically given me."

"Might I inquire about the reasons, Jim?" Danilov asked. "Or was it just on general principle?"

"I had a hunch."

Danilov let out a long breath. "No arguing with those," he said after a moment. "They've saved both our lives often enough before now."

"And it turns out to have been a good thing, in retrospect. It proves I was correct to be concerned about leaks of information from—" Even now Jim could hardly bring himself to say "Starfleet." "From Earth."

Dan sat back and looked at him. "No one but Fleet should have known where *Bloodwing* was going to be, or when," Jim said, "and regardless, there were seven Romulan vessels waiting for us there, cloaked. If Ael had been on site when originally scheduled, she would be dead now."

"Not a captive?"

"I doubt it. No one offered us the opportunity to surrender her. They just attacked."

"Your presence there might have affected their plans."

"That's occurred to me. But it doesn't matter, Dan. *Bloodwing*'s commander wouldn't have allowed herself to be taken alive. She would have fought until her ship was destroyed to prevent the Sword, or herself, falling into their hands."

"You're sure of that?"

"Yes."

"You're sure," Danilov said, looking steadily at Jim, "that your thinking on this particular subject is clear?"

"Dan," Jim said, nettled, " 'this particular subject' is a non-subject. My 'thinking' as regards Commander t'Rllaillieu is clear enough for my first officer, who is something of an expert on the clarity of thought, and my CMO, who is something of an expert on humans in general, and me in particular." Danilov's gaze dropped. "The commander is a courageous and sometimes brilliant officer who, at the cost of her own career, sought us out and gave us valuable information which kept the balance of power from being irreparably destroyed. If the effectiveness of that intervention has been rendered short-lived by subsequent events, well, such things happen. If one of *us* had done the things she's done, he or she would have been loaded down with enough decorations to make the wearer fall face forward on trying to stand. But because she's from an unfriendly power, no one seems willing to take what she's done at face value."

There was a short silence. "The point is," Danilov said, "she's a Romulan. And Romulans plot."

Jim got up and started to pace. "Dan, with all due respect, you know as well as I do why you were so glad to get away from that desk in San Francisco. Politics! Romulans have politics just as we do, though possibly in a more complex mode. But this time, politics is failing, as it sometimes does, to keep this culture's internal conflicts from erupting into a war that affects others outside it. Including us. And we still have a problem at our end, because somehow very detailed information about our reactions to this situation is leaking out of Starfleet and getting to the Romulans—going straight to where it can do the most harm." Jim paused and gripped the back of his chair, leaning on it. "Something has to be done, and fast. Otherwise, when hostilities do break out, we're going to be in serious trouble."

Danilov sat back. "Your concern," he said, "is noted and logged."

"Which reassures me. But what's being *done* about it?"

Danilov just looked at him for a moment. "Jim, I can't discuss it."

Which meant he either knew something was being done, or knew that nothing was. "It's going to impair our conduct of this operation," Jim said, "if our personnel can't be sure that details of where they'll be aren't being piped straight through to the people who're going to be shooting at them."

"You leave the conduct of the operation with me," Danilov said, "since that's where Starfleet has placed it." The look he gave Jim implied that even enduring comradeship would not be allowed to interfere with some things.

Jim let the pause stretch out. "Yes, sir."

Danilov let out a long breath and reached out to pick up the smooth gray soapstone bear, turning it over in his hands. "Aside from that for the moment, Jim, message traffic has become an issue. It's way, way up on the Romulan side. We don't even need to be able to read those messages to know that a massive mobilization is under way, and to understand perfectly well where it's pointing."

"Lieutenant Commander Uhura tells me that Starfleet message traffic has also been reaching unusual levels," Jim said, sitting down again.

Danilov nodded. "Yes. With that in mind, we're carrying some material for you that Starfleet didn't want to send out through the ether. Strategy briefings, general intelligence from inside the Imperium . . . other information."

"They *are* afraid that some of our codes have been broken."

Danilov put the bear back down on his desk. "Yes. Some have been allowed to go 'stale' on purpose, for use when we *want* traffic to be intercepted. We've hand carried in two new encryption systems for you; all the rest of the ships in the task force have them already. You're to have your science officer install them immediately. One of them is for use now, the other is to be held."

"For when war breaks out . . ." Jim said.

Danilov looked at Jim with great unease. "No one in Fleet is saying that word out loud," he said. "But you don't have to be a telepath to hear people thinking it."

"And another thing about message traffic," Jim said. "Are you sure the monitoring stations are functioning properly? Those Romulan ships shouldn't have been able to cross the Zone, cloaked or not, without being detected by the monitoring web. Are some of those satellites malfunctioning? Have they been sabotaged? Or have the Romulans come up with a cloaking device that not even the monitoring stations' hardware can detect?"

Danilov frowned, shook his head. "It's being looked into, Jim. We're carrying a specialist communications team that will be performing advanced remote sensing and diagnostic routines to see what the story is when we get close enough to the Zone. For the moment, we're treating the information as reliable once it's been corroborated by other intelligence sources."

Jim nodded. He took out the data solid he had brought with him and passed it across the desk to the commodore, who put it on the reading pad. A little holographic text window leaped into being, scrolling down some of the contents with a soft chirring sound.

"While we're on the subject of things better not pumped into the ether at the moment," Jim said, "on this solid is our most recent work on the Sunseed project, including a way to tune starships' shields in order to screen out the worst of the artificial ion storm effect. I think this should be passed immediately to every other Starfleet vessel within range . . . and the preferred method of passing it should be by hand carry rather than broadcast."

Danilov looked at the text a moment longer, then nodded and touched the reading plate. The "window" disappeared with a chirp. "We'll pass it to them tomorrow," he said, turning the solid over in his hands.

"More material should be forthcoming shortly," Jim said. "But this kept our rear ends out of the sling at 15 Tri. Please make sure everyone takes it seriously."

"All right." Danilov looked up again. "There's no doubt that your forethought pulled this one out of the fire, Jim. It was a nasty situation, elegantly handled. But I should warn you, there'll still be some at Fleet who construe this kind of order juggling as an indication of someone trying to see how much he can get away with . . ."

"You're saying," Jim said, "that they're looking for proof of loyalty via blind obedience. Not the best place to look for it, Dan. But even if they *are* presently wasting their time worrying about minor issues like that, I don't think they'll have leisure for it much longer."

"No," Danilov said, "not once things get started tomorrow morning." He brought his standard desk viewer around toward him and glanced at it. "The first nonofficial meeting happens tomorrow morning. *Lake Champlain* and *Hemalat* have gone ahead to meet the Romulans and bring them in to RV Tri; we expect to hear that they've made contact in a few hours. Tomorrow afternoon, our ships' time, we'll be arriving at the rendezvous point. That evening, we have a social event to allow for some early assessments and to let both sides synchronize the meeting schedule—no one wants to be up in the middle of their own night while the other side is fresh. And then the main session gets under way, and we find out how much trouble we're really in."

"While behind us, on both sides, the eagles gather . . ." Jim frowned. "A lot of chances for things to go wrong, Dan. Somebody on one side or the other jumps the gun, and the shooting starts . . ."

"If any of my commanders do any such thing," Danilov said, "I will have their hides for hangings."

"A pity you can't enforce something similar on the Romulans," Jim said.

"We will play by the rules," Danilov said. "What the Romulans will do, the event will show."

Jim's smile was both grim and amused. "That's almost exactly what Ael said . . . You should come over and meet her this evening."

"I will," said Danilov, "once we're under way. I wouldn't mind getting out of this general area, just in case anyone else turns up."

"That's another concern, Dan. On that solid I gave you there's a 3-D analysis I did earlier. Later on you should take a look at it—"

"Why not now?" Danilov said. He put the solid down on the reader plate again and touched another control. Jim's hologram of the area where Empire, Imperium, and Federation all met now sprang into life in the air.

Jim's smile was annoyed. "Dan, it's just not fair that you have all these slick new gadgets when *I*—"

"Now, now," Danilov said, "thou shalt not covet thy neighbor's ship."

"Yes, well. But my neighbor's weaponry," Jim said, "is another matter."

Danilov smiled at that as he rotated the hologram. "Yes, *Sempach is* loaded for bear, isn't she? I've been wishing for a chance to use what she's got. Now I wish I didn't have to . . . and I'm becoming increasingly sure I will."

He paused, looking at the hologram. "You think there might be a multiple-location breakout."

"It's occurred to me."

"Fleet's been thinking that way too." Danilov looked at the hologram, sighed, and reached sideways to pick up his bear again, turning it over and over in his hands. "And there sit the Klingons. Or rather, they haven't been sitting; they've been running amok in the Romulan fringe systems—smash-and-grab stuff, asset-stripping the furthest planets."

"Suggesting they know the Romulans are going to make a big move now and won't bother defending targets that distance makes difficult to support."

"It does suggest that, doesn't it," Danilov said. "Hints and suggestions . . . I'd give a lot for some recent hard data from a source I trust."

"You may get some of that shortly."

"I desperately hope so." He turned away from the hologram and put the bear aside. "Well, is there anything else?"

Jim and the commodore looked at each other somewhat somberly as Jim stood up. "As regards Starfleet's concerns about me," Jim said, "you don't believe them, Dan, do you? You know me better than that."

Danilov didn't say anything for a long moment. "Look, Jim," he said finally, "people change. We're scattered all over the galaxy, all of us, for prolonged periods of time, in strange and sometimes disturbing circumstances. Starship captains are selected for stability, we both know that. But there's a galaxy full of unknowns out there, not to mention the ones at the bottom of the human mind . . . and things that can't always be predicted do happen. In a ship of this class, it's hard to avoid thinking frequently of Matt Decker."

"Matt was a one-off."

"Garth of Izar."

"That wasn't his fault. The alien treatment that saved his life—"

"Ron Tracey."

Jim grimaced.

"Jim," Danilov said, "we may or may not be a breed apart, but when starship commanders go off the rails, we do it spectacularly. Now, don't mistake me. I know perfectly well you're not likely to do anything like what Matt did. But every heart has its weaknesses, and conflicting loyalties can crucify a man faster than anything else."

"You can tell the fleet admiral," Jim said, standing very straight, "that my loyalties to the Federation and to Starfleet are quite clear, in accordance with my oaths to both those organizations. Starfleet Command should relieve me immediately if they think otherwise. But I will fight such a course of action, for they have *no* evidence whatsoever to back up any such suspicions. And I will win that fight."

Danilov looked at him steadily. "They sent you ahead to warn me, didn't they?" Jim said.

"I volunteered to make this side trip when I saw which way the wind was blowing back on Earth," Danilov said after a moment. "We've known each other a good while, Jim. You were the most ornery ensign a first-time lieutenant ever had to keep in order. But you wouldn't lie to a shipmate then, and I don't believe you'd lie to a fellow officer now. Indeed, you weren't all that good at lying when you had to."

"Possibly the root of this whole problem," Jim said softly, remembering how he had flinched, long ago, at reading the sealed orders from Starfleet that finally sent *Enterprise* into the Neutral Zone under the command of a captain who had to seem to be losing his marbles. *And as for this time . . .*

"Yes. You know the truth, and I'm sure you're telling it to me. But, Jim, you understand . . . *they* have to be sure."

"I understand," Jim said. "But it doesn't make me any happier about it, at a time like this, to find them so damned uncertain."

"No one promised us these jobs were necessarily going to make us happy all the time," Commodore Danilov said. "And our superiors are as mortal as we are, and as fallible."

"They are?" Jim said. "There go all my illusions."

Danilov chuckled. "Jim, our three ships will leave immediately for the task force rendezvous point at RV Tri. *Nimrod* will join us in a couple of hours, and *Ortisei* shortly thereafter. We should find *Hemalat* and *Lake Champlain* waiting for us with the Romulans. *Speedwell* has another errand and may arrive a little late. A little before we arrive at RV Tri, *Ortisei* will escort *Bloodwing* out of the area. Together they'll stay some light-years out of detection range until and unless they're called in."

"I'll pass that on to Commander t'Rllaillieu," Jim said.

"Will she cooperate?" Danilov said, looking closely at him again.

"She will," Jim said. "But I must tell you that she's already made it plain she has no intention of freely giving herself up to the Romulans if they ask for her."

"That could be a problem."

"It has to be one that Starfleet's anticipated. And it's a problem only if they decide they want to hand her over to the Romulans. Which, taking that into account"—he nodded at the hologram hanging in the air, burning in red, blue, and green—"isn't going to keep them from going to war now. Not after what they did at 15 Tri."

Danilov looked at the hologram. "I wish I could be sure," he said. "The Federation isn't. Part of our job here is to find out whether this war really has to happen."

"You may find out the answer," Jim said, "by being in the first battle, Dan."

"We're prepared for that," Danilov said. "But just as prepared to walk away, if there's any way to have peace break out instead."

"Amen," Jim said, reaching down to the desk and lifting his glass.

They knocked their glasses together and tossed off the remainder of the brandy. Jim put his glass down as Danilov did. "Jim," Danilov said. "I know what shape of orders they cut you. Please . . . be careful . . . because you're being closely watched."

*By you, old friend,* Jim thought. "Thanks for the warning," he said as Danilov stood. "No, it's all right, Dan. I can find my way out."

Danilov sat down again, throwing him an amused look. "Later, Jim."

He left Danilov there looking at the holographic representation of the Triangulum spaces, and only got lost once on his way back to the transporter room.

Rihannsu song spoke wistfully enough of the ancient morning and evening stars, the old ships, long fallen from orbit. *Nowadays, though,* Teleb tr'Sathe thought, *we have only the one . . . but it's better by far.* Often enough, when on leave on ch'Rihan, he had looked up from some balmy beach or forest path and tracked it across the night sky. Right now he could not see it, but that was only natural: he was in it. *But not for long!*

Teleb turned from the wide plasteel port looking down on ch'Rihan and gazed back across the loading bay. It was a space half a *stai* wide, one of twenty docking and loading facilities arranged around a vast spherical central core that was big enough to take even the largest of Grand Fleet's starships. Ur-Metheisn was probably one of the biggest orbital ship-servicing facilities anywhere in known space; even the Klingons and the Federation had nothing to match it. They preferred smaller facilities, more spread out among their colonies. The Rihannsu school of thought preferred larger central facilities, "hubs," and this was the first and greatest of them: Sunside Station, the undisputed ruler of the skies over ch'Rihan. From it all the defense satellites were controlled and coordinated; from it the Fleet's ships were dispatched all over the Empire, executing the decisions made by the great-and-good down in the dome. This was the beating heart of the Grand Fleet, and the kindly Elements had seen fit to drop Teleb right into the middle of it, his captain-apprenticeship successfully passed and himself newly promoted, the pins now bright on his collar, with his own cruiser *Calaf* poised graceful and nearly ready to go outside the docking and loading tube, and the prospect of battle in the offing. Life could not have looked brighter to him if Teleb had stared straight at the sun.

For the moment, he was doing what his mentor-captain had advised him—standing by and letting his crew get on with their jobs—though he would have much preferred to be right in the middle of them, hustling the loading crew, watching every detail. The excitement was definitely getting the better of him now. *Artaleirh!* When Teleb had seen the orders, he had nearly begun to sing with the sheer excitement of it all. Artaleirh was a vital system, and the news of the rebellion there had shocked and horrified him. But there would not be a rebellion for much longer. The sight of six cruisers in their skies would shortly remind those people of their proper loyalties. *But if it doesn't*—Teleb frowned. He didn't much care for the idea of having to make war on other Rihannsu. Weren't there Klingons and Feds enough to destroy? But there was no place for rebellion if the Empire was to remain strong in the face of her enemies elsewhere in the galaxy. *I am the servant of the Senate and the Praetorate,* he thought. *I am the strong arm of the Empire. I am a captain in Grand Fleet, and I will carry out my orders and win victory over the Empire's enemies, within it or without it, at whatever cost!*

Then Teleb grinned. "Adolescent effusions." That was what his mentor-captain Mirrstul had called such statements, though she had been kindly enough about it. Well, she had a right to her opinions. She was a doughty warrior and a brilliant tactician. But he could not imagine her ever having been young. As for himself, while he had his youth, he was not going to waste it on too much somberness.

Teleb leaned against the bulkhead with his arms folded, watching one of the specialist loading crews bringing in the last batch of photon torpedoes, trundling them quickly down the huge loading tube into *Calaf*'s lower weapons bay. He glanced at the chrono woven into his uniform sleeve. *Almost ready,* he thought. Teleb wanted very much to be the first to have the honor of reporting his ship ready to take off on this mission. *A few breaths more, then I will take my bridge and be the first to make the announcement—*

Then he caught sight of a tall dark shape walking quickly across the floor of the vast bay toward him, and he smiled slightly. Full dress uniform, glittering in black-gold and black; on departure day, you would never see Jisit in anything else. She was trying hard to look sober and serious, as befitted one setting out on an important mission, but such a demeanor always sat oddly on her as far as Teleb was concerned. His memory always overlaid them with the image of Jisit as she had been on that outrageous party night after her return from her first campaign, completely sozzled on ale, wearing a strange pointed hat with a tassel and singing "The High Queen's Bastard Daughter" to her crew and his in a key yet to be discovered by any other sentient being.

"Well, Captain tr'Sathe," she said, coming up to him and giving him two breaths' worth of bow.

"Well, Captain t'Nennien," he said, and gave it right back to her, to the very fraction of a second.

Then they both burst out laughing and collapsed into one another's arms. "Are you excited?" she hissed into his ear. "I can't bear it. I think I'll scream."

"Don't. They'll think you're singing again."

She laughed even harder and held him away. "Beast!"

"Guilty," Teleb said. "Is *Teverresh* ready?"

"Two loads to go yet, and my master engineer is complaining about retuning the warp drive before we leave. You'll beat me again, you fiddly little *neirrh*."

He grinned. "I must keep you in your place somehow."

"Oh, and what would that be?"

"Behind me."

"Behind your back, you mean." The grin went a little more sober. "But that way, with me and *Teverresh* there, maybe no one will stab you in it. It's not a safe place we're going, Teleb. Artaleirh has gone quiet."

"Oh?"

She shook her head. "The time limit on the ultimatum expired two hours ago. They made no answer to the Senate's last warning. We will have to implement our orders to the full."

Teleb sighed. "Are they all gone mad? With the Klingons running about savaging everything they can, this is no time to renounce the Empire's protection."

"Mad or not, we will call them back to their proper loyalty," Jisit said, ". . . or relieve them of it and take it on ourselves."

"And win glory . . ."

"I don't know about the glory," Jisit said, "but we'll carry out our orders, make our frontiers safe, and uphold the rule of law. That's good enough for me. Maybe pick up a few points toward my next promotion." She poked him none too gently in the shoulder. "And as for you,

*you* stay out of trouble when we get there. It would be embarrassing for me to have to save you again, now that they've finally trusted you with *Calaf* without old Mirrstul looking over your shoulder."

"What do you mean, save me *again?*" But Teleb's chrono chirped softly. "That's it," he said, glancing over at the loading tubes. The Sunside-based loading crews were leaving, pushing the last of the floater pallets in front of them. "I should go."

"Go on," Jisit said, "and I'll resume reminding you of the Elements' own truth, which you are pleased to refuse to see, after this operation's over. Mind your crew now, Captain!"

"You mind yours, Captain," he said. She turned, but he caught her by the hand and she paused. He bowed over that hand, low enough to breathe softly on the back of it.

She smiled, gripped the hand as he straightened. "Message me tonight, after we make warp."

"I will."

She turned and headed away across the loading bay, and Teleb hurried across to *Calaf*'s loading tube to make one final check on the condition of the weapons hold before going up to his bridge. He was humming the first line of "The High Queen's Bastard Daughter" as he went up the tube ramp into *Calaf*'s belly, and away to his first real war.

Jim was still thinking about *Sempach*'s weapons when he got back. The thought led to the idea that he'd like to look over her warp engines at some point, and that thought reminded him of something else. He paused in the corridor and hit a comm button. "Bridge."

*"Bridge. Chekov here."*

"Mr. Chekov, is Mr. Spock on the bridge?"

*"He is on a scheduled break, Captain. I believe he has gone down to the main mess."*

"Very well," Jim said. "Coordinate with the helm officer on *Sempach;* then notify *Bloodwing* we're setting course for RV Trianguli and implementing immediately."

*"Aye, aye, sir,"* Chekov's voice came back.

"Kirk out."

Jim headed off down the corridor, caught a turbolift, and made his way down to the mess. There he found not only Spock but also McCoy, both finishing their lunches at one of the tables nearest the wall, both reading from electronic clipboard-padds as they did. Spock glanced up. "Captain—" he said.

"Finish your lunch, Mr. Spock, there's no rush about anything." Jim went over to the hatch and got himself a chicken sandwich and a cup of coffee, then sat down with them.

"How was your meeting with the commodore?" McCoy said, pushing his clipboard away.

Jim made a rather wry face. "Affable enough. But Fleet is antsy, as I expected, about our association with *Bloodwing* . . . even though they suggested we renew it. Suspicions rear their ugly heads." He sighed, shook his head, and bit into his sandwich.

McCoy snorted. "Invisible cat syndrome."

It took a moment of dealing with the sandwich before Jim could respond. "What?"

"As regards the commander, anyway."

Spock glanced over at McCoy. "If I remember correctly, the paradigm was first used by a religious apologist on Earth in the early twentieth century."

"That's right. Say somebody comes along," McCoy said, "and points at a chair and says to you, 'There's an invisible cat in that chair.' Now, *you* know the person's nuts. You say to them, 'But there's nothing there. The chair's empty.' Their response is, 'And isn't that exactly how it *would* look if there were an invisible cat in the chair? See, you've proved my point.' "

"*Argumentum ex fallacio,*" Spock said.

"In your case, Jim—" McCoy had the grace to look just slightly abashed. "Well, come on. The source of all this trouble is that your opposite number's female. Bearing in mind some of your past behavior— not that I'm casting any aspersions, mind you—what *are* they supposed to think?"

Jim made a wry face. "This is just another way of saying it's all my own fault, isn't it?"

Spock addressed himself with renewed interest to his salad. "Jim," McCoy said, "they'll think what they think. You're not going to be able to change it, so you may as well just get on with what you were going to do anyway. How was the rest of your meeting?"

"Troubling," Jim said. He paused as a group of six or seven crewmen came into the mess and took a table, then headed for the food dispensers. "I think they're expecting the balloon to go up with a bang sometime after the talks with the Romulans, but no one seems to be clear about just when, or what will trigger it."

"I bet half of them are just hoping it doesn't happen, somehow," Bones said. "That the Romulans will just back down."

That thought had occurred to Jim, and it was making him nervous. He drank some coffee. "This time, I think that would be a serious miscalculation," he said. "Spock, I know perfectly well we run frequent readiness checks on all the weapons systems and the engines, but I want Scotty to use this next day or so to go over absolutely everything defense-oriented with a fine-tooth comb. Tell him to co-opt as much assistance from less busy departments aboard ship as he feels he needs to make sure that everything—*everything*—is in working order."

"Yes, Captain."

Jim finished his coffee and put the cup aside. "We also have some new cryptographic equipment or routines, or both, to be installed in the comm system and the main computer; they'll be coming over from *Sempach*. Which reminds me. Those automations Ael wanted you to have a look at? You never did report on those."

"It was not a very pressing matter, Captain. I wrote you a report, which you may not yet have seen."

Jim did his best to look unconcerned, but he knew he had been letting his paperwork slip a little lately. "Um. Well, what's the verdict?"

Spock put aside his empty bowl of salad and steepled his fingers. "I was able to assist them in several areas where newer programming and hardware needed to be restructured to interleave correctly with other, older control programs and routines," Spock said. "*Bloodwing*'s personnel have been most ingenious, and I should also say innovative, in compensating for their present lack of manpower. But here and there conflicts had occurred, since some of the newer programming was done by crewmen with less expertise than might have been desired, and the automation reprogramming had extended to almost every system aboard the ship."

"Almost?"

"There was one notable exception," Spock said. "The ship's engines did not appear on the list of augmented systems which I was asked to examine."

Jim thought about that for a moment. "Well, they didn't lose too many people from their engineering department during the trouble, as I remember. And tr'Keirianh is a fairly hands-on sort, from what I can make of him. Maybe he's uneasy about allowing such a crucial system to be automated."

"It could be, Captain," Spock said. "It could also be that there was something involving *Bloodwing*'s engine systems that the commander or the master engineer did not care to have me see."

Jim took another swig of coffee, considering that briefly. "Any evidence to support such a conjecture?"

"Little, and that circumstantial," Spock said. "Should another opportunity arise to investigate this, however, I confess I might attempt to do so."

"Curiosity, Mr. Spock?" Jim said.

Spock raised an eyebrow.

"Well, never mind it for now," Jim said. "Though if the opportunity arises this evening to do a little discreet inquiry, feel free." He sighed. "I won't be down in rec for long. I've got to start getting caught up on my paperwork. Meanwhile, when Ael and her people come by this evening to meet the commodore, see to it that each of them has an escort permanently within eyeshot. Security is going to become more of an issue now."

"I will see to it, Captain," Spock said. "Have you any preferences as to who should be assigned to the commander?"

Jim considered for a moment. "Now that you mention it . . ."

The darkness of the caverns, when the lights were turned down to their lowest, often seemed to amplify every sound, every breath. So it seemed very loud to Mheven when her mother spoke up suddenly out of what ought to have been her sleep.

"I hear," said Rrolsh. "I'm going out."

Mheven was at first not sure she hadn't been dreaming the words, for she had been thinking them, on and off, for nearly the past twenty days, since she came back from a mission. *Is it really that long,* she thought, *that we have been down in this darkness? It seems like a thousand years.* The sun— she dreamed about that too, golden in an emerald sky, but she knew she was not going to see it anytime soon. Up there, in the light and the air, more light than just the sun's was raining down on the fertile land. The sky was still filled with ships raining down fire. The crops were all surely burned now, the forest blanketing these hills all charred, if what had happened to the city had been any indication.

"Mother," Mheven said to the unseen presence across the room, "you're half asleep. You know they've been scanning the surface constantly. Anyone who goes out will be caught and interrogated, and they'll discover where we are. Then all this will be for nothing."

A faint sound of bedding being discarded drifted across the darkness of the cavern. Mheven sighed and fumbled for the little battery lamp.

At her touch it glowed up to its preset level: low. No one down here wasted power. Since the destruction of the concealed solar arrays in the last spate of bombing, there had been none to spare. Mheven looked across the low-ceilinged little rest-cave and saw what she expected: the water trickling down its dank walls, the supplies of food and water and materiel stacked up in their crates at the back of the cave, and the beautiful, drawn, tired, aging face of her mother popping suddenly out of the cold-tunic she was hurriedly pulling over her head. That grim face looked at her; those eyes, fierce and eager, looked into hers.

"You can't hear it?" she asked.

"Hear what?"

"I'm going out!"

Her mother scrambled up out of the bedroll and headed for the sleeping cave's entrance, which had someone's blanket hung up over it as a screen against the lights always burning on the other side. Mheven sighed and pulled on her own tunic. Kicking her bedroll aside, she went after her mother.

The main cavern, even with the tiny lights that were all the group now allowed itself, was still spectacularly beautiful. There had been a time when people had come from all over this part of the Empire to see these caverns, a natural wonder as astonishing in their way as the fire-falls at Gal Gath'thonng on ch'Rihan; possibly the biggest natural caverns in all the Empire's worlds, but no one knew for sure, because no one had ever completely explored them in all the time the planet Ysail had been colonized, a matter of several hundred years. The caverns stretched beneath the smaller of the planet's two continents, Saijja, from the cliffs of Eilmajen in the east nearly to Veweil in the west, and they were so deep and complex that they had never even been completely mapped. Scanners could not reach so deep, not even the powerful ones used from space.

The refugees had picked this spot for their labors because it was one of the deepest caverns and because it was unknown to outsiders. Though in more peaceful times tourists had constantly been passing through one part or another of the Saijja Caverns, there had always been parts of the cavern complex that no tourist had ever been shown: the spelunkers' secrets, the private delights of those inhabitants of the planet who made it their business to come here every chance they got in leisure time, exploring a frontier that was not infinite but that would certainly take thousands of years to discover fully.

This one, the greatest cavern to be found for several hundred miles in any direction, was called Bheirsenn—"bright in the night," in the local dialect. When the lights were on, it was bright indeed; a vast bubble of air trapped in the depths of the planet, roughly a mile and a half in diameter, ceilinged in terrifyingly huge and glittering stalactite chandeliers of limestone, calcite, and quartz crystal. That impossibly distant ceiling shone bright as a hazy sky when the great high-intensity lights were on. They were not on much lately, what with the power crisis, but even with the lights dimmed, the distant pendant crystalline stalactites glittered faintly like faraway galaxies, like the points of stars. It was a space difficult for even the most ground-shy Rihannsu to feel claustro-phobic in, one of awe-inspiring beauty.

And it was also a perfect place for making weapons of all kinds, espe-cially bombs. From the great main cavern, hundreds of smaller caves budded off in clusters and chains, a labyrinth that only those who lived there could ever master. Working separately, the technicians and the people whom they had trained occupied small, dense-walled stone rooms in which they could work with deadly explosives and other dan-gerous technologies without being concerned about triggering a cata-clysm. The whole group, totaling about five hundred people, had been down here for almost a year now. They had slipped away with their families and even their pets when the government had declared Ysail to be a "primary resource world." Others, at a distance, might have been fooled about what this meant, but the Ysailsu knew all too well. The Empire had seized all the industry on their planet. Then, when there was bitter protest at this, they had sent ships from Grand Fleet, carrying troops from the army and intelligence, to round up the population of a couple of cities and send them off to work camps, expecting the rest to settle down and do as they were told.

It had not worked out that way, for over the centuries the Ysailsu had developed what the Empire considered an irrational attitude: they thought *they* owned their world. The small population of the planet rose in nearly simultaneous rebellion. Immediately after that, the Em-pire began bombing it—very selective bombing, of course, concentrat-ing on the cities and taking care to do no harm to industrial resources. The Ysailsu, though, partaking in full of the legendary stubbornness of their parent species, had decided that if *they* could not profit from the industries they had spent hundreds of years building, then neither would the Empire. Led by a group of thoughtful and angry guerrillas, the Ysailsu took all the food, water, spare parts, power sources, and sup-plies of every kind that they could find, and went to ground in the caves en masse. They scattered themselves across the underside of their smaller continent, made themselves at home, and began blowing up their factories themselves.

All this, as well as the smoking cities and the ground shuddering with explosions, now seemed as distant to Mheven as a dream. The workers and fighters down here did not hear or feel the explosions. The caves were far too deep. There was no way the Empire could find them, and even if it did, no way it could reach them without dropping atomics on them, and since the Empire theoretically wanted to use the planet for something else later, even *they* would not have been that crazy.

*Crazy* . . . thought Mheven, concerned, watching her mother make her way into the dim light of the main cavern, heading for the little makeshift workspace where Ddoya had his "office." Ddoya tr'Shelhnae was as much of a leader as their group had, the one to whom everyone brought their problems, the one to whom the once-a-tenday gathering turned for suggestions and direction. He had been a doctor once, and he was one of the original group of guerrillas who had convinced the population to use the strength that the Element Earth had given them as they descended into it and sheltered in it. Earth—the quietest Element and maybe the most taken for granted, but possibly the most powerful. He had more than a little of that Element in his own makeup, Mheven thought. He was a quiet man, slow, thoughtful, but eloquent; as with the ground when it quaked, when Ddoya spoke, you paid attention.

Her mother headed across that big space toward him, where a little light shone in his workspace. Elements only knew when the man slept; Mheven sometimes suspected him of having a clone or two stashed in one of the caves. Now she could just make him out, small, burly, and dark, sitting in his workspace, bent over something, as she hurried along in her mother's wake. Various other people were up and around, heading here and there in the cave, about their business. They watched Mheven heading after Rrolsh, and even in the dimness she caught some smiles from them. Living here was like living in the bosom of a large and un-avoidable family, or a small town. Everybody knew everything about everybody soon enough, and everybody knew that Rrolsh had something rare: the visionary gift, which sometimes made her a little strange.

Mheven blushed but kept on going after her mother and finally caught up with her at the "door" of the workspace, which was just another blanket, one of four thrown over a cubical pipe-metal framework. It was fastened up at the moment, and Ddoya looked up at the two of them from the round, silvery thing he was holding in his hand.

"This isn't your shift, as a rule," he said. "Is there some problem?"

Mheven blushed again.

"Ddoya," Rrolsh said, "I heard something. Something's going to happen."

"What?"

Rrolsh looked frustrated. "I don't know for certain," she said. "But it's imminent."

He raised his eyebrows. "I could wish," Ddoya said, "that our distant ancestors had left us some instructions about what to do with such talents as yours when they crop up, for I'm sure I don't know what questions to ask you to help you be more definite. Nonetheless, we'll go on alert, if you feel the need, Rrolsh. I haven't forgotten that last incident with the government courier."

Rrolsh sighed and shook her head, looking suddenly weary. "It's not that close," she said. "Or . . . it's not that serious. I can't tell which. I only caught a feeling, a word . . ."

"Well, let it rest for the moment," he said. He looked past her at Mheven. "Meanwhile," he said to her, "we have another attack group going out in a few days. We should send some of these with them for testing. But I'd like you and your people to double-check these first."

Mheven was one of the group's engineers. Once her forte had been medical machinery, which was how Ddoya had recruited her. Now she had acquired a rather more destructive specialty, and what he held intrigued her. She held out her hand, and Ddoya passed the object to her. It was a flattened ovoid of silvery metal, about the thickness of her hand.

"Implosion charge?" Mheven said, turning it over.

"Combined implosion-disruption," said Ddoya. "Remember the old dissolution fields that the warships used to use?"

"The ones that would unravel a metal's crystalline structure."

"That's right. An overlooked technology, but surprisingly suitable to

being packed down small, these days, with the new solid-phase circuitry. This one goes off in two stages. The dissolution field propagates
first, and then the imploder collapses the deranged matter. One of
these"—he took it back from her carefully—"will scoop out a spherical
section from a building, or a bridge, or a ship, something like twenty
*testai* in diameter." He smiled grimly.

"How many do we have?"

"Five so far."

"I want to go along," Mheven said.

"Check with Ussi," Ddoya said. "She's coordinating. Was there anything else?"

Mheven shook her head.

"No," her mother said. "Ddoya . . . thanks."

"Don't thank me. I know it's difficult for you, and you bear this burden, and work as hard as any of us, as well."

A few others, faces Mheven recognized but was too tired to greet,
were drifting over. Mheven sketched a wave at them, linked her arm
through her mother's, and started back toward their rest-cave.

"I embarrass you," said her mother.

"Not seriously."

"I wonder what it was like, in the old days," Rrolsh said, sounding
wistful. "When there were talents in the ships, and telepaths, people for
whom seeing more than one world, hearing more than spoken voices,
was normal."

"Maybe someday we'll find out again," Mheven said. Hope was
good. Any distraction, sometimes, was good for turning one's mind
from the idea that one might be living in a cave making bombs only
until something went wrong, everything was found out, and they were
all hunted down and killed. "Maybe someday the Empire will just give
up and—"

Her mother stopped and stood still. Mheven turned to her, and in
the dimness she could just see her lips move. Then Rrolsh let go of her
and turned back the way they had come. She went straight back to
Ddoya, who, with the two people to whom he was talking, looked up at
her, surprised.

"I heard it clearly this time," her mother said. "I heard it! Just a whisper in the darkness. It said *lleiset.*"

The others looked at each other, not knowing what to say.

*Freedom . . .*

Ddoya turned the new charge over and over in his hands, then looked up at her.

A soft *queep* from a small console on the floor beside his chair brought all their heads around. Eyes widened. Ddoya, in particular, looked at the thing as if he expected the little square console to stand up and bite him in the leg.

"Ddoya," said one of the fighters standing nearby, a man named Terph, "they can't be here yet. It's too soon."

"It could be a trick," said Lais, the other.

Silence, and then another *queep.*

The five of them looked at one another. No more sound was forthcoming, for the sound was the one realtime noise made by the narrow-bandwidth subspace transmitter-receiver until it was instructed to play. The receiver did not produce output in realtime. It took a coded digital squawk no longer than a millisecond, decompressed it, decoded it, and played it on command, recording and sending outgoing messages the same way. It was how their group kept in touch with the hundreds of others scattered through the caves, and they did not overuse it for fear of detection.

Ddoya got off his chair, knelt down beside the transmitter-receiver. He touched its controls in a coded sequence, and the transmitter's decode lights went on.

*"The ships are coming,"* whispered the voice from the narrow-bandwidth subspace transmitter. *"Repeat, the ships are coming. This is a multiple sighting, multiple confirmed. Relief will be with you within ten standard days. Events to follow will most likely cause the Fleet to withdraw. Prepare to emerge in force. More details are packed with this squirt. Unpacking now."*

Ddoya looked up at them his stolid face suddenly alight with excitement. For a few moments he was as speechless as the rest of them. "Well," he said finally. "We'd better get everyone together to discuss this in the morning. Meanwhile, let's get back to planning the next raid."

They smiled at one another, a little more fiercely than usual. Mheven looked over at her mother and smiled. "So you were right," she said. "We *are* going out. All of us. But meantime, let's get caught up on our sleep."

They walked off together. But this time, as they went, Mheven's heart was pounding. Enough of her people had died waiting for this day when it would start, when they would not be fighting alone. Enough of them had died trying to bring it about. She herself might yet die in these next few days. But all the same, she smiled. And as she and her mother slipped back into the darkness of their sleeping place, Mheven wasn't entirely sure she didn't hear the same whisper.

*Freedom . . .*

In the rec room that evening, Ael looked up out of the great windows at the stars pouring past and let out a small sad breath. The time when she might freely enjoy this spectacular view was swiftly coming to an end. *Soon enough,* she thought, *I will be staring into a tactical display again, concentrating on objects moving in space much more slowly, relatively speaking, than the stars. I should enjoy this while I can . . . as far as possible.*

She glanced around. All about her, various crewpeople sat and chatted, or gamed, as usual. Off in a small conversation pit nearby, Scotty and tr'Keirianh and K's't'lk were conversing with energy, occasionally waving hands or jointed glittering limbs in gestures strangely reminiscent of those which young Khiy and Mr. Sulu had been using the other day. Lieutenant Commander Uhura was leaning over the back of one of the settles that formed the back of the pit, asking K's't'lk something. The answer came back in a bright spill of music, but oddly, with no words that Ael could hear. Curious, Ael started strolling their way, and a discreet rumbling accompanied her, like a boulder trying to roll along without making too much of a racket.

Ael had to smile, though the smile was doubtless somewhat edged with irony for a perceptive viewer. "Mr. Naraht," Ael said, "this duty must be a trial for you. Doubtless there are many more interesting things for you to be doing."

"Not at all, Commander," the Horta said, shuffling his fringes about a little as he came up alongside her. "Everything here is interesting."

"Surely you are putting a brave face on it," Ael said.

"Madam," Naraht said, "if you've ever lived in the crust of a planet with nothing to do but eat rock, and nothing to do after that but listen to your ten thousand siblings eat rock, and then listen to them talking about *having* eaten rock—after a while, *anything* else is interesting." His translator module emitted that rough, gravelly sound that seemed to be laughter, and his fringe tendrils shivered. "And when you notice that weird creatures who *don't* eat rock, or even talk about it much, are wandering around the place, they and their affairs are likely to become, by comparison, very interesting indeed."

Ael raised her eyebrows at that. Amid some human and Rihannsu laughter, she saw Uhura straighten up and head off purposefully, as if in search of something. "Might you not be overstating the case, Lieutenant? Most of us think our ordinary home life is boring. And your people, Mr. Spock tells me, are a most intelligent and complex species."

"Far be it from me to argue with Mr. Spock," Naraht said. "My mother would come down on me like a ton of ore if she found out. But, Commander, intelligence doesn't necessarily imply culture."

Ael chuckled. As they came up to the conversation pit, Ael leaned against the back of one of the higher-backed semicircular settles on one side, glancing down with slight affection at tr'Keirianh. He was oblivious, concentrating on something Scotty was saying to K's't'lk. ". . . downright heretical, lass," Scotty said, "in the merely physical sense rather than the physics one."

K's't'lk sighed a long, jangling sigh, like a set of wind chimes out of sorts. "The distinction is strictly artificial," she said. "Or rather, it's a perception problem. The law of general relationships says—" She started singing again, a very bright precise sequence of notes. When she finished, after about ten seconds, tr'Keirianh, sitting with his head tilted slightly to one side, said, "I believe I nearly heard it that time. Perhaps the difficulty is with the way our people handle tonalities. But I am no musician. I never had any interest in music when I was younger, and nowadays I have little time, though I admit the inclination is forming—"

"For what, Giellun?" Ael said.

Her master engineer looked up at her with some amusement. "The

commander is teaching us the basic elements of Hamalki physics nota-
tion, *khre'Riov,*" he said. "Or trying to."

" 'Tis an exchange program, Commander," Scotty said. "She'll teach
us this, and we'll teach her poker."

"And Khiy and Aidoann and I will teach her *aithat,*" tr'Keirianh said.

Ael shook her head. "Elements send we all have time for all this," she
said, "but, Mr. Scott, of your courtesy, what in the worlds is 'poker'?
The translator suggests an iron stick. But I think I have found one of its
blind spots; I don't think you speak of such."

A slow grin began to spread over Mr. Scott's face. "Poker is a game,"
he said.

Giellun's expression became somewhat more wicked. "If I understand Mr. Scott's description correctly," he said, "it is, like *aithat,* a way
of equalizing the distribution of the crew's pay throughout the ship."

"Ah, me," Ael said. "Given our current circumstances, perhaps this
would be useful." Though she wondered, for *aithat,* a gambling game
based on the careful calculation of odds and the distribution of counters
and tiles of fixed value among the players, already served that purpose.
"But it is not a strategy game then, like your *schhess.*"

"Not in the same way—"

"Oh, I'm sorry, Commander, am I interrupting something?" Uhura
said from behind Ael.

Ael turned. "Not at all," she said, and then blinked in surprise, for
Uhura was carrying a *ryill,* a particularly handsome one, maybe a century or so old, to judge by the patina on the inlaid wood, and well-cared
for. "Air's name, where did you come by such a fine instrument?"

"The lute is Mr. Spock's," Uhura said. "He lends it to me occasionally. I was hurting my throat trying to match some of these higher notes
K's't'lk's been producing, and if I want to learn how to at least commu-
nicate date and time coordinates in Hamalki, I need to be able to produce the sounds some other way, for practice purposes anyway." She sat
down in the pit next to K's't'lk and began tuning the *ryill* for the octave
she wanted. "The physics I'm in no hurry about, but the syntax and
structure of the language shouldn't be too far beyond me. K's't'lk, would
you give me one more example of the one you did just before I left?"

K's't'lk emitted one short burst of sound, a chord, followed by a short phrase that seemed to be in a major key, about five seconds long. Uhura finished adjusting the *ryill*'s drone control and then mimicked the phrase. The tone of the *ryill* was excellent. Ael suspected that her estimate of its age was correct, for it was using the relatively old form of solid-state audio inlays, which gave a warmer, more intimate sound to the bass "stringing."

"Very close," K's't'lk said. "Einstein might not understand it, but I do. Add a note a fourth above the high note in the drone."

Uhura played the sequence again. "There you are," K's't'lk said.

Scotty was shaking his head. "Lass, if they'd put $E=mc^2$ to me that way when I was young," he said, "no telling where I'd be now."

"In a first chair at the Mars Philharmonic, possibly," K's't'lk said, and laughed. "Not that we couldn't still have used you in that capacity on Hamal. Sometimes I think Bach was one of us who took a very wrong turn and got born on Earth by accident . . ."

"Did I miss the folk singing?" said a voice from behind Ael. She smiled and turned to see the captain there.

"We are folk," tr'Keirianh said, "but the commander here has been doing most of the singing."

K's't'lk chortled again and then launched into a long syncopated phrase full of sudden leaps up and down a very oddly assembled chromatic scale. Ael glanced at tr'Keirianh, curious to see if he made anything of it; to her it sounded like someone dropping a box of broken glass. Uhura frowned and started repeating the phrase, more hesitantly than the last time. The captain raised his eyebrows. "Marsalis?"

"Hawking," K's't'lk said. "The equation for working out the rate of evaporation of black holes."

"I should know better than to ask," the captain said. "Commander, might I borrow you for a moment?"

She inclined her head to him, then raised a hand to tr'Keirianh and the others and stepped away. Behind her, K's't'lk was saying, "All right. Here's an easy one—"

"What was that?"

"The formula for Planck time."

"Can I have that again? I missed it . . ."

Ael walked back in the direction of the great windows with the captain. Mr. Naraht remained behind for the moment. Very quietly, the captain said, "I just wanted to let you know that I've had one more word with the commodore. Unfortunately, he's not willing to be swayed on this. Starfleet is very insistent that you be taken out of the area while negotiations are ongoing."

"Well, I suppose I can understand that," Ael said. "But of course it will not be *Enterprise* that accompanies us."

"No," Jim said, "of course not. *Ortisei* will go with you."

"Well," said Ael, "once again I show myself a prophetess, though in these circumstances it takes little accomplishment to manage it." She glanced up at the great windows again. "But I appreciate your effort on our behalf. We will, at least, be able to keep in touch in the usual fashion."

"I'm going to have to be careful about that," the captain said. "Communications to and from all our ships are likely to be carefully watched, I think, and clandestine messaging could be misunderstood."

Ael nodded.

"Either way, we'll see to it that very frequent reports of the meetings, and anything else germane, reach you every day. And one other thing. The Romulan group has now been met by the first two escort ships. We'll all be at the rendezvous point within five hours."

Ael nodded again. "I will remain here just a little while longer," she said, "and then head back to *Bloodwing*. There is still a great deal to make ready."

He nodded too, looking tired—more tired than she could remember seeing him since the two of them had been surrounded by the blood and phaser fire of Levaeri V. *He feels the weight of what is about to happen,* she thought, *and the fear, even as I do. I wish I could give him some assurance of how things will go, but that is not in my power. Any more than it is in his gift to give such assurances to me.*

"I have a ton of paperwork to deal with," the captain said, "and I've been getting behind. Bearing in mind what we're going to be going into, I'd better get it sorted out before things heat up." He looked up again, met her eyes. "Commander, should I not see you again before things start . . ."

She bowed to him, three breaths' worth, then straightened. "No long farewells as yet, Jim," she said, then had to smile. She had never quite got used to calling him that with a straight face.

The captain grinned at her, understanding. Then he departed, lifting a hand in casual salute to the commodore across the room. That man's eyes went from the captain to Ael, rested on her a moment, then turned away again to the windows and the view of the ships pacing *Enterprise* through the night. Ael looked at the commodore for a few seconds longer. He was a likable man, Ddan'ilof, but cautious, reserved, like one new to high command and still slightly nervous of its weight and pressures; also a man who, it was plain, did not trust her. Ael had caught one or two glimpses of him looking at her and the captain while they had been speaking, once or twice, earlier this evening—not being obvious about it, but watching them all the same, with a quiet, assessing look.

Her own crew had thrown her a few looks like that over the past couple of months. They hadn't voiced any suspicions, naturally, but the looks had been there. Even after everything *Bloodwing* had been through under her command, it still came hard for Rihannsu to trust aliens, and the closer they became, in some cases, the harder her crew seemed to find it to trust them. There was irony in it, for *Bloodwing* had suffered more from the treachery of other Rihannsu than from any alien. Command back on the Homeworlds, and various members of her own crew, had been blades enough in Ael's side, and in the sides of those aboard *Bloodwing* who had honored their oaths, held their *mnhei'sahe,* and served her until Levaeri V and past it, out into the darkness of uncertainty and homelessness. Now they were the crew of a ship without a fleet, and a commander without rank. *And yet they serve me,* she thought, *while wondering if they may still be further betrayed by their own.*

*While I wonder if I may be so betrayed as well . . .*

The heavy rumbling sound came up slowly behind her as Ael looked up at those big windows. The stars poured by, and far nearer than they, two of the three other starships presently accompanying *Enterprise* rode off her starboard, sleek and silent and dangerous-looking in the shifting starlight shimmering on their hulls. It was not as if *Enterprise* did not have the same general look, but to Ael, at least, she no longer *seemed* dangerous.

*And that perception,* she thought, *may eventually prove fallacious. Beware . . .*

The rumbling died back to a faint shuffle. From across the room there was another bright spill of notes, scaling quickly upward into a kind of melodious crash, followed by Uhura's and tr'Keirianh's and Mr. Scott's laughter. *Time to go,* Ael thought, *while I am still in good cheer.* She glanced down. "Mr. Naraht," she said, "perhaps you would be good enough to accompany me down to the transporter room."

"My pleasure, madam."

She had to chuckle, for he actually said *llhei,* bypassing the translator installed in his voder pack. "Very strange it is," she said as they left together and headed for the cargo lifts at the end of the corridor, "to find the seeming essence of Earth so mutable. Do you study languages, then, as well as sciences?"

"It's all part of biomaths, Commander," the lieutenant said. "Life needs language to understand itself, and the more language, the better. The translator is a tool, but sometimes it's more fun to get straight down into the matrix of thought and wallow—even if it does taste strange at first." There was a pause. "As for stone being so immutable, what about magma, then?" No question; the voice was smiling. "That's one of the few things I miss. It's been an age since I had a swim."

Ael stared at him as they went. "In *lava?*"

"We had a swimming hole," Naraht said. "When we were big enough, our mother took us. Oh, that first dive into the fire . . ." As they paused outside the lift, Naraht shivered all over, and Ael realized with astonishment that the gesture was one of sheer delight. "How scared we all were. And how silly we were to be scared. It stung a little, but it was worth it."

She got into the turbolift, and Mr. Naraht, with some difficulty, shuffled in behind her. The doors shut. "Deck nine," she said, and off it went, obedient. "Lieutenant," Ael said, "I ask you to forgive me if I transgress. But your people are a wonder to me—as if you were an aspect of my own folk's way of looking at the universe, of one of the Elements, indeed, suddenly come real. And it makes me wonder, how do *your* people see that universe? Not the physical parts of it, I mean. What lies beneath?"

He shuffled around a little, turning, almost as if to look at her. "It's odd you should phrase it that way," Naraht said. " 'Beneath.' We know well enough what's at the heart of our planet—of most planets. The pressure, the heat and density. But what if that were an idiom for something else? A heat that scorches but doesn't burn—the pressure so great it becomes total, the whole weight of being pressing down, with yourself at the center of it, accepting it, thereby defining it, creating it, eternal. The inexpressible richness, the transcendent temperature, down there in the deepest places beneath and within, the depth that never ends, increasing, crushing us into reality—" He paused, as if to recover himself. The diffidence Ael was used to hearing in his voice had been missing. "I'm still learning the language for this," Naraht said then. "I may be learning it for hundreds of years, while I talk to other people, learning what they think . . . so I can better find out what I think. It's frightening, a little, like that first jump into the lava. Afterwards you wonder why you waited so long, but it's still hard to go where your fears take you. Or where they would, if you let them." He paused. "Sometimes I think that's why I came here," Naraht said, more quietly. "I was afraid of the emptiness—first the air, and then the dark above it, the places where almost nothing was solid. But I said to myself, 'I'll jump anyway . . .'"

Ael nodded. "I see," she said. And after a moment she said, "I was half afraid to come here once, too. But I had no choice."

"Only half?" Naraht said.

Ael chuckled at that. "Earth you are indeed," she said, "and as such you see through stone readily enough with time. This noble ship—how I regretted, once, walking its corridors while being unable to bring it home to the Imperium in triumph as a prize of war."

"But that changed," Naraht said.

"It did," Ael said. Not even to him, personified Element or not, would she say just how. But what she now valued most about the *Enterprise*—most paradoxically, with an eye to the ship's many past encounters with

*Bloodwing*—was its sense of being a sort of haven of peace. Though of course there were parts of it she still found most uncomfortable to be in; sickbay, particularly, and—

Ael swallowed. "Stop," she said. The lift paused. "Destination?" it said.

"Madam?" Naraht said. "Is there a problem?"

Ael stood there, turning the idea over in her head for a moment. To her horror, she could find no good reason to reject it. "Mr. Naraht," she said, "perhaps we might make one stop before we leave."

"Certainly, Commander."

"Deck five," Ael said.

Off the lift went again, and presently its doors opened. Having had the idea, now Ael stood there frozen for several seconds. Embarrassment, though, finally moved her. She got out, Naraht rumbling along behind her, and stood in the corridor for a moment to get her bearings; it had been a different lift she had used the last time. Then she walked down the corridor, her heart pounding, to the door she remembered all too well.

Naraht did not comment, simply shuffled himself up against the wall to wait. Ael touched the signal beside the door.

"Come," said the voice from inside.

She went inside; the door closed behind her.

Spock looked at her in considerable surprise and got up from the seat behind his desk, where he had been sitting with fingers steepled, gazing at something on the desk viewer that Ael could not see. "Commander," he said.

"Mr. Spock," Ael said, "I have interrupted you at meditation, I see. Please forgive me." She turned to go.

"There is no need," Spock said. "The meditation was not formal. How may I assist you?"

Ael opened her mouth, but could find nothing to say.

If this astonished her, she could only wonder what Spock must think of it. He showed no sign of surprise, though, and merely pulled out a chair from the other side of the desk. "Please, Commander," he said, "sit down."

Ael sat in that chair, though it cost her some effort. She had sat in it once before, and the memory was still not scarred over sufficiently to touch without discomfort.

Her eyes slid up to the S'harien hanging on the wall, a curve of darkness all too like the one across the chair in her cabin, which she could feel looking at her, these days, more than ever. *There is your excuse,* her mind whispered to her. *Your last chance—*

"I have a problem, Mr. Spock," Ael said. "I have put off dealing with it for some time. It occurs to me that the most likely solution is unique, and that you possess it."

"A description of the problem would assist me," Spock said.

Ael swallowed again. "Starships," she said, "are not the only hardware my people have purchased from the Klingons of late."

"It would be only logical to assume as much," Spock said.

"Indeed. After Sunseed and the DNA acquisition project were stolen, there appeared a sudden enthusiasm for that piece of equipment known as the mind-sifter. It apparently has become very popular among the intelligence forces of the Two Worlds, for Rihannsu have no defense against it. And even though our own Fleet sees to it that those of us who command are given buried mental protections similar to your own command conditioning, even those would not suffice to protect us against the Klingon tool."

Spock nodded. "I believe your assessment is correct."

"One must plan for all eventualities," Ael said. "Worse may yet come to worst. Logic suggests that circumstance or accident might yet cause me to fall into their hands."

"I cannot deny that, Commander."

"Spock," Ael said, "I will be open with you. The stakes in this game have greatly increased since I first began to play. Where only my own life was involved, and those of *Bloodwing* who have sworn themselves to me with full knowledge of the continuing risk, I have been willing to depend on my own resources. But now many more people, well-intentioned but perhaps ill-informed of the dangers of aligning themselves with me, are becoming involved, and I must hold them in mind as well. I have no desire to betray those on the Hearthworlds and among the colonies whom I know are engaged in the struggle about to begin. Yet I may not be able to avoid doing so, if my enemies succeed in preventing me from ending my life before they do their will with me. Should this happen, those who would continue the fight after my death would have no chance to do so. My destruction would mean theirs as well, and that of their families and very likely even their acquaintances. Therefore . . ."

Spock waited.

"I would ask," Ael said, "whether there is among the mind disciplines one you might be able to teach me quickly, one that would allow me to make that end if other, more straightforward means are denied me. Or one that simply would make information I hold forever inaccessible to those who would use it against the ones who would continue the fight. I understand that this might be impossible . . ."

"Speed and the disciplines are usually incompatible, Commander," Spock said. "However . . ."

Now it was her turn to wait. She was afraid, but she would not allow fear to dictate her actions. Her need, or rather the need of those who looked to her to be protected from the Empire, was too great.

Spock was very still. At last he turned back to her. "Commander," he said, "it is possible that you might be taught. There is one condition in which speed does not obtain as an issue."

Ael swallowed. "Mind-meld," she said.

A silence fell again.

"I remember," Ael said, "the technique that you mentioned Captain Suvuk of *Intrepid* had used after being captured by the personnel at Levaeri V, to prevent my people extracting his command codes from him. *Kan-sorn.*"

"It could be taught," Spock said. "But there are other disciplines that might benefit you more, most specifically against interrogation. I have had some personal experience in this regard."

And then he was silent again.

"But there is a problem," said Ael.

"There are certain . . . ethical constraints," Spock said. "There are constraints against teaching the disciplines, any of them, to those who have not committed themselves to—"

"Surak's strictures for peace," Ael finished for him, softly, and smiled a rather ironic smile. "Always Surak comes between our peoples, at the end." She stood up, glancing once again at the S'harien that hung on the wall, and turned away. "Mr. Spock, I am sorry to have interrupted you to no purpose. Please excuse me."

She was moving toward the door when he put out a hand and touched her arm. The sudden unexpectedness of it shocked Ael to the core. She stood as still as if she had been struck so.

The hand that Spock had raised now fell. "It has occurred to me," Spock said, very low, "more than once, of late, that there may be more than one road to peace."

Ael looked up into that still, unrevealing face and thought she saw more revealed there than Spock intended. "If I err in my judgment," Spock said, "the price will be mine to pay, for a lifetime. Yet you too have paid a high price for your actions of late, yet have not regretted them."

"Imprecision, Mr. Spock," Ael said softly. "Bitterly indeed I have regretted my actions—some of them. Yet given the chance to repeat those actions, I would not do otherwise. Could not. *Mnhei'sahe* is its own reward—though sometimes that reward cuts deep. But what use is a sword that will not cut?"

It was Spock's turn now to glance up at the S'harien, then back at her. "I do not think I err," Spock said. "Commander, if you consent to this—"

She sat down again, trying to find calm. Spock slowly clasped his hands and stood still for a moment, the expression starting to go inturned; but his eyes were dark with concern, with final warning. "I must apologize to you in advance for any discomfort I cause you and for any lack of clarity in the transmission," he said. "I am not trained in the teaching of these techniques, though others have trained me in them. It is possible I will blunder."

"I have no concern in that regard," Ael said. Nonetheless, she was holding herself very still, determined not to tremble.

*It is absurd. We have done this before. There was no harm done.*

*And I trust him.*

He circled around behind the chair where she sat. This was the

worst part, and Ael fought for calm. Very precisely his fingers positioned themselves over her nerve junctions, then touched her face. Ael
took one long, shuddering breath and closed her eyes as, very slowly,
another view of the world began overlaying itself on her own.

*My mind to your mind. My thoughts . . . to your thoughts.*

It had seemed impossible before, terrible, like insanity encroach-
ing—another's voice in her own mind, another presence that spoke
with her own voice, somehow thinking thoughts that were not hers.
But they were slowly becoming hers. Slowly the sense of difference between herself and the other was dwindling. The back of her mind
shrieked in protest at the loss of difference, but Ael was in no mood for
it, and the terror receded.

*. . . easier this time . . .*

*Yes,* the answer came. *Our minds are drawing together.* She could feel the
congruencies establishing themselves, similarities interlocking, differences respected and incorporated into the nearly established wholeness.
*Closer still*—the whole compacting, slipping into phase—

*Our minds are one.* As if she needed telling now, with the flare of
union, the astonished fire of synapses momentarily blinding her, a storm
of thought and memory, the two streams of thought rushing together
like two rivers in spate, eddies whirling and pouring into one another, a
great rush of starfire and darkness, knowledge and uncertainty—

She saw now why her people had lost this art so long ago. Had the
people of the Crossing, so enamored of pride, individuality, difference,
their own chosen insularity from the rest of the species they left behind, come to reject this forced sharing-of-being as too high a price?
Too undermining to the cherished sense of lonely individuality? For
here, despite the vast gulf that separated her life from this other one,
her upbringing and tendencies and her whole cast of mind, what was
plain here was how alike, how very *alike* she and this other were, a great
wash of similarities and resonances had risen to drown the differences.
And the question arose before her: *Why in the Elements' names did we give
this up? Why did we walk away?*

*First see where you are. What must be done will become plain.*

She stood in a darkness that shivered around its edges with red fire, and occupying the heart of the darkness was her other self's mind as it might appear in its solitary state, a cool but frighteningly complex weave of intellection, logic, and peace all interleaved with and woven into an equally complex, barbed, interconnected tangle of emotion, passion, and old buried violence. The logic was not an overlay, but a network, a matrix in which the older, dangerous substrates were embedded, held and managed, broken up and made relatively safe— though preserved for when they might be needed. This dangerous landscape leveled itself out before her as she gazed, while the force that held it all inside, the mind and will that bound it all up, watched to see what she would do.

She stepped out into it, over it, knowing that in so doing she would lay herself progressively more bare. The raging heat and aridity at the heart of that other worldview smote her with every step, tyrannous, partly a longing recollection of Vulcan's terrible heat, partly a paradigm for revelation, disclosure, layers of meaning burning and peeling away, revealing what lay beneath.

She gasped, but nonetheless moved forward over that dark and savage landscape, gazing down into its fires, and not so much seeing what lay within, but being seen by the source of the fires looking up and out at her. It perceived the image of Rihannsu space wrapped around her like a cloak, a great sweep of thousands of cubic light-years held all in mind despite its size, for after many years' service she knew it intimately. All that immense darkness was strung through with the implication of forces moving, men and minds and ships, though the knowledge was fragmentary, and all that space seemed to burn now with the sense of frustration at what was missing, what needed yet to be known. More was coming—when would it come?—it was not enough.

*The anger will keep you from seeing clearly what must be done. You must let it go.*

She pushed herself through the stifling heat and the darkness, feeling the layers of her own anger and terror burning away. It came hard, but for her people, for her own people on *Bloodwing* and for the innocents on ch'Rihan and ch'Havran and the colony worlds, she must have this, would have this, no matter how she suffered.

As if from out of the fires beneath her the glimpse erupted into her consciousness: the furious faces, shouting into hers, and at the edges of her mind, something tearing, pressing in, ripping at her as if with hooks.

She staggered on, unable to believe the intensity of the pain. It came and went in great bouts and waves, every one leaving the mind tenderer than the one before, and with an awful feeling of being raped, intruded into, that most intimate and secret place torn at and gored, ultimate violation—

*Do not allow the circumstances to distract you. The mind-sifter is simply a mechanism that performs mind-meld without permission. It can be defeated in two ways. The first, by disengaging the pain, by denying it permission. The second requires a higher level of accomplishment. The first is accomplished by completely mastering the emotion: distaste, anger, but mostly fear.*

She shuddered all over. *There. You see how the fear of what the pain will do is as bad as the pain itself, if allowed to persist. But both can be mastered—*

—there again, the leering faces, roaring with amusement, the questions, like hot iron, like cruelly spiked and unbearably heavy weights, pressing in intolerably from every side. She cried out in anguish. It seemed worse to feel it through him, with the experience reflecting back and forth inside their joined mind, doubled, quadrupled, than it would have felt had it simply been happening to her. She fought back against what was happening, tried to hold the pain at a distance.

*You are reacting incorrectly.* His instructor, or him? There was no telling; that meld was this meld . . . *This is not about resistance. The pain is part of what is really happening. To deny the truth is illogical. To accept it is the beginning of mastery. The pain must be accepted, and mastered, second by second, each second anew.*

She struggled along through the ever-increasing burning, and suffered with him as he tried to achieve mastery in this most terrible situation, tried, failed. But tried again. And failed again, and tried again. And this time achieved it, finding his composure and adapting the techniques his instructor had shown him so long ago, not trying to stop the pain but accepting it wholly, including it, letting it pass through him, like a phaserblast through air; it vanishes, and the air closes around its path and is the air again, unbroken, untroubled. A flood of near disbelief, following the first second that the technique worked. But it *had* worked, though the next second the pain reasserted itself in all its fury. Again the air opens, includes it, lets it go by; and there is no pain. Again the pain; the air lets it pass; there is no pain . . .

*There is no pain.*

She fastened on that phrase, hope flaring in her, for now she felt his experience as he did, knew for sure that he had done it, had survived, and with his mind and his secrets intact. *But there is more to it than that,* the other self said. *The words do not describe what you are making happen, but what has* already *happened. Resistance is not how the pain is overcome. Resistance implies that there* exists *something else that must second by second be resisted. This phenomenology will defeat you, leaving you at the mercy of the pain. But to master the pain, it must be included, accepted. Then it vanishes, then there truly is no pain.*

*Understood.*

*Is it indeed? Let us see.*

*Sickbay—*

Her mind went up in a flare of anguish and fear. She would not look at that. *I have paid that price. I pay it again every day. I will not pay in that coinage now!*

*Then prevent this.*

The terrible pain came and tore at her part of the joined mind, efficiently, fiercely—though not mercilessly. It was not a machine, though it was acting like one, for her sake. And she knew, too, as she strove to deal with the pain, that whatever she might say, *he* was paying in such a coinage. To some extent, every mind-meld recalled every other. She heard echoes: *if only I could forget . . . to the death, or life for both of us! . . . cry for the children, weep for the murdered ones! . . .* and many another. And they were all cries of pain. *Ah, it is ill named mind-meld,* Ael thought in anguish. *Heart-meld would be closer.*

*The children.* That echo, wordless, seemed somehow more immediate than the others. There had been some resonance between the mother Horta and her children, even while they were still in the egg, that her other self had sensed without clearly understanding. Were Hortas at all telepathic? Possibly no more so than humans or Rihannsu, but suddenly Ael perceived the lake of lava burning against the darkness of the Horta homeworld's great depths, and saw the skin of cooling stone across the top of it hardening, going cold and dark, and then breaking and shattering with the flow of the lava beneath it, cracks widening, the liquid fire oozing up, cooling and darkening again. That was the path she had to traverse, the paradigm through which she had to move. The lava was the pain, which always would break through. But the pain itself could be subverted again and again, the energy diverted from it, so that it would go cold; and over that surface one could safely walk.

She swallowed, feeling the rising tide of agony. *Or instead, one might accept it wholly,* she thought. *How often have I pushed it aside, for the sake of duty . . . or fear?*

*No more.*

She walked out to where the lava crust broke, and the terrible scorching heat of it blasted up at her from the molten stone, blazing, so that her skin went tight with it and her eyes stung, watering terribly.

*No more . . .*

And she leaped.

*Sickbay.*

The rage, the pain, the agony, more intense than she had ever felt before, than she had ever *allowed* herself to feel before, now swallowed her whole in a blaze of white-hot fire that molded itself to her like a terrible new flesh, devouring the flesh beneath it. *My son . . .*

*Not my son! He could not have betrayed—*

*—weep for the children!—*

The lava finished burning her flesh away, charred her bones, eating inward . . .

*What did I do wrong? How has he done this to them, to me?!*

*—cry for the murdered ones!—*

*Dead at my hand. Not his own. Mine. I am responsible.*

*—eyes burning, skull alight, the brain flashing into final fire—*

*Oh my Element, would that I had died instead of him!*

There was nothing left of her. It was over.

*Sorrow . . . for the end of things.*

Finished . . .

. . . when she noticed that the pain was gone, and she was swimming in blazing light that blinded her, but hurt her not at all.

And then she was alone.

She blinked. Behind her, she heard someone move—*felt* him move, without having to look. It was Spock, coming around to face her, leaning against the desk.

"It is done," he said. He straightened, trying to look casual about it, but she knew perfectly well what effort the last few minutes had cost him. They had felt like years.

For her own part Ael wiped her face and sat still for several moments, trying to find her composure again. "You are a harsh teacher, Mr. Spock," Ael said.

He shook his head. "On the contrary, Commander. I merely showed you the path. You walked it . . . and further than the need of the moment required."

"I would not be sure of that," Ael said.

"I would."

She could find no answer. "The paradigm you chose was an unusual one," Spock said, "but since it was of your choosing, I believe it will serve you well. Recall it to yourself daily, by way of reinforcing it. Meanwhile, if circumstances allow, a second session within several days might be wise, in order to check that the routine has been correctly installed and implemented."

She was half tempted to laugh, hearing him speak as dryly of her mind as of a computer into which he had been loading new software. But the metaphor was probably apt. "As you say, that will be as circumstances permit. But for the moment . . ."

Ael got up slowly, a little stiff from sitting a long time tensed in that chair. She cast around in her mind to see how things felt. Her sense of herself was normal again, save for that thin persistent thread of connectedness between them, carrying at the moment no overheard content, no remotely sensed imagery—just the knowledge that it was *there*. Last time it had faded quickly; this time she was not quite sure how long it might remain.

Words to describe any of the many things she presently felt eluded her utterly. All Ael could do was bow to him and hold the bow—as she had for Jim, but for different reasons—three full breaths' worth. She might have held it longer, but she felt his fingers brush her arm, and she straightened.

He had neither moved nor reached out to her. As Ael looked up at him again, she caught an echo, so indistinct she thought she had not been meant to hear it, and very distant. *touching . . . never touched . . .* "Use it well, Commander," Spock said. "Or rather, so live and prosper that you need never use it at all."

Ael went out and found Mr. Naraht waiting for her. She smiled at him with more than the usual affection, though she did not tell him why. When the *Enterprise*'s transporter room glowed out of existence to be replaced by *Bloodwing*'s, suddenly the weariness hit her full force, and she stumbled down off the pads like one caught between dream and waking. The doors opened, and Aidoann was there. She opened her mouth to say something, but she checked herself and came forward hurriedly to take Ael by the arms and steady her. *"Khre'Riov,"* Aidoann said, and then more softly, "Ael, in Fire's name, what's come to you? You look like you've seen a ghost."

Ael shook her head and tried to laugh, but a weak, shaky laugh it was that came out. "So I have," she said. "I may yet see many more such, but they and I will hereafter learn to be more at peace with one another, perhaps." She straightened up, and this time her voice found something of the accustomed steadiness again. "However that may be, the living will be enough trouble for us in the next while, cousin—so let's go finish setting our ship in order. In just a few hours, the enemy will be at the gate . . ."

# Chapter Seven

RV Trianguli was an A3 giant, something of a loner as stars went. It had no planets—just an asteroid belt about 14 AU out—and its only other claim to fame was its classification as a star of the delta Scuti type, a variable with a difference. *Enterprise* came coasting in past its radiopause, the primary's actinic blue-white fire blazing with ever-increasing brilliance on her hull, and on those of *Sempach* and *Nimrod* to either side. The increase in the brilliance was not entirely because they were coming closer to it: as they approached, the star could be seen to be gently swelling. Somewhere out there, at a comfortable distance from the star, the Romulans were waiting with the other Federation starships, and Jim found himself hoping the sight of RV made them twitch. It certainly had that effect on *him*.

Jim was coming back up from engineering on the way to the bridge when he met Spock at the turbolift. "Anything from *Hemalat* or *Lake Champlain?*" he asked as they got into the lift.

"They are in position, and the Romulan vessels are all present and accounted for," Spock said. "Bridge. Apparently the initial meeting went without incident; translator upgrades were exchanged."

"Good. See to it that Uhura gets what she needs."

"Additionally," Spock said, "*Ortisei* and *Bloodwing* have left for the neighborhood of 38 Tri . . . though officially, of course, we do not know that is where they have gone."

Jim nodded. "Any new insights into your, ah, 'meeting' with her?"

Spock looked thoughtful. "Not as such. But regarding your interest in the ship movements and planetary mobilizations I perceived in her memory—there is no possibility of error as regards their genuineness, Captain."

"Unless she's being deluded about them too."

"I rate that probability as very low."

"How low? Zero?"

Spock gave Jim one of those "you know better than that" looks. "Sorry, Mr. Spock," Jim said, "but the stakes are a lot higher than usual this time out. I need to know how strong a hand I'm betting on."

"I would say the odds on the commander being correct in her particulars are significantly better than those for drawing to an inside straight," Spock said, "as I observed you doing at the open game in the recreation room nine days ago. With predictable results."

"Ouch," Jim said. There seemed no point in mentioning that it had seemed like a good idea at the time. "Noted and logged."

The lift doors opened. "Captain," Uhura said, "*Speedwell* has arrived. The 'neutral ground' vessel is coming in with her."

"Oh, the Lalairu ship," Jim said. The Romulans had been somewhat uneasy about meeting with the Federation delegation on a Starfleet vessel or Federation world, and—though he would not have said so out loud—Jim suspected the Federation complement had similar concerns about walking into a Romulan ship. Therefore both sides had agreed that the actual meetings would take place aboard a vessel of the Lalairu, an independent "family" of species who favored the traveling lifestyle—a species well known for not favoring any one large interstellar bloc over another, and for going their own way, neutral but most seriously armed, preferring to take care of themselves in the empty spaces rather than depend on the protection of federations or empires. The Lalairu had been willing to assist the two parties and had had a ship out this way. Jim was particularly fascinated by this aspect of the meetings; he had never seen a Lalairu ship, though like most other people he had heard about them.

Now *Enterprise* coasted in close to that brilliant sun, ten million miles out or so, and away past it again, as RV Trianguli continued to swell, like some huge creature taking in a breath, and taking it in, and taking it in . . . Jim looked at it on the bridge viewscreen with faint unease as he sat down. "That's not a star that could be successfully seeded, is it, Spock?"

Spock, standing behind the center seat for the moment, raised his eyebrows. "It would be a problematic endeavor, Captain," he said. "While it is in the 'possible' range as far as stellar class is concerned, the mere fact of its variability would complicate matters considerably. Add to the equation the nature of its variability—three different 'variation' cycles running at once, so that its luminosity increases and decreases by a full magnitude every thirty-three hours, by two-tenths of a magnitude every five hours, and by six-tenths of a magnitude every fourteen hours—" He shook his head. "This star's upper atmosphere is already unstable enough. I would be forced to conclude that anyone willing to tamper with it could be judged suicidal."

"We'll hope everybody else sees it your way, Mr. Spock," Jim said softly. "All the same . . ." He trailed off. There were plenty of other Starfleet vessels here, but he would be keeping an eye on that star regardless.

The star fell away behind them, and Mr. Sulu changed the view for one forward. Way out in the system one could barely make out a faint dusting of light, a long thin diffuse band stretched across the darkness: the star's asteroid belt, a densely populated region indeed to judge by the fact that it could be seen at all at this distance, with so little magnification. "Was that a planet once, do you think?"

"There has been no research done that I am aware of," Spock said, heading over to his scanner and bending to peer down into it, "but the conjecture would not be out of the bounds of possibility. Though it is rare for delta Scuti stars to produce planets at all. The question of greatest interest would be, if it *had* been a planet, what caused the fragmentation?" He worked with the scanner for a moment, then said, "Total mass of material in present orbit would suggest a planet originally about twice the size of Earth, or two-thirds that of Vulcan. Composition mostly the lighter elements. To judge by a sampling of the residue, the core was small and low in metals. More like Vulcan than Earth." Spock straightened up again, looking at the viewscreen, where that dust of light was beginning to resolve itself into a chain of faint, faint sparks. "Whatever happened to it would have been a major event. I would hope there might be time to investigate further."

Another gleam of light showed up off to one side of the forward view: the characteristically brief but splendid light trail of a starship dropping out of warp and "braking" hard, the superluminal particles she had carried with her inside her warp field now hitting the inflexible barrier of $c$ and destroying themselves in a brief and furious deceleration rainbow as the field collapsed. As she approached, Jim counted four nacelles—another *Constellation*-class ship. It was *Speedwell,* a shade late, as Danilov had predicted, but in good enough time.

"*Speedwell* is hailing us, Captain," Uhura said.

"Put them on."

The viewscreen shimmered into a view of the new arrival's bridge. In the center seat sat a handsome woman of medium height and build, with short, fluffy silver hair, a round, cheerful face, and the devil in her blue eyes. Jim stood up, as much out of respect as for the fact that the newcomer was a woman, and said, "Captain Helgasdottir."

"*Captain Kirk,*" Birga Helgasdottir said, inclining her head to him a little. *"A pleasure to meet you at last. Even if we do have to do it here at the back end of nowhere."*

"If nothing else," Jim said, "the background won't be boring."

*"No, I'd have to agree with you there. I look forward to having the leisure to get to know you better. Meanwhile, Captain, I have someone here who wanted to greet you before we met the rest of the group and got down to business."* She glanced to one side.

A big, burly man in the restrained silver-gray of the Federation's "commissioned" diplomatic corps stepped into view. Jim was surprised. "Ambassador Fox!" he said. "Don't tell me you're finally *finished* at Eminiar VII."

The man actually laughed, a sound Jim wouldn't have thought he had in him when they first met. Robert Fox looked much as he had when he had first become involved in the negotiations between Eminiar and Vendikar, though perhaps a little more silvery at the temples and a little wearier. As far as Jim knew, he had been stuck for at least the last few years in a bout of shuttlecraft diplomacy between the two worlds that had looked like it would become a permanent thing. *"Finished?"* he said. *"Captain, I'm pretty good at my job, but not that good. I've been training my replacement for a while now. Apparently the Federation thought this would be a good time to see if he's learned anything, and to send me off for a change of pace."*

"You'll get that," Jim said, "in spades. How are things going between Eminiar and Vendikar?"

*"Oh, they've got a ways to go yet before people from either side feel comfortable going for vacations on each other's planets,"* Fox said, sounding rueful. *"But it's no surprise. All those centuries of war have left them with a lot of pain. The hostilities proper may be over, but the hostility isn't. They have a lot to unlearn."*

"But they're on their way."

*"They are,"* Fox said. *"When they found out where I was going, though, they specifically asked me to greet you for them."*

Jim put his eyebrows up at that. "How would they have known *I'd* be here?"

Fox smiled slightly. *"Where the Romulans are involved,"* he said, *"I don't think anyone would expect this particular meeting to happen without you and* Enterprise *at least somewhere in the background—if not rather more centrally placed. Even though the news that's gotten out to the public services has been somewhat, shall we say, controlled, there's a lot of speculation out there at the moment. And some people are guessing right about what's happening."*

Jim nodded. "Well, Ambassador," he said, "I hope we have some time to sit down and talk between actual proceedings."

*"I suspect we will. Captain?"* Fox turned to Helgasdottir.

She turned her attention back to the viewscreen from the yeoman who had just presented her with a padd of orders to sign. *"Well, Captain, we'll see you in a few hours at the informal session. We need to clear in the vessel we've been escorting."*

"Certainly, Captain. Until later."

The screen flicked back to the view of the stars again, and the asteroid belt now even closer, as Sulu dumped *Enterprise*'s speed right down to impulse. *Speedwell* matched her, alongside, and Jim sat back down.

Spock came down to stand behind the center seat. "I must confess it is something of a surprise to see *Speedwell* here at all," he said. "Her late engagements at 302 Ceti and the Anduath uprising were a considerable distance away."

"You have a talent for understatement, Mr. Spock," Jim said. "But somehow it's not a surprise to me." *The eagles are gathering,* Jim thought. *Danilov and Helgasdottir here together, they could have had a war all by themselves. And probably would, if allowed.*

Jim looked at the screen, where the asteroids were now a chain of tiny stars. One of the documents Ael had left for him to look at had been a list of the major names likely to be appearing for the Romulans in the discussions about to start, and with few exceptions the only balance for which they seemed to have been chosen was one which weighed down hard on one side against the Federation in every way that mattered. Poor Fox was going to have his work cut out for him.

The bridge doors opened and McCoy came in, stepping down to stand off to one side of the center seat. "Is everybody here who's supposed to be here?" he said.

"So *Sempach* says, Doctor," Spock said, "though it will be a few seconds yet before we have visual without magnification." He stepped back to his scanner and looked down into it. "There are six Romulan vessels in system, IDs coming in now—" He broke off.

Jim turned around. "Something quite massive dropping out of warp," Spock said. "Very close."

The viewscreen blazed with rainbow light as a shining ovoid shape came plunging in along the vector *Speedwell* had used, bremsstrahlung fire sleeting and sheeting away from it, dying back to leave only the fierce sheen of RV's light on what was now revealed as a great, sleek, egg-shaped hull. Behind Jim, McCoy's hands tightened on the back of the center seat.

"What in Beelzebub's name is *that?*" McCoy said.

The huge thing decelerated hard and fast, and seemingly without effort, slipping up to ride behind and above *Speedwell* and matching her speed and *Enterprise*'s perfectly. It was like being paced by a small moon. "That," Jim said, "is the neutral vessel. The Lalairu ship."

It filled the entire viewscreen in aft view; a massive and perfectly symmetrical "egg" of plasteel, which reflected the glare of RV Tri in some places and let it through, somewhat diminished, in others. "Look at the size of that thing!" McCoy said in a hushed voice. "I bet it gets to be neutral anywhere it wants. How many crew are *in* there?"

"I don't know how many of them are crew as such," Uhura said, "but there are about nine thousand entities aboard, of all kinds of species. Then again the Lalairu aren't a single species, anyway, but a family . . . and by their standards, that's probably not so much a ship as a city. It IDs itself as *Mascrar*."

"I hope they do not expect us to take care of them if trouble breaks out," Chekov muttered.

"On the contrary, Mr. Chekov," Spock said, "the Lalairu are most likely more heavily armed than any of us, and 'if trouble breaks out' they will take whatever measures are necessary to see that it does not affect them."

*Mascrar* continued to follow behind them, demure but impossible to ignore, and the *Enterprise* slipped in closer to where the other ships were awaiting her. Well this side of the asteroid belt, there were *Lake Champlain* and *Hemalat* hanging in the darkness, with *Sempach* and *Nimrod* decelerating to take a stand with them. And there, at a little distance, were the Romulan ships.

Jim got up from the center seat again and folded his arms, looking at them. "One quarter impulse, Mr. Sulu," he said. "Bring us in to park with the others."

"Aye, sir."

"Is it just me," McCoy said from behind him, "or do those ships look bigger than the ones we've seen before?"

"Some of them," Jim said, "yes." It looked to Jim as if someone in the Romulan space services had decided it was time to update their "signature" design somewhat. In the newer ships—*replacements,* Jim thought rather unrepentantly, *for ones we blew up at Levaeri V*—someone had taken the original flattish bird-of-prey design and decided to go for curves instead of angles. The curves drooped downward, as did the bows of the ships, giving them a look that still made you think of some big predatory bird, but one with a more lowering, dangerous quality to it. Jim smiled a little grimly. Whoever had been at work on these ships knew one of the rules of starship design: if you were designing warships as such, you should try to make them look to your enemy like something he or she would prefer not to tangle with. Worse, for someone who knew the old bird-of-prey designs, these suggested that the designers were hinting at some kind of secret—one that was not going to be in *your* best interests. And these were not merely takeoffs on Klingon ship design, either; this particular look bore a different kind of threat.

"Interesting," Spock said. "This transitional design would seem to suggest that they too are experimenting with warp field augmentation . . ."

"Better than our newer ships, you think?" Jim said.

"It is difficult to tell at first glance," Spock said. "Certainly we are meant to think so." He was already stepping back to his scanner to get some readings. "But the hull design is suggestive . . . And here are the ship IDs for you, Captain. *Gorget* is that largest one, and its companion of the same class is *Thraiset*. The others are *Saheh'lill, Greave, Pillion,* and *Hheirant.*"

They were mostly new names to Jim. But a lot of the older Romulan ships with which he was familiar, ships with which he and *Enterprise* had skirmished in the past, were gone following the events of the last few months—the notable exception being *Bloodwing*.

Jim went back to the center seat and glanced at McCoy in passing. "Is this pre-meeting formal dress?" the doctor asked, rubbing his neck meditatively.

"Afraid so, Bones," Jim said as he sat down again. "It's the tight collars for both of us."

"As long as it's nothing tighter," Bones said, looking at the Romulan ships with slight unease. "Though last time we met, they were more likely to shoot me than hang me, as I remember."

"The Lalairu take their neutrality very seriously, Doctor," Jim said. "If the Romulans tried to kill you, they'd almost immediately have cause to be extremely sorry."

"Not half as sorry as *I* would be," McCoy muttered.

Uhura looked up at that. "The city manager of *Mascrar,* the Laihe as it calls itself, would like to meet briefly with the Federation negotiating team and the captains of the on-site ships about an hour before the first informal meeting with the Romulans, Captain. Just to restate the conditions under which the negotiations are taking place and to clear up any last-minute difficulties."

"That's fine, Uhura," said Jim. "Tell it we'll be there." He got up and headed for the lift. "I may as well go get changed."

The Lalairu vessel turned out to be as spectacular inside as outside. Because of all the species that made up the Lalairu extended family, their architecture was a farrago of the styles and mannerisms of many worlds, sometimes bizarrely blended, sometimes welded into a surprisingly effective unity, considering the unlikeness, or unlikeliness, of the component parts when taken separately. The city inside the egg-shaped structure was arranged around a core "spindle" that ran from one end to the other of the ovoid, and buildings—spires and domes and arches of every shape and kind—were arranged right around that cylinder, so that the huge airy inside of the egg looked as if someone had stuffed a bottle-brush into it. Everything glittered with light, not just from RV Trianguli but from the interior lights inside the outer shell that came on to maintain minimum light levels for the parts of the city that were rotating into darkness.

The building where the captains and the Federation team were meeting was at the far end of one spindle, near the top of a spire that jutted from the end of it. As they materialized inside it, McCoy was muttering, "Don't know how this thing stays where it *is,* Spock. You'd think it would have to be fastened somewhere."

"Doubtless it is secured, Doctor," Spock said, "but by inertial pressors and other such non-visible mechanisms. There are, after all, Hamalki among the Lalairu, not to mention Sulamids and members of other species that have great reputations as builders and engineers." Jim glanced around him at the space in which they now stood—a circular room about fifty meters in diameter, completely surrounded by floor-to-ceiling windows, and containing what seemed to be a small forest of trees reaching to within several meters of the ceiling, some twenty meters up. The ceiling proper glowed with warm, golden artificial light suggestive of a K- or G-type star. In the middle of the "forest" was a large, irregular circle of various kinds of comfortable seating, in muted colors. At the center of the circle stood the Laihe.

Jim made his way over to it with the other captains and their executive crew. The Laihe was a humanoid, though an unusual one—most likely a member of a species native to a low-gravity world, to judge by its extreme slenderness and its height, nearly three meters. Its skin was ebony black, its eyes and long shaggy mane of hair a gold that almost perfectly matched the color of the ceiling light, and it was clothed in a coverall of some material that managed to look more like topaz-colored glass than anything else, transparent in some places and translucent in others, but not the usual ones. As the Federation group approached, it bowed to them, a graceful, curving gesture that took its head right down to the ground and up again to look at them with those golden eyes.

"Gentlebeings, you are welcome to the city *Mascrar*," the Laihe said. "I am the city manager."

"May we ask how we should properly address you?" said Commodore Danilov.

"We give up personal names during our term of office. Laihe is the only name I have right now—besides the ones people call me in the course of business." The Laihe produced an expression which by hominid standards would pass for a smile, but was so edged with irony that Jim suspected that in emergencies it could be used to shave with. "In any case, I thank you for agreeing to meet with me before the main event begins. Will you all sit?"

Everyone sorted themselves out into the kind of seating that best fitted their physiology. "I just wanted to make sure that we had everyone's understanding of the physical arrangements for the discussions," the Laihe said, seating itself also. "For the time being we would ask your group of ships to stay on the opposite side of our city from the one where the Romulans are orbiting. There have occasionally been breakdowns in communication in such circumstances, and when discussions of such delicacy are in train, for the sake of our own reputation as facilitators, we prefer that the aggressor be easily determined from the start—by putting ourselves in the line of fire, and thereby ensuring we are best able to judge from which direction fire initially came." It smiled that barbed smile again. "Naturally we will respond robustly to any such occurrence. I mention it merely in passing, since you obviously would not be the cause of such a situation."

"Of course not," Commodore Danilov said. Jim had to smile slightly, for he had a strong feeling that the Laihe had used exactly the same wording with the Romulans. "And we appreciate your willingness to assist both sides in this matter."

"You are most welcome," the Laihe said. "The formal discussions are scheduled to begin ten standard hours from now, in another part of this building, which is our 'city hall.' Coordinates will be provided for you, and we will pass a broadcast of the proceedings to each ship for dissemination to involved personnel. If the various captains will coordinate with our communications center and sort out the details, I would take it very kindly. Meanwhile, is there anything with which the city can assist you? Do you have everything you need to carry out your business here?"

There were murmurs of thanks and polite refusal from most of the captains. Jim glanced around and said, "Laihe, I would appreciate an exchange of ship's libraries, if possible."

"My pleasure," the Laihe said. "There is no higher aspiration than the preservation and distribution of knowledge." It smiled again, a less barbed look this time. "But then I am a Telkandai, and I *would* say that. I will gladly coordinate with your science officer in this matter."

"Thank you, Laihe."

"Is there anything else, gentlemen and ladies? No?" The Laihe rose again. "Then let us repair to the informal meeting. Your opposite numbers will be arriving there now. The transporter pads are over this way."

It led them through several small spinneys of trees into a niche where a good-sized multiple transport pad was sited, and led the first group of Starfleet officers onto it. Jim hung back a little, letting them go with the Laihe, and as they shimmered away, Bones leaned a little closer to him and muttered, "Was that a *warning,* you think?"

"A tactful one, anyway," Jim said. His mind was on something he had been reading the night before, and the warning struck him as unusually apropos. "They're not a trigger-happy people, at any rate. I wouldn't be overly worried, Bones. They've never been involved in the beginning of a war."

"First time for everything," McCoy muttered as they stepped up onto the pads themselves.

The shimmer took them out of the "forest" room and into a place where the lighting was dimmer, more subtle. Jim stepped down off the pads . . . and took a long breath.

The word *room* would have been a poor description for where they were now. The place stood at the top of the spire—the very top. It was surrounded by inward-leaning walls of something transparent—clearsteel, glass, or plex—from the floor to the spearing ceiling. The view beyond was of the stars and nothing else. The outer walls of the city-ship at this end had, for the moment at least, lost their reflective quality, and the stars showed through clearly. They circled around the cynosure of the peak-spire as if around a polestar. No matter how angry or nervous any being had been on entering that room, it had to stop and gaze up, and if it had so much as a breath of wonder in it, it would stop and let that breath out, for the view was dazzling.

Jim let his own breath out, very impressed indeed. Then he looked across the huge room and saw the Romulans there, waiting.

They were gathered fairly close together, as if trying to present a united front. Some of them were glaring at the Federation people; others looked nonchalant. Some were sneaking repeat glances at that amazing view. They were all splendidly dressed, some in formal robes and cloaks along vaguely Vulcan lines, others in the dark uniforms of the Romulan armed forces or space forces—tunics and breeches or skirts or kilts of various lengths, usually topped with diagonal or vertical sashes of subtly glittering colors. Jim knew enough about Rihannsu uniform conventions after consulting with Ael to realize that some of the people here were very senior indeed, in either the military or civilian mode. They were apparently intent on not insulting anyone by sending negotiators of inadequate rank.

"Buffet tables over there look pretty good," McCoy said. "Do we have to wait for introductions or something?"

"I am sure the Laihe would have mentioned such a necessity," Spock said. "I would guess you may by all means feel free to go indulge your appetites."

Bones snorted. "Thanks a lot." He paused, then smiled slightly. "Think I'll mosey on over there and annoy a couple of people."

"Oh?" Jim said. "Doctor, don't get us off to a bad start here. Who did you have in mind?"

"See that tall lady in the dark robe with the green sash?" Jim nodded. The woman was easily one of the tallest members of the group of about twenty. She was striking, with high cheekbones and long, very dark red hair, and looked like a candidate for the recently vacated position of Wicked Witch of the West.

"The sash," McCoy said, "is for a blood feud presently ongoing. With *you,* Jim. That's the wife of *Battlequeen*'s late commander. A Praetor, and hence pretty much at the head of the line of people who wanted to see what color my liver was, a month or so ago. Hloal t'Illialhlae, her name is."

Jim nodded. He remembered her from McCoy's report, and now privately thought that he had not understated the woman's potential dangerousness. It was always unwise to assume too much about facial expressions across hominid species, but humans and Rihannsu were alike enough in some regards that Jim was pretty sure t'Illialhlae did not have his best interests, or *Enterprise*'s, at heart. "If she hands me a drink," he said softly, "I'll let you scan it first."

"I fear the Lalairu would not appreciate that, Captain," Spock said. "They have guaranteed our safety while we are under their roof."

"I'll grant you, it's some roof," McCoy said, glancing up. "But all the same, I won't let her serve the punch while *I'm* nearby. Speaking of which . . ."

He headed off across the room. Jim, for his own part, glanced around among the final group of Federation people arriving, and as Ambassador Fox headed past Jim toward the Romulan delegation, Jim suddenly caught sight in the ambassador's group of a face he had been expecting to see, though he hadn't been sure of exactly when. A small man with sandy hair and a wrinkled, genial face, wearing a beige and brown singlesuit that looked as if it had been applied to him with a shovel, and carrying the unmistakable telltale of a big book under one arm. The sharp eyes in that face caught Jim's and lit up.

"Sam!"

Samuel T. Cogley, Esquire, headed across the acreage of floor toward Jim, reached out, and shook him vigorously by the hand. "Been too damn long," he said. "Too long by half. Hello there, Mr. Spock! Nice to see you. How are you, Jim?"

"Concerned by the circumstances and the surroundings," Jim said as they walked off a little way, and he nodded for Spock to come with them, "but otherwise, fine. How've you been?"

"Oh, a little busy, working on this case," said Cogley. "After all, asylum law was hardly a specialty for me. But it's like anything else—you start getting interested, and then it's too late . . ."

Jim chuckled. When it had become obvious how things were going, he had strongly suggested to Ael that she was going to need some form of help on the Federation side that did not have phasers attached to it. "Certainly," she had said, "if you know someone who handles lost causes . . ." Jim had grinned and immediately sent off a message to the best handler of lost causes he knew.

Afterwards he'd gotten a sneaking feeling that Starfleet might have preferred some other defender at these proceedings, but there was nothing they could do about it when Sam Cogley volunteered his services. Merely knowing and having successfully defended James T. Kirk was not enough to disqualify a counselor who was known for many other successful if positively quirky defenses here and there in Federation space. In fact, there were certainly people in Fleet who would have taken Cogley's involvement as a sign that the best had been done—was being done—for Ael, and they were perfectly willing to let him go ahead, since the chances were better than even that the best might not be good enough.

"Have you had a chance to look over the preliminary paperwork?" Jim said.

Sam put his eyebrows up. "I've done better than that," he said. "I did opening submissions earlier today."

*"What?"*

Sam smiled slightly and steered Jim and Spock toward one of the great windows. "There's already been an initial session," Cogley said, very quietly. "It's usually the case in proceedings like this. The diplomats involved, the real ones or their representatives rather than the negotiators of title, try to get together and do a little sorting out before the official sessions start. Fox sent an assistant in early with instructions; the Romulans did the same. Establishing ground rules, feeling out the sentiments of the other party . . . the usual."

"Without telling *us?*" Jim muttered.

"It's how business gets done," Sam said.

Jim let out a long breath. "Well, we're just here as enforcement, really," he said. "I suppose it shouldn't surprise me that we hear about things a little late."

"That's true. But I'll keep you posted as best I can," Sam said. "Though we don't want to spend too much time together in public, so let's keep this brief. Anyway, things are already going moderately well. I was able to throw a few procedural *sabots* into the machinery earlier. Though apparently that suits Fox's intentions at the moment."

"Diplomacy," Spock said, "is after all the art of prolonging a conflict."

"Prolonging it at the jaw-flapping stage, instead of the photon torpedo and phaser stage," Sam said, "yes, indeed. If today's been anything to go by, we're doing well in that regard. We spent the better part of an hour just attempting to settle whether Commander-General t'Rllaillieu was extraditable."

Jim was slightly surprised. "I would have thought she was."

"Oh, that wouldn't be at all certain." Sam smiled with pure enjoyment. "See, the concept of extradition requires *ab initio* that the two jurisdictions agree in recognizing the action in question as a crime. Not the action as a *class,* mind you, the Federation side rejected that out of hand."

"You mean you rejected it and they jumped on the bandwagon."

"When the band's playing the right tune," Cogley said, "sometimes it's hard to resist. But the Federation's reaction to what happened at Levaeri V, when the Romulans started complaining to them about the de-

struction of their ships and their space station and its personnel, was
fairly straightforward. Their immediate counterquestion was: 'Well,
what were you doing with all that Vulcan brain tissue? Oh, and now that
we think of it, exactly what were you doing with the Starship *Intrepid?*'"
Sam grinned. "From the Starfleet point of view, there wasn't any crime
committed. *Enterprise* and *Inaieu* and the other ships went in to recover
our hijacked personnel and materials. Then the Romulans said, 'But this
woman has stolen one of our starships. We want it back.' 'Ah,' Starfleet
says, through Fox and his cronies, 'but she's applied for political asylum
here, stating that what she did was an act of resistance against a corrupt
government, and that she used no more than reasonable force to allow
her and her crew to escape. And naturally all her crew have filed for asylum as well, and are backing her up in their testimony.'"

Jim said nothing for the moment. The reality was a little more hazy,
for Ael had applied for nothing, as he understood it. Starfleet's agreement with her that she could take refuge in Federation space had been
an informal one. *They wanted to pump her for information about the Imperium,*
Jim thought, *and didn't find her terribly forthcoming at that point, so they never
went any further in formally confirming the privilege.* It was a matter that had
made Ael, as Jim understood it, somewhat uncomfortable—not that she
would ever reveal that discomfort to Starfleet. But now apparently
someone had produced documentation to suggest that a request for asylum had been formally made and accepted. Or else someone had implied that such documentation existed.

*Very, very interesting . . .*

"Look, Sam," Jim said, "stay in touch. We're not going anywhere,
and I'll really be wanting to hear your slant on this thing as it unfolds."

Sam nodded, glancing sideways to see Commodore Danilov rather
stiffly and quietly greeting Hloal t'Illialhlae, who herself seemed to be
concentrating on keeping her face an absolute mask as she spoke. She
might as well not have bothered; the way she was holding the rest of
her body suggested her loathing and fury all too clearly. "I can understand that," he said. "I'll do what I can for you, and for her. But one
thing, Jim. If there are going to be any sudden moves, let me know."

Jim nodded. "Do my best."

Sam took himself away toward Fox's group. Jim looked after him as he went, and said to Spock, "I didn't see what the book was."

Spock's expression was difficult to read. "It was *The Lives of the Martyrs.*"

Jim let out a breath. "Huh," he said. "Well, come on, Mr. Spock. Let's eat, drink, and be merry, for tomorrow—"

Spock favored him with a look suggesting that he found the quote profoundly inappropriate.

They headed for the buffet tables nonetheless. Jim was aware that it would probably be unwise for him to make a first move toward the Romulans. Like the other captains, he was aware that he was here on sufferance—for the rest of the negotiations he and the others would be aboard their ships, since their presence at the proceedings would certainly have been seen as potentially provocative by one side or the other. For the moment, Jim busied himself briefly with making a small tidy sandwich with some grilled and "pulled" stayf—heaven only knew where the Lalairu were getting stayf; for all Jim knew, they were cloning it themselves—and watching what McCoy would have referred to as "the group dynamic."

It was uncomfortable. At first the two groups did not have much to do with each other; each stayed mostly gathered to itself, looking at the others and making no overt move toward them. *Caution, or xenophobia, under the guise of nonintrusiveness,* Jim thought. *Or a desire to have a more structured environment in which to meet than this . . .* But the Lalairu were making no attempt whatever to bring the two sides together. Possibly they might have thought it a violation of their neutral role. Or perhaps they were simply wise enough to realize that sooner or later, curiosity would do for both sides what amity would have done in a less loaded situation.

Fox, for his own part, was talking to a small, slender man in Romulan ground-forces uniform whom Jim did not recognize. He committed the man's face to memory for the moment—dossiers with pictures and vids would doubtless be making the rounds shortly—and turned his attention elsewhere, to that tall, striking woman t'Illialhlae, again. It was truly astonishing how hostile she could look, how deadly. *If she bit me, I'd want shots right then,* he thought, trying to remember whether Ael had said anything about her. He couldn't remember offhand, but the thought of shots suddenly made him wonder what McCoy was up to. And come to think of it, where was Spock? He had drifted off while Jim was assembling his second sandwich.

Before he got started looking around, Jim moved over to one of the tables where drinks were laid out, picked up a decanter, and was pouring himself a small tot of Romulan ale when he felt a shadow fall over him. He looked up.

Blocking the starlight was one of the tallest Romulans he had ever seen, a big bear of a man in an older-style military uniform with a sort of floor-length dark green tabard over it. The man had short bristly hair and a craggy, fierce, broken-nosed face. He was looking at Jim with an expression that, while hostile, seemed to embody an amiable kind of hostility, like that of one who admired the handsome colors of a bug prior to stepping on it.

Jim straightened up and reacted to the look the only way he could, holding up the crystal decanter from which he had been pouring. "Ale, sir?"

Those dark, angry eyes widened a little, and then the man bowed to him a little and said, "I take that very kindly." He held out his glass.

"Say when."

The man looked at him oddly. "Why?"

"I'm sorry, sir. I mean, tell me how much of this you'd like."

The rough face split in a grin. "More than it would be wise for me to drink, at the moment. Half the glass, if you would."

Jim poured, privately considering that the day he drank that much of the blue stuff at one sitting would only be the day on which McCoy finally worked out the bugs in the removable-brain routine for humans. He briefly considered topping up his own glass and ditching it after he and this man parted company, then shrugged and put the decanter down.

Jim raised his glass. "Your health," he said.

The Romulan studied him. "That's something it surprises me that you would wish for."

"Common courtesy," Jim said, "would seem to suggest it. Other healths used by officers of previous services"—he smiled—"would seem to be inappropriate here."

"And what healths would those be?"

"Well, a typical one, in armed services where the officers did not usually advance much in position in peacetime, would be, 'To a sudden plague or a bloody war.'"

There was a pause, and then a great guffaw of laughter. It startled Jim, for he had never heard such a sound from a Romulan before. He had to laugh too, just at the sound of it; it was infectious.

"Maybe," the Romulan said, "maybe I see what the damned traitress sees in you."

"You have the advantage of me, sir," Jim said, borrowing Bones's phrase. "I don't know your name."

"Gurrhim tr'Siedhri, they call me."

*Aha,* Jim thought, for that was a name he had heard in passing from Ael. The dossier on him would make interesting rereading, later, in view of this meeting. He looked thoughtfully at the Praetor's uniform. "Space services, perhaps?"

"Only long ago," tr'Siedhri said, "when they were differently constituted than they are now." Was that a breath of anger behind the nostalgia? "Now I am just a farmer."

Jim had to grin at that. "With all due respect, sir, I don't think it was talk about farm subsidies that brought you here."

Tr'Siedhri's eyes widened, and he produced that roaring laugh again. Heads turned around the room, and astonished eyes were fixed on them from here and there. Jim, looking past tr'Siedhri for a second, caught a glance from the t'Illialhlae woman. For once she had forgotten to keep her face still. Her glance at tr'Siedhri's back suggested she would like to see some edged implement buried in it—deep. "Why, here's fine news," said tr'Siedhri, "that you know our local business, *my* local business, so well. The Praetorate must after all be as riddled with spies as they've been claiming. Indeed the odds are short that there's anyone here who's not a spy of some kind."

The phrase "guilty as charged," used as a joke, occurred to Jim, but he decided it would be unwise to use it at the moment. "There must be *someone* normal here," he said instead.

"*Au,* the odds are still short," said tr'Siedhri. "Has anyone here *not* in the military ever held an honest job? No, it's just me, I fear, and little what's-her-name there, the housekeeper-as-was: Arrhae i-Khellian as she is now."

"Meaning that she 'was' something else?"

"Perspicacious," Gurrhim said. "But we won't speak of it. No, she's noble now, that's all that counts. They can't take that from her, not even if they kill her. Once a Senator in ch'Rihan, always one—while you breathe, anyway."

"Breath," Spock said from behind the captain, "can be as precious a commodity for a Senator, then, as votes?"

The Praetor looked at Spock with another of those what-a-shiny-bug expressions. "Now here's a wonder," he said, "for who would have thought a Vulcan had any tittle of wit about him? But you too are slightly out of the ordinary as we reckon things. Votes, yes, Commander. The Senate depends on them. On our level of the House, we're Praetor-blood as soon as we're born. A sad state of affairs. No need or reason to prove oneself worthy of the position . . . just heredity on your side, and that as fickle and unpredictable an ally as it is for everyone else. Time passes, inbreeding sets in, the vigor of noble old houses runs out of their descendants like blood from a slit vein . . ." He shook his head. "Nothing is as it was when we were young."

It was a complaint Jim had heard often enough before, but rarely with such a clear sense that the person voicing it was grandstanding, and to some purpose. He wondered what the purpose might be, for this man, who as he understood it had a fearsome reputation as a warrior in the ground forces when he was young, and later made the difficult transition to the Fleet with distinction, reaching Ael's rank before being called to the Praetorate and resigning all but a reserve commission. "Time, then, for the Elements to move toward reunion?" he asked.

The look tr'Siedhri gave Jim was amusing. "Not just yet," he said. "A few things to do before then . . . about which we will no doubt be speaking shortly."

"Not 'we,' I think," Jim said. "I am far less senior than some of the people here, Praetor. One of our poets better described my present role, I fear: 'They also serve who only stand and wait.'"

A small smile, a subdued expression, was the response, and it looked odd on this man, who seemed constructed for the big gesture and the exercise of power on a large scale. "Somehow," Gurrhim tr'Siedhri said, "I do not think you will be kept waiting long."

He lifted his glass. "Live well," he said, and tossed the ale back in one gulp. Jim blinked.

The Praetor assumed a thoughtful expression. "Not a bad week, that," he said, and picked up the decanter. "May I top you up?"

Jim let him do it, aware of Spock's look resting on him and on the glass, and considered that prolonging this exchange would probably be worth the headache later. Anyway, McCoy could always slip him something to detoxify him a little; if anyone knew how to treat a Romulan ale overdose, considering recent history, it was McCoy.

"I should ask my friend to join me," Jim said, attempting to put off for a few seconds at least the prospect of doing to this glassful what tr'Siedhri had just done.

"Oh," tr'Siedhri said, "surely a Vulcan would not—"

"Surely," Spock said, "not."

"It was my other friend I was looking for," Jim said, turning away a little desperately. He was just going to have to drink the stuff down; there was no way out of it.

"Indeed?" tr'Siedhri said, looking past Jim.

Jim turned and saw McCoy. And someone else.

The doctor was not ten meters away, looking absently at the stars through the nearby wall. In front of him, making her way from one group of Romulans toward another, as calm and unconcerned as a cloud passing in front of the moon, a handsome, dark-haired Rihannsu woman passed him by in a drift of robes that shimmered like midnight silk. The long, dark, delicate scarf trailing sashwise over her shoulder and floating gently behind her now slipped lazily down her back and whispered to the shining white floor, pooling there as still as a shadow gone truant.

"Our other 'normal' one," tr'Siedhri said, too softly for anyone but Jim to hear.

McCoy heard the susurrus of the falling scarf, reacted with slight surprise, bent down, and picked it up. He strolled after her, and the sound of his footsteps brought her around.

"Sorry, ma'am," McCoy said, "you dropped this."

All this was happening, relatively speaking, away at the edge of things, but Jim, stealing a glance around the room, saw that some other eyes were now turned that way. One tall, thin woman by the door, in a long, relatively simple dark robe that would have passed for a very stylish evening dress in Earth society at the moment, was watching Senator i-Khellian very closely from behind a small knot of Rihannsu who were talking energetically about something else, oblivious to McCoy and the Senator.

McCoy slipped the delicate silk through his hands once and then presented it to the lady, as if it were more a weapon than an ornament of dress. The Senator looked quizzically from it to McCoy, and her expression took on an air of faint distaste as she looked him up and down. "It is not as if I don't have enough of them to be able to afford to lose one now and then," she said to him, very coolly, "and do not need to ask *you* to bring them back to me. Indeed, the last time we met you were more eager to throttle me than to be of any assistance. This is a pleasant change. May it be the herald of other unexpected civilities."

She reached out and took the scarf from him, draping it over one forearm and giving him a nod of dismissal. McCoy's bow was exactly that of a Southern gentleman being correctly polite to a lady who is being very correct with him. "At your service, ma'am," he said, and waited for her to turn away before doing so himself.

Off she went in her cloud of dark silk, and McCoy turned back toward the buffet table, seeing Jim and Spock there, and their sudden companion. He ambled over toward them, nodded to the Praetor, and picked up a glass. "Captain," he said, "Mr. Spock."

"And so this is the other criminal," said tr'Siedhri mildly. "Now my evening is complete, at least unless t'Rllaillieu should put in an appearance. Gentlemen, live well." He raised his glass and drained it again.

Jim did the same, only hoping that this time his eyes wouldn't water. As usual, the hope was in vain.

"Doctor?" said the Praetor, as McCoy filled his own glass.

"Here's mud in your eye, sir," McCoy said, and knocked his straight back without having to be coached. A moment later he took a long breath and said, "You people are masochists."

"*Au*, no. Sadism, more usually, is our people's vice," said the Praetor. "This is merely self-abuse. Gentlemen."

He gave the three of them just the slightest bow and went off toward the middle of the room, where various Rihannsu were talking quietly with Ambassador Fox. Jim glanced around and could see nothing of the tall woman who had been watching Senator i-Khellian; everyone else seemed to be looking everywhere else.

McCoy, meanwhile, was watching him with some slight concern. "You," he said, "are going to have a head on you the size of a Rigelian's in about an hour if you don't get back to the ship and have a dose of Old Doc McCoy's Famous Patent Nostrum for Overindulgence by the Diplomatically Minded."

"Believe me, Bones, it was on my mind," Jim said with feeling, for his eyeballs were starting to feel as if they were vibrating slightly in his head. "Let's go do it now."

"Not at all," McCoy said. "Rude to leave the party so soon. Give it half an hour or so, then you two go down to sickbay. I'll follow."

Spock put an eyebrow up. "The doctor is merely attempting to be left alone with the buffet. Or to run a covert physical on me a month early."

"You just keep believing that, Mr. Spock," McCoy said. "And as for the illicit pleasures of the table, which you are so far above, *I* saw what you were doing to that *plomeek* dip. Don't try to deny it."

They strolled off under the stars.

Half an hour later Jim and Spock were in sickbay, waiting impatiently. McCoy came in about ten minutes after they arrived, having stopped at his quarters to get rid of his dress uniform. "Damn thing's like being in traction," he said as he came through the doors. "Don't know why the

surgeon general's office hasn't challenged the dress uniform on human-
itarian grounds before now. Here."

He put out his hand to Spock, who held out a hand, slightly startled.
McCoy dropped two tiny data chips into it. "They were stuck to her
scarf, under the roll of the hemming. Almost missed them."

"Someone was watching her make the pass," Jim said. "Tall, dark-
haired woman, black robes."

"Green eyes? Kind of a high coloration for a Romulan?" McCoy
said. "Uh-oh. I think I may know that one. She must have been keeping away from me, or I would have spotted her for sure. She's intelligence, Jim."

"Wonderful," Jim said. "Spock?"

The Vulcan was looking closely at the chips. "It is one of the high-
density solid media," he said, "but not the newest. I will take them up
to the bridge and see what they contain."

"I think I have a good guess," Jim said.

"Tried them in the reader in my quarters," McCoy said. "Both of
them were gibberish."

"They will not be for long," Spock said. "Captain, if you will excuse
me . . ." He headed out.

"Bones," Jim said, trying not to sound too plaintive, "there's a little
man in my head rehearsing the percussion line for the 'Anvil Chorus.'
Could you please . . ."

"Yeah, me too, just keep your tunic on." McCoy sat down behind his
desk and began rummaging through it for a particular hypospray. He
glanced up. "Jim," he said, "I'm kind of worried about Terise. Her
cover was never meant to stand this kind of scrutiny."

"It withstood enough scrutiny to allow her to be elevated to the Senate, Bones . . ."

"In a hurried way," McCoy said, finding the hypo he wanted and
getting up, "and with a lot of emotional overreaction going on in the
upper levels of the government at that point, and the need to make a
hero out of somebody, yes. But now there's going to be time for more
detailed investigation. Both back on ch'Rihan and on the ship that
brought her here, which has to be crawling with intelligence operatives.

Every word she says is going to be scrutinized." He slid open one of his meds cabinets and started going through it. "And she's here in the first place, you can bet, because someone high up in the government has decided to use her to find out what someone else high up in the government is doing during these talks. No matter what she says or does, she's going to be in danger."

"She's a very intelligent young woman, if what you told us is true," Jim said. "We're going to have to assume that she's capable of taking care of herself."

"She's more than half Rihannsu, by choice," McCoy muttered as he came up with the vial he wanted. "I'm just hoping that's going to be enough. She's swimming with the sharks for real at the moment, and there's nothing we can do to help."

"Meanwhile," Jim said, "Spock'll see what he can make of what she gave you."

"Yeah, well, what surprises me is that there should be two of those things. One I can understand. The second one is—what? An afterthought? A revision?"

"We'll know pretty soon. *Ow!*"

"Sorry, I have to do this bolus. Timed release won't help with what you drank." McCoy reversed the hypo and gave himself a spray in the arm. "*Ow!* Lord, that smarts."

"Crybaby."

"Now sit down," McCoy said. "Even Spock isn't going to be able to decode those chips in five minutes." He went over to the food slot and had it produce a pitcher of cold water and a couple of glasses. "And then tell me what that Praetor said to you . . ."

# Chapter Eight

Eisn was just risen, and so was tr'Anierh when he heard the flitter landing outside his study and sighed. He was barely dressed and had only just had morning-draft, and here the man was already. "Who would be a Praetor of the Empire?" he muttered. "All my influence and I can't even keep one of my peers out of my house until I've broken fast . . ."

He heard the door open, and the poor opener's faint protest. Down the hall he could hear Urellh pounding his way, noisy as a herd of *hlai*. Then the study door flew open, and in Urellh came bustling, all good cheer, actually rubbing his hands together. *Why does he never storm into Arhm'n's house this way?* tr'Anierh thought wearily. *Or perhaps he does, and I am merely his second stop today. Oh, happy Arhm'n, to be rid of him already . . .*

"The earliest reports have come back," Urellh said. "Matters are going well."

Tr'Anierh sat down again behind the desk as he watched Urellh pace up and down the room. The man was unable to sit still when he was excited; it was astonishing that he had been able to keep people from knowing what he was thinking when he was still in the Senate. *Except that most of the Senators of his time were as dim as he,* tr'Anierh thought. "So what have you heard?"

"In the initial meeting they glossed over the attack at 15 Trianguli," Urellh said. "It was not without mention, of course, but they are so nervous as to the result of the negotiations that they have not put nearly as much weight on it as they might have. It goes very well indeed."

"Was the woman there?" said tr'Anierh, moving over to the bookshelves to start putting away the volumes he had been using the night before.

"No, she had been sent off somewhere out of the way," said Urellh, producing his first frown of the morning. "More's the pity. But she is not far, our people there think. They have begun remote sensor sweeps to locate her ship."

Tr'Anierh nodded. "I would not hope for too much success too quickly in that regard," he said, "but we will see what the scans reveal. They may become incautious of her while they try to prolong the talks to see what else they can discover about our situation."

"They will have just been given more to chew on than they will like," Urellh said, "and their minds should be more on others' troubles than on ours." He looked abnormally pleased.

That by itself bothered tr'Anierh, for he had recently come into rather more information than he wanted about some of Urellh's doings and had been puzzling over what to do with it. "Well," he said, "that is as well. We would not want them paying too much attention to our own preparations just now."

"They would be paying less attention still had those seven ships not been where they were not wanted," Urellh said. But he said it with much less venom than tr'Anierh would have expected. "However, it turns out that that ill-thought-out venture has perhaps done us a favor. There were folk aboard a few of those ships who might have done us a disservice had they returned." He was frowning now. "The less comfortable and aggressive some elements of the other power blocs in the Senate feel at the moment, the better I like it."

Tr'Anierh took a long breath. "I have been meaning to talk to you about this," tr'Anierh said, "and this is probably as good a time as any." He had been thinking of how to phrase this for some days; now he threw all those ideas away as useless temporizing. "As regards those disturbances on the outworlds . . ."

Urellh's frown got more threatening. "They are unimportant. A seasonal manifestation."

"I am not so sure of that," tr'Anierh said. "Urellh, I have seen clearly enough how intelligence has been trying to manage this business, and the tactic is not working. I was willing enough to give it a chance to produce a positive result, but it has not done so. We should not be hunting those people down. The more intelligence does so, the more foolish they look, especially when those they are hunting escape them and spread the word. And if our people in the outworlds are indeed growing dissatisfied with our rule, we should be working to find out why, and to put the problem right."

Urellh looked at him as if he had grown another head. "What should be done," he said, "is what *is* being done. They are being told what we require of them, and how to obey. If they do not obey, the results will be predictable. That predictability is what keeps them in order—"

"It is *not* keeping them in order," tr'Anierh said, turning on Urellh with a suddenness that actually made the man take a step backward. "I have other sources of news than those you see fit to allow around you, Urellh. A thousand dead on Jullheh three days ago in the rioting; the government buildings set alight on Saulnrih, and half the state's spacecraft there destroyed or stolen in a night. This is a new definition of *order!* The men and women in those seven ships had friends, and now they are stirring up others on their behalf."

Urellh glared at him. "That," he said, "is your problem to deal with, of your making, not mine. If I were of a suspicious turn of mind, I would think perhaps you sent those people into harm's way specifically to produce this result."

Tr'Anierh's face went hard as he took a couple of steps toward the other. "You would think hard before you made that claim as a certainty," he said softly, "for it would be the Park for you then, for certain. I am one of the Three, Urellh, whether you like the fact or not, whether you think the number too large or not. You had best study to resign yourself more completely to that fact." Urellh's face closed over as if he did not care, and he held his ground, but tr'Anierh was not fooled. "And as for your earlier accusations, I have only one thing to say. What about Eilhaunn, Urellh? How was it that the Klingons happened on *that* world at just such a time? Apparently knowing everything about where its defenses were—and what defenses it had?"

Urellh did not even have the grace to look embarrassed. "I know well enough that one of your creatures was responsible for that. Where does that leave you now with the Elements, after such behavior toward 'My people, whom I rule'?" There was no use trying to contain his scorn anymore. "Driven off as slaves now, sold to Klingon worlds, into lives of abuse and scorn, if lives they have at all! How have you protected *them?*"

"If it was not that world," said Urellh, "it would soon enough have been another. The Klingons were coming *anyway,* tr'Anierh! They would have struck deeper into our spaces, and found richer prey, richer worlds, ones more important to us, had the beasts not had a bone thrown them—something to satisfy their own command, something that would not affect our own security too deeply. Now they are stripping Eilhaunn, yes, but little enough they'll find for their pains. No industry to speak of, nothing of worth but slaves—and a long way to come for just those! *That* they will notice. They will think again before their next raid, for such poor payment. And they have shown their side of the board, in doing so. Now the Federation are looking their way, when once they had been concentrating wholly on us. That will cool their ale for them. No, we have lost a few lives, and gained many. And gained time, which is more precious than lives right now, for even though we seem to have acquired an early advantage in the talks, the game is still delicately balanced—"

Tr'Anierh looked at Urellh through his carefully suppressed distaste and anger and thought, *The package. Where is it now? More, who does know where it is?* It was something he dared not ask about directly. To show interest at all would be to show his own side of the board, and where his counters lay. "I am still not sure I care for the physical circumstances," he said. "The Lalairu cannot be trusted not to interfere, and the Federation has begun to move much more significant assets into that area, as we know. Those six ships all by themselves—"

"Are enough to keep the Federation and the Starfleet people busy for the moment," Urellh said lightly, having apparently regained his composure. "Too busy to see the seventh that passes, if all goes well. If it does . . . then all our problems will be over, quite soon."

Tr'Anierh nodded, trying to look casual about it, trying to look as if the momentary unease had blown past him now. "Well," he said, "then all the trouble and disruption will have been worth something after all. And once it finally happens, the outworlds will fall into line quickly enough. The traitress's allies will be either destroyed or powerless, and the Klingons will swiftly enough learn to lie quiet lest they receive such a package themselves."

"I thought you would see sense eventually," Urellh said. Tr'Anierh held his face still until Urellh turned, for even now the man had no sense of his own arrogance and how transparent it was. "We have an early session today . . ." He was already halfway to the door.

"I know. I will be there."

Urellh went out without closing the door, as usual. Softly tr'Anierh crossed to it, shut it, and began to walk slowly toward the windows again, looking out at the expanse of reinforced pavement, with flitters and small courier craft parked on it, that ran up against the distant wall.

*He is too intent on his own vision,* tr'Anierh thought, *to see or allow the validity of any other. I wish he were merely mad; he might be turned from this course if he were. But he is all too sane.*

*Now all that remains to be seen is whether I can make Arhm'n aware of the danger, and get him to turn my way rather than Urellh's.*

And there was the other image, the image of the destruction of whole worlds. That was on his mind more or less constantly now, coming between him and his sleep and making the light of Eisn and the very greenness of the sky look uncertain in his eyes. Tr'Anierh shivered. *Even the news of this thing,* tr'Anierh thought, *should be enough to strike fear into them. Knowing we have such a device, the Federation would not then dare move against us. We would have leisure enough to restore order in our own good time.*

*But one way or another . . . they must know about it.*

Tr'Anierh looked around the comfortable room, the shelves of books, almost properly organized now, the beautiful table with its delicate inlay over which he idly brushed his fingers. He thought of what lay outside that door, these windows—people and machines and wealth, the accessories of power, hard-earned over many years, all marshaled and ready to do his bidding. All he had to do to stay where he was, to keep what was his, was keep silent.

Let matters take their course. Do nothing. Nothing would happen to him. He was, after all, one of the Three.

*Yet . . .*

*Are there things worth giving up all this for?* There had seemed to be, when he was younger. Was that simply a stage that he had grown out of? He would have thought so. But now old doubts and fears that tr'Anierh had not felt for years were assailing him, and, having long ago given up the discipline of struggling with them every day, he was losing this struggle now.

The inlay in the table caught his eye again as his fingers brushed it, that one long stanza from "The Song of the Sun":

> I am They; I am the light of their shining:
> save by me, how shall you see and behold
> Them?
> How shall anything else be seen
> save by the light of Their burning?
> How shall the shapes of things be known
> except that Truth burning give light thereto:
> how shall reality be disclosed
> without Them burning Themselves away?
> Fused, the atom dies, yet by its dying we see,
> Day by day, as the light
> boils up from the depths of the starheart:
> if the Elements for your sake
> so burn themselves to nothing,
> how much more you for each other?
> How are you less than They?

He turned, looked out at the lawn. The sound of Urellh's departing flitter had almost faded to nothing against the normal morning city sounds. Things grew very quiet, very still, as tr'Anierh looked out into the burgeoning day, at Eisn's amber sunlight striking in sideways and casting long shadows from the trees that surrounded the compound. The shadows, to his dismay, looked more real than the light; the light looked temporary, endangered, ephemeral.

Tr'Anierh turned and headed quickly out of the room.

Aboard the *Enterprise,* Spock had returned to sickbay, not in a matter of minutes, but after nearly an hour. He dropped a small data solid on the desk. Jim picked it up and turned it over in his hands. "The cryptography," Spock said, "decoded correctly, but I wished to take some extra time to be sure of the encoded signatures associated with the material." He looked grave.

"And?" Jim said.

"They were both genuine. But the material is, to put it mildly, explosive. It comes in two different sets, as you will have gathered from the two chips. One set of data purports to be from another Federation operative on ch'Rihan, who I fear we may assume has come to what the doctor would doubtless describe as 'a bad end.'"

"And just how can we assume that?" McCoy asked.

"Because I have run a syntactic and stylistic analysis on that entire set of data, Doctor," Spock said. "Even within a single short letter or message, each unique writer has specific telltales, stylistic tendencies from sentence structure to punctuation, that can serve as a guide to the genuineness of the text as a whole. In this case, there are alterations to the operative's text, in a style that differs quantifiably, to no less than an eighty-four percent certainty, from its main body. The immediate suggestion, to my mind at least, is that the material was taken from this operative under, shall we say, less than optimum circumstances, and altered afterward so that we should accept it as genuine. Mostly the data has to do with troop and ship movements in the parts of Romulan space closest to the Neutral Zone, and if my conjectures as to the purposes of those who altered it are correct, we are meant to believe that the Rihannsu are not preparing for any major offensive, or rather not one against us, but for a 'police action' against rebellious elements within the Imperium."

"The intel people are going to want to make up their own minds about that," Jim said.

"Yes, Captain. But I would guess that their analysis will not be very different from mine." Spock folded his arms and leaned back. "The other set of data—" He looked at McCoy. "Doctor, I have read Lieutenant Commander Haleakala-LoBrutto's initial report on her stay on ch'Rihan, but you have had more recent contact with her. I would appreciate your input as to whether you note stylistic changes in the content. I do not, however."

"I'll look at it right away, Spock. But what's the story?"

"It is a remarkable one." Spock's expression, to Jim's eye at least, got much graver. "There would seem to be some truth in the first data set's report of rebellion among the Romulan Empire's worlds. There is indeed such rebellion. But it is far worse than we have expected. The commander has not overstated the case in the slightest; possibly she has understated it, and the first report may have acknowledged rebellion in the first place because it has become impracticable to continue disguising or suppressing the truth. Various of the outermost worlds, which normally have a somewhat less stringent level of government imposed on them by the Senate and Praetorate—for the good reason that it is logistically more difficult to exert such control over great distances—are beginning to move to assert what on Earth once would have been called UDI . . ."

"Unilateral declarations of independence," Jim said softly.

"Yes, Captain. The rebellious factions have correctly assessed the central government's position. It is now too busy handling internal problems closer to home, similar rebellions and disaffections, and most lately the matter of the commander and the lost Sword, to effectively crack down on the worlds farthest away. According to the news which Lieutenant Commander Haleakala-LoBrutto has been given to pass on to us, these more distant colony worlds have become themselves disaffected over recent years by the Rihannsu government's decision to withdraw its protection from them while continuing to demand ever higher taxes and conscription. And on some of the most distant worlds, where the families who settled were those of the engineers and pilots of the old-generation ships, the disaffection is strongest and is now erupting into the open. On those worlds, so the lieutenant commander says she has been told, the leaders of the movement—if that is the word for it, its organization being loose—have spent years amassing the capital, resources, and manpower to secretly begin building great ships again."

"Secretly?" Jim said. "That must take some doing, with their bureaucracy. But what kind of 'great ships'?"

McCoy was already shaking his head. "Knowing those people," he said, "knowing what I heard about the Ship-clans while I was there—they won't just be generation ships, this time. They'll be multipurpose . . ."

"Warships, then," Jim said.

Spock nodded. "The outworlds are now intent on their freedom. Their people would largely prefer to remain Rihannsu. But as such, they are also pragmatists, and they know the present government will not let them go without a fight. They are preparing to fight for their worlds' freedom, and if they cannot achieve this, they intend to lead their people out into the long night again, and never return."

Jim swallowed. It was nothing less than the beginning of the disintegration of an empire that Spock was discussing so calmly, but Jim knew all too well from history that where one empire fell, another would rush in to fill the vacuum unless something happened to stop the process.

"Several of the great ships are complete already, apparently," Spock said. "They have been built in orbit and concealed in the asteroid belts of several of the colony worlds where the Rihannsu government's surveillance is poorest. Several more will be ready soon. And meanwhile, as a result of this—for the leading minds in the movement have seen to it that the news has seeped out—thousands of Rihannsu have begun demonstrating in the cities of the outworlds. And there has been considerable civil disorder associated with the demonstrations, along with destruction or theft of government property. This is information which has apparently been suppressed by the authorities on ch'Rihan until now. Lieutenant Commander Haleakala-LoBrutto says that they have had less success suppressing the larger-scale demonstrations on ch'Havran, but the government continues to attempt to deny what is going on, or to pretend that it is unimportant. Some of the Praetorate know the truth, and have spoken it, but they are not popular."

Jim thought of the great bear of a man who had towered over him, looking at him so curiously, so speculatively. He wondered if he now understood something of the reason why. "Spock," he said, "doesn't Gurrhim tr'Siedhri have Ship-clan connections?"

"Indeed he does, Captain. Normally someone with such close ties would not survive long in the Praetorate, but his hereditary rights to the title cannot be denied, and he wields considerable power because of extensive land holdings on both ch'Rihan and ch'Havran, but more so on the latter world, which also has Ship-clan ties of its own which ch'Rihan does not. He would be seen by the other Praetors, particularly by the 'ruling' three, as at least potentially subversive, and a danger to them, but so far they have not found a way to reduce his 'dangerousness.' "

"Short of killing him," McCoy said, "which is something that does happen to you sometimes in Rihannsu politics." He folded his arms, leaned back. "I'd watch how I drank, if I were him, and who poured it out of what bottle."

"And Ael . . ." Jim said.

"Ael," Spock said. "There are apparently many among the Ship-clans who see her as someone they can use as a banner, a rallying point."

"Knowing the commander," McCoy said, "I'm not sure who would be using whom, exactly."

"She would certainly be willing to use this kind of force if it was offered to her in alliance," Jim said. "But is it really enough, do they really have the resources, to unseat an empire? Spock?"

"The lieutenant commander's data has numerous lacunae," Spock said. "The data apparently came to her in some haste, and she passed it on the same way to her superiors in Starfleet Intelligence—whom it will only now be reaching. But the kind of uprising presently taking place is unprecedented in the history of the Imperium. Whatever the final outcome, the Romulan Star Empire as we have known it is about to change forever."

"This is news we've got to get to Ambassador Fox," Jim said, getting up. "He would get it from intel himself, anyway, but not as quickly. Talk about timely . . ."

"It is," McCoy said. "In the case of the first set of information, of course, the timeliness is obviously planned."

"Yes. Now we've got to figure out which way they think we're going to jump as a result of it." He headed out. "Spock? Let's go see if the ambassador's available."

He wasn't, but this hardly came as a surprise to Jim, considering what the events of the next day were going to entail. All they could do was leave a copy of the information and a précis with Fox's assistant at his office aboard *Speedwell,* and head back to *Enterprise* to wait for the proceedings to commence. Jim went to bed and dreamed uneasily of things exploding in the darkness, and of the light of the nearby star suddenly beginning to balloon out at him in the unnerving way it had at 15 Tri.

He was up earlier than necessary and found Spock already on the bridge. "Did you sleep at all last night?" Jim said.

"No more than need required," Spock said, rather absently, as he was looking down his scanner at the moment. "There have been other matters in need of my attention."

Jim sat down at the helm and rubbed his face. "Anything interesting?"

Spock straightened up and stepped down toward the center seat, where he stood looking at the viewscreen. It was showing *Mascrar* and not much else, which was no particular surprise, considering the thing's size. "The Romulan vessels," he said, "have been evincing a considerable amount of scan activity since they arrived."

Jim made a face. "Looking for Ael, I bet."

"It would seem a logical conclusion," Spock said. "Though one might reasonably expect them to be more circumspect about it."

Sulu looked over his shoulder. "Maybe they think there's no point in trying to hide it at all," he said, "since the level of surveillance around them is going to be so high anyway, and also it's what everyone would *expect* them to be doing."

Spock let out what would have sounded like a sigh of mild frustration in a human. "It can often be difficult to tell what a Romulan is thinking," he said, "even in mind-meld. Or rather, what he means by what he is thinking." He kept gazing at *Mascrar* as if attempting to see through it into the Romulan ships and possibly into their crews' brains.

"Well, keep an eye on them," Jim said and stretched. Behind him the turbolift doors opened, and Uhura came in. "You're on shift early, Commander."

She gave him a smile that suggested she knew his reason for having jumped his own on-shift time by an hour or so. "If I've got to be on tenterhooks about what's going on over there, sir," Uhura said, "I may as well be that way up here as at breakfast. And up here I won't drink so much coffee."

Jim gave her an ironic look as Spock went back up to his station. "Well, let me give you something to do besides contemplate your blood caffeine level, then. Spock, those new comm ciphers are in place, aren't they?"

"The ones for use at the present time," Spock said, "yes, Captain."

"Good. Uhura, are you certain that they're properly implemented?"

"I ran them through a full test cycle last night," Uhura said. "Everything seemed fine."

"Good. Then hail *Ortisei* for me, would you? I wouldn't mind a word with Captain Gutierrez."

"Yes, Captain."

Jim sat and watched *Mascrar* rotating gently for a few moments. *It's not like we wouldn't have suspected they'd be looking for her,* he thought. *They obviously want advance notice of her coming into range. The only question is, What use of that information are they preparing to make? They wouldn't dare try to attack her under all our noses. They're seriously outgunned . . .*

*. . . aren't they?*

"*Ortisei* is answering, Captain," said Uhura.

"On screen," Jim said.

*Mascrar* disappeared, to be replaced by the bridge of another starship of *Enterprise*'s class. In its center seat sat a big, broad-shouldered man with broad, open features and very cool eyes; longish auburn hair was neatly bound back while he was in uniform. "Afterburner," Jim said, "how are things?"

Captain Harold Gutierrez sat back in the center seat, stretched his arms out in front of him with the fingers interlaced, and cracked his knuckles. *"Dead quiet at the moment,"* he said, *"but in this neighborhood you'd expect that. How're things closer in to the primary?"*

"Heating up," Jim said. "I won't spoil any surprises for you, but you should expect a package from Fox and the team this morning. Some interesting reading in there."

*"I just bet."* Gutierrez made a slightly sour face, and Jim controlled the urge to smile. This was another of the commanders in Starfleet who had acquired something of a reputation for quick action in a crisis, and a gift for finding a crisis to exploit, so much so that Jim could en-

tirely understand why Fleet hadn't wanted him here on site with both Helgasdottir and Danilov: fighting would have broken out spontaneously, as unavoidable as the results when you mix nitric acid and glycerin. *"So when do the fireworks start?"*

"They've already started, I'm told. Major formal 'representations' will be made shortly, but both sides already know what these are, apparently. What we're going to be expecting is reactions to the representations. Which is why I thought I'd call."

*"So I suspected. No, everything's fine here, Jim,"* Gutierrez said. *"All's quiet on Bloodwing. I spoke to Commander t'Rllaillieu about half an hour ago, in fact."*

"And?"

*"No problems,"* Gutierrez said, *"except that I think she'd dearly love to present herself right in front of her people's noses to see how far out of joint they get."*

"I can imagine. Well, don't let it happen without Danilov saying the word," Jim said, "or we're all going to be in the soup together. Meanwhile, how's the new baby?" *Ortisei* was Harry's second command; *Raksha* had been decommissioned out from under him because of advancing age and a warp engine that kept malfunctioning when no one could figure out why.

*"She's a honey,"* Harry said. *"The rough edges are pretty much sanded off now. My chief engineer thinks we can start doing some customizing now."*

"Uh-oh," Jim said. "Keep a close eye on her. You never know what they're going to install down there when you're not looking."

Harry snorted. *"As if I get a say. But she and the commander were swapping busted-engine stories, and—"*

Jim shook his head, smiling. "Trouble already. Well, look, Harry, while you're keeping an eye on the two of them, don't neglect your sensors to the outward. My science officer tells me that certain ships not a million kilometers from here are doing a lot of scanning."

*"Theoretically we should be well out of range,"* Harry said, *"but I'll have Mr. Mitchelson peel a few extra of his eyes and see if he notices anything unusual. It's not like there haven't been occasional breakthroughs in scanning technology in the last five or ten years."*

"Good. Call and let us know if you find anything of interest. And give my best to the commander when you speak."

*"Will do, Jim.* Ortisei *out."*

The screen flickered, then went back to its view of *Mascrar.*

Uhura had one hand to the transdator in her ear. She turned toward Jim and said, "Captain, the formal opening proceedings are about to start. Mr. Freeman has rigged the big holo display down in rec for viewing, but I imagine there'll be a lot of off-duty people watching down there, and it might get crowded. Shall I put it up on the screen for you here?"

"Nothing else to watch but the scenery," Jim said. "Please do."

The room to which the viewscreen cut was another of those with floor-to-ceiling windows, all looking out into space—another room in the "city hall" spire of *Mascrar*—but this one contained nothing else but the biggest circular table Jim had ever seen, easily thirty meters across. More properly, it was not a circle, but a ring, empty in the center so that assistants could come and go with padds and paperwork and so forth. On one side of it were the Rihannsu, nearly fifty of them all told, the last of them seating themselves now. Opposite them the Federation delegation sat, nearly as many—if not exactly as many, Jim thought. He let his eyes slide around to the background of the view that the Lalairu camera was giving them and caught a glimpse of Sam Cogley back there, and not too far from him, though well separated from him by an empty "neutral" space, a slender, handsome woman now dressed in dark clothes much less formal than the ones she had been wearing the previous evening. Arrhae i-Khellian. He was very glad to see her there, looking untroubled—though, heaven knew, appearances could be deceiving. At least she seemed to be in no immediate trouble with the dark-featured intelligence operative whom McCoy had reported was watching her. *Let's hope it stays that way.*

The opening comments from both sides went on for half an hour or so, from Ambassador Fox on the Federation side and Gurrhim tr'Siedhri on the other, before things started to heat up, and Jim watched it all, becoming increasingly concerned. The atmosphere in the room looked leisurely enough as the two elder statesmen went on in turn about mutual respect and past misunderstandings. But Jim could feel the tension as plainly as if he were sitting there in the middle of those people, all so busy looking statesmanlike, when Hloal t'Illialhlae stood up to read the official Rihannsu position paper. *They already know they're going to get an answer they won't like,* Jim thought, *and they're beginning to consider just what they're going to do about it.*

Hloal t'Illialhlae was reading the position paper from a padd on the table in front of her. Why she was reading it standing wasn't entirely clear to Jim. *Just that the gesture itself is threatening? Or because she looks more impressive that way? Or is there some other cultural thing?* But she was wearing just a shade of a smile, and the look of it troubled Jim obscurely. *"We desire, as you do,"* she was saying now, *"to bring an end to the unfortunate conflicts between our peoples which have troubled the tranquillity of our spaces and yours for a number of years, distracting all our attention from matters of more importance. The final resolution of these conflicts may most swiftly be brought about by the acknowledgment and implementation of the following four points. First: the abolition of the so-called Neutral Zone and the declaration by the Federation of what is true and known to be true, that these spaces have been, are, and will remain in perpetuity the territory of the Rihannsu Star Empire, and the surrender to our authority of all the surveillance facilities, known as monitoring outposts, in that zone of space. Second: the public acknowledgment by the Federation of previous thefts of vital technology and intellectual property from our territory, vessels, and citizens, including the cloaking device stolen from the vessel ChR 1675 Memenda, and certain research materials formerly located at Levaeri V before the unprovoked attack on and looting of that facility, and a public apology for those thefts, accompanied by an undertaking never to use or develop the technologies or materials acquired in those thefts. Third: the immediate return for trial of the woman Ael i-Mhiessan t'Rllaillieu, formerly a commander-general in the Space Forces of the Rihannsu Star Empire, and self-acknowledged traitor to the Empire, though our government has chosen to relinquish any claim on the antiquated vessel that she stole, and has graciously chosen to commute to perpetual banishment the sentence of death passed on her crew, personages who have proved themselves unfit for further service in our military services by reason of allowing themselves to be duped by the aforesaid t'Rllaillieu and made accomplices in her crimes against the Empire. And fourth: the immediate return of the cultural artifact which the aforesaid t'Rllaillieu stole, variously known as the Fifth Sword of S'harien, the Sword of S'task, or the Sword in the Empty Chair."*

She sat down again, looking most poisonously demure. Jim sat there listening to the little rustle of reaction going through the room, and for his own part was amazed by the tone of calm threat and absolute insolence. *You'd think they already had a big force sitting on the moon, dictating terms, while they got ready to drop something large and nasty on the Earth.* "Huh," said McCoy's voice, ironic, from behind the center seat.

Jim glanced over his shoulder. "Didn't hear you come in."

"Nope. I see, though," Bones said, "that a couple of the pawns have been knocked off the board already."

Jim nodded. There had been no mention of the return of *Bloodwing* or her crew. "Somehow, though," Jim said, "I don't think Starfleet is going to agree to hand the Neutral Zone over to them."

McCoy shook his head. "No, or the Sunseed routines, either."

Jim nodded again. Fox was standing up to speak, now, and not bothering with a padd. *"I thank the noble Praetor for her clarification of the Imperium's intentions,"* he said, *"and intend to respond in kind. Certainly much time and energy has been spent pursuing courses of action which have caused difficulty to both the Star Empire and the Federation, and any reasonable being would consider it prudent to seek to resolve these outstanding issues between us and move on into positions of greater interstellar security, always remembering that we are not the only two major powers to be reckoned with in the present scheme of things."*

Did Gurrhim and a few of the other Romulans blink at that bit of frankness? Jim looked closely at them and couldn't be sure. *"As regards the Star Empire's four points,"* Fox said, *"first: any change in the status of the Neutral Zone would have to be taken after a period of extensive consultation with the various inhabited planets in the area and a thorough investigation into the various consequences of such a change in the status of the area. Needless to say, so major a change would require some while to implement properly, with an eye to guaranteeing the continued peace and security of the star systems in this area, and the logistics of the change would need careful coordination among the interested parties. Regardless, the Federation will give this proposal careful consideration and will reply in more detail in due course."*

McCoy snorted softly. *"As regards the second point,"* Fox went on, *"the Federation fully understands the concern that unauthorized intrusions into Rihannsu space cause the Star Empire. The Federation has suffered various similar intrusions into its own space of late, and is well acquainted with the annoyance secondary to the loss of valuable equipment and personnel, as well as the loss of face which is invariably associated with such tragedies."* That had an effect: Hloal t'Illialhlae turned a most astonishing jade color and stirred in her chair as if about to leap out of it. *"However, the Federation has no desire to reopen old wounds at this time, or, for that matter, to inflame new ones, and is minded to let bygones be bygones in this regard. I am, however, empowered to say that the Federation will consider such gestures toward truth and reconciliation in tandem with the Rihannsu Star Empire's own consideration of such gestures, and stands ready to make a simultaneous public announcement at such a time as the Empire is prepared to do so in regards to its own previous incursions. Third—"*

The hellish image of the chromosphere of 15 Trianguli rose up in front of Jim, and the memory of seven ships chasing *Enterprise* and *Bloodwing* around it and out into the cold again. His back itched as if the sweat were running down it all over again as they ran for their lives. "That's *it?*" Jim said. *"That's* all he's got to say about—"

"Shh," McCoy said.

"I can't *believe* this!"

*"—as regards the former commander-general Ael i-Mhiessan t'Rllaillieu, the United Federation of Planets is presently engaged in discussions intended to clarify her legal position with regard to her presence and possible rights under law in Federation space. Until such clarification is available, I regret that no statement can be made regarding her disposition. Additionally, and in regard to your fourth point, since there is some uncertainty regarding her whereabouts, it is at this time difficult to say whether the artifact about which you are inquiring is actually in her possession or not. Needless to say, it is the Federation's wish that any artifact of cultural value should be restored to its proper place as soon as the facts of the case have been understood and evaluated by those most closely involved, and we would hope that such an evaluation could occur at the earliest possible date."*

And Fox sat down.

Jim just sat there, speechless. The only satisfaction he got for the moment was that the Romulans were doing the same.

After a moment, Hloal t'Illialhlae leaned across the table and looked hard at Fox. *"When,"* she said, *"might we reasonably expect this 'legal clarification' to be forthcoming?"*

*"I expect it within thirty-six of our hours,"* Fox said promptly, *"and I would hope your schedule allows you to remain here that long, so that whatever the nature of the clarification, we may then expedite further talks arising from it."*

Jim wasn't entirely sure he liked the sound of that.

*"We will return,"* said t'Illialhlae, *"in thirty-six hours, then."* She stood up, as did all her delegation. *"But, Ambassador Fox, you must understand our position. If we do not achieve satisfaction on all four points by that time, the results will be unfortunate."*

Fox and the people on the Federation side all stood up as well. *"Intemperate action without the advice and consent of one's superiors is always unfortunate,"* Fox said. Jim raised his eyebrows at that, for it was astonishing how so cool and seemingly casual an utterance could seem suddenly edged with threat. *"We look forward to meeting with you again, thirty-six hours from now."*

The Romulans filed out, eldest first, as was their habit, though there was something of a clear space between Hloal t'Illialhlae and everyone else, as if not even her own people cared to get too close. Shortly the screen showed only an empty room, and Uhura killed that view, leaving Jim looking at the serenely rotating bulk of *Mascrar* again.

Sulu blew out a long breath but said nothing. Jim swung around in the center seat to look over at Spock, who was turning back to look down his scanner as if he had been watching nothing of more moment than one of Mr. Freeman's rechanneled ancient videos down in the rec room. Uhura just shook her head a little and then put her hand to her transdator, listening.

"That was the ambassador's aide," she said. "There'll be a briefing for the negotiating team and the ships' captains in about eight hours. Apparently Fox expects the talks with the main body of Romulan negotiators and observers to resume again later this afternoon, regardless of what we just saw."

Jim nodded, trying to get a grip on himself and slowly finding it.

McCoy let out a long breath, looking at the screen again. "At least he stood up to tell them that last part."

"It does mean something, then . . ."

"You don't fight your enemy sitting down," McCoy said. "Challenges are always delivered standing, unless you so despise the enemy that you don't feel you need to do them that honor, or you foresee an outcome where you needn't have bothered to extend the courtesy, because they're not going to be alive long enough for it to matter." He shook his head. "At least Fox understands the nuances."

"I certainly hope he does," Jim said. "The good ambassador isn't without his occasional blind spot, as we've seen." The memory of the near disaster that had been triggered by Fox's actions when *Enterprise* had ferried him to Eminiar VII was all too vivid in Jim's mind. He was willing to cut the man some slack; while his actions on behalf of the Federation there had been somewhat ham-handed, there had never been any doubt but that his intentions had been good. But good intentions were not always enough. Fox's insistence on *Enterprise* remaining in the system even though the Eminians had warned her off resulted in the ship being declared "destroyed" in the virtual war between Eminiar and Vendikar. It was only smart action by Scotty, then in command while Jim, Spock, and the rest of the landing party were being held prisoner on the planet, that had kept the ship from really being destroyed, and had bought the landing party the time to escape, change the odds, and effectively end the war.

That had been a while ago, though. People did change and learn. Jim had heard of no further disasters with Fox's name attached to them. *And Starfleet must think he's the best we've got at the moment,* Jim thought. He hoped with unusual fervor that they were right.

He also wondered what one who understood the nuances better than anyone on the Federation side was making of it all . . .

"Captain," Ael said, allowing herself to start to sound irritated, "you must not so misconstrue me. This is *not* a matter of whim, but one of personal honor, and as such cannot be deprioritized. Indeed, I had not thought your people went in much these days for instruments of torture, but I see I have yet much to learn." She leaned forward in her command chair and gave Captain Gutierrez, on the viewscreen, a fierce look. Behind her was a soft rustling of uniforms and creaking of chairs as a shift change took place—Aidoann and the day crew coming on—

but it was happening much more quietly than usual. Ael's people were listening with an intensity that suggested they were very interested, or very amused, or both.

"*Commander,*" said Captain Gutierrez, moving uncomfortably in his own center seat, "*please, it's just a figure of speech. I simply mean that we cannot turn up in the neighborhood of* Mascrar *without security precautions first being in place.*"

"There are six Federation starships there, two of them most outrageously overweaponed, if I understand even the public specs for *Sempach* and *Speedwell,*" Ael said, "not to mention *Mascrar,* which is closer in strength to a planetary-level defense installation. How much more security could you need?"

She shook her head at him as he started to speak. "Captain, my people have been foully maligned!" Ael said. "It is an act of dishonor for me to sit here and keep mum, as if fear or shame motivated me! *Mnhei'sahe* requires that I return with all due speed to defend my people's reputations as reasoning, thinking beings. Not to mention the reputation of *Bloodwing,* a vessel worthy of a better assessment than 'antiquated'!" She let the scorn show a little.

"*Oh, come on, Commander. We have a saying: 'Sticks and stones may break my bones, but words will never hurt me.'*"

She shook her head in mock wonder. "Such violence in idiom surprises me from the representative of a purportedly peaceful people."

"*Commander, it's a* children's *saying. It means—*"

"Elements protect me from your children, then!"

Aidoann, behind her, cleared her throat softly. Ael glanced at her and shook her head. It was a planned interruption, but it was not needed at the moment.

Gutierrez looked put out. "*It means that just because they call your ship names, that's no reason to overreact—*"

"Indeed? I seem to remember that Captain Kiurrk's crew once nearly precipitated a diplomatic incident because some Klingon called the *Enterprise* a 'garbage scow.'"

"*That was different,*" Gutierrez said. "*If the captain—*"

"Sir," Ael said. "The insult that has been leveled at my crew is not one

I can let slide. I swore to be their good lady and to lead them faithfully and well. Their long loyalty to me requires I take action to defend them. Even your culture, surely, supports the right to directly confront one's accusers when accusations so unbearable are made! Now, Captain, you must call the commodore, or whoever else you feel you must consult about this matter, and see to it that whatever 'security measures' are required are put swiftly in place—for I will *not* linger here another two days while that slander on my crew lies smarting in my mind, and those who committed it sit about congratulating themselves. One standard day I give you. Then I will make my way back to the location of the talks . . . with you or without you. And we shall see what happens then."

Gutierrez swallowed again. Ael thought with secret amusement that she could almost hear him swallow, the only sound on her bridge except for the soft purr of the life-support systems and the occasional *beep* or *tck* of a touched control or closing circuit.

*"Commander,"* Gutierrez said, *"you know I can't permit that."*

The temptation to say *And how will you stop me?* was strong, but would have been unwise. It would have made him start thinking too actively about ways to do so. "Perhaps you cannot," Ael said, "but a good way to see that it does not become an issue is to speak to the commodore immediately. We will talk again when you have done so."

She glanced over at tr'Hrienteh and flicked the finger of one hand up the other wrist. Tr'Hrienteh killed the connection. "Answer no hails from *Ortisei* for the next four hours or so," Ael said, "and raise the shields. I will speak no more to Captain Gutierrez until he has better news for me."

Aidoann swung down from the engineering station, where she had been running some engine checks. *"Khre'Riov,"* she said, "you can't think that any of us take Hloal's mouth-wind at all seriously."

*"Au,* not at all," Ael said. "But Captain Gutierrez does not know that. Nor do I mean him to." Nonetheless she sat back in her hard command seat and smiled. "All the same, I find our good fortune hard to believe. Their arrogance has made them foolish, Aidoann. We lie here sinking in deep water, and they throw us a line, giving us an excuse to be right where we want to be."

"Always assuming, *khre'Riov,* that it was not their intent to play us so."

Ael cocked an eye up at Aidoann. "This cautious tone becomes you, cousin; you are growing into the habits of command. But the thought occurred to me some while ago." She leaned back, crossing her legs and making herself as comfortable as she could in that hard seat. "Yet I do not credit it. They are too far from remembering how true honor motivates action to use it effectively as a trap. When we do appear, and what must happen, happens, it will have been their own foolishness that brings it down on their heads. Meanwhile, we must prepare ourselves. We may have to move more quickly than in just one standard day. I must see tr'Keirianh immediately." She got up. "Call the engine room and tell him I am on my way. I want to see those new propulsion models, for my heart tells me that in some hours, we will need them."

In the neighborhood of RV Trianguli, aboard *Sempach,* the scheduled briefing between the negotiating team and the top-level officers of the starships on site had been going on for half an hour or so. Ambassador Fox had finished delivering the précis of the negotiations that had led to the morning's "public" session, and a shorter one of the afternoon's work. Now he pushed the padd away and sat back in his chair at the briefing-room table, as the stars slid slowly past the window and the great bulk of *Mascrar* began to slip into view.

"It's actually going relatively well," he said, "despite the apparent ultimatum we were offered. It's standard enough tactics in talks like this to go 'hard' after the opposing party gives you a 'soft' response to the initial proposals—or what are supposed to be the initial ones. You'll all have noticed that the initial Romulan official proposal was a lot milder than expected on the issues that really concern us, though more robust in other areas. The Neutral Zone, specifically."

From where he sat between Spock and McCoy, Jim looked up as sunlight reflected from *Mascrar* began to flood into the room. "It's the 'softness,'" Jim said to Fox, "that is concerning me at the moment. I would have liked to see the incident at 15 Trianguli discussed in rather greater detail."

Danilov looked over at Fox, then at Jim. "That," he said, "is a matter which Starfleet Command has decided not to press any further, with a view to advancing other discussions considered more pertinent at the moment."

Spock glanced in Jim's direction. Jim folded his arms so that he wouldn't start drumming his fingers on the table. "Commodore," Jim said, "with all due respect, this does *not* strike me as a way for Starfleet to improve or augment the respect with which its ships are treated when they travel into debatable space."

"Captain," said Danilov, "I know what you're thinking. You were the one stuck in a tough place and getting shot at. But you got out of it with your skin intact, as you usually do—and now we have other fish to fry."

*Oh no,* Jim thought. He had always been warned of what happened when a ship started to become legendary for something. Soon it started to be taken for granted that the ship would always do what it had managed, sometimes by the skin of its teeth, to do until then.

"Commodore, I'm sorry, but I have to emphasize this," Jim said. "What if some other ship, not *Enterprise* with her admittedly laudable record for getting out of trouble, had happened into the situation we found waiting for us at 15 Tri? And had not come out of it? It would unquestionably have been a *casus belli.* But because we escaped, through good luck and bloody-mindedness, the subject is just going to be allowed to fall by the wayside?"

Danilov looked at Jim and said nothing. "They are going to draw certain inevitable conclusions from this," Jim said. "And the wrong ones. That we are so afraid of going to war that we will make considerable concessions to avoid it. Giving Romulans this idea is a major error. The location of the encounter is no accident, but the encounter itself is a message written in letters half a light-year high. They were not merely testing our preparedness in that part of space, but seeing whether we would call them on it. We didn't. We've apparently bent over backwards to let them weasel out of it! And now they have the answer they want. They've seen that they can commit a major breach of the treaty, an attack on a ship nominally under Federation protection, fairly deep in our space, and get away with it."

"Permission to speak freely," Danilov said softly, "granted."

Jim fell silent.

"Captain," Danilov said, "you're overstating the case. Fifty planets are not the same as one ship. Those worlds are populated by Federation citizens—"

"Was *Bloodwing* granted free passage through Federation space, or not?" Jim said. "Were her people given asylum here, or not?"

Around the table, some of the most senior officers looked at one another uncomfortably. Jim knew why, for the legal position was still being "clarified" at the Federation High Council level, and no one wanted to commit themselves without having at least a clue of which way the Council would jump. *Politics!* Jim thought, and looked at Danilov. Danilov returned his gaze, his face not changing.

"The camel's nose is in the tent, gentlemen," Jim said. "And the rest of it is going to follow. I must protest the way the negotiations are going in the strongest possible terms."

He looked at Fox.

"It seems we're fated to be on the wrong side of these arguments, Captain," Fox said. "My instructions from the Federation Council are very clear, and they give me little latitude for improvisation in some regards, no matter what my personal feelings on the subject might be."

There it was, as clear as his position would let him say it: *I don't approve either, but I have my job to do.* Jim breathed out.

"Ambassador," said Captain Helgasdottir, "allow me to say a word here."

All heads turned to her. Birga Helgasdottir pursed her lips and folded her hands together.

"I agree with Captain Kirk," she said. "If this matter of the incursion at 15 Trianguli is not pressed with the Romulans now, and vigorously, we are all going to suffer for it later."

Danilov gave Captain Helgasdottir a look not quite as annoyed as the one he had given Jim. "I'm sorry to find opinion so divided," he said, "when for the time being, the execution of policy must continue to go the way it's presently going. We must wait the forty or so hours left us, let this move of the game play itself out, and see how the Romulans react. There have been some early indications of a softening in their position; we'll see what further ones turn up tomorrow, after subspace messages have had time to make their way home to the Empire and back here again. But the whole situation is riding on a knife-edge at the moment, and if any evidence of divisions among us reaches the other side, it could wreck everything. I expect you all"—he glanced around the table—"to conduct yourselves accordingly."

Helgasdottir was wearing a tight look that suggested clearly enough to Jim how little she liked this, but she nodded. The other starship captains—the tall blond Centauri, Finn Winter of *Lake Champlain,* and the slender dark-maned Caitian, Hressth ssha-Aurrffesh of *Hemalat*—nodded too. They kept their faces neutral, but Jim got the strong feeling that neither of them felt any happier about this than he and Helgasdottir did. *They know,* Jim thought, *it could be them all alone out in the dark the next time . . .*

The meeting went on for a little while more, mostly dealing with administrative business and the movement of various supplies and resources among the gathered ships; it was unusual enough for so many Starfleet vessels to meet away from a starbase or between scheduled resupply or careening stops. Finally, Danilov stood up and said, "That's all for now, ladies and gentlemen. Dismissed." As the group rose with him, he glanced at Jim. "Captain Kirk, would you stay a moment?"

Jim stayed where he was; the room emptied.

When the door finally shut, Danilov sat down again. "Jim," he said, "I need a favor from you."

"Permission to speak freely?" Jim said.

"Granted."

Jim took a long breath, then let it out again. "Forget it," he said. "What is it you need, Dan?"

"I need you to send a message to the commander," he said, "telling her at all costs to stay where she is for the moment."

*I wondered how long she was going to maintain her position. Now, is this one of her sudden hunches . . . or something more concrete?* "What's the story at your end, Dan?" Jim said. "Not the cover story—the real one. I have to know."

"Things are moving, Jim. We may be able to defuse this war without any major concessions. But if, as you say, one nose is already in the tent, two is going to be just one too many."

"Have you heard from Starfleet about her status?"

"No. But the Romulans are already arguing about their own position, and the two major forces in the negotiations are sitting on information from the Hearthworlds that's making them lean toward changing their minds."

"I take it that this information has come from the inside . . ."

"You know our source," Danilov said. "Or McCoy does. An uprising is getting started on another of their colony worlds, a major one, Artaleirh. The asteroid belt around the primary there is the main source for high-quality dilithium crystals in the Imperium, and the planet itself has a great deal of heavy and high-tech industry. The Romulans could lose the system and not be crippled if it came to that, but its position is strategically critical for them. Artaleirh is far enough away from the center of things that they're concerned that the Klingons might make a move on the system from one or another of several former Rihannsu worlds they've recently occupied. But it's also close enough to ch'Rihan and ch'Havran that a failure to respond to the threat would be read as a sign of weakness by both their own people and the Klingons."

He pushed back a little in his chair, stretching, frowning. "Jim, this is distracting their attention powerfully at the moment. This whole expedition after Ael and the Sword has always been a fishing expedition for them, a way to justify what they've been planning to do anyway. But now dealing with Artaleirh is much more imperative. They're already at each other's throats about it. If we just sit right where we are, Fox says, and keep staring, and don't blink, they'll blink first and use Artaleirh as an excuse to pull back from the brink. But it's imperative that nothing else distract them right now—and most definitely not Ael. Even she'll have to admit that."

*I wonder,* Jim thought. "She has her own oaths, to her crew," he said, "which, to her, sometimes transcend even the disciplines of her own service. I've been in a situation like that myself, and was fortunate enough to have Fleet come down on my side, eventually." He did not add that it had taken no less a being than T'Pau of Vulcan to get them to do so. "But I would have done what I did regardless, and Ael is capable of the same level of resolve. I can give her advice, but I can't guarantee the results."

"I'm not asking you to. But Jim, please do this for me."

He stood there for a moment more, thinking about it. "All right," Jim said.

"Thank you, Jim."

*Enterprise*'s captain fixed the commodore-in-command with a cool look. "You don't need to thank me," Jim said. "My oaths are in place. This is a duty matter. If you want to take it as a favor for a friend, that's your prerogative. But I may ask for that favor back sometime soon, and I just hope your duty won't get in the way."

Danilov simply looked at him. "We'll have to see," he said, "won't we?"

Jim nodded and went out.

"They're coming," said the scan technician, whose name Courhig could never remember.

Courhig tr'Meihan began to shake, and just stood still for a few moments until he could control that. Finally he felt himself steady down, his breathing begin to sort itself out. The image was indeed clear enough in the display—six Grand Fleet light cruisers, in formation, cruising slowly into the system. Courhig glanced around him at the people looking over his shoulders at the jury-rigged display and coordination panel, the hundred other people crammed together there in the big, bare, empty hangar—men and women, young and old, bulky enough already in their pressure suits. It was for all the world as if there was no room for them to spread out. But they were hungry for closeness, all of them, at the moment. None of them had any idea how much longer they were likely to live.

"All right," Courhig said to them. "You all know what you have to do?"

Nods, murmurs of agreement. "Wait till we give you the signal," Courhig said. "Don't hurry the moment until we're certain the handlers have consolidated their control. If any of you have signal failures, abort immediately and get out of the way so that we can try to destroy whichever ship isn't responding to what we do. We can't afford to take the chance of one of these vessels escaping with news of what's happened."

Everyone nodded. They had heard it all a hundred times before, in simulations and in trials, but they knew he had to say it again.

"Then go," Courhig said. "And Elements with you all."

"You also," some of them murmured. Then all the pilots and crews turned and headed out the pressure door, into the big airlock where their helms were racked.

That door sealed behind them, and to Courhig's ears the hiss of it was like someone's last breath. "I wish I could go with them," he said.

Behind him, Felaen stood with her arms folded, watching the displays. "We've had this discussion," she said. "You started this, and so we need you to talk to the government later—assuming that any of us survive the next thirty hours. Now just sit quiet and bear it."

He nodded. Felaen was his second-in-command mostly because she was the only one who could speak unpalatable truths to him and not be affected, or even particularly impressed, by attempts to pull rank on her afterward. There was, at the end of the day, no effective way to pull rank on one's wife.

"Gio—" he said to the tech.

"Gielo," said the tech, and laughed. It was about the tenth time it had happened.

"Gielo, sorry."

"Here's the ecliptic view, sir." The man touched several controls, and the main display, at the center of the cluster of nine, showed the outside view—the glitter of the asteroid belt seen from inside, a wide spatter of light fining down to a hard sharp glitter of it arcing away through space, toward the sun. The sensor was attached to a tower on top of the hollowed-out asteroid in which the hangar and the ships now departing were sheltered, one of hundreds that had been adapted over the past couple of centuries for storage and temporary docking. As Courhig watched, starlight shimmered above the asteroid's horizon, but he could see nothing else, and had been lucky to see that. The cloaked smallships were away, carrying with them the weapons that, if the simulations had not misled them, would start the process of making Ar-taleirh truly free.

Courhig found it entirely appropriate, as he stood there clenching his fists from tension and watching the display, that the technology on which those weapons were based was a spin-off from the automated rock-handling setup that had been originally invented on Artaleirh for use in this asteroid belt. Since the "handlers" had become affordable, relatively few miners bothered to actually go out in ships and wrestle with rocks anymore, now that they could sit in a comfortable room on a planet or inside an asteroid and do the wrestling from there with me-chanical arms and eyes. Cheap subspace radio relaying solved the time-delay problem for those who had preferred to continue work after relocating to Artaleirh, though there were some few who still liked to stay out in the belt. For those, old habits and lifestyles died hard. Some of those old hands were the ones who were sitting at consoles elsewhere inside this rock, using virtual-reality controls to manage the handlers—the little machines that, themselves hidden with the new multiphasic cloaking device, were now making their way on detection-baffled im-pulse toward vessels that thought themselves invisible and, therefore, invulnerable.

Courhig watched the display that showed the tactical and tracking information. There, about five million *stai* from the asteroid belt, came the cruisers, still coasting in in formation, maintaining radio silence, looking Artaleirh over carefully from a safe distance. And meanwhile, on the other scan screens, six different readouts showed six different handlers closing in on the shimmers in space that hid the six Grand Fleet light cruisers as they braked down. One after another, as the min-utes crept by, each shimmer, in its own display, suddenly gave way to views of field-attenuated, shimmery sunlight on starship hulls: the han-dler vehicles, precisely matching velocities with their targets, dropping slowly and gently through their cloaking fields, unseen themselves, moving closer to the vessels' hulls.

*Easy,* Courhig thought, *easy!* It would be too awful, after all this money spent, all this planning, all this time, to have their tactics be-trayed by mere sound. But the men and women controlling the handlers were expert at maneuvering on impulse, and with the most exquisite softness, the first handler touched down on its target ship's hull and clamped tightly onto it.

Courhig and Felaen went tense, waiting for alarms, some sign of trouble. But there was none. These ships were cloaked; they thought themselves invisible, and therefore were blind to what was about to happen to them.

"They're scanning now," said the tech.

Courhig bit his lip, held himself still. This would be the last test.

"No result apparent," said the tech. "No change in course. They haven't noticed anything."

"All right," Courhig said, as one after another of the cloaked drones sat down on its target, and finally they were all in place. "Are the crews all ready?"

"All ready, *llha.*"

"Then tell the virtual warriors to turn the handlers loose." *And Earth and Fire both be with the little metal creatures.*

Courhig turned his attention to the first of the handlers to come down on one of the cruisers. He could see nothing of what it was doing; its hemispherical shape was blocking his view. But underneath it he knew that the dissolution charge was being released. That would unravel the crystalline structure of a section of the ship's hull about a cubit in diameter. A fraction of a second after that, before the hull pressure changed at all significantly, the sealing "bell" would come down over the new aperture, snugging down tight and preventing any further change in pressure. And out of the sealing bell, the "smart" cabling would come worming its way down into the 'tween-hulls space, sniffing out what it was programmed to seek: the ship's energy and communications system.

Courhig clenched his hands hard, trying not to panic. This had always been the most uncertain part of the operation in their simulations. Yet in some ways it was the simplest, for the people who had designed it were, some of them, people who had built ships for Grand Fleet in their time—and they had chosen for exploitation one of the simplest and most sensible parts of starship design. In the years since the development of silicate-based conduction conduits, Rihannsu power networks for starships had been built with what was called multiple redundancy; any cabling could carry any signal, electrical or optical. As a result, the ship's cabling network now functioned like the pathways in the brain. If one path was disabled or destroyed, a message, command, or impulse could route around the "dead" spot and get where it was going some other way. The same system carried computer linkages, comms, anything vital.

Now, though, that strength was about to be turned into a deadly weakness.

Courhig watched as the blank subscreen for that particular handler stayed blank. It was blank for a long time. *What's keeping it? Is the routine failing? Have they changed frequencies, or systems, or—* But the screen lit, then, a sudden blast of code scrolling down it, garbage characters that confirmed that the handler cable had tapped into one of the ship's networking trunks and only needed to get into synch.

Other subscreens in other displays began to show similar screenfuls of code. Courhig gulped, daring to think that it was actually going to work. The starships' computers had been programmed to protect themselves, logically enough, from commands that came from outside, from other systems. But they could not defend against ones that seemed to come from inside the ship, using the vessel's own circuitry and networking systems, seeming to belong to one of the ship's own computer terminals. The ship did not keep secrets from itself—or not for long.

Courhig watched the first handler's programming go looking for the first piece of information it had been instructed to find and disable. Self-destruct—"Encoded," Felaen whispered, as a string of garbage characters appeared. Courhig nodded

Then the code flashed into a string of intelligible letters and numbers. Courhig breathed out. Encrypted the information might have been, but the computer also had to store the information on how to decrypt it. Otherwise it would be useless. "Let me talk to the virtual pilots," Courhig said.

"You're on."

"Is everything going all right?" Courhig said.

The voice of Kerih, one of the oldest of them and the chief "brain" behind the handlers' programming, came back over comms. *"So far,"* he said, *"we're into three of the systems. Four. Five and six should follow shortly."*

"Don't wait for them," Courhig said. "Lock down the self-destruct systems right away."

*"Doing that,* llha."

"Then lock their helms and weapons systems," Courhig said. "Comms too. I don't want any warnings getting out."

There was a pause. Courhig stared nervously at the subscreens showing the handlers' output. All but one of them was showing results; that one was still dark.

*"Done,"* the report came back after a moment. *"All but six."*

"What's the matter with that one?"

*"Don't know yet,* llha," said Kerih. *"Got visual from three of the other five, though."*

"Good. Let me see it, and trigger the first five's invader control systems," he said. "Knock out their crews."

And now all he and Felaen could do was wait, watching repetition after repetition of the same scene: narrow views of Rihannsu officers hammering on unresponsive consoles, staggering down the corridors of their ships, trying to defend themselves and their shipmates against something they couldn't understand, then falling to the decks, overcome. Courhig should have felt triumphant, but instead he felt faintly sick. At least the crews had not needed killing, but these people had honestly—he assumed—been trying to do what they thought was their duty. When they were sent home after everything was finally settled—assuming that the Artaleirhin as a people, and Artaleirh itself, would survive long enough to send them back—all too likely the loyalty of the light cruisers' crews would be questioned, and a lot of them might be court-martialed and shot. Killing them cleanly might have been kinder. But that would have meant destroying the ships, and that Courhig would not do. Except . . . there was still that sixth subscreen, still dark. "Kerih, *what about six?*"

*"That's* Calaf," Kerih said, sounding unnerved. *"I just took down self-destruct and comms. Just in time too, though I don't think they got any messages out. But there's another problem—they rerouted invader control away from us somehow."*

*"Taif,"* Courrig said bitterly. He had been afraid of this. "Leave the ships locked on course out of the system for the moment," he said. "We'll have to clean them out later. Retask the smallship crews to *Calaf.* Tell them to board and neutralize the crew."

*"Got that."*

Courhig steadied himself on the back of Gielo's chair and swallowed hard. *Neutralize. What a nice word for it.* "I wish I were there," he said.

Felaen said nothing, just put her hands on his shoulders from behind and watched him. The five screens that were showing them images showed no new ones: only collapsed people, sleeping in smoky corridors, as they would do for hours. The ships would be followed out of system by other smallships, stopped, boarded, and their crews removed. New crews would shortly be put aboard. That in itself was a mighty success. But meantime there was still that last screen, just a stream of text . . .

It went dark.

There was a long silence.

*"Kerih?"* Courhig said, his voice cracking. "What happened?"

A pause. *"The first two smallships made contact with* Calaf *and started forcing her hull,"* he said. *"But somebody inside managed to override the weapons lockdown and detonated the whole complement of photon torpedoes."*

"Oh, Elements . . ." Courhig covered his face with his hands. "Which smallships?"

*"Pirrip and* Fardraw," Kerih said. *"Some damage to the others. Pressure leaks . . . nothing major."*

Rhean, and Merik and Tuhellen, and Emmiad with her laughing eyes, and Wraet and Sulleen . . . Courhig wiped his eyes. *They knew the risks, though. They were eager. There was no way I could have stopped them.*

*Too late now.*

"Do you know what went wrong with that last handler?" Courhig said finally.

*"Some indications. Be hard to know for sure, now."* Kerih sounded bitter. *"But next time we won't start operations until all the handlers are live and answering properly."*

"If there is a next time," Courhig said. "Grand Fleet's not as stupid as the government, alas. They'll work out a defense against this approach as soon as they understand what happened. Meanwhile, we have a little while to exploit it—maybe as long as a month. Till then, we have other business." He turned to Felaen. "Are the message teams ready?"

She had been bending over another console, and now straightened up. "Already starting work," she said. "They'll be using the handlers to pull these five ships' last three days' communications and using them to fabricate reports of what they're 'doing' now that they're in system. With luck we can keep the deception going for a few days—enough for us to consolidate our position. Enough time for other things to happen."

He nodded. "Well," Courhig said, "let's pray that they do. Pray to all Elements that she gets here in a hurry. And that other help arrives hard on her heels . . . for if it doesn't, we've got no other hope."

After seeing Danilov, Jim spent the next couple of hours in his quarters, looking again at the slowly rotating map on the viewscreen at his desk. The computer had rendered the map in 3-D and had added some of the star names and statuses that had come from Ael's information. The dry Federation/new-Bayer names and catalog numbers of the stars within the boundaries of the Neutral Zone were now augmented by Rihannsu proper names. Apparently their astronomers did not go in much for cataloging by numbers, a cultural habit based in respect for the Elements and for stars and planets as "personifications" of Fire and Earth. Jim's attention was very much on what he had defined earlier as the "second breakout" area, the part of Romulan space closest to both the Klingons and the Federation, and the stars there: Orith, Mendaissa, Uriend, Artaleirh, Samnethe, Ysail. Many of them had been tagged with colors meant to show that they were being fortified, that substantial ship squadrons had been moved there in recent days or weeks.

"Computer," he said.

*"Working."*

"Add data on most recent Federation/Starfleet ship and troop disposi-
tions."

Various small stars of colored light added themselves to the ones already present in the viewer. Jim had to squint a little at the display.
Most of the additions were closer to the area where the talks were now
being held than to the space around 15 Tri. Jim swallowed.

*Even if Fox and the intelligence people put this most recent info from Ael to-
gether with theirs,* he thought, *it's almost too late. And if the Romulans have our
information, it* is *too late. They'll see that Starfleet has placed its ships too far
away from the "second breakout" area to stop them when they move, or to keep
them from moving in the first place.*

*Only a miracle can keep this war from happening now.*

Jim got up, breathed out, and stood behind the desk, looking at
nothing in particular. *And secretly,* he thought, *I've been expecting a miracle,
just like everyone else.*

Jim stepped around the desk and went to the shelf where he kept his
very few real books. Sam Cogley had taught him this particular liking,
one he had been selectively indulging ever since they met, and now he
reached for the book Sam had given him when they parted company
after the court-martial. *Strange choice,* Jim had thought at the time, as he
took the old volume down and riffled through the pages. But as he had
read it he'd come to the conclusion that Sam had chosen wisely. Any
starship captain was, after all, a kind of descendant of the people in these
pages, journeying through a landscape as strange and unpredictable as
theirs, and usually doing it with just as little backup. Now the pages fell
open at the spot Jim had thought of more than once today, the story of
another negotiation between distrustful parties, a long time ago.

. . . and Arthur warned all his host that an they see any sword
drawn, "Look ye come on fiercely, for I in no wise trust Sir Mordred." In like wise Sir Mordred warned his host. And so they met,
and wine was fetched, and they drank. Right soon a little adder
came out and stung a knight on the foot. And when the knight
saw the adder, he drew his sword to kill it. When the host on both
parties saw that sword drawn, then they blew trumpets and horns,

and shouted grimly. Thus they fought all the day, and never stinted until many a noble knight was laid to the cold earth. . . .

Jim let out the long breath that he had been holding, thinking of the tension in that meeting room this morning, the sense of people wanting a fight and intent on getting on with it, though not without first allowing this little local drama to play itself out, so that everyone would be able to say, *We did everything we could, of course no one wants war, but you see how it is, we had no choice!* There had been the same sense of awful inevitability about the First World War and the Eugenics Wars on Earth, and most of the great battles that had followed, right down to the last big one with the Klingons. *A shame peace isn't as inevitable,* Jim thought.

*But it can be. It has to be.*

*Someone just has to set out to make it that way.*

He went back to the desk, the book still in his hand, and sat looking for a long time at the image slowly rotating on the viewer's screen.

"Computer," he said at last, into the heavy, waiting silence.

*"Working."*

"New message. When complete, lock under voiceprint access, encrypt, and send."

*"Ready."*

"Begin message. Emphasize. Hold your position. Do not proceed until you hear from me. Close emphasis. The short delay may prove vital for all of us. End message. Send immediately according to routine AR-2."

*"Working. Routed to communications . . . Message sent."*

Jim sat back and let out a long breath.

*Now the only question is, What will she do?*

# Chapter Nine

When the door chimed one more time, that evening, Arrhae looked up in resignation. Earlier this evening, after the meeting of the whole negotiating group, had come yet another visit from tr'AAnikh—in a much more subdued mood than the last time, and proffering an apology. She noticed that he would not come too close to her. That, at least, made Arrhae smile. But all that while she had been nervous, for she still had not managed to identify where the bugging devices in her suite might be. She had sent tr'AAnikh away, her excuse being that she refused to accept his apology as yet—though this had left her in a foul mood, for she disliked having to act so disagreeable.

Now she got up with a frown and went to the door. Intelligence, no doubt, in the form of the miserable t'Radaik, with another of her obscure errands. She paused by the door, breathed out. "Who comes?" she said.

"A friend," said a big, deep voice.

Her eyes widened. She knew that voice, but there was no reason in space or beyond it for its owner to be outside *her* door. Nonetheless, she waved the door open.

He stood there, a little shadowy in the hallway's late-evening-scheme lighting, but unmistakable: Gurrhim tr'Siedhri. He sketched her a brief bow, one which he did not have to give her at all, and said, "Perhaps the Senator might have time to speak to me."

She stood aside, and he slipped in; the door shut behind him. Arrhae waved it locked. He stood by the couch, and she blinked to see that he was actually waiting for her to sit first.

She did so, and for confusion's sake retreated into *hru'hfe* mode, saying, "May I give you something to drink, Praetor? I have here some excellent ale—"

"I take that kindly, but there is no need, and little time." He reached under his tabard.

Arrhae froze. What he brought out, though, was no weapon. It was a small sphere of dark-green metal, with several recessed touch-patches set into it, matte finish against the sheen of the rest of it. He set it down on the low table in front of the couch, and it balanced on one of the recessed patches and began to make a very small, demure humming sound. One of the patches on the side glowed a soft blue.

"It is a personal cloak," he said. "It has been set to blank out my life-sign readings; it is now also jamming whatever listening and scanning devices may have been operating in this area."

Arrhae looked at it with astonishment. Like everyone else, she had heard of such things, but had never thought to see one. Such devices were of fabulously advanced technology and expensive beyond belief, the sort of thing that only the government could afford for its own agents—it having been careful to make such technology illegal except when purchased by a government agency.

Tr'Siedhri caught Arrhae's look and gave her a dry one back. "If there is not the occasional advantage to being offensively rich," Gurrhim said, "it would be a sad thing. With this in operation, no one will know I am here. Whatever intelligence operatives are eavesdropping on you at this moment, if any, will neither see nor hear anything that occurs in here for what I intend to restrict to a very short period. They will almost certainly attribute the brief failure of their equipment to a malfunction, for this whole ship has been riddled with such; so that it would be ready for this mission, its final stages of construction were hurried through much too quickly." He smiled. "And I count it unlikely that anyone will come down here to visit. That would make it too plain that you, like everyone else aboard, were being watched, and the intel folk do so like to believe that no one knows what they are doing."

"I hope you are right," Arrhae said. "Meanwhile, the Praetor's confidence honors me. Perhaps he will extend it a little—to the reason for his visit."

"Madam, you needn't be so formal with *me*," said Gurrhim. "I am a farmer, and you are . . . an intelligent young woman whom events have raised to her proper level."

"Flatterer," Arrhae said.

He grinned, and his amiably ugly face went a little feral. "Truth sometimes wears a skewed look," he said, "while being no less true. To business, young Senator. Artaleirh is in rebellion. They have declared their independence, and have also declared for the traitress."

Arrhae held very still, watching his eyes. *"Artaleirh?"* she said, taking care to sound surprised, for it was no surprise to her; the chip that tr'AAnikh had passed to Arrhae had mentioned there was trouble there. But it had not been explicit about what kind, nor had it mentioned that the planet's leadership was rising in support of Ael. That a first-generation colony world barely thirty light-years from Eisn was rebelling in so spectacular a fashion would be a blow to the Imperium indeed. "And how does this strike you?"

"As predictable," he said, "but what strikes me more is the reaction of others to the same news."

*He means tr'Anierh; he would hardly be discussing the matter with me otherwise.* For a moment Arrhae was irrationally distracted by a soft ticking from the heating vessel that kept water hot for herbdraft on her sideboard. But she came back to herself hurriedly. Carefully Arrhae said, "My political patron receives my reports without comment. He does not share his ideas on their content with me."

"No, that would hardly be his style," Gurrhim said. "He may use others as his sounding boards, but what song the *ryill* will produce after those first few testing notes, that information tr'Anierh keeps very much to himself. Such was his style in sending you here as observer. Doubtless you will have been reporting to him the reactions of others to the events now unfolding—doubtless mine as well."

It was hard to know what to do about such unadorned bluntness, a great rarity in Rihannsu of such rank. "That would seem to be a reasonable expectation on your part," Arrhae said, still watching him carefully.

Gurrhim laughed at her, though it was not an unkindly laugh. "Well," he said, "the private meeting of the senior negotiators after our whole-group meeting today was unusually lively because of this news.

Hloal thought she was the only one who had heard, and thought to wrest control of the meeting to herself with it. But so many of us have come here carrying the wherewithal, in software or hardware, to carry on our business privately . . ." His smile grew ironic. "I am sure *Gorget*'s poor crew would not know where to begin if told to track down every illicit sending or receiving device aboard, or to start trying to decode all the different kinds of encrypted messages presently flowing in and out of here."

"'Us,'" Arrhae said, concentrating on staying calm. "So you, too, have received word from outside . . ."

"*Ie,*" he said, "and found myself in an interesting position. For the Artaleirhin have asked me to take their part and to approach the traitress on their behalf, making her aware of the support which they offer her."

"But how would you . . ." Arrhae trailed off. She could feel herself going cold, and probably pale as well. *He knows who I am. He* knows . . .

"Additionally," Gurrhim said, the smile going colder now, "Hloal and her faction have found out about the Artaleirhin's message to me. It is the excuse they have been waiting for. They will certainly kill me tonight, or try to, and dead or alive, I will be charged with treason."

The sweat broke out all over her, no stopping it. "Praetor," she said, "if this is so, then even if that does what you say it will"—she glanced at the sphere—"you may have doomed us both by coming here."

"I think not," Gurrhim said. "I think you are safe. Though Hloal and her cronies hope to upset the balance enough to oust at least one of the Three, they cannot possibly hope to do so with all of them . . . and tr'Anierh is the moderate, the balancing figure between the other two, the one most likely to survive the turmoil now beginning. An attack on you would be an attack on him. But my own fate is certainly in the balance, and who can say how it will rise or fall? So this information now passes to you, to put into your master's hand as a weapon, or to let fall unused. But consider carefully the circumstances, in either case. More—"

He bent close, as if they could even now be overheard. "Hloal and the others of her party are sure that *Bloodwing*'s commander is either already on her way back or preparing to set out. I do not know where they get this information, but they are very sure, and indeed they have so laid their nets that it seems she *must* come back. They think they have played her skillfully. We shall see. But sooner or later she must return, and some of them are intent on striking at her immediately, by surprise, meaning to take her or kill her as soon as she comes. The arguments are going on right now, and though I cannot say how long they will take, I can see already which side is likely to win, for word will shortly come from ch'Rihan to put an end to the arguing. The commanders of our ships will be instructed to take *Bloodwing*'s commander and the Sword if they can; if they cannot, they will simply destroy her and her ship, no matter how the Federation ships or Lalairu try to prevent it. And some other stroke is planned as well, something terrible, something meant to pass unnoticed in the stour that will break out when they attack her. She must be warned, Arrhae; *they* must be warned. For there is no honor in destroying an unprepared enemy."

She swallowed once, hard, at the sound of her name. Rihannsu were chary about the use of own-names outside of family. When one appeared in conversation, it was best to listen, for one way or another, blood would likely be involved.

"Why do you come to *me* with this information?" Arrhae said.

Gurrhim gave her a sidelong look. "Has not all the world and its wife already seen you talking to Mak'khoi, by the very orders of the intelligence folk here?" he said. "Why will anyone think, should you find a moment to speak to him again, or send him a message, that it is not again at their orders?"

"*One* of them will know it is not," Arrhae said. "T'Radaik."

"I count that as of no importance," Gurrhim said. "You will find a way to work around her. In your past life you will have found ways to do all manner of things without your master knowing. Why else, if you will forgive me for speaking of it, is a good *hru'hfe* so valued, except that in the leanest times there is somehow always food on the table, and no one ever accused of theft?"

The words "past life" had made her go hot and cold within seconds, in a rush of terror. That was passing now, but still Arrhae was not sure what he knew and didn't know, and half afraid to find out for sure. "Feeling as you feel about *Bloodwing*'s commander," Arrhae said at last, "—or as you allow others to think you feel—why have the Artaleirhin come to *you* with this information, this request?"

"Partly because there are Ship-clan sympathizers among them," Gurrhim said, "and my loyalties are known. Partly because we have other connections. Much dilithium has been quietly diverted from its source in the Artaleirh system to other worlds farther out, for other purposes, with the help of trading companies on ch'Havran and elsewhere which I control. But more likely because the Artaleirhin know me to be, in my way, as they are: like a *shaill* of mixed blood, short, scrappy, and hard to ride, but more robust than the narrow-muzzled, thin-legged breeds that the purebreds have become in this latter day, creatures that have to be cosseted and fed their meat chopped up in little pieces. They know I have been doing in my lands, insofar as possible when one actually lives on one of the Hearthworlds, as *they* have been trying to do, farther away: running their lives as they wish to, with an eye to old law, local ways, commonsense justice. The Artaleirhin have become increasingly used to making their own way, and now they wish to do so as a freer people, in association with an empire, but not anymore as its subjects or slaves. They see *Bloodwing*'s lady as a way out of their troubles. They are willing to be a sword in her hand . . . for a while. At least they are willing to gamble, with their lives, that she will be useful to them."

She was tempted to smile at his old-fashioned manners. Nothing would bring him to speak Ael's name, which had been thrice written and thrice burned, and so did not exist, even though he was apparently willing to deal with her, even at one remove. "Why do you bring this news to me and not some other?" Arrhae said at last. "For all the sensibleness of your answer, I do not think it is merely a matter of Mak'khoi."

"No," Gurrhim said, standing. "It is because I feel you are one of very few people here who did not come with a preordained agenda. Oh, I know you are tr'Anierh's creature, or must seem to be. But you seem to *me* to be in a position—and of a disposition—to judge rightly.

One who will know what properly to do with this information to make the greatest difference. From what I hear, and what little I have seen of you, you seem like one who truly loves our worlds—our worlds as they ought to be, as they were once and can be again, and would be willing to risk something of value for them. *Mnhei'sahe*," he said, "you understand that, I think."

She nodded, uncertain why her eyes were starting to fill.

"And you do not flinch when you hear the word," Gurrhim said with satisfaction. "I take that as a good sign." He bent over to pick up the cloaking device, turned it over in his hands, pressed one of the patches on it.

Then he put it, heavy and cool, in her hands. "It has selfed to you, now, and will know your body readings and mask them," Gurrhim said. "It will extend range to cover me out to the lifts, then collapse the field when I am out of range. This patch"—he turned the sphere over—"will access the documentation. Hide it away, now, and do not use it unless you are in great need. Quiet night to you."

And he turned and left. Astonished, Arrhae watched him out the door, holding the thing close to her body.

Then she swallowed and hurried away to find a place to hide the cloaker, already composing in her mind her message to McCoy and trying to work out how in the worlds she was to get it to him.

Disruptor fire and phaser fire whined all around her, the deck shook with yet another explosion, and the air stank of burning plastic and scorched metal—and the other smell, the one she had not ever wanted to scent again: blood, Rihannsu and human, shed, mixed, burning. But there was no avoiding it, and the more she had tried to, the more the certainty of this moment had been pursuing her. *Better to get it over with.* She put her hand out behind her for one more phaser to set on overload and throw down that corridor, but no one put one into her hand. She turned to look over her shoulder at him.

He was not there. No one else was, either. No one stood behind her, no one waited to back her up in that charge around the corner and down the last corridor that lay between her and her desire. She was all alone. Her heart beat wildly. Mockingly, a voice said to her, *If I must go alone . . .* Her own voice.

Her eyes flew open. She saw only darkness.

The terminal on her desk chimed softly, and the sound of it reminded her when and where she was. Ael let out a breath, listened for a moment more to her heart hammering away in her side, and then sat up on her hard couch, pushing the silks away. For a moment she sat there with her fists clenched. Then she got up, made her way to the desk in the darkness, and touched the display.

*"Ae."*

"Khre'Riov," tr'Hrienteh's voice said, *"I am sorry to wake you, but you insisted."*

"I did, and I am glad you did. Who is it from?"

*"One of the go-betweens."*

She sighed. "Send it here, if you would. Then I will come up to the bridge. No point in my seeking more sleep this shift."

*"I can give you something, if you like—"*

Ael shook her head. "I would only fret my way through it. Better to save the drugs for when we truly need them."

*"Very well, khre'Riov,"* The voice was the one tr'Hrienteh used when she was humoring a difficult patient, and Ael had to chuckle at the sound of it, for she had been hearing it a great deal recently.

"I am all right," she said. "I will be with you shortly."

*"Out,"* tr'Hrienteh said.

Ael sat down behind the desk and waited for the message to display its usual multiple screenful of gibberish. "Analyze," she said to the computer, "and decrypt."

Obediently it did so. The message was unusually brief, even by the standards of the communiqués that came from this particular source.

SIX FLEET LIGHT CRUISERS DISPATCHED TO ARTALEIRH NOW OFFICIALLY RECOGNIZED AS "MISSING." NINE GRAND FLEET VESSELS HAVE BEEN RECALLED FROM PATROL ROUTES IN THE ZONE NEAREST LAESSIND / RV TRIANGULI AND ARE NOW PROCEEDING TO ARTALEIRH

TO INVESTIGATE/INTERVENE. ACCORDINGLY, *TYRAVA* HAS DEPARTED TO MEET THEM.

ADVISE IMMEDIATELY AS TO YOUR INTENTIONS.

She swallowed. This was it at last, the hinge moment on which everything would ride. Her heartbeat had been slowing, but now it began to speed again.

Ael held very still and looked across her quarters at the chair by the wall and the barely seen shadow that lay across its arms.

"Computer," she said, "record reply. I will come immediately. Will advise as to transit time. End message. Encrypt."

And there her voice failed her.

*"Send?"* the computer said.

Her mouth was dry. "Send."

The computer acknowledged the order, but she barely heard it. Ael got up and went to the 'fresher, put herself into it on its shortest cycle, and barely noticed that either. A few minutes later she was uniformed, out of her quarters, and on the way to the bridge.

Tr'Hrienteh was still there, working at the comms board. "I begin to think," Ael said as she swung down from the lift to where the master surgeon sat, "that you are starting to enjoy this job."

Tr'Hrienteh looked up at her. "I will enjoy it more profoundly still when my replacement is fully trained," she said, "but even he has to sleep occasionally. What orders, *khre'Riov?*"

"Get me *Ortisei,* if you would be so kind," Ael said, sitting down in her command chair. "We shall see if time has brought Captain Gutierrez wisdom."

A glance at tr'Hrienteh's expression told Ael what the surgeon thought of that possibility as she made the connection. A second or so later, the front viewscreen lit to show Ael the captain's center seat, and Gutierrez in it, looking weary. "Captain," Ael said, "a fair morning to you—assuming that our schedules are still running somewhat in tandem."

*"Somewhat,"* Gutierrez said. *"I've been trying to reach you for some time. Is there a comms problem?"*

"I will investigate," Ael said, "for we have had our share of those."

And that at least was true, if not specifically in this case. "Have you spoken to the commodore?"

"*I have.*"

"That is well," Ael said, "for I can wait no longer; we must return to RV Trianguli."

"*The commodore,*" Gutierrez said, "*when I spoke to him six hours ago, instructed me to attempt to dissuade you from making such a move right now.*"

"You may try, but you will achieve no result you desire, Captain. I am sorry."

Gutierrez looked at her in silence for a moment. "*That being the case,*" he said then, "*Commodore Danilov has instructed me to accompany you wherever you go. If you would have your navs officer coordinate with mine, we can leave immediately for RV Tri, if you insist on going now, and be there within two standard hours.*"

"I do insist," Ael said. *But how interesting. Either Ddan'ilof has realized that he sent too few ships with* Bloodwing *to enforce any order, or someone in Starfleet or elsewhere has become willing to allow this matter to come to a swifter conclusion. I suppose I should be grateful that for once we agree . . . but it is unusual . . .*

She glanced at Khiy. "Arrange matters with *Ortisei*'s helm officer immediately," she said. "And meanwhile, Captain, I thank you for your assistance. Is there anything else needs saying before we go?"

He gave her what for a human was a fairly dry look. "*Don't do anything cute.*"

"Why, Captain, if I understand your idiom correctly, you have nothing to fear. Returning to RV Trianguli is all I desire." *For the moment . . . until what waits there has been dealt with. And after that, we will not linger.*

"*I'm delighted to be able to oblige you,*" Gutierrez said. He glanced at his helm officer. "*Feeding you coordinates now, Commander. If you would pace us at warp seven?*"

"So ordered. I thank you, Captain." She gave him about a finger-joint's-depth of bow and then glanced sideways at tr'Hrienteh, who killed the connection.

"And now for it," Ael said, straightening, as the warp drive came on line and Khiy took *Bloodwing* out along the course indicated. "All crew to alert stations. Run the priming checks on the weapons systems but do not bring them up to hot status, not yet. Shields up, and have the cloak ready, but do not under any circumstances implement it until I give the word."

She glanced around her cramped little bridge and saw everyone bending to their instruments with the familiar looks of concentration, and a little more besides: excitement. It was beginning to stir in her, as well. "Aidoann," she said, "I have a few things to set in order. I will be in my quarters for a short time, and then down in engineering, if you need me."

"Yes, *khre'Riov,*" Aidoann said and smiled with that feral little look of eager preparedness that Ael had come to depend on over time. It was very unlike Tafv's old calm, which had always set in harder the more excited he got.

She sighed. *Very unlike.* And she thought, as she got into the lift, *How strange. This is the first time I have thought of him today. Not so long ago he would have been my first thought after waking.*

*He is finally beginning to slip away from me.*

*But is this a bad thing?*

In her quarters, Ael moved around, putting away those few things she had taken out of their storage cupboards over the past couple of days' quiet time—the clumsy cast-ceramic bird figurine Tafv had made as a present for her when he was little, the old hard-copy notebook from her days in the Colleges of the Great Art—and folded away the couch. Then she slipped around to sit at the desk again, and found the terminal's screen blinking with the notifier herald that indicated another message waiting for her. Apparently it had been waiting long enough that the audio signal had turned itself off.

"Analyze," she said, "and decrypt."

The characters on the screen descrambled themselves, leaving her looking at another very short message. It was from Jim.

For once the name did not bring the customary smile to her lips as she read the message. Ael leaned on her elbows, laced her fingers together, leaned her chin on them, and looked at the screen.

*It is not too late to change my mind. Though doubtless it would irk poor Gutierrez, despite the fact that we would be following Ddan'ilof's wishes.*

Yet here she could see the commodore's hand at work, and she did not trust his motives. She trusted Jim's, but at the same time the captain was subordinate to Ddan'ilof, and had little choice about obeying his orders. Though if the captain agreed with the commodore's reasons . . .

After a moment Ael unlaced her fingers and reached out to touch the comms control on the display. But then she stopped herself.

*They do not know what I know about Artaleirh . . . or about* Tyrava. *And I have already told those who are waiting for us that I am on my way.*

*I cannot do as he asks. And just now, I dare not tell him why. It must wait.*

"No reply. Store," she said.

*"Stored."*

Ael stared at the blanked screen for a moment more, and then got up and went out, making for the engine room and one last consultation with tr'Keirianh.

In the dim late-night lighting of the corridor aboard *Gorget,* Arrhae pressed the door signal one more time. She was starting to get impatient, and letting it show for the benefit of any scanner. She was just lifting a fist to bang on the door when it slid open.

Tr'AAnikh stood there in rather charming disarray, barefoot, breeches pulled on hastily, and one of his sleeping silks draped around his torso for modesty's sake. His eyes widened at the sight of Arrhae. She swept straight past him into his cubbyhole, taking it all in at a glance—in fact, it was hard not to, it was so small: couch-pallet, silks, clothes cupboard, a very minimal 'fresher. As the door shut she turned to face him again, wearing an expression of careful disdain. "I have decided," Arrhae said, "how I may after all allow you to do me a service as penance for your recent crude behavior."

"You have? I mean, ah, yes, you have," tr'AAnikh said, running a hand through his hair as if trying to push it into some kind of order, and failing.

"Yes. Now straighten up and attend me, tr'AAnikh. You have been running documents back and forth several times each day from your mistress's office to Ambassador Fox's, I understand."

"Yes, noble *deihu,*" he said, looking more bemused every moment.

"Very well. It will be morning in a matter of an hour or so aboard their ships. I require you to deliver this package to the ambassador's office for me, along with whatever else you would normally be taking there on your first errand."

She thrust the film-wrapped box she had been carrying at him, and tr'AAnikh took it and stared at it. "What is it, noble lady?"

"As if that's any of your business," Arrhae said. "Or as if I need to explain myself to such as you. It's a flask of ale. I was rather abrupt with the poor doctor the other evening—more so than necessary, in the face of what he intended as a courtesy. And good behavior should be reinforced, even when it's aliens and barbarians evincing it. He has a taste for ale, apparently, and I've enough of the stuff in my suite to swim in if I chose. I can easily enough spare him a bottle. So see to it that this comes to him without delay. The ambassador's assistant will manage it."

"Uh," tr'AAnikh said.

*"Without delay,"* Arrhae said, her eyes locking with his, "or you'll smart for it. Your mistress asked me how I wanted you punished for your behavior. I've given her no answer yet. If you prove dilatory in this, I'll think of something with great speed. Now be about it."

And very, very slightly, as he bowed to her, she winked at him.

The bow got caught for just a fraction of a second, then went deep. "Noble *deihu*, I will attend to it instantly," tr'AAnikh said.

Arrhae sniffed and swept out of the tiny cabin, hearing behind her, as the door closed, the sound of someone starting very hurriedly to get dressed.

*Now,* she thought as she made her way casually back to her suite, *the matter is in the Elements' domain. Let Them speed the message to where it needs to be . . .*

She had barely made it inside and shut the door before a dreadful noise erupted in her suite, and as far as she could tell, everywhere in the ship. Her first horrified thought was that she was already betrayed, that someone had scanned that bottle preparatory to beaming it out. Ffairrl came immediately out of his little galley-room, where he had been preparing breakfast.

"What in the worlds *is* that?" Arrhae said, not having to work very hard to sound frightened.

"Security alert," Ffairrl said. "The level just below battle stations." He looked pale.

And then the terminal on the desk in her office started chiming urgently for attention.

Arrhae swallowed once, then went in and touched it awake. "I-Khellian," she said.

"Deihu—" The face looking at her from the screen was one she did not know, a young man with light hair, but the uniform was intelligence green-sashed black. *"Are you all right? Is everything well there?"*

"Yes, everything is fine, except for that dreadful noise," Arrhae said. "What's amiss?"

*"Someone has shot the Praetor Gurrhim tr'Siedhri,"* the young officer said. *"We are checking on everyone in the delegation while the ship is searched for the perpetrator and the weapon. Please stay in your quarters until the search is complete,* deihu, *and assist the search party when they arrive."*

"Of course. But the Praetor, is he . . ."

*"Living still. He is in the infirmary. But his injuries are severe, and the surgeons are uncertain whether they can save him . . ."*

"Thank you," Arrhae said, and touched the connection off.

She looked up and saw Ffairrl looking in the office door at her. Her mind was in turmoil. "You heard that?" she said.

"I could not help it, noble *deihu*."

"Terrible," she said. "Terrible . . ." She walked out into the main room again, while one thought burned hot in her brain: *Whoever tried to kill him will find it all too easy to finish the job in the infirmary—assuming the surgeons themselves are not even now being told to do so, by action or inaction. Either way, he will not survive if he remains aboard* Gorget.

She poured herself a cup of herbdraft from the sideboard. "My appetite will be worth nothing until this searching is over," she said. "This will suffice me for now. Meanwhile, Ffairrl, will you do something for me?"

"Certainly, noble *deihu*."

"I am minded to accept young tr'AAnikh's apology now," she said. "He has shown himself contrite enough that I can afford to be gracious about his lapse. You know where his quarters are?"

"I can find them, *deihu*."

"Go do so, then, and tell him he may wait on me without delay as soon as he has completed the other errand I gave him. Say just that to him."

Ffairrl bowed. "I will deliver your message exactly so, *deihu*." He made for the door.

"Oh, and Ffairrl—" He paused. She smiled very slightly, with a conspiratorial look. "When he arrives, I will wish to be private with him for an hour or so. See to it."

"But, lady, if the searchers come while—"

"Certainly nothing is going to happen until they have left," Arrhae said, sounding scornful. "On *that* you may depend. Now go."

He went.

Arrhae glanced at the cupboard. The little cloaking sphere lay in a bottom drawer, under a pile of bodysilks. *Where can I possibly hide it so they will not find it? If they—*

The door signal went off.

She got up and went to answer it. The door slid open to reveal six people, three men and two women in the gray-on-black of ship's security, and one in intel black and green, all bearing various kinds of scanning equipment. "Noble *deihu*," the intel officer said, "we beg your pardon, but we—"

"Yes, yes, come in and get it over with," Arrhae said, "so that I can get back to my firstmeal before it grows cold."

They filed in and walked around the room, which soon filled with the hum and buzz of their scan equipment. Arrhae sat down and drank her draft and pointedly ignored them all, fighting not to look as nervous as she felt, while they went into Ffairrl's little galley, all over her suite and into her bathroom, scanning every piece of furniture in the place, and every drawer and cupboard. But the moment she was dreading, the sound of one of their scanners going off as it discovered something suspicious, never came. Finally one of them opened the clothespress and started scanning in there, and when he was finished, even started opening the drawers.

*Now or never.* Arrhae looked over at him, the last one left looking for anything; the rest were gathered together in the middle of the room, comparing readings, plainly having had only negative results. In a voice dripping with lazy scorn, Arrhae said, "If with all your high-priced machinery you have found nothing, I think you may safely leave off pawing through a Senator's intimates, fellow. Unless you and your comrades prefer to find yourselves pawing through something far less attractive, on your account, when we get back home . . ."

The security man, who had been about to open that last drawer, started straight up as if shocked. "Close that up straightway," the intelligence officer said, irritated, "and come along. *Deihu,* a thousand pardons for troubling your morning."

And out they went.

Arrhae sat right where she was for a few seconds, trying to find her composure again. *It not only kept poor Gurrhim from being detected,* she thought, *but it has protected itself from detection as well.*

The small relief did nothing to assuage her greater concern. *Well. If this does not qualify as a great need . . .* For something in her was saying, *Keep that man alive. Whatever you do, keep him alive!*

Arrhae got up, waved the door locked, and went to get the sphere. For the next little while she sat in the bathroom with the door closed, hurriedly speed-reading her way through the holographic projection it produced of its documentation. And by the time the door signal went again, she was ready.

She stuffed the sphere into her breeches pocket and went to answer the door. Tr'AAnikh was standing there, looking somewhat apprehensive.

"*Deihu . . .*" he said.

"Come in," Arrhae said. "And sit down. We must have a talk . . ."

The building in which the Senate kept its administrative offices was only across the Avenue of Processions from the great domed building itself, but even so close, no whisper of the noise of reconstruction came through the plasteel of the window that made up one whole wall. Everything was silent in the small, bare retiring room where the three men now stood. It looked as if it should have echoed, for there was not so much as a stick of furniture in it, and the floor and walls were bare. But every word spoken sounded almost painfully anechoic due to the damping devices in operation. No force known to Rihannsu science could see or hear what was happening in that room . . . which was the way the three men wanted it.

"We should at least get it back."

"There's no *point* in it now, Arhm'n! It's a liability. Trying to save it will only multiply the chances that she'll somehow escape alive. And we cannot permit that now. We have to kill her immediately, while we have the chance."

"I'm not saying *that's* a bad idea. You know how I feel, Urellh! But the Sword—"

"It no longer *matters.* There's far worse to deal with now. If we're concerned about keeping our people in line, well, the Klingons will be giving us more than enough fuel for that fire momentarily. Maybe it's a blessing in disguise; nothing unifies a people like a good war, eh? But whatever happens, if we are not to have Artaleirh, *they* certainly cannot be permitted to have it. The place is going to be destroyed anyway; it makes little odds which of us does it now. No news will come from there to ch'Rihan and ch'Havran that we don't permit to come . . . and after the fact, we can present that news any way we like. But there's time to worry about that later."

"My people in the Fleet will handle it. But the Sword—"

"Let it be *lost,* for Fire's sake, Arhm'n! It's *her* the damned Artaleirhin are after, not what she stole. She is poison, that woman! Kill her now before she becomes some kind of symbol for noble rebellion."

"Before the sickness spreads any further," said the third man. "And the Sword is also likely to be contaminated forever after by its association with her; it will be no more use to us as a symbol. The news of its loss can be managed, too. As that of tr'Siedhri's death, when that finally happens."

"Damn the man, is he unable to cooperate with *anything?* I thought he would have died by now—"

"Still 'critical,'" Urellh said. "Well, he can't last long in *Gorget*'s infirmary; he needs surgical routines with which they're not equipped to provide him. And their master surgeon knows which way the wind is blowing; he'll do nothing heroic. Never mind Farmer Gurri—he's paid for his treason, and he'll soon be mucking out the Elements' stables. As for t'Rllaillieu, Arhm'n, capture and trial are now the wrong way to handle her. She must die immediately, before she can do any more damage."

There was a long silence. Arhm'n looked at tr'Anierh.

"Expediency," tr'Anierh said, "I think, requires this of us now. This unrest is caused—and spread—by uncertainty. The best way to settle the unrest is by providing the rebels and would-be rebels with a certainty they cannot contest: that she is finally gone, forever, beyond any possibility of rescue, exculpation, or pardon. Let us make it unanimous, Arhm'n. In the present circumstances, we three must not be seen to be divided. Too much rests on it."

The silence stretched out.

"Tell them to go ahead with it, then," Arhm'n muttered. He stood watching them taking the scaffolding away from the great dome across the way. "Problems may be multiplying at the moment, but shortly their number will decrease by one . . . one very *large* one."

Sleep forsook Jim early that morning, after only a few hours, and would not come back. The clock was ticking toward Fox's deadline, and the tension ruined his sleep. By the time he had breakfast and got up to the bridge, it was still only seven hours until the meeting at which Ael's status would be clarified, and everything would blow up, one way or another. And there had been no answer from Ael, even though Jim knew she might send none even if she agreed with him. Her concerns about the security of information on her own ship could well be behind the silence.

On the bridge, Mr. Spock was standing at his viewer, looking down it steadily, making delicate adjustments at one side of it, and he did not look up at the sound of the lift doors opening and shutting. Jim went and sat down in the center seat, and when the morning duty yeoman came to him with the order-of-the-day padd, he said softly, "How long has he been at it, Nyarla?"

The tall, dark-haired yeoman glanced over at Spock and said as softly, "At least since I first came in, Captain—three hours and fifty-four minutes ago."

Jim nodded as he looked down the padd and initialed the bottom of it. A Syan had a circadian-based clock in her head as accurate as Spock's, for different reasons, so the phrasing was nothing unusual. But her presence here was. "You're not supposed to be on for a couple of hours yet," Jim said.

She raised her eyebrows. "After I finish budding," she said, "I'm always on edge. Present circumstances . . ."

"Understood," Jim said, and handed her back the stylus and the padd. "Did that go smoothly, by the way?"

"No problems, Captain," Nyarla said. "Except, as usual, the new personality is starting to complain about wanting her own quarters." She put up her eyebrows, looking resigned. "Same as always. 'Twelve's a crowd . . .'"

"Well, let the doctor know if it starts to be a problem."

"I will, sir." She headed for the turbolift. Jim raised his eyebrows, once again making a mental note to ask McCoy exactly how he dealt with a crewmember who budded off a new subsection of her brain, and hence a new personality, every eight months or so. Though probably McCoy would refuse to tell him much, on confidentiality grounds.

Sulu came in as Nyarla went out. He relieved the duty helmsman and started checking out his console. Jim glanced over his shoulder and saw that Scotty's station was empty. "Commander, has Mr. Scott come on duty yet?" he said to Uhura.

"Came in and went out again half an hour ago, Captain," she said. "He's down in engineering with K's't'lk and a couple of his staff, going over some new Sunseed numbers, he said."

Jim nodded. Everything running with the usual efficiency, but a little ahead of schedule. *Everybody else around here is getting as twitchy as I am,* he thought. *It can be a good thing . . . within reason. If the tension gets so great that it starts affecting response times . . .*

Spock straightened up, though he was still looking down at the scanner as if he distrusted what he had been seeing. Jim glanced back at him. "The Romulans still busy with their long-range scanning, Mr. Spock?"

"They are," Spock said. "But that is not my concern at the moment."

"It's not?"

Spock left the science station and came down to stand by the center seat. "The scanning I have been monitoring is of a sort I have not seen in previous encounters with Romulan vessels," he said. "It suggests they may have made some theoretical breakthroughs in their understanding of the nature and structure of subspace, and further analysis will be interesting. I have begun work on such analysis. But while monitoring the scanning activity, I also detected some interesting energy readings from two of the ships, *Pillion* and *Hheirant*."

"Interesting? In what way?"

Spock raised his eyebrows. Jim had seen this expression before; it was that of a Vulcan who cannot admit to annoyance, but is experiencing it nonetheless. "Our own scans seem to be detecting power generation from within both *Pillion* and *Hheirant* considerably in excess of what ships of their size should require either for maximum projected propulsion or for maximum weapons use, or, for that matter, for both together. And if this were not in itself cause enough for interest, I am unable to determine from exactly what system aboard these ships the power in question is being generated, except that it does not appear to be directly associated with their engine rooms."

"Some kind of weapon we haven't been told about?" Jim said.

Spock let out a breath. "Insufficient data," he said. "Our own scans are not proving as efficient as they should, especially considering that we are at such close range. I have recalibrated our scanners twice within the last three hours, with only marginal improvement in the resulting scans."

"And it's nothing to do with *Mascrar* being in the way?"

"No, Captain."

Jim thought for a moment. "Some variant on the cloaking device?"

"That is a theory that had occurred to me, Captain, but the typical waveform signature of the cloaking device we know is missing. That does not, of course, rule out the possibility that a new one has been developed, and there are some waveforms presenting in the scans from *Pillion* and *Hheirant* that I do not recognize, but there is as yet no evidence to support the conjecture that they are associated with new cloaking technology. They could, for example, be parasitic on the ships' communications systems. But unless I can improve the quality of our own scanning, there is no way either to confirm this or to rule it out."

Jim's attention went to the main viewscreen. He could just catch sight of one of *Gorget*'s long, swept-back nacelles below the curve of *Mascrar.* "There's a lot of new technology out there," he said. "Some of it has plainly been brought to impress us."

"But what I am picking up is not associated with the newer ships, Captain. *Pillion* and *Hheirant* are two of the older *K'tinga*-class models."

"Well, stay on it, Mr. Spock. I'll be interested to see what you find."

Spock nodded and went back up to his science station. The turbolift doors opened, and McCoy came ambling in. "I don't suppose," he said, "that anything's happened to make them have that meeting early."

"What do *you* think?" Jim said.

"Well, hope springs eternal . . ."

"Oh, Doctor," Uhura said, "while you're here—a message just came in for you from *Speedwell,* from the ambassador's office."

"For me?" McCoy said. "What the heck do they want from me?"

"It's nothing they want *from* you. They have something *for* you. A package. It came over from *Gorget,* apparently, with this morning's documents exchange."

Jim looked at McCoy, wondering. McCoy raised his eyebrows. "Did they scan it? Do they have any idea what it is?"

"The ambassador's assistant says it checks clean for explosives or other dangerous devices. He says it's a bottle."

McCoy smiled slightly. "Ale, I bet," he said. "Shows you what the explosives scan's worth. Ask them to beam it over, would you?"

"They'll be doing that shortly."

"Fine, I'll go on down and get it."

Uhura chuckled then. "My, we're busy this morning. Captain, I have Commodore Danilov waiting for you, scrambled."

"Put him on," Jim said.

The screen flickered, and there was Danilov, looking pleased. *"Jim,"* he said, *"I wanted to thank you again for that message you sent."*

"No need, Commodore," Jim said, rather surprised.

"*I disagree,*" Danilov said. "*We just got in a message from one of the Zone monitoring stations. Long-range scan shows that a number of Romulan vessels that were patrolling the other side of the Neutral Zone near here have pulled out.*"

*So Fox was right,* Jim thought. *They're starting to blink.*

*Or so it seems.*

"*There's something else you should know about,*" Danilov said. "*Apparently things are breaking apart somewhat among the Romulan negotiation team. One of the Praetors, Gurrhim tr'Siedhri, is in the infirmary aboard* Gorget, *subsequent to an assassination attempt.*"

"Good Lord," Jim said. "How is he?"

"*No details,*" Danilov said. "*Fox thinks this is symptomatic of a serious split among the senior negotiators. We'll see what happens at the meeting later.*"

"Have we heard back from Earth yet about Ael?" Jim said.

"*We have,*" Danilov said. "*Later, Jim.* Speedwell *out.*"

The screen flicked back to its view of *Mascrar* and the other vessels orbiting on this side with *Enterprise.* Jim sat back in the center seat and let out a breath of exasperation. *I am* not *cut out for this diplomatic work,* he thought.

Nonetheless, he settled in to wait.

Half an hour or so later, McCoy was leaning against the console in transporter room two, trying to control his impatience and failing. "What's *keepin'* those people?" he said.

"Something to do with the assassination attempt aboard *Gorget,*" said the transporter chief. "None of the diplomatic people are where they'd usually be. The transporter chief over on *Speedwell* says she sent most of the ambassador's people over to *Mascrar.* The rest could have used another transporter."

"Typical," McCoy muttered. He reached out to the comm button, hit it. "*Speedwell,* this is McCoy aboard *Enterprise.* Can somebody please track down this package or bottle or whatever it is that the ambassador's office is holding for me? I have other things to do today . . ."

"*Hold on a moment, Doctor,*" said a somewhat bored male voice. Then another voice, a female one, said, *"Chief Perelli, shuttle bay. We've got a kind of long box here. It's annotated as 'bottle' on the docs manifest the courier brought over this morning."*

"That's sounds like what we're after. Would you run it up here?"

*"Sure thing. Sorry for the delay, Doctor. This is medicinal, right?"*

McCoy grinned. "If you get a chance to come over here, I'll let you see *how* medicinal."

A few minutes later there was a sparkle on one of the frontmost transporter pads, and a box wrapped in silvery prismatic plastic appeared. "Thanks, Chief," McCoy said, going over to pick it up.

"Hey, don't *I* get any?"

"Come see me when you're off duty. You're due for your multipox inoculation anyway; you can have that at the same time."

"Uh . . . thanks."

McCoy chuckled as he made his way out of the transporter room and back to sickbay. Slender, curly-haired Lia Burke, the head nurse, met McCoy going out as he came in, and glanced at what he was holding. "Oh, you got your bottle, finally."

"Yes. And you can't have any."

"Hmph."

"While on duty," McCoy added belatedly as the door closed behind her. He went to his desk and picked up a phaser scalpel lying there, and started to use it delicately on the end of the package. The wrapping shriveled away, revealing a prosaic box. He upended it, looking for the opening. He found the seal and ran a thumbnail along it.

The side of the box opened up. Inside there was something silky and black, with a faint touch of fragrance about it, a warmly herbal scent. McCoy looked at it with a moment's affection, but the warmth suddenly faded as he considered what this might mean.

He pulled the long, diaphanous scarf out of the box from around the bottle for which it had been used as wrapping, and ran it quickly through his hands. There was nothing hidden in the seams this time. But it was a message nonetheless.

McCoy picked up his medical scanner from the instrument tray nearby and ran it down the length of the scarf, just to make sure. Nothing.

Then he reached into the box and pulled out the bottle. The ale in it was unusually blue, the sign of a good "vintage," at least a couple of weeks old. More, it had that slight cloudiness of *really* good Romulan ale, an indication that all the fruit solids hadn't been filtered out of it. *Also,* McCoy thought, as he ran the scanner over the bottle, *it makes it that much harder to see anything that might be inside.*

The medical scanner chirruped twice, the alert sound it made when it found embedded data content in a sample but couldn't immediately read it.

McCoy's eyes widened. He took himself and the bottle out of sickbay in a hurry, heading for the bridge.

Spock was still staring down his scanner. Jim was wondering if this wasn't beginning to get a little obsessive. Still, there had been enough times before when Spock had focused on a problem until he wore himself thin, and his persistence had wound up being the only thing that saved *Enterprise* and everyone in her—one more aspect of her charmed life, too easily overlooked when outsiders examined the legend. Jim sat back and sighed. "Uhura—" he said.

"Another hour yet till the meeting, Captain." She sighed too.

He had to smile. "Spock," he said, "find anything worthwhile yet?"

Spock shook his head without looking up from the scanner. "Their long-range scans continue. Over the past twenty minutes I have seen that odd waveform again in several brief bursts, each several seconds long, from what seem to be two different sources associated with *Pillion* and *Hheirant.* But then the traces faded out entirely. I am at a loss to understand it. I begin to wonder whether I am detecting some sort of malfunction, except that—"

The turbolift doors opened. "Mr. Spock! Here! Quick!"

Jim turned around, surprised to hear McCoy so out of breath. Spock had looked up from his scanning with a rather severe expression, for McCoy was standing there next to him, holding a bottle of something blue. "Doctor," Spock said, "this is hardly the time or the place—"

"Spock," McCoy growled, "I've always thought you needed a humoroplasty, but by God as soon as I have two seconds to rub together,

I'm going to change your surgery status from elective to required." He
shoved the bottle at Spock. "Now in the name of everything that's holy,
scan this thing and find out what it *says!*"

Nonplussed, Spock took the bottle and looked it over, then sat it on
his science console and touched several controls. He put up one eyebrow.
"There is a picochip attached under the stopper," Spock said, and hurriedly touched several more controls in sequence. "Reading now . . ."

The screen nearest his station filled with gibberish, which then
started to resolve itself.

He stared at it, then turned toward the center seat. "It is from Lieutenant Commander Haleakala-LoBrutto," Spock said. "She reports that
the Romulans intend to attack and destroy *Bloodwing* immediately on
her return to the system—"

"Warp ingress, Captain," Sulu said urgently. "Two vessels going subluminal, ten light-seconds out."

"Uhura, copy that message to *Speedwell* and the other ships right away!"
Jim said. "Mr. Sulu, take us out toward the ingress point, full impulse. Put
it on screen. Mr. Chekov, ready phasers and photon torpedoes."

"Enterprise," Danilov's voice said over the comm link, *"where do you
think you're going? Hold your position—"*

"Read your mail, Dan!" Jim said. "Mr. Chekov—"

"Phasers ready, Captain. Photon torpedoes loading."

"Mr. Sulu, what are the Romulans doing?"

"Nothing, Captain. Holding position. No evidence of weapons activity."

"There is more to the lieutenant commander's message, Captain,"
Spock said. "She warns of an imminent clandestine attack of a major
and devastating nature on Federation space."

"Mr. Chekov, raise shields." But Jim's attention was distracted by an
alarm indicator that suddenly began to flash at Sulu's position at the
helm console. Sulu, busy with taking *Enterprise* away from *Mascrar* and
the rest of the Federation task force without immediately exposing her
to the Romulans on the other side of the habitat, glanced at it and said,
"Intruder alert, Captain!"

The intercom whistled. *"Bridge,"* Scotty's voice said, *"we've got someone beaming aboard from one of the other ships. The transport signature's Romulan!"*

"Shields!"

"Up now, Captain."

*Too late,* Jim thought. "Scotty, where's the intruder beaming to?"

*"Transporter room two."*

"Seal that deck off. Get a security detail down there on the double." He gripped the arms of the center seat, resisting the urge to jump up and see what the hell was going on. "Mr. Sulu, are we secure now?"

"Yes, Captain. Heading for the ingress point. Two ships coming in, decelerating from warp, down to about point two *c* now."

On screen, with magnification, you could just see them, two sparks coasting inward in RV Trianguli's hot blue light. "Uhura," Jim said, "send to both ships. *Ortisei, Bloodwing,* break away, you are about to come under attack!"

"Enterprise," came another voice. It was the city manager from *Mascrar,* sounding rather alarmed. *"You are not scheduled to leave formation at this time, and your movements and signals may be misconstrued—"*

"Captain, I am picking up impulse engine activity out there," Chekov said, working over his console. "But all ships in the system are in position and accounted for, none of them can be producing it!"

"The new waveform I detected earlier is associated with the impulse engine readings," Spock said suddenly. "I believe your conjecture was correct, Captain. The source of the readings is accelerating toward *Ortisei* and *Bloodwing.* But there is still a peculiarity." Spock stared down his scanner, manipulating it. "I cannot tell whether it is one impulse engine or two. It is ghosting, phasing in and out."

"Mr. Chekov, lock weapons on that impulse engine reading and prepare to fire. Try to refine the scan, though! Mr. Sulu—"

*"Enterprise, I warn you, if you open fire, we will act to enforce the neutrality of the space around us!"*

*"Mascrar,* scan ahead of us, it's not *our* fire you need to be worrying about! What about that impulse engine, attached to a ship that we can't see? Sulu, position!"

"Four light-seconds out at bearing one one five mark six, Captain. Closing on *Ortisei* and *Bloodwing*."

"Oh, my God," McCoy said softly. "This is it."

"*Security to Captain Kirk,*" a voice said. "*Lieutenant Harmon here.*"

"Report!" Jim said.

"*Three Romulans have beamed aboard, Captain,*" said Harmon. "*All male. All three are wounded, two severely. Those two are unconscious. The conscious one is asking specifically for Dr. McCoy.*"

"Get them straight down to sickbay," McCoy said. "I'll meet you there. Uhura, page Dr. M'Benga and have him report there immediately. Sickbay, Burke!"

"*Burke here, Doctor.*"

"Incoming wounded. Romulan. Break out the Vulcaniform trauma packs. You're going to have a security team in there in about three minutes, and I'll be there in about five. Triage the wounded, stabilize them, and activate scrub fields as necessary." And he was gone.

Jim turned his attention back to the screen. There was nothing to be seen out in the starry darkness but *Bloodwing* and *Ortisei,* coasting in. "The other Federation vessels are going to alert status," Chekov said. "Shields going up. Romulan vessels are doing the same. Their weapons systems are heating up—"

*And when the host on both parties saw that sword drawn* . . . But if the sword was *not* drawn, lives were going to be lost. He knew it. "*Ortisei!*" Jim said. "Afterburner, can you see the impulse reading approaching you? Fire at it, it's going to attack!"

"*Bloodwing* is breaking away," Sulu said. "The vessel running on impulse is changing course to intercept."

"Both *Ortisei* and *Bloodwing* have raised shields," Chekov said. "Weapons systems aboard *Bloodwing* coming on line—"

"*Enterprise, I have orders not to fire unless fired upon,*" Gutierrez's voice came back. "*You have the same orders, Jim. I can see a faint impulse track, all right, but there's no sign of any cloaking device in use—*"

"I am a fool," Spock said.

The statement was so bald and so flat that even in these circumstances, Jim had to glance over at Spock in astonishment. "What?"

"I have misread data which has been in front of me for many hours," Spock said, his voice tight. "The name *Pillion*, Captain! It is not just a name. It could be taken for such, for the Romulans often name ships after the accoutrements of an armed warrior: *Gorget, Helm,* and so on. A pillion is a saddle. But it is also an extra pad fastened behind a regular saddle so that another rider can use the same conveyance. To ride pillion is to ride two on a mount."

Jim's eyes widened. "Oh, my God," he said, turning back to the screen.

"The impulse signature is changing," Sulu said. "Two signatures, Captain, not one. One heading toward *Ortisei* now!"

"*Pillion* has been carrying at least one second vessel, which remained cloaked even though the primary one was uncloaked and visible," Spock said. "They must have achieved a major breakthrough in the design of the cloaking device to be able to produce such an effect, especially one that would withstand visual and scan inspection at such close range. That is the vessel responsible for the attack we have just seen."

Jim swallowed. This information alone qualified as one of the triggers that would activate his sealed orders, but he had little time to spare for that issue now. *Ortisei* and *Bloodwing* were getting closer. "The impulse sources continue to accelerate," Chekov said. "One is now within conventional phaser range of *Ortisei*. Captain, shall I fire?"

He stared at the screen. It had never occurred to him that the sword to be drawn would be in *his* hand. He opened his mouth to tell Chekov to fire.

In the space between *Ortisei* and *Bloodwing,* the stars suddenly began to shimmer.

And *Bloodwing,* as she curved away, fired her phasers, nearly point-blank, right at *Ortisei.*

Between the two of them, where space had been shimmering, only one spread of torpedoes had time to come blasting out from the little half-decloaked ship before it blossomed into a tremendous explosion. *Bloodwing* twisted and arced away from the explosion and the remaining torpedoes, and on the other side, *Ortisei,* having just begun an evasive maneuver, shuddered and sideslipped as the force of the explosion hit her shields.

And everything started to happen at once. All the Romulan ships but *Gorget* left their positions on the far side of *Mascrar* and started to move with increasing speed toward *Bloodwing*. *Bloodwing,* recovering from her evasive maneuvers, threw herself straight at the Romulan vessels, firing.

"Captain!" Chekov said. "The torpedoes that the cloaked vessel launched—*they're coming back!*"

"Evasive," Jim said.

"They appear to be tracking *Bloodwing,*" Spock said. "Difficult to determine whether they are targeting the ship's ID, or just her engine type."

*Bloodwing* streaked past *Ortisei,* which was drifting now, a terrible flickering running up and down her starboard nacelle. The torpedoes followed, and the Romulan vessels, seeing her coming, scattered . . .

. . . but not fast enough. One torpedo, its tracking computers possibly confused by all the other Romulan engines in the area or deranged by the explosion of the originating vessel when it first fired, slammed into *Thraiset,* whose shields flared into a globe of fire and then collapsed. A second torpedo coming right behind the first one hit *Thraiset* amidships, and the ship instantly bloomed into a white fury of fire as its antimatter catastrophically annihilated.

*"Brace for impact!"* Jim yelled. Even with shields up, *Enterprise* rocked and plunged as the shock wave from the matter-antimatter annihilation hit her. The lights wavered and the artificial gravity flickered once or twice, but not severely enough to throw people around. "Damage report!"

Spock was reading his console. "Reports coming in from decks six, eight, nine, forward," he said. "Some injuries, no major structural damage. Shields down to sixty percent, they will take some time to recharge—"

Jim's heart was pounding. It was a captain's worst nightmare, everything happening at once, no way and no time to limit the damage. *Ortisei* was still drifting, the discharge-flicker around her nacelle gone now. *"Ortisei* is evacuating her crew to *Mascrar,"* Uhura said. "Matter-antimatter containment is holding, but they're not taking any chances."

That at least was some consolation. "Mr. Sulu, go after those torpedoes," Jim said, "before this whole part of space turns into a free-fire zone! Mr. Chekov, phasers!"

"Ready, Captain," Chekov said. But past *Ortisei,* Jim could see *Saheh'lill* and *Greave* curving around again past *Mascrar,* firing at *Bloodwing* as she passed . . .

. . . and *Saheh'lill*'s phasers hit *Speedwell. Speedwell*'s shields took the fire and held. She flung herself away from the Romulan vessel, forbearing to fire even though orders would have permitted it. *Saheh'lill* curved back toward *Mascrar,* low over the city's surface, very low, still firing, trying to reach *Bloodwing* while she was at close range.

A terrible lance of fire suddenly blasted out from *Mascrar* and struck *Saheh'lill* full on. The Romulan ship simply vanished in it, together with its explosion, its only remnant a long lingering streak of excited ions in the space through which the beam had struck.

Sulu threw *Enterprise* past *Mascrar* in *Bloodwing*'s wake, and the view on the main screen gyred and pinwheeled wildly as Sulu rolled the ship hard on her longitudinal axis, and then up and over in a variant of the ancient Immelmann. Chekov pounced on his console, and then did it again, and two of the torpedoes following *Bloodwing* blew up, small bright clouds of expanding fire in the night. But another one, corkscrewing in pursuit as she did, missed *Bloodwing* as she suddenly straightened and ran straight at *Greave,* firing. *Hheirant,* now plunging away from *Mascrar* and toward *Enterprise,* took the torpedo on her shields. They flickered, went down; she started losing acceleration, limped away.

"How many of those things left?" Jim said.

"Two, Captain. Still tracking *Bloodwing.* She's coming around tight to try to deal with them."

Close by, *Sempach* was closing with the damaged *Hheirant.* "*Hheirant,*" Jim heard the comms officer aboard *Sempach* hailing them, "do you have casualties, can we assist—"

*Hheirant* fired on *Sempach.*

The flagship took the fire on her shields. A long moment's pause . . .

*Pillion* dived in from the other side and began to fire on *Sempach* as well, while *Hheirant* continued firing.

*Sempach* yawed hard forward, quickly as a coin being flipped, and her phasers lanced out repeatedly at *Pillion* en passant. *Pillion*'s shields went down under the onslaught, and after a moment she broke off attack and fled out of range. *Hheirant,* though, could not do the same, and as the phasers raked her, she blew.

Once again *Enterprise* and the other ships shuddered and wallowed in the shockwave of the detonation. It passed, and people let go of whatever they had been using to brace themselves and stared at the screen.

*Gorget* was fleeing, plunging away from RV Trianguli out into the darkness; she cloaked herself and vanished. *Pillion* streaked off in her wake and a second later was also gone.

*Bloodwing* went after, vanishing as well.

The bridge went very quiet.

"They are all headed toward the Neutral Zone," Spock said. "Projected courses appear to indicate the first two vessels are headed for the Eisn system."

"Back to ch'Rihan," Jim said softly. "So much for diplomacy. Status of the other ships?"

"*Sempach* has some structural damage, but it does not seem severe. *Ortisei* has no power and has lost pressure in much of her secondary hull; she has been almost entirely evacuated except for a skeleton engineering crew who are trying to stabilize her warp core. *Lake Champlain* is nowhere to be found, though a debris cloud nearby strongly implies that she was destroyed during the engagement. *Hemalat*'s primary hull seems to have taken a hit from a torpedo; she has no warp capacity. Estimated time of repair thirty-six hours. *Nimrod* is not reporting, probably due to communications problems—her readings are otherwise normal. *Speedwell* is reporting that her shield generators took damage during the attack, and shields cannot be raised."

"Enterprise!"

It was Danilov's voice. "On screen," Jim said.

Danilov was sitting there in a bridge full of smoke, flickering fire, and outcries. *"Captain Kirk,"* he said, *"you are ordered to pursue* Bloodwing *and bring her back to Federation space."*

"That may prove difficult, Commodore."

"Do *it,"* Danilov said. *"You know what you stand to lose if you don't."*

Jim had a pretty good idea. "One thing, Commodore. What is the Federation's stance as regards the commander's request for asylum?"

*"They granted it."*

Jim raised his eyebrows. "Probably just as well we never had a chance to tell the Romulans so," he said. "A fight could have broken out."

Danilov looked grim.

"As regards *Bloodwing,* Commodore," Jim said, "what if her commander declines to cooperate?"

*"Then you are to return to RV Trianguli immediately for debriefing and reassignment."*

There were about thirty things that could mean. "Yes, sir," Jim said.

*"You are to state that you understand my orders and will comply with them fully and without reservation."*

The silence got long. Then Jim turned around to look at Uhura. "What happened to the signal, Commander?" he said.

They exchanged a long look. After a second, she glanced down at her console. She didn't do anything that Jim could see, but she said, "We seem to have lost it, Captain."

When she looked up at him again, her expression was too neutral to read.

"Thank you, Uhura," Jim said. "That will be all for the moment." He turned away, looking at Spock.

"Captain . . ." Spock said.

"Mr. Spock," Jim said, "I will want to see you in my quarters briefly in about half an hour. Mr. Sulu, set a course matching *Bloodwing*'s. Pursue her, at warp eight. If you need more speed to catch her, use it. Estimated time to intercept?"

"Twenty minutes, Captain, if we're on the right course. She may have altered."

"Make that an hour from now in my quarters, Mr. Spock. Uhura, hail her, and at the very least get a course update from her if she's not willing to decloak. Sickbay!"

Sickbay had been in turmoil when McCoy got there. The place was full of security personnel who were holding phasers on three people, all on diagnostic beds now. Lia was working busily over one of the two prone forms, getting the scrub field set over him. Another nurse, big, broad-shouldered, mustached Tom Krejci, was tending to the second patient, a young man sitting up in bed and holding a sterile pad over a disruptor wound on his head. *Only a graze,* McCoy thought, for anything better targeted would have burst the young man's head like a rock dropped on a melon. "Put those things down," McCoy said to the security people, "I know this boy, this is tr'AAnikh. He's all right. Tom, what did you give him?"

"Ten mils of orienthrin for the shock, and fifty mikes of entrivate-B for pain relief."

"Give him another five of orienthrin, to be on the safe side." McCoy lifted the sterile pad, looked quickly under it. "Then get busy regenerating that; shouldn't take you more than five minutes. Make sure you keep that protoplaser set below three—Romulan dermal perfusion's a little more leisurely than ours."

"Right, Doctor."

"Okay, son," McCoy said to tr'AAnikh, replacing the sterile pad, "you just hold that there a couple minutes more. Here, have some ale."

Tr'AAnikh sat looking in astonishment at the bottle McCoy had shoved at him as the doctor moved over past the second diagnostic bed. The figure lying there was half draped under a silvery heatcon blanket. Without turning away from the sterile field she was working under, Lia said, "I'm sorry, Doctor. He was already gone when they brought him in. Massive internal disruptor injuries."

McCoy nodded, pulled the blanket up to cover the face, then turned to look over Lia's shoulder at the occupant of the third bed. "He'll be ready for you in about two minutes," she said, her attention focused on the hologram of the patient's organs that had formed under the sterile field cowl. "Nearly stable enough to start work. Dr. M'Benga's on his way."

"Good." McCoy pulled off his duty tunic, chucked it into a nearby clean-or-recycle chute and turned back to the diagnostic bed where tr'AAnikh was sitting. "How'd you get over here in the first place?" McCoy asked, taking the high-sleeved surgical tunic that Krejci handed him and pulling it on. "I don't imagine they let you just waltz in and beam out of there without any authorization."

"The Senator helped us," tr'AAnikh said. "Senator Arrhae i-Khellian. She gave us a device that let us get to the infirmary on *Gorget* and get the Praetor out without the alarm being raised. Then Hhil and I went to the transporter room with the Praetor. The guards there tried to stop us . . ." He looked sorrowfully at the blanket-shrouded form on the next bed.

"They failed," McCoy said, hurriedly sealing up the surgical tunic, "and I suspect that's going to be worth something shortly. But I'm truly sorry about your friend."

"He knew this might happen, and he was prepared for it," tr'AAnikh said. "He and I both wanted to help the commander, and the captain . . . and the Senator said this was the best way to do it."

"I hope she's right," McCoy said. "You lie back and rest now." He turned back to Burke. "Lia, is he ready?"

"All set, Doctor. Recorders are running. Field's on invasive visual."

"Right. What have we got?"

Under the sterile field's archlike canopy, and over the patient's ravaged chest, a holographic representation of the contents now superimposed itself, the tissues of the various organs and systems differentiated by shade and intensity of color. Shadowy forms of organs missing or damaged overlaid themselves on the originals. Right now the respiratory and cardiac systems were outlined and highlighted in strident red, indicating both massive trauma and failure status, and showing some big initial forcefield bypasses that Burke had installed to keep the vascular flow going around the patient's heart. "Extensive dorsal supradermal and infradermal burns," Burke said. "I've been infusing adjusted saline by inguinal veinpak to compensate. Extensive crenation of superficial muscular and fascial tissue secondary to disruptor damage. I've debrided the blasted tissue, saved some noncrenated tissue for cloning— it's in the hopper now and first divisions are ongoing. The rest can wait. A lot of intestinal damage, but nothing serious once he's stable. No major bleeding, and I stopped the leakage from the mesentery. The big problem's the heart, as you can see. Someone over there's a good shot."

"Too damn good," McCoy said, looking at the holographic image of the heart. It was a mess, already once partially exploded by disruptor fire, and roughly patched by the Romulan surgeons—they had merely butted the tears in the ventricles together with mechanical crimps and sealed them with inorganic adhesives, and the patching was rapidly coming undone without any replacement connective tissue to keep it in place. *Give them the benefit of the doubt—they may have planned surgery later.* But now the heart had a new set of tears in it from the attack that had just happened. *So. Save or replace?* "Mmm. Primary-degree disruption involvement to upper simulpericardium, anterior atrium, superior diaphragmatic stosis, secondary-degree damage to centricardium, upper right ventricle, upper left ventricle, medial upper ventricular septum." *And look at it, they left all this exploded cellular material in place at the edges. That would never have healed. I know they can do better than this! Did someone over there not want him to survive? Well, tough luck.*

"The AV and periHV rhythms in the heart muscle have gone sporadic," Burke said. "They're full of transient conduction spikes due to enzyme flooding, and the new tears are pulling the old ones open. It won't hold long; it's going to rip itself apart again, if it doesn't stop first."

"Damn," McCoy said softly. "Patching this is going to be a nightmare. Still, we can't risk an artificial heart under the circumstances." Especially since, if things got lively out there and the ship lost power while maneuvering, a heart made of nothing but forcefields would do the Praetor no good at all. "Let's rebuild this on the double, and get a spare growing." McCoy poked a spot with the guide protoplaser. "There's the AV node. Lia, harvest me some tissue from there. And for God's sake don't let it stop contracting! I don't want to have to waste time jump-starting it later—"

From the nearby instrument tray, Burke picked up what McCoy routinely referred to as the "magic wand," a foot-long chromed instrument that liaised with the pattern buffer of the surgical transporter under the diagnostic bed. She slipped the wand into the hologram, focused the harvesting field into it in the form of a little sphere of yellow light, used the control on the side of the wand to enlarge the sphere a little, then tightened the sphere's volume down again. "That enough?"

"Hell, take the whole thing. It's not doing him any good at the moment."

The sphere sparkled with transporter effect and vanished, taking the tissue with it into the waiting container of growth medium. "Tom?" Burke said.

"I'll take care of it."

*"Sickbay!"* said Jim's voice out of the air.

"McCoy here."

*"Report, Bones."*

*She's right, it won't hold,* McCoy thought as he spotted the aneurysm forming in the equivalent to the vena cava, swelling out and out like a blown balloon. *Oh no, you don't!* Sweat burst out on his forehead as he grabbed the "guide" protoplaser that Lia handed him, set it for "vascular" and "designate," and swiftly traced a glowing path through the hologram from about two centimeters above the aneurysm to about three centimeters below it. The surgical support system built into the sterile field cowl immediately emplaced a small tubular forcefield into that spot inside the patient, and "marked" it in glowing red for reference. Just as the forcefield patch snugged down and mated to the vessel at the cellular level, the aneurysm blew like a badly patched tire, dark green blood flooding the forcefield segment and turning it brown-black. *Lord, that was close.*

He swallowed, his mouth briefly too dry to speak. "Three people down here, Jim. One dead. One alive and known to me, not seriously injured. One in pretty bad shape—that's the Praetor, Jim. Big hole in his gut. Heart's all ripped up. But we're in luck," McCoy added, glancing at one of the readouts in the visualization hologram. "He's a pretty regulation T-positive. I was wondering whether some fraction changes had crept into Romulan serology over time, but it seems not . . ."

*"Aren't the T-types rare?"* Jim said.

The door hissed as M'Benga came hurrying in, took in the scene at a glance, and immediately started pulling off his duty tunic. "Relatively speaking," McCoy said. "But we'll be okay for a while. I have enough synthetic cuproplasm from the reserve stock we keep down here for Mr. Spock to keep Gurrhim's plasma balance acceptable, while we clone the extra fractions needed from the samples Ambassador Sarek left us. M'Benga, you sterile?"

"Five seconds more."

"Good. I'm playing Little Dutch Boy here at the moment, and there are better things for me to be doing. Come reroute these damn bleeders before one of them blows sky high the way the cava just tried to. Every vessel in here's been weakened by the disruptor blast, and we're going to have to fuse in physical replacements for all the majors in the next five minutes." M'Benga slipped in opposite him across their patient, next to Burke. "I want you to 'plast the ones I'm force-patching just as soon as I finish each one.

"Spock, would you be willing to go on marrow stimulants for a couple of days if we need some more whole blood?"

*"Certainly, Doctor."*

"Good. Stop in and see me later. I've got my hands full right now . . ." He slapped the guide protoplaser into Dr. M'Benga's outstretched hand, picked up another one, and started patching another major vein. "Lia, get me eight pieces of ten-by-ten idioplast and slot them into the transporter pad for Dr. M'Benga's protoplaser, and after that, prep eight more. Then stick two units of cuproplasm into the patient to start with, and prepare three more; he's exsanguinating like mad. And beam out that serosanguinous fluid in the peritoneum before he drowns in it!"

"Right. *Tom?*"

"Got it. Our other patient's okay, I'll circulate. Here's the cuproplasm. The AV's cloning."

"What did they do to this man besides shoot him?" M'Benga said softly, starting to patch another of the bursting major coronary vessels.

"Precious little," McCoy muttered. "Which may have been their intention. Because, good God, man, I would have thought those people's medicine was a little more sophisticated than *this*. Look at those burns. Is laser cautery and autografting the best they can do? Got to do something about that after we tend to the major organs. Lia, there's another leak in here, he's losing what blood pressure he has, *hurry up!*"

"Plasm's running, Doctor—"

"Start another, and *find that leak!*"

*"Bones,"* Jim's voice said, *"will he live?"*

"Maybe. Depends on him. I'll let you know. But meanwhile we should be grateful that whoever tried to kill him was in so much of a hurry. Now let me get on with this!" McCoy finished patching another of the vessels attached to the heart.

"That's the other three big vessels idioplasted," M'Benga said. "The fuse is good and tight. Want me to 'plast that one?"

"Yes, and then start regenerating the nerves while I re-butt those tears in the ventricle and weld them," McCoy said, using the protoplaser to mark two torn pieces of tissue and touching the control that would make the pressor function in the manipulation field pull them together. In the holographic image they met, and he drew the protoplaser down the juncture. Granular scar tissue grew and spread between them in its wake, welding them together. "Then start resealing the simulperi-cardium. We've got to get this thing going again real quick."

M'Benga was silent for a moment, then swore under his breath. "The nerves aren't responding."

"Goddam alien myelin! Never mind, right now we'll concentrate on the mechanical aspects." He started sealing another tear in the upper left ventricle. "Will you look at the thickness of this heart muscle? Let's hope it's diagnostic of more kinds of strength than one, because it'd be real annoying to lose this man in post-op. Meanwhile, if we patch it right, it may actually hold. Tom, *let's go, we need more idioplast here!*"

"*Bloodwing*'s responded, Captain," Uhura said. "But just with her course. Mr. Sulu has it now."

"She's accelerated to warp nine, Captain," Sulu said. "Heading deep into Romulan space—what we would call the neighborhood of 450 Arietis."

Jim shook his head. "Well, don't lose her, Mr. Sulu. Match it."

"*We may ha' no choice but to lose her after a while,*" Scotty said from engi-neering. "*We canna maintain warp nine for long.*"

"Warp ten now, Captain," Sulu said, shaking his head. "Sir, she shouldn't be capable—"

*She sure wasn't at 15 Tri,* Jim thought. "*Bloodwing!*"

No reply.

"*Bloodwing,* reply!"

Nothing.

Jim's face set hard. "Mr. Spock—"

"Enterprise," Ael's voice said, "*apologies for the delay. We had a technical problem. Are you intact?*"

"Yes. But others aren't. Ael, where the hell are you going?"

"*Not to ch'Rihan, if that is what you thought,*" Ael said. "*I have no interest in chasing* Gorget *and* Pillion *just now, though I confess to interest in the new technology* Pillion *used to attack us. But for now we can safely let them go. Those who attacked us have paid the price. Meanwhile, I have an urgent appointment in the Artaleirh system. What I must know is, are you coming?*"

"You'd better believe it," Jim said. "I am not letting you out of my sight. And when you finish whatever it is you have in mind at Artaleirh, you are coming back to Federation space with me . . . or else."

"*When we are done at Artaleirh, Captain, I will gladly come back with you, if you still insist. And if, by that point, Starfleet does. But for the next sixteen hours, which is the time it will take us to get there at this speed, let us allow the matter to rest. We have trouble enough ahead of us.*"

"Which is another thing. Scotty, can we *do* sixteen hours at this speed?"

Scotty sounded annoyed. "*With adequate warning, aye. And with constant attention. But we'll suffer some failures and burnouts as a result, and we'll need downtime afterwards, a couple of days' worth for sure. And are we expected to fight when we get wherever we're going?*"

"*Of a certainty,*" Ael said calmly. "*There are nine Grand Fleet vessels meeting us there. None of them, I think, are expecting* Enterprise, *but when they see* Bloodwing, *they will certainly be intent on destroying it, and I feel sure they will try to extend the courtesy to you as well.*"

Scotty was muttering under his breath. Jim could hardly blame him. "I take it, though," Jim said, "that you're expecting help of some kind."

"*Yes,*" Ael said. "*This will be a major engagement, and if conducted properly, it may much shorten this war. I rejoice that you will be present, for your appearance will give the Rihannsu fleet as much pause as the presence of all the other ships that will be arrayed against them.*"

It was flattery of the most outrageous kind. Still, flattery had to contain a kernel of truth in order to work at all. Jim smiled through the anger . . . just a little. "And another thing," Jim said. "Since when can *Bloodwing* maintain this kind of speed? What the devil have you done to your engines?"

*"Well,"* Ael said, *"since we left home space, Master Engineer tr'Keirianh has been experimenting with a propulsion concept our people came up with a while ago. Grand Fleet had abandoned it as too dangerous an idea and sent it back to the researchers for more work. But you know how engineers are, once a better way of doing something is suggested to them. Tr'Keirianh simply could not let it be, and eventually he found a way to make it work. If one creates a small local singularity and connects it to the warp engines—"*

"Oh, no," Jim said softly, and rubbed his forehead gently, where the headache was already starting. Practically in unison with him, *"Oh, no!"* Scotty said, from down in engineering.

*"Why?"* Ael said. *"Have your people had problems with such a thing? It certainly is somewhat experimental, and it will take a good while yet to work all the bugs out of it. The singularity has a tendency to fail without warning. But K's't'lk said—"*

"Uh-oh," Jim said. *Bugs indeed!*

*"What's the matter? K's't'lk says that the design is one which her people have been using for some years. She had a look at what tr'Keirianh had done and changed a couple of connections in his basic design, but that was all."*

*"He would have worked it out in a month or so anyway, at the rate he was going,"* K's't'lk said, from down in engineering. *"All I had to do was show him the equivalent system in my own ship. He sorted out the details very quickly."*

"Ael," Jim said, "why didn't you tell me you had this?"

*"Because for a good while it refused to work except intermittently,"* Ael said. *"When we tried to use it at 15 Trianguli, it failed us when we greatly needed it. But today, at least, it is working. How much better it might work yet remains to be seen. Theoretically it could be pushed as high as warp thirteen. Maybe even more. For the meantime, though, we will hold it at nine, so that you can keep up."*

Jim raised his eyebrows. "Nice of you, Commander. I have a few things to deal with here. Would you excuse me for a little while?"

*"Certainly, Captain. Bloodwing out."*

He stood up from the center seat and rubbed his face for a moment. "Mr. Sulu," he said, "if she does anything sudden, I want to know immediately."

"Yes, sir."

He turned to look at Spock. Spock was bent over his scanner again. "Spock," Jim said, "what is it now?"

"Captain, I am once again picking up that peculiar waveform we detected earlier."

"*What?* Don't tell me another cloaked Romulan ship is on our tail."

Spock straightened, looking surprised. "Not at all, Captain. The waveform is presently coming from sickbay."

Jim's eyes widened, and he headed straight for the turbolift. "Mr. Sulu, you have the conn. Come on, Spock, let's see what gives. Then you and I need to go down to my quarters."

An hour later they were still there, and Jim was just putting a data solid away in the little safe near his desk. Spock stood to one side, turning over and over in his hands the little green metal sphere that the young Rihannsu officer tr'AAnikh had handed over to them.

"So you see my problem," Jim said softly to Spock as he touched the buttons to reprogram the combination and lock the safe.

"Yes, Captain," Spock said. "It is considerable."

"I'll be informing McCoy about this as soon as he's out of surgery," Jim said. "But I'm afraid the orders don't permit me to confide in the crew . . . at least not yet. We may have problems."

"It is always difficult to predict the future with any accuracy," Spock said, "but I suggest that you may be overestimating the severity of this problem."

"I just hope you're right. Meantime . . ." He looked at the little sphere. "What can you make of that?"

"I believe it will prove very useful," Spock said. "Further analysis will reveal whether its technology can be exploited on a larger scale. If, as I think—"

The intercom whistled. Jim hit the control on his desk. "Kirk here."

"*A message has come in from Starfleet Command, Captain, via relay from RV Trianguli.*"

"Yes?"

"*It's Code One, sir.*"

Jim swallowed.

"I'll be right up."

On *Bloodwing*'s bridge, everything was very quiet. Ael sat there with only tr'Hrienteh for company, looking out as the stars poured past them in the darkness.

"It is," tr'Hrienteh said, "a normal physiological reaction to the stress of battle, Ael. You know that."

"Of course I know it," Ael said. "But surely it is folly to reject sorrow simply because one has just had a victory." She sighed. "Such as it is. What of poor *Lake Champlain,* then? Its crew did not think to die on this mission. And as for those who sought, however indirectly, to protect us, this is a sad repayment of their wish to do us justice. Yet at the same time, our own people broke their own truce at the first second they could . . . and if one will deal with such folk, well, that has its dangers. If the Federation was not clear about that before, they are now."

She looked grimly out at the stars. But the grimness could not hold; the sorrow came back to replace it.

Tr'Hrienteh shook her head. "There is no harm in second thoughts, *khre'Riov.*"

"As long as I do not act on them," Ael said. "I have chosen this path. To turn from it because of pity for blood shed now will make that bloodshed worthless. I must go all the way through, for their sakes, for the sake of all those who will shortly die; else it means nothing."

She stood up. "Ask the crew to assemble in the workout room," she said. "This will only take a few minutes. But there may not be time when we reach Artaleirh."

Jim and Spock stood looking over Uhura's shoulder at the screen, where the text version of the message was scrolling. Its detail filled the whole screen, but one part of it mattered most.

. . . PREVIOUS ATTACKS ON FEDERATION VESSELS AND IN-CURSIONS INTO FEDERATION SPACE. NEGOTIATIONS REGARDING THESE INCURSIONS HAVE FAILED, AND

HAVE BEEN FOLLOWED BY A NEW INCURSION OF A ROM-
ULAN TASK FORCE INTO THE SPACE NEAR 15 TRIANGULI.
THESE HOSTILE ACTIONS HAVE LEFT US NO ALTERNA-
TIVE BUT TO DECLARE THAT AS OF THIS DATE, A STATE
OF WAR EXISTS BETWEEN THE UNITED FEDERATION OF
PLANETS AND THE ROMULAN STAR EMPIRE.

Jim's mouth was dry. "I hoped we would never have to see this again," he said softly. It had been the Klingons the last time Code One came through, and there had been more than enough deaths in that awful time, enough destruction and terror, before the Organians had abruptly brought that war to a close. This time, though, they showed no sign of interfering. Jim wondered one more time whether this meant the Organians were either gone or merely bored with dealing with lesser races, or whether humans and Romulans did not have the kind of joint future—bizarre as it sounded right now—which they had predicted that Klingons and humans would someday have. *I think we're on our own this time,* he thought. *But will we have the sense to end it as quickly as we can, or will we all get stuck again in the old habit of killing "aliens" for fun?*

There was no way to tell. The only thing that was certain was that the Second Romulan War had begun.

In the workout room, with its hung-up floor mats and its floor scuffed and scarred from thousands of games and bouts, all of Ael's little crew were waiting for her when she came in. They stared at her, for she was, for the first time, not in uniform. She was dressed all in pale silver-gray—breeches, tunic, boots—like one going to a wedding or a funeral, and in her hand she held the Sword.

She slipped it out of the scabbard and glanced at Aidoann, who stood off to one side. The blade glinted in the hard light of the room as she tossed the scabbard to Aidoann. Her second-in-command caught it.

"Too long this mighty heirloom has lain hidden," Ael said. "But, for life or death, it will do so no more. I will not sheathe it again until we are done, or our work is done. Ships the Imperium has spent, lives they have spent, and what little honor they had left they have spent hunting the Sword. Now the Sword shall come hunting them. Let us see how well they like it."

The cheer from them nearly deafened her as Ael left the workout room and made her way back up to the bridge. There she laid the Sword naked over the arms of her command seat, and stood behind it a moment, looking out at the main viewscreen's image of the stars.

Then Ael went out, and the Sword lay alone in the stillness and the starlight, with the cold, still, blue-shifted fires streaking and glittering on its blade.

To be continued in

# The Empty Chair

on sale now . . .

# GLOSSARY

*Translator's Note:* This glossary is not intended to be exhaustive, but rather merely a general guide to various terms of interest. In many places translations are approximate due to inadequate equivalents in the translating language.

*aefvadh*—"Be welcome."

*aehallh*—monster-ghost. An illusory creature: cognate to "nightmare" in Terran tradition, a creature that "rides" the dreamer to his perdition. Also, the "image" or illusion that one being has of another; as opposed to the true nature of the being in question.

*Ael*—proper name, fairly common on ch'Havran. "Winged." In other usage an adjective with connotations indicating a creature that moves quickly, gives one little time to make out details.

*afw'ein*—reason, as in use of one's faculties, rather than as the "excuse" one contrives to explain one's behavior.

*Aidoann*—proper name, uncommon. "Moon."

*aihai*—plains, plain country. Flatlands: cognomen "prairie."

*aihr*—"this is." Indicative noun prefix or infix.

*Arrhae*—proper name, der. "arrhe," q.v.

*arrhe*—worth-in-cash. Originally derogatory (a servant who performed the duties of slaves below his/her rank; modified to be "a servant more worthy of higher position than those awarded it").

*au'e*—"Oh yes." (Emphatic from "oh *yes!*")

*auethn*—advise me—answer a query.

*ch'Havran*—(planet) "of the Travelers."

*ch'Rihan*—(planet) "of the Declared."

*daise*—prefix; chief, principal, senior, foremost (etc.).

*daisemi'in*—chief among several (choices, candidates).

*deihu*—"elder"; a member of the Senate; regarded as an equivalent to the Terran "Senator": cf. Latin "senex."

*Eisn*—"homesun." The G9 star 128 Trianguli.

*Eitreih'hveinn*—the Farmers' Festival.

*enarrain*—senior centurion; colonel of infantry, commodore of Fleet forces. Minimum rank at which the officer may command more than his own vessel.

*erei'riov*—subcommander; captain of infantry, lieutenant commander of Fleet—usual rank for a first officer.

*erein*—antecenturion/subcenturion (translation sources vary); officer-cadet of infantry, ensign of Fleet forces.

*fvai, fvaiin*—child's riding-beast and house-pet (in larger houses) analogous to the Terran Oligocene-period *Mesohippus* in size—that of the Holocene-period *C. familiaris inostranzewi* (Great Dane)—though only approximate appearance.

*fvillha*—Rihannsu analogue to Terran "praetor": originally a judicial-level official with some executive powers (now much expanded). Cf. *fvillhaih,* "Praetorate."

*galae*—fleet; most specifically, space-fleet, since the battles of Rihannsu history were principally land-based. However, there was a later, enthusiastic adoption of massed airpower in both the offensive and defensive modes, and it is here, rather than in naval tradition, that the term has its origins.

*haerh, haerht*—cargo space, cargo hold.

*haudet'*—fr. *haud,* writing, and *etrehh,* machine. Computer printout: sometimes, screen dump as well. Cf. *hnhaudr,* "data transfer": direct protocol transfer from one computer to another.

*Havranha, Havranssu*—native(s) of the planet ch'Havran.

*Hellguard*—872 Trianguli V, a failed colony planet hastily and incompletely evacuated after "the Second Federation Encroachment."

*hfai, hfehan*—bond-servant; one earning a wage but without the liberty of changing employers at will.

*hfihar, hfihrnn*—House(s); noble families, not dwellings.

*hlai, hlaiin*—large flightless birds farmed for their meat; similar to the Terran ostrich, *Struthio camelus.* The very largest ones are also sometimes tamed for children to ride. This, however, renders their meat unusable.

*hlai'hwy, hlai'vna*—"held" and "loose" *hlai;* domesticated and wild (game) birds.

*hna'h*—activation-imperative suffix: e.g. "Fire!" "Energize!" "Go!"

*hnafirh*—"see," but not an active verb: passive with an implication that someone else must cooperate in the act by imparting or sharing information. Cf. *hnafirh'rau,* "Let me/us see it."

*hnafiv*—"hear," as above: *hnavif'rau,* "let me/us hear it."

*hnoiyika, hnoiyikar*—predator, similar to the Terran weasel *mustela frenata*—but 4 feet long, excluding tail, and 3 feet tall at the shoulder. Notorious for their vicious habits and insatiable appetites.

*hrrau*—at/on/in: a general locative particle or infix.

*hru'hfe*—Head-of-Household. The senior servant among domestic staff, appointed as overseer and servants' manager.

*hru'hfirh*—Head-of-House, euph. "The Lord." Most senior member of a noble family.

*h'ta-fvau*—"To last-place, immediate-return!" (Come back here!)

*hteij*—transporter, transmat. Not considered as a reliable form of travel, most of the time (possibly understandable, considering that the technology is purchased second-hand from the Klingons).

*hwaveyiir*—"command-executive center"; the flight bridge of a ship, as opposed to the combat-control area. (See *oira.*)

*hwiiy*—"You are": sometimes imperative.

*ie'yyak-hnah*—"Fire phasers!"

*iehyyak*—"multiple" rather than "several" phasers, especially in reference to shipboard phaser-banks.

*khellian*—arch. "hunter"; also the name of a minor Praetorial house.

*khoi*—"switch off," "cease," "finish."

*khre'riov*—commander-general; equivalent to a colonel of infantry or a commodore of Fleet forces.

*kllhe*—the annelid worm, introduced to domestic *hlai*-pens, which ingests the acidic dung and thus processes it to usable fertilizer. Also an insult.

*kll'inghann*—the Klingon people (However, see *lloannen'mhrahel.*)

*Levaeri V*—fifth planet of the Levaeri system (identified with 113 Tri): site of an orbital station at which various biological researches were conducted until the destruction of the base by Federation forces and the renegade ship *Bloodwing.*

*lhhei*—"Madam."

*llaekh-ae'rl*—"laughing-murder"; the practice or *kata* forms of a common Rihannsu unarmed combat technique. Provenance of the name is uncertain.

*llhrei'sian*—diarrhea as a result of mild food-poisoning; a term exactly equivalent to "the runs," "the Titanian two-step," "the (any number of edible objects) revenge."

*llilla'hu*—that will do, "That's just enough": barely adequate, sufficient.

*lloann'mhrahel*—the United Federation of Planets; however, the word translates most accurately as "Them, from There" (as opposed to "Us, from Here"). The Klingons, once encountered, were promptly named *khell'oann-mhehorael* (More of Them, from Somewhere Else).

*lloann'na*—catchall title for a UFP member, translating exactly as "a/the Fed."

*lloannen'galae*—Federation fleet, battlegroup, task force; the word has aggressive connotations which do not differentiate between warships and unarmed civilian vessels, but then the Rihannsu have seldom seen the need to regard other ships than theirs as other than potential enemies.

*mnek'nra, mnekha*—"well, good, correct, satisfactory." Inferior-superior and superior-inferior modes, respectively.

*mnhei'sahe*—the Ruling Passion: a concept or concept-complex which rules most of Rihannsu life in terms of honor. *Mnhei'sahe* is primarily occupied with courtesy to the people around one: this courtesy, depending on circumstances, may require killing a person to do him honor, or severely disadvantaging oneself on his behalf. There are many ramifications too involved to go into, but generally *mnhei'sahe* is satisfied if all the parties to an agreement or situation feel that their "face" or honor is intact after a social (or other) transaction. NB: The concept has occasionally been mistranslated as implying that a given action is done "for another person's good." This is incorrect; such a concept literally does not exist in Rihannsu. One does things for one's own good—or rather, the good of one's honor—and if properly carried out, the actions in question will have benefited the other parties in the transaction as well.

*nei'rrh*—small birds, similar in size and flight characteristics to the Terran hummingbirds (fam. Trochilidae), with a poison-secreting spur on the upper mandible of the beak. Also an insult, referring to a person annoying or dangerous out of all proportion to their size, status, or (usually) worth.

*neth . . . nah'lai*—either . . . or.

*nuhirrien*—"look-toward"; the quality of charisma or mass attractiveness.

*oal'lhlih*—"announce the presence/the arrival."

*oira*—"battle-control"; aboard warbird-class and smaller ships this is the same bridge-deck (see *hwaveyiir*) as the standard flight-control area, although rigged for combat; but on the larger, Klingon-built *Akif* and *K't'inga*-class vessels the word refers to a separate, heavily armored area deep in the command prow.

*qiuu, qiuu'n (oaii)*—all, everything, "the lot."

*Ra'kholh*—Avenger. A popular ship-name in the Rihannsu Fleet.

*rekkhai*—"sir"; inferior-superior high-phase mode.

*rha, rh'e*—"indeed," "is that so" (colloq. vulg. "oh yeah?").

*rrh-thanai*—hostage-fostering. Sometimes the making of peace by the exchange of children, each to be brought up in the other's tradition to further understanding and harmony; sometimes the exchange is to simply provide leverage and a surety of good behavior: "Don't do this, or your son/daughter will die." Fosterings often start in one context and wind up in another.

*S'harien*—lit. "pierceblood"; the name, in Old Vulcan, chosen by pre-Sundering Vulcan's most famous swordsmith as a reaction against the teachings of Surak: the name was also given to his swords.

*siuren*—"minutes"; or at least, the Rihannsu equivalent, actually equal to 50.5 seconds.

*sseikea*—a scavenger, analogous to the Terran hyena *Crocuta crocuta* and employed as an insult in the same way.

*ssuaj-ha*—"Understood!" (Inferior-superior mode.)

*ssuej-d'ifv*—"Do you understand?" (Superior-inferior mode.)

*sthea'hwill*—"I request (an action) be done at once." (Superior-inferior, courteous mode.)

*ta krenn*—"Look here, look at this."

*ta'khoi*—"Screen off." Usage for voice-activation equipment and (if used to another person) very explicit superiority.

*ta'rhae*—"Screen on." (See above.)

*th'ann, th'ann-a*—"a/the prisoner."

*thrai, thraiin*—predator, analogous to the Terran wolverine *Gulo luscus;* and possessed of similar legendary traits for persistence, vengeful stubbornness, and ferocity.

*tlhei*—"my word"; occasionally as in "my (given) Word" but more usually "my command/order/bidding."

*urru*—"go to . . ." A non-mode imperative, which (if circumstances permit) can be used from low to high as well as the more usual vice versa.

*vaed'rae*—"Hear me/attend me." More imperative than "listen," and more formal.

*vah-udt*—"What rank?" "Who are you (to be asking/doing this)?"

*vriha*—highest, most superior.

*yhfi-ss'ue*—"travel-tubes"; the public transport system, of five rail-mounted cars, powered by electromagnetic linear motors, carrying 20 persons in an enclosed weatherproof tube.

# AFTERWORD

To tell you the truth, as regards the Rihannsu . . . it all started with *Coriolanus*.

I have dearly loved Shakespeare since I first stumbled on his plays as one of the first books I was "allowed to read" after I'd read through everything in the basement children's section of the library in the town where I grew up. (Though, to tell you the truth, I was already reading the upstairs stuff anyway, whether they allowed me to check it out or not; the librarian upstairs was usually too busy to notice when a kid crept up the cellar steps and into the stacks to liberate a copy of *To Kill a Mockingbird* or Hamilton's *The Roman Way*.)

I still reread the plays at least once a year, straight through, to reground myself in a very special part of the English language and its history. I was rereading the plays again just after finishing my first *Trek* novel, *The Wounded Sky,* and at the time making an attempt to get friendly with some of the material I'd read years before but hadn't much cared for. One of these plays was *Coriolanus*. On first reading, I liked that one about as much as I'd liked *Titus Andronicus:* not very. On earlier readings, the protagonist had seemed like an idiot, so desperately hung up on his own class-oriented sense of honor that he could turn against his native city, even his family, primarily for the sake of assuaging his pleb-bruised ego. On the post–*Wounded Sky* rereading, that opinion had deepened a little, but the play still didn't particularly jump onto my top-ten list.

There were also other things going on. Having finished *Sky* and having been promptly invited by my then-editor at Pocket to do another *Trek* book if I liked, I'd been thinking about exactly what to do. The Klingon language had been making its first splash in the public consciousness around then, and I mentioned the possibility of taking on another of *Trek*'s favorite species in that idiom: the Romulans. My editor shook his head and suggested that there wouldn't be much of a demand for a Romulan dictionary, as the initial Klingon one seemed to be running rather slow in terms of sales. "But if you want to do a novel about the Romulans . . ." he said.

I'd thought about that for a while, principally in terms of the challenge. From canonical first-series *Trek,* we knew little enough about the Klingons; we knew far less about the Romulans. "Can I do some culture building," I said, "the way John M. Ford's done with the Klingons?" My editor checked with Paramount, and a while later came back to me to say, "Sure, go ahead, knock yourself out."

So I started thinking about what that people's history might look like. There were some hints in the episode "Balance of Terror" (reinforced later in "The *Enterprise* Incident") about a possible connection to the Vulcans, but beyond that, little to go on except a sense—as much conveyed by the actors' performance as by script content—of an honorable people, dignified, private, even secretive, and somehow with an air of being strangely threatened; dangerous and powerful enough, but also seeming to prefer remaining in the shadows. That whole patchy gestalt began to churn around in the back of my head, in company with the basic question that every wise psychiatric nurse learns to ask herself about the motivations and actions of a client: *How do you raise someone so that they turn out like this?*

It was in this context that I was immersed while I was reading *Coriolanus.* The connection I was hunting for, however, the key to the book I was about to write, didn't happen immediately. After a few weeks I finished up with Shakespeare and went on to other reading, including a very favorite book, Ursula K. Le Guin's *The Left Hand of Darkness.* And everything was going along as usual in the chilly and familiar territory of the planet the Terrans call Winter until the disgraced and exiled "prime minister" of the nation of Karhide, Estraven, finds himself in a situation where he thinks: "I knew it was time to turn to my enemies, for there was no more good in my friends."

*Click!*

Sometimes a book will not coalesce properly in my mind until a core appears around which it can form. I had been looking for my main character, the one who could best express why Romulans were the way they were—tough work, when I wasn't myself sure as yet. But suddenly the character was there, in generalities if not in detail: someone who was going to leave the Romulan Empire behind and turn to the Federation—and someone who would ironically be doomed forever after, even under the best of circumstances, to be considered a traitor not just by one side, but by both. And not too long after that, the character quite abruptly coalesced around the likeness of another of my early *Trek* editors, Mimi Panitch—a small, slender woman with long dark hair and sharp eyes.

That was that. That was Ael—though I didn't know her name for a good while, as her world started building itself around her. Echoes of *Coriolanus* swiftly began to run all through that book as I outlined it—a sense of someone forced to turn her coat and change her loyalties, not because of ego issues or a desire for vengeance, but by her culture's steady drift away from the certainties that had once made it a noble thing, despite the unease and fear that had driven it (as I pretended) from its original home.

I found myself with other problems, though. I have to admit right here that I hadn't originally thought her character would be female. But there Ael was, and sitting in the center seat of the vessel which would oppose her and *Bloodwing*—on and off—was a man with something of a reputation among the ladies. How was James T. Kirk going to react to being thrown together with a woman who (for maximum effect) had to have come close enough to killing him at least once or twice? How was he going to like her sitting in his center seat, while *he* sat in the *Enterprise*'s brig? I kept finding myself muttering, as I wrote, "There's gonna be *trouble . . . !*" Yet at the same time, there was the temptation to increase that trouble, to make Ael give him as difficult a time as possible. Too few women in *Trek*'s history had ever at that point given Kirk a real run for his money, either tactically, intellectually, or emotionally. It would be a lot of fun to see how it worked out. . . .

So in that book went, and a while later, there came a request for a sequel. That was the story that became *The Romulan Way,* a novel famously written extremely late (I really hadn't expected to get involved in story-editing a cartoon series that year, but it had happened; nor had I expected to wind up writing an episode of *Star Trek: The Next Generation,* but that happened too . . .) and written at great speed, during my honeymoon (I really hadn't expected to have marriage provide me with a fellow writer who could so accurately ace my style; there are still people who aren't sure which parts of that book Peter wrote and which I did, which suits both of us fine. The outline was mine—that's all you really need to know). The title probably makes it plain that Edith Hamilton's great cultural examinations *The Greek Way* and *The Roman Way* were still on my mind. As a sort of homage to Hamilton, I threw in another female character, Terise Haleakala-LoBrutto—a lady willingly immersed neck-deep, and perhaps dangerously deeper, in an alien culture she has come to love.

After that book went in, there followed something of a hiatus at the Rihannsu end of things, partly due to relocation overseas and an increased concentration on book and television work on the European side of the world. While I had long planned the end of Ael's story—and after *TNG,* was already thinking about ways in which her worlds could be reconciled with the image of the Romulan worlds which was then becoming canon in TV *Trek*—I'd come to assume that there would be no particular interest at either Paramount's or Pocket's end in continuing the series. It came as something of a shock, therefore, when yet another *Trek* editor, John Ordover, emailed me and asked me to come in one more time and finish Ael's story. I started that process, but once more life intervened: film work yet again threw the wrench so thoroughly into all my other writing that it was a number of years before I could get back to grips with Ael, *Bloodwing,* and the significantly escalated problems of the Rihannsu Star Empire. I do at least have something to show for that interference: the miniseries that Peter and I were working on almost constantly between 1999 and 2005, *Dark Kingdom: The Dragon King,* will have aired on the Sci-Fi Channel by the time anyone reads this. But I want everybody who waited so patiently (and sometimes not so patiently) to understand how thoroughly I regret the long delay between the publication of *Swordhunt* and *Honor Blade* and the story's conclusion in *The Empty Chair.* Lennon was absolutely right, and would probably forgive me the paraphrase: life is indeed what happens when your publisher's made other plans. I just want to thank Marco Palmieri once again for his help and thoughtfulness while he took one arm and I took the other and we dragged Ael (figuratively, at least) kicking and screaming into the Senate chambers and her people's history.

So now, with regret, it becomes time for me to say my last goodbyes to these characters. They've been excellent companions through many hours spent in that dark place in the back of the writer's brain, where drama plays itself out in a hundred different forms before finally suffering itself to be pinned down on paper. I'm going to miss them. But it's time now for them to be out on their own . . . so keep an eye on them for me.

And the only thing that remains to be said is this:

No, I will *not* tell you what "Jim" means. Because if you just spend a little time thinking about it . . . you'll know.

Diane Duane
County Wicklow, Ireland
the Nones of March, 2006

# ABOUT THE AUTHORS

**Diane Duane** has been making her living writing fantasy and science fiction for more than a quarter century, and has written for *Star Trek* in more media than anyone else alive. Born in Manhattan, a descendant of the first mayor of New York City after the Revolutionary War, she initially trained and worked as a psychiatric nurse; then, after the publication of her first book in 1979, spent some years living and writing on both coasts of the U.S. before relocating to County Wicklow in Ireland, where she settled down with her husband, the Belfast-born novelist and screenwriter Peter Morwood. Her work includes more than forty novels—a number of which have spent time on the *New York Times* bestseller list—and much television work, including story-editing stints on the DiC animated series *Dinosaucers* and the BBC educational series *Science Challenge,* a co-writer credit on the first-season *Star Trek: The Next Generation* episode "Where No One Has Gone Before," and (most recently) another on the Sci-Fi Channel miniseries *Dark Kingdom: The Dragon King,* written in collaboration with her husband. When not writing, she conducts an active online life based around her weblog (http:dianeduane.com/outofambit), her popular "Young Wizards" novel series (http:www.youngwizards.com), and her European recipe collection (http:www.europeancuisines.com), while also stargazing, cooking, attempting to keep the cats from eating all the herbs in the garden, and trying to figure out how to make more spare time.

**Peter Morwood** was born in Northern Ireland, and has been writing fantasy and science fiction for more than twenty years, with one solo Star Trek novel, *Rules of Engagement,* to his credit—this possibly making him the only *Trek* novelist with fighter-pilot training. His first fantasy series, *The Book of Years,* was reissued in the U.S. in 2005; his first live-action miniseries, *Dark Kingdom: The Dragon King* (co-written with wife Diane Duane, in association with director Uli Edel) aired on the Sci-Fi Channel in March of 2006. He's currently working on the fifth volume of *The Book of Years,* the third in *The Clan Wars* series, as well as a new fantasy-historical novel and screenplays for a feature film and a second miniseries.